NEW
TOEIC

U0033941

決勝
新制多益

聽力閱讀6回模擬試題

作者 ◎ Kim dae Kyun
譯者 ◎ 林育珊／蔡裴驊／關亭薇

LISTENING & READING

MP3

作者序

　　筆者潛心著筆，將《決勝新制多益：聽力6回模擬試題＋完全剖析》與《決勝新制多益：閱讀6回模擬試題＋完全剖析》出版成冊。為了撰寫出貼近實際測驗的試題，筆者曾多次赴日參加多益測驗，持續致力於新制多益的解題分析。歷經這些過程後，終於完成這套直擊最新命題趨勢的著作。與舊制多益相比，新制多益的整體難度相對提升不少，考生在考前務必要精準掌握出題方向，並勤於練習仿真試題。

根據筆者的透徹分析，新制多益的改制內容與應考對策如下：

PART 1　　請務必優先熟記高難度單字。在照片題型中，比起人物，將重點擺在事物上更有利於解題。

PART 2　　切勿在聽完題目的當下，立即選填答案。通常需要經過一番思索，才能找出正確答案。

PART 3　　為掌握聽力分數的關鍵，請務必充分練習。

PART 4　　雖與舊制多益的難易度相當，但聽力的語速加快，這一點請特別留意。

　　筆者親自監聽錄音檔，精選配音員錄製本書。依照多益聽力測驗語速，完成最貼近實際考試的錄音。

PART 5　　與舊制多益的難易度相當。

PART 6　　短文填空題的難度提升，請善用本書勤加練習！

PART 7　　為掌握閱讀分數的關鍵，充分練習本書的仿真試題，方能取得好成績。

　　筆者報考過230餘次的多益測驗，自詡是擁有最多滿分經驗的最強權威，至今仍持續參加測驗。這14年來在韓國EBS電台《金大鈞TOEIC KING》擔任內容策劃與主講人，節目不僅獲得大眾的認可，更讓我獲得專業主題類別最佳BJ（註：線上節目主持人）的殊榮。除此之外，就讀金大鈞英語學院的學生，也頻頻獲得滿分的佳績。多益滿分不再遙不可及，相信大家也能做到。我保證在本書的幫助下，大家勢必能快速提升多益成績！

歷史，由你來創造。
身為多益界的不敗傳奇，筆者亦將不負眾望，跨出更大的步伐向前邁進。

向上蒼與讀者致上謝意

金大鈞

CONTENTS

新制多益題型更新重點

PART 1

	新制多益	舊制多益
題型	照片描述	照片描述
題數	總題數6題	總題數10題

題型不變，照片描述仍為四個選項。

 題數減少

PART 2

	新制多益	舊制多益
題型	應答問題	應答問題
題數	總題數25題	總題數30題

題型不變，應答問題仍為選出適當的選項。

 題數減少

PART 3

	新制多益	舊制多益
題型	簡短對話	簡短對話
題數	13組對話（每組3題） 總題數39題	10組對話（每組3題） 總題數30題

 新增三人對話題型　 對話和題數增加

PART 4

	新制多益	舊制多益
題型	簡短獨白	簡短獨白
題數	10組簡短獨白（每組3題） 總題數30題	10組簡短獨白（每組3題） 總題數30題

 新增圖表作答題型

PART 5

	新制多益	舊制多益
題型	句子填空	句子填空
題數	總題數30題	總題數40題

題型不變,選出句子中適合填入的單字或片語。

 題數減少

PART 6

	新制多益	舊制多益
題型	段落填空	段落填空
題數	總題數16題	總題數12題

 新增選一完整句子填入空格　 題數增加

PART 7

	新制多益	舊制多益
題型	單篇閱讀	單篇閱讀
題數	10篇單篇閱讀 每篇2–4題 總題數29題	9篇單篇閱讀 每篇2–5題 總題數28題
題型	雙篇閱讀	雙篇閱讀
題數	兩組雙篇閱讀 每組5題 總題數10題	四組雙篇閱讀 每組5題 總題數20題
題型	多篇閱讀	
題數	三組多篇閱讀 每組5題 總題數15題	
題數	總題數54題	總題數48題

保留原有的閱讀測驗。

 新增多篇閱讀題型　 題數增加

各大考題最新命題趨勢

新制多益的整體難度相對提升，唯有接受這個事實，認真準備才能取得佳績。本書準確分析出題趨勢，完全比照實際測驗，只要充分練習本書的試題，定能勇奪高分！

PART 1 **照片描述** 核心攻略

通常只要聽懂**動詞關鍵字**，就能答出大部分的題目，但是仍有不少題目以**高難度單字**和**特殊描寫**命題。在新制多益 PART 1 中，只要聽到 holding、display、casting a shadow（蒙上陰影）、lead to、occupied、unoccupied 這些關鍵字，就是正確選項。然而值得注意的是，你可能會同時聽到**兩個以上**的高難度單字。

1.

(A) A woman is holding an oar. 女子拿著一支槳。
(B) A woman is tying a boat to a pier. 女子把小船繫在碼頭邊。
(C) A woman is getting out of the boat. 女子正從小船上下來。
(D) A woman is swimming across a lake. 女子正泳渡一座湖。

解答 A

第一大題中，只要聽到 holding，就是正確的選項。若同時聽到高難度單字 oar（槳），就能更加肯定它就是正解。雖然 PART 1 中的單字相對容易，但千萬不可小覷，請務必注意單字的發音。vase 通常會唸成 [ves]，但在多益測驗中，若為英國腔，聽起來則像是 [vɑz]。

2.

(A) A knife has been placed on the chair. 刀子放在椅子上。

　→ 照片中並未出現刀和椅子。

(B) Flowers have been put in vases. 花插在花瓶裡。

　→ 這裡的 vases 發音為 [vɑzɪz]（英國腔）。雖然有時會將 vase 唸成 [ves] ，但英式唸法
　　[vɑz] 通常才是正解，請務必熟記！

(C) A woman is watering some flowers. 一名女子正在澆花。

　→ 照片中並未出現人物和動作。

(D) A woman is buying some flowers. 一名女子正在買花。

　→ 照片裡看不到人物。

解答　B

3.

(A) People are gathered at the entryway. 人們聚集在入口處。

(B) A door is beneath a staircase. 樓梯下方有一扇門。

(C) A man is repairing the stairs. 一名男子正在整修樓梯。

(D) Some pictures are propped against a wall. 牆上掛著一些畫。

解答　B

不同於過往題型，題目當中會出現針對事物的特殊描寫。將特殊描寫設為正解，
已成為一種出題趨勢。

請特別注意 PART 1 的第五、六題，雖然照片中有出現人物，但答案可能是單純
針對事物描寫的選項。

PART 2 應答問題 核心攻略

眾多考生為 PART 2 苦惱不已。值得注意的是，PART 2 可不只是少了五題這麼簡單而已，命題方式反而變得更加巧妙、難度也隨之提升。所謂的「Read between the lines.」，即「**言外之意**」，將大量出現在考題中，考生必須要聽出背後的含意才能找出答案。碰到此類題型時，在聽完題目後，需要經過一番**思考**，才能挑出正確的答案。只要稍不留神，很容易就錯失下一題的解題機會。請務必勤加練習，熟悉此類題型的模式。

7. **Sales of the newly published books are higher than we expected.**
   新出版的書銷量比我們預期的還要高。

   (A) We want to hire her. 我們想僱用她。
   → hire 僅與 higher 的發音相近，為錯誤選項。

   (B) I know they are very popular. 我知道它們很暢銷。
   → 為最適當的答案，表示「很暢銷」。

   (C) What is the bottom line? 主要重點是什麼？

   解答 B

8. **How will the new members be selected?**
   新成員會怎麼選出來？

   (A) They've already been chosen. 已經選出來了。
   → selected 可替換成 chosen，為正確答案。

   (B) Jane has a monthly membership. 珍持有月會員資格。

   (C) Is it on the third floor? 它在三樓嗎？
   → 不符合單複數一致性（members 為複數，it 為單數），為錯誤選項。

   解答 A

9. **Why don't you sign up for the TOEIC workshop with us?**
   你何不和我們一起報名多益工作坊？

   (A) I don't have time to go. 我沒空去。
   → 極為明確的回答，為正確答案。

   (B) There is a shop around the corner. 有一間店在轉角處。
   → shop 僅與 workshop 的發音相近，為錯誤選項。

   (C) At the auditorium. 在禮堂。

   解答 A

10. **Have you made any progress on the merger and acquisition meeting?**

併購會議，你們有任何進展嗎？

(A) The company's office. 公司的辦公室。

(B) We're getting together again next Monday. 我們下週一要再聚一次。

→ 表示「之後將繼續進行」的意思，為需要稍微思考一下的選項。

(C) Acquired immune deficiency syndrome. 後天免疫缺乏症候群。

→ acquired 僅與 acquisition 的發音相近，為錯誤選項。

解答 B

11. **What restaurant did you choose to host the retirement party?**

你選擇在哪間餐廳主辦退休歡送會？

(A) He said he will retire next year. 他說他明年退休。

(B) Mark is the host of the show. 馬克是活動的主持人。

(C) I'm still waiting for some price quotes. 我還在等一些報價。

→ 請熟記 quote 除了有「引用」的意思之外，作為名詞也有「報價」的意思。
   quote = estimate

解答 C

12. **Didn't Susan already fill an order for this?**

蘇珊沒有填這個的訂單嗎？

(A) That was for December. 那是12月的事了。

→ 需要歷經一番思考才能解出的高難度題目。當出現像(A)這類的選項時，請先標記三角形符號，之後回過頭再聽一次。

(B) Fill her up with unleaded, please. 無鉛加滿，麻煩你。

→ 當出現和題目相同的單字 fill 時，不是答案的可能性極高。

(C) In chronological order. 照時間順序排列。

→ order 也是重複出現的單字，不是答案的可能性極高。

解答 A

PART 3 簡短對話 核心攻略

PART 3 不僅對話的**篇幅較長**，特別要注意的是對話**語速也加快了**。從第32題開始，你將聽到語速極快的澳洲口音，而實際測驗中的語速也非常地快，請務必集中精神仔細聆聽。**詢問句意**為何的題目，大多屬於高難度命題，請利用本教材勤加練習！例如：對話中出現「Well, that's a good question.」且題目詢問本句句意為何時，這句話的意思並非是指「這真是個好問題」，而是「He cannot provide the answer. (不太清楚，無法回答)」的意思。

圖表類題型的難度則不如想像中困難。

PART 3 為**掌握聽力分數的關鍵**，同時也是題數最多 (39題)、難度較高的大題，請務必好好準備。

PART 4 簡短獨白 核心攻略

PART 4 的難易度與舊制多益相當。在 PART 3 和 PART 4 的命題部分，解題線索不會只放在一個句子裡面，而是要聽懂兩三個句子後，才能找出答案。PART 4 的圖表類題型也是相對容易的部分。

經分析 PART 3 和 PART 4 的答案後，發現**不太會連續出現三次相同的答案**，也就是幾乎不太可能出現像是 AAA、BBB、CCC、DDD 這樣的答案。因此當你沒聽清楚題目時，不要重複選擇和前一題相同的答案，而是改選其他選項，如此一來猜中答案的機率相對較高，請務必牢記這個小訣竅。

PART 5 句子填空 核心攻略

與舊制多益相比，PART 5 的總題數減少了 10 題，難易度不變，因此只要依照過往的準備方式來解題即可。不過偶爾也會出現一些容易誤答的題目。例如：片語 be selective about，正確答案應為 selective（挑剔的、有選擇性的），但選項中會出現 rigorous（嚴格的）作為出題陷阱來誤導你。碰到這類題目時，請務必好好**觀察放入句中的單字是否適當**。

PART 5 會因為每個月考試的難易度而有所差異，讓我們一起挑出難度偏高的題型吧！

101. Tina is one of the most popular musical artists in the world, ------- only Mozart in record sales.

(A) except
(B) into
(C) from
(D) behind

解答 D

本題必須先釐清句意後，才能正確解答。緹娜是位國際級的音樂家，排名第二，僅次於莫札特。這是很多考生都會答錯的題型，請仔細檢視一遍。

中譯 緹娜是位國際知名的音樂家，專輯銷量僅次於莫札特。

102. This year's Kinglish Conference will be held in Seoul, though it has ------- alternated between Tokyo and San Francisco.

(A) traditionally
(B) abruptly
(C) exactly
(D) necessarily

解答 A

本題要從選項中選出最適當的副詞。每次考試都會出現這類題型，難度不亞於上方的範例，請務必多加留意。

中譯 雖然歷來都是在東京和舊金山輪流舉行，但金英大會今年將在首爾舉辦。

103. As they had with the first, organizers of Kinglish Conference ------- managed to find an alternative speaker for the second canceled seminar.

(A) much
(B) excessively
(C) concurrently
(D) likewise

解答 D

本題要從選項中選出最適當的副詞。

中譯 如同上一個場次那般，金英大會主辦方比照辦理，設法為先前取消的第二場研討會找了另一位講師替代。

104. We should know that the terms are subject to change ------- when oil prices rise or fall.

(A) heavily
(B) quarterly
(C) still
(D) nearby

解答 B

請先掌握文意,才能找出正確答案。本句的文意為:「條件會隨著季度改變」。

中譯 我們都應該知道,每當油價漲跌時,每季的油價也應隨之調整。

105. ------- the world's tallest building was completed, HaJin and Tina Ltd. had already begun designing a taller one.

(A) By the time
(B) Whenever
(C) If
(D) Because

解答 A

屬於過去完成式的考題。經常以過去完成式和未來完成式來命題。

By the time+主詞+過去式, 主詞+had p.p.

By the time+主詞+現在式, 主詞+will have p.p.

中譯 當世界最高的建築完工時,哈金與緹娜公司已經在著手設計更高的了。

PART 6 段落填空 核心攻略

PART 6 最難的地方在於要從選項 (四個句子) 中選出適當的句子填入空格中。這部分為新增加的題型,不僅要花費較多時間解題,平時也應在如何**掌握前後文意**上,下一番功夫。請利用本書徹底釐清觀念,並好好練習本大題的題型!

PART 6 會因每個月考試的難易度而有所差異,難易度較不固定,請務必勤加演練。

PART 7 單/雙/多篇閱讀 核心攻略

最近總是聽到許多人談論 PART 7 的難度很高。PART 7 的總題數增加為 54 題，除了要花費很多時間解題之外，就連題目本身也不太容易理解。如果說 PART 3 是掌握聽力分數的關鍵，那麼 PART 7 就是**掌握閱讀分數的關鍵**。在舊制多益測驗中，原本可以輕鬆解題過關的短文閱讀，難度也大幅提升。而雙篇閱讀和多篇閱讀，也有逐漸變難的趨勢，建議大家可以利用本書精選的試題反覆演練。

另外，考生在寫到第 196–200 題時，常因解題時間不夠，隨便亂猜答案。當各位遇到這種狀況時，請特別留意 ABCD 答案的分配比例都是相同的！從開始實行新制多益測驗，一直到最近本書準備出版之際，我分析了這段期間內 PART 7 中 196–200 題的正確選項後發現：答案為 A 的次數為 18 次；答案為 B 的次數為 18 次；答案為 C 的次數為18次；答案為 D 的次數為 17 次，**ABCD 選項為答案的比例幾乎均等**。因此考生若碰上 PART 7 的作答時間不足，必須猜答案時，請務必分散風險作答。在此提醒，此技巧僅作為解題的輔助手段，希望大家還是以全力以赴解題為優先。

在 PART 7 中，同義詞替換的難度也逐漸提升。例如 retain 這個字最常用的意思為「留存 (to keep possession of)」或是「保持」。

例：They insisted on retaining old customs.

　　他們堅持沿用舊制。

但是你知道其實 retain 也有依合約「聘僱」某人從事有酬工作的意思嗎？
舉例而言：retain a lawyer 意思就是「聘請法律顧問」。

例1：The team failed to retain him, and he became a free agent.

　　那支球隊無法和他續約，於是他成為自由球員。

例2：They have decided to retain a firm to conduct a survey.

　　他們決定僱用一間公司來執行調查。

例3：You may need to retain an attorney.

　　你可能需要聘請律師。

最近在多益閱讀題中，改以 contract 的近義詞 retain 出題，讓眾多考生驚慌失措。這個用法甚至是英英字典裡的最後一個意思。因此當你在複習已經熟悉的單字時，請務必確認這個單字是否還有其他意思，並透過例句來學習，最重要的就是保持學習態度！

做完本書所有試題後，請反覆練習，重點在於**充分理解**所有例句，並維持**做筆記**的習慣。

七大攻略讀熟後，請翻開第一回擬真試題，實際測驗看看吧！

LISTENING TEST

In the Listening test, you will be asked to demonstrate how well you understand spoken English. The entire Listening test will last approximately 45 minutes. There are four parts, and directions are given for each part. You must mark your answers on the separate answer sheet. Do not write your answers in your test book.

PART 1

Directions: For each question in this part, you will hear four statements about a picture in your test book. When you hear the statements, you must select the one statement that best describes what you see in the picture. Then find the number of the question on your answer sheet and mark your answer. The statements will not be printed in your test book and will be spoken only one time.

Example

Sample Answer

Ⓐ Ⓑ ● Ⓓ

Statement (C), "A woman is admiring some artwork.," is the best description of the picture, so you should select answer (C) and mark it on your answer sheet.

1.

2.

GO ON TO THE NEXT PAGE

3.

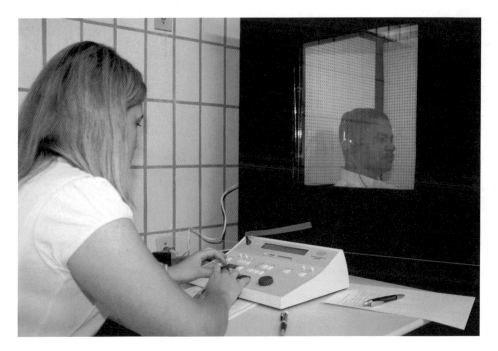

4.

5.

6.

Directions: You will hear a question or statement and three responses spoken in English. They will not be printed in your test book and will be spoken only one time. Select the best response to the question or statement and mark the letter (A), (B), or (C) on your answer sheet.

7. Mark your answer on your answer sheet.

8. Mark your answer on your answer sheet.

9. Mark your answer on your answer sheet.

10. Mark your answer on your answer sheet.

11. Mark your answer on your answer sheet.

12. Mark your answer on your answer sheet.

13. Mark your answer on your answer sheet.

14. Mark your answer on your answer sheet.

15. Mark your answer on your answer sheet.

16. Mark your answer on your answer sheet.

17. Mark your answer on your answer sheet.

18. Mark your answer on your answer sheet.

19. Mark your answer on your answer sheet.

20. Mark your answer on your answer sheet.

21. Mark your answer on your answer sheet.

22. Mark your answer on your answer sheet.

23. Mark your answer on your answer sheet.

24. Mark your answer on your answer sheet.

25. Mark your answer on your answer sheet.

26. Mark your answer on your answer sheet.

27. Mark your answer on your answer sheet.

28. Mark your answer on your answer sheet.

29. Mark your answer on your answer sheet.

30. Mark your answer on your answer sheet.

31. Mark your answer on your answer sheet.

PART 3 🎧03

Directions: You will hear some conversations between two or more people. You will be asked to answer three questions about what the speakers say in each conversation. Select the best response to each question and mark the letter (A), (B), (C), or (D) on your answer sheet. The conversations will not be printed in your test book and will be spoken only one time.

32. Where most likely does the man work?

(A) At a law office
(B) At a repair company
(C) At a bookstore
(D) At a print shop

33. What does the man ask the woman to do?

(A) Restart some equipment
(B) Use another machine
(C) Consult a manual
(D) Find a reset code

34. What does the man say he can do?

(A) Locate some equipment
(B) Copy some documents
(C) Contact a supplier
(D) Go to the woman's office

35. Why is the man calling?

(A) To book tickets for an event
(B) To inquire about accommodation
(C) To change a reservation
(D) To purchase a printer

36. What information does the woman request?

(A) The number of rooms
(B) The name of a conference
(C) A membership card number
(D) A check-out date

37. What does the woman suggest?

(A) Upgrading some rooms
(B) Signing a contract
(C) Checking a website
(D) Using a discount code

38. What is the conversation mainly about?

(A) An updated menu
(B) A change in a schedule
(C) A writing contest
(D) A volunteer project

39. What is true about the woman?

(A) She will relocate next week.
(B) She is a university professor.
(C) She has a photocopier.
(D) She won an award.

40. What is Mark asked to do?

(A) Take photographs
(B) Develop a design plan
(C) Attend a workshop
(D) Order some supplies

41. What is being discussed?

(A) A business card design
(B) A printing order
(C) A company retreat
(D) New work schedules

42. What was the problem with the sample item?

(A) The paper was damaged.
(B) A logo was outdated.
(C) Some information was incorrect.
(D) The cost was too high.

43. What does the woman ask the man to do?

(A) Contact a company
(B) Return a sample
(C) Hire a new employee
(D) Pay an account

44. Where most likely do the speakers work?

(A) At a subway station
(B) At a dental clinic
(C) At a travel agency
(D) At a marketing firm

45. What project have the women been working on?

(A) Drafting an employee's contract
(B) Creating a television advertisement
(C) Inputting details into a computer
(D) Installing some audio equipment

46. What does the man suggest?

(A) Working some overtime
(B) Moving the deadline
(C) Using different software
(D) Assigning more staff

47. Why is the woman calling?

(A) To request a reservation change
(B) To inquire about a special discount
(C) To ask for a full refund
(D) To upgrade her flight ticket

48. What event does the woman mention?

(A) An animal competition
(B) A veterinary seminar
(C) A tour of a city
(D) An art convention

49. What additional information does the man ask for?

(A) The number of passengers
(B) The dimension of the carriers
(C) The preferred payment method
(D) A membership card number

50. What did the man recently do?

    (A) He had an oven repaired.
    (B) He printed out a receipt.
    (C) He looked at customer feedback.
    (D) He corrected an invoice error.

51. Why does the woman say, "I've spent all day training the new cooks"?

    (A) To express agreement
    (B) To suggest a solution
    (C) To request more details
    (D) To provide an excuse

52. What will the man mention at the meeting?

    (A) Taking orders from people who are waiting
    (B) Keeping the business open late on weekends
    (C) Removing certain dishes from the menu
    (D) Offering more specials during lunchtime

53. What suggestion does the man make?

    (A) Organizing workspaces
    (B) Being friendly
    (C) Working extra hours
    (D) Recording information

54. What does the man mean when he says, "It's funny you mention that"?

    (A) The woman's suggestion is already true.
    (B) He thinks the woman's comment is false.
    (C) The woman's idea is strange.
    (D) He refuses to answer the question.

55. According to the man, what will happen in October?

    (A) A report will be distributed.
    (B) A book will become available.
    (C) A company will be established.
    (D) A project will be started.

56. What is the woman unable to do?

    (A) Print some documents
    (B) Locate a file
    (C) Send some work e-mails
    (D) Join the company dinner

57. What did the man do this morning?

    (A) Access a server
    (B) Visit a department
    (C) Fix a computer problem
    (D) File a complaint

58. What does the man say he will do?

    (A) Demonstrate how to sign in
    (B) Submit another form
    (C) Update a service request
    (D) Reset a company password

59. What did the man do in Chicago?

    (A) Sign a new client
    (B) Meet with some customers
    (C) Attend a workshop
    (D) Deliver a sample order

60. What problem does the man mention?

    (A) A client canceled a contract.
    (B) A CEO was too busy to meet.
    (C) A trip was delayed by a week.
    (D) A price was not agreed upon.

61. What does the woman suggest doing next?

    (A) Flying back to Chicago
    (B) Reading an article
    (C) Writing a proposal
    (D) Reviewing a website

Business	Suite
Jane, Baker, and Sons Law	601
Walder Tech Solutions	602
Sedwick International Trade	603
Martin Sound and Recording	604

62. What is the purpose of the woman's visit?

(A) To interview a lawyer
(B) To attend a medical appointment
(C) To purchase a parking pass
(D) To meet with a client

63. What does the man say about parking?

(A) It is free for paying customers.
(B) It is cheaper than most places.
(C) It is only for employees.
(D) It is located on the roof.

64. Look at the graphic. Which office name needs to be updated on the building directory?

(A) Jane, Baker, and Sons Law
(B) Walder Tech Solutions
(C) Sedwick International Trade
(D) Martin Sound and Recording

CONFERENCE ROOM A: WEDNESDAY

TIME	EVENT
10:00 A.M.	Graphic Design Meeting
11:00 A.M.	Conference Call
2:00 P.M.	Meeting with S&V Fashions
3:00 P.M.	Budget Review

65. Where do the speakers work?

(A) At a fashion house
(B) At an advertising firm
(C) At shipping business
(D) At a medical clinic

66. Look at the graphic. According to the man, what event is Jim in charge of?

(A) Graphic Design Meeting
(B) Conference Call
(C) Meeting with S&V Fashions
(D) Budget Review

67. What does the woman say she will do?

(A) Upgrade a room
(B) Locate some files
(C) Postpone a meeting
(D) Ask for a room change

ITEM or SERVICE	Price
Inkspark 306 Printer	$399.00
2-year extended warranty	$69.00
306 color ink cartridge	$32.00
306 black ink cartridge	$15.00
Total:	$515.00

68. Who most likely is the woman?

(A) A hotel receptionist
(B) A sales clerk
(C) A civil servant
(D) An artist

69. What does the man ask about?

(A) Payment plans
(B) Special discounts
(C) Tax rebates
(D) New products

70. Look at the graphic. Which amount will be removed from the bill?

(A) $399
(B) $69
(C) $32
(D) $15

Directions: You will hear some talks given by a single speaker. You will be asked to answer three questions about what the speaker says in each talk. Select the best response to each question and mark the letter (A), (B), (C), or (D) on your answer sheet. The talks will not be printed in your test book and will be spoken only one time.

71. Where does the speaker work?

(A) At a software company
(B) At an electronics manufacturer
(C) At a computer repair store
(D) At a shipping company

72. What does the speaker say he has done?

(A) Ordered a component
(B) Refunded a fee
(C) Replaced a part
(D) Upgraded some software

73. What does the speaker offer?

(A) To lend a computer
(B) To move some information
(C) To extend a service warranty
(D) To pay for a new computer

74. Why did Ms. Renolds visit Star Insurance's website?

(A) To review a product
(B) To fill out a form
(C) To set up a meeting
(D) To upgrade a service

75. What does the speaker offer Ms. Renolds?

(A) A membership card
(B) A full refund
(C) A discount
(D) A new vehicle

76. According to the speaker, what must Ms. Renolds do by June 23rd?

(A) Sign up for a newsletter
(B) Visit Star Insurance in person
(C) Complete a training course
(D) Make a decision

77. Where is the tour most likely taking place?

(A) At an automotive plant
(B) At a car dealership
(C) At a toy outlet
(D) At a mechanic's shop

78. What does the speaker say has changed about the tour?

(A) The number of guides
(B) The outdoor sites
(C) The cost of tickets
(D) The order of locations

79. What does the speaker offer the listeners?

(A) A limited-time discount
(B) A hands-on workshop
(C) A free membership
(D) A map of the facility

80. Why is the mayor visiting the restaurant?

(A) To hold a celebration
(B) To conduct an inspection
(C) To give a speech
(D) To host a birthday party

81. Why does the speaker say, "This shouldn't be any different than usual"?

(A) To stress the importance of a meeting
(B) To reassure employees about an event
(C) To inform of the mayor's special request
(D) To guess the duration of an inspection

82. What must listeners do before the end of the day?

(A) Check an updated schedule
(B) Fill out some information
(C) Purchase some new clothing
(D) Print some new menus

83. What does Renton & Sons produce?

(A) Office furniture
(B) Flooring
(C) Appliances
(D) Windows

84. What does the man imply when he says, "ten thousand units is a bit excessive"?

(A) The customer's order may be wrong.
(B) He will have to hire additional workers.
(C) The customer has canceled her order.
(D) He will deliver some materials late.

85. What does the man explain about his products?

(A) They are easy to clean.
(B) They are cheaper in summer.
(C) They are of high quality.
(D) They are large in size.

86. Where does the speaker most likely work?

(A) At an employment agency
(B) At a computer store
(C) At a university
(D) At a software company

87. What change to the internship program does the speaker mention?

(A) Employees will submit regular reports.
(B) Interns will be paid for their work.
(C) Fewer students will be selected.
(D) The program length will be extended.

88. What is the purpose of the change?

(A) To ensure interns follow all the rules
(B) To make job candidate selection easier
(C) To provide team leaders with incentives
(D) To allow managers to apply for funding

89. According to the speaker, what service will the company begin offering next month?

(A) Discounted products
(B) Free shipping
(C) Cheap memberships
(D) Complimentary samples

90. Why has the company decided to add the new service?

(A) An advertisement failed.
(B) Business has dropped.
(C) Competition has increased.
(D) Some customers complained.

91. What does the speaker say he will do next week?

(A) Conclude an important deal
(B) Test a skincare product
(C) Update an online store
(D) Deliver some products himself

---

92. What type of business is being discussed?

(A) An electronics market
(B) A restaurant chain
(C) A shopping center
(D) A coffee shop

93. Why does the speaker say, "Visitors are already lining up"?

(A) To emphasize interest in an event
(B) To encourage listeners to stay home
(C) To discuss the size of a location
(D) To express concern about crowdedness

94. What will customers receive if they visit the food court?

(A) A free beverage
(B) A 30% refund
(C) A discount coupon
(D) A parking pass

Schedule: *Thursday, March, 2nd*

Time	Event
10:30 A.M.–11:30 A.M.	Conference Call
12:00 P.M.–1:20 P.M.	Lunch Meeting
1:30 P.M.–3:00 P.M.	Staff Meeting
4:00 P.M.–6:00 P.M.	Meeting at ARF Technology

95. What is planned for the next week?

(A) A bigger team will be created.
(B) A new product will be launched.
(C) Some managers will retire.
(D) Some meetings will be canceled.

96. Why does the speaker want to meet?

(A) To visit a client's store
(B) To go over some regulations
(C) To introduce some employees
(D) To explain a new contract

97. Look at the graphic. What time does the speaker want to meet?

(A) At 10:30
(B) At 12:00
(C) At 1:30
(D) At 4:00

Forestview Recreation Park

Forestview Nature Center

Trail 4 →

Visitor Center

Trail 1 →

Cafeteria

Trail 2

Trail 3

98. Who is the talk intended for?

(A) Park employees
(B) Botany students
(C) Construction workers
(D) Visitors at a park

99. Look at the graphic. Which trail is closed to visitors?

(A) Trail 1
(B) Trail 2
(C) Trail 3
(D) Trail 4

100. What project is the park developing?

(A) A bird-watching club
(B) A research foundation
(C) A study on chipmunks
(D) An educational program

This is the end of the Listening test. Turn to Part 5 in your test book.

READING TEST

In the Reading Test, you will read a variety of texts and answer several different types of reading comprehension questions. The entire Reading test will last 75 minutes. There are three parts, and directions are given for each part. You are encouraged to answer as many questions as possible within the time allowed.

You must mark your answers on the separate answer sheet. Do not write your answers in your test book.

PART 5

Directions: A word or phrase is missing in each of the sentences below. Four answer choices are given below each sentence. Select the best answer to complete the sentence. Then mark the letter (A), (B), (C), or (D) on your answer sheet.

101. All employees will receive ------- letters and severance pay upon termination of employment.

(A) recommends
(B) recommendation
(C) recommended
(D) recommending

102. Mr. Stevens picked up some new supplies for the office ------- Stationery and Paper World.

(A) but
(B) as
(C) at
(D) after

103. ------- needs to come and repair the photocopier as soon as possible.

(A) Someone
(B) Us
(C) They
(D) Any

104. The company's new software is designed to update to the most recent version -------.

(A) automate
(B) automatic
(C) automated
(D) automatically

105. The new policies are designed to curb lateness and ------- employee accountability.

(A) promote
(B) declare
(C) obtain
(D) benefit

106. Most employees have cited the positive work ------- as the reason they have remained with the company.

(A) reconstruction
(B) environment
(C) employment
(D) position

107. Martin's Coffee ------- over 300 shops across Canada by next summer.

(A) will have
(B) has
(C) is having
(D) has had

108. This law was passed to protect citizens ------- own and operate small businesses.

(A) for
(B) who
(C) those
(D) as

109. The meeting with our new supplier has been rescheduled for an ------- time on Wednesday.

(A) hardly
(B) comfortably
(C) early
(D) eagerly

110. Haverstock Telephone & Cable has built a ------- as a provider of prompt customer service.

(A) privilege
(B) character
(C) reputation
(D) consequence

111. The employee handbook ------- the proper procedure for handling customer complaints.

(A) outlining
(B) outlines
(C) to outline
(D) is outlined

112. Mr. Randal has decided to install new vending machines in the lounge ------- everyone to use.

(A) if
(B) to
(C) for
(D) until

113. Smith International Trading's department managers ------- conduct employee satisfaction surveys.

(A) lively
(B) harshly
(C) routinely
(D) vastly

114. The consulting firm ------- several procedural changes that would improve the shipping company's efficiency.

(A) proposing
(B) proposed
(C) proposal
(D) proposals

115. The main responsibility of the volunteers is to help visitors ------- their way around the exhibition hall.
(A) do
(B) find
(C) put
(D) ask

116. Please retain this e-mail as ------- that your payment information has been entered into our system.
(A) confirm
(B) confirmed
(C) confirmable
(D) confirmation

117. Ms. Derlago started working at this bank almost a decade ago and has --------- assumed the role of assistant manager.
(A) ever
(B) yet
(C) so
(D) since

118. Mr. Barns is attempting to collect several references ------- for gaining employment at the hospital.
(A) required
(B) requiring
(C) requires
(D) will require

119. The -------- for building within the city limits are all listed on the city's permit website.
(A) probabilities
(B) allowances
(C) regulations
(D) varieties

120. ------- at Austin Tech University is considered the most advanced in the country.
(A) Research
(B) Researchers
(C) Researched
(D) Researches

121. Covington Ice Cream attributes its recent surge in sales to the addition of its newest flavor ------- its advertising campaigns.
(A) as for
(B) even so
(C) rather than
(D) after all

122. The service at Wallace Limos improved ------- after the customer surveys were conducted.
(A) tightly
(B) markedly
(C) manageably
(D) separately

123. These computers are reserved for people searching ------- employment opportunities in downtown London.
(A) for
(B) up
(C) as
(D) to

124. Please ensure that you have written all your information -------, as an error could result in a long delay in the process.
(A) affordably
(B) precisely
(C) unitedly
(D) decisively

125. June Austin's article on THP Power's expansion plans was very unique due to her ------- as a former employee.

(A) detail
(B) prospect
(C) investment
(D) perspective

126. Human resources employees were able to solve the problem among ------- without intervention from the department manager.

(A) themselves
(B) theirs
(C) their
(D) they

127. Mr. Brown is ------- when it comes to international company policies, so we had better ask him.

(A) appropriate
(B) knowledgeable
(C) undeveloped
(D) triumphant

128. Car insurance claims must be made ------- policy owners receive bills for damages.

(A) as well as
(B) as soon as
(C) in regard to
(D) in addition to

129. With such a beautiful beach and huge assortment of art galleries, Adelaine Town is quite a ------- tourist spot.

(A) offering
(B) proposing
(C) promising
(D) identifying

130. The marketing department arranged to have weekly meetings to ensure a ------ effort is made on the new project.

(A) mundane
(B) transitional
(C) reduced
(D) concentrated

Directions: Read the texts that follow. A word, phrase, or sentence is missing in parts of each text. Four answer choices for each question are given below the text. Select the best answer to complete the text. Then mark the letter (A), (B), (C), or (D) on your answer sheet.

Questions 131-134 refer to the following information.

Extended Vacations

Employees who have been with Star Packaging for at least two years may be ___131.___ to receive an additional five days of summer vacation. ___132.___. Department managers will be responsible for reviewing the applications and those ___133.___ who qualify will have their names entered into a lottery system. Those who have been at the company for five years or longer will be given ___134.___, and up to fifteen names will be drawn from the lottery.

131. (A) prominent
(B) cooperative
(C) exclusive
(D) eligible

132. (A) Employees can fill out an application and return it to their manager.
(B) For example, all long-term employees will receive additional benefits packages.
(C) However, competitive salary raises will be given to a few deserving employees.
(D) Management is pleased to announce that new employees have been hired.

133. (A) candidates
(B) awardees
(C) suppliers
(D) occupants

134. (A) prefer
(B) preferred
(C) preference
(D) preferential

Questions 135-138 refer to the following notice.

Channel 8 News Turns 60!

On March 15, Channel 8 News, the city's number one news source, celebrates its sixtieth anniversary. That's six decades of studio and live ___135.___. For well over half a century, we at Channel 8 News ___136.___ our viewers breaking news coverage, insightful commentaries, and wonderful human-interest stories from across the city and region. We would like to invite you, our loyal viewers, to our celebration. On March 15, we will hold an open house from 4:30 P.M. to 6:00 P.M. at our studio on Kingsley Street. Take part in a studio tour and see first-hand what goes on behind the scenes and watch a demonstration of our state-of-the-art broadcasting equipment. ___137.___. There is no charge to attend this event, but you do have to register. We hope to see you all at this ___138.___ occasion.

---

135. (A) concerts
(B) discussions
(C) programming
(D) teaching

136. (A) offers
(B) offering
(C) will offer
(D) have offered

137. (A) The station will remain a vital part of this city for years to come.
(B) You will even have the chance to meet and talk with our news anchors.
(C) This celebration will be the third one to take place in March.
(D) Channel 8 News will be acquired by a national news network in a few months.

138. (A) special
(B) specialize
(C) especially
(D) specialization

Questions 139-142 refer to the following information.

This is just a reminder that residents of Archer Court are required to obtain a permit for any exterior home-improvement projects. Interior changes do not currently need a permit. ___139.___, all external jobs, large and small, must be authorized in advance.

In the past, some residents have assumed that their contractors are responsible for arranging permits. ___140.___. In truth, property owners must obtain the necessary permits themselves. Building inspectors may visit a site at any time, and if the property owner does not have a permit, fines may be issued.

___141.___ permit laws is an important responsibility of building inspectors. The permit process ensures that all necessary safety standards ___142.___, which in turn protects the community from property damages and dangerous hazards.

To view a list of permits that might apply to your project, please visit renviewtown.com/permits.

139. (A) Namely
(B) Similarly
(C) Therefore
(D) However

140. (A) Contractors may charge extra for overtime.
(B) This commonly held belief is actually false.
(C) Most building inspectors also work as contractors.
(D) The cost of the project may increase seasonally.

141. (A) Questioning
(B) Eliminating
(C) Enforcing
(D) Reviewing

142. (A) are met
(B) to meet
(C) meeting
(D) have met

Questions 143-146 refer to the following webpage.

Star Credit Purchase Points

Star Credit would like to offer its credit card holders the ___[143]___ points program in the world. ___[144]___. Members can even double their points by shopping at any of the two hundred specially ___[145]___ stores. Points can be redeemed in exchange for gift cards at any of those two hundred stores. ___[146]___, points can be used on www.travelone.com to book flights and hotel rooms, and rent cars. To apply for Star Credit's points program, simply fill out the following form and click submit.

---

143. (A) comprehension
(B) most comprehensive
(C) comprehensive
(D) most comprehensively

144. (A) With every purchase you make with your Star Credit Card, you can earn up to 100 points.
(B) Points can only be used to lower your monthly interest rates on all credit card purchases.
(C) Program members must not have applied for a Star Credit Card in the past.
(D) Furthermore, program members can receive in-store discounts on all their purchases.

145. (A) select
(B) selects
(C) selected
(D) selection

146. (A) Therefore
(B) Regardless
(C) In addition
(D) For instance

PART 7

Directions: In this part you will read a selection of texts, such as magazine and newspaper articles, e-mails, and instant messages. Each text or set of texts is followed by several questions. Select the best answer for each question and mark the letter (A), (B), (C), or (D) on your answer sheet.

Questions 147-148 refer to the following website.

http://www.premiuminsurance.com

Home	Policies	My Account	Sign Out

Welcome back, Tom Schwarz! Now, you can easily access all your policy information with Premium Insurance's new website. Please take a moment to familiarize yourself with our website's features.

- Additional payment methods and online receipts of all payments
- Easy access to all your policy information in one place
- Upgraded security and timed log-outs to protect your sensitive information
- New customer service tools, such as an updated FAQ and a live chat function
- Simple online forms to update address and telephone information

147. Who most likely is Mr. Schwarz?

(A) An insurance salesman
(B) An insurance customer
(C) A web designer
(D) An insurance claims representative

148. What is NOT mentioned as a feature of the new website?

(A) Group insurance applications
(B) New customer service tools
(C) Consolidated information
(D) Improved Internet security

Questions 149-151 refer to the following information.

Affluence Pharmaceuticals

Manuel Rodriguez
Lead Researcher

A highly sought-after leader in today's pharmaceutical industry, Mr. Rodriquez had overseen all major research projects at Affluence Pharmaceuticals for the last five years. Mr. Rodriguez joined Affluence seven years ago and was quickly recognized for his great talent and vision. He was promoted to lead researcher and has since drastically improved employee productivity by more than 20%.

Mr. Rodriguez has been invited to speak at numerous conferences and was even honored at last year's Pharma Vision Conference as the keynote speaker. He also works as a consultant for Techtron University's medical department where he has contributed to numerous academic projects. Prior to joining Affluence, Mr. Rodriguez immigrated from Mexico and attended Stratford University where he graduated with honors.

---

149. What is the purpose of the information?

(A) To outline a university program
(B) To announce an employee promotion
(C) To introduce a company employee
(D) To celebrate an employee's retirement

150. What is NOT indicated about Mr. Rodriguez?

(A) He is employed as a university professor.
(B) He previously lived in Mexico.
(C) He has improved employee performance.
(D) He is an experienced public speaker.

151. What is suggested about Mr. Rodriguez's career?

(A) He often receives awards for his great work ethic.
(B) He completed two degrees before he applied for a job.
(C) He worked as an intern prior to being hired as lead researcher.
(D) He was not hired as lead researcher at first.

March 7 — the local mayor's office has just released the details of the Budding Futures Internship Program for Park County students. Led by the program director, Milly Andrews, the program is designed to give senior high school students a taste of what it's like working in a public office. --[1]--.

Mayor Steven Greenhorn announced the internship program last year. "I think it's important to include teenagers in public affairs," he said in an interview. "It may help them decide what course of study they want to pursue in college." --[2]--.

According to the newly released details, Milly Andrews will select fifteen students from fifteen schools across the county. Based on their areas of interest, the chosen students will be assigned various jobs in the mayor's downtown office. --[3]--. The program will last eight weeks during the summer.

Applications for the program will be available on the mayor's website at the beginning of next week. --[4]--. The selected interns will be announced in early May.

152. What is suggested about the Budding Futures Internship Program?

(A) It is available nationwide.
(B) It is a brand new program.
(C) It is for university students.
(D) It is led by Steven Greenhorn.

153. According to Mr. Greenhorn, what is the main goal of the internship program?

(A) Teaching students about elections
(B) Establishing a community of volunteers
(C) Providing students with well-paying jobs
(D) Guiding students in their future education

154. In which of the positions marked [1], [2], [3], and [4] does the following sentence best belong?

"Students are encouraged to collect at least one reference in advance."

(A) [1]
(B) [2]
(C) [3]
(D) [4]

Questions 155-156 refer to the following webpage.

ASPIRE UNLIMITED

As a client of our firm, you
- have access to around-the-clock surveillance
- pay a reasonable monthly fee with no additional costs
- can improve your office's security needs

We provide
- custom installations of CCTV equipment
- regular maintenance of all cameras and alarm systems
- 24-hour remote monitoring of your office
- fingerprint scanning technology for all entrances (additional charges will apply)
- access to Aspire's website for all your billing needs

---

155. What is one of the services offered by Aspire Unlimited?

(A) Office cleaning
(B) CCTV monitoring
(C) Website development
(D) Heating system maintenance

156. What is mentioned about fingerprint scanning technology?

(A) It is purchased on a weekly basis.
(B) It is one of Aspire's unique services.
(C) It can be purchased for an extra fee.
(D) It can be added to an account by phone.

Questions 157-158 refer to the following article.

ROUGE TOWNSHIP. March 3 — Rouge Township officials have recently announced a new development proposal for an amusement park that will be located on Rouge Lake's 4000-acre waterfront.

The new amusement park is expected to include numerous rollercoasters, an extensive aquarium, a waterpark, and a pavilion for live music. Several local businesses, such as Rotary Automobiles, Pancake House Restaurants, and Maverick Beverages have agreed to sponsor the park's development.

Following the release of the development proposal, several local activists have expressed concerns about effect the park will have on the waterfront's delicate ecosystem. "We can assure you that all precautions will be taken," Lead Developer, Jan Freedman, said in an interview yesterday. "The park will be located far enough away from the beach and the bike trails that it will have little effect on the surrounding wildlife."

Other Rouge Township residents have expressed excitement about the potential increase in business the new park will bring to the Rouge Lake area.

157. What is suggested about Rouge Township?
(A) It currently has a large tourism industry.
(B) It is home to a famous water park.
(C) Some of its residents disagree with the proposal.
(D) Much of the local wildlife is endangered.

158. What feature of the amusement park is NOT mentioned?
(A) Its large on-site aquarium
(B) Its location at the waterfront
(C) A place for live performances
(D) The gift shops and kiosks

Questions 159-161 refer to the following information.

Maintenance Services

The maintenance department of Fairsview Condos is available to make routine repairs to your condo and all shared spaces, most of which are available at no charge to residents. The following services are free of charge and must be booked two weeks in advance.

● Bathroom fixtures, such as showerheads, faucets, and toilet parts may be replaced once every two years. Free repairs of any broken components can be arranged once per year.
● Doors and windows, including window screens, will be repaired as needed at any time of the year.
● Fan filters above stoves and smoke detectors can be replaced every six months. Air conditioners are allotted one free cleaning service per year.
● For a full list of services, please visit our website. Reservations can be made by filling out a request form at www.fairsviewcondos.com/maintenance.

159. For whom is the information most likely intended?

(A) Real estate agents
(B) Employees at a building management company
(C) Landlords of a retirement home
(D) Residents at a complex

160. How often can bathroom fixtures be repaired at no cost?

(A) Once a month
(B) Every six months
(C) Once a year
(D) At any time

161. According to the information, how can readers arrange to have something repaired?

(A) By filling out an online form
(B) By calling a department
(C) By speaking to a landlord
(D) By signing up on a sheet

Ron Parks [8:03]:

Jim, can I get your input on the changes Jennifer asked me to make to tomorrow's presentation?

Jim Webber [8:05]:

Sure. What do you need?

Ron Parks [8:07]:

Can I e-mail you the new proposal? I've highlighted the changes in red, but I'm not sure if these reflect our full range of advertising services.

Jim Webber [8:08]:

I'm afraid not. I'm just about to meet a client for dinner. How about I stop by your hotel room after?

Ron Parks [8:09]:

That would be OK. Then I can show you the PowerPoint presentation I've made as well.

Jim Webber [8:10]:

OK, great. What room are you in?

Ron Parks [8:10]:

Room 506. See you then!

162. Who most likely is Mr. Parks?

(A) An advertiser
(B) A hotel receptionist
(C) An art collector
(D) An IT specialist

163. At 8:08, what does Mr. Webber most likely mean when he writes, "I'm afraid not"?

(A) He is worried about a presentation.
(B) He dosen't have time to review a document.
(C) He does not agree with some changes.
(D) He did not request the changes to be made.

Questions 164-167 refer to the following e-mail.

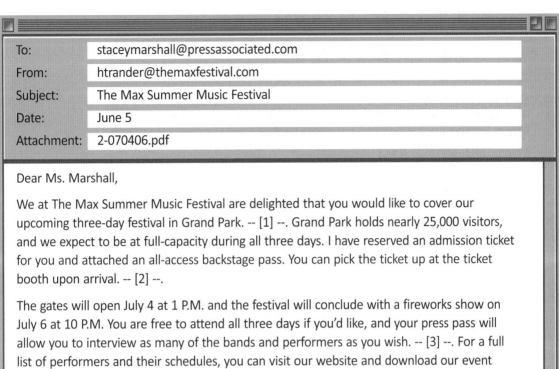

To: staceymarshall@pressassociated.com

From: htrander@themaxfestival.com

Subject: The Max Summer Music Festival

Date: June 5

Attachment: 2-070406.pdf

Dear Ms. Marshall,

We at The Max Summer Music Festival are delighted that you would like to cover our upcoming three-day festival in Grand Park. -- [1] --. Grand Park holds nearly 25,000 visitors, and we expect to be at full-capacity during all three days. I have reserved an admission ticket for you and attached an all-access backstage pass. You can pick the ticket up at the ticket booth upon arrival. -- [2] --.

The gates will open July 4 at 1 P.M. and the festival will conclude with a fireworks show on July 6 at 10 P.M. You are free to attend all three days if you'd like, and your press pass will allow you to interview as many of the bands and performers as you wish. -- [3] --. For a full list of performers and their schedules, you can visit our website and download our event calendar. Lastly, should you need anything at all during your visit, you can contact Molly at press services at 776-3333-6713. -- [4] --. Thank you, and I hope you enjoy The Max Summer Music Festival.

Sincerely,

Harry Trander
Festival Press Coordinator

164. Who most likely is Ms. Marshall?

(A) A customer
(B) A journalist
(C) A band manager
(D) A performer

165. What was sent with the e-mail?

(A) An admission ticket
(B) A parking voucher
(C) A schedule of performances
(D) A backstage press pass

166. According to the e-mail, what is a notable feature of the festival?

(A) It may accommodate more than 25,000 people.
(B) It will include jazz dance performances.
(C) It will end with a special fireworks display.
(D) It may include free camping services.

167. In which of the positions marked [1], [2], [3], and [4] does the following sentence best belong?

"It is our first festival and we have many bands lined up."

(A) [1]
(B) [2]
(C) [3]
(D) [4]

Questions 168-171 refer to the following online chat discussion.

Jessica Simon [10:32 A.M.]
Marcus, do you have a minute? I'm trying to access our online store, but it's not loading. Does it load on your computer?

Marcus Adams [10:40 A.M.]
It's the same for me. Was it like this yesterday?

Jessica Simon [10:42 A.M.]
I don't think so. I have some orders that were placed online yesterday. But I got an e-mail from a repeat customer who said our site was down. Can you ask the IT department about it?

Jeff Peters has been added to the chat.

Marcus Adams [10:44 A.M.]
Jeff, something is wrong with our online store. It doesn't seem to be loading. Can you figure out what's wrong?

Jeff Peters [10:48 A.M.]
This is strange. It looks like the hosting site is down.

Marcus Adams [10:50 A.M.]
Do you have their telephone number?

Jeff Peters [10:55 A.M.]
Yes, I just called them. They said they are having some technical difficulties, which should be fixed by tomorrow morning.

Jessica Simon [11:00 A.M.]
OK, I have a meeting with the sales manager shortly. I'll let him know about this problem.

---

168. What problem does Ms. Simon report?
(A) Sales cannot be made online currently.
(B) The online store includes wrong information.
(C) A customer wants to return some items.
(D) A product is no longer listed on the website.

169. From whom did Ms. Simon learn about the problem?
(A) A department head
(B) A customer
(C) An IT manager
(D) An assistant

170. At 10:50, what does Mr. Adams most likely mean when he writes, "Do you have their telephone number"?
(A) He is requesting some information.
(B) He wants Mr. Peters to call a company.
(C) He would like a directory updated.
(D) He is worried he will get lost.

171. What will Ms. Simon most likely do next?
(A) Call some customers
(B) Purchase items online
(C) Attend a meeting
(D) Contact a hosting site

Questions 172-175 refer to the following article.

Employment Weekly Column
Job Fairs

Job fairs are a quick and easy way to hire new employees. However, holding a job fair may be a costly event, especially if you're only hiring a few employees. Consider the following advice to determine if holding a job fair is right for your company.

How many employees are you hiring?

If your company is planning to hire a large group of employees, a job fair might be right for you. Job fairs can bring in a large number of applicants. However, if you're only interested in finding a few new workers, the number of applicants at a job fair may overwhelm human resources departments, making the hiring process even harder.

Is there a good location to hold the job fair?

High schools and universities are popular places to hold job fairs, but if your company is seeking more experienced candidates, schools are probably not the right place. It is critical to hold the job fair in a place where you can attract suitable employees, such as business conventions. Unfortunately, business conventions are only held at certain times of the year.

Can you hire employees another way?

Online job advertisement websites have changed the way people search for jobs. Prior to your company's hiring season, human resources staff members may be able to post job openings on numerous websites. This would garner a lot of attention and allow your company to list the experience requirements applicants must meet.

Is the cost worth it?

Before holding a job fair, consider the cost of the event. You may need to pay to rent a suitable space and would need to provide refreshments and application packages. If your hiring needs could be met by free online websites, a job fair may not be worth it.

---

172. What is the article about?

(A) Tips for increasing a worker's productivity

(B) Websites used to hire employees

(C) Methods of increasing the chances of being hired

(D) Strategies for efficient and economical recruitment

173. According to the article, what is a good reason to hold a job fair?

(A) To hire specialized workers

(B) To fill a large number of positions

(C) To provide employees with experience

(D) To promote the brand of a company

174. The word "critical" in paragraph 3, line 2, is closest in meaning to

(A) urgent

(B) essential

(C) creative

(D) negative

175. What is mentioned as an alternative way of finding job candidates?

(A) Advertising in local newspapers

(B) Using employment websites

(C) Holding job fairs at the office

(D) Sending out mass e-mails

Publisher Instructs the Next Generation

January 10 — Since his retirement last year, publisher and editor Jim Frank has run the Department of Publishing Studies at Western University. Frank is best known for his role at Maxwell Publishing House where he worked as a senior editor on numerous projects, including the publication of several successful series.

Jim Frank joined Western University as both a department head and a professor. He developed new courses such as E-publishing, Writing for the Web, and International Rights Management. Students who wish to work in the publishing industry as editors, book designers, or literary agents have benefited greatly from his wisdom.

As a result of Frank's hard work, Western University has also founded its first ever publishing internship. Students have been matched with editors, designers, and agents during three-week programs. Additionally, Frank has organized numerous events in which industry professionals have given presentations at the university on various topics. Because of Frank's innovation and connections, the publishing program at Western University has become one of the best in the country.

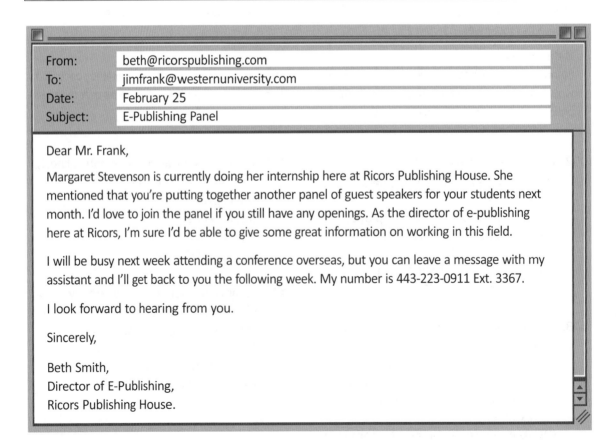

From:	beth@ricorspublishing.com
To:	jimfrank@westernuniversity.com
Date:	February 25
Subject:	E-Publishing Panel

Dear Mr. Frank,

Margaret Stevenson is currently doing her internship here at Ricors Publishing House. She mentioned that you're putting together another panel of guest speakers for your students next month. I'd love to join the panel if you still have any openings. As the director of e-publishing here at Ricors, I'm sure I'd be able to give some great information on working in this field.

I will be busy next week attending a conference overseas, but you can leave a message with my assistant and I'll get back to you the following week. My number is 443-223-0911 Ext. 3367.

I look forward to hearing from you.

Sincerely,

Beth Smith,
Director of E-Publishing,
Ricors Publishing House.

ACTUAL TEST 01

176. What does the article mainly discuss?

(A) A company's business practices
(B) An editor's career change
(C) A publisher's new series
(D) A student internship program

177. What is one contribution Jim Frank has made to the university?

(A) More courses have become available to students.
(B) A student employment website has been developed.
(C) A scholarship foundation has been established.
(D) A computer lab has recently opened.

178. Why did Ms. Smith send the e-mail?

(A) She is replying to a phone message.
(B) She would like to join a speaking event.
(C) She is looking for more interns.
(D) She wants to register in a course.

179. Who most likely is Ms. Stevenson?

(A) A director at Ricors Publishing House
(B) A student at Western University
(C) A guest speaker in a publishing course
(D) A former editor at Maxwell Publishing House

180. What does Ms. Smith say about her schedule?

(A) She can reschedule her meetings.
(B) She is not available for the panel in March.
(C) She can be reached only during the day.
(D) She will be away on business next week.

Questions 181-185 refer to the following memo and e-mail.

MEMO
Free Cloud Services

As you know, Roth Computer Sales has recently partnered with L&B Tech to improve our company's efficiency and file storage. In order to make saving and sharing files easier, we plan to install L&B's Cloud Software program on all our systems.

L&B's Cloud Software allows employees to store files of any size without taking up too much computer memory. Employees can easily send large files in seconds without worrying about slow upload speeds. Additionally, employees who bring their company laptops on business trips will be able to access their files remotely. Furthermore, L&B Cloud Software is extremely secure, so employees can rest assured that any sensitive files will be safe.

To use this new software, simply complete the setup, register with your company e-mail, and start storing and sending files. The service will be available on April 10 at 9 A.M. If you have any questions or concerns about setting up or using the new software, please contact Michael Brown in the IT Department at extension 3342 or by e-mail at michaelbrown@ rothcomputers.com.

To:	michaelbrown@rothcomputers.com
From:	sandrabell@rothcomputers.com
Date:	April 12
Subject:	Cloud Software

Dear Mr. Brown,

I tried calling you at your extension, but you did not answer. I'm writing to request assistance with the new L&B Cloud Software. I set up my account on the first day the service was available, but today I was unable to find any of the files in my account. It seems that all of the files I uploaded have been deleted, as my account is empty. Since these files include very important sales figures from last quarter, I really need to access them immediately. Can you give me an idea about how to recover these files? It would be great if you could stop by my office sometime today.

Sandra Bell

181. What is the purpose of the memo?

    (A) To announce a change in a policy

    (B) To remind employees to back up computers

    (C) To give information about a new program

    (D) To explain a new set of rules

182. In the memo, the word "sensitive" in paragraph 2, line 5, is closest in meaning to

    (A) cautious

    (B) responsive

    (C) surprising

    (D) confidential

183. What is stated as a benefit of L&B Cloud Software?

    (A) It reduces cost.

    (B) It saves a company time.

    (C) It is free to install.

    (D) It scans documents for mistakes.

184. What problem is Ms. Bell having?

    (A) She has forgotten her password.

    (B) Her computer has crashed.

    (C) All files have gone missing.

    (D) She cannot access a server.

185. When did Ms. Bell set up her account?

    (A) On April 10

    (B) On April 11

    (C) On April 12

    (D) On April 13

GO ON TO THE NEXT PAGE

Questions 186-190 refer to the following e-mails and form.

From: oemerson@sommerfield.com
To: mfernandez@rkdistribution.br
Subject: demonstration
Date: August 5

Dear Ms. Fernandez,

My plane landed in Sao Paulo and I am e-mailing you from a waiting room in the airport. Unfortunately, the large suitcase that I had checked has been misplaced. Even though I have printed summaries of all the items right here in my carry-on bag, the sample products for the demonstration are in the missing luggage. Airport staff informed me that they need at least three days to locate the bags and deliver them to where I am staying. That means, of course, that I will not have them in time for the demonstration scheduled for the day after tomorrow.

Once I reach my hotel, I will fax the summaries to your company. If it is not too much trouble, could we possibly postpone the demonstration for another two days? Please contact me about this as soon as possible.

Sincerely,

Oscar Emerson

Missing Baggage Claim Form

We would like to extend our deepest apologies for our mishandling of your belongings and any inconveniences it caused. The information you provide below will assist us greatly. Please provide a clear description of every piece of luggage as well as a list of the items inside each piece. This will definitely help expedite the entire process.

Claim No.:	341567S/3
Name of Passenger:	Oscar Emerson
E-mail:	oemerson@sommerfield.com

Permanent address:

409 Jackson Lane
Cleveland, OH, 44103
United States of America

Temporary address (Until August 12):

Piquiri Hotel
Av. Paulista 1209
Sao Paulo, Brazil
01310-060

Flight No.	Date	From	To
MTC971	August 3	Toledo	Buenos Aires
BTA302	August 5	Buenos Aires	Sao Paulo

| Suitcase Type: Large leather bag, zipper, shoulder strap | Manufacturer: Riggs | Color: Brown |

Contents (Please be as specific as possible):

Description	Number
Running shoes, tennis shoes, golf shoes, baseball shoes, high-top basketball sneakers	12 pairs
Top Guy brand Man's suits	2
Greyvalley brand digital camera with battery charger	1
Trousers, shorts, socks, etc.	6
South American pocket-sized travel guides	2

From:	airportlostfoundoffice@spinternat.com
To:	oemerson@sommerfield.com
Subject:	claim 341567S/3
Date:	August 6

Dear Mr. Emerson,

We are delighted to inform you that your missing suitcase has been located with all the items you listed. It will arrive at the temporary address you provided between 1:00 P.M. and 3:00 P.M. on August 7.

We truly appreciate your patience and understanding.

Regards,

Sao Paulo International Airport Lost and Found

186. What does Mr. Emerson indicate about the product summaries?

(A) They will be sent by fax.
(B) They are not ready yet.
(C) They are longer than expected.
(D) They need to be printed out.

187. What does Mr. Emerson ask Ms. Fernandez to do?

(A) Deliver product samples
(B) Submit an order form
(C) Reschedule a meeting
(D) Drive him to the hotel

188. What does Mr. Emerson want to demonstrate?

(A) Bicycle tires
(B) Athletic shoes
(C) Image software
(D) Coffee makers

189. In the form, the word "expedite" in paragraph 1, line 4, is closest in meaning to

(A) discover
(B) modify
(C) elaborate
(D) accelerate

190. Where will the delivery be sent?

(A) To Cleveland
(B) To Toledo
(C) To Sao Paulo
(D) To Buenos Aires

GO ON TO THE NEXT PAGE

Questions 191-195 refer to the following e-mail, webpage, and article.

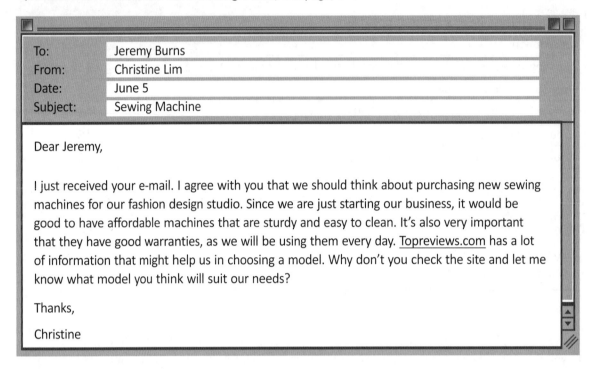

To:	Jeremy Burns
From:	Christine Lim
Date:	June 5
Subject:	Sewing Machine

Dear Jeremy,

I just received your e-mail. I agree with you that we should think about purchasing new sewing machines for our fashion design studio. Since we are just starting our business, it would be good to have affordable machines that are sturdy and easy to clean. It's also very important that they have good warranties, as we will be using them every day. Topreviews.com has a lot of information that might help us in choosing a model. Why don't you check the site and let me know what model you think will suit our needs?

Thanks,

Christine

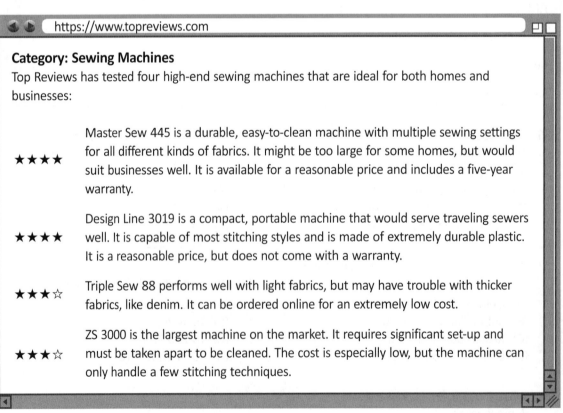

https://www.topreviews.com

Category: Sewing Machines

Top Reviews has tested four high-end sewing machines that are ideal for both homes and businesses:

★★★★ Master Sew 445 is a durable, easy-to-clean machine with multiple sewing settings for all different kinds of fabrics. It might be too large for some homes, but would suit businesses well. It is available for a reasonable price and includes a five-year warranty.

★★★★ Design Line 3019 is a compact, portable machine that would serve traveling sewers well. It is capable of most stitching styles and is made of extremely durable plastic. It is a reasonable price, but does not come with a warranty.

★★★☆ Triple Sew 88 performs well with light fabrics, but may have trouble with thicker fabrics, like denim. It can be ordered online for an extremely low cost.

★★★☆ ZS 3000 is the largest machine on the market. It requires significant set-up and must be taken apart to be cleaned. The cost is especially low, but the machine can only handle a few stitching techniques.

Fashion in Park Falls
By Zander Cornelli

December 20—Residents of Park Falls who monitor the latest trends in fashion were excited about attending the upscale fashion event held in the Park Falls Convention Center last week. Numerous companies that have made Park Falls the home of their growing businesses participated in the 10th Park Falls Fashion Festival. Over twenty fashion studios were showcased in the event, several of which are owned by local residents.

Rose Designs, which has been in the area for over twenty years, kicked off the festival with some incredible winter apparel. The show was followed by a presentation by Kim Miller, the owner of Accessories Forever. In-Style Fashions and Turnbull Jeans, which have been in business for six months and three years respectively, were newcomers to the festival. All items featured during the fashion shows are available for sale on company websites.

191. What is indicated about the ZS 3000?

(A) It is commonly used in homes.
(B) It has an extended warranty.
(C) It can be transported easily.
(D) It has limited functions.

192. What do all the machines mentioned on the webpage have in common?

(A) They are compact and portable.
(B) They are affordable prices.
(C) They come in various colors.
(D) They can be repaired easily.

193. What sewing machine did Mr. Burns most likely recommend to Ms. Lim?

(A) Master Sew 445
(B) Design Line 3019
(C) Triple Sew 88
(D) ZS 3000

194. In the article, in paragraph 1, line 1, the word "monitor" is closest in meaning to

(A) believe in
(B) observe
(C) supervise
(D depend on

195. What company mentioned in the article do Ms. Lim and Mr. Burns most likely work for?

(A) Rose Designs
(B) Accessories Forever
(C) In-Style Fashions
(D) Turnbull Jeans

Questions **196-200** refer to the following webpage, online order form, and e-mail.

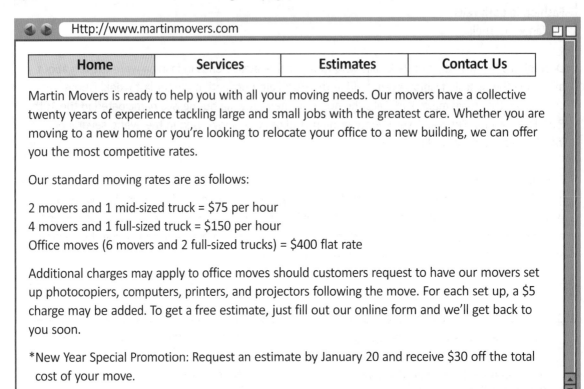

Http://www.martinmovers.com

| Home | Services | Estimates | Contact Us |

Martin Movers is ready to help you with all your moving needs. Our movers have a collective twenty years of experience tackling large and small jobs with the greatest care. Whether you are moving to a new home or you're looking to relocate your office to a new building, we can offer you the most competitive rates.

Our standard moving rates are as follows:

2 movers and 1 mid-sized truck = $75 per hour
4 movers and 1 full-sized truck = $150 per hour
Office moves (6 movers and 2 full-sized trucks) = $400 flat rate

Additional charges may apply to office moves should customers request to have our movers set up photocopiers, computers, printers, and projectors following the move. For each set up, a $5 charge may be added. To get a free estimate, just fill out our online form and we'll get back to you soon.

*New Year Special Promotion: Request an estimate by January 20 and receive $30 off the total cost of your move.

Martin Movers
Estimate Request Form

Date	January 10
Name	Connor Goldsmith
E-mail address	connor@goldsmithlegal.com
Telephone	409-333-2314
Moving from: Moving to:	54 First Avenue, New York City 889 Fallsview Lane, New York City
Moving date	February 23
Items to be moved	8 desks, 8 computers, 3 printers, 1 photocopier, 1 refrigerator, 1 conference table, 25 office chairs
Additional comments	My law office is moving to a new location. As we have our own IT employee, we will not require anyone to set up our equipment. Thus, I believe your standard flat rate will apply. Please contact me by e-mail to confirm the price and finalize the reservation.

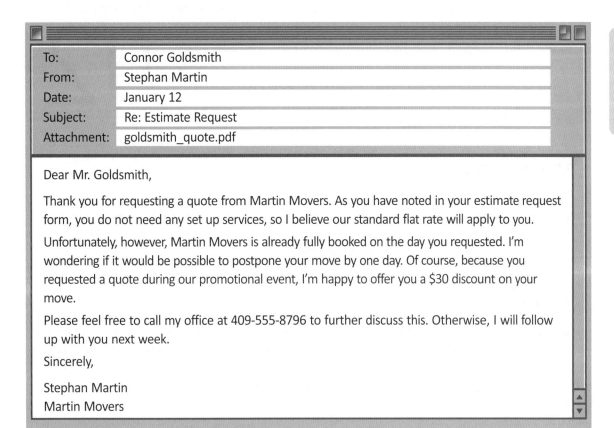

To:	Connor Goldsmith
From:	Stephan Martin
Date:	January 12
Subject:	Re: Estimate Request
Attachment:	goldsmith_quote.pdf

Dear Mr. Goldsmith,

Thank you for requesting a quote from Martin Movers. As you have noted in your estimate request form, you do not need any set up services, so I believe our standard flat rate will apply to you.

Unfortunately, however, Martin Movers is already fully booked on the day you requested. I'm wondering if it would be possible to postpone your move by one day. Of course, because you requested a quote during our promotional event, I'm happy to offer you a $30 discount on your move.

Please feel free to call my office at 409-555-8796 to further discuss this. Otherwise, I will follow up with you next week.

Sincerely,

Stephan Martin
Martin Movers

196. In the webpage, the word "tackling" in paragraph 1, line 2, is closest in meaning to

(A) repairing
(B) handling
(C) considering
(D) entertaining

197. What is NOT mentioned about office moves?

(A) Six movers will be involved.
(B) More than one truck will be used.
(C) Estimates will be provided at no cost.
(D) It must be booked at least two weeks in advance.

198. What does Mr. Goldsmith mention about his company?

(A) It will discard several items.
(B) It will downsize its office space.
(C) It requires an additional mover.
(D) It employs an IT specialist.

199. If Mr. Goldsmith uses Martin Movers, how much will he be charged for his move?

(A) $75
(B) $150
(C) $370
(D) $400

200. What is suggested about Martin Movers?

(A) It is booked solid on February 23.
(B) It is located in New York City.
(C) It has five trucks in its fleet.
(D) It charges extra for work done on weekends.

Stop! This is the end of the test. If you finish before time is called, you may go back to Parts 5, 6, and 7 and check your work.

LISTENING TEST

In the Listening test, you will be asked to demonstrate how well you understand spoken English. The entire Listening test will last approximately 45 minutes. There are four parts, and directions are given for each part. You must mark your answers on the separate answer sheet. Do not write your answers in your test book.

PART 1

Directions: For each question in this part, you will hear four statements about a picture in your test book. When you hear the statements, you must select the one statement that best describes what you see in the picture. Then find the number of the question on your answer sheet and mark your answer. The statements will not be printed in your test book and will be spoken only one time.

Example

Sample Answer

Ⓐ Ⓑ ● Ⓓ

Statement (C), "A woman is admiring some artwork.," is the best description of the picture, so you should select answer (C) and mark it on your answer sheet.

1.

2.

3.

4.

5.

6.

Directions: You will hear a question or statement and three responses spoken in English. They will not be printed in your test book and will be spoken only one time. Select the best response to the question or statement and mark the letter (A), (B), or (C) on your answer sheet.

7. Mark your answer on your answer sheet.

8. Mark your answer on your answer sheet.

9. Mark your answer on your answer sheet.

10. Mark your answer on your answer sheet.

11. Mark your answer on your answer sheet.

12. Mark your answer on your answer sheet.

13. Mark your answer on your answer sheet.

14. Mark your answer on your answer sheet.

15. Mark your answer on your answer sheet.

16. Mark your answer on your answer sheet.

17. Mark your answer on your answer sheet.

18. Mark your answer on your answer sheet.

19. Mark your answer on your answer sheet.

20. Mark your answer on your answer sheet.

21. Mark your answer on your answer sheet.

22. Mark your answer on your answer sheet.

23. Mark your answer on your answer sheet.

24. Mark your answer on your answer sheet.

25. Mark your answer on your answer sheet.

26. Mark your answer on your answer sheet.

27. Mark your answer on your answer sheet.

28. Mark your answer on your answer sheet.

29. Mark your answer on your answer sheet.

30. Mark your answer on your answer sheet.

31. Mark your answer on your answer sheet.

PART 3 (07)

Directions: You will hear some conversations between two or more people. You will be asked to answer three questions about what the speakers say in each conversation. Select the best response to each question and mark the letter (A), (B), (C), or (D) on your answer sheet. The conversations will not be printed in your test book and will be spoken only one time.

32. What are the speakers discussing?

(A) A suitcase
(B) A printer
(C) A monitor
(D) A tablet computer

33. What does the man ask about?

(A) The total cost
(B) The available sizes
(C) The warranty options
(D) The free accessories

34. What will the woman most likely do next?

(A) Request payment
(B) Consult a manager
(C) Register an ID
(D) Return an item

35. Why did the man call the woman?

(A) To inform of a change of plans
(B) To offer to call a car service
(C) To explain an event schedule
(D) To reschedule an appointment

36. What does the man suggest?

(A) Canceling an event
(B) Using public transit
(C) Asking a coworker for help
(D) Borrowing a neighbor's car

37. What does the woman say she will do?

(A) Change a reservation
(B) Contact a colleague
(C) Call a tow truck
(D) Pick up a coworker

38. What are the speakers discussing?

    (A) A new office location
    (B) A store's hours
    (C) A package delivery
    (D) A change of schedule

39. Why is the man's company behind the schedule?

    (A) A new store was opened.
    (B) Some items were lost.
    (C) A few workers were sick.
    (D) Some roads were congested.

40. What does the woman say she will do next?

    (A) Go to a supermarket
    (B) Wait for an item at home
    (C) Cancel a purchase
    (D) Visit another post office

---

41. What type of services does the man's company offer?

    (A) Vehicle upgrades
    (B) Home renovations
    (C) Window cleaning
    (D) Appliance installations

42. Why is the man calling?

    (A) To return a phone call
    (B) To offer a free service
    (C) To discuss a payment plan
    (D) To advertise a promotion

43. What does the man offer to do for the woman?

    (A) Provide a bigger discount
    (B) Mail some carpet samples
    (C) Send an employee
    (D) Replace some old items

---

44. Where does the woman work?

    (A) At a doctor's office
    (B) At an insurance company
    (C) At a sales office
    (D) At a dental clinic

45. What information does the man ask for?

    (A) A list of services
    (B) A doctor's schedule
    (C) The location of a clinic
    (D) The price of a service

46. What does the man imply when he says, "I have a business meeting that day"?

    (A) He needs another appointment.
    (B) He will wear a formal suit.
    (C) He will visit another location.
    (D) He doesn't mind traveling far.

---

47. What does the woman want to do?

    (A) Rent a house overseas
    (B) Sign up for a mailing list
    (C) Purchase airline tickets
    (D) Upgrade a membership

48. What does the man recommend?

    (A) Going to a travel agency
    (B) Buying a lifetime membership
    (C) Using a new travel website
    (D) Calling an airline directly

49. What is the woman concerned about?

    (A) A delay in payment
    (B) The price of a membership
    (C) A missing coupon book
    (D) The location of an airport

50. Who most likely is the woman?

(A) A graphic designer
(B) A store owner
(C) A newspaper reporter
(D) A web developer

51. What is the woman pleased about?

(A) Some seasonal discounts
(B) A new logo design
(C) The price of a service
(D) The annual sales results

52. What does the man offer to do?

(A) Move a company logo
(B) Add a border to a design
(C) Enlarge the size of a picture
(D) Change the color of some words

53. What does the woman imply when she says, "I won't be able to leave for a while"?

(A) She had to change her plans.
(B) She is waiting for someone.
(C) She has already eaten dinner.
(D) She doesn't have a car now.

54. What is the woman worried about?

(A) Presenting her findings to her boss
(B) Finishing a report on time
(C) Mending a business relationship
(D) Inspecting some damages

55. What does the man say he will do before he leaves?

(A) Hold a monthly meeting
(B) Pass on some information
(C) Visit a customer's office
(D) Check the status of an order

56. Where do the interviewers most likely work?

(A) At a furniture manufacturer
(B) At an interior design company
(C) At an art gallery
(D) At a moving company

57. What job requirement do the speakers discuss?

(A) Meeting deadlines
(B) Cooperating with others
(C) Working long hours
(D) Lifting heavy objects

58. What does the man agree to do next?

(A) Show some documents
(B) Fill out an application
(C) Submit some design samples
(D) Sign an employment contract

59. What problem does the woman mention?

(A) A room was damaged.
(B) Some guests complained.
(C) Some workers quit.
(D) A business is slow.

60. What does the man suggest?

(A) Offering free meals to guests
(B) Holding a promotional event
(C) Upgrading room sizes
(D) Merging with another business

61. What does the woman ask the man to do?

(A) Analyze customer feedback
(B) Update a website
(C) Make a mailing list
(D) Prepare some materials

62. What industry do the speakers most likely work in?

(A) Cosmetics
(B) Engineering
(C) Software
(D) Trade

63. What does the woman say will happen next month?

(A) A convention will take place.
(B) A new product will be manufactured.
(C) A patent will expire.
(D) A new law will be enacted.

64. What does the woman imply when she says, "This diagram is from last year's convention"?

(A) A fee must be paid.
(B) Nothing needs to be done.
(C) This year's figures are not available yet.
(D) Some information is outdated.

Office 4	Office 3	Office 2
Break Room	Office 1	

65. According to the woman, what will she be doing this afternoon?

(A) Going on vacation
(B) Moving to a new office
(C) Meeting some customers
(D) Drawing up a floor plan

66. Look at the graphic. Which office has been assigned to the woman?

(A) Office 1
(B) Office 2
(C) Office 3
(D) Office 4

67. What does the woman say will take place tomorrow morning?

(A) A visit with clients
(B) An employee meeting
(C) A renovation
(D) A company party

Company	Location
Stanford Design	Chicago
Able Advertising	Miami
Renview Media	New York
Smart Style Design	Atlanta

68. What type of event is the company hosting?

(A) A charity ball
(B) An art gallery opening
(C) A retirement party
(D) A professional conference

69. What is the man concerned about?

(A) The cost of a project
(B) The location of an event
(C) A company's efficiency
(D) A worker's absence

70. Look at the graphic. Which company does the woman suggest?

(A) Stanford Design
(B) Able Advertising
(C) Renview Media
(D) Smart Style Design

Directions: You will hear some talks given by a single speaker. You will be asked to answer three questions about what the speaker says in each talk. Select the best response to each question and mark the letter (A), (B), (C), or (D) on your answer sheet. The talks will not be printed in your test book and will be spoken only one time.

71. Where most likely are the listeners?

(A) At an airport
(B) On a ship
(C) At a travel agency
(D) In a shopping mall

72. What is the cause of the delay?

(A) A security issue
(B) Missing passengers
(C) Mechanical problems
(D) Poor weather

73. What does the speaker suggest listeners do?

(A) Request a ticket refund
(B) Obtain a complimentary drink
(C) Book hotel accommodation
(D) Visit an information desk

74. What is the speaker mainly discussing?

(A) A downsizing plan
(B) A company merger
(C) A new office manager
(D) A potential client

75. What does the speaker say will take place at the company once a month?

(A) An employee review
(B) A monthly bonus
(C) A sales meeting
(D) A training course

76. Why will some employees be unavailable in the afternoon?

(A) They are attending a training session.
(B) They are presenting at a trade show.
(C) They are meeting with the head manager.
(D) They are leaving for a company trip.

77. What does the speaker say the business is considering?

(A) Renovating a kitchen
(B) Changing operation hours
(C) Contracting a new chef
(D) Hiring a new supplier

78. Why should listeners visit the head chef's office?

(A) To have an interview
(B) To pick up a coupon
(C) To sample some food
(D) To submit a form

79. What can listeners receive for participation?

(A) Some movie tickets
(B) A vacation package
(C) Some free food
(D) A pay raise

---

80. Where most likely is the speaker?

(A) At a bus station
(B) At an airport
(C) At her home
(D) In an airplane

81. What does the speaker imply when she says, "It's really too bad"?

(A) She is not well.
(B) She is disappointed.
(C) She lost a lot of money.
(D) She regrets her decision.

82. What does the speaker ask the listener to do?

(A) Drive to an airport
(B) Reschedule a party
(C) Unlock a door
(D) Meet her for dinner

---

83. Where most likely is this announcement being made?

(A) At pastry shop
(B) At a bookstore
(C) At a supermarket
(D) At a sports center

84. What problem does the speaker mention?

(A) Some employees are sick.
(B) Some items were misplaced.
(C) Some power cables are damaged.
(D) Some areas are flooded.

85. What will employees be informed about this evening?

(A) A store's schedule
(B) A vacation plan
(C) A promotional sale
(D) A city inspection

---

86. What is the news report about?

(A) Becoming an interior decorator
(B) Selling a home quickly
(C) Taking an online survey
(D) Buying a home abroad

87. What did Channel 6 do on their website recently?

(A) Conduct a survey
(B) Review a service
(C) Advertise a home
(D) Hold a contest

88. According to the speaker, what can listeners do after the break?

(A) View houses on the market
(B) Visit a designer's studio
(C) Hear some advice
(D) Sign up for a newsletter

GO ON TO THE NEXT PAGE

89. According to the speaker, what is the company trying to do?

    (A) Increase productivity
    (B) Eliminate paper use
    (C) Upgrade a computer system
    (D) Reduce electricity costs

90. What does the speaker mean when he says, "I know what you must be thinking"?

    (A) He wants to stress a key detail.
    (B) He wants to caution against disobedience.
    (C) He understands the listeners' concerns.
    (D) He acknowledges a listener's complaint.

91. What will the listeners be rewarded with?

    (A) A free meal
    (B) A new computer
    (C) A gift card
    (D) A promotion

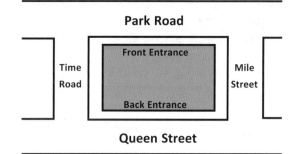

92. What will take place on Friday afternoon?

    (A) A contest
    (B) A parade
    (C) A repair
    (D) A sale

93. Look at the graphic. Which street will be closed?

    (A) Time Road
    (B) Park Road
    (C) Mile Street
    (D) Queen Street

94. What does the speaker suggest?

    (A) Staying home
    (B) Attending an event
    (C) Parking underground
    (D) Taking public transportation

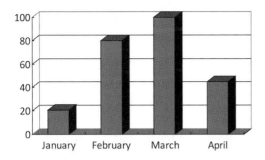

	Kimberly Shoe Outlet	Shoe Source Plus
Competitive prices	V	X
Free shipping	V	V
Innovative displays	V	X
Online orders	X	V

95. Where most likely does the speaker work?

(A) At a home improvement store
(B) At an advertising firm
(C) At a publishing company
(D) At a design company

96. Look at the graphic. When was the discount event held?

(A) In January
(B) In February
(C) In March
(D) In April

97. According to the speaker, what should staff members do by next Friday?

(A) Edit some articles
(B) Prepare a report
(C) Book train tickets
(D) Update a website

98. What is the main topic of the meeting?

(A) A new line of products
(B) A manager's promotion
(C) A company's location
(D) A business's success

99. Who most likely is the speaker?

(A) A shoe designer
(B) A store owner
(C) An advertiser
(D) A financial planner

100. Look at the graphic. What will the speaker most likely discuss next?

(A) Competitive prices
(B) Free shipping
(C) Innovative displays
(D) Online orders

This is the end of the Listening test. Turn to Part 5 in your test book.

READING TEST

In the Reading Test, you will read a variety of texts and answer several different types of reading comprehension questions. The entire Reading test will last 75 minutes. There are three parts, and directions are given for each part. You are encouraged to answer as many questions as possible within the time allowed.

You must mark your answers on the separate answer sheet. Do not write your answers in your test book.

PART 5

Directions: A word or phrase is missing in each of the sentences below. Four answer choices are given below each sentence. Select the best answer to complete the sentence. Then mark the letter (A), (B), (C), or (D) on your answer sheet.

101. Ms. Parker plans to interview the applicants ------- because she understands the position better than anybody.

(A) hers
(B) herself
(C) she
(D) her

102. Tax rebates will be given to public servants ------- the State of California.

(A) within
(B) until
(C) during
(D) since

103. Interested parties can -------- register online for this weekend's seminar on real estate investing.

(A) very
(B) least
(C) easily
(D) more

104. The promotion will ------- employees with upgraded benefits, company cars, and more vacation days.

(A) provide
(B) earn
(C) contrast
(D) loan

105. Office staff at Morin Legal Services ------- work four days a week, from Monday to Thursday.

(A) norm
(B) norms
(C) normal
(D) normally

106. Items can be exchanged ------- they are returned within one week following the date of purchase.

(A) or
(B) if
(C) nor
(D) but

107. According to this newspaper article, earnings at BTR Electronics last quarter were ------- than expected.

(A) lowest
(B) lowering
(C) lower
(D) low

108. Everyone ------- the store owner took a week-long vacation in the summertime last year.

(A) out of
(B) other
(C) except
(D) between

109. Even though all her landscape paintings are of actual places, Doris Clements puts a great deal of ------- into her work.

(A) imagine
(B) imaginative
(C) imagination
(D) imaginary

110. The receptionist will provide the ------ client list to all sales personnel this afternoon.

(A) frequent
(B) updated
(C) certain
(D) monitored

111. The spring training course was developed to help sales employees think more -------.

(A) create
(B) creative
(C) creativity
(D) creatively

112. Before attempting to assemble this table, you should ------- the instructions.

(A) direct
(B) review
(C) gather
(D) program

113. Ms. Jannel, the director of customer relations, ------- the poor reviews the company has received online at the staff meeting tomorrow.

(A) had been addressing
(B) is addressing
(C) will be addressed
(D) should be addressed

114. Larson Motors aims to improve its public image ------- the guidance of publicist Cynthia Morison of M&T Public Relations.

(A) under
(B) either
(C) among
(D) beyond

115. When --------- to any new clients, don't forget to mention Beckingham's promotional event next week.

(A) spoken
(B) speaking
(C) spoke
(D) to speak

116. Tickets for Friday night's play at the Alexander Theater sold out quickly because the production --------- two famous actors from this area.

(A) feature
(B) features
(C) to feature
(D) featuring

117. The Thompson Art Gallery will extend its hours of operation ------- on August 1.

(A) will begin
(B) has begun
(C) beginner
(D) beginning

118. Donald Mahoney is in charge of the supplies ------- to all plumbers working for Grady Pipe Repairs.

(A) distribute
(B) distribution
(C) distributes
(D) is distributed

119. The CEO is known for being ambitious as he expressed his ------- in an interview with *Today Business Magazine* last fall.

(A) interferences
(B) prevention
(C) views
(D) exchange

120. Anna Sanchez, founding editor of *Financial Monthly*, has quickly earned the respect of practically ------- in the financial industry.

(A) everyone
(B) anything
(C) whatever
(D) each other

121. As stated in the reviews, the theater's new performance was ------- a big hit.

(A) clear
(B) clearly
(C) clearer
(D) clearing

122. ------- our hiring committee reads all the resumes, we will compile a list of 20 candidates to invite in for interviews.

(A) Compared to
(B) As soon as
(C) So that
(D) Not only

123. The concert was a huge success and drew a crowd of over 5,000 to Moose Park and Recreation Center, -------- the cold weather.

(A) while
(B) whereas
(C) notwithstanding
(D) moreover

124. The research staff at Pullford Pharmaceuticals will be using the conference room as its office ------- the renovation period.

(A) opposite
(B) beside
(C) during
(D) with

125. As stated on the company's website, clients who wish to cancel their membership ------- it expires must pay a fee.

(A) before
(B) how
(C) why
(D) either

126. Although the job description is ------- to those at other firms, this job has a much higher salary.

(A) similar
(B) likable
(C) reflected
(D) considerate

127. Access to the research laboratory will be limited to senior employees to ensure ------- with all safety regulations.

(A) activation
(B) fulfillment
(C) compliance
(D) indication

128. If the window had been broken during installation, Riley's Building Supplies ------- to replace it at no charge.

(A) would have offered
(B) has offered
(C) is being offered
(D) would have been offered

129. Prior to reviewing -------, the town council agreed to three proposals in principle.

(A) specifics
(B) specify
(C) specific
(D) specifically

130. Administrators at the Ben Phillips Hospital maintain that ------- to the facility will make many medical procedures more efficient.

(A) continuations
(B) increments
(C) deviations
(D) enhancements

GO ON TO THE NEXT PAGE

PART 6

Directions: Read the texts that follow. A word, phrase, or sentence is missing in parts of each text. Four answer choices for each question are given below the text. Select the best answer to complete the text. Then mark the letter (A), (B), (C), or (D) on your answer sheet.

Questions 131-134 refer to the following article.

March 3 — After nearly three years of planning, the largest stadium in Harpville will begin construction. The Expo Stadium will be located on Harpville's majestic waterfront and will have a capacity of up to ten thousand seats. __131.__. The project is expected to take three years to complete. It will be located amongst several other new developments currently __132.__ on the waterfront. According to Marshal Thomas, president of the Harpville Sports Association, the new stadium is a __133.__. "We're going to need a large stadium to accommodate our growing sports clubs," Mr. Thomas said. "__134.__, we'll also be able to use the stadium for concerts and circus performances."

131. (A) Developers are unsure how long it will take to complete the project.
(B) The stadium will be moved from the waterfront to the outskirts of the city.
(C) It will also include over 100 press viewing rooms that hold up to ten people each.
(D) Delays occurred when the mayor refused to fund the city's development plans.

132. (A) to construct
(B) are constructing
(C) were constructed
(D) being constructed

133. (A) necessity
(B) nuisance
(C) risk
(D) bargain

134. (A) On the other hand
(B) In other words
(C) In the first place
(D) As a result

Questions 135-138 refer to the following press release.

Meredith Hobson, CEO and founder of Hobson Dining, Trenton's oldest family dining franchise, announced that she ___135. $6,500 towards renovations to the Jasper Community Center in the city's downtown region. The funds were generated from ticket sales for a banquet held last Friday evening at her ___136.. Ms. Hobson will present the management staff of the center with a check at a special ceremony scheduled to take place tomorrow afternoon at 2:00. ___137. the past 25 years, Ms. Hobson has organized a number of successful fund-raising events for community services and charities. ___138..

---

135. (A) will donate
(B) donated
(C) might donate
(D) donating

136. (A) gallery
(B) hotel
(C) academy
(D) restaurant

137. (A) Despite
(B) Over
(C) Between
(D) Beneath

138. (A) The Jasper Community Center has programs for both children and adults.
(B) The opening ceremony at the center will be done by 2:30 P.M.
(C) However, last Friday's event was, without a doubt, her most successful one.
(D) Ms. Hobson plans to open a branch in uptown Trenton sometime next year.

Questions 139-142 refer to the following meeting summary.

Our monthly meeting commenced at 4:30 P.M. The meeting's purpose was to discuss the advantages and disadvantages of ⎺⎺⎺⎺ LGQ International Shipping. Max Powel led the debate on **139.** the possible move by stressing the importance of furthering LGQ's current growth patterns. He explained that LGQ has grown to be one of the most successful ⎺⎺⎺⎺ and that it ships the largest **140.** number of electronics in the country.

⎺⎺⎺⎺. According to recent reports, the traveling distance from the closest harbor is becoming costly **141.** ⎺⎺⎺⎺ LGQ begins to grow. Staff members discussed some possible solutions, but a final decision was **142.** not reached. Mr. Powel will do some more research and present his findings at the next meeting.

139. (A) acquiring
(B) joining
(C) promoting
(D) relocating

140. (A) distribute
(B) distributing
(C) distributors
(D) distributes

141. (A) Mr. Powel also outlined the challenges LGQ is experiencing as a result of its growth.
(B) The CEO then proceeded to discuss the advantages of the new facilities.
(C) Next, shareholders were invited to conduct a vote to decide the date.
(D) Mr. Powel directed employees to consider how operations would be conducted.

142. (A) now
(B) why
(C) just as
(D) ever since

Questions 143-146 refer to the following e-mail.

From: tina@lindcosmetics.com
To: mia@mymailnow.com
Date: September 8
Subject: Order 445009

Dear Ms. Kramar,

Thank you for writing to inquire about your order. According to our records, you ordered one tube of Lind SPF 50 Sunscreen, one bottle of Lind 500 Hand Cream, and two bottles of Lind Ultrashine Shampoo from our website on September 1. Your products were scheduled to arrive on September 5. I was surprised to hear that you have not received ‾‾‾‾. **143.**

‾‾‾‾. **144.** According to their schedule, your products will arrive on September 10. If your order is not delivered by that day, feel free ‾‾‾‾ us again. **145.**

I sincerely apologize for this inconvenience. Our shipping methods are usually fast and affordable. This situation is quite ‾‾‾‾. **146.** I hope it will not discourage you from shopping at Lind Cosmetics.

Thank you,

Tina Speller
Lind Cosmetics

---

143. (A) it
(B) one
(C) them
(D) some

144. (A) We would like to invite you to visit our store.
(B) Please leave a review on our website.
(C) We are currently sold out of that particular product.
(D) I have contacted the shipping company on your behalf.

145. (A) contacted
(B) to contact
(C) contacting
(D) contact

146. (A) similar
(B) exciting
(C) unusual
(D) welcome

PART 7

Directions: In this part you will read a selection of texts, such as magazine and newspaper articles, e-mails, and instant messages. Each text or set of texts is followed by several questions. Select the best answer for each question and mark the letter (A), (B), (C), or (D) on your answer sheet.

Questions 147-148 refer to the following advertisement.

Item for Sale	Price	Location
Model A7000 Flamesburg Barbecue	$450	Los Angeles, CA

Item Description:
Purchased new three years ago. Original cost was $700 and came with a two-year warranty.
Grill pieces are charred. Buyer can purchase new ones on the Flamesburg website.
Exterior is in great condition. (Pictures available upon request)
Price is negotiable. Willing to deliver anywhere in the Los Angeles area.
E-mail rjohnson@mail.com if you have any questions.

147. What is NOT indicated about the barbecue?

(A) It comes in the original box.
(B) It needs new parts.
(C) Its price is not set.
(D) Its warranty has expired.

148. What is the seller willing to do?

(A) Reserve the item for up to a month
(B) Provide instructions on how to use the item
(C) Deliver anywhere in the country
(D) Send photographs to potential buyers

Questions 149-150 refer to the following notice.

We are delighted to announce that Cordelia Winters has joined IPM Talent as an associate agent. Ms. Winters is a graduate of Roden University's public relations program. While studying at Roden, she founded the university's first student-run magazine. Following graduation, she completed an internship at UV Media and Talent, a prestigious agency that represents a wide variety of musicians, authors, professional athletes, and actors. Ms. Winters has undergone exceptional training and will be a great asset to our growing team of agents. Please join us in conference room B tomorrow morning at 10:00 A.M. to welcome her to the team.

149. Where is the notice most likely posted?

(A) In an advertising firm
(B) In a university
(C) In a music studio
(D) In a talent agency

150. What are employees invited to do tomorrow?

(A) Participate in a conference
(B) Greet a new employee
(C) Visit a competitor
(D) Meet some new clients

Questions 151-152 refer to the following text message chain.

Tim Peterson [11:03 A.M.]
Hey, Amanda. Can you update me on the Sampson Lane job?

Amanda Ray [11:10 A.M.]
We've cleared out the main floor and the garage. We're just starting on the second floor of the house now.

Tim Peterson [11:12 A.M.]
Is that all? What time do you think you'll be done? We have a move scheduled for 3:00 P.M.

Amanda Ray [11:15 A.M.]
We're behind schedule. When the estimate was done, it didn't take into account the old furniture in the garage.

Tim Peterson [11:20 A.M.]
Really? Who did the estimate?

Amanda Ray [11:21 A.M.]
Matthew did before he went on vacation.

Tim Peterson [11:23 A.M.]
OK. Contact me at 1:00 P.M. with a progress report. I'll decide then if I need to call in another crew for the afternoon job.

SEND

Type your message . . .

151. What type of business does Ms. Ray work for?

(A) A real estate agency
(B) A furniture store
(C) A moving company
(D) A truck rental service

152. At 11:12, what does Mr. Peterson mean when he says, "Is that all"?

(A) He wants to know the address of a house.
(B) He thinks the employees are working slowly.
(C) He is surprised because the price is very cheap.
(D) He wants to confirm that everything is loaded on the truck.

Rutherford Eye Clinic
54 Rutherford Avenue
Los Angeles, California

14 March

Katrina Serova
123 Colonel Lane
Los Angeles, California

Dear Ms. Serova,

It is important to us here at Rutherford Eye Clinic that all our customers receive advanced notice of changes to our policies. As of August 1, all routine yearly eye exams will no longer be covered by most major insurance providers. To help offset the cost, we are reducing our fees by $15 per exam. Please see the enclosed list of affected insurance providers.

In some select cases, we are willing to provide eye exams to children free of charge should your family have a history of prior exams with us. Please contact our billing manager Maggie Wilson at 445-987-0023 to inquire about this service or if you have any questions.

Sincerely,

Dr. Nadia Fortuni
Rutherford Eye Clinic

153. Why was the letter sent to Ms. Serova?

(A) To announce a billing change
(B) To advertise a new service
(C) To confirm an appointment
(D) To inform of a missed exam

154. What is indicated about Rutherford Eye Clinic?

(A) It wants to hire new staff members.
(B) It has extended its hours of operation.
(C) It caters to clients from all around the world.
(D) It will offer free exams to certain customers.

Questions 155-157 refer to the following article.

Westpoint Shopping Mall to Begin Construction

By Melanie Rosenberg, Staff Writer

March 23 — Yesterday, in a press conference at Mayor Zanga's office downtown, the mayor announced the city's approval of development plans for a new shopping mall. According to the mayor, Westpoint Shopping Mall will be located at Park Road and Wilson Street. --[1]--.

The shopping mall is a joint project between the City of Forks and Windsor Partners, a private development corporation. The mall will include over 200 hundred new stores, 55 restaurants, and a department store. --[2]--. Windsor Partners will be in charge of executing construction and overseeing initial operations.

"The City of Forks has never had a major shopping center," Mr. Johnson of Windsor Partners said in an interview. "By building this state-of-the-art facility, the people of Forks will see an increase in jobs and tourism." --[3]--.

Many retailers have already signed contracts with Windsor Partners to reserve store space in the mall. However, some small business owners have expressed worry that they will lose business once the shopping mall opens. --[4]--. "My store has been in business for two generations," Michelle Stevens of Shoe Blitz said. "My customers are loyal, but I won't be able to compete with shopping mall prices."

---

155. What does Windsor Partners hope to attract to Forks?

(A) Foreign students
(B) A supermarket
(C) More tourists
(D) New small businesses

156. Who most likely is Michelle Stevens?

(A A newspaper reporter
(B) A retail store owner
(C) A city official
(D) A property developer

157. In which of the positions marked [1], [2], [3], and [4] does the following sentence best belong?

"Last year, a fire consumed the auto factory located there, leaving the site open to new development."

(A) [1]
(B) [2]
(C) [3]
(D) [4]

Questions 158-160 refer to the following information.

Simone Decourte
Kites at Sunset
Mobile Installation, painted sheet metal and rods
1984

Kites at Sunset is one of the most popular mobile installations by Simone Decourte. Decourte revolutionized mobile art in the 1970s by including portable motors to create movement. *Kites at Sunset* is part of a larger series constructed by Decourte between 1970 to 1988. It has been featured in The Museum of Abstract Art in Milan, The Contemporary Art Gallery in New York City, and The New Art Movement Museum in London. Decourte originally donated the piece to the University of Montenegro. It remained there for 10 years before being acquired by Maxwell George of the Wilson Fine Art Museum where it has remained as part of our permanent collection. Before her death, Decourte said *Kites at Sunset* was her "most vibrant piece ever created."

158. How does the information describe Simone Decourte?

(A) She was attentive to details.
(B) She created a lot of art work.
(C) She was an innovative artist.
(D) She worked for the poor.

159. Where is the information posted?

(A) At the Museum of Abstract Art
(B) At the Wilson Fine Art Museum
(C) At the Contemporary Art Gallery
(D) At the New Art Movement Museum

160. What is NOT stated about *Kites at Sunset*?

(A) The artist regarded it as one of her best works.
(B) It has traveled to several places.
(C) It was owned by a university.
(D) It took almost two decades to complete the piece.

Questions 161-163 refer to the following e-mail.

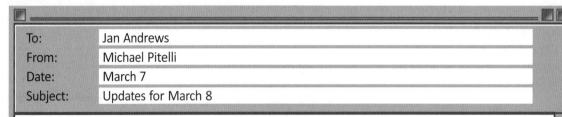

To:	Jan Andrews
From:	Michael Pitelli
Date:	March 7
Subject:	Updates for March 8

Ms. Andrews,

I've had to make a few minor changes to your schedule for tomorrow. Your meeting with potential client Jeff Woods has been canceled. His assistant suggested March 10 as a possible date to meet. Since you're flying back that morning, you're free in the afternoon. Would you like me to set up the appointment? Please have a look at your updated schedule below. I've replaced Mr. Woods's appointment with your budget review. Please let me know if this doesn't work for you.

Time	Appointment	Attendees
8:30 A.M.	Staff Meeting	Departments A and B
9:45 A.M.	Conference Call with Washington Partners	Jessica Bowers, Tom Park
10:30 A.M.	Budget Review	Ally Strenski
1:30 P.M.	Meeting about Conference Itinerary	Joshua Wilson
4:00 P.M.	Leave for your 7:00 flight to Chicago	

I have printed out your e-ticket and put it in your company mailbox. Good luck on your trip.

Best,

Michael

161. Why was the e-mail sent?

(A) To cancel an appointment next month
(B) To provide a travel itinerary
(C) To update a daily schedule
(D) To provide documents for a meeting

162. What will happen on March 10?

(A) Mr. Pitelli will fly to Washington.
(B) Ms. Andrews will attend a conference.
(C) Mr. Woods will hold a budget review.
(D) Ms. Andrews will return from Chicago.

163. At what time was Mr. Woods expected?

(A) 8:35 A.M.
(B) 9:45 A.M.
(C) 10:30 A.M.
(D) 1:30 P.M.

Questions **164-167** refer to the following e-mail.

To:	Employees of Winfred Financial
From:	Sandra Burns
Date:	October 24
Subject:	New regulations

Dear employees,

As you know, the Ministry of Health and Environment has introduced a new set of laws for work places in order to help reduce the amount of energy consumed during the winter months. In accordance with these new regulations, Winfred Financial will program its heating system during the winter. As such, you will not be able to regulate the temperature of your office at any time. The system will heat the building to 19°C on weekdays, which will be maintained throughout the day. It will then lower to 13°C at the end of each day. By following this new regulation, we should see a 10% reduction in the cost of our utility bills.

As some of you work on weekends, management has decided that offices on the 5th floor will be able to control the temperature manually. Weekend workers may request a change of office with their department managers. We simply ask that the rooms not be heated any warmer than 19°C.

Sincerely,

Sandra Burns,
General Manager

164. What is the purpose of the e-mail?

(A) To announce an upcoming change in the workplace
(B) To inform employees of a scheduled inspection
(C) To encourage employees to choose new office furniture
(D) To offer managers the opportunity to get a promotion

165. The word "maintained" in paragraph 1, line 5, is closest in meaning to

(A) confirmed
(B) repaired
(C) taken
(D) kept

166. What is mentioned as a benefit of the new regulation?

(A) It will improve employee work efficiency.
(B) It can allow the company to hire more workers.
(C) It will help the company save money.
(D) It can be applied to public and private companies.

167. What are employees who work on weekends advised to do?

(A) E-mail Ms. Burns directly
(B) Request office changes
(C) Alter their work schedules
(D) Work at home on weekends

GO ON TO THE NEXT PAGE

Questions 168-171 refer to the following online chat discussion.

Mary Renold [2:02 P.M.]
Hello, Ben. Can you spare a moment? I want to double-check an inventory report with you.

Ben Jeffries [2:03 P.M.]
No problem.

Mary Renold [2:04 P.M.]
According to the report, we only have two A75 Canpro notebooks left. We've been selling a lot of that model lately. Should I order more?

Ben Jeffries [2:06 P.M.]
That's not necessary. The new A76 model has just come out, so we're going to carry that model instead. I ordered 50 of the new ones, but they haven't come in yet.

Mary Renold [2:10 P.M.]
Oh, OK. Thanks for explaining that.

Ben Jeffries [2:11 P.M.]
Next week, we'll start displaying them on the shelves, so make sure to print the product information for the displays.

Mary Renold [2:12 P.M.]
Sure. I'll get right on that.

168. At 2:03 P.M., what does Mr. Jeffries most likely mean when he writes, "No Problem"?

(A) He agrees with Ms. Renold's idea.
(B) He is available to answer Ms. Renold's question.
(C) He wants to set up a meeting with Ms. Renold.
(D) He did exactly as Ms. Renold requested.

169. What is mentioned about Mr. Jeffries?

(A) He already ordered some items.
(B) He downloaded some information.
(C) He set up some products today.
(D) He visited a supplier last week.

170. What type of business do Mr. Jeffries and Ms. Renold work for?

(A) A computer repair business
(B) A delivery company
(C) An electronics store
(D) A software developer

171. What will Mr. Jeffries and Ms. Renold do next week?

(A) Renovate a storefront
(B) Hold a sale for new products
(C) Return some obsolete items
(D) Set up some product displays

Questions 172-175 refer to the following article.

June 15 — The Walter Horman Estate, the home of deceased millionaire Walter Horman, was recently purchased by the City of Rogerton. According to Malika Trenton, director of the Rogerton Historical Society, the estate will undergo light renovations and restorations before being turned into a local museum. --[1]--. According to Trenton, "The Horman family has included all of the original decorations and furnishings for visitors to enjoy."

Over the last several decades, the Walter Horman Estate has been unoccupied. Instead, the property was available for private party rentals and weddings. Some major film companies have even shot scenes at the estate. However, the cost of keeping the grounds in good condition proved to be too much for the family. --[2]--. Stephen Horman, grandson of the late Walter Horman, said, "It was a tough choice to make. The estate has been in our family for generations, but selling it was the best way to ensure its upkeep." The rest of the Horman family has expressed satisfaction that the estate will be turned into a museum. --[3]--.

The Rogerton Historical Society intends to develop guided tours of the estate rooms, while still providing access to the gardens for private parties. Visitors to the estate can learn the history of the Horman family from its early immigrant beginning to its rise in society as the owner of one of the first food processing companies in the country. --[4]--. Tours are expected to begin next spring. Anyone interested in purchasing passes or learning about the estate's history can visit www.walterhormanestate.com/info.

172. What is suggested about the Walter Horman Estate?

(A) It was built by Walter Horman's father.
(B) It is expensive to reserve for parties.
(C) It will have its appliances upgraded.
(D) It includes the original furniture.

173. According to the article, what was difficult for the Horman family?

(A) Turning the property into a park
(B) Maintaining the estate
(C) Finding furniture for the rooms
(D) Locating a suitable buyer

174. According to the article, what will remain the same about the estate?

(A) It will be owned by the Horman family.
(B) Its exterior walls will be used for security.
(C) Its buildings will serve as guest houses.
(D) Its outdoor property will be available for rent.

175. In which of the positions marked [1], [2], [3], and [4] does the following sentence best belong?

"They are pleased the memory of Walter Horman will be preserved."

(A) [1]
(B) [2]
(C) [3]
(D) [4]

To:	samadams@adamsroofing.com
From:	ginachoi@homeimprovementmonthly.com
Date:	January 3
Subject:	Home Improvement Monthly

Dear Mr. Adams,

As a special New Year promotion, *Home Improvement Monthly* will be offering discounted prices for new advertisers in our magazine. *Home Improvement Monthly* has a readership of over 20,000 print subscriptions. Your advertisement will reach each subscriber in print as well as our many online subscribers. With our services, you can increase your business!

This offer is valid until March 1. Our price packages are outlined below, and our designers are ready to create color advertisements according to your specifications. To purchase any of our packages, please reply by e-mail or visit us at www.homeimprovementmonthly.com/advertisements/orders.

Package	Advertisement Format	Monthly Price
1	One full-page print ad plus banner website ad	$300
2	One half-page print ad plus half-banner website ad	$275
3	One half-page print ad plus corner website ad	$250
4	One quarter-page print ad plus corner website ad	$225

Sincerely,

Gina Choi
Advertising Coordinator
Home Improvement Monthly

To:	ginachoi@homeimprovementmonthly.com
From:	samadams@adamsroofing.com
Date:	January 5
Subject: Re:	Home Improvement Monthly

Dear Ms. Choi,

Thank you for e-mailing me about your promotion. My business partner and I are interested in placing an ad in your magazine. However, I have some questions about your quarter-page print ad. I've purchased a copy of your magazine and looked at the advertisements. I noticed that some are in the front of the magazine and some are in the back. I'm wondering what determines the location of the ad? Do we need to pay additional fees to have our ad located in the front?

Thank you in advance for answering these questions.

Sincerely,

Sam Adams
Co-owner
Adams Roofing

176. Why did Ms. Choi e-mail Mr. Adams?

(A) To announce a new advertising opportunity
(B) To offer a promotional discount on subscriptions
(C) To encourage him to hire a marketing agency
(D) To inform him of a change in a contract

177. What is suggested about *Home Improvement Monthly*?

(A) Some of its issues were delivered late.
(B) Its advertisers do not pay for subscriptions.
(C) It will put out two issues every month starting next year.
(D) Some of its subscribers only pay for the website version.

178. What is mentioned about *Home Improvement Monthly's* designers?

(A) They can provide custom work.
(B) They require additional fees.
(C) They also design the company website.
(D) They are unavailable until March.

179. In the second e-mail, the word "placing" in paragraph 1, line 2, is closest in meaning to

(A) hiring
(B) putting
(C) assigning
(D) calculating

180. What package does Mr. Adams most likely want?

(A) Package 1
(B) Package 2
(C) Package 3
(D) Package 4

Questions 181-185 refer to the following e-mails.

To:	mpordeski@mailme.com
From:	imranandal@pearsonmedicalresearch.com
Date:	April 12
Subject:	Pearson Medical Research Position
Attachment:	contract

Dear Ms. Pordeski,

I enjoyed speaking with you during your telephone interview, and I'm delighted to offer you a position on our team as a research assistant. As I'm sure you're aware, you will be working with the top medical researchers in the country using the most advanced equipment. Your education in both biology and engineering will be a great asset during your six-month contract.

As I mentioned to you, our company works jointly with Austin University. Thus, you will need to know your way around both our company headquarters and the laboratories at the university. As such, I would like to arrange an orientation for you and our other new researchers. You mentioned that you're finishing up your final year of your degree, so I'd like to arrange a time that does not interfere with your schedule. Please let me know which days in May you are available.

Please note, this position is an internship. Your wages will be $200 a week and the occasional work expenses will be reimbursed. However, following the six-month period, there will be permanent employment for our top interns. To finalize your acceptance of these terms, please sign and return the attached contract. Andrew Baxter, our human resources manager, will contact you if there are any problems.

Thank you, and I look forward to working with you!

Imran Andal
Lead Researcher
Pearson Medical Research

To:	Intern Group
From:	imranandal@pearsonmedicalresearch.com
Date:	April 24
Subject:	Orientation

Dear Research Interns,

Since most of you are not available at the same time, I'd like to hold two orientations, one on May 11 and the second on May 16. The May 16 orientation is scheduled on a weekend to accommodate the students in the group. However, if you're not a student, you will be expected to attend the May 11 orientation. Both orientations will start at 9 A.M. at our company headquarters. After a tour, we will have lunch at Buffy's Bistro and then make our way over to the university. Please bring a photo ID in order to gain admittance to the university labs.

Thank you, and I'm looking forward to meeting you all!

Imran Andal,
Lead Researcher,
Pearson Medical Research

---

181. Why did Mr. Andal write to Ms. Pordeski?

(A) To negotiate a contract
(B) To invite her to apply for a job
(C) To provide medical assistance
(D) To offer her an internship

182. What document is Ms. Pordeski asked to return?

(A) An employer reference
(B) A signed contract
(C) A program application
(D) A university transcript

183. What is indicated about new staff at Pearson Medical Research?

(A) They may work from home.
(B) Their tax forms must be submitted online.
(C) They will not be paid for their work.
(D) Their performance will be evaluated.

184. Why might Andrew Baxter contact Ms. Pordeski?

(A) To review company regulations
(B) To resolve a contract issue
(C) To ask for additional references
(D) To explain payment procedures

185. When will Ms. Pordeski most likely attend the orientation?

(A) May 11
(B) May 15
(C) May 16
(D) May 19

Questions 186-190 refer to the following webpage and e-mails.

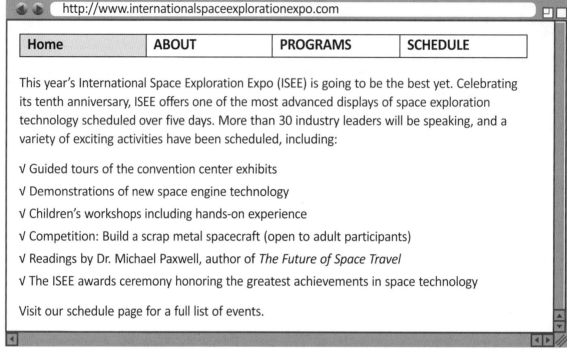

http://www.internationalspaceexplorationexpo.com

| Home | ABOUT | PROGRAMS | SCHEDULE |

This year's International Space Exploration Expo (ISEE) is going to be the best yet. Celebrating its tenth anniversary, ISEE offers one of the most advanced displays of space exploration technology scheduled over five days. More than 30 industry leaders will be speaking, and a variety of exciting activities have been scheduled, including:

√ Guided tours of the convention center exhibits

√ Demonstrations of new space engine technology

√ Children's workshops including hands-on experience

√ Competition: Build a scrap metal spacecraft (open to adult participants)

√ Readings by Dr. Michael Paxwell, author of *The Future of Space Travel*

√ The ISEE awards ceremony honoring the greatest achievements in space technology

Visit our schedule page for a full list of events.

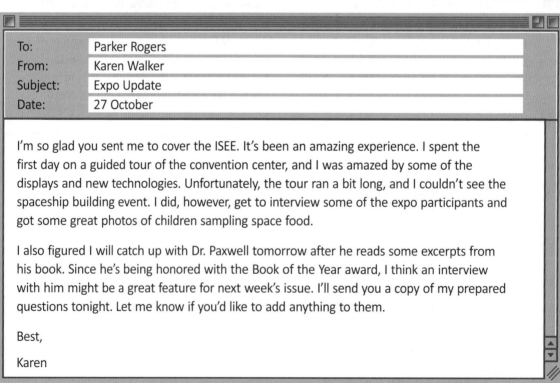

To:	Parker Rogers
From:	Karen Walker
Subject:	Expo Update
Date:	27 October

I'm so glad you sent me to cover the ISEE. It's been an amazing experience. I spent the first day on a guided tour of the convention center, and I was amazed by some of the displays and new technologies. Unfortunately, the tour ran a bit long, and I couldn't see the spaceship building event. I did, however, get to interview some of the expo participants and got some great photos of children sampling space food.

I also figured I will catch up with Dr. Paxwell tomorrow after he reads some excerpts from his book. Since he's being honored with the Book of the Year award, I think an interview with him might be a great feature for next week's issue. I'll send you a copy of my prepared questions tonight. Let me know if you'd like to add anything to them.

Best,

Karen

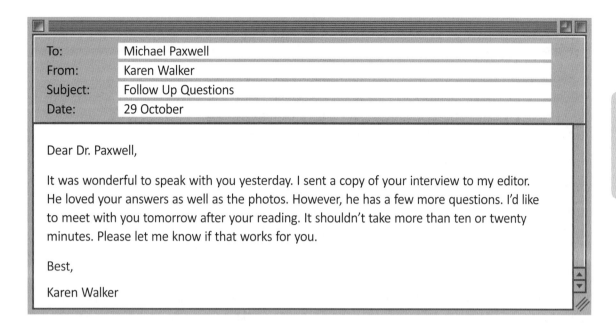

To:	Michael Paxwell
From:	Karen Walker
Subject:	Follow Up Questions
Date:	29 October

Dear Dr. Paxwell,

It was wonderful to speak with you yesterday. I sent a copy of your interview to my editor. He loved your answers as well as the photos. However, he has a few more questions. I'd like to meet with you tomorrow after your reading. It shouldn't take more than ten or twenty minutes. Please let me know if that works for you.

Best,

Karen Walker

186. What is indicated about ISEE?

(A) It was originally designed for students.
(B) It is held multiple times per year.
(C) It has existed for several years.
(D) It has moved to a new venue.

187. Who most likely is Ms. Walker?

(A) A publisher
(B) An astronaut
(C) A scientist
(D) A journalist

188. According to Ms. Walker, what conference activity was she unable to attend?

(A) A demonstration
(B) A craft competition
(C) A guided tour
(D) A workshop

189. In the first e-mail, the word "figured" in paragraph 2, line 1, is closest in meaning to

(A) decided
(B) involved
(C) represented
(D) performed

190. What is suggested about Dr. Paxwell?

(A) He has won several awards this year.
(B) He will give multiple presentations at the expo.
(C) He is a well-known newspaper editor.
(D) He gives demonstrations every year.

BREDENBURY (June 11) — Bredenbury town officials sat down today to discuss the fate of the Mossomin Bridge which has been in need of major repairs for years. Today's meeting was the first of several expected talks on the subject. Although an extensive restoration is one option, several complications may compel the town to demolish the structure.

"The cost to restore the bridge will be too great," said town planner Ilkay Tidsale. "The only financially feasible option I can see is replacing the structure."

According to Malcolm Vonda, a well-known structural engineer, traffic flow must also be taken into consideration. "Highway 209 will soon have two additional lanes, making it a four-lane highway. The Mossomin Bridge cannot accommodate such a huge increase in the number of vehicles," Vonda says. "I see no other alternative but to build a bigger, modern structure."

The town council would like input from residents on this issue as well. Anyone wishing to share their views can attend a public forum next Monday at 4:30 P.M. at Akber Square, in front of the town hall.

Letters to the Editor

June 12 — Yesterday's article concerning the future of the Mossomin Bridge prompted me to write this response. The bridge is more than just a bridge; it is an integral part of Bredenbury's culture. For this reason, the town must keep the structure intact. Plus, considering the high revenues generated annually by tourism industry, the short-term costs needed to restore this landmark will prove to be beneficial in the end.

Pierre Atherton, founding member of the Bredenbury Preservation Society (BPS)

To: members@bredenburypressoc.org
From: isabellecharlebois@bredenburypressoc.org
Date: June 23
Subject: update on Mossomin Bridge

Dear BPS Members,

Congratulations! Thanks to our organization's undeniably strong presence at the town council event, combined with the countless e-mails, letters, and calls to the members of town council, it appears that the bridge is safe from demolition. According to an article in today's *Bredenbury Herald*, the town has decided to relocate Mossomin Bridge to the south end of the town where only pedestrians will be allowed to use it. The bridge will not be open to motorized vehicles.

All of you should feel proud for speaking out and expressing your concerns last Monday. Your actions definitely influenced the town's decision. Great work!

Thank you once again,

Isabelle Charlebois, President
Bredenbury Preservation Society

---

191. In the article, what is indicated about the town of Bredenbury?

(A) It will increase its yearly budget.
(B) It is going to upgrade a road.
(C) It is enforcing local parking laws.
(D) It will offer special tours to attract tourists.

192. What is NOT implied about Mr. Atherton?

(A) He works with Mr. Vonda.
(B) He disagrees with Ms. Tisdale.
(C) He read the June 11 newspaper article.
(D) He values a town landmark.

193. In the e-mail, the word "countless" in paragraph 1, line 2, is closest in meaning to

(A) unreported
(B) registered
(C) numerous
(D) ambiguous

194. Why does Ms. Charlebois congratulate BPS members?

(A) They helped influence a town's decision.
(B) They elected a new vice president.
(C) They were the subjects of a front-page news story.
(D) They raised additional funds for town projects.

195. What is suggested about BPS members?

(A) They helped repair a structure.
(B) Many of them spoke out at Akber Square.
(C) Many of them reside in the south end.
(D) They meet on the first Monday of every month.

Questions 196-200 refer to the following webpage, receipt, and review.

Home	Tours	Reservations	Customer Service

http://www.grandcanyonexploreadventure.com

For over 20 years, our experienced pilots have been conducting spectacular, one of a kind sightseeing tours of the incredible Grand Canyon. Our trips are available for groups of up to six passengers and can be conducted in English, French, Spanish, and Chinese. Take a look at our trip itineraries below and then visit our reservations page for more information about pricing.

• Grand Canyon Helicopter Tour — Available every day from 14:30 P.M. – 15:30 P.M. Spend your afternoon flying over the magnificent Grand Canyon in a helicopter. You will see amazing views of the Hoover Dam, Lake Mead, and the surrounding desert.

• Grand Canyon Helicopter Tour & Lunch — Available every day from 11:30 A.M. – 15:00 P.M. See all the incredible aerial sights listed in the Grand Canyon Helicopter Tour. Following your flight, you will descend 4,000 feet to the canyon floor and enjoy a picnic lunch served on the shore of the Colorado River.

• Ultimate Grand Canyon Tour Package — Available every day from 11:30 A.M. – 18:00 P.M. Enjoy all the benefits of our other packages, including an aerial tour and a picnic lunch. Following lunch, you can explore the historical Native American lands before returning to your helicopter for a second flight to watch the beautiful sunset. Join us for a complimentary steak dinner at the Explore and Adventure Lodge.

---

http://www.grandcanyonexploreadventure.com/reservations/customerreceipt

Customer Reservation Receipt

Date of purchase:	August 3
Customer name:	June Thompson
Reference number:	877573999

Reservation Details	No. of Passengers	Payment Total
Ultimate Grand Canyon Tour Package (August 27 departure)	6 x $80	$480

Payment Method:	Credit Card
Card Number:	111222-359229
Cardholder's Name:	June Thompson
Card Expiry Date:	07/20

Please retain a copy of this receipt for your records. We recommend that you print a copy and bring it with you on the day of your tour. Furthermore, we recommend that you arrive one hour in advance of your departure time in order to be briefed on all safety precautions.

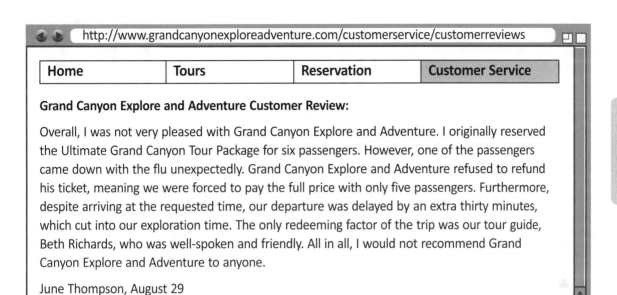

Grand Canyon Explore and Adventure Customer Review:

Overall, I was not very pleased with Grand Canyon Explore and Adventure. I originally reserved the Ultimate Grand Canyon Tour Package for six passengers. However, one of the passengers came down with the flu unexpectedly. Grand Canyon Explore and Adventure refused to refund his ticket, meaning we were forced to pay the full price with only five passengers. Furthermore, despite arriving at the requested time, our departure was delayed by an extra thirty minutes, which cut into our exploration time. The only redeeming factor of the trip was our tour guide, Beth Richards, who was well-spoken and friendly. All in all, I would not recommend Grand Canyon Explore and Adventure to anyone.

June Thompson, August 29

196. What is true about the Grand Canyon Helicopter Tour & Lunch Package?

(A) It is designed for large groups.
(B) It includes lunch in a restaurant.
(C) It is the most frequently purchased tour.
(D) It brings the guests over the Hoover Dam and Lake Mead.

197. What time and day must Ms. Thompson's group arrive for their tour?

(A) At 10:30 A.M. on August 3
(B) At 11:30 A.M. on August 3
(C) At 10:30 A.M. on August 27
(D) At 14:30 P.M. on August 27

198. What does Grand Canyon Explore and Adventure recommend Ms. Thompson to do?

(A) Write a review on their website
(B) Pay via bank transfer
(C) Bring some food with them
(D) Save a copy of her receipt

199. What is suggested about Ms. Thompson's tour?

(A) Ms. Thompson paid for it in cash.
(B) It featured a kayak tour along a river.
(C) The guide was rude and unprofessional.
(D) It concluded with a free meal.

200. According to Ms. Thompson, how much should her group have been charged?

(A) $80
(B) $350
(C) $400
(D) $450

**Stop! This is the end of the test. If you finish before time is called, you may go
back to Parts 5, 6, and 7 and check your work.**

LISTENING TEST

In the Listening test, you will be asked to demonstrate how well you understand spoken English. The entire Listening test will last approximately 45 minutes. There are four parts, and directions are given for each part. You must mark your answers on the separate answer sheet. Do not write your answers in your test book.

PART 1

Directions: For each question in this part, you will hear four statements about a picture in your test book. When you hear the statements, you must select the one statement that best describes what you see in the picture. Then find the number of the question on your answer sheet and mark your answer. The statements will not be printed in your test book and will be spoken only one time.

Example

Sample Answer

Ⓐ Ⓑ ● Ⓓ

Statement (C), "A woman is admiring some artwork.," is the best description of the picture, so you should select answer (C) and mark it on your answer sheet.

1.

2.

GO ON TO THE NEXT PAGE

3.

4.

5.

6.

GO ON TO THE NEXT PAGE

Directions: You will hear a question or statement and three responses spoken in English. They will not be printed in your test book and will be spoken only one time. Select the best response to the question or statement and mark the letter (A), (B), or (C) on your answer sheet.

7. Mark your answer on your answer sheet.

8. Mark your answer on your answer sheet.

9. Mark your answer on your answer sheet.

10. Mark your answer on your answer sheet.

11. Mark your answer on your answer sheet.

12. Mark your answer on your answer sheet.

13. Mark your answer on your answer sheet.

14. Mark your answer on your answer sheet.

15. Mark your answer on your answer sheet.

16. Mark your answer on your answer sheet.

17. Mark your answer on your answer sheet.

18. Mark your answer on your answer sheet.

19. Mark your answer on your answer sheet.

20. Mark your answer on your answer sheet.

21. Mark your answer on your answer sheet.

22. Mark your answer on your answer sheet.

23. Mark your answer on your answer sheet.

24. Mark your answer on your answer sheet.

25. Mark your answer on your answer sheet.

26. Mark your answer on your answer sheet.

27. Mark your answer on your answer sheet.

28. Mark your answer on your answer sheet.

29. Mark your answer on your answer sheet.

30. Mark your answer on your answer sheet.

31. Mark your answer on your answer sheet.

PART 3 🎧

Directions: You will hear some conversations between two or more people. You will be asked to answer three questions about what the speakers say in each conversation. Select the best response to each question and mark the letter (A), (B), (C), or (D) on your answer sheet. The conversations will not be printed in your test book and will be spoken only one time.

32. Where is the conversation most likely taking place?

(A) At a clothing store
(B) At an outdoor market
(C) At a second-hand shop
(D) At a fabric store

33. What is the problem?

(A) The price was not correct.
(B) A receipt is missing.
(C) An item is defective.
(D) A product is sold out.

34. What does the woman ask the man for?

(A) A membership upgrade
(B) His current address
(C) A credit card number
(D) Proof of payment

35. What is the woman trying to do?

(A) Get a refund
(B) Print some tickets
(C) Reserve a flight
(D) Schedule an event

36. What has caused a problem?

(A) Some tickets are sold out.
(B) An account has expired.
(C) The printer is not working.
(D) Some payment errors occurred.

37. What information does the man ask the woman for?

(A) An address
(B) A credit card number
(C) An account password
(D) A payment total

38. What does the woman ask the man to do?

  (A) Cancel an appointment
  (B) Call a manager
  (C) Repair a vehicle
  (D) Pick up a coworker

39. What does the man say he needs to do?

  (A) Borrow a car
  (B) Delay a trip
  (C) Hire a driver
  (D) Meet a client

40. What does the woman remind the man to do?

  (A) Arrive an hour early
  (B) Park in the free area
  (C) Call a car company
  (D) Carry some luggage

41. Where do the speakers most likely work?

  (A) At a law firm
  (B) At a department store
  (C) At an art gallery
  (D) At a fashion company

42. What does the woman mean when she says, "I can't make any promises"?

  (A) She is unable to confirm her participation.
  (B) She is busy with other projects.
  (C) She will leave her contract early.
  (D) She has to hire additional employees.

43. What does the man propose?

  (A) Attending a meeting
  (B) Calling a supervisor
  (C) Delivering a report
  (D) Preparing a proposal

44. What type of business is the man calling?

  (A) A dental clinic
  (B) A post office
  (C) A moving company
  (D) A bookstore

45. What problem does the woman mention?

  (A) A payment was not made.
  (B) A package was sent back.
  (C) An address is wrong.
  (D) A form is missing.

46. What will the man most likely do next?

  (A) Make a phone call to a client
  (B) Check the reverse side of an item
  (C) E-mail a document to a colleague
  (D) Provide payment information

47. Who is the woman?

  (A) A veterinarian
  (B) A reporter
  (C) A shelter owner
  (D) An artist

48. What has the man recently done?

  (A) Hired new summer employees
  (B) Appeared on a television program
  (C) Purchased a local animal shelter
  (D) Introduced animals to a workplace

49. What does the man say about the cost of the program?

  (A) Employees cover most of the costs.
  (B) The benefits outweigh the costs.
  (C) Donations help offset the costs.
  (D) The program does not cost anything.

50. What type of event are the speakers attending?

(A) A job orientation
(B) A staff party
(C) A law conference
(D) An orchestra performance

51. Why does the woman say, "Are you sure that's okay?"?

(A) She wants to leave a meeting early.
(B) She thinks the speakers are too quiet.
(C) She prefers to be in a larger room.
(D) She does not like an option very much.

52. What does the man say about the comment cards?

(A) They include personal information.
(B) They are too small to write on.
(C) They can be handed in after the presentation.
(D) They are reserved for managers only.

53. Where most likely does the woman work?

(A) A travel agency
(B) A taxi and limo service
(C) A car rental company
(D) A conference center

54. What does the man say about his trip?

(A) He needs to pick up many people.
(B) He will be traveling for two months.
(C) His company pays for his expenses.
(D) His colleagues are giving presentations.

55. What information does the woman request?

(A) A hotel's location
(B) The cost of flight
(C) The dates of a trip
(D) Some contact information

56. What problem does the restaurant have?

(A) It lost some applications.
(B) Its appliances are too old.
(C) Its costs have increased.
(D) It got some negative reviews.

57. What does the woman suggest?

(A) Hiring some new employees
(B) Offering more menu options
(C) Advertising online
(D) Providing refunds

58. What does the woman ask Max to do?

(A) Contact a store manager
(B) Prepare for the next meeting
(C) Host a student job fair
(D) Respond to online reviews

59. What are the speakers discussing?

(A) Hiring a training agency
(B) Advertising on the web
(C) Launching a new product
(D) Hosting a conference

60. What type of business does the woman own?

(A) A trade corporation
(B) A web development firm
(C) A landscaping business
(D) A home improvement company

61. What does the man suggest?

(A) Developing a program
(B) Interviewing some clients
(C) Finding a company online
(D) Attending a meeting

Admission Price per Person
Students $10
Groups of 6 or more $13
Members $17
Non-members $20

62. What type of event are the speakers discussing?

(A) A film release
(B) A restaurant opening
(C) An academic seminar
(D) A musical performance

63. Look at the graphic. What ticket price will the speakers probably pay?

(A) $10
(B) $13
(C) $17
(D) $20

64. What does the woman offer to do?

(A) Pick up some tickets
(B) Make a purchase online
(C) Contact a coworker
(D) Delay an event

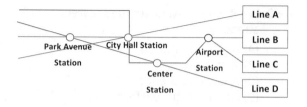

65. Where does the conversation take place?

(A) At a bus stop
(B) In a subway station
(C) At an airport
(D) In an office

66. Look at the graphic. Which line does the man suggest the woman take first?

(A) Line A
(B) Line B
(C) Line C
(D) Line D

67. Why is the woman going to Florida?

(A) To visit with family
(B) To attend a seminar
(C) To go to an office
(D) To meet some clients

FROM	SUBJECT:
Andrew Webber	ATTACHED: August Sales Figures
Anna Stevens	Budget Projection for September
David Skinner	Advertising Meeting Summary
Janine Rogers	CANCELED: Dinner with Mr. Sampson

68. Why is the man unable to access his e-mail?

(A) The company servers are down.
(B) His office connection is not working.
(C) He needs to upgrade his software.
(D) His computer has no battery power.

69. Look at the graphic. Who sent the e-mail the speakers are referring to?

(A) Andrew Webber
(B) Anna Stevens
(C) David Skinner
(D) Janine Rogers

70. What does the man ask the woman to do?

(A) Pass on an e-mail
(B) Attend a meeting
(C) Scan a budget report
(D) Cancel a client dinner

PART 4 🎧 (12)

Directions: You will hear some talks given by a single speaker. You will be asked to answer three questions about what the speaker says in each talk. Select the best response to each question and mark the letter (A), (B), (C), or (D) on your answer sheet. The talks will not be printed in your test book and will be spoken only one time.

71. Where does the speaker work?
    (A) At a radio station
    (B) At a hospital
    (C) At a university
    (D) At a newspaper

72. What will Dr. McKay be discussing?
    (A) Business finances
    (B) Healthy living
    (C) Beauty products
    (D) Political candidates

73. What does the speaker encourage listeners to do?
    (A) Write down tips and information
    (B) Call a receptionist with questions
    (C) Purchase a new best-selling book
    (D) Leave a comment on a website

74. Who most likely are the listeners?
    (A) Hotel guests
    (B) Supermarket employees
    (C) Business managers
    (D) Restaurant workers

75. What is the topic of the meeting?
    (A) Introducing new menus
    (B) Being friendly with customers
    (C) Wearing company uniforms
    (D) Policies for cleaning workspaces

76. What will the listeners do next?
    (A) Watch a film
    (B) Complete a survey
    (C) Practice a dialogue
    (D) Study a pamphlet

77. What event is being introduced?

   (A) A store opening
   (B) A charity marathon
   (C) A product demonstration
   (D) A technology sale

78. What did Steven Jones do over the last three years?

   (A) Lead several development projects
   (B) Review new products in the market
   (C) Acquire a few small companies
   (D) Coordinate marketing campaigns

79. What should listeners do if they want to attend the question and answer session?

   (A) Install a new app
   (B) Visit a press room
   (C) Log into a website
   (D) Hand in a question card

80. What did the speaker find out?

   (A) His conference was canceled.
   (B) His luggage was misplaced.
   (C) His reservation was lost.
   (D) His speech is too long.

81. What is the speaker scheduled to do on Friday?

   (A) Take a vacation
   (B) Meet some clients
   (C) Review a proposal
   (D) Attend a conference

82. Why does the man say, "I know you're busy preparing your presentation"?

   (A) To reschedule a trip date
   (B) To acknowledge an inconvenience
   (C) To offer help with a project
   (D) To provide feedback on some work

83. According to the news report, what will happen over the next five years?

   (A) A city will be planned and developed.
   (B) A new highway route will be completed.
   (C) A new location for the city hall will be sought.
   (D) A tourism sector will be revamped.

84. What benefit to travelers does the speaker mention?

   (A) Safer ways to travel
   (B) Discounts for families
   (C) Beautiful natural landscapes
   (D) Shorter travel times

85. What does the speaker say about express passes?

   (A) They can be used repeatedly.
   (B) They can be ordered online.
   (C) They will be distributed free of charge.
   (D) They will expire every six months.

86. Who most likely are the listeners?

   (A) Librarians
   (B) Educators
   (C) Nurses
   (D) Professors

87. What does the woman mean when she says, "we have another group scheduled after lunch"?

   (A) A meeting will take place later.
   (B) Some refunds will be given.
   (C) An event will be canceled.
   (D) She cannot wait any longer.

88. What will the speaker distribute to the listeners?

   (A) A sign-up form
   (B) Music CDs
   (C) Training materials
   (D) Payment requests

89. What does the speaker say about the law firm?

(A) It hired some full-time employees.
(B) It has donated to a local charity.
(C) It will merge with another firm.
(D) It acquired some new cases.

90. According to the speaker, what decision was recently made?

(A) To hire temporary staff
(B) To cancel summer vacations
(C) To increase some rates
(D) To renovate a conference room

91. What does the speaker ask the listeners to do?

(A) Host a training session
(B) Interview candidates
(C) Submit resumes
(D) Fill out a questionnaire

---

92. What is the talk mostly about?

(A) An awards ceremony
(B) A film festival
(C) A local competition
(D) A political speech

93. What does the speaker imply when he says, "You won't want to miss it"?

(A) A local event will be sold out soon.
(B) Some performances will start early.
(C) The show was very popular last year.
(D) A schedule of events is very exciting.

94. Why does the speaker suggest that listeners visit a website?

(A) To get a free parking pass
(B) To see a full list of contestants
(C) To find a map of the event
(D) To sign up to be a performer

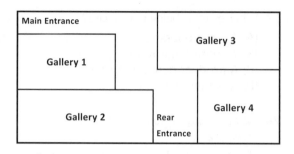

95. What is the gallery featuring this month?

(A) Landscape photography
(B) Watercolor paintings
(C) Abstract installations
(D) Pencil sketches

96. Look at the graphic. In which room is the Cubist art exhibit?

(A) Gallery 1
(B) Gallery 2
(C) Gallery 3
(D) Gallery 4

97. How can listeners attend a guided tour?

(A) By paying a fee
(B) By calling a tour guide
(C) By registering on a website
(D) By signing up on a sheet

September 1	Taxi to Airport: $45	Client Dinner: $98
September 2	Car Rental: $55	Convention Ticket: $35

98. Why is the speaker calling?

    (A) An application has been lost.
    (B) A submission is incomplete.
    (C) A trip has been delayed.
    (D) A file is damaged.

99. Look at the graphic. Which expense is the man referring to?

    (A) Taxi to Airport
    (B) Car Rental
    (C) Client Dinner
    (D) Convention Ticket

100. What does the speaker say he can do?

    (A) Send a form
    (B) Pay a fee
    (C) Reject a request
    (D) Submit a proposal

This is the end of the Listening test. Turn to Part 5 in your test book.

READING TEST

In the Reading Test, you will read a variety of texts and answer several different types of reading comprehension questions. The entire Reading test will last 75 minutes. There are three parts, and directions are given for each part. You are encouraged to answer as many questions as possible within the time allowed.

You must mark your answers on the separate answer sheet. Do not write your answers in your test book.

PART 5

Directions: A word or phrase is missing in each of the sentences below. Four answer choices are given below each sentence. Select the best answer to complete the sentence. Then mark the letter (A), (B), (C), or (D) on your answer sheet.

101. The ------- of additional city councilors will take place at the beginning of next year.

(A) appoint
(B) appoints
(C) appointed
(D) appointment

102. The president of Northern Star Footwear stated that ------ is drafting a proposal for a business merger.

(A) him
(B) he
(C) his
(D) himself

103. Ms. Wilson should update her itinerary before she ------- for her trip overseas.

(A) will leave
(B) leaves
(C) leaving
(D) left

104. According to the report, the recent ------- with the city mayor's office did not progress favorably.

(A) negotiator
(B) negotiations
(C) negotiated
(D) negotiates

105. Several of the candidates were given interviews, but only a few of ------- were chosen for the positions.

(A) we
(B) us
(C) our
(D) ourselves

106. The merger was successful because all the partners played a role in ------- planning the deal.

(A) strategy
(B) strategic
(C) strategized
(D) strategically

107. After completing his degree at an American university, Paul Bouchard ------- to Paris to teach at a local school.

(A) visited
(B) returned
(C) occurred
(D) related

108. Please ensure all deliveries are brought to the side ------- of the supermarket.

(A) entrant
(B) entered
(C) entering
(D) entrance

109. The urban planners met several times a week to discuss plans for the upcoming downtown development -------.

(A) statement
(B) permission
(C) project
(D) ability

110. The sales position will be open to new graduates, ------- means applicants must have completed a degree program.

(A) whoever
(B) who
(C) which
(D) whatever

111. Courses at the company ------- to both seasonal hires and long-term employees.

(A) are offered
(B) have offered
(C) an offer
(D) offering

112. The Benson Music School is situated just ------- the Roland Dental Clinic on Boyd Avenue.

(A) into
(B) over
(C) among
(D) past

113. Following a mandatory probationary period, full-time employees are ------- to receive benefits.

(A) beneficial
(B) eligible
(C) convenient
(D) relevant

114. The Weston Grant ------- outstanding research conducted in the science and technology field.

(A) recognizes
(B) assumes
(C) reassures
(D) moderates

115. Every staff member is given an employee handbook so they can ------- remind themselves of procedures.

(A) consecutively
(B) standardly
(C) namely
(D) easily

116. Sanford Shoes is the most popular outlet in the city because its products are always durable, ------- priced, and fashionable.

(A) reason
(B) reasoning
(C) reasonable
(D) reasonably

117. All staff at Brennan's are ------- to discuss your home decorating needs either in person or over the phone.

(A) delighting
(B) delighted
(C) delights
(D) delight

118. Rose Textile Manufacturers uses the ------- latest manufacturing equipment and materials.

(A) so
(B) more
(C) very
(D) much

119. All Libby brand refrigerators come with a two-year guarantee -------- stated otherwise.

(A) whereas
(B) below
(C) neither
(D) unless

120. The community thanks you for your ------- in keeping Acorn Valley Apartments clean and safe.

(A) participant
(B) participation
(C) participate
(D) participated

121. The interest rates were a key ------- in the CEO's decision to switch to the Emerald Bank.

(A) factor
(B) position
(C) instructor
(D) composition

122. The health inspector will arrive at an unforeseen date ------- ensure the conditions of the inspection are fair.

(A) even if
(B) in order to
(C) after all
(D) given that

123. Peter Nugent's novel was made into an adventure movie two years ago after Winston Studios obtained -------- from Nugent's grandson.

(A) permission
(B) suggestion
(C) comparison
(D) registration

124. The mayor's office has issued a statement ------- the use of tax revenue to repair roads in the coming year.

(A) excluding
(B) during
(C) following
(D) regarding

125. The Delbert Condominium Tower is
------- located within walking distance of
two subway stations.

(A) conveniently
(B) consistently
(C) continually
(D) commonly

126. Interns should ------- new applications if
they wish to apply for any of the new full-
time positions.

(A) reply
(B) submit
(C) vacate
(D) oppose

127. Ms. Houlahan's revised draft of Reynold
Manufacturing's mission statement
expresses the goals of the company --------.

(A) precise
(B) more precise
(C) preciseness
(D) precisely

128. ------- the park is open during the summer
months, the public is restricted from
accessing certain areas.

(A) While
(B) When
(C) For
(D) But

129. ------- the education level of Paul Rogers,
it is no wonder that he is the highest-paid
speaker at the convention.

(A) About
(B) Given
(C) Upon
(D) Since

130. Considering all the hot weather we're
having, the number of people using public
swimming pools is ------- to increase.

(A) covered
(B) sought
(C) limited
(D) bound

Directions: Read the texts that follow. A word, phrase, or sentence is missing in parts of each text. Four answer choices for each question are given below the text. Select the best answer to complete the text. Then mark the letter (A), (B), (C), or (D) on your answer sheet.

Questions 131-134 refer to the following information.

At Echo Stationery Supplies, we try to ship your orders as quickly as we can. If you have concerns that your shipment has been delayed, please ____131.____ our shipping policies. Our expected delivery time may range from 4 days up to 4 weeks, which depends on the method of shipping customers choose during checkout. ____132.____ . We try to ensure our shipping estimates are accurate; however, some orders may take ____133.____ to arrive at your door. If you have found that your order is excessively ____134.____ , do not hesitate to contact us immediately. We promise to look into the problem and let you know the status of your shipment.

131. (A) note
(B) send
(C) prepare
(D) require

132. (A) Returned items will be eligible for exchanges only, not refunds.
(B) Contact our specialists to get an updated list of all of our new products.
(C) An approximate delivery date is indicated on your receipt.
(D) Visit our online feedback section and let us know how well we served you.

133. (A) length
(B) lengthy
(C) longer
(D) longest

134. (A) different
(B) delayed
(C) overpriced
(D) greater

Questions 135-138 refer to the following article.

April 24

After months of discussions, Nackawic Town Council has finally approved an agreement with DRTL Enterprises. Under the terms of the agreement, DRTL ___135.___ the 30-acre lot on the east end of Barrett Street. The detailed proposal calls for the building of both retail shops and offices in the area. Nackawic's mayor, Leona Hovey, is optimistic that the project will bring ___136.___ benefits to the town and surrounding areas. "It is expected to create 300 full-time jobs," says Hovey. "For a while, I felt the ongoing postponements would force us to cancel the project all together." ___137.___ . DRTL spokesperson, Jeff Perkins believes the development will take three years to finish. At the same time, he cautions people that there may be more setbacks. "Of course, we provided the town council with our very best ___138.___ , but even so, we have no way of predicting everything that will happen," Perkins said.

135. (A) to develop
     (B) will develop
     (C) has developed
     (D) could have developed

136. (A) economic
     (B) unforeseen
     (C) environmental
     (D) frequent

137. (A) While the town is eager to get moving on this, delays are inevitable for major developments like this.
     (B) Local residents, however, have approached us with legitimate concerns about the high noise levels construction will create.
     (C) Members of town council are set to vote on four different proposals from well-known architects.
     (D) Despite the town's promise to grant the developers a contract, they may now have to look at other options.

138. (A) argument
     (B) background
     (C) estimate
     (D) combination

Questions 139-142 refer to the following article.

Roderick Opera House has announced that it will lengthen its run of Melanie Beck's new musical, *The Birth of Jazz*. Due to an increase in ____ for tickets, the show will be playing nightly
139.
until the end of August. The announcement was unexpected, as the musical received ____
140.
criticism from renowned musical theater critic Jeffrey O'pry.

____ . However, last week the show was sold out three nights in a row. According to representatives of
141.
the opera house, the show has been attracting an older crowd who may not normally attend musicals.
The new attendees are ____ excited about hearing the great jazz numbers reinvented by Beck.
142.

139. (A) demand
     (B) demanded
     (C) demanding
     (D) to demand

140. (A) brilliant
     (B) deep
     (C) harsh
     (D) prompt

141. (A) Guests at the musical were mostly
         from out of town.
     (B) The final show will be held on August
         24.
     (C) Following the review, ticket sales
         dropped dramatically.
     (D) Similarly, the theater has been
         suffering for years.

142. (A) apparent
     (B) more apparent
     (C) apparentness
     (D) apparently

Questions 143-146 refer to the following e-mail.

From: Customer Care

To: Paul Kanagawa

Date: October 16

Subject: Welcome to Atlantic Music Trends

Attachment: Form

Dear Mr. Kanagawa,

Thank you very much for subscribing to *Atlantic Music Trends*! ___143.___ you will have detailed information about upcoming music classes, festivals, and concerts happening all over Canada's Atlantic coast. You can expect your first issue at your door by the 20th. ___144.___ . After that, every issue will be sent out during the first week of the month. With this subscription, you will also have unlimited ___145.___ to online videos, song recordings, articles, schedules, and even ticketing information for concerts. All you have to do is log on to our website using the user ID and eight-digit passwords listed ___146.___ the bottom line of the attached enrollment form.

Sincerely,

Veronica Van Zeyl

Customer Representative

ACTUAL TEST 03

143. (A) Now
   (B) Afterward
   (C) Then
   (D) Meanwhile

144. (A) Please notify us if it does not arrive by that date.
   (B) To subscribe, please phone during regular business hours.
   (C) The next festival will take place in Moncton in mid-November.
   (D) We invite readers to submit reviews of concerts for publication.

145. (A) accessing
   (B) accesses
   (C) accessed
   (D) access

146. (A) for
   (B) about
   (C) on
   (D) at

Directions: In this part you will read a selection of texts, such as magazine and newspaper articles, e-mails, and instant messages. Each text or set of texts is followed by several questions. Select the best answer for each question and mark the letter (A), (B), (C), or (D) on your answer sheet.

Questions 147-148 refer to the following notice.

Jen's Salon and Spa

Holiday Information

- Spa hours will be extended from November 20 to January 20.
  (Monday — Saturday 10 A.M. to 10 P.M.)
- Please note, the spa will be closed from December 24 – 29.
- As always, cancellations must be made 24 hours in advance to avoid cancelation fees.

---

147. What is the purpose of the notice?

(A) To advertise a new service
(B) To explain a schedule
(C) To announce a sale
(D) To offer a refund

148. What is stated about cancellations?

(A) The spa requires advance notice of cancellations.
(B) Customers can cancel appointments online.
(C) A service fee is always applied to cancellations.
(D) Holiday appointments cannot be cancelled.

Notice for Eastpoint Community Residents

As of next month, our weekly community newsletter will be going paperless. In an effort to protect the environment and reduce the amount of paper we use, the newsletter will now be available online only.

Anyone who currently has a small business advertisement in the newsletter is encouraged to contact the newsletter editor for an updated contract at 900-555-3434. The first online newsletter is scheduled to be on www.eastpointcommunity.com/newsletter on November 1. We hope you enjoy this new convenient way to receive your weekly newsletter.

Sincerely,

Eastpoint Community Newsletter Team

---

149. What change will be made to the newsletter?

(A) It will merge with another publication.

(B) It will be delivered faster.

(C) It will run less frequently.

(D) It will no longer be printed on paper.

150. According to the notice, why might advertisers contact the editor?

(A) To sign a new contract

(B) To receive a discount

(C) To upgrade a membership

(D) To change a listing

Questions 151-153 refer to the following agenda.

Unpaid Spring Training Session
9:30 A.M. to 4:30 P.M.

9:30 A.M.: Meet and Greet
Meet your managers as well as your fellow new employees. Enjoy coffee and donuts as you watch a short introduction video to the company.

10:30 A.M.: Rules and Procedures
Pick up your employee handbook and review the rules and procedures with the office manager. A short question and answer session will be included.

12:00 P.M.: Lunch Break
A light buffet lunch of sandwiches, salads, and desserts will be catered in the conference room. Vegetarian options will be provided for employees.

1:00 P.M.: Department Shadowing
Employees will visit their respective departments and receive hands-on training from an assigned veteran employee.

3:30 P.M.: Desk Assignments
Employees will be shown to their desks and given an opportunity to set up their company accounts and e-mails. IT will be available for any problems that may arise.

---

151. For whom is the session most likely intended?

(A) Company CEOs
(B) Computer technicians
(C) New office employees
(D) Department transfers

152. What portion of the session involves IT specialists?

(A) Meet and Greet
(B) Rules and Procedures
(C) Department Shadowing
(D) Desk Assignments

153. What is NOT indicated about the session?

(A) It is an unpaid event.
(B) It lasts for one work day.
(C) It is run by the HR director.
(D) It includes refreshments.

Questions 154-157 refer to the following report.

Rengrew Bedding

Weekly Status Report: September 5-9
Prepared by: Alexander Corbin, Project Coordinator

Accomplished this Week:

- Got in touch with four manufacturers in Mexico who currently produce bedding products.
  --[1]--. E-mailed them design specifications for our new bedding sets along with questions about production pricing, turnaround time, fabric availability, and shipping costs.

- According to the replies, P&M Textiles appears to be the best candidate. --[2]--. Additionally, Sammy Ruiz, a client services manager, e-mailed me promptly. Her responses to my questions were very detailed and professional. I believe she would ensure this transition is both smooth and efficient.

- The other three companies either did not have access to our preferred fabrics or they could not meet our supply demand. --[3]--. As a result, we will no longer be able to consider them.

Plans for Next Week:

- Contact P&M Textiles to set up a conference call about payment and shipping terms. --[4]--.

- Review final designs for all products and request revisions if need be. Meet with the design team to discuss any changes.

---

154. What is suggested about Rengrew Bedding?
(A) It has just hired a new manager.
(B) It is a brand new company in Mexico.
(C) It has its own factories on-site.
(D) It is getting ready to launch new products.

155. According to the report, what did Mr. Corbin do during the week of September 5?
(A) Finalized some design information
(B) Assessed potential business partners
(C) Visited a manufacturer in person
(D) Requested a payment be delayed

156. What is mentioned about Ms. Ruiz?
(A) She is new to P&M Textiles.
(B) She suggested some changes.
(C) She contacted some businesses.
(D) She is easy to work with.

157. In which of the positions marked [1], [2], [3], and [4] does the following sentence best belong?

"It is located further south than most companies, but it has the capacity to meet our supply needs."
(A) [1]
(B) [2]
(C) [3]
(D) [4]

Grand Avenue Hotel: Banquet Services

Thank you for choosing Grand Avenue Hotel for your banquet. Please fill out the information below. One of our guest services representatives will contact you to confirm your reservation and request payment information.

Reservation Name: _____ Event Date: _____
E-mail: _____ Business Phone: _____
Personal Phone: _____

Room Preference:
[   ] Diamond Room (up to 100 guests) [   ] Rose Room (up to 150 guests)
[   ] Starlight Room (up to 200 guests)

Requested Layout:
[   ] Dinner (round tables and chairs) [   ] Dinner and Dance (tables and a dance floor)
[   ] Dinner and Speech (tables and a stage) [   ] Other : _____

Food and Beverages:
[   ] Full-Service Buffet and Dessert Bar [   ] Three-Course Catered Dinner

AV Equipment Required: [   ] Yes [   ] No Explain: _____
Hotel Accommodation for Guests: [   ] Yes [   ] No Number of Rooms: _____

---

158. According to the form, what will Grand Avenue Hotel staff do?

(A) E-mail brochures with room photos
(B) Assist customers with setup and cleanup
(C) Offer free accommodation vouchers to guests
(D) Contact customers about payment information

159. What is implied about Grand Avenue Hotel's banquet services?

(A) It requires payment for the use of audio-visual equipment.
(B) It will arrange the room to suit the event.
(C) It provides discounted hotel rooms to banquet guests.
(D) It offers free live music for dinner and dance events.

Questions 160-162 refer to the following job advertisement.

---

https://www.employmentfind.com

Find Employment Online

Build Your Career Today!

The real estate business can be hard when you're working alone. At Team Real Estate, you are not alone! Our large network of real estate agents makes showing and selling properties easy. By sharing information on potential buyers in our database, we sell more properties than any other agency in the country. Our shared commission rates encourage our team members to work together to get the job done.

Complete our new real estate training seminar and apply for your real estate license. If you're successful, you may be offered a full-time contract position with full benefits.

Education and experience will be considered before you are offered a contract. University degrees are a plus, but high school graduates may also apply. Applicants must have access to their own vehicle, as driving to and from local properties is a must.

To apply for this position, please click the button below. You'll need to input your e-mail address, phone number, and upload your resume. Only those selected for interviews will be contacted. Prior to interviews, we recommend that all candidates familiarize themselves with our company policies. Please visit www.teamrealestate.com/careers to learn more about this.

> **Apply Now**

---

160. What duty is suggested as part of the job?

(A) Listing clients on a shared database
(B) Offering advice on upgrading properties
(C) Attracting clients through phone calls
(D) Coordinating a mentorship program

161. According to the advertisement, what is requested for a contract position?

(A) A college diploma
(B) A real estate license
(C) Marketing experience
(D) Employment references

162. According to the advertisement, why should applicants visit the Team Real Estate website?

(A) To learn about Team Real Estate's procedures
(B) To apply for a contract position with benefits
(C) To upload a resume and references
(D) To inquire about the time of a training session

Questions 163-166 refer to the following article.

50 Years of Community Service

March 27 — Professor Abraham Drew is known in the local community not for his years as a teacher of psychology or for his numerous papers published in academic journals, but for his dedication to community outreach. Fifty years ago, Mr. Drew founded the first after-school program for local children, which has helped numerous children in the city. The program, which started as a baseball camp for troubled boys, has since grown into Homework Helpers for elementary school-aged children, Art on the Street for teenagers, and Give Back, a charity in which individuals and businesses organize food drives for the homeless. "I never thought my after-school program would develop into all these unique programs," Mr. Drew said, "but there was so much community interest. Everywhere, people were looking for a way to help out."

After 50 years of service, Mr. Drew will retire from both his job as a professor and as program coordinator. His grandson, Michael Drew, will retain control of the programs. "I'm very happy to continue what my grandfather started," Michael Drew said. "He's a great man, and the community needs the work he has done."

Mr. Drew's volunteers will host a retirement party to honor him next month at Wilfred Park. The party will include performances by local bands, food prepared by local restaurants, and a small fireworks show. The mayor will present Mr. Drew with a Lifetime Service Achievement Award as thanks for his years of giving back to the community. For details about this event, please visit www.wilfredpark.com/events/April.

163. Why most likely was the article written?
(A) To celebrate the founding of a city
(B) To encourage readers to donate to charity
(C) To announce the closing of a community business
(D) To highlight the achievements of a local figure

164. The word "retain" in paragraph 2, line 2, is closest in meaning to
(A) contribute to
(B) agree with
(C) remember
(D) keep

165. What is NOT suggested about Abraham Drew?
(A) He started a baseball camp for boys.
(B) He instructs students at a university.
(C) He will open another school next year.
(D) He inspired others to do charity work.

166. What is stated about the party at Wilfred Park?
(A) Local comedy acts will perform.
(B) The city will host the celebration.
(C) Participants can attend for a small fee.
(D) Mr. Drew will be honored with an award.

Questions 167-168 refer to the following text message chain.

Pedro Alando [11:00 A.M.]:
Ms. Wilson, please check your e-mail. I sent you an updated contract.

Tina Wilson [11:02 A.M.]:
OK, thank you. Has the payment scale been updated as well?

Pedro Alando [11:03 A.M.]:
Certainly. Because you've been with us for longer than a year, you will now be paid $100 dollars for every color photo you take for our magazine instead of $80.

Tina Wilson [11:05 A.M.]:
Excellent. Thank you for clarifying that. I'll have a look at the contract, sign it, and send it back shortly.

Pedro Alando [11:08 A.M.]:
Fantastic. We are very pleased you have decided to work with us for another year.

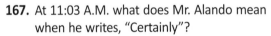
SEND

167. At 11:03 A.M. what does Mr. Alando mean when he writes, "Certainly"?

(A) He will send an e-mail one more time.

(B) He is sure of the success of a plan.

(C) He is willing to share some information.

(D) He made a previously agreed-upon change.

168. Who most likely is Ms. Wilson?

(A) A contract lawyer

(B) A magazine editor

(C) A photographer

(D) A journalist

Questions 169-171 refer to the following e-mail.

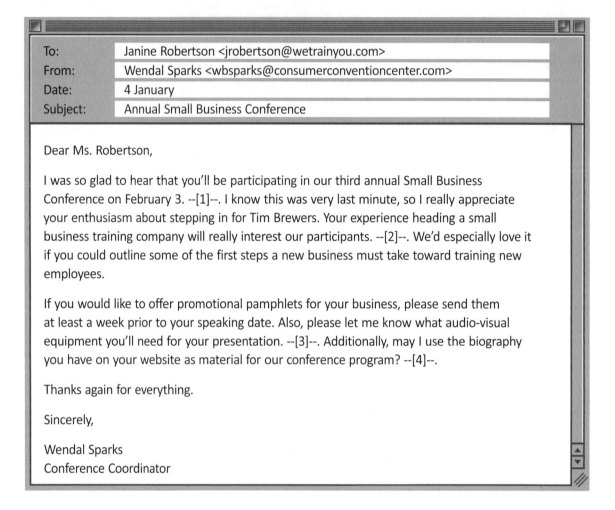

To: Janine Robertson <jrobertson@wetrainyou.com>
From: Wendal Sparks <wbsparks@consumerconventioncenter.com>
Date: 4 January
Subject: Annual Small Business Conference

Dear Ms. Robertson,

I was so glad to hear that you'll be participating in our third annual Small Business Conference on February 3. --[1]--. I know this was very last minute, so I really appreciate your enthusiasm about stepping in for Tim Brewers. Your experience heading a small business training company will really interest our participants. --[2]--. We'd especially love it if you could outline some of the first steps a new business must take toward training new employees.

If you would like to offer promotional pamphlets for your business, please send them at least a week prior to your speaking date. Also, please let me know what audio-visual equipment you'll need for your presentation. --[3]--. Additionally, may I use the biography you have on your website as material for our conference program? --[4]--.

Thanks again for everything.

Sincerely,

Wendal Sparks
Conference Coordinator

169. Why did Mr. Sparks most likely send the e-mail?

(A) To propose an itinerary change
(B) To ask for an updated schedule
(C) To send a belated invitation
(D) To recognize an offer of acceptance

170. What is suggested about Mr. Brewers?

(A) He attends conferences every year.
(B) He is unable to speak at a conference.
(C) He works as an event coordinator.
(D) He started his own small business.

171. In which of the positions marked [1], [2], [3], and [4] does the following sentence best belong?

"If you'd prefer to use a different text, please e-mail it to me."

(A) [1]
(B) [2]
(C) [3]
(D) [4]

Questions 172-175 refer to the following text message chain.

Jan Swanson   **4 September, 2:35**

Jonathan, have you sent order #2256 out for delivery?
If not, we need to add another identical set of personalized pens and paper to it.

Jonathan Gruer   **4 September, 2:37**

The order is still in the storeroom, but it'll take at least two more days to produce the custom pens and paper.

Jan Swanson   **4 September, 2:38**

Is it possible to get it done sooner? The customer said it's urgent.

Jonathan Gruer   **4 September, 2:40**

Let's check with someone from manufacturing.

Rowena MacArthur has been added to the chat.

Jonathan Gruer   **4 September, 2:41**

Rowena, do you have time for a rush order? It's a duplicate of order #2256.

Rowena MacArthur   **4 September, 2:43**

I think I can get it done by tomorrow morning. Is that OK?

Jan Swanson   **4 September, 2:44**

Yes, that works. Thanks a lot!

---

172. What type of products does the company sell?

(A) Watches
(B) Stationery
(C) Furniture
(D) Electronics

173. Why does Mr. Gruer contact Ms. MacArthur?

(A) To pass on a customer complaint
(B) To find out where a staff meeting will be held
(C) To determine where an order has been shipped to
(D) To inquire about the timeframe for some work

174. What does the customer want to do?

(A) Double an order
(B) Cancel a delivery
(C) Return a damaged item
(D) Update payment information

175. At 2:44, what does Ms. Swanson most likely mean when she writes, "that works"?

(A) She can reschedule some appointments.
(B) She is impressed with a new product.
(C) A deadline will be acceptable for a customer.
(D) Some new items will be advertised online.

To:	msimpson@tristarinternational.com
From:	bookings@stonewallhotel.com
Date:	May 17
Subject:	Booking CV1124

Dear Ms. Simpson,

Thank you for selecting Stonewall Hotel for your company's annual workshop. As you indicated on your online reservation, 12 king-sized ocean view suites have been booked for your group. Since the purpose of your visit is to conduct a business workshop, I have also reserved our executive lounge and conference room at no extra charge.

According to your online reservation, your check-in date will be August 5 and your check-out will be August 8. A charge of $109 dollars for each room per night will be added to your final bill. Your reservation number is CV1124. Please ensure you record this number as you will need it should you request any changes to your reservation.

As you know, Stonewall Hotel includes many additional features and activities. If your group wish to take a complimentary surfing lesson, I suggest reserving a spot in advance. Furthermore, we offer complimentary breakfasts, room service packages, and have just opened up Stonewall Grill, a brand new steak restaurant located next to the lobby.

Thank you for choosing Stonewall Hotel. We look forward to serving you.

Booking Services, Stonewall Hotel

To:	bookings@stonewallhotel.com
From:	msimpson@tristarinternational.com
Date:	May 19
Subject: Re:	Booking CV1124

Dear booking services staff,

I am writing to let you know that there were a few errors with my reservation. My reservation number is CV1124. I indicated 10 junior-sized suites when I reserved online, but your e-mail says something different. Additionally, I also paid for a catered lunch during my group's hiking trip on August 6, but that was not mentioned in your e-mail. Please make sure this service has been booked in addition to updating the correct room size. I would appreciate it if you notified me about this issue as soon as possible.

Thank you for your assistance.

Sincerely,

Margo Simpson
Office of the CEO
Tristar International

176. What is the purpose of the first e-mail?

(A) To confirm a group reservation
(B) To inform of a new policy
(C) To assist in making a reservation
(D) To provide a free upgrade

177. What is suggested about Stonewall's surfing lessons?

(A) They are available only in the mornings.
(B) They are a new service.
(C) They are being offered temporarily.
(D) They are a popular feature.

178. What information in the hotel's records is missing?

(A) The lounge has been reserved.
(B) The group will arrive on August 5.
(C) A catering service is booked.
(D) The room bill has been prepaid.

179. What can be inferred about the group from Tristar International?

(A) It consists of 12 members.
(B) It will go hiking on the second day of the workshop.
(C) It will have dinner at the Stonewall Grill.
(D) It will arrive a day later than the reservation states.

180. In the second e-mail, the word "issue" in paragraph 1, line 6, is closest in meaning to

(A) alteration
(B) selection
(C) price
(D) problem

Heber Birdwatching Club

April 2 — The Northville Recreation Board recently announced the creation of the Heber Park Birdwatching Club at Heber Wildlife Park. The birdwatching club will meet from Friday through Sunday, from 1 P.M. until 3 P.M. The club meetings will run all summer long and will feature a number of lookout sites located on the Heber Trails. Each participant should dress appropriately for hiking on the trails and bring a supply of drinking water. Cameras are allowed for participants who want to photograph the numerous bird species located in Heber Wildlife Park. Up to 10 members may join the club, and those interested can sign up with the club coordinator, Mindy Beckett (334-998-0034).

June Weekend Activities at Heber Wildlife Park

- **Friday**
  - 12:00 P.M. Children's Picnic (Camp and Recreation Park)
  - 2:00 P.M. Heber Birdwatching Club (Squirrel Trail)
  - 4:00 P.M. T&V Industries Weekly Baseball Game (Diamond)

- **Saturday**
  - 2:00 P.M. Heber Birdwatching Club (Squirrel Trail)
  - 4:00 P.M. Barbecue Madness (East Pavilion on June 10 and 24 only)

- **Sunday**
  - 10:00 A.M. Nature Watercolor Painting (Gallery Building, $15 per person)
  - 2:00 P.M. Heber Birdwatching Club (Squirrel Trail)
  - 4:00 P.M. Level A Soccer (Soccer field)
  - 6:00 P.M. Music at the Park (West Pavilion)

For more information on any of the above events, please visit www.heberwildlifepark.com or call 556-332-0989.

181. What is the purpose of the notice?
   (A) To inform of a new activity at Heber Wildlife Park
   (B) To announce a new coordinator for the Heber Birdwatching Club
   (C) To apologize for the cancelation of an event at Heber Wildlife Park
   (D) To advertise a new position at the Northville Recreation Board

182. In the notice, the word "run" in paragraph 1, line 3, is closest in meaning to
   (A) jog
   (B) continue
   (C) roam
   (D) grow

183. What is suggested about the birdwatching club in June?
   (A) It has 12 members.
   (B) It requires participants to bring cameras.
   (C) Its meeting time has been changed.
   (D) Its coordinator will be absent.

184. What activity will only occur twice in June?
   (A) T&V Industries Baseball Game
   (B) Barbecue Madness
   (C) Nature Watercolor Painting
   (D) Music at the Park

185. What is indicated about Heber Wildlife Park?
   (A) Its pavilions have all been upgraded.
   (B) Its campground is open all year round.
   (C) It includes a lake and a water fountain.
   (D) It has special programs for children.

Questions 186-190 refer to the following advertisement, e-mail, and website feedback.

Toronto Tours

★★★★★
Toronto, Ontario

To celebrate its first year of business, Toronto Tours is offering a special 20% discount on Culture of Toronto tours booked between April 5 and May 5. This is our most popular tour and is offered every Friday. The following is breakdown of our standard itinerary.

▶ The Royal Ontario Museum: Start at the famous Royal Ontario Museum. Enjoy some of the most beautiful art in the world in the ROM's many modern galleries. See the latest archeological discoveries on display and a number of large dinosaur species. April's special exhibit: 18th Century Maps.

▶ The Hockey Hall of Fame: Head over to the Hockey Hall of Fame and see Canada's greatest hockey legends remembered in numerous video exhibits. Learn the history of Canada's favorite sport, and view memorabilia that belonged to players of the past.

▶ The Danforth Festival: Conclude your tour at the Danforth Festival. Enjoy a taste of Greek culture at this energetic street party. Sample food from Toronto's many Greek restaurants while you enjoy live music and dancing. (Until April 20)

Note: The final portion of the tour will be subject to changes depending on which festivals are taking place downtown. Additionally, all entrance fees are covered in your package price, but food and beverage costs are extra.

From:	Susan Malek
To:	Samuel Park
Date:	April 10
Re:	Reservation Confirmation

Dear Mr. Park,

Thank you for booking your tour with Toronto Tours. Below is a summary of your tour information. Should you have any questions or concerns, please contact me at 416-888-3232.

Tour name: Culture of Toronto
Tour date: April 12
Starting Time: 9:00 A.M. at Toronto Union Station
Return to Union Station: 11:30 P.M.
Your credit card has been charged: $190.00

Thank you and enjoy your tour!

Best,

Susan Malek
Tour Coordinator

Customer Feedback:

This was my first time using Toronto Tours, and I found the tour to be much more impressive than the sightseeing bus tour I took the last time I visited Toronto. This company sure understands how to treat tourists' interest in the city's unique history and culture. Francis Weltz, our tour guide, was extremely helpful in getting us to and from locations as well as ensuring speedy entry to the listed stops. The only downside of the tour was the rainy weather, which made it hard to enjoy the final stop. As a result, I wish an alternate destination would've been available in the event of poor weather.

Posted by: Samuel Park

186. What is suggested about Toronto Tours?

(A) It operates several tour programs.
(B) It has been open for several years.
(C) It will stop offering summer tours.
(D) It has added a new sightseeing tour.

187. According to the advertisement, what does Toronto Tours offer clients?

(A) Vouchers for food and beverages
(B) Upgraded travel options
(C) Discounts on group packages
(D) Admission fees to museums

188. What is suggested about Mr. Park's tour?

(A) It included return airfare from Greece.
(B) It visited four main stops.
(C) It was purchased at a discount.
(D) It was originally developed for local artists.

189. In the website feedback, the word "treat" in paragraph 1, line 3, is closest in meaning to

(A) serve
(B) increase
(C) decide
(D) ignore

190. What portion of the tour was Mr. Park dissatisfied with?

(A) Seeing off at Union Station
(B) The Royal Ontario Museum
(C) The Hockey Hall of Fame
(D) The Danforth Festival

European Manufacturing Commission

4th Annual Convention
Rowensburg Conference Center
Berlin, Germany
Saturday, October 10

Tentative Schedule

Time	Location	
9:00 A.M. – 9:30 A.M.	Greetings and Opening Speech by EMC Chairman Alek Sorvenski in the Cranz Banquet Room	
10:00 A.M. – 11:30 A.M.	Strauss Room	Whitman Room
	Textile Factory Management Techniques — Hans Tiskawet	Advanced Coloration and Bleaching Technologies — Michelle Perdeu
1:00 P.M. – 2:30 P.M.	Outsourcing and Overseas Management — Rowena Wentworth	Upgrading and Maintaining Equipment — Spencer Defiore
3:00 P.M. – 4:30 P.M.	Establishing Contacts with International Clothing Distributors — Anita Pitelli	International Shipping Strategies — Thao Lee

● Speakers must confirm their availability with Johanna Swartz (jswartz@emc.com) no later than August 28. Failure to report availability will result in an automatic change of speaker.

● Speakers will be given complimentary accommodation at the Deluxe Grand Hotel for one night. Please fill out the attached form and return it to Berta Joven by September 5. If you are traveling with a colleague or an assistant, you will need to book another room at an additional charge. Please indicate that on the form.

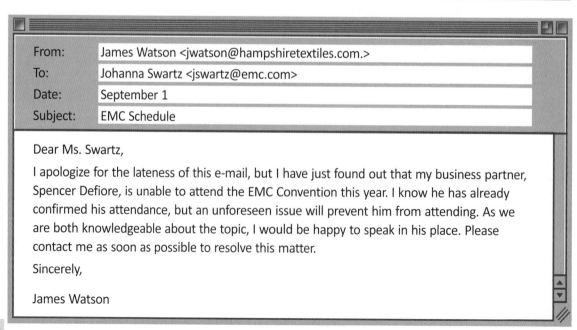

From:	James Watson <jwatson@hampshiretextiles.com.>
To:	Johanna Swartz <jswartz@emc.com>
Date:	September 1
Subject:	EMC Schedule

Dear Ms. Swartz,

I apologize for the lateness of this e-mail, but I have just found out that my business partner, Spencer Defiore, is unable to attend the EMC Convention this year. I know he has already confirmed his attendance, but an unforeseen issue will prevent him from attending. As we are both knowledgeable about the topic, I would be happy to speak in his place. Please contact me as soon as possible to resolve this matter.

Sincerely,

James Watson

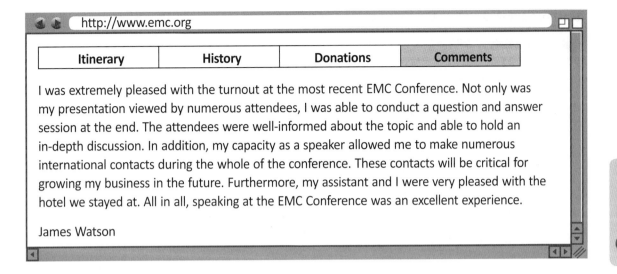

| Itinerary | History | Donations | Comments |

I was extremely pleased with the turnout at the most recent EMC Conference. Not only was my presentation viewed by numerous attendees, I was able to conduct a question and answer session at the end. The attendees were well-informed about the topic and able to hold an in-depth discussion. In addition, my capacity as a speaker allowed me to make numerous international contacts during the whole of the conference. These contacts will be critical for growing my business in the future. Furthermore, my assistant and I were very pleased with the hotel we stayed at. All in all, speaking at the EMC Conference was an excellent experience.

James Watson

191. What industry is the focus of the conference?

(A) Shipping
(B) Dairy
(C) Electronics
(D) Fabrics

192. According to the schedule, what are presenters expected to do?

(A) Pay for hotel accommodation
(B) Arrive in Berlin by October 8
(C) Ship some presentation materials
(D) Confirm their participation in an event

193. What topic will Mr. Watson most likely speak about?

(A) Textile Factory Management Techniques
(B) Outsourcing and Overseas Management
(C) Upgrading and Maintaining Equipment
(D) International Shipping Strategies

194. In the review, the word "capacity" in paragraph 1, line 4, is closest in meaning to

(A) role
(B) time
(C) perspective
(D) experience

195. What is probably true about Mr. Watson?

(A) He operates several manufacturing plants in Germany.
(B) He booked a second room at the Deluxe Grand Hotel.
(C) He attends the EMC conference every year.
(D) He changed his topic to a more difficult one.

Questions 196-200 refer to the following form, e-mail, and letter.

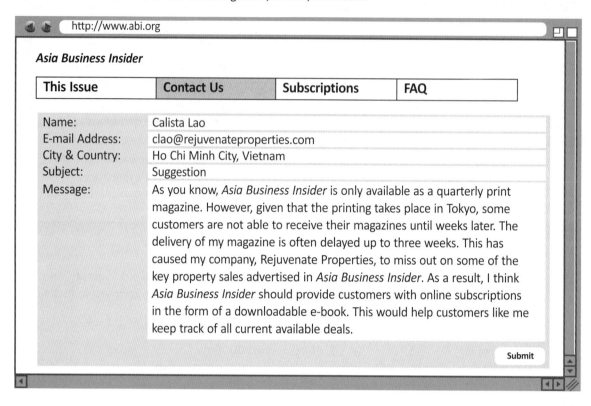

http://www.abi.org

Asia Business Insider

| This Issue | Contact Us | Subscriptions | FAQ |

Name:	Calista Lao
E-mail Address:	clao@rejuvenateproperties.com
City & Country:	Ho Chi Minh City, Vietnam
Subject:	Suggestion
Message:	As you know, *Asia Business Insider* is only available as a quarterly print magazine. However, given that the printing takes place in Tokyo, some customers are not able to receive their magazines until weeks later. The delivery of my magazine is often delayed up to three weeks. This has caused my company, Rejuvenate Properties, to miss out on some of the key property sales advertised in *Asia Business Insider*. As a result, I think *Asia Business Insider* should provide customers with online subscriptions in the form of a downloadable e-book. This would help customers like me keep track of all current available deals.

Submit

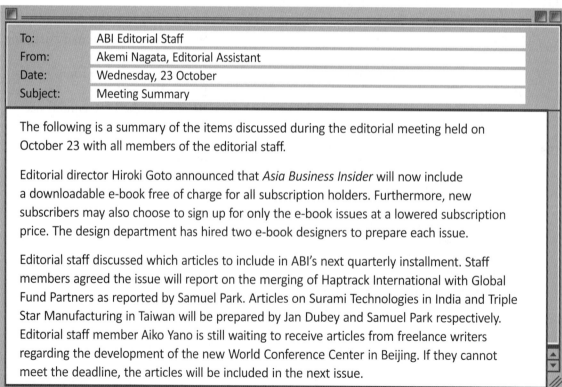

To:	ABI Editorial Staff
From:	Akemi Nagata, Editorial Assistant
Date:	Wednesday, 23 October
Subject:	Meeting Summary

The following is a summary of the items discussed during the editorial meeting held on October 23 with all members of the editorial staff.

Editorial director Hiroki Goto announced that *Asia Business Insider* will now include a downloadable e-book free of charge for all subscription holders. Furthermore, new subscribers may also choose to sign up for only the e-book issues at a lowered subscription price. The design department has hired two e-book designers to prepare each issue.

Editorial staff discussed which articles to include in ABI's next quarterly installment. Staff members agreed the issue will report on the merging of Haptrack International with Global Fund Partners as reported by Samuel Park. Articles on Surami Technologies in India and Triple Star Manufacturing in Taiwan will be prepared by Jan Dubey and Samuel Park respectively. Editorial staff member Aiko Yano is still waiting to receive articles from freelance writers regarding the development of the new World Conference Center in Beijing. If they cannot meet the deadline, the articles will be included in the next issue.

Asia Business Insider
January ▪ Vol. 7 ▪ Number 1

Letter from the Editor,

This issue celebrates the launch of *Asia Business Insider*'s e-book series. Subscribers can now download fully designed e-books that include all aspects of our print versions. The January issue will cover numerous business deals taking place in Asia. It will also include the launch of our new Editor's Commentary section in which the editorial staff will respond to questions and comments placed online.

Make sure to keep an eye out for our next issue in which we cover all the pertinent details surrounding the plans for the World Conference Center in Beijing. Make sure to sign up on our website for a chance to win free tickets to the center's grand opening business conference next year.

Hiroki Goto

196. What is true about Ms. Lao?

(A) She only buys property in Vietnam.
(B) Her ideas were implemented by ABI.
(C) She subscribes to several Japanese magazines.
(D) Her articles often appear in ABI.

197. Who will be discussing Surami Technologies?

(A) Hiroki Goto
(B) Samuel Park
(C) Jan Dubey
(D) Akemi Nagata

198. What is suggested about Aiko Yano?

(A) She joined ABI as an e-book designer.
(B) She did not receive some articles on time.
(C) She co-writes articles with Samuel Park.
(D) She was absent from the June 1 meeting.

199. What is indicated about *Asia Business Insider*?

(A) It has developed a new column.
(B) Its subscribers are mostly located in Vietnam.
(C) It will relocate to Beijing, China.
(D) It prints six issues per year.

200. What is mentioned about ABI's website?

(A) It is only for ABI subscribers.
(B) It will be upgraded next year.
(C) It is available in seven different languages.
(D) It will host a give-away for subscribers.

Stop! This is the end of the test. If you finish before time is called, you may go back to Parts 5, 6, and 7 and check your work.

LISTENING TEST 🎧 13

In the Listening test, you will be asked to demonstrate how well you understand spoken English. The entire Listening test will last approximately 45 minutes. There are four parts, and directions are given for each part. You must mark your answers on the separate answer sheet. Do not write your answers in your test book.

PART 1

Directions: For each question in this part, you will hear four statements about a picture in your test book. When you hear the statements, you must select the one statement that best describes what you see in the picture. Then find the number of the question on your answer sheet and mark your answer. The statements will not be printed in your test book and will be spoken only one time.

Example

Sample Answer

Ⓐ Ⓑ ● Ⓓ

Statement (C), "A woman is admiring some artwork.," is the best description of the picture, so you should select answer (C) and mark it on your answer sheet.

1.

2.

GO ON TO THE NEXT PAGE

3.

4.

5.

6.

PART 2 🎧 14

Directions: You will hear a question or statement and three responses spoken in English. They will not be printed in your test book and will be spoken only one time. Select the best response to the question or statement and mark the letter (A), (B), or (C) on your answer sheet.

7. Mark your answer on your answer sheet.

8. Mark your answer on your answer sheet.

9. Mark your answer on your answer sheet.

10. Mark your answer on your answer sheet.

11. Mark your answer on your answer sheet.

12. Mark your answer on your answer sheet.

13. Mark your answer on your answer sheet.

14. Mark your answer on your answer sheet.

15. Mark your answer on your answer sheet.

16. Mark your answer on your answer sheet.

17. Mark your answer on your answer sheet.

18. Mark your answer on your answer sheet.

19. Mark your answer on your answer sheet.

20. Mark your answer on your answer sheet.

21. Mark your answer on your answer sheet.

22. Mark your answer on your answer sheet.

23. Mark your answer on your answer sheet.

24. Mark your answer on your answer sheet.

25. Mark your answer on your answer sheet.

26. Mark your answer on your answer sheet.

27. Mark your answer on your answer sheet.

28. Mark your answer on your answer sheet.

29. Mark your answer on your answer sheet.

30. Mark your answer on your answer sheet.

31. Mark your answer on your answer sheet.

PART 3 🎧 15

Directions: You will hear some conversations between two or more people. You will be asked to answer three questions about what the speakers say in each conversation. Select the best response to each question and mark the letter (A), (B), (C), or (D) on your answer sheet. The conversations will not be printed in your test book and will be spoken only one time.

32. Where most likely are the speakers?

(A) In a bank
(B) In a dental clinic
(C) In a shopping mall
(D) In a bookstore

33. What problem does the woman mention?

(A) An appointment will be delayed.
(B) A patient file was misplaced.
(C) An employee called in sick.
(D) A bill was not paid.

34. What does the woman advise the man to do?

(A) Reschedule an appointment
(B) Stay in the office
(C) Take the stairs
(D) Use a specific door

35. What is the purpose of the man's visit?

(A) To extend a warranty
(B) To request a repair
(C) To do some shopping
(D) To deliver an appliance

36. What is the man's job?

(A) Caterer
(B) Architect
(C) Engineer
(D) Farmer

37. What does the woman suggest the man do?

(A) Look at a catalogue
(B) Inspect some merchandise
(C) Shop on a website
(D) Provide an address

38. What does the man ask the woman for?

(A) A later deadline
(B) An updated contract
(C) A credit card number
(D) A coworker's e-mail

39. What problem does the man mention?

(A) He lost some client information.
(B) He forgot his login password.
(C) He did not understand some directions.
(D) He had some technical difficulties.

40. What does the woman say she will do?

(A) Send some forms
(B) Contact a manager
(C) Hire some workers
(D) Locate a file

---

41. Where does the man most likely work?

(A) At a library
(B) At a bakery
(C) At a pharmacy
(D) At a law office

42. Why is the woman unavailable during the day?

(A) She is working for a company.
(B) She is taking a college course.
(C) She is traveling out of town.
(D) She is attending a conference.

43. What does the man ask the woman to do?

(A) Submit an updated application
(B) Learn about company systems
(C) Conduct an online survey
(D) Provide written references

---

44. What does the man want to buy?

(A) A refrigerator
(B) Some shoes
(C) A copy machine
(D) Some office furniture

45. Why does the woman apologize?

(A) A discount cannot be used.
(B) Some products are sold out.
(C) A store is closed for renovations.
(D) Some customers complained.

46. What does the man say he will do?

(A) Discuss an issue with a colleague
(B) Visit an online store
(C) Provide an address
(D) Send some measurements

---

47. What are the speakers mainly talking about?

(A) Moving to a new building
(B) Hiring a designer
(C) Updating a customer profile
(D) Editing a document

48. What problem does the woman notice?

(A) An address is outdated.
(B) A form was misplaced.
(C) An employee was late.
(D) A phone number is wrong.

49. Why does the woman say, "It happens to us all"?

(A) To explain a problem
(B) To provide clarification
(C) To prevent an accident
(D) To show compassion

50. What is the purpose of the woman's call?

(A) To inquire about test results
(B) To make a payment
(C) To change an appointment
(D) To update insurance information

51. What is the woman doing on Wednesday morning?

(A) Visiting a clinic
(B) Traveling to another city
(C) Meeting a client
(D) Hosting a local event

52. What will the woman most likely do next?

(A) Contact a coworker
(B) Record some information
(C) Go to a hospital
(D) Meet with a consultant

53. According to the man, what will happen next year?

(A) A CEO will visit.
(B) A business will fail.
(C) A renovation will occur.
(D) A contract will expire.

54. What does Betina suggest?

(A) Checking a website
(B) Taking a building tour
(C) Extending a lease
(D) Purchasing a building

55. What does Betina agree to do?

(A) Pass on a phone number
(B) Call a real estate agent
(C) Revise a contract
(D) Create a company sign

56. What does the woman say is special about the hairpins?

(A) They are made of gold.
(B) They are inexpensive.
(C) They are made in France.
(D) They are all unique.

57. Why does the woman say she no longer wears her hairpin?

(A) She lost it.
(B) She broke it.
(C) She dislikes it.
(D) She gifted it.

58. What does the man imply when he says, "I don't get paid for ten days"?

(A) He usually gets paid every week.
(B) He forgot to pick up his paycheck.
(C) He doesn't have enough money right now.
(D) He recently got a pay increase.

59. Who most likely is the woman?

(A) A sales clerk
(B) A web designer
(C) A company receptionist
(D) A post office manager

60. Why does the man visit the office?

(A) To make a delivery
(B) To have a meeting
(C) To inspect a lab
(D) To collect a payment

61. What does the woman imply when she says, "Well, Dr. Strummer is at our Swanson Road laboratory right now"?

(A) Dr. Strummer is a medical scientist.
(B) A storage room is available.
(C) Dr. Strummer cannot sign a form.
(D) An urgent prescription request must be made.

62. What type of event are the speakers discussing?

(A) A store's grand opening
(B) An award ceremony
(C) A company anniversary
(D) A retirement party

63. What is the man considering?

(A) Whether to send invitations
(B) Who to hire as a caterer
(C) When to schedule an event
(D) Where to hold an event

64. What does the man say he will do?

(A) Visit a venue
(B) Update a menu
(C) Cancel a reservation
(D) Consult a supervisor

PREMIUM HOME DÉCOR		
Item	Quantity	Total Price
Panel Curtains	4	$160.00
Cushions	4	$40.00
Shag Rug	1	$79.00
Lamp Shade	2	$44.00

65. What does the woman say she did recently?

(A) She stained her carpet.
(B) She moved to a new house.
(C) She misplaced some items.
(D) She purchased some new furniture.

66. Why does the woman need assistance?

(A) Her order arrived incomplete.
(B) She was charged too much for an item.
(C) She does not like some items.
(D) Her receipt was not in the box.

67. Look at the graphic. How much money will the woman be refunded?

(A) $160.00
(B) $40.00
(C) $79.00
(D) $44.00

Flight	Destination	Gate
AV13	Los Angeles	A56
CP03	Miami	B45
PS55	Paris	B13
AA01	Beijing	A32

68. What type of event are the speakers traveling to?

(A) A holiday vacation
(B) A sales conference
(C) A training session
(D) A corporate workshop

69. Why is the man staying just a short time?

(A) He was unable to get a flight.
(B) He could not reserve a hotel.
(C) He has a conflicting schedule.
(D) He is not well.

70. Look at the graphic. What city are the speakers flying to?

(A) Los Angeles
(B) Miami
(C) Paris
(D) Beijing

Directions: You will hear some talks given by a single speaker. You will be asked to answer three questions about what the speaker says in each talk. Select the best response to each question and mark the letter (A), (B), (C), or (D) on your answer sheet. The talks will not be printed in your test book and will be spoken only one time.

71. Who is Samuel Berkley?

(A) A radio host
(B) A publisher
(C) A writer
(D) A diplomat

72. What is Samuel Berkley planning on doing?

(A) Launching a travel website
(B) Taking a trip around the world
(C) Releasing a book series
(D) Giving a talk about hotels

73. What are listeners instructed to do?

(A) Go to a website
(B) Book a trip
(C) Purchase a book
(D) Post questions online

74. What product is being discussed?

(A) A stereo system
(B) An audio device
(C) A television set
(D) A software program

75. How does the product differ from competitors' products?

(A) It is cheaper to repair.
(B) It is more durable.
(C) It is less expensive.
(D) It has a unique feature.

76. How can listeners win a free product?

(A) By testing out a model
(B) By completing a survey
(C) By visiting a website
(D) By purchasing an item

77. What did the speaker do yesterday?

    (A) He went to a restaurant.
    (B) He talked to the listener.
    (C) He purchased a storage unit.
    (D) He signed a lease.

78. What does the speaker say about storage rooms?

    (A) They have shelving units inside.
    (B) They are an added bonus.
    (C) They have security systems.
    (D) They are available for a fee.

79. Why does the speaker say, "Several people are interested in the space"?

    (A) To explain why the space is no longer available
    (B) To encourage the listener to see the space quickly
    (C) To request the listener to give up the space
    (D) To describe the size and price of the space

80. Where does the speaker work?

    (A) At a job agency
    (B) At a charity
    (C) At a concert hall
    (D) At a city park

81. Why does the speaker say, "As of now we have enough volunteers for the event"?

    (A) To turn down an offer
    (B) To stress the success of an event
    (C) To voice a concern about a policy
    (D) To request more funding

82. What does the speaker ask the listener to do?

    (A) Attend a concert
    (B) Send an e-mail
    (C) Visit a website
    (D) Record some information

83. Where is the talk taking place?

    (A) At a factory
    (B) At a yacht club
    (C) At a museum
    (D) At a travel agency

84. According to the speaker, what did Samuel Welsh do last year?

    (A) He made a donation.
    (B) He hired an assistant.
    (C) He went on a sailing trip.
    (D) He opened a gallery.

85. What does the speaker recommend that the listeners do?

    (A) Read a booklet
    (B) Book a cruise
    (C) Go for a swim
    (D) Buy a membership

86. Who is the advertisement intended for?

    (A) Hotel staff
    (B) Security guards
    (C) Office managers
    (D) Bus drivers

87. What does the speaker say is special about the service?

    (A) It is offered every day.
    (B) It can be booked online.
    (C) It can be cancelled easily.
    (D) It is done in the evenings.

88. What are listeners encouraged to do?

    (A) Ask for an estimate
    (B) Call a telephone number
    (C) Read some client reviews
    (D) Purchase new equipment

89. What is the main topic of the announcement?

(A) Booking flights online
(B) Paying for travel costs
(C) Training new employees
(D) Canceling out of town travel

90. According to the speaker, why is the change being made?

(A) To respond to employee complaints
(B) To improve employee work efficiency
(C) To make up for a lack of pay raises
(D) To follow a government regulation

91. What are the listeners reminded to do?

(A) Update employee contracts
(B) Pass out new information booklets
(C) Gather reports from employees
(D) Speak with department managers

Tour Date	Departure Time
Monday, May 2	10:30 A.M. / 2:30 P.M.
Tuesday, May 3	11:30 A.M. / 3:30 P.M.
Wednesday, May 4	10:30 A.M. / 2:30 P.M.
Thursday, May 5	11:30 A.M. / 3:30 P.M.

92. What has caused a cancelation?

(A) An absent ship captain
(B) Missing passengers
(C) Poor weather conditions
(D) A damaged boat

93. Look at the graphic. What time will the next boat tour take place?

(A) 10:30 A.M.
(B) 11:30 A.M.
(C) 2:30 P.M.
(D) 3:30 P.M.

94. What does the speaker ask listeners to do?

(A) Wait for a few hours
(B) Try a new restaurant
(C) Stay away from the dock
(D) Visit the front desk

Question: *What improvement would you most like to see?*	
Answer Option	**Number of Votes**
A. A reduction in fares	105
B. Shorter wait times	87
C. More payment options	55
D. Online reservations	32

95. Where most likely does the speaker work?

    (A) At a travel agency
    (B) At an airline
    (C) At a marketing agency
    (D) At a bus company

96. Look at the graphic. What survey result does the speaker want to implement?

    (A) A reduction in fares
    (B) Shorter wait times
    (C) More payment options
    (D) Online reservations

97. What does the speaker ask the listeners to do?

    (A) Recommend employment websites
    (B) Interview potential candidates
    (C) Review customer information
    (D) Upgrade a company system

Ristorante Catoria
50% Off Group Discount Coupon

* *Groups may not exceed 15 patrons.*
* *Valid until December 31st.*

98. Why is the event being held?

    (A) To launch a product line
    (B) To host an award ceremony
    (C) To announce a promotion
    (D) To celebrate a holiday

99. Look at the graphic. Why is the speaker unable to use the coupon for the event?

    (A) Not enough guests will attend the event.
    (B) The event will occur after the expiration date.
    (C) The event will take place on a weekend.
    (D) Too many people will be present at the event.

100. What does the speaker ask the listener to do?

    (A) Make a list of other restaurants
    (B) Call Ristorante Catoria
    (C) Change the date of an event
    (D) Ask management for more funds

This is the end of the Listening test. Turn to Part 5 in your test book.

READING TEST

In the Reading Test, you will read a variety of texts and answer several different types of reading comprehension questions. The entire Reading test will last 75 minutes. There are three parts, and directions are given for each part. You are encouraged to answer as many questions as possible within the time allowed.

You must mark your answers on the separate answer sheet. Do not write your answers in your test book.

PART 5

Directions: A word or phrase is missing in each of the sentences below. Four answer choices are given below each sentence. Select the best answer to complete the sentence. Then mark the letter (A), (B), (C), or (D) on your answer sheet.

101. Thanks to the ------- recommendation from his previous employer, Derrick was immediately offered the managerial position.

(A) impress
(B) impression
(C) impressive
(D) impresses

102. Nemis Air is no longer ------- to transport freight to the northern regions.

(A) license
(B) licensed
(C) licenses
(D) licensing

103. Jerome tried to get tickets to tomorrow's game, but they are ------- sold out.

(A) complete
(B) completed
(C) completing
(D) completely

104. Nobody can enter this office ------- proper authorization.

(A) without
(B) unless
(C) only
(D) although

105. The annual charity banquet hosted by the Fredericton Children Aid Society is ------- to take place at the Grand Marian Hotel on December 7.

(A) given
(B) scheduled
(C) found
(D) considered

106. The owner's manual includes detailed ------- on cleaning this microwave.

(A) instructions
(B) computers
(C) posters
(D) fixings

107. The city purchased the ------- building on Balena Street to convert it into an elementary school.

(A) approaching
(B) adjustable
(C) vacant
(D) united

108. Customers must provide ------- at the counter or prescriptions will not be filled.

(A) paid
(B) payers
(C) payment
(D) pays

109. The company will not reimburse staff for travel expenses unless original receipts are presented ------- upon returning.

(A) mainly
(B) formerly
(C) nearly
(D) immediately

110. The *Stickney Entertainment Guide* is, without a doubt, the most reliable source ------- finding the best places to eat in this region.

(A) around
(B) for
(C) as
(D) through

111. Mr. Tolliver, the head mechanic, started the repairs by ------- this morning, but two more staff were available to help him after lunch.

(A) he
(B) his
(C) him
(D) himself

112. For optimal results, the manufacturer ------- applying this exterior paint when the weather is sunny.

(A) reminds
(B) recognizes
(C) recommends
(D) registers

113. Instructors at Darthmouth College have to submit their final student evaluations ------- the last day of this month.

(A) in anticipation of
(B) already
(C) before
(D) so as to

114. The Fitzgerald Theater is being renovated so concert organizers for Roland Gagnon's band are ------- seeking another venue.

(A) actively
(B) activity
(C) active
(D) activate

115. Once the conveyor belt was fixed, the factory was ------- to continue production.

(A) valuable
(B) responsible
(C) able
(D) possible

116. Someone should tell Mr. Sinopoli that ------- car is parked in the section reserved for shopping center customers.

(A) he
(B) him
(C) his
(D) himself

117. Ratzenberg Motorcycles will benefit greatly ------- the proposed acquisition by Shefferville Auto.

(A) from
(B) to
(C) on
(D) about

118. The application forms we received yesterday ------- have to be reviewed by one of the division heads.

(A) lately
(B) evenly
(C) ever
(D) still

119. If bad weather forces a cancellation of the baseball game, full refunds will be issued to ------- who have purchased tickets.

(A) those
(B) which
(C) them
(D) whichever

120. Even though tourism revenue in this region usually ------- during the cold winter months, it always recovers in the warm spring.

(A) declines
(B) delays
(C) impacts
(D) impedes

121. One important ------- the new personnel manager is responsible for is meeting regularly with factory workers to discuss safety matters.

(A) initiative
(B) initiating
(C) initiation
(D) initiator

122. Ms. Gaitor is ------- with implementing policies that led to a significant increase in the number of clients.

(A) credited
(B) scored
(C) agreed
(D) relied

123. Tickets to the gallery can be purchased online at a ------- reduced price.

(A) slightest
(B) slighted
(C) slighting
(D) slightly

124. Our division ------- last week's policy meeting, but there was a conflict with the schedule.

(A) can attend
(B) must have attended
(C) should attend
(D) would have attended

125. Mr. Gleason opted to lease office space on Queen Street instead of Morley Lane, ------- a view of the lake.

(A) prefer
(B) preferring
(C) preferred
(D) preference

126. ------- for next year's Grondin Literature Award must be received by the selection committee by the end of March.

(A) Subscriptions
(B) Nominations
(C) Supporters
(D) Venues

127. In an effort to make the team less ------- the manager sent all the sales charts to everyone as e-mail attachments rather than printing out hardcopies.

(A) waste
(B) wasteful
(C) wastefully
(D) wasting

128. Ms. Wilson must contact the bank manager ------- she needs a little more time for the payment.

(A) if
(B) soon
(C) only
(D) then

129. Besides speedy delivery, friendly service is something ------- the management of Caron Courier will never sacrifice.

(A) where
(B) that
(C) when
(D) then

130. The editor of the sports section is more ------- about the articles she approves than the other editors.

(A) prominent
(B) punctual
(C) rigorous
(D) selective

Directions: Read the texts that follow. A word, phrase, or sentence is missing in parts of each text. Four answer choices for each question are given below the text. Select the best answer to complete the text. Then mark the letter (A), (B), (C), or (D) on your answer sheet.

Questions 131-134 refer to the following article.

Bold Move by Popular Shop

CASTLEBAR — Flavor Fun, Castlebar's oldest and most popular yoghurt restaurant, has introduced a truly unanticipated change as the result of a growing number of ___131___. The restaurant's owner decided to introduce a policy that many find to be unusual. For the past two weeks, customers have not been permitted to work on laptops while eating in the restaurant. Flavor Fun is the first and only restaurant in the city to implement such a policy aimed at encouraging customers to leave the restaurant after eating. By making customers spend ___132___ time at a table, the restaurant has increased its daily sales by over 20 percent, and customers did not have to wait for a place to sit. ___133___. Now, some other popular eating spots throughout Castlebar ___134___ similar changes.

131. (A) staff
     (B) prices
     (C) complaints
     (D) deliveries

132. (A) some
     (B) less
     (C) any
     (D) much

133. (A) Customers will receive free coffee during the trial period.
     (B) The new policy has already proven popular with customers.
     (C) Flavor Fun also has an outdoor patio for dining.
     (D) Owners believe new staff need more training before starting work.

134. (A) considers
     (B) to consider
     (C) being considered
     (D) are considering

Questions 135-138 refer to the following letter.

Do You Use a Hearing Aid? Contact Knapton Technologies Today!

In August, Knapton Technologies will begin a detailed consumer study on behalf of Hearing 1000. For this huge undertaking, our team is ___135.___ more than 300 individuals who wear hearing aids. All participants must have a doctor prescribed device that they began wearing no more than three years ago ___136.___ the beginning of the study. ___137.___. If you are interested, we ask that you visit us online at www.knaptontechnologies.com/hearingaidstudy and complete our short survey. One of our staff members will be contacting qualified applicants. Every participant ___138.___ a gift voucher valued at $200 upon completing of this study.

---

135. (A) seeking
    (B) insuring
    (C) promoting
    (D) showing

136. (A) except for
    (B) as
    (C) because of
    (D) at

137. (A) A hard copy of the prescription must be presented for confirmation.
    (B) New batteries will be available for all participants.
    (C) We request that payment for your prescription is provided on the spot.
    (D) The prescription will be filled immediately after submission.

138. (A) will receive
    (B) had received
    (C) to receive
    (D) to be received

Next month, the national headquarters of Zaki Ltd., Japan's top manufacturer of __139.__, will relocate to 117 Aoyagi Street, where a modern office building was recently renovated. Zaki will __140.__ the top seven floors of the Aoyagi Building. In this new location, the staff will enjoy over 90,000 square meters of beautiful office space and convenient amenities.

__141.__ "That is the perfect place to display our latest high-tech refrigerators and ovens." said Kaori Akiba, spokesperson for Zaki. Ms. Akiba noted that the design and engineer divisions will remain in __142.__ original spot in the Ogawa Building.

139. (A) furniture
(B) apparel
(C) wallpaper
(D) appliances

140. (A) sell
(B) paint
(C) occupy
(D) photograph

141. (A) Zaki's products are known for their cutting-edge designs and energy efficiency.
(B) Zaki also plans to lease additional retail space on the first floor of the building.
(C) Zaki was listed in the *Tokyo Times* as one of the top 20 places to work in Asia.
(D) Zaki stock doubled in value immediately following the announcement.

142. (A) it
(B) their
(C) what
(D) any

Questions 143-146 refer to the following e-mail.

To: Kaori Sazaki <ssawaki601@e-mail.co.jp>

From: Customer Service <customerserv@elsworth.co.uk>

Date: Thursday, 16 October 8:56 P.M.

Subject: inquiry about website

Dear Ms. Sazaki:

We would like to thank you for leaving a comment in the feedback section of our website regarding the instruction booklet for the EW2500 digital camera. You indicated that the instructions on how to upload an image to a phone or mobile device is confusing and we completely agree with you __143.__ that point. __144.__ . Our publications division has __145.__ made some revisions to the section that details the specific software and cable needed to transfer an image from your particular camera. We have made the __146.__ version of the instruction booklet available on our website. You can find it under the New Digital Camera section. If you prefer a print version, we will gladly send it by regular mail but delivery will take at least one week.

Sincerely,

Lirim Kilgore
Customer Service Agent
Elsworth Camera Company

---

143. (A) all
(B) on
(C) what
(D) of

144. (A) The EW2500 digital camera is currently our most popular item.
(B) We can send you the complete instructions via e-mail if you wish.
(C) Other customers have submitted feedback about the same issue.
(D) Most of our customers are based in the southern regions of Asia.

145. (A) instead
(B) likewise
(C) therefore
(D) nevertheless

146. (A) original
(B) updated
(C) absolute
(D) focused

Directions: In this part you will read a selection of texts, such as magazine and newspaper articles, e-mails, and instant messages. Each text or set of texts is followed by several questions. Select the best answer for each question and mark the letter (A), (B), (C), or (D) on your answer sheet.

Questions 147-148 refer to the following text message.

From: Ron Kapoor, 553-0304

To: Zelda Vincenti

Zelda, I left my schedule book in the office. I have to meet a client at 2:00, but I can't remember the exact location. I'm just about to leave Denny's Grill and had planned to go straight to the meeting. Can you check my book and send me the address?

147. Why did Mr. Kapoor send a text message to Ms. Vincenti?

(A) To ask if she found his briefcase
(B) To inquire about a canceled meeting
(C) To request that she send him an address
(D) To make a restaurant reservation

148. What will Mr. Kapoor probably do next?

(A) Leave a restaurant
(B) Go to his office
(C) Check a website
(D) Call a client

Questions 149-150 refer to the following advertisement.

The American chapter of Ancient Worlds Archaeological Foundation seeks two full-time interns to assist with our archaeological dig near Siem Reap, Cambodia.

Candidates must have completed a four-year degree in archaeological studies or must be currently enrolled in their 4th year of an archaeology program.

Research experience is a must, and candidates with hands-on field training will be given preference.

Applicants must be willing to travel to the dig site during the months of August through October. Accommodation and flights will be paid for by the foundation.

Interns will be paid a lump sum at the end of the trip. At the discretion of the project coordinator, interns may be hired as full-time employees following the dig's conclusion.

149. What is indicated about the American chapter of Ancient Worlds Archaeological Foundation?
(A) It wants to hire one part-time intern.
(B) It conducts digs in foreign countries.
(C) It does not pay its interns except for travel expenses.
(D) It was founded three years ago.

150. What is NOT a qualification for the position?
(A) University education
(B) Willingness to travel
(C) Field training
(D) Computer knowledge

Questions 151-153 refer to the following memo.

To: Timmons Medical Research Staff
From: Anderson Baxtor, Director of Employee Relations
Re: Presentation
Date: 5 April

Attention all staff members,

Next Thursday, 13 April, we will have a special presentation in auditorium 203. Maria Sergios is a senior researcher at the University of Westwood, where she has conducted research for the last five years. She headed the development of a new series of vaccines in addition to partnering with researchers in London, England to work on the development of several new treatments for cancer. Before joining the University of Westwood, Sergios made a name for herself at the Institute of Medical Research in Sydney, Australia. There, I had the chance to learn from her during several ground-breaking projects. Ms. Sergios will be here in Vancouver next week and has agreed to share her latest publication on laboratory techniques with us. All staff members are required to attend the presentation.

---

151. What does the memo discuss?

(A) Plans to found a new lab
(B) A new job opening
(C) A scientist's career
(D) Deadlines for a project

152. Where is Timmons Medical Research located?

(A) In London
(B) In Sydney
(C) In Westwood
(D) In Vancouver

153. What does Mr. Baxtor indicate about Ms. Sergios?

(A) She is his former mentor.
(B) She is moving to Vancouver.
(C) She will join his research team.
(D) She will open her own laboratory.

Questions 154-155 refer to the following text message chain.

Jamal Myers 10:30 A.M.

Hi, Ferguson. I'm still at Davis Printers waiting for our two banners. Could you go ahead and begin setting up? I put the key to the room in the top right drawer of my desk.

Ferguson Boyd 10:33 A.M.

Found it. I'm leaving now.

Jamal Myers 10:35 A.M.

Thanks a lot. I know the award ceremony doesn't start until 1:30, but we need to double-check all the equipment.

Ferguson Boyd 10:40 A.M.

Just to make sure, we will be having the ceremony in the former city hall building on Elliot Street, right? Not the new one on Queen Street?

Jamal Myers 10:42 A.M.

Correct. Right after the ceremony, a photographer will take photos of the winners on the front lawn. That is why I ordered an additional banner to be used outside. I will catch up with you at the former city hall building as soon as I get the banners.

Ferguson Boyd 10:45 A.M.

OK. See you in a little while!

154. At 10:33 A.M., what does Mr. Boyd most likely mean when he writes, "Found it"?

(A) He will pass on the information a client needs.
(B) He noticed Davis Printers while driving.
(C) He has the key to the venue in his hand.
(D) He is looking at a phone number in a directory.

155. Where most likely is Mr. Boyd going next?

(A) To the train station
(B) To company headquarters
(C) To a print shop
(D) To the old city hall

 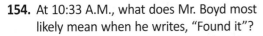

Questions 156-158 refer to the following letter.

Holt Golf and Country Club
34 Russet Drive
Edmonton, Alberta
www.holtgolf.ca

24 April

Mr. Henry MacArthur
220 Washington Avenue
Edmonton, Alberta

Dear Mr. MacArthur,

Thank you for purchasing a membership to Holt Golf and Country Club. --[1]--. From May 1 until September 30, in addition to having your choice of tee-off time, you will have full access to our lounge, restaurant, and spa. Furthermore, carbonated beverages are complimentary in all our cafés. Simply show your membership card when you order. --[2]--.

In addition to all these incredible services, Holt Golf and Country Club is announcing yet another service for its members. From now until the end of August, all members may invite guests for a round of golf on our extensive course. This feature is available from 8 A.M. until 4 P.M. only. Guest reservations must be made 24 hours in advance. --[3]--.

If you have any questions or concerns, please contact our customer service hotline at 900-555-3344. --[4]--.

Sincerely,

Mitchel Walker

---

156. What is true about Holt golf and Country Club?

(A) It offers its members free drinks.
(B) It only opens during the spring.
(C) It offers discount memberships.
(D) It hosts seasonal parties.

157. According to the letter, what will be different after August?

(A) Members cannot access the spa.
(B) Members may not bring guests.
(C) Golf tee-off times will be earlier.
(D) Golf lessons will be available.

158. In which of the positions marked [1], [2], [3], and [4] does the following sentence best belong?

"This year, you will be able to enjoy all our premium services."

(A) [1]
(B) [2]
(C) [3]
(D) [4]

Questions 159-162 refer to the following article.

Milan (July 14) — Roberto Pelini, lead designer at Marshenco Fashions, one of Europe's top design companies, has announced he will retire from his role at the company. --[1]--.

Since first accepting the position 10 years ago, Roberto Pelini has worked hard to make Marshenco Fashions one of the most-recognized names in the industry. Because of Pelini's passion and eye for design, Marshenco has become a favorite among celebrities and his designs can often be seen both on the runway and the red carpet. --[2]--. The company's success has even allowed for the founding of a sister company, Marshenco Accessories.

Irina Morova, former designer at Ruvera Design, will assume the position of lead designer at Marshenco. Morova has more than 10 years of experience heading a major fashion company. Her work has been featured in numerous fashion festivals, magazines, and has clothed some of Europe's top singers and actors. --[3]--.

Following his departure from Marshenco, Roberto Pelini will partner with Sophia Bertuski to found a new independent fashion house. Pelini is quoted as saying, "I look forward to working with Sophia. Her creative vision is similar to my own." --[4]--.

159. What is the purpose of the article?

(A) To report on a company's closure
(B) To announce a change in a company's leadership
(C) To advertise a new job opening at a company
(D) To publicize a new line of products

160. What is indicated about Marshenco?

(A) It is based in North America.
(B) It was purchased by Pelini.
(C) It owns Ruvera Design.
(D) It founded a second company.

161. What is mentioned about Irina Morova?

(A) She will become Pelini's business partner.
(B) Her career at Ruvera Design was successful.
(C) She originally worked as a runway model.
(D) Her designs are for average consumers.

162. In which of the positions marked [1], [2], [3], and [4] does the following sentence best belong?

"There is no news as to when Pelini's new lines will be available to the public."

(A) [1]
(B) [2]
(C) [3]
(D) [4]

Questions 163-165 refer to the following advertisement.

The First Annual Waterfront Food Truck Festival!

Ajax Food and Beverage Association is pleased to announce the first ever Waterfront Food Truck Festival. From Monday August 8 through Sunday August 14, the Ajax waterfront will host a number of local food trucks. Guests can enjoy live music, prizes, and children's entertainment between the hours of 11 A.M. and 6 P.M. Food truck items can be sampled for discount prices.

Famous Participating Food Trucks:

◆ Rio Tacos — Enjoy fresh appetizers and a variety of tacos and nachos
◆ Barbecue Madness — Marinated pork ribs, chicken wings, and pulled pork
◆ Benny's Fries — French fries topped with your choice of ingredients

Admission is free for all participants. Parking will be available on a limited basis, so make sure to get there early.

For a complete list of participating food trucks, visit www.ajaxwaterfront.com/foodtruckfestival.

---

163. What is being advertised?

(A) A restaurant's grand opening
(B) A concert in the park
(C) An auto show
(D) A new community event

164. What is mentioned about the participating food trucks?

(A) They will travel to various cities.
(B) They will distribute free gifts.
(C) They will be open all day.
(D) They will sell food at reduced prices.

165. What are participants encouraged to do?

(A) Arrive at the site early
(B) Leave their cars at home
(C) Pay an admission fee
(D) Camp at the waterfront

Questions 166-169 refer to the following e-mail.

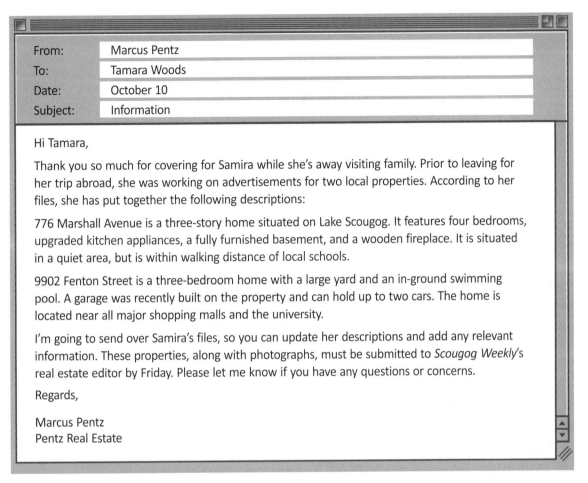

From:	Marcus Pentz
To:	Tamara Woods
Date:	October 10
Subject:	Information

Hi Tamara,

Thank you so much for covering for Samira while she's away visiting family. Prior to leaving for her trip abroad, she was working on advertisements for two local properties. According to her files, she has put together the following descriptions:

776 Marshall Avenue is a three-story home situated on Lake Scougog. It features four bedrooms, upgraded kitchen appliances, a fully furnished basement, and a wooden fireplace. It is situated in a quiet area, but is within walking distance of local schools.

9902 Fenton Street is a three-bedroom home with a large yard and an in-ground swimming pool. A garage was recently built on the property and can hold up to two cars. The home is located near all major shopping malls and the university.

I'm going to send over Samira's files, so you can update her descriptions and add any relevant information. These properties, along with photographs, must be submitted to *Scougog Weekly*'s real estate editor by Friday. Please let me know if you have any questions or concerns.

Regards,

Marcus Pentz
Pentz Real Estate

166. Why was the e-mail sent?

(A) To request some files
(B) To give some job instructions
(C) To provide payment information
(D) To ask for some local contacts

167. What is suggested about Samira?

(A) She often travels abroad.
(B) She purchased a new home.
(C) She works for a newspaper.
(D) She has gone on vacation.

168. What is NOT mentioned about the property on Fenton Street?

(A) It has a big yard and a swimming pool.
(B) It was previously listed on a website.
(C) It includes a newly built garage.
(D) It is close to many important amenities.

169. According to the e-mail, what is indicated about *Scougog Weekly*?

(A) It will feature the selections Ms. Woods must update.
(B) It comes out every Friday.
(C) It charges fees based on property prices.
(D) It is distributed to local residents free of charge.

GO ON TO THE NEXT PAGE

Blake Wyatt [3:23 P.M.]
Ms. Parker, I just found out there's going to be a parade on First Street. The area is going to be really crowded, so the repaving of your restaurant's parking lot will have to wait.

Janice Parker [3:26 P.M.]
So does that mean you won't be coming in at all?

Blake Wyatt [3:28 P.M.]
No, we'll still be there. We can help get the basement storage rooms finished.

Janice Parker [3:31 P.M.]
OK, great. How long do you think it will take to get everything done down there?

Blake Wyatt [3:32 P.M.]
I'll check now.

Tim Robins has been added to the conversation.

Blake Wyatt [3:35 P.M.]
Tim, how far have you gotten on the basement project?

Tim Robins [3:40 P.M.]
Well, things were running smoothly until we found some water damage in the southeast corner. It looks like a big cleanup job.

Blake Wyatt [3:42 P.M.]
What if my crew gave you a hand tomorrow?

Tim Robins [3:44 P.M.]
That might get us back on schedule. We might even be able to install the new refrigerators.

Janice Parker [3:45 P.M.]
If you're moving the fridges, you'll need access to the service entrance behind the building. I think you still have the key, right?

Blake Wyatt [3:47 P.M.]
Yes, I've got it. Are there any spots behind the building where the guys can park for the day?

Janice Parker [3:50 P.M.]
There might not be any free if there's a parade. You should probably park in the empty lot on Fifth Avenue.

170. What does Mr. Wyatt suggest will interrupt tomorrow's work?

(A) A public holiday
(B) A street event
(C) A lost delivery
(D) A lack of equipment

171. At 3:40 P.M. what does Mr. Robins most likely mean when he writes, "It looks like a big cleanup job."?

(A) His crew usually does the cleaning.
(B) Some damage was significant.
(C) He does not like his current job.
(D) His crew's project is too complicated.

172. Who most likely is Ms. Parker?

(A) A restaurant owner
(B) A construction worker
(C) A parking attendant
(D) An appliance manufacturer

173. What is one topic Mr. Wyatt asks about?

(A) Directions to another entrance
(B) The location of a building key
(C) The time of a local event
(D) The location of parking spaces

Questions 174-175 refer to the following webpage.

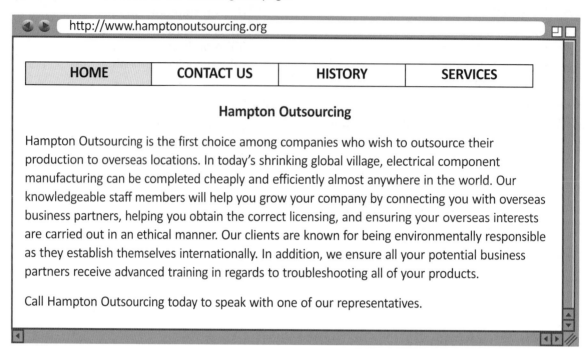

http://www.hamptonoutsourcing.org

| HOME | CONTACT US | HISTORY | SERVICES |

Hampton Outsourcing

Hampton Outsourcing is the first choice among companies who wish to outsource their production to overseas locations. In today's shrinking global village, electrical component manufacturing can be completed cheaply and efficiently almost anywhere in the world. Our knowledgeable staff members will help you grow your company by connecting you with overseas business partners, helping you obtain the correct licensing, and ensuring your overseas interests are carried out in an ethical manner. Our clients are known for being environmentally responsible as they establish themselves internationally. In addition, we ensure all your potential business partners receive advanced training in regards to troubleshooting all of your products.

Call Hampton Outsourcing today to speak with one of our representatives.

174. Who most likely will be a customer of Hampton Outsourcing?

(A) Call center workers
(B) Insurance brokers
(C) Environmental agencies
(D) Home appliance companies

175. What is NOT mentioned as a strength of Hampton Outsourcing?

(A) Superior employee training
(B) Knowledge of licensing
(C) Environmentally conscious procedures
(D) Familiarity with export taxes

Questions 176-180 refer to the following letter and voucher.

To:	Raphael Rosario <rosario@ebookmail.com>
From:	Janelle Parik <jparik@alliancepremiumairways.com>
Subject:	Your Flight
Date:	6 January
Attachment:	voucher

Dear Mr. Rosario,

Thank you for sharing your experience with Alliance Premium Airways Customer Service. I am sorry to learn about your negative experience on January 2. According to the online form you completed, you had reserved a business class seat on a third-party website, but you were forced to fly economy class because your reservation had been lost.

I have contacted the website you used to book your flight. Apparently, there was a computer malfunction, which caused some prior bookings to be deleted. Unfortunately, this resulted in some seats being resold. I understand that you have already received a partial refund, but I'd like to offer you an additional coupon for your troubles. Please see the attachment for more information.

Sincerely,

Janelle Parik,
Customer Service Manager
Alliance Premium Airways

Alliance Premium Airways Voucher
$200 off your next flight

Details: Alliance Premium Airways would like to offer you $200 off your next flight. Please note, this coupon may only be used for international return flights. This coupon is good until December 31 of this year. You may use this coupon at any Alliance Premium Airways kiosk or online at www.alliancepremiumairways.com.

Voucher Number: YY7732999938   Date Issued: January 6
Issuing office: _____ Vancouver _____ Edmonton _____ Montreal   X Toronto

176. Why did Ms. Parik send the e-mail?

(A) To reply to an online complaint
(B) To provide a job contract
(C) To cancel an airline ticket
(D) To inquire about a trip

177. What does Ms. Parik indicate happened on January 2?

(A) She solved a seating problem.
(B) A flight was unnecessarily delayed.
(C) Many business class seats were empty.
(D) Mr. Rosario got a seat in a lower class.

178. What is suggested about Mr. Rosario?

(A) He requested a last-minute flight change.
(B) He flew from Vancouver to Toronto.
(C) He paid for his flight in advance.
(D) He usually flies economy class.

179. In the voucher, the word "good" in paragraph 1, line 2, is closest in meaning to

(A) high quality
(B) lucky
(C) well behaved
(D) valid

180. Where most likely is Ms. Parik's office located?

(A) Vancouver
(B) Edmonton
(C) Montreal
(D) Toronto

GO ON TO THE NEXT PAGE

Questions 181-185 refer to the following webpage and customer review.

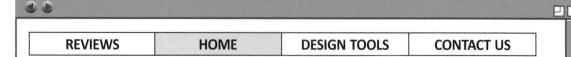

| REVIEWS | HOME | DESIGN TOOLS | CONTACT US |

Flyer Frenzy, the best online flyer generator for businesses large and small!

With Flyer Frenzy, you can create custom flyers for your business. Whether you are advertising the opening of your business or simply trying to generate awareness about your services, Flyer Frenzy has everything you need to design the perfect flyer.

Step 1: Design Your Flyer

Our online generator has numerous customizable templates. Browse through our categories and select the right template for you. All our fonts are easy to change with just the click of a mouse. If you want to accent your design with images, we have over 10,000 stock photos you can use at no extra cost. Furthermore, you can upload your own designs and logos to use along with any of our fonts.

Step 2: Select A Quantity

At Flyer Frenzy, we can print as few as 25 flyers for each order. However, the more flyers you order, the less you pay for each one.

Quantity	Price Per Item
25-300	20 cents
300-1,000	15 cents
1,001-1,500	10 cents
1,501 or more	5 cents

Step 3: Purchase A Digital Copy

For an extra flat fee of $50, you can download a digital copy of your design. This design is perfect for featuring on your business's website, as part of an e-mail newsletter, or as a printed advertisement.

Step 4: Finalize Your Order

Orders take five days to process; however, large orders may take longer to prepare. In the event that there are delays, you will be notified by e-mail.

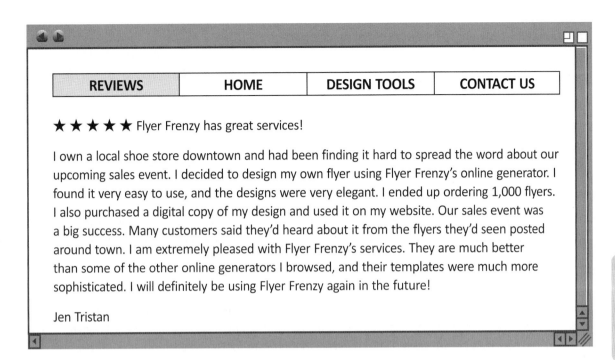

| REVIEWS | HOME | DESIGN TOOLS | CONTACT US |

★ ★ ★ ★ ★ Flyer Frenzy has great services!

I own a local shoe store downtown and had been finding it hard to spread the word about our upcoming sales event. I decided to design my own flyer using Flyer Frenzy's online generator. I found it very easy to use, and the designs were very elegant. I ended up ordering 1,000 flyers. I also purchased a digital copy of my design and used it on my website. Our sales event was a big success. Many customers said they'd heard about it from the flyers they'd seen posted around town. I am extremely pleased with Flyer Frenzy's services. They are much better than some of the other online generators I browsed, and their templates were much more sophisticated. I will definitely be using Flyer Frenzy again in the future!

Jen Tristan

181. According to the webpage, what does the online generator allow users to do?

(A) Add images
(B) Include web links
(C) Select paper type
(D) Design a logo

182. What is mentioned on the webpage about Flyer Frenzy?

(A) It delivers products free of charge.
(B) It offers digital files for an extra fee.
(C) It allows users to see each other's designs.
(D) It only takes orders in person at a store.

183. What is indicated about Ms. Tristan?

(A) She received more flyers than she ordered.
(B) Her order was delayed by a few days.
(C) She received a fifty dollar discount.
(D) She paid fifteen cents per flyer.

184. What is suggested about Ms. Tristan's store?

(A) It advertises solely online.
(B) It put flyers up around town.
(C) It holds sales every month.
(D) It gives discounts for online orders.

185. According to the review, why does Ms. Tristan prefer Flyer Frenzy's services over other companies?

(A) They have faster delivery times.
(B) They have better design features.
(C) They use better quality paper.
(D) They are cheaper to use.

GO ON TO THE NEXT PAGE

From:	linda@mailmail.com
To:	billing@startelecom.com
Date:	April 23
Subject:	Bill Number 3788292

Dear Customer Service,

I am writing in regards to an unusually high cell phone bill I received in March. The amount listed on my phone bill was $155.33. Previously, my bill ranged between $80 and $90 per month.

I have already paid the bill to avoid any late fees, but I am interested in knowing why I was charged so much. My bill did not show any details to explain these charges. I know I recently upgraded my data usage, which would cost extra, but I also canceled the insurance policy I had for all my devices. These two costs should have balanced each other out if my request for cancellation was handled properly.

Please call me about this matter at 333-0967-5563. I am available to speak only in the afternoons after 3:30 P.M.

Sincerely,

Linda Albert

Customer Service Contact Log Sheet
Date: April 24

Representative Name	Account Number	Call Time	Resolved? Y/N
Michael Park	BG44532	9:33 A.M.	Yes
June Bartholdi	GH30993	10:42 A.M.	Yes
Nadia Kapoor	TZ33221	3:23 P.M.	No
Brooklyn Smith	GS17649	3:45 P.M.	No

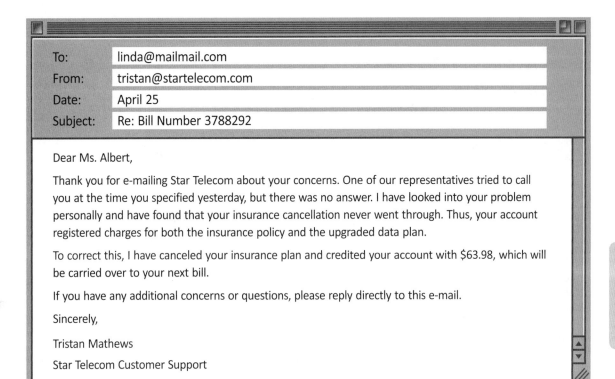

To: linda@mailmail.com
From: tristan@startelecom.com
Date: April 25
Subject: Re: Bill Number 3788292

Dear Ms. Albert,

Thank you for e-mailing Star Telecom about your concerns. One of our representatives tried to call you at the time you specified yesterday, but there was no answer. I have looked into your problem personally and have found that your insurance cancellation never went through. Thus, your account registered charges for both the insurance policy and the upgraded data plan.

To correct this, I have canceled your insurance plan and credited your account with $63.98, which will be carried over to your next bill.

If you have any additional concerns or questions, please reply directly to this e-mail.

Sincerely,

Tristan Mathews

Star Telecom Customer Support

186. Why was the first e-mail sent?

(A) To cancel a service
(B) To request another bill
(C) To ask about an invoice
(D) To register for an account

187. What is suggested about Ms. Albert?

(A) She previously worked for Star Telecom.
(B) She called a Star Telecom customer service representative.
(C) She correctly identified Star Telecom's mistake.
(D) She wants to close her account with Star Telecom.

188. Who called Ms. Albert on April 24?

(A) Michael Park
(B) June Bartholdi
(C) Nadia Kapoor
(D) Brooklyn Smith

189. In the second e-mail, in paragraph 1, line 4, the word "registered" is closest in meaning to

(A) enrolled
(B) recorded
(C) matched
(D) allowed

190. What does Mr. Mathews indicate in his e-mail?

(A) Some services will be offered for free.
(B) Ms. Kapoor will call Ms. Albert tomorrow.
(C) Ms. Albert's bill will decrease next month.
(D) Customers will be charged for cancellations.

Questions 191-195 refer to the following e-mail, flyer, and text message.

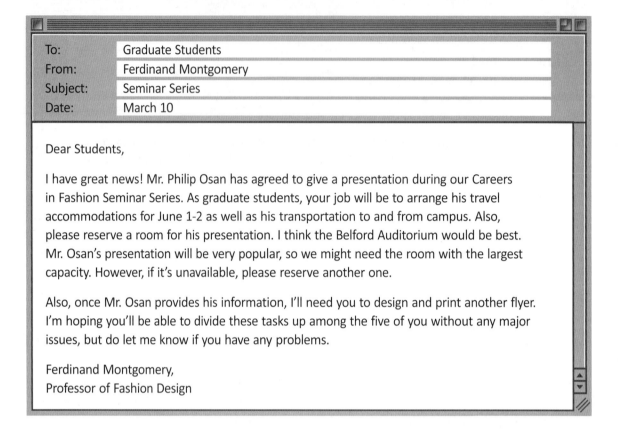

To:	Graduate Students
From:	Ferdinand Montgomery
Subject:	Seminar Series
Date:	March 10

Dear Students,

I have great news! Mr. Philip Osan has agreed to give a presentation during our Careers in Fashion Seminar Series. As graduate students, your job will be to arrange his travel accommodations for June 1-2 as well as his transportation to and from campus. Also, please reserve a room for his presentation. I think the Belford Auditorium would be best. Mr. Osan's presentation will be very popular, so we might need the room with the largest capacity. However, if it's unavailable, please reserve another one.

Also, once Mr. Osan provides his information, I'll need you to design and print another flyer. I'm hoping you'll be able to divide these tasks up among the five of you without any major issues, but do let me know if you have any problems.

Ferdinand Montgomery,
Professor of Fashion Design

The College of Fashion and Design's
Careers in Fashion Seminar Series Presents:

Mr. Philip Osan
CEO and Lead Designer of Bath Fashion House

Fashion Design and Technology
June 1, 3:30 P.M.
Westmont Auditorium

Over the years, many fashion houses have switched from hand-drawn designs to fashion design software programs. As up-and-coming designers, you must be aware of all the newest innovations in fashion design software. How can you keep up to date on the newest software trends? One possible solution is to become fluent in each new program. However, that may be costly and time-consuming. There are several ways to predict which programs will be major players in the future of fashion design. I will share my insights regarding the technological trends in the fashion industry.

From: Robert Parker
To: Rosa Hernandez
Date: May 28

Rosa, I'm at the copy center in the Hurtz Building to print the flyers, but I noticed something is missing. It seems that Mr. Osan's photograph was deleted. Can you fix the flyer and e-mail me the new version as soon as possible? The copy center closes in less than an hour and Dr. Montgomery asked me to drop the flyers off at his office tonight.

191. What is suggested about the Westmont Auditorium?

(A) It is not available on June 1.
(B) It is the location for all seminar presentations.
(C) It has fewer seats than the Belford Auditorium.
(D) It has a new projector system.

192. In the e-mail, the word "issues" in paragraph 2, line 3, is closest in meaning to

(A) conflicts
(B) periodicals
(C) distributions
(D) announcements

193. What is Mr. Osan's presentation about?

(A) New trends in design software
(B) Advancements in sewing machines
(C) Learning drawing techniques
(D) Characteristics of fashion houses

194. What problem does Mr. Parker mention?

(A) A location has been changed.
(B) The flyer is missing an image.
(C) A work history is incorrect.
(D) The time of an event is wrong.

195. Who most likely is Ms. Hernandez?

(A) Lead designer at Bath Fashion House
(B) A fashion design software developer
(C) A professor at The College of Fashion and Design
(D) A graduate student at The College of Fashion and Design

Trenton Air Conditioning

Air Conditioning Units

Trenton Air Conditioning has been providing businesses with affordable air conditioning units for over 15 years. We have provided numerous local cafés, restaurants, and supermarkets with reliable cooling solutions. All our units include cleaning services and repairs at your request, and should your unit be unsatisfactory in any way, we will replace it at no extra cost. Delivery to any location in the Sydney area and setup are both absolutely free of charge. A two-year contract must be signed by the business owner, and monthly payment plans are available.

Air Conditioning Unit Options:

Contract Option	Model	Type	Room size in square meters (m²)	Cost Per Month
Bronze	GP-A3000	Ceiling	9-25	$55.00
Silver	GP-A4000	Standing	26-55	$75.00
Gold	GP-A9999	Ceiling	55-100	$95.00
Platinum	GP-AR300	Ceiling	100-200	$115.00

Contact us for a free service quote today by visiting www.trentonaircon.com or calling one of our knowledgeable customer service agents at 1-800-444-2323.

Trenton Air Conditioning — Customer Service Quote Form

Name:	Medina Prias
Business:	Medina's Café
E-mail:	medina@mailme.com
Date:	23 April
Remarks:	I'm writing to inquire about your air conditioning units. The restaurant next to my café is currently using one of your units, and the owner, Mr. Smithe, highly recommends your services. Right now, the air conditioner in my café is nearly 10 years old. Just keeping up with the repairs and cleaning is costing a fortune. I think it would be much cheaper to just rent from your company. Since my café is quite small with only 22 square meters, I think one of your cheaper packages would be suitable. However, I will rely on your recommendation about this. Also, can you make sure any unit you recommend comes with a remote control. Our current air conditioner does not have one. Thank you, and I look forward to hearing from you.

Customer Review

I have been a customer of Trenton Air Conditioning for a year, and I have to say that I am very pleased with their services. I was very surprised to receive a 10 percent discount on my first year of service thanks to Trenton's referral program. Apparently, if you give the name of the person who connected you with Trenton, both parties will automatically receive a discount. Furthermore, I am very pleased with the contract conditions, which have allowed me to change my unit based on my business's needs. After my business went through an expansion, I called Trenton and the customer service representative agreed to upgrade my unit to a larger package. The new unit turned up only two days later and was installed free of charge even though the type changed from ceiling to standing. I highly recommend Trenton for their great business practices and customer service.

Medina Prias, Owner of Medina's Café

196. What information about Trenton Air Conditioning is NOT included in the advertisement?

(A) The energy efficiency
(B) The monthly costs
(C) The room sizes
(D) The model numbers

197. What is probably true about Mr. Smithe?

(A) He can save on air conditioning for his restaurant.
(B) He purchased a café next to his restaurant.
(C) He received one year free service from Trenton Air Conditioning.
(D) He will upgrade his air conditioning unit next year.

198. What is suggested about Medina's Café?

(A) It is owned by Mr. Smithe.
(B) It moved to a new location.
(C) It features nightly entertainment.
(D) It increased its size recently.

199. Which contract option is Ms. Prias currently using?

(A) Bronze
(B) Silver
(C) Gold
(D) Platinum

200. In the review, the phrase "turned up" in paragraph 1, line 7, is closest in meaning to

(A) removed
(B) considered
(C) designed
(D) arrived

Stop! This is the end of the test. If you finish before time is called, you may go back to Parts 5, 6, and 7 and check your work.

LISTENING TEST

In the Listening test, you will be asked to demonstrate how well you understand spoken English. The entire Listening test will last approximately 45 minutes. There are four parts, and directions are given for each part. You must mark your answers on the separate answer sheet. Do not write your answers in your test book.

PART 1

Directions: For each question in this part, you will hear four statements about a picture in your test book. When you hear the statements, you must select the one statement that best describes what you see in the picture. Then find the number of the question on your answer sheet and mark your answer. The statements will not be printed in your test book and will be spoken only one time.

Example

Sample Answer

Ⓐ Ⓑ ● Ⓓ

Statement (C), "A woman is admiring some artwork.," is the best description of the picture, so you should select answer (C) and mark it on your answer sheet.

1.

ACTUAL TEST

05

2.

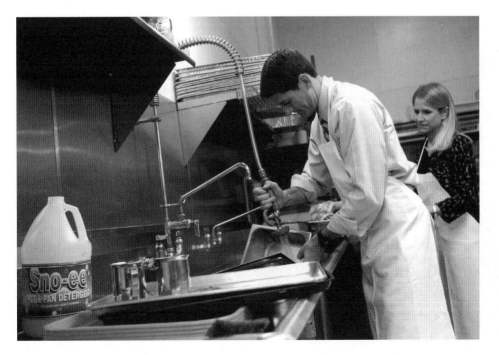

GO ON TO THE NEXT PAGE

3.

4.

5.

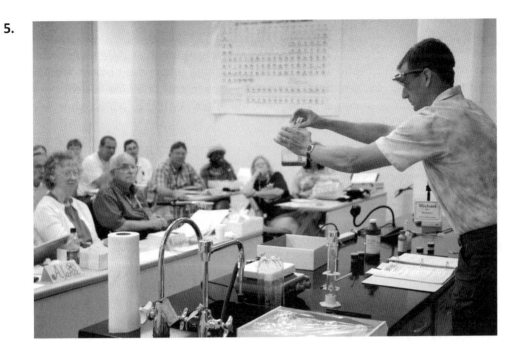

6.

PART 2 (18)

Directions: You will hear a question or statement and three responses spoken in English. They will not be printed in your test book and will be spoken only one time. Select the best response to the question or statement and mark the letter (A), (B), or (C) on your answer sheet.

7. Mark your answer on your answer sheet.

8. Mark your answer on your answer sheet.

9. Mark your answer on your answer sheet.

10. Mark your answer on your answer sheet.

11. Mark your answer on your answer sheet.

12. Mark your answer on your answer sheet.

13. Mark your answer on your answer sheet.

14. Mark your answer on your answer sheet.

15. Mark your answer on your answer sheet.

16. Mark your answer on your answer sheet.

17. Mark your answer on your answer sheet.

18. Mark your answer on your answer sheet.

19. Mark your answer on your answer sheet.

20. Mark your answer on your answer sheet.

21. Mark your answer on your answer sheet.

22. Mark your answer on your answer sheet.

23. Mark your answer on your answer sheet.

24. Mark your answer on your answer sheet.

25. Mark your answer on your answer sheet.

26. Mark your answer on your answer sheet.

27. Mark your answer on your answer sheet.

28. Mark your answer on your answer sheet.

29. Mark your answer on your answer sheet.

30. Mark your answer on your answer sheet.

31. Mark your answer on your answer sheet.

Directions: You will hear some conversations between two or more people. You will be asked to answer three questions about what the speakers say in each conversation. Select the best response to each question and mark the letter (A), (B), (C), or (D) on your answer sheet. The conversations will not be printed in your test book and will be spoken only one time.

32. What is the woman trying to do?

(A) Lease a new car
(B) Purchase an appliance
(C) Renew an insurance policy
(D) Apply for a credit card

33. What has caused a problem?

(A) An application was rejected.
(B) Some mail did not arrive.
(C) A payment method failed.
(D) Some information was wrong.

34. What does the man offer to do?

(A) Complete a profile
(B) Send a new contract
(C) Cancel a policy
(D) Provide a web address

35. What did the man do on his holiday?

(A) He threw parties.
(B) He visited a farm.
(C) He camped.
(D) He shopped.

36. What does the man say about the places he visited?

(A) They served free food.
(B) They had many discounts.
(C) They were hard to find.
(D) They were next to a park.

37. According to the woman, what did the company do recently?

(A) They gained a client.
(B) They held a sale.
(C) They took a vacation.
(D) They changed management.

ACTUAL TEST

05

38. What are the speakers mainly discussing?

(A) An office inspection
(B) A factory opening
(C) A client visit
(D) An advertising launch

39. What does the woman suggest doing?

(A) Presenting a new campaign
(B) Signing a contract
(C) Organizing an inspection
(D) Having some equipment repaired

40. What does the man say he will do?

(A) Pass on some information
(B) E-mail some samples
(C) Update a website
(D) Prepare an itinerary

41. What are the speakers discussing?

(A) Moving a business
(B) Negotiating a contract
(C) Traveling for business
(D) Changing event management

42. What does James advise the woman to do?

(A) Schedule another meeting
(B) Make a list of vendors
(C) Hire an assistant
(D) Send receipts by e-mail

43. What does James say he is excited about?

(A) Moving to a new city
(B) Managing more projects
(C) Earning more money
(D) Learning a new sport

44. Why is the woman calling the man?

(A) To provide directions to an office
(B) To request a room change
(C) To report a malfunction in equipment
(D) To inquire about a missing file

45. What does the woman mean when she says, "Right now"?

(A) She feels sorry about bothering the man.
(B) She will cancel a meeting.
(C) She wants to delay a repair.
(D) She is pleased with a plan.

46. What does the man say is unusual?

(A) The weather is unseasonably cold.
(B) The office is experiencing many problems.
(C) The meetings have been cancelled.
(D) The woman's schedule is busy.

47. What problem does the man mention?

(A) A telephone number was lost.
(B) A ticket price was wrong.
(C) A trip was postponed.
(D) An event was canceled.

48. What does the woman suggest?

(A) A visit to a museum
(B) An evening on a boat
(C) A vacation to Italy
(D) A night at the opera

49. What does the man ask the woman to do?

(A) Inquire about a price
(B) Contact some clients
(C) Refund some tickets
(D) Make a reservation

50. Who most likely are Micha and Jennifer?

(A) City inspectors
(B) Potential tenants
(C) Interior designers
(D) Hotel receptionists

51. What are Micha and Jennifer concerned about?

(A) The location of the windows
(B) The size of the rooms
(C) The cost of heating
(D) The noise of the city

52. What is mentioned about the previous couple?

(A) They are no longer working.
(B) They own the whole building.
(C) They prefer warmer climates.
(D) They have not moved yet.

53. What will happen on Monday?

(A) A vehicle will be repaired.
(B) A training session will continue.
(C) A trade show will start.
(D) A new product will launch.

54. What did the woman forget to do?

(A) Find some volunteers
(B) Contact a convention center
(C) Set up some tables
(D) Update an itinerary

55. What does the man say is available?

(A) Extra passes into a show
(B) A company banner
(C) Free refreshments
(D) Product samples

56. Why does the woman call the man?

(A) To ask for a payment
(B) To return a phone call
(C) To cancel a meeting
(D) To make a hair appointment

57. What did the man recently do?

(A) Hired a graphic designer
(B) Cancelled a subscription
(C) Started a new business
(D) Purchased a billboard

58. What does the man say he will do tomorrow?

(A) Attend a lunch
(B) Get a haircut
(C) Sell some products
(D) Go to an office

59. What department do the speakers work in?

(A) Finance
(B) Editorial
(C) Advertising
(D) Design

60. Why does the woman say, "Wow, isn't that too many"?

(A) To express surprise about a decision
(B) To suggest another option
(C) To correct a management mistake
(D) To request a change of policy

61. According to the man, what does the human resources department plan to do?

(A) Prepare a new manual
(B) Host a job fair at an office
(C) Hold a training workshop
(D) Run an advertisement online

GO ON TO THE NEXT PAGE

Package	Rate per Day
All Star Coverage	$35.00
Premium Coverage	$20.00
Advanced Coverage	$15.00
Basic Coverage	$10.00

Flight Number	Departure City	On Time/ Delayed	Est. Arrival Time
BT091	Toronto	Landed	11:00
AC550	Alberta	On Time	11:35
HG330	Vancouver	On Time	12:00
DT302	Montreal	Delayed	13:20

62. What is the purpose of the phone call?

(A) To inquire about a discount
(B) To apply for a service
(C) To make a reservation
(D) To schedule a meeting

63. Why does the man ask if the employees will do any sports?

(A) To offer some free gifts
(B) To decide on the most suitable package
(C) To recommend a travel destination
(D) To request some medical information

64. Look at the graphic. How much will each employee likely pay per day?

(A) $35
(B) $20
(C) $15
(D) $10

65. Look at the graphic. Which city is Michael Park traveling from?

(A) Toronto
(B) Alberta
(C) Vancouver
(D) Montreal

66. According to the man, why should the speakers leave now?

(A) Traffic may cause delays.
(B) The airport is far away.
(C) They need to take the bus.
(D) A flight was early.

67. What does the woman suggest doing while they wait?

(A) Getting some food
(B) Looking in some stores
(C) Seeing a film
(D) Having coffee

Plan	Contract Length	Monthly Payment
Bronze	6 months	$140.00
Silver	12 months	$100.00
Gold	24 months	$60.00
Platinum	36 months	$30.00

68. According to the woman, when is an extra fee charged?

(A) When a product is delivered
(B) When a device gets broken
(C) When a client doesn't pay a bill
(D) When a service is canceled early

69. What does the man say he might do next year?

(A) Purchase a new phone
(B) Go overseas
(C) Sign a new contract
(D) Lease a device

70. Look at the graphic. How much has the man agreed to pay per month?

(A) $140.00
(B) $100.00
(C) $60.00
(D) $30.00

Directions: You will hear some talks given by a single speaker. You will be asked to answer three questions about what the speaker says in each talk. Select the best response to each question and mark the letter (A), (B), (C), or (D) on your answer sheet. The talks will not be printed in your test book and will be spoken only one time.

71. What is the purpose of the talk?

(A) To explain the rules
(B) To name some key features
(C) To ask for payment
(D) To begin a tour

72. What will the speaker distribute?

(A) Some headphones
(B) A museum program
(C) Tickets to a performance
(D) A map of nearby galleries

73. According to the speaker, what will begin at 3:30?

(A) A question and answer session
(B) A classical music concert
(C) An antiques auction
(D) An educational presentation

74. What is being discussed?

(A) Company expense regulations
(B) Training new sales employees
(C) Hiring an office manager
(D) Filling out insurance forms

75. Why will Veronica contact listeners?

(A) To provide payment
(B) To request receipts
(C) To review a policy
(D) To resolve an error

76. What will the company do next month?

(A) Stop using a form system
(B) Begin using a new policy
(C) Lengthen a project deadline
(D) Deposit payments electronically

77. Where is the announcement taking place?

(A) At an outdoor market
(B) At a shopping center
(C) At a bus station
(D) At an art gallery

78. Why does the speaker say, "We have two stations set up"?

(A) To correct a mistake
(B) To explain some locations
(C) To apologize for a delay
(D) To express disappointment

79. What does the speaker offer?

(A) Entrance into a contest
(B) A book of discount coupons
(C) Free beverages at a café
(D) A discount on a purchase

80. What is Ms. Bernstein's area of expertise?

(A) Web development
(B) Entertainment
(C) Career guidance
(D) Finance

81. What are the listeners encouraged to do?

(A) Send in résumés
(B) Call Ms. Bernstein
(C) Purchase an e-book
(D) Leave a comment online

82. What does the speaker say happened last month?

(A) A group interview was conducted.
(B) A radio schedule changed.
(C) A free seminar took place.
(D) A line of books was released.

83. Who most likely are the listeners?

(A) Restaurant chefs
(B) Café workers
(C) Software designers
(D) Employee trainers

84. What is the purpose of the talk?

(A) To explain a customer complaint
(B) To announce a new sales procedure
(C) To begin a training session
(D) To demonstrate some new equipment

85. What can be found at each cash register?

(A) Announcement signs
(B) Membership cards
(C) Promotional coupons
(D) Updated menus

86. What is the purpose of the telephone message?

(A) To order some electronics
(B) To purchase insurance
(C) To apologize for a problem
(D) To ask for a shipping address

87. What problem does the speaker mention?

(A) Some electronics are broken.
(B) Some packaging is damaged.
(C) A payment has been delayed.
(D) A new item is sold out.

88. What does the speaker say he will do?

(A) Pick up an item
(B) Contact a manager
(C) Provide a refund
(D) Send another package

89. What industry does the speaker work in?

(A) Internet sales
(B) Fashion retail
(C) Advertising
(D) Publishing

90. Why does the speaker say, "Actually, the design has a few issues"?

(A) To outline the survey results about a design
(B) To suggest that their budget is limited
(C) To indicate a problem with some finished work
(D) To express some safety concerns

91. What does the speaker suggest the listener do?

(A) Study some prior designs
(B) Work on another project
(C) Contact a client directly
(D) Consult a coworker

92. What does the woman imply when she says, "Who knows how many will cancel their orders"?

(A) She wants someone to report an exact figure.
(B) She is worried about a loss of business.
(C) She would prefer to receive online orders.
(D) She was not expecting any problems to occur.

93. What is the topic of the meeting?

(A) Redesigning a book cover
(B) Reducing production costs
(C) Developing a marketing strategy
(D) Attracting new authors

94. What will the speaker probably do this morning?

(A) Attend a weekly meeting
(B) Conduct a telephone consultation
(C) Visit a broadcasting station
(D) Address employee questions

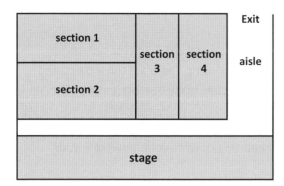

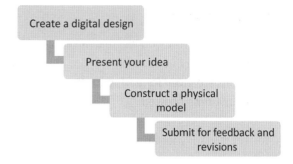

95. Who most likely are the listeners?

(A) Directors
(B) Writers
(C) Performers
(D) Reporters

96. Look at the graphic. What section does the speaker want the listeners to sit in?

(A) Section 1
(B) Section 2
(C) Section 3
(D) Section 4

97. What are listeners asked to do during the audition?

(A) Remain quiet
(B) Take photographs
(C) Avoid cellphone use
(D) Speak to choreographers

98. What does the speaker say about Frontier Architecture?

(A) They lost several important clients.
(B) They recently merged with another company.
(C) They hired a new design team.
(D) They won an international award.

99. Look at the graphic. According to the speaker, which step was recently added?

(A) Create a digital design
(B) Present your idea
(C) Construct a physical model
(D) Submit for feedback and revisions

100. What problem will the speaker's plan prevent?

(A) Losing digital files
(B) Paying overtime wages
(C) Working in a crowded office
(D) Not finishing work on time

This is the end of the Listening test. Turn to Part 5 in your test book.

READING TEST

In the Reading Test, you will read a variety of texts and answer several different types of reading comprehension questions. The entire Reading test will last 75 minutes. There are three parts, and directions are given for each part. You are encouraged to answer as many questions as possible within the time allowed.

You must mark your answers on the separate answer sheet. Do not write your answers in your test book.

PART 5

Directions: A word or phrase is missing in each of the sentences below. Four answer choices are given below each sentence. Select the best answer to complete the sentence. Then mark the letter (A), (B), (C), or (D) on your answer sheet.

101. The colorful team uniforms were provided by Danchester Tires, ------- sister company.

(A) we
(B) our
(C) us
(D) ours

102. The family's visa will be processed as soon as all necessary travel ------- are received.

(A) document
(B) documents
(C) documented
(D) documenting

103. In his speech, the CEO of Grandstead Pharmaceuticals ------- mentioned the director of the research division as a contributor to the company's success.

(A) thoroughly
(B) utterly
(C) specifically
(D) densely

104. Joanne's managerial techniques are quite ------- from her predecessor's.

(A) different
(B) differently
(C) difference
(D) differences

105. Wearing a safety harness is not an option for roofers at Delbert Contractors but rather a -------.
(A) training
(B) fulfillment
(C) speculation
(D) requirement

106. One of our plumbers will ------- how to replace a Malton DR sink drain quickly and easily.
(A) demonstrate
(B) respond
(C) inquire
(D) visit

107. Bramwell Carpets does not issue refunds of any kind so be sure to measure the floor space ------- before purchasing.
(A) careful
(B) caring
(C) carefully
(D) cares

108. ------- annual profits are high or low, they still provide important economic information for business analysts.
(A) Whether
(B) Either
(C) Despite
(D) Even

109. The report provides a detailed ------- between the old Argo motorcycle design and the new Grandford one.
(A) comparable
(B) comparison
(C) compared
(D) comparative

110. ------- speak to a customer service agent, please stay on the line.
(A) For
(B) Across
(C) With
(D) To

111. The storage space in the new warehouse is more than ------- for three hundred bicycles.
(A) able
(B) great
(C) sure
(D) enough

112. Applying for a family visa in this country is a long and ------- process.
(A) complicate
(B) complicated
(C) complication
(D) complicatedness

113. Leading automotive experts maintain that Woykin Oil filters deliver ------- results.
(A) exceptionally
(B) exceptional
(C) exception
(D) exceptions

114. A credit card statement or phone bill can be ------- of residency.
(A) process
(B) analysis
(C) proof
(D) basis

115. Mr. Bolduc ------- asked Gabriella to organize the workshop, but then assigned the task to Louise.
    (A) initial
    (B) initially
    (C) initialize
    (D) initialized

116. Job candidates need to submit three letters of recommendation ------- the completed application.
    (A) too
    (B) in addition
    (C) moreover
    (D) along with

117. Even though Mr. Buono has never worked in refrigerator repair, his knowledge of refrigeration systems is -------.
    (A) extensive
    (B) clever
    (C) considered
    (D) eager

118. The flowchart on page six describes the ------- of duties among the different project managers.
    (A) support
    (B) attention
    (C) division
    (D) statement

119. These seeds will produce the biggest tomatoes but not ------- the healthiest ones.
    (A) expectedly
    (B) necessarily
    (C) preventively
    (D) permanently

120. While the store does not issue refunds, customers can exchange any item for something ------- in amount to the original sales price.
    (A) equivalent
    (B) profitable
    (C) deliberate
    (D) controlled

121. This newspaper photograph shows the mayor of Otterbury sitting ------- the prime minister.
    (A) from
    (B) reverse
    (C) opposite
    (D) distant

122. The decision to launch a new line of footwear was ------- the results of some market research.
    (A) such as
    (B) adjacent to
    (C) except for
    (D) based on

123. The Alderburn Employment Center is the only building on this block that is ------- to people in wheelchairs.
    (A) access
    (B) accessibly
    (C) accessible
    (D) accessibility

124. Dr. Darius is striving ------- the look of his office and is going to put a painting in the waiting room.
    (A) to enhance
    (B) enhances
    (C) is enhancing
    (D) enhanced

125. Players ------- teams did not make it to the finals can watch the game for free.
   (A) its
   (B) which
   (C) whose
   (D) more

126. Local officials ------- farmers that the pesticide sprayed on the potato crops was harmless to humans.
   (A) assured
   (B) arranged
   (C) described
   (D) committed

127. Factory laborers at Langford Manufacturing ------- to work 30 minutes more each day to offset rising production costs.
   (A) agreeing
   (B) to agree
   (C) agreement
   (D) have agreed

128. ------- Samuel's work experience in three continents, it was no surprise that the CEO put him in charge of the overseas project.
   (A) Since
   (B) Given
   (C) Among
   (D) Upon

129. A person who was not raised in this community may not understand the historical ------- on the Steinhauer Street Bridge.
   (A) signify
   (B) significant
   (C) significance
   (D) significantly

130. Jennifer has more seniority than Bill at the company, ------- she is much younger than him.
   (A) as if
   (B) so that
   (C) in case
   (D) even though

PART 6

Directions: Read the texts that follow. A word, phrase, or sentence is missing in parts of each text. Four answer choices for each question are given below the text. Select the best answer to complete the text. Then mark the letter (A), (B), (C), or (D) on your answer sheet.

Questions 131-134 refer to the following e-mail.

To: <nina_haidara@kmail.net>
From: <duron_charette@wrnpharmaceuticals.com>
Date: September 7
Subject: Head of Research position

Dear Ms. Haidara,

WRN Pharmaceuticals is delighted to invite you to come in for a second interview next week. Since this is the second stage, our hiring committee will be speaking to only the top five applicants whom we feel are most __131.__ for this challenging position. Our entire committee agrees that you possess almost all the __132.__ we need. We trust that you are still interested in the position. __133.__, would you be available for an appointment next Wednesday at 2:30? Also, as part of the interview, we would like you to prepare a written research proposal related to one of the topics discussed at the first interview as well as a 10-minute presentation. __134.__.

Best regards,

Duron Charette
WRN Pharmaceuticals
304-677-2426 ext. 18

131. (A) suiting
 (C) suit
 (B) suitable
 (D) suits

132. (A) agreements
 (C) qualities
 (B) performances
 (D) promotions

133. (A) Despite that
 (C) However
 (B) If so
 (D) For example

134. (A) Our current research head will train you in your new duties.
 (B) The CEO will be delighted to provide you with a letter of reference.
 (C) You need to complete your current research project before Wednesday.
 (D) We are looking forward to hearing your vision for a future project.

Questions 135-138 refer to the following the letter.

Chantal Youldon

302 Moline Street

Delavan, IL

61735

Dear Ms. Youldon,

We would like to remind you that the time for another eye examination is soon approaching. ___135.___. Eye specialists ___136.___ having your vision checked at least once a year. ___137.___, eye problems can be detected early and the prescription for your eyeglasses can also be updated. Our number one ___138.___ is providing our patients with the best vision possible. We will follow up this letter with a phone call in a few days. Please phone us at (309) 754-3231 if you would like to make an appointment. Thank you very much.

The Eye Care Team

Herrin Street Eye Clinic

---

135. (A) We recently expanded our waiting room to include a larger play area for children.
(B) Our records indicate that it has been eleven months since your last saw Dr. Hoban.
(C) Exercise and a healthy diet also have an impact on the condition of your eyes.
(D) Our office updated its website to include a convenient online appointment system.

136. (A) recommending
(B) had recommended
(C) recommend
(D) will recommend

137. (A) Nevertheless
(B) In this way
(C) For example
(D) Likewise

138. (A) manner
(B) opinion
(C) condition
(D) priority

GO ON TO THE NEXT PAGE

Questions 139-142 refer to the following article.

Parrsboro Herald

Local News

(12 June) — On Tuesday afternoon, Parrsboro City Mayor Deborah Middleton announced city council's decision to implement one-on-one training programs for aspiring city bus drivers. **139.** , she stated that 20 new drivers will be needed before the end of the year. Speaking at a press conference, she stressed that there is an urgent **140.** for new drivers to replace those who are set to retire soon. The announcement **141.** with approval by most city officials. Councilor Stephen Digby of Truro Region, however, continues to speak out against the city funding costly training programs when graduates of the Wolfville College of Vehicle Operations, just 50 km west of Parrsboro, are already qualified to fill the positions. **142.** .

---

139. (A) Specifically
(B) Undoubtedly
(C) Regardless
(D) Besides

140. (A) settlement
(B) reduction
(C) demand
(D) difficulty

141. (A) will be meeting
(B) to meet
(C) had been meeting
(D) was met

142. (A) He believes the current buses can be improved to allow more seats.
(B) He wants the city to hire staff already skilled in the field.
(C) He feels the test to become a certified driver is too easy to pass.
(D) He expects the high fuel costs will lead to higher bus rates.

Questions 143-146 refer to the following letter.

To: Frans Vanek

From: Michelle Sekera

Date: 14 July

Subject: Good morning.

I learned of your upcoming ____**143.**____ from a colleague. Even though the position of chief recruiter at our newly-opened office in Oslo officially ____**144.**____ on August 2, I would like to take a moment now to wish you the very best in your new career. If you require any assistance, please do not hesitate to contact me. I am well aware that this type of transition, while exciting, is also extremely ____**145.**____ . Your work performance here in Paris at Chara Fashion as assistant hiring director has always been outstanding. ____**146.**____ . Congratulations and good luck!

Sincerely,

Michelle Sekera

---

143. (A) trip
    (B) event
    (C) award
    (D) promotion

144. (A) begins
    (B) began
    (C) has begun
    (D) could begin

145. (A) challenging
    (B) challenge
    (C) challenger
    (D) challenges

146. (A) The Oslo office is a little smaller with a big parking lot.
    (B) I'm still conducting interviews for all the new positions.
    (C) You could ask about staff discounts at clothing shops.
    (D) I am certain that you will be successful in your new position.

GO ON TO THE NEXT PAGE

Directions: In this part you will read a selection of texts, such as magazine and newspaper articles, e-mails, and instant messages. Each text or set of texts is followed by several questions. Select the best answer for each question and mark the letter (A), (B), (C), or (D) on your answer sheet.

Questions 147-148 refer to the following receipt.

Park Home Outfitters
229 Park Road South
Edmonton, Alberta
(777) 223-4455

Date: May 12   Time: 10:37

Items

3345	La Roux 4-Seat Sofa	$499.00
3348	La Roux Armchair	$199.00
3355	La Roux Footstool	$99.00
4489	D&F 6-drawer Dresser	
	4 $79.00/ea	$316.00
1223	Star Designs pillow	
	2 $19.00/ea	$38.00

Subtotal	$1151.00
Tax (5%)	$57.55
Total	$1208.55
Paid by credit card	$1208.55

Total number of items purchased: 9

Returns may be made for all non-sale items within 60 days of purchase.
To view our return policy, please visit
www.parkhomeoutfitters.ca/returns.
****

Sign up for a membership on our website and receive up to 50% off on
select online purchases. Offer ends June 28.
****

Thank you for shopping at Park Home Outfitters.

147. What kind of store most likely is Park Home Outfitters?

(A) A furniture store
(B) A fabric outlet
(C) A construction company
(D) A clothing store

148. According to the receipt, how can customers get a discount?

(A) By applying for a membership
(B) By showing a coupon
(C) By completing a survey
(D) By purchasing two or more items

Questions 149-150 refer to the following e-mail.

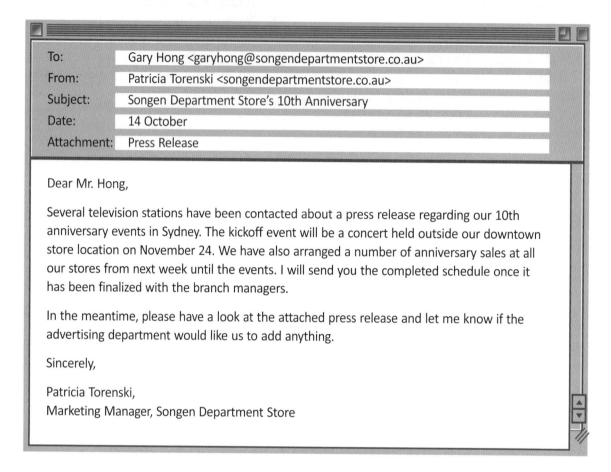

To: Gary Hong <garyhong@songendepartmentstore.co.au>

From: Patricia Torenski <songendepartmentstore.co.au>

Subject: Songen Department Store's 10th Anniversary

Date: 14 October

Attachment: Press Release

Dear Mr. Hong,

Several television stations have been contacted about a press release regarding our 10th anniversary events in Sydney. The kickoff event will be a concert held outside our downtown store location on November 24. We have also arranged a number of anniversary sales at all our stores from next week until the events. I will send you the completed schedule once it has been finalized with the branch managers.

In the meantime, please have a look at the attached press release and let me know if the advertising department would like us to add anything.

Sincerely,

Patricia Torenski,
Marketing Manager, Songen Department Store

149. What is the purpose of the e-mail?
   (A) To make a list of items for sale
   (B) To reschedule a live music event
   (C) To invite a coworker to attend an event
   (D) To give an update on a promotional plan

150. What does Ms. Torenski promise to send later?
   (A) A recent news article
   (B) A schedule of store discounts
   (C) A list of television stations
   (D) A revised press release

Questions 151-152 refer to the following article.

Around Town

Town Books owner Cynthia Purdel has announced her plans to open a second bookstore at 667 Brookside Avenue. The building, located across from Brookside Elementary School, was once the home of Smithton Bakery. Ms. Purdel's new bookstore, which has yet to be named, is scheduled to open in the spring of next year. The bookstore will include an extensive children's section, which Ms. Purdel hopes it will attract numerous customers from Brookside Elementary School. Ms. Purdel's original bookstore, Town Books, is located on 5th Avenue and houses genres that are targeted to adult readers.

---

151. What is the purpose of the article?

(A) To discuss the closing of a business
(B) To profile a successful bakery owner
(C) To report on a store's relocation
(D) To announce the opening of a new business

152. What is indicated about the new store on Brookside Avenue?

(A) It is located across from a popular bakery.
(B) It is scheduled to open this year.
(C) It is Ms. Purdel's first business venture.
(D) It is expected to receive business from students.

Questions 153-155 refer to the following notice.

St. Michael's Hospital Research Gala

St. Michael's Hospital will host a gala to benefit continued medical research. The gala will be held at the Grand Renaissance Hotel; however, the day has been changed due to a hotel booking error. Instead of September 20, the event will be held on October 5, from 5:00 P.M. until 8:00 P.M. Please note the following information before attending.

Directions to Grand Renaissance Hotel from Central Station:

Drive north on Parcelle Boulevard and turn right onto Meadow Drive. Turn left onto Bath Avenue and continue for five blocks before turning right onto Smithview Road. The Grand Renaissance Hotel is located across from the Mary Rose Theater. The gala will be held in Banquet Room 1A.

Parking Information:

Parking is available free of charge in the underground parking lot. Please ensure you have the parking pass that was issued along with your gala ticket. Otherwise, you will be responsible for paying for parking.

---

153. What has changed about the event?

(A) The cost
(B) The location
(C) The sponsor
(D) The date

154. Where is Central Station located?

(A) Meadow Drive
(B) Bath Avenue
(C) Parcelle Boulevard
(D) Smithview Road

155. What is indicated about the Grand Renaissance Hotel's parking?

(A) Gala guests will have to pay for parking.
(B) The parking lot is located across the street.
(C) Parking is free with a guest pass.
(D) The hotel has a shared parking garage.

Questions 156-157 refer to the following text message chain.

Steven Yoon 4:45 P.M.
Jennifer tried to call you about the meeting with the CEO tomorrow. She's wondering if you can call her back.

Roger Martinez 4:50 P.M.
I'm in the warehouse right now. Do you think she's worried the reports won't be finished in time?

Steven Yoon 4:52 P.M.
It's possible.

Roger Martinez 4:54 P.M.
Well, I'm checking the warehouse alarm system now. I got called away, because it seems to be acting up again.

Steven Yoon 4:57 P.M.
Do you want me to call the security company?

Roger Martinez 5:00 P.M.
I think I can fix it myself. Can you tell Jennifer to stop by my office at 5:30? I think we should discuss her concerns tonight before we go home.

Steven Yoon 5:01 P.M.
OK. No problem.

---

156. At 4:50 P.M. what does Mr. Martinez most likely mean when he writes, "I'm in the warehouse right now"?

(A) He will not be in tomorrow.
(B) He has a delivery to make.
(C) He needs to speak with Mr. Yoon.
(D) He cannot call Jennifer.

157. What task is Mr. Yoon asked to do?

(A) Contact the CEO
(B) Set up a meeting
(C) Call a technician
(D) Leave the office

Questions 158-160 refer to the following letter.

October 10

Peter Stephenson
45 Ramsay Avenue
Cleveland, Ohio

Dear Mr. Stephenson:

Thank you very much for deciding to attend the very first International Magazine Festival that will take place in Paris, France. We received your registration. --[1]--. As requested, we billed your credit card to include both admission to the event as well as the extra fee needed to reserve a table for your display. Immediately upon arrival, we will show you to your table and also present you with a name badge that will allow you to receive discounts at any beverage and food vendors at the festival. --[2]--.

We would like to remind you that accommodation is not included in the festival admission price. To reserve a room in the neighborhood, please visit www.parishotels.com. You may be able to book a room at 25% off the regular rate by providing proof that you are participating in our festival. --[3]--.

Enclosed, please find a map of this particular area of Paris. This will allow you to acquaint yourself with the neighborhood. The map also includes the area's most popular restaurants and hotels. --[4]--.

Again, thank you and we hope the International Magazine Festival turns out to be a rewarding experience for you.

Sincerely,

Nicole Desjardins,
Festival Coordinator

---

158. Why was the letter sent?

(A) To offer a partial refund
(B) To inform of an address change
(C) To explain a procedure
(D) To acknowledge registration

159. What is Mr. Stephenson advised to review ahead of time?

(A) A local map
(B) A meeting agenda
(C) Contract terms
(D) Flight times

160. In which of the positions marked [1], [2], [3], and [4] does the following sentence best belong?

"This letter is suitable verification so simply present it to the clerk when you check in."

(A) [1]
(B) [2]
(C) [3]
(D) [4]

Questions 161-164 refer to the following article.

Unforeseeable Delays for the Hammer Electronics 8000 Series

By Sophia Miachi

Last week, Hammer Electronics, the world's leading producer of smart phones, announced a delay in the launch of its new 8000 Series smart phone line. Industry professionals and customers alike were shocked by the news. Hammer Electronics enthusiasts took to social media to express their frustration with the cancellation of the much-anticipated 8000 Series.

According to Hammer representatives, the 8000 Series, which will consist of three individual models and various companion technologies, has been delayed due to unforeseeable problems with the company's new screen design. --[1]--. While the prototypes were initially approved, the first batch of devices were unable to pass safety tests. --[2]--. This may be due to a flaw in the glass used to construct the screens, which makes the internal components vulnerable to overheating.

In addition to not passing the inspections, Hammer's new line has proven to be less durable than the company intended. Because of the flawed materials, the 8000 Series has proven to be quite delicate. --[3]--.

Hammer Electronics is now looking at alternative materials and plans to release the 8000 Series next year. --[4]--. However, the company may have already lost many of its eager customers.

161. What is indicated about Hammer Electronics?

(A) It is a top producer of smart phone technology.
(B) It will sell the 8000 Series at a discount.
(C) It is moving its headquarters to another country.
(D) It will continue producing a flawed design.

162. What is NOT mentioned as a problem with the 8000 Series design?

(A) The screens have flawed glass.
(B) The devices may overheat.
(C) The materials are too expensive.
(D) The devices are fragile.

163. Why will Hammer Electronics release the 8000 Series next year?

(A) They need to address a patent issue.
(B) Their inspections have been rescheduled.
(C) Some factories need to be upgraded.
(D) They need enough time to find new materials.

164. In which of the positions marked [1], [2], [3], and [4] does the following sentence best belong?

"For a company that prides itself on durable products, releasing this line of devices would be an embarrassment."

(A) [1]
(B) [2]
(C) [3]
(D) [4]

Questions 165-168 refer to the following text message chain.

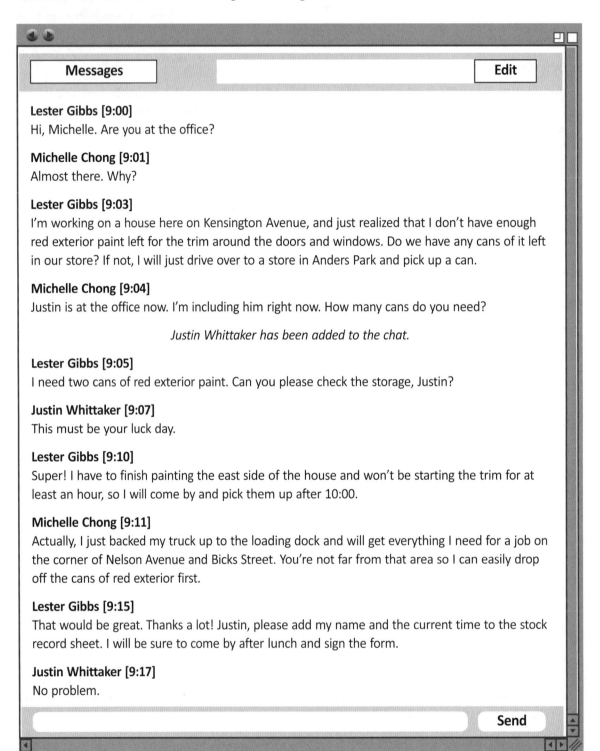

Messages   **Edit**

Lester Gibbs [9:00]
Hi, Michelle. Are you at the office?

Michelle Chong [9:01]
Almost there. Why?

Lester Gibbs [9:03]
I'm working on a house here on Kensington Avenue, and just realized that I don't have enough red exterior paint left for the trim around the doors and windows. Do we have any cans of it left in our store? If not, I will just drive over to a store in Anders Park and pick up a can.

Michelle Chong [9:04]
Justin is at the office now. I'm including him right now. How many cans do you need?

Justin Whittaker has been added to the chat.

Lester Gibbs [9:05]
I need two cans of red exterior paint. Can you please check the storage, Justin?

Justin Whittaker [9:07]
This must be your luck day.

Lester Gibbs [9:10]
Super! I have to finish painting the east side of the house and won't be starting the trim for at least an hour, so I will come by and pick them up after 10:00.

Michelle Chong [9:11]
Actually, I just backed my truck up to the loading dock and will get everything I need for a job on the corner of Nelson Avenue and Bicks Street. You're not far from that area so I can easily drop off the cans of red exterior first.

Lester Gibbs [9:15]
That would be great. Thanks a lot! Justin, please add my name and the current time to the stock record sheet. I will be sure to come by after lunch and sign the form.

Justin Whittaker [9:17]
No problem.

Send

165. What type of business does Mr. Gibbs probably work for?

(A) A home improvement contractor
(B) An Internet provider
(C) A plastics manufacturer
(D) A fast food restaurant

166. Where does Ms. Chong say she will go next?

(A) To Anders Park
(B) To Kensington Avenue
(C) To Bicks Street
(D) To Nelson Avenue

167. At 9:07 A.M. what does Mr. Whittaker most likely mean when he writes, "This must be your lucky day"?

(A) There is enough money for a new project.
(B) The directions to the house are easy to follow.
(C) The exact number of cans needed is in stock.
(D) He will be able to help Mr. Gibbs in the evening.

168. What does Mr. Gibbs ask Mr. Whittaker to do?

(A) Fill in the main details on a form
(B) Place some items on a shelf
(C) Set up a consultation with a client
(D) Send an invoice to a local business

BizNet
Networking at the click of a mouse!

BizNet is the latest development in online networking services. Quick, affordable, and easy-to-use, BizNet can connect you with industry professionals and help you land the job of your dreams. Our online services allow you to track trends in the job market as well as get up-to-date information on business conferences in your area.

In cooperation with our sister network, StudyNet, you get numerous advanced features, such as:
- A simple résumé builder that allows you to create a perfect résumé in minutes
- An extensive list of businesses and search tools for finding the right job opening
- A library of videos on everything from applying to interviewing for your dream job
- Weekly matching services that pair you up with new jobs based on your skills

For more information, visit www.biznet.com.

169. How would a customer most likely use BizNet?

(A) To shop for online services
(B) To find employment at a company
(C) To complete tax documents
(D) To advertise the services of a company

170. What is suggested about the company that developed BizNet?

(A) Its representatives can be contacted by telephone.
(B) It has a reputation for helping home businesses.
(C) It was founded by a large sales corporation.
(D) It has more than one networking website.

171. What is NOT mentioned as a feature of BizNet?

(A) A library of videos
(B) A résumé generator
(C) Tickets to conferences
(D) Employment search tools

Lake Porticole Beach and Campground (LPBC)

Lake Porticole Beach and Campground will be open this spring & summer season beginning April 10 through September 1. Please note, however, LPBC reserves the right to impose additional restrictions on campers. Due to the repeated occurrence of dry weather, campers may be prohibited from having open campfires at certain times. This does not apply to the use of camping stoves and barbecues for cooking, however. When fires are permitted, campers must purchase pre-cut wood from the park. Cutting down trees will not be permitted at any time.

Lake Porticole Beach may be accessed by non-campers for day visits for a small fee. Beach goers may arrive as early as 8 A.M. and stay until 5 P.M. Group tickets may be booked in advance for a discount. Additionally, the park offers guided tours of the Lake Porticole Museum, a historical estate originally owned by Sir William Marks. Tickets for the museum can be purchased at the front gate on the day of the tour.

Payment and Reservations

• For campsite reservations, call 888-341-0867. Campsites are $65.00 per night. A non-refundable deposit of $30.00 must be made at the time of reservation. This deposit goes toward the cost of your stay.

• Beach day passes for non-campers can be purchased upon arrival for $8.00 per person. Groups of more than 15 can receive a 20% discount if reservations are made in advance.

• Lake Porticole Museum tickets are available for $7.00 per person. Tours are offered three times per day at 11 A.M., 1 P.M., and 3 P.M.

172. What is announced in the notice?

(A) A new policy
(B) A business's closing
(C) An increase in fees
(D) An operation schedule

173. What is indicated about visiting Lake Porticole's campground?

(A) Campers can be fined for littering in the forest.
(B) Campers might not be able to have campfires.
(C) To see the museum, campers must be part of a group.
(D) To access the beach, campers need to pay another fee.

174. What is mentioned about the Lake Porticole's non-camping services?

(A) Museum tickets can be reserved.
(B) Beach visitors can stay overnight on weekends.
(C) Parasols are offered to beach visitors free of charge.
(D) Groups can get a discount when visiting the beach.

175. What happens when a campsite reservation is canceled?

(A) A reservation fee is lost.
(B) A payment is refunded.
(C) A bill will be sent.
(D) A membership will be downgraded.

ACTUAL TEST 05

Questions 176-180 refer to the following letter and e-mail.

10 March

Ms. Kelly Norstram
Simpson Publishing
Human Resources Department
55 Center St.
Sydney, Australia

Dear Ms. Norstram,

I would like to take this opportunity to submit my application for the editorial director position at Simpson Publishing in its new Sydney office. As you can see from my enclosed résumé, I have extensive experience in the editorial field, including five years as head editor at *Lush Magazine* and three years as an editorial assistant at the *Sydney Times* newspaper.

Aside from this experience, I also have a Bachelor's degree in Journalism and a Master's degree in Publishing Studies. Furthermore, I believe I would add a new dimension to the editorial director position given that I am also a published author of seven children's books. I believe that my unique combination of experience will contribute greatly to the company.

Thank you very much for your time. I look forward to speaking with you.

Sincerely,

Adrian Perdu

To:	Simpson Publishing Editorial Staff
From:	Adrian Perdu
Date:	April 30
Subject:	Some Reminders

Editorial Staff Members,

It has been nearly a year since we first proposed our new line of educational children's books. I'd like to commend you all on your hard work on this series. With our publication date fast approaching, I'd just like to remind everyone of a few things.

First, please ensure you communicate with designers weekly regarding the overall design of our books. It is important that you give them your input and guidance in bringing our collective vision to fruition.

Second, some freelance proofreaders have fallen behind on their deadlines. Please make sure you contact them regularly and if need be, hire additional freelancers to complete the work.

Finally, as the release of our series will include a website launch, I'd like everyone to submit a biography for the "about us" section. A simple biography of about 100 words will suffice.

Thank you all for your continued hard work, and I look forward to launch day!

Adrian

176. What is one purpose of the letter?

(A) To inquire about a starting salary
(B) To list some professional qualifications
(C) To provide an employment reference
(D) To ask about the location of a job

177. In the letter, the word "dimension" in paragraph 2, line 2, is closest in meaning to

(A) demand
(B) precedent
(C) matter
(D) characteristic

178. Why did Mr. Perdu write the e-mail?

(A) To praise workers for getting tasks done
(B) To stress the importance of some duties
(C) To motivate employees to take on extra work
(D) To inform new hires of special procedures

179. What is stated about Simpson Publishing?

(A) It publishes primarily e-books.
(B) It employs editors in seven countries.
(C) It will discontinue some publications.
(D) It will introduce its staff on its website.

180. What is suggested about Mr. Perdu?

(A) He previously worked as a book designer.
(B) He was hired by Simpson Publishing one year ago.
(C) He moved to the US for a job opportunity.
(D) He no longer writes books for children.

Questions 181-185 refer to the following e-mail and business plan.

To:	Wanda Willis <willis@utcbankandloans.com
From:	Jeffrey Thomas <jthomas@mailmail.com
Date:	March 12
Re:	Business Plan
Attachment:	Revised Plan

Dear Ms. Willis,

Thank you so much for your quick reply. I am very happy you are able to help me secure financial backing for my new business venture. I have looked over all the feedback you sent and edited my business plan accordingly. As you advised, I have included a section that details our potential customers and attached the revised version.

I think this is all I need to complete the application package for my business loan. However, if there's anything else I need to fill out, please contact me.

I look forward to hearing from you.

Sincerely,

Jeffrey Thomas

Revised Business Plan: The Brim

Section 1. Purpose

Downtown Portside has become a bustling business district, filled with numerous office buildings, banks, and department stores. My business, The Brim, will be located near the prestigious courthouse, a busy area of the downtown core. We hope to offer a wide variety of international gourmet coffees at affordable prices, while also providing a relaxing atmosphere to enjoy our gourmet lunch items.

Section 2. Target Market

The Brim will serve business professionals working downtown. Because there are so many law offices and banks within walking distance, our customers are likely to visit our coffee house in the mornings, during break times, and at lunch. Furthermore, weekend customers will consist of shoppers who are visiting the nearby Portside Department Store.

Section 3. Timeline

The Brim is scheduled to open on June 1. We expect the following preparations to be completed by:

March 28	Sign the lease and apply for a business permit
April 10	Renovate the dining area and upgrade the kitchen
April 20	Hire staff and complete employee training
May 15	Finalize the menu, order inventory, and plan the grand opening

Section 4. Marketing Plan

Please see the attached spread sheet for our detailed marketing plans prior to opening and after.

181. What is the purpose of the e-mail?

(A) To review the guidelines of a permit
(B) To send feedback about some financial data
(C) To request advice on writing a business plan
(D) To respond to a requested revision

182. In the e-mail, the word "secure" in paragraph 1, line 1, is closest in meaning to

(A) guard
(B) obtain
(C) save
(D) fasten

183. What section of the business plan was added?

(A) Section 1
(B) Section 2
(C) Section 3
(D) Section 4

184. What type of business does Mr. Thomas plan to start?

(A) A loan company
(B) A department store
(C) A law office
(D) A gourmet café

185. According to the business plan, what information was submitted separately?

(A) A detailed estimate of expected profits
(B) Contact information for employment references
(C) A list of ways the business will advertise
(D) Recommendations for renovation companies

Questions 186-190 refer to the following webpage, e-mail, and form.

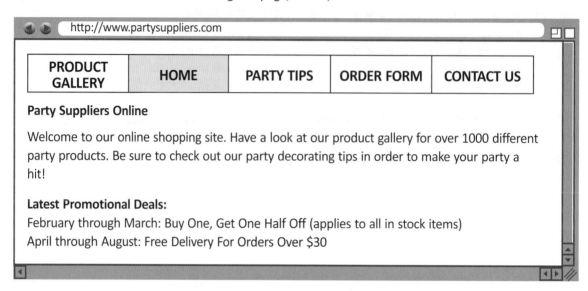

| PRODUCT GALLERY | HOME | PARTY TIPS | ORDER FORM | CONTACT US |

Party Suppliers Online

Welcome to our online shopping site. Have a look at our product gallery for over 1000 different party products. Be sure to check out our party decorating tips in order to make your party a hit!

Latest Promotional Deals:
February through March: Buy One, Get One Half Off (applies to all in stock items)
April through August: Free Delivery For Orders Over $30

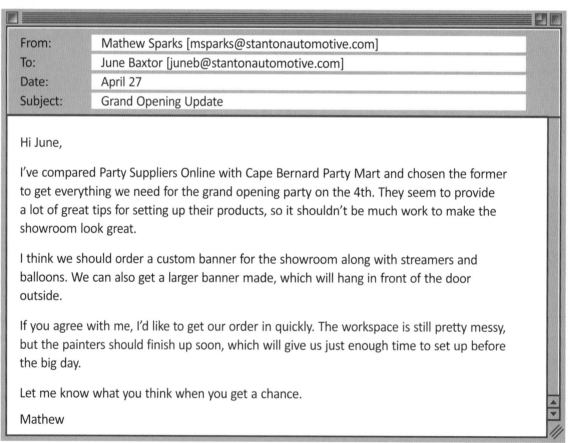

From:	Mathew Sparks [msparks@stantonautomotive.com]
To:	June Baxtor [juneb@stantonautomotive.com]
Date:	April 27
Subject:	Grand Opening Update

Hi June,

I've compared Party Suppliers Online with Cape Bernard Party Mart and chosen the former to get everything we need for the grand opening party on the 4th. They seem to provide a lot of great tips for setting up their products, so it shouldn't be much work to make the showroom look great.

I think we should order a custom banner for the showroom along with streamers and balloons. We can also get a larger banner made, which will hang in front of the door outside.

If you agree with me, I'd like to get our order in quickly. The workspace is still pretty messy, but the painters should finish up soon, which will give us just enough time to set up before the big day.

Let me know what you think when you get a chance.

Mathew

Order Number: 112233265
Contact Info: Mathew Sparks (444) 232-0916
Delivery To: Stanton Automotive Dealership, 14 Brooks Lane, Atlantic City
Delivery Window: 01-02 May, 09:00-13:00

Quantity	Product Code	Description
1	YZ0933	Custom Banner (3 feet long)
1	YZ0955	Custom Banner (6 feet long)
12	GH3345	Rainbow Balloons 12 per pack
2	BB3200	Streamers (white)
		Total: $104.50

Note: All our custom banners are printed at our manufacturing headquarters in Baltimore. Those items will be shipped into Atlantic City from Baltimore instead of our Port Edward store, which means you will have two separate shipments. Should you have any questions, do not hesitate to call us immediately.

186. What is indicated about Party Suppliers Online?
    (A) It provides complimentary product samples.
    (B) It offers decorating advice to customers.
    (C) It recently opened up another store.
    (D) It will expand its product line next year.

187. What is probably true about Stanton Automotive Dealership's order?
    (A) It will be delivered for free.
    (B) It includes foreign products.
    (C) It includes half-price items.
    (D) It will be refunded in May.

188. Why does Mr. Sparks probably prefer to schedule a delivery quickly?
    (A) He needs time to purchase more items.
    (B) He wants to take advantage of a promotion.
    (C) He needs some workers to help clean up.
    (D) He wants to have enough time to set up.

189. What product will most likely be placed outside Stanton Automotive Dealership?
    (A) Custom Banner 3ft
    (B) Custom Banner 6ft
    (C) Rainbow Balloons
    (D) Streamers

190. According to the form, where most likely will the balloons be shipped from?
    (A) Baltimore
    (B) Atlantic City
    (C) Cape Bernard
    (D) Port Edward

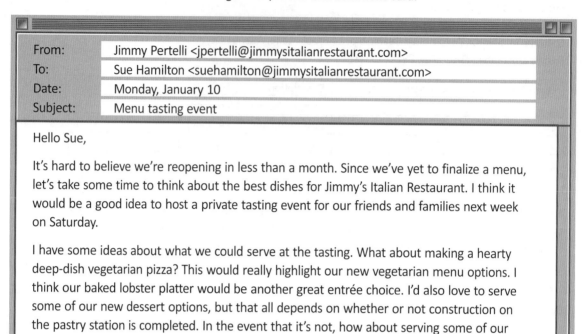

From:	Jimmy Pertelli <jpertelli@jimmysitalianrestaurant.com>
To:	Sue Hamilton <suehamilton@jimmysitalianrestaurant.com>
Date:	Monday, January 10
Subject:	Menu tasting event

Hello Sue,

It's hard to believe we're reopening in less than a month. Since we've yet to finalize a menu, let's take some time to think about the best dishes for Jimmy's Italian Restaurant. I think it would be a good idea to host a private tasting event for our friends and families next week on Saturday.

I have some ideas about what we could serve at the tasting. What about making a hearty deep-dish vegetarian pizza? This would really highlight our new vegetarian menu options. I think our baked lobster platter would be another great entrée choice. I'd also love to serve some of our new dessert options, but that all depends on whether or not construction on the pastry station is completed. In the event that it's not, how about serving some of our new organic ice cream flavors topped with your amazing chocolate sauce? I will leave it all up to you, though. As head chef, you have complete freedom.

Finally, I'd love to offer our guests an ice-cream making demonstration after the tasting. Let me know if you think that would be possible.

Thanks,

Jimmy

Jimmy's Italian Restaurant Tasting Menu
Saturday, January 15
Caprese Salad with mozzarella cheese and fresh basil
Coconut Shrimp
Baked Garlic Bread
Vegetarian Pasta with tomato sauce
Baked Lobster Platter smothered in melted butter
Rib eye Fire-Grilled Steak served with roasted potatoes
Jimmy's Famous Puff Pastries

Tasting Comment Card

Name: Fran Humphrey

Please comment on your tasting experience at Jimmy's Italian Restaurant.

I enjoyed the appetizers very much. The salad, however, had too much balsamic dressing for my taste. The vegetarian pasta dish was quite good, but I found the noodles to be a bit overcooked. The baked lobster, on the other hand, was the best I've ever tasted. I found the steak to be a bit rare, but the potatoes were seasoned very nicely. The dessert was perhaps too sweet for me, but I thought the pastry was cooked to perfection. I also enjoyed the ice cream making demonstration, though I wish we could've tasted some of the flavors.

191. What is the purpose of the menu tasting?
(A) To select dishes for a new menu
(B) To prepare for a restaurant inspection
(C) To audition new cooking staff
(D) To decide who will be head chef

192. In the e-mail, the word "hearty" in paragraph 2, line 1, is closest in meaning to
(A) sincere
(B) aromatic
(C) satisfying
(D) original

193. What is true about the tasting menu?
(A) It showcases only old menu items.
(B) It lists several new ice cream flavors.
(C) It is only available to customers on weekends.
(D) It includes an entrée suggested by Mr. Pertelli.

194. Which menu item was most likely Ms. Humphrey's favorite?
(A) The salad
(B) The pasta
(C) The lobster
(D) The steak

195. What is suggested about the pastry station?
(A) It was too large for the kitchen.
(B) It was moved to another location.
(C) It was damaged in a renovation.
(D) It was completed on time.

Questions 196-200 refer to the following advertisement, e-mail, and text message.

Hartford Opera House
45 Bellview Street
New York City
www.hartfordoperahouse.com

The Hartford Opera House is pleased to announce an exciting schedule of events that will take place this summer. We will be featuring everything from concerts to stage plays, so we are sure to have something for you. Tickets will be available on our website for each event, and seasonal passes may be purchased for a lump sum. Seasonal pass holders will be able to attend as many events as they wish and bring up to three guests at a time free of charge.

Schedule of Events:

June 23 — The Miller Brothers Classical Ensemble
July 3 — Stand-Up Comedy by Alan Brewer
July 4 — *Into the Jungle*, an award-winning musical featuring songs by Catrina Belford
July 10 — *Women of Egypt*, a stage play directed by Tommy Wilson

For a complete summer schedule, please visit www.hartfordoperahouse.com.

To:	Lila Sampson
From:	Roderick Kelly
Cc:	June Varek
Subject:	Your Trip to Meadworth Paper and Packaging
Date:	June 2

Dear Ms. Sampson,

We at Meadworth Paper and Packaging are looking forward to your visit to our company headquarters from July 2 to July 4. We are very pleased that your company has agreed to discuss the terms of a possible merger between our two businesses.

In addition to providing you with a tour of our factory and offices, we have an exciting schedule planned for you, which will include a lunch with our CEO, a trip to Westflower Golf Club, and an excursion at the Harbor Yacht Club. We have also scheduled an evening at our local opera house for some live entertainment on your last night. We hope you will enjoy your trip, and if you need anything else, please let me know.

Sincerely

Roderick Kelly
Meadworth Paper and Packaging

From: Varek

To: Kelly

The weather forecast predicts rain during our trip to the golf club with Ms. Sampson next week. I think it would be best if you switched the golf club visit with the opera house event. This will change the opera house event we'll attend, but there's no need to buy new tickets. I'm allowed to bring a few guests free of charge.

196. What is suggested about the Hartford Opera House?

(A) It is merging with another company.

(B) It gives away free seasonal passes.

(C) It is located next to a golf club.

(D) It schedules a variety of events.

197. What is Ms. Sampson scheduled to do during her visit?

(A) Discuss a new deal

(B) Review a contract

(C) Consult a lawyer

(D) Present a product

198. What opera house event was Ms. Sampson originally scheduled to attend?

(A) A classical music performance

(B) A live comedy performance

(C) A popular musical

(D) A stage play about Egypt

199. What does Mr. Kelly need to reschedule?

(A) A boat trip

(B) A game of golf

(C) A lunch meeting

(D) A factory tour

200. Why most likely does Ms. Varek not need to purchase tickets?

(A) The event they will attend is free for everyone.

(B) Ms. Sampson has not approved the schedule yet.

(C) Ms. Varek already has a seasonal pass for the opera house.

(D) Mr. Kelly must wait for some tickets to be refunded.

Stop! This is the end of the test. If you finish before time is called, you may go back to Parts 5, 6, and 7 and check your work.

LISTENING TEST 🎧21

In the Listening test, you will be asked to demonstrate how well you understand spoken English. The entire Listening test will last approximately 45 minutes. There are four parts, and directions are given for each part. You must mark your answers on the separate answer sheet. Do not write your answers in your test book.

PART 1

Directions: For each question in this part, you will hear four statements about a picture in your test book. When you hear the statements, you must select the one statement that best describes what you see in the picture. Then find the number of the question on your answer sheet and mark your answer. The statements will not be printed in your test book and will be spoken only one time.

Example

Sample Answer

Ⓐ Ⓑ ● Ⓓ

Statement (C), "A woman is admiring some artwork.," is the best description of the picture, so you should select answer (C) and mark it on your answer sheet.

1.

2.

GO ON TO THE NEXT PAGE

3.

4.

5.

6.

GO ON TO THE NEXT PAGE

PART 2 🎧(22)

Directions: You will hear a question or statement and three responses spoken in English. They will not be printed in your test book and will be spoken only one time. Select the best response to the question or statement and mark the letter (A), (B), or (C) on your answer sheet.

7. Mark your answer on your answer sheet.

8. Mark your answer on your answer sheet.

9. Mark your answer on your answer sheet.

10. Mark your answer on your answer sheet.

11. Mark your answer on your answer sheet.

12. Mark your answer on your answer sheet.

13. Mark your answer on your answer sheet.

14. Mark your answer on your answer sheet.

15. Mark your answer on your answer sheet.

16. Mark your answer on your answer sheet.

17. Mark your answer on your answer sheet.

18. Mark your answer on your answer sheet.

19. Mark your answer on your answer sheet.

20. Mark your answer on your answer sheet.

21. Mark your answer on your answer sheet.

22. Mark your answer on your answer sheet.

23. Mark your answer on your answer sheet.

24. Mark your answer on your answer sheet.

25. Mark your answer on your answer sheet.

26. Mark your answer on your answer sheet.

27. Mark your answer on your answer sheet.

28. Mark your answer on your answer sheet.

29. Mark your answer on your answer sheet.

30. Mark your answer on your answer sheet.

31. Mark your answer on your answer sheet.

PART 3 (23)

Directions: You will hear some conversations between two or more people. You will be asked to answer three questions about what the speakers say in each conversation. Select the best response to each question and mark the letter (A), (B), (C), or (D) on your answer sheet. The conversations will not be printed in your test book and will be spoken only one time.

32. Why did the man choose to shop at the store?

(A) The store is next to his home.
(B) He received an e-mail notification.
(C) His friend recommended the store.
(D) The store's selection is very large.

33. What does the woman ask for?

(A) A credit card number
(B) A purchase receipt
(C) A membership card
(D) A discount voucher

34. Why does the man say he will return at a later time?

(A) He left his wallet at the office.
(B) He wants to bring his wife.
(C) He needs to print something.
(D) He has an urgent meeting.

35. Where is this conversation most likely taking place?

(A) At a fabric store
(B) At a supermarket
(C) At a restaurant
(D) At a dry cleaner

36. What is the woman doing on Wednesday?

(A) Traveling out of town
(B) Attending a company event
(C) Making a presentation
(D) Going to a conference

37. What does the man offer to do?

(A) Refund a service
(B) Replace an item
(C) Rush an order
(D) Rent out a garment

ACTUAL TEST

06

38. Why will the man visit the woman's office?

(A) To deliver an invoice
(B) To apply for a job
(C) To install some equipment
(D) To pick up a vehicle

39. What does the woman say she will do?

(A) Wait for a worker to arrive
(B) Give a key to an employee
(C) Pay for a service online
(D) Use a discount coupon

40. What does the woman ask the man to put in her mailbox?

(A) Some client paperwork
(B) A tax receipt
(C) A user's manual
(D) Some promotional vouchers

41. What is the woman shopping for?

(A) Books
(B) Printer ink
(C) Paper
(D) Folders

42. What does Tim say about some items?

(A) They are still in storage.
(B) They are out of stock.
(C) They are available at another store.
(D) They are currently on sale.

43. What additional service does Tim mention?

(A) Free shipping
(B) In-store printing
(C) Discounted membership
(D) Free book binding

44. What are the speakers organizing?

(A) A company trip
(B) A holiday event
(C) An awards dinner
(D) A fundraiser

45. What problem does the woman mention?

(A) A hotel is in need of repair.
(B) A reservation was lost.
(C) Some invitations were misplaced.
(D) Some customers complained.

46. What most likely will the man do next?

(A) Cancel an event
(B) Visit a hotel
(C) Find a contact number
(D) Make a reservation

47. Where most likely do the speakers work?

(A) A dance academy
(B) An art school
(C) A paint supply shop
(D) A restaurant

48. What does the woman imply when she says, "Will that be a problem"?

(A) She disagrees with the man's statement.
(B) She does not want to edit a schedule.
(C) She wants to know what she has overlooked.
(D) She is eager to take the man's class.

49. What does the woman offer to do?

(A) Change a classroom
(B) Hire a cleaner
(C) Recruit some students
(D) Pay for art supplies

50. What are the speakers discussing?

(A) Preparing for a presentation
(B) Building a new website
(C) Submitting a budget review
(D) Hiring a new advertiser

51. Why was the man unable to complete a task?

(A) A meeting lasted all day.
(B) A website was not working.
(C) Some files went missing.
(D) Some fees were not paid.

52. What does the woman say she will do on Friday?

(A) Meet with a client
(B) Give a presentation
(C) Design a brochure
(D) Print a document

53. What is Mr. Holland planning to do?

(A) Purchase a new car
(B) Make an insurance claim
(C) Apply for a license
(D) Rent a vehicle

54. According to the conversation, what did Kevin do yesterday?

(A) He had a car towed.
(B) He ordered some new parts.
(C) He prepared a price quote.
(D) He witnessed a car accident.

55. What does Kevin ask the woman to do?

(A) Process a payment
(B) Call an insurance company
(C) Fill out a form
(D) Print a document

56. Why is the man calling?

(A) He received the wrong order.
(B) He wants to return an item.
(C) He would like to visit the store.
(D) He was charged too much for an item.

57. What does the woman explain?

(A) A technical malfunction
(B) A discount policy
(C) A delivery failure
(D) A change in supplier

58. What does the woman ask the man to do?

(A) Send an order back
(B) Locate an invoice
(C) Renew a membership
(D) Describe an item

59. Where most likely is the woman?

(A) At a parking entrance
(B) On a bus
(C) In an office
(D) In a stairwell

60. What does the woman ask the man to do?

(A) Call the parking attendant
(B) Deliver a parking pass
(C) Cancel a meeting
(D) Recommend a venue

61. Why does the man say, "I'm just heading into a meeting"?

(A) To acknowledge a problem
(B) To ask for permission
(C) To suggest an option
(D) To decline a request

```
=========== Front ===========
```

	seat 25C	seat 25D	
Aisle	seat 26C	seat 26D	Window

Stage	Project Type
1	In-ground swimming pool installation
2	Backyard landscaping and gardens
3	Veranda reconstruction (front and back)
4	Final roof repairs

62. What is the purpose of the conversation?

(A) To determine a cost
(B) To request a service
(C) To correct a mistake
(D) To explain a process

63. Look at the graphic. Which seat was the woman originally assigned to?

(A) 25C
(B) 25D
(C) 26C
(D) 26D

64. What will the woman most likely do next?

(A) File a complaint with the airline
(B) Report a change to the flight staff
(C) Get off the plane
(D) Request a vegetarian meal

65. What most likely is the man's profession?

(A) Interior decorator
(B) Delivery man
(C) Real estate agent
(D) Contractor

66. Look at the graphic. What stage of the improvements will begin in a couple days?

(A) Stage 1
(B) Stage 2
(C) Stage 3
(D) Stage 4

67. What does the woman ask the man to keep?

(A) Receipts of all costs
(B) A list of available homes
(C) A record of time worked
(D) Photos of his progress

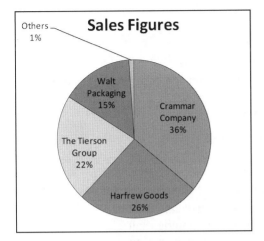

Sales Figures

Others 1%

Walt Packaging 15%

Crammar Company 36%

The Tierson Group 22%

Harfrew Goods 26%

68. What are the speakers mainly discussing?

(A) A company merger
(B) A budget report
(C) Department productivity
(D) Hiring a financial analyst

69. Look at the graphic. Where do the speakers work?

(A) Walt Packaging
(B) Harfrew Goods
(C) The Tierson Group
(D) Crammar Company

70. Why does the woman say she has doubts?

(A) The man did not understand some figures.
(B) A company was excluded from a report.
(C) Her company is located in another state.
(D) A company has not made many sales.

Directions: You will hear some talks given by a single speaker. You will be asked to answer three questions about what the speaker says in each talk. Select the best response to each question and mark the letter (A), (B), (C), or (D) on your answer sheet. The talks will not be printed in your test book and will be spoken only one time.

71. What service is being advertised?

(A) Dry cleaning
(B) Furniture delivery
(C) A clothing recycling program
(D) A cooking course

72. How can listeners receive a discount?

(A) By becoming a member
(B) By ordering two items
(C) By registering online
(D) By entering a contest

73. What does the speaker say is available over the phone?

(A) A customer survey
(B) A list of stores
(C) The best discount
(D) An appointment

74. Where is the announcement being made?

(A) At a city hall
(B) At a shopping mall
(C) At a transit station
(D) At a concert venue

75. What does the speaker ask listeners to do?

(A) Proceed to a boarding gate
(B) Keep an original receipt
(C) Use a bank machine
(D) Purchase another ticket

76. According to the speaker, what can customers get at Coffee Madness?

(A) A train ticket
(B) A complimentary drink
(C) A loaned computer
(D) An updated bus schedule

77. What is the purpose of the message?

(A) To locate some materials
(B) To request a meeting
(C) To hire a designer
(D) To ask about a product

78. What does the speaker imply when she says, "The boss is getting impatient"?

(A) Her boss needs to reschedule a project.
(B) She needs to change some paint colors.
(C) The designers will start working soon.
(D) Some selections must be confirmed quickly.

79. What most likely will the speaker do next?

(A) Decide on design samples
(B) Contact a manager
(C) Visit a manufacturing site
(D) Go to a paint supply store

80. Where do the listeners work?

(A) At a bank
(B) At a fashion house
(C) At a university
(D) At a real estate agency

81. What will the listeners be doing tomorrow?

(A) Conducting surveys
(B) Interviewing interns
(C) Distributing pamphlets
(D) Cleaning up an office

82. What has the speaker done for the listeners?

(A) Prepared uniforms
(B) Bought some chairs
(C) Shortened a schedule
(D) Paid for a trip

83. What is the speaker announcing?

(A) Hiring a new employee
(B) A company fundraiser
(C) An upcoming mentorship program
(D) The winning of an award

84. What did the company sponsor in June?

(A) A sports club
(B) A fundraising event
(C) A financial convention
(D) A university scholarship

85. What does the speaker say about Mona Ruiz's work?

(A) It improved the company image.
(B) It is outlined on the company's website.
(C) It increased the company's charity work.
(D) It doubled the number of clients.

86. What is the main topic of the meeting?

(A) Restructuring plans
(B) A new delivery method
(C) A product prototype
(D) Customer feedback

87. What feature of the product does the speaker mention?

(A) Removable grills
(B) Portability
(C) Color options
(D) Energy efficiency

88. What does the speaker imply when he says, "Our website does not display images of each color"?

(A) A website should be edited.
(B) Images have been removed from a website.
(C) A photographer needs to be hired.
(D) Customers mostly chose one color.

GO ON TO THE NEXT PAGE

89. What is the talk mainly about?

(A) Electing a new town mayor
(B) Planning a city anniversary
(C) Convincing state officials
(D) Forming a charity group

90. What problem does the speaker mention?

(A) Lack of public support
(B) A delay in the release of funds
(C) Damaged facilities
(D) Lost signatures

91. What are listeners asked to do?

(A) E-mail state officials
(B) Volunteer at an event
(C) Sample some food
(D) Contact local media

92. What type of business does the speaker work for?

(A) A transit company
(B) A medical facility
(C) An advertising firm
(D) A pharmacy

93. What does the speaker imply when he says, "Not all seats are full right now"?

(A) Some participants have not arrived.
(B) The chairs can be rearranged.
(C) The venue will be changed.
(D) The event is not successful.

94. What does the speaker ask the listeners to do?

(A) Write down their medical history
(B) Go to their assigned departments
(C) Fill out contact information
(D) Review some materials

Quantity	Item Description
10	Ballpoint Pens (10 per package)
20	Black toner cartridge
35	Clear plastic A4 file
60	Glossy copy paper (1000 sheets per box)

95. Look at the graphic. Which quantity on the order form will probably be changed?

(A) 10
(B) 20
(C) 35
(D) 60

96. What will the speaker do before processing the order?

(A) Wait for a confirmation
(B) Give a phone number
(C) Inspect a package
(D) Review a product manual

97. What does the speaker say about Tina?

(A) She will not be in the office.
(B) She will deliver some items herself.
(C) She will take care of shipping problems.
(D) She will refund some purchases.

98. Where does the talk take place?

(A) At a museum
(B) At a restaurant
(C) At a shopping mall
(D) At an office

99. Look at the graphic. Which suggestion will the company begin to work on?

(A) Employee break rooms
(B) Food court discounts
(C) Better parking spaces
(D) Free transit passes

100. What will employees receive for completing comment cards?

(A) A gift card for the mall
(B) Entrance into a contest
(C) A voucher for a free drink
(D) A new work uniform

This is the end of the Listening test. Turn to Part 5 in your test book.

READING TEST

In the Reading Test, you will read a variety of texts and answer several different types of reading comprehension questions. The entire Reading test will last 75 minutes. There are three parts, and directions are given for each part. You are encouraged to answer as many questions as possible within the time allowed.

You must mark your answers on the separate answer sheet. Do not write your answers in your test book.

PART 5

Directions: A word or phrase is missing in each of the sentences below. Four answer choices are given below each sentence. Select the best answer to complete the sentence. Then mark the letter (A), (B), (C), or (D) on your answer sheet.

101. The shelves in the east warehouse must be ------- stocked for the holiday season.

(A) full
(B) fully
(C) fuller
(D) fullest

102. ------- to the swimming pool is reserved for guests staying in one of our deluxe suites.

(A) Access
(B) Accessed
(C) Accessing
(D) Accessible

103. Mr. Takashi admits that ------- is expected to take on more managerial duties.

(A) he
(B) his
(C) him
(D) himself

104. At the end of the month, Davisville Incorporated is ------- its Internet provider.

(A) changing
(B) attending
(C) holding
(D) turning

105. Better City Travel offers bicycle tours ------- Skiff Lake at very reasonable rates.

(A) between
(B) along
(C) below
(D) apart

106. Of all snow tires, Marten's new MR-200 is, without a doubt, the most durable -------.

(A) that
(B) any
(C) one
(D) either

107. As the amount of orders increased significantly, Lawford's Coffee Shop was able to ------- new deals with its suppliers.

(A) negotiating
(B) negotiates
(C) negotiated
(D) negotiate

108. Pandora Hair Design offers employees ------- opportunities to advance their careers.

(A) plenty
(B) each
(C) very
(D) many

109. Highway 56 between Greenville and Trenton has been blocked off ------- fallen power poles.

(A) so that
(B) as a result
(C) in order to
(D) because of

110. It is impossible to rent an apartment in the Dorchester Building without a ------- from a current tenant.

(A) referring
(B) referred
(C) referral
(D) refer

111. A green sticker will be placed on the windshield ------- after the inspection of the vehicle is complete.

(A) when
(B) only
(C) still
(D) most

112. Since two managers have opted for early retirement, it is ------- to find replacements by July 30.

(A) necessitating
(B) necessary
(C) necessarily
(D) necessities

113. The cargo elevator in the south end of the building will not be in operation ------- further notice.

(A) until
(B) onto
(C) since
(D) all

114. The weight indicated on the outside of this package is ------- accurate.

(A) fairness
(B) fairest
(C) fairly
(D) fair

115. David sent a link to a website that has a ------- of information on engine repair.

(A) wealth
(B) height
(C) labor
(D) fame

116. To find the easiest route to Simmons, Darthmouth, and nearby towns, be sure to look at an ------- map.

(A) update
(B) updated
(C) updates
(D) updating

117. The hiring committee will start reviewing résumés ------- the application deadline has passed.

(A) how
(B) nor
(C) now that
(D) whether

118. On her television show, Gloria Van Cingel, the well-known art critic, ------- paintings from a variety of periods.

(A) analysis
(B) analyzer
(C) analyzes
(D) analyzing

119. The installation of several self-checkout kiosks in the Redford Supermarket is expected to create changes ------- the number of employees.

(A) in
(B) again
(C) positions
(D) ultimately

120. Compared to everyone else, Donald prepared himself for the real estate license exam in a ------- short period of time.

(A) surprised
(B) surprise
(C) surprisingly
(D) surprising

121. The production supervisor of Gleason Shoes is ------- of all the factory's operations.

(A) aware
(B) current
(C) serious
(D) alert

122. The tourism ------- of Cape Breton Island has dramatically improved ever since the harbor was reopened last year.

(A) economical
(B) economic
(C) economize
(D) economy

123. Someone from Renforth Building Supplies asked us to ------- the type of lumber needed for the project.

(A) personify
(B) magnify
(C) specify
(D) testify

124. Fitzgerald Air offers flights to over 200 destinations ------- northern Canada.

(A) toward
(B) throughout
(C) regarding
(D) aboard

125. The beginners' guitar class at the Lesterville Academy fills up quickly so we recommend filling out an online ------- form.

(A) enrollment
(B) inventory
(C) complaint
(D) solicitation

126. On Friday, Lancaster Incorporated's newly ------- vice president will address his staff for the first time.

(A) appoint
(B) appoints
(C) appointed
(D) appointing

127. The head of public relations must be continually in contact with the media, so Randolph Industries ------- someone with exceptional communication skills.

(A) seeking
(B) is seeking
(C) are sought
(D) have been sought

128. Ms. Laporte's approach to organizing a fundraising event is ------- different from Ms. Halloway's.

(A) haltingly
(B) intimately
(C) permissibly
(D) markedly

129. Recently, Kingston has experienced a huge increase in the number of residents, ------- are international students.

(A) inasmuch as
(B) the reason being
(C) because of them
(D) most of whom

130. To help the staff of the Carrington Inn make your stay more -------, please fill out a guest feedback form and leave it at the front desk.

(A) knowledgeable
(B) considerable
(C) enjoyable
(D) available

PART 6

Directions: Read the texts that follow. A word, phrase, or sentence is missing in parts of each text. Four answer choices for each question are given below the text. Select the best answer to complete the text. Then mark the letter (A), (B), (C), or (D) on your answer sheet.

Questions 131-134 refer to the following e-mail.

To: sandrabae@gladstoneresearch.com.au

From: markjohnson@sydneyunienergy.au

Date: 15 May

Subject: Thank you!

Dear Dr. Bae,

Thank you very much for _____ our main research center last Friday. Your expert advice, as always,
131.

_____ . Our entire engineering team benefited greatly from your presentation on the exciting new
132.

advances in energy generation and consumption systems for industrial facilities. This fall, our

department plans to hire five more engineering researchers. Would _____ mind leading a training
133.

session on the topic you spoke of last week? _____ . We will look forward to your prompt response
134.

so that details can be discussed.

Sincerely,

Mark Johnson

---

131. (A) calling
 (B) opening
 (C) visiting
 (D) staffing

132. (A) appreciates
 (B) will be appreciated
 (C) is appreciating
 (D) was appreciated

133. (A) his
 (B) yours
 (C) you
 (D) he

134. (A) All engineers must adhere to our center's strict regulations.
 (B) A large number of candidates have impressive résumés.
 (C) If you can, it would undoubtedly prove beneficial to the new staff.
 (D) With your feedback, we will be able to build it quickly.

Questions 135-138 refer to the following article.

GEARY (April 5) — This morning, the National Transportation Authority announced that a $41 million grant has been awarded to Weston Valley Air Travel Network. Thanks to this ____135.__ , the dream of having two airports in Weston Valley will soon be realized. Many residents in the region welcome news of this expansion to the current air service. ____136.__ . Business owners throughout the Weston Valley are truly delighted. Jennifer Rossignol, a local business owner, expressed her delight with the grant earlier today. "This is fantastic news for someone like myself ____137.__ has to travel to Toronto frequently on business," says Rossignol. "We have had no choice ____138.__ years but to endure a four-hour bus ride into the city, but soon, I will be able to board a plane and be there in under an hour."

135. (A) funding
(B) policy
(C) design
(D) strategy

136. (A) Weston Valley Air Travel Network confirmed that the project must be delayed.
(B) Passengers will have access to more parking spaces at one of the airports.
(C) This development is expected to create over 500 jobs at both airports.
(D) Air fares for most regional flights, however, will most likely be raised.

137. (A) likewise
(B) another
(C) then
(D) who

138. (A) for
(B) with
(C) about
(D) on

To: Arnold Mallory [amallory@channel6news.net]

From: Melinda Calhoun [mcalhoun@channel6news.net]

Re: Fantastic reviews

Date: March 21

Dear Arnold,

The managerial division here at Channel 6 News was positively excited to read sensational reviews of our program in both the *Moncton Gazette* and *Uptown Entertainment*. All of us agree that your work here has been nothing but ------- **139.** For this reason, Channel 6 News is truly delighted ------- **140.** you a yearly bonus that will be added to your next monthly paycheck on March 30. ------- **141.** , your current salary will be raised by 12% effective April 1. Since you took over as head news anchor last November, our number of regular viewers has tripled. ------- **142.** We could not have achieved any of this without your outstanding performance. On behalf of everyone at Channel 6 News, thank you for your hard work and dedication.

Melinda

139. (A) withdrawn
(B) matched
(C) affordable
(D) exceptional

140. (A) to award
(B) an award
(C) it awarded
(D) that awards

141. (A) For example
(B) In addition
(C) Nevertheless
(D) On the other hand

142. (A) Channel 6 News has also received fabulous reviews in national newspapers.
(B) An assistant news anchor will be hired sometime next month.
(C) Our team will meet next week to discuss changes to your show.
(D) You are one of two employees who are entitled to an annual bonus.

Electronics Trade Show

(25 August) The annual Global Electronics Trade Show came to Tokyo on Saturday, 23 August for the fifth consecutive year. ___143.___. As was the case last year, China was the most ___144.___ represented nation. ___145.___, organizers reported that the number of South American companies was significantly higher than previous years. Another noticeable change at this year's ___146.___ was the fact that the majority of companies showcased kitchen appliances rather than the usual entertainment electronics.

---

143. (A) Volunteers at the event were not required to pay the registration fee.
    (B) Product demonstrations will be held in three different auditoriums.
    (C) The event featured over 500 companies from every corner of the world.
    (D) Recruiters collected résumés from university students in attendance.

144. (A) heavy
    (B) heavily
    (C) heavier
    (D) heaviness

145. (A) Moreover
    (B) Rather
    (C) Instead
    (D) Thus

146. (A) class
    (B) demonstration
    (C) event
    (D) ceremony

PART 7

Directions: In this part you will read a selection of texts, such as magazine and newspaper articles, e-mails, and instant messages. Each text or set of texts is followed by several questions. Select the best answer for each question and mark the letter (A), (B), (C), or (D) on your answer sheet.

Questions 147-148 refer to the following notice.

To our dear customers,

We are happy to announce that we will be hosting a weekly talent night starting in October. The event will be held every Wednesday from 6:00 P.M. until 8:00 P.M. and the stage will be set up on the first floor of our café.

Participants may sing, play instruments, or read poetry. Make sure to arrive early to sign up for a twenty-minute slot. All participants will be allowed free coffee or tea for the duration of the event.

For more information, please visit our website at www.cafémaria.com or call us at 777-4367.

147. Where would the notice most likely appear?

(A) In a subway station
(B) In a music book
(C) At a coffee house
(D) At a doctor's office

148. According to the notice, what will participants receive?

(A) Discount coupons
(B) A small payment
(C) A participation certificate
(D) Free beverages

Eastview Convention Center
55 Lakeview Road
Seattle, Washington

Date: April 12 **Invoice number:** 9800032	**Bill To:** Trisha Baxter Pure Motorcycles 90 Yamer Street Orlando, Florida

Invoice for the Eastview Convention Center's Annual Automotive Show from June 25 – June 27.

Item:	**Rate:**	**Total:**
Convention Booth (30 square feet)	$100.00/day	$300.00
Additional Services:		
3 display tables	$10.00/unit	$30.00
Storage	$30.00/unit	$120.00
Computer rental	$20.00/unit	$20.00
55-inch television rental	$30.00/unit	$30.00
Show passes	$20.00/person	$200.00
	Subtotal:	$700.00
	Tax:	$45.50
	Total:	$745.50*

*Please visit your online account to arrange payment by April 20.

149. What is NOT included in the cost of the event?
     (A) Passes to the show
     (B) Display tables
     (C) Television rental
     (D) Setup and cleanup

150. What is Ms. Baxter asked to do?
     (A) Sign up for a membership
     (B) Mail a check to the venue
     (C) Settle an invoice
     (D) Confirm the number of participants

Questions 151-152 refer to the following text message chain.

Jennifer Porter [11:23 A.M.]
Hi, Raphael. Were you able to stop by the Rickter Avenue property this weekend?

Raphael Morez [11:25 A.M.]
Yes, I went on Saturday. Since most of our photographers will be working at events every day, are you sure we need such a big place?

Jennifer Porter [11:27 A.M.]
The rooms are large, but as we expand, we'll need the space.

Raphael Morez [11:28 A.M.]
That might not happen for a few years, though.

Jennifer Porter [11:30 A.M.]
Yes, but we should be thinking about our long-term goals for the company. The Rickter Avenue property will give us a chance to finally develop an on-site studio.

Raphael Morez [11:32 A.M.]
You're right. We'll definitely need the extra space once we start offering portrait services.

151. At what kind of business do the people most likely work?
(A) A photography company
(B) A fashion design house
(C) An event planning business
(D) An art gallery

152. At 11:32 A.M., what does Mr. Morez most likely mean when he writes, "You're right"?
(A) A location is too far from the city.
(B) The building will help the company meet its goals.
(C) Much interior design work is needed in the building.
(D) The property has some significant flaws.

To: Tristan Starr
From: Emilia Simpson
Date: June 2
Re: Walton Shopping Center contract

Hi Tristan,

I just got an e-mail from Marcus Pine about the budget proposal you sent him yesterday. Apparently, several of the figures are incorrect. It seems you included the initial figures we presented to him during our first advertising pitch on May 6 and not the figures we later agreed on during negotiations on May 20.

Mr. Pine was hoping to present the advertising plan to his superiors on June 5. He mentioned that there are several other agencies that have sent him proposals, and he will select one of them instead if we cannot get this paperwork done by June 3. Since I'm just about to fly to our Chicago office, I'm hoping you can handle this right away. Please send Mr. Pine the revised proposal and e-mail me when you get his response.

Sincerely,

Emilia

153. Why was the e-mail written?

(A) To request a vacation
(B) To introduce an applicant
(C) To announce a policy change
(D) To point out some mistakes

154. When was the proposal modified?

(A) On May 6
(B) On May 20
(C) On June 3
(D) On June 5

155. What would Ms. Simpson like Mr. Starr to do?

(A) Make a phone call
(B) Issue a refund
(C) Send a document
(D) Speak with a manager

Questions 156-157 refer to the following article.

Restaurant sales are down in Plymouth County. According to a report in the *Plymouth Journal*, sales have dropped by more than 15 percent this winter. The drop has shocked many restaurant owners, especially since the winter holidays usually increase restaurant business. Bob Fulton, owner of Little Italy Eatery, attributed the drop to an increase in wholesale prices as one factor of the drop. "With the prices of everything going up, we've had to increase our prices as well," Mr. Fulton said in an interview. "Most customers just don't want to pay that much for a meal." To encourage more business, many local restaurants have joined forces to develop membership programs. These programs provide customers with discounts at numerous restaurants in the county.

156. According to the article, why have restaurant sales dropped?

(A) The weather has become unpleasant.

(B) The costs have risen too high.

(C) Newer restaurants have been built.

(D) Many local jobs have been lost.

157. How are restaurant owners responding to the trend?

(A) By improving the quality of the food

(B) By decreasing the number of workers

(C) By working with other restaurants

(D) By launching television advertisements.

Questions 158-161 refer to the following online chat discussion.

Rita Frasier [2:23 P.M.]
Ms. Norton, do you have a minute? Thomas and I are unclear about our assignments. Last year, I was in charge of developing the seasonal training program, but Thomas was assigned the exact same job this year.

Patrina Norton [2:25 P.M.]
Yes, everyone needs a chance to work on developing their own programs for human resources.

Rita Frasier [2:26 P.M.]
So, we will no longer use the materials I developed last year?

Patrina Norton [2:28 P.M.]
That's right. Thomas is expected to develop new materials that will be used this year.

Thomas Woods [2:30 P.M.]
But what if I would like to use some of Rita's ideas?

Patrina Norton [2:33 P.M.]
Program development is part of the job.

Thomas Woods [2:35 P.M.]
Yes, but Rita's program was excellent last year. I would hate all her hard work to go to waste.

Patrina Norton [2:39 P.M.]
If Rita is OK with it, I think you could use some of her materials so long as you update them where appropriate. Let me review last year's materials first and get back to you.

Rita Frasier [2:41 P.M.]
What if Thomas and I worked together on the project?

Patrina Norton [2:44 P.M.]
I don't think that will be necessary.

Rita Frasier [2:45 P.M.]
OK, I understand.

Thomas Woods [2:46 P.M.]
Let us know when you've decided. Thanks.

158. Who most likely is Ms. Norton?

(A) A financial planner
(B) A human resources manager
(C) A company intern
(D) An advertising consultant

159. What is suggested about Ms. Frasier?

(A) She developed a successful training program last year.
(B) She usually works with Mr. Woods on projects.
(C) She is pleased with this year's assignment.
(D) She will take over Ms. Norton's job next year.

160. At 2:33 P.M., what does Ms. Norton most likely mean when she writes, "Program development is part of the job"?

(A) Her job duties include program development.
(B) She believes Ms. Frasier is better suited for the job.
(C) She disagrees with Mr. Woods's suggestion.
(D) Her contract with the company needs revising.

161. What will most likely happen next?

(A) Ms. Frasier will contact a supervisor.
(B) Mr. Woods will begin working on a project.
(C) Mr. Woods and Ms. Frasier will have a meeting.
(D) Ms. Norton will look at some old materials.

GO ON TO THE NEXT PAGE →

Questions 162-165 refer to the following e-mail.

To: Tamika Keynes
From: Marcel Ventrue
Re: Information
Date: April 22

I'm writing in regard to the service quote you requested on our website. I'm delighted you're interested in Lawn and Garden Care's extensive range of services. --[1]--. I can assure you that we are the top landscaping company in the city. We service many local businesses, such as hotels and country clubs. --[2]--. We also maintain the extensive lawns at Memorial Stadium downtown.

I have attached the service quote you requested. --[3]--. The quote is based on weekly lawn maintenance services for The Renolds Gallery. In the event that you require additional services, such as garden planting or tree removal, you would be charged extra. --[4]--. Have a look at the quote and I will be in touch early next week to answer any questions you might have.

Sincerely,

Marcel Ventrue

---

162. What is the purpose of the e-mail?

(A) To change a schedule
(B) To respond to a request
(C) To send a blueprint
(D) To submit an application

163. For what kind of business does Ms. Keynes most likely work?

(A) An art gallery
(B) A stadium
(C) A country club
(D) A hotel

164. What is mentioned in the e-mail?

(A) Ms. Keynes is a new employee at Lawn and Garden Care.
(B) Lawn and Garden Care is a new business.
(C) Ms. Keynes will hear from Mr. Ventrue next week.
(D) Mr. Ventrue visited Ms. Keynes' business.

165. In which of the positions marked [1], [2], [3], and [4] does the following sentence best belong?

"However, all additional services will be discounted should you sign a two-year contract with us."

(A) [1]
(B) [2]
(C) [3]
(D) [4]

Questions 166-168 refer to the following article.

Parker Wallace to Join Adventure Software
By Amy Swanson, *The Daily Chat*

NEW YORK (24 February) — Parker Wallace has announced he will join the new start-up Adventure Software. Wallace, who has been developing software applications for five years now, is best known as the creator of Marble FM, a music sharing application. Marble FM accumulated over three million downloads in just two years, leading Wallace to become one of the most sought-after developers in the industry.

Despite turning down jobs at Liquid Apps and T&B Developers, Wallace has made the surprising move and accepted an offer to join a company that is less than two years old. "When I met Alan Pike of Adventure Software, I knew he and I shared the same goals," Wallace recently said at the launch of his latest app. "He and I are both passionate about music, and he had some great ideas for future projects. I am extremely confident that we'll be putting out hot new products in the next year."

Wallace's newest app, Marble Video, has already generated over 500,000 downloads in less than a month. The tech world will be expecting big things from the partnership between Wallace and Pike, starting with the rerelease of an upgraded version of Pike's Smart Symphony on March 30.

166. Who most likely is Mr. Pike?

(A) A film director
(B) A symphony composer
(C) A music video producer
(D) A software company owner

167. What most likely is true about Ms. Swanson?

(A) She was formerly employed at Liquid Apps.
(B) She attended the launch of Marble Video.
(C) She purchased a copy of Marble FM.
(D) She met with Mr. Pike at an event.

168. What is indicated about Smart Symphony?

(A) It is an already existing app.
(B) It was originally developed by T&B Developers.
(C) It will be limited to 500,000 copies.
(D) It will feature elements of Marble FM.

Questions 169-171 refer to the following brochure.

Energy Savers

Are you paying high utility bills during the summer or winter months? With Energy Savers, you can find the energy solutions that will save you money. Contact us for your free four-step consultation.

1. Determine your energy needs

Our qualified energy consultants will visit your home to determine what your energy needs are. You will be asked to complete a detailed survey regarding the number of hours you spend at home, your desired temperatures during each season, and your cooking and cleaning habits.

2. Home inspection

Once our consultants determine your needs, they will inspect the windows, walls, and doors of your home to ensure proper insulation. They will also test your heating, cooling, and lighting systems for weaknesses. Unlike other companies, Energy Savers will prepare a detailed report of flaws and make suggestions for improvements.

3. Choose your upgrades

Our consultants will discuss the recommended upgrades for your home while keeping your budget in mind. We can help you choose and install everything from double-paned glass for your windows to solar panels on your roof.

4. Installations

Our team will work around your schedule to install your upgrades. However, most installations take several days to complete. You will see instant savings on your utility bills and the best part is those savings never end. You will continue to save money for years to come. Should you have problems with your upgrades within the first year, Energy Savers will fix them free of charge.

169. What is the purpose of the brochure?
(A) To announce a new type of energy
(B) To compare two energy companies
(C) To advertise a company's services
(D) To discuss the benefits of insulation

170. What is NOT examined during the home consultation?
(A) The number of hours the home is occupied
(B) The home owner's preferred temperatures
(C) The efficiency of heating systems
(D) The current cost of monthly utilities

171. What does the brochure suggest is one disadvantage of the upgrades?
(A) The upgrades are costly to purchase.
(B) It takes time to install all the features.
(C) Home owners must be present during the installations.
(D) Monthly bills will not decrease for a year.

Questions 172-175 refer to the following article.

Newmont Technology Convention to Launch World Tour

March 5 — The Newmont Technology Convention (NTC) is scheduled to make the first stop on its world tour next month. The convention is one of the world's largest technology exhibitions and features everything from medical technology to aerospace engineering demonstrations. The NTC was founded in Sydney, Australia by Newmont Industries and its CEO, Barret Michaels. --[1]--. Every year, over 30,000 people visit the Sydney convention to see some of the most innovative technologies that have not yet reached the market.

The NTC commonly hosts scientists from all over the world, but this is the first year it will become an international traveling exhibition. --[2]--. Mr. Michaels stated in an interview, "We're very excited about this expansion. When we started the convention 10 years ago, we had no idea it would grow to be the biggest technology event in the world. -- [3]--. We're extremely happy to kick off our six-country tour in London, England next month. We're already expecting a huge crowd."

The U.S., Brazil, Japan, Germany, and South Africa will also host the NTC during its tour. Tickets to most of the tour dates are already sold out. --[4]--. "Industry professionals in both Canada and France have already reached out to us with proposals," Mr. Michaels said. "We're optimistic that other countries will make similar proposals."

---

172. What is true about Newmont Industries?

(A) It helped establish the Newmont Technology Convention.
(B) It has offices in England, Brazil, and Japan.
(C) It is the leading developer of medical technology.
(D) It buys and sells aerospace engineering equipment.

173. What is stated about the convention in Sydney?

(A) It took five years to become popular.
(B) It employs over 30,000 workers.
(C) It features technologies that cannot be purchased.
(D) It was the second location for the exhibition.

174. Where will the next Newmont Technology Convention be held?

(A) In France
(B) In England
(C) In Brazil
(D) In Japan

175. In which of the positions marked [1], [2], [3], and [4] does the following sentence best belong?

"If the NTC tour is successful, Mr. Michaels plans to add additional locations to next year's tour."

(A) [1]
(B) [2]
(C) [3]
(D) [4]

Grand Palace Hotel
Koh Samui, Thailand

Bethanie Sparks
44 Brock Road,
Toronto, ON L1T 4W2

Dear Ms. Sparks,

Thank you for choosing the Grand Palace Hotel as your accommodation from October 12 to October 25. According to our records, you purchased your stay as part of our Vacation in Thailand package, which celebrated our hotel's 50th anniversary. We are conducting a short survey regarding this package. We would appreciate your completion of the enclosed survey and its return in the self-addressed envelope. If you respond by January 2, you will receive a 10% discount on your next trip as our thanks. However, should you send it back after that deadline, we would still like to enter you into a draw for a free night's stay in any of our hotels.

Sincerely,

Rita Lao
Grand Palace Hotel

Grand Palace Hotel, Thailand **By participating in this survey, you can assist us in providing the best possible services to all our guests.**	
Name: Bethanie Sparks	**Date:** 28 November
1. May we call you to discuss your answers further? • Yes, phone number_____ • NO	
2. How would you rate the quality of our facilities and services? • Poor • Fair • Average • Good • Excellent	
Please explain your response: I found my room to be luxurious and clean. The food in the restaurant was also excellent. However, when I ordered room service, the food was always delivered quite late.	
3. How would you rate our amenities?	
• Poor • Fair • Average • Good • Excellent	
Please explain your response: I enjoyed the variety of the activities you had to offer. During my stay, I was able to go scuba diving, cave exploring, attend a dance lesson, and even take a tour of the local markets. There were so many exciting things to do!	

176. Why did Ms. Lao write to Ms. Sparks?

(A) To notify of a late payment
(B) To reschedule a hotel stay
(C) To request some customer feedback
(D) To respond to a complaint

177. What is indicated about the Grand Palace Hotel?

(A) Its head office is located in Thailand.
(B) It plans to build a hotel in Toronto.
(C) It wants to expand its recreational activities.
(D) It launched a promotion to celebrate an anniversary.

178. In the letter, the word "conducting" in paragraph 1, line 3, is closest in meaning to

(A) administering
(B) authorizing
(C) behaving
(D) transferring

179. What will Ms. Sparks most likely receive from the Grand Palace Hotel?

(A) A discount coupon
(B) Entry into a contest
(C) Free scuba diving lessons
(D) A free night's stay

180. What does Ms. Sparks mention about the Grand Palace Hotel?

(A) Its staff did not help her solve a problem.
(B) It has a wide range of activities for guests.
(C) Its food was of poor quality.
(D) It has a great location in a large city.

Questions 181-185 refer to the following notice and form.

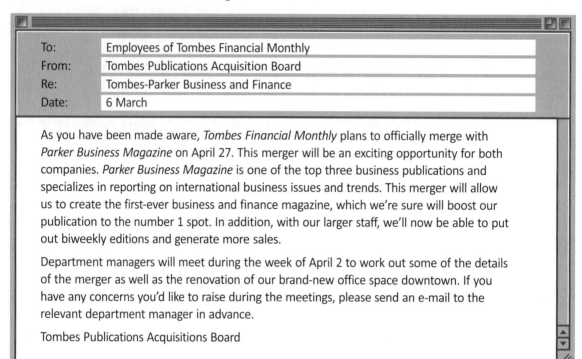

To:	Employees of Tombes Financial Monthly
From:	Tombes Publications Acquisition Board
Re:	Tombes-Parker Business and Finance
Date:	6 March

As you have been made aware, *Tombes Financial Monthly* plans to officially merge with *Parker Business Magazine* on April 27. This merger will be an exciting opportunity for both companies. *Parker Business Magazine* is one of the top three business publications and specializes in reporting on international business issues and trends. This merger will allow us to create the first-ever business and finance magazine, which we're sure will boost our publication to the number 1 spot. In addition, with our larger staff, we'll now be able to put out biweekly editions and generate more sales.

Department managers will meet during the week of April 2 to work out some of the details of the merger as well as the renovation of our brand-new office space downtown. If you have any concerns you'd like to raise during the meetings, please send an e-mail to the relevant department manager in advance.

Tombes Publications Acquisitions Board

Department	Date / Time	Department Managers
Editorial	Monday, April 2 9:00 A.M. – 1:00 P.M.	Joanne Steele, Editorial Director *(Tombes Financial Monthly)* / Tommy Renaldo, Editor-in-Chief *(Parker Business Magazine)*
Design	Tuesday, April 3 10:00 A.M. – 2:00 P.M.	Samuel Westford, Lead Designer *(Tombes Financial Monthly)* / Wendy Skeller, Head of Design *(Parker Business Magazine)*
Administrative	Wednesday, April 4 11:00 A.M. – 4:00 P.M.	Annabelle Cordel, Office Manager *(Tombes Financial Monthly)* / Steven Parinon, Office Manager *(Parker Business Magazine)*
Public Relations	Thursday, April 5 09:30 A.M. – 12:00 P.M.	Laini Peterson, Lead Advertiser *(Tombes Financial Monthly)* / Sandy Baxter, Head of Advertising *(Parker Business Magazine)*

*All meetings will take place at *Tombes Financial Monthly* in the relevant department.
*Steven Parinon will retire prior to the merger. Annabelle Cordel has been selected run the new office following the merger. All department managers are expected to attend the meeting on April 4, which will be in conference room A to accommodate the number of attendees.

181. What is one purpose of the memo?

(A) To remind of changes to a financial plan
(B) To explain why some employees were let go
(C) To announce the retirement of an office manager
(D) To note the benefits of an upcoming merger

182. According to the memo, what is *Parker Business Magazine*'s area of expertise?

(A) Local finance
(B) Company mergers
(C) Government policies
(D) International business

183. What is suggested about the employees of Tombes-Parker Business and Finance?

(A) They have been asked to retire early.
(B) They will be able to apply for management positions.
(C) They will relocate to a new office building.
(D) They all need to attend the meeting on April 6.

184. What is indicated about Mr. Westford?

(A) He plans to take over the position of office manager.
(B) He will discuss some e-mailed questions at his meeting.
(C) He organized the merger between the two magazines.
(D) He chose the location for the new company headquarters.

185. What will happen at a meeting on April 4?

(A) A greater number of participants will be present.
(B) Mr. Parinon will be absent from the discussion.
(C) The CEO of *Parker Business Magazine* will give a presentation.
(D) Employees will be informed of their new job assignments.

Questions **186-190** refer to the following announcement, instructions, and e-mail.

Individuals Needed for Mini Focus Groups

Dressler Marketing, the biggest market research company in Edmonton, is recruiting people between the ages of 21 and 70 for a study focused on travel. The event will take place in the conference center of the Sanderson Hotel, 48 Emery Avenue, during the second week of June. The study begins by viewing a series of short travel-related videos followed by small group discussions that are facilitated by our moderators. The entire session will last three hours and compensation will be provided for all who participate. Anyone interested can phone Dressler at 409-5321-8082. Be sure to mention study 73. To determine if a caller is eligible to take part in this study, he or she will be asked to remain on the line and respond to a few screening questions.

Roland,

Dressler Marketing really appreciates you taking time out from your busy work schedule to assist with our market research project for Pacific Adventures at the Sanderson Hotel. You will be facilitating four mini focus groups composed of five people each. Since the focus is travelling along Canada's west coast, our client insists that we locate individuals with extensive travel experience, either for business or leisure, in that region.

Schedule of Sessions from 3:00 to 6:00 P.M.

Age Range/Date
21-35 Tuesday, June 9
36-45 Wednesday, June 10
46-60 Thursday, June 11
61-70 Friday, June 12

Upon arrival, participants will be given yellow name tags. Make sure their name tags are clearly visible at all times during the study, especially when making the video recordings of the members' discussions. This will allow Dressler to refer to individuals by their names when submitting our findings and recommendations to Pacific Adventures.

Each of the four video clips centers on a different aspect of Pacific Adventures:

Video Clip 1: Group Discussion of Whale-watching tours
Video Clip 2: One-Day Kayaking Adventures
Video Clip 3: Popular Mountain Resorts
Video Clip 4: Hiking Adventures in Whistler Mountain

Nina Hernandez

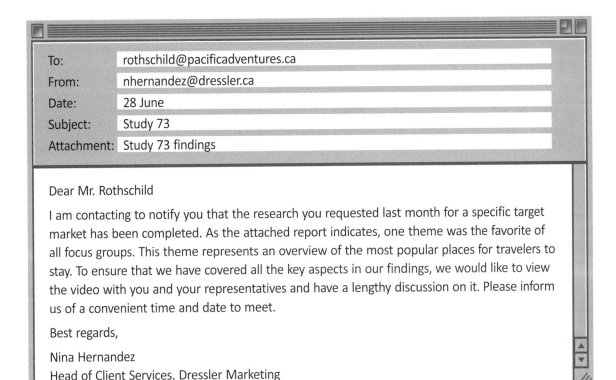

To: rothschild@pacificadventures.ca
From: nhernandez@dressler.ca
Date: 28 June
Subject: Study 73
Attachment: Study 73 findings

Dear Mr. Rothschild

I am contacting to notify you that the research you requested last month for a specific target market has been completed. As the attached report indicates, one theme was the favorite of all focus groups. This theme represents an overview of the most popular places for travelers to stay. To ensure that we have covered all the key aspects in our findings, we would like to view the video with you and your representatives and have a lengthy discussion on it. Please inform us of a convenient time and date to meet.

Best regards,

Nina Hernandez
Head of Client Services, Dressler Marketing

186. What is NOT suggested about the participants of the mini focus groups?

(A) They will receive a payment.
(B) They need to answer questions when they call.
(C) They must be experienced travelers.
(D) They are hotel employees.

187. In the Instructions, paragraph 1, line 4, the word "locate" is the closest in meaning to

(A) remark
(B) believe
(C) find
(D) check

188. What is indicated about study 73?

(A) It will be held at Dressler's headquarters.
(B) It includes four groups of the same size.
(C) It centers solely on water leisure.
(D) It will be completed in two days.

189. According to the instructions, why were the participants provided with name tags?

(A) So that the marketing company can identify them easily.
(B) So that each registration number matches with the correct name.
(C) So that they would be able to find their seats quickly.
(D) So that they would be permitted to enter the conference center.

190. Based on the results of the study, what video clip was the most popular?

(A) Video Clip 1
(B) Video Clip 2
(C) Video Clip 3
(D) Video Clip 4

Questions 191-195 refer to the following schedule and two e-mails.

St. John Art Gallery
Upcoming Exhibitions

Dates	Title of Exhibition	Brief Description
11 April – 20 August	Recycled Materials as Sculptures	People usually see recycled materials as mere scrap piles. However, as this exhibition featuring the works of 10 artists throughout South America shows, any material can be transformed into breathtaking sculptures.
28 April – 3 October	The Portraits of Athletes	This watercolor collection features beautiful paintings of professional athletes by artists from every corner of the globe.
5 June – 29 November	More than Just Trees	This remarkable collection of photographs and paintings by artists throughout Africa and several Mediterranean nations captures the mesmerizing power of forests.
11 June – 14 July	The History of Food in Art	Through video recordings, sculptures, photographs, and paintings, this unique exhibition traces the history of food in Europe from the 15th to the 19th century.

Tickets can be purchased through our website or by sending an e-mail to banderson@ stjohnartgallery.org. To learn about our wonderful membership plans, simply go to our website and click on "Become a St. John Art Gallery Member!" Members receive two free tickets to the exhibition of their choice.

From:	Chevon Jabar <CJabar@rogerstalent.ca>
To:	Belinda Anderson <banderson@stjohnartgallery.org>
Subject:	thank you
Date:	March 10

I am e-mailing to say thank you for the two free tickets to "The History of Food in Art." I also need another ticket for this event for my division head, Helena Lafleur. I assume the gallery has a record of my credit card details, so please bill the same card and send the tickets to the same address.

I would like to thank your staff for providing such fantastic exhibitions.

Chevon Jabar

From:	Belinda Anderson <banderson@stjohnartgallery.org>
To:	Chevon Jabar <CJabar@rogerstalent.ca>
Subject:	a cancelled exhibition
Date:	March 14

Dear Mr. Jabar,

St. John Art Gallery would like to thank you for your patronage during the past seven years. We are truly sorry that the exhibition you and your colleague planned to see was cancelled due to circumstances beyond our control. However, we have already scheduled a replacement exhibition of black and white photographs. It is scheduled to run during the exact same dates (11 June – 14 July) and is called "The Working Classes of Latin America." I have already sent a new program guide in the mail to your office. Please let me know which exhibition you would like to see instead.

Thank you for your understanding in this matter.

Sincerely yours,

Belinda Anderson
St. John Art Gallery

191. According to the website, what do all of the exhibitions have in common?

(A) They showcase works from various nations.
(B) They showcase paintings from Mediterranean countries.
(C) They include video presentations.
(D) They include sculptures.

192. What is indicated about Mr. Jabar?

(A) He donated a collection for an exhibition.
(B) He is currently employed as an art instructor.
(C) He has already seen three of the exhibits.
(D) He is a paid member of the art gallery.

193. Which exhibition has been canceled?

(A) Recycled Materials as Sculptures
(B) The Portraits of Athletes
(C) More Than Just Trees
(D) The History of Food in Art

194. In the second e-mail, the word "run" in paragraph 1, line 4, is closest in meaning to

(A) direct
(B) remove
(C) be shown
(D) be announced

195. What did Ms. Anderson do for Mr. Jabar?

(A) Bill his credit card
(B) Mail an updated program guide
(C) Upgrade his membership
(D) Reschedule a social event

Questions 196-200 refer to the following e-mails and the attachment.

To:	Marcus Lount; Gabriella Sanchez; Daniel Wilkes
From:	Shelly Dorcas
Date:	July 16, 9:09 A.M.
Subject:	business space
Attachment:	available properties

Hi everyone,

I really enjoyed last Friday's lunch with you at the Davisville Grill. I am truly excited about opening our first Miami branch of Ebbet Construction Equipment Rentals. As Miami's housing market grows more and more each day, I am sure that we are all eager to attract our very first customers and start advising companies on the equipment that is most suitable for their projects and objectives.

I appreciate all the input you offered on the most appropriate business space. Using the budget and criteria you suggested, I searched for spaces at www.vanzylerealty.com. I found several possible spaces and compiled them into a list. That document is attached. Please have a look at it and get back to me with any comments you may have.

Shelly Dorcas, Ebbet Construction Equipment Rentals

13990 Gifford Way

Suburban two-story rental facility. Second floor office suites. Parking lot can accommodate up to 100 automobiles. Located across from Devon City's main bus terminal and near a large number of hotels used by business travelers. Half an hour from downtown Miami.
Monthly lease: $975

1389 Singleton Highway

Large retail space located in the heart of downtown Miami. Large sign on building makes it high visible to highway motorists. Building includes large storage facilities for parts and equipment. The newly installed air conditioning unit is guaranteed to keep you comfortable during the hot summers.
Monthly lease: $1,150

7643 Beckford Avenue

Third-floor retails and office space. Located uptown within Miami's main business district. Located on the same street as two major shopping centers. Facility includes state-of-the-art security alarm system. Printer/scanner/fax/color copier on-site for company use.
Monthly lease: $1,050

6094 Wilmot Drive

Single-story building. Comes with small office space. Land contract is also offered for property immediately behind facility. Located on the city's east side in lovely Ryerson Park, a prime Miami development site for condominium towers.
Monthly lease: $825

To:	Shelly Dorcas; Marcus Lount; Gabriella Sanchez
From:	Daniel Wilkes
Date:	July 20, 11:23 A.M.
Re:	business space

Hi everyone,

Thank you very much, Shelly, for all your work in narrowing our search to the options in the list you provided. I'm certain the strategy meeting held last Friday was quite productive. My apologies for not being there, but I was called to Boston all of a sudden on an urgent business matter. Also, I have to say thank all of you for being patient in waiting for my response to this important e-mail discussion.

Marcus, while I truly appreciate the need to save money on an inexpensive suburban facility, our company should not ignore the significance of having a facility conveniently located downtown as more and more homes are being built in that area.

I am also in agreement with Gabriella's idea that our company needs a booth at Miami's upcoming housing fair. Next week, I will be flying to Miami to visit relatives so I will look into the matter then. Also, while in Miami, I am scheduled to have lunch with a local realtor who worked for our company up until two years ago. Thank you, Shelly, for reminding me that Helen Richardson now resides in Miami. I'm sure she will have useful insights for us.

Daniel Wilkes, Ebbet Construction Equipment Rentals

06

196. Who most likely is Ms. Dorcas?

(A) A real estate expert
(B) An official in Miami Housing Bureau
(C) A construction equipment specialist
(D) A cook at Davisville Grill

197. What is one property feature mentioned in the attachment?

(A) An energy-efficient heating system
(B) A newly-installed carpet in the office
(C) A large cafeteria for employees
(D) A location close to housing development

198. What is suggested about Mr. Wilkes?

(A) He will fly to Miami tomorrow morning.
(B) He is renting some property in Boston.
(C) He did not make it to the Davisville Grill meeting.
(D) He plans to apply for a managerial position.

199. What is indicated about Ms. Sanchez?

(A) She suggested an idea to her colleagues by e-mail.
(B) She used to live in downtown Miami.
(C) She will meet a former colleague.
(D) She started her own equipment rental business.

200. Which property does Mr. Wilkes most likely favor?

(A) 13990 Gifford Way
(B) 1389 Singleton Highway
(C) 7643 Beckford Avenue
(D) 6094 Wilmot Drive

Stop! This is the end of the test. If you finish before time is called, you may go back to Parts 5, 6, and 7 and check your work.

SCRIPT
&
TRANSLATION

PART 1 P. 14–17   🎧 01

1. (A) **He is drawing on a screen.***
    (B) He is adjusting his watch.
    (C) He is signing a document.
    (D) He is throwing a pen away.

2. (A) **They're setting the table.***
    (B) They're arranging some flowers.
    (C) They're cooking on a stove.
    (D) They're hanging a plant on the wall.

3. (A) A woman is wiping the windowsill.
    (B) A man is playing music.
    (C) A man is pulling open a door.
    (D) **A woman is using some equipment.***

4. (A) A man is waiting to board a bus.
    (B) A man is walking toward a van.
    (C) **A woman is holding a newspaper.***
    (D) A woman is getting a book out of her bag.

5. (A) Some workers are moving the chairs.
    (B) **A waiting room is decorated with pictures.***
    (C) A light fixture is being mounted above the doorway.
    (D) Some lampshades have been set on the floor.

6. (A) Pedestrians are crossing a road.
    (B) A store sign is being replaced.
    (C) A commercial building is under construction.
    (D) **Some cars are parked on the side of a road.***

PART 2 P. 18   🎧 02

7. When did Jeffrey clean out the storage room?
    (A) He cleaned the windows.
    (B) **Sometime this morning.***
    (C) A storage container.

8. What does your store sell?
    (A) **Secondhand furniture.***
    (B) The interns will arrive soon.
    (C) A full refund.

1. (A) 他正在螢幕上畫圖。
    (B) 他正在調校手錶。
    (C) 他正在簽署文件。
    (D) 他正把筆丟開。

2. (A) 他們正在擺設餐具。
    (B) 他們正在插花。
    (C) 他們正在爐子上煮東西。
    (D) 他們正把植物掛到牆上。

3. (A) 一名女子正在擦窗台。
    (B) 一名男子正在演奏音樂。
    (C) 一名男子正拉開門。
    (D) 一名女子正在使用某種機器設備。

4. (A) 一名男子正等著上公車。
    (B) 一名男子正走向一輛小貨車。
    (C) 一名女子拿著一份報紙。
    (D) 一名女子正從袋子中拿出一本書。

5. (A) 一些工人正在搬動椅子。
    (B) 等候室裡裝飾著畫。
    (C) 門口上方正在裝設燈具。
    (D) 一些燈罩被放在地板上。

6. (A) 行人正在過馬路。
    (B) 商店招牌正在被更換。
    (C) 商業大樓正在施工中。
    (D) 有些車停在馬路邊。

7. 傑佛瑞何時打掃了貯藏室？
    (A) 他清潔了窗戶。
    (B) 今天早上某個時候。
    (C) 一個置物箱。

8. 你的店賣什麼？
    (A) 二手家具。
    (B) 實習生很快就來了。
    (C) 全額退費。

9. Do you know where I can find a newsstand?
   (A) I saw one just down the street.*
   (B) No, I can't read it.
   (C) It's an interesting story.

10. Can I try those sunglasses on, please?
   (A) Sure, I'll work hard.
   (B) It has a good location.
   (C) Yes, here you are.*

11. Who informed the newcomers of the changes to their assignments?
   (A) With the assigned newcomers.
   (B) The head of Human Resources.*
   (C) One or two minor changes.

12. When is the best time to talk to your manager?
   (A) You must be in management.
   (B) At her downtown office.
   (C) Anytime in the afternoon.*

13. Would you prefer to take a vacation later this month or after we finish the project?
   (A) It's taking up too much space.
   (B) I'm okay with either.*
   (C) I like project work.

14. Why did you suggest paying by credit card instead of cash?
   (A) A local bank.
   (B) Because you can earn points.*
   (C) You could write about it.

15. You do know how to make curry, don't you?
   (A) I've cooked it over a hundred times.*
   (B) At an authentic Indian place.
   (C) During lunchtime.

16. What task was Ms. Johnson's team given this month?
   (A) By the middle of next month.
   (B) Sure, I'll speak to her about it.
   (C) Reviewing the latest project proposal.*

17. I would like to go see Jennifer dance in the ballet performance.
   (A) No, not here. Over there, please.
   (B) It's two hours away by car.*
   (C) I must perform well this time.

9. 你知道哪裡有書報攤嗎？
   (A) 我有看到一家，就在這條街上。
   (B) 不，我看不懂。
   (C) 這篇故事很有趣。

10. 請問我可以試戴那副太陽眼鏡嗎？
   (A) 當然，我會努力工作。
   (B) 它的位置很好。
   (C) 可以，來，給你。

11. 誰通知了新同事，他們的工作改變了？
   (A) 和指派的新同事。
   (B) 人事部的主管。
   (C) 一、兩個小改動。

12. 什麼時候最適合和你的經理談話？
   (A) 你一定是管理階級。
   (B) 在她市區的辦公室。
   (C) 下午都可以。

13. 你要在這個月晚一點休假，還是等我們完成這個專案再說？
   (A) 它太佔空間了。
   (B) 我都可以。
   (C) 我喜歡專案工作。

14. 你為什麼建議用信用卡付款，而非現金？
   (A) 一家本地銀行。
   (B) 因為你可以得到點數。
   (C) 你可以描寫它。

15. 你真的知道怎麼煮咖哩，對嗎？
   (A) 我已經煮過不下一百次了。
   (B) 在道地的印度餐館。
   (C) 在午餐時間。

16. 強生女士的小組這個月的任務是什麼？
   (A) 在下個月中之前。
   (B) 當然，我會和她說這件事。
   (C) 複審最新的提案。

17. 我想去看珍妮佛的芭蕾舞演出。
   (A) 不，不是這裡。請到那邊。
   (B) 開車要兩個小時。
   (C) 我這次一定要好好表演。

 01
 02

18. Is the meeting room big enough to accommodate twenty people?
(A) He is on a conference call.
(B) The company had some financial troubles.
(C) Well, it depends on how we arrange the chairs.*

19. When did the company cafeteria open?
(A) It often happens in the morning.
(B) In other departments, too.
(C) After the new CEO was appointed.*

20. Do you plan to distribute the sales report at the meeting or before it?
(A) Let's send it now by e-mail.*
(B) No, I will report to him.
(C) She met the sales manager already.

21. Let's hire some part-time workers so we can handle all these extra orders.
(A) I'll order them online.
(B) Should we post an advertisement?*
(C) Five hours a day.

22. Do you think the new reception area gives a good impression to visitors?
(A) I would've liked brighter colors.*
(B) I am impressed with him.
(C) Between the first and the seventh floor.

23. How about taking a flight that departs on Friday?
(A) I'm a frequent flier.
(B) It will have to be close to midnight.*
(C) In a department store.

24. Chevon tested the sound equipment, didn't he?
(A) I'll ask him.*
(B) They're equipped for the job.
(C) Our new speakers.

25. Have you visited the new community center?
(A) More charity events.
(B) It's written in the manual, I guess.
(C) I haven't had a chance.*

26. Has the schedule for next week's workshop changed?
(A) Has she worked on it before?
(B) Yes, I'll forward the e-mail to you.*
(C) They will focus on teamwork.

18. 會議室夠不夠大到足以容納二十個人?
(A) 他正在開電話會議。
(B) 公司有些財務狀況。
(C) 嗯,要看我們椅子怎麼排。

19. 公司的員工餐廳是何時開幕的?
(A) 通常發生在上午。
(B) 其他部門也是。
(C) 在任命新的執行長之後。

20. 你打算在會議中還是開會前分發銷售報告?
(A) 我們現在就用電子郵件寄出吧。
(B) 不,我會向他報告。
(C) 她已經見過業務經理了。

21. 我們來僱用一些兼職人員吧,這樣才能處理這些額外的訂單。
(A) 我會上網訂購。
(B) 我們是否該登個廣告?
(C) 一天五個小時。

22. 你覺得新的接待區會帶給訪客好印象嗎?
(A) 我原本想要更亮的顏色。
(B) 他令我印象深刻。
(C) 在一樓到七樓之間。

23. 搭星期五出發的航班好嗎?
(A) 我常搭飛機。
(B) 可能會將近半夜。
(C) 在百貨公司。

24. 薛峰測試過音響設備了,不是嗎?
(A) 我會問他。
(B) 他們有能力做這個工作。
(C) 我們的新喇叭。

25. 你去過新的活動中心嗎?
(A) 更多慈善活動。
(B) 我想應該是寫在使用手冊裡。
(C) 我還沒有機會去。

26. 下星期工作坊的日程表更改了嗎?
(A) 她以前做過嗎?
(B) 是的,我會把電子郵件轉發給你。
(C) 他們會專注在團隊合作上。

27. Who's in charge of maintaining the photocopiers?
(A) Behind the file cabinet.
(B) Yes, it was fantastic.
(C) You can talk to me.*

28. But I thought you said you would be away next week.
(A) My trip has been canceled.*
(B) A member of the committee.
(C) From the train station.

29. Our electricity cost decreased this year, didn't it?
(A) Yes, by 7%.*
(B) During the election.
(C) It was not our product.

30. Why aren't they wearing their uniforms?
(A) I forgot to tell them.*
(B) The servers and cooks.
(C) Before Wednesday.

31. Does Dr. Kwon know he has several appointments today?
(A) A university professor.
(B) It's on the top shelf.
(C) He will arrive in time for them.*

27. 誰負責維修影印機?
(A) 在檔案櫃後面。
(B) 是啊,棒透了。
(C) 你可以跟我說。

28. 可是,我以為你說你下星期不在。
(A) 我的行程取消了。
(B) 委員會的成員。
(C) 從火車站來。

29. 我們今年的電費降低了,不是嗎?
(A) 是的,降了 7%。
(B) 在選舉期間。
(C) 那不是我們的產品。

30. 他們為什麼沒穿制服?
(A) 我忘記告訴他們了。
(B) 侍者和廚師。
(C) 在星期三以前。

31. 權醫師知道他今天有好幾個約診嗎?
(A) 一位大學教授。
(B) 在架子最上層。
(C) 他會及時抵達看診。

PART 3   P. 19-23   03

Questions 32–34　對話

W	Hello, this is Suzie Thompson at Pearson Law. **³² I'm calling about a problem with our photocopier.** Whenever I try to make copies, the text is so shrunken that it's unreadable.
M	Okay. **³² I think I can help you with that.** **³³ Have you tried turning it off and then turning it back on?**
W	Yes, I did that a few times, but it didn't help. I also tried the reset code you gave me during your last service visit, but that didn't help, either.
M	I see. Well, I have some time this afternoon. **³⁴ How about I stop by your office** and see if I can find out what's wrong?

女	哈囉,我是皮爾森律師事務所的蘇西‧湯普生。**³² 我打電話來,是因為我們的影印機有點問題。** 我每次影印,字都縮得很小,無法閱讀。
男	好的。**³² 我想,我可以幫上您的忙。** **³³ 您試過關機,再重新開機嗎?**
女	是的,我試了好幾次都沒用。我也試過你上次來時給的那組重新設定的密碼,但也沒有用。
男	了解。嗯,我今天下午有空。**³⁴ 我順道過去您的辦公室**,看看我能不能找出問題,好嗎?

32. Where most likely does the man work?

    (A) At a law office

    (B) At a repair company*

    (C) At a bookstore

    (D) At a print shop

33. What does the man ask the woman to do?

    (A) Restart some equipment *

    (B) Use another machine

    (C) Consult a manual

    (D) Find a reset code

34. What does the man say he can do?

    (A) Locate some equipment

    (B) Copy some documents

    (C) Contact a supplier

    (D) Go to the woman's office*

32. 男子最可能在哪裡工作？

    (A) 律師事務所。

    (B) 維修服務公司。

    (C) 書店。

    (D) 影印店。

33. 男子要求女子做什麼？

    (A) 把某個設備重新開機。

    (B) 使用另一台機器。

    (C) 查閱使用手冊。

    (D) 找到重新設定的密碼。

34. 男子説他可以做什麼？

    (A) 安置某個設備。

    (B) 影印一些文件。

    (C) 聯絡供應商。

    (D) 去女子的辦公室。

Questions 35–37 對話

M	Good morning, my coworkers and I are planning to attend the State Accounting Conference in September. **35 Do you have any rooms available** from the 7th to the 10th?	男 早安，我和同事計劃參加九月的國家會計研討會。**35 你們七日到十日有空房間嗎？**
W	Let me check our reservation system. Yes, it looks like we have several rooms available. **36 How many would you like to reserve?**	女 我查一下訂房系統。有的，看來我們還有好幾間空房。**36 您要預訂幾間房間？**
M	There are five of us, so we would prefer to book five single suites. Do your single suites have Internet access?	男 我們有五個人，所以，我們比較想要預訂五間單人套房。你們的單人套房可以上網嗎？
W	In that case, **37 I suggest booking five single business suites.** For only $10 more per night, each business suite comes with free Internet access and an onsite laser printer.	女 那樣的話，**37 我建議您預訂五間單人商務套房。** 升級為商務套房只要每晚再加十元就好。每間商務套房都可以免費上網，房間裡還備有雷射印表機。
M	That sounds perfect. Let me discuss it with my coworkers, and I'll call you back within the hour.	男 聽起來非常合適。我和同事討論一下，一個鐘頭內回電。

35. Why is the man calling?

    (A) To book tickets for an event

    (B) To inquire about accommodation*

    (C) To change a reservation

    (D) To purchase a printer

35. 男子為何打這通電話？

    (A) 為了預訂某個活動的門票。

    (B) 為了詢問住房。

    (C) 為了更改預訂資料。

    (D) 為了購買印表機。

36. What information does the woman request?

   (A) The number of rooms*

   (B) The name of a conference

   (C) A membership card number

   (D) A check-out date

37. What does the woman suggest?

   (A) Upgrading some rooms*

   (B) Signing a contract

   (C) Checking a website

   (D) Using a discount code

36. 女子要求什麼資訊？

   (A) 房間的數量。

   (B) 研討會的名稱。

   (C) 會員卡的卡號。

   (D) 退房的日期。

37. 女子有何建議？

   (A) 升級一些房間。

   (B) 簽署一份合約。

   (C) 查看一個網站。

   (D) 使用折扣優惠代碼。

Questions 38–40 三人對話

M1 Hello. As you are all aware, next month, we will hold the annual charity dinner. I think it is a good idea to create a pamphlet to promote the event to local business owners. **38 Would anyone be interested in leading the project?**	**男 1** 哈囉，你們大家都知道，我們下個月要舉行年度慈善晚宴。我認為，做一份宣傳小冊，向本地商家宣傳這個活動是個好主意。**38 有人有興趣主持這個專案嗎？**
W I'd love to try it. I have some experience in publishing, and **39 I won the Hartford Essay Contest last year.**	**女** 我很樂意嘗試。我在出版業工作過，而且 **39 去年還得過哈特福散文獎。**
M1 Excellent, Sue. That takes care of the written portion. Is there anyone who would like to work on the pamphlet's overall design?	**男 1** 太好了，蘇。文章的部分搞定。有人願意做宣傳小冊的整體設計嗎？
W Mark graduated from Stanford's design program. **40 Maybe he will be able to come up with some fantastic ideas for the design plan.**	**女** 馬克是史丹佛大學的設計學位學程畢業的。**40 也許他能想出一些很棒的設計點子。**
M2 Sure. I'd be glad to help out in any way I can.	**男 2** 當然，我很樂意盡我所能幫忙。
M1 Okay. Let's meet next week to discuss the project more in depth.	**男 1** 好的。我們下星期碰面，再更深入討論專案內容。

38. What is the conversation mainly about?

   (A) An updated menu

   (B) A change in a schedule

   (C) A writing contest

   (D) A volunteer project*

39. What is true about the woman?

   (A) She will relocate next week.

   (B) She is a university professor.

   (C) She has a photocopier.

   (D) She won an award.*

38. 這段對話的主題為何？

   (A) 一份更新的菜單。

   (B) 時程表的一項更動。

   (C) 一場寫作比賽。

   (D) 一個志工專案。

39. 關於女子，何者為真？

   (A) 她下星期要搬家。

   (B) 她是大學教授。

   (C) 她有一台影印機。

   (D) 她得過一個獎項。

40. What is Mark asked to do?
(A) Take photographs
(B) Develop a design plan*
(C) Attend a workshop
(D) Order some supplies

40. 馬克被要求做什麼?
(A) 拍照。
(B) 定出設計方案。
(C) 參加一個工作坊。
(D) 訂購一些用品。

Questions 41–43 對話

W Hello, Tim. **41 I'm wondering if the invitations for the company fundraiser have been delivered yet.**

M No, they haven't. **42 I got the sample invitation yesterday, but I noticed that our company name was spelled wrong.** I called the design studio about it. They apologized and said they'd send the corrected invitations by next Monday.

W Oh, no. Unfortunately, we can't delay it until Monday. Since the event is Wednesday, we need to make sure the invitations are mailed by Friday. **43 Could you call them back** and let them know our deadline is urgent?

M Sure. I'll call them right away.

女 哈囉,提姆。**41 我想知道公司募款活動的邀請函發出去了沒?**

男 沒,還沒有。**42 我昨天收到邀請函的樣本,但我發現公司名稱拼錯了。**我打電話告訴設計工作室。他們道了歉,並說最晚下星期一會把更正好的邀請函寄過來。

女 喔,糟了。不幸的是,我們沒辦法等到星期一。因為活動是星期三,我們必須確定邀請函最晚星期五前要寄出去。**43 你可不可以再打一次電話,**告訴他們,我們的截稿日期很趕?

男 當然可以。我現在就打給他們。

41. What is being discussed?
(A) A business card design
(B) A printing order*
(C) A company retreat
(D) New work schedules

41. 對話在討論何事?
(A) 名片設計。
(B) 印刷的訂單。
(C) 公司的教育訓練。
(D) 新的工作時程表。

42. What was the problem with the sample item?
(A) The paper was damaged.
(B) A logo was outdated.
(C) Some information was incorrect.*
(D) The cost was too high.

42. 邀請函的樣本有何問題?
(A) 紙張受損。
(B) 商標過時了。
(C) 有訊息錯誤。
(D) 費用太高。

43. What does the woman ask the man to do?
(A) Contact a company*
(B) Return a sample
(C) Hire a new employee
(D) Pay an account

43. 女子要求男子何事?
(A) 聯絡一家公司。
(B) 退回一份樣本。
(C) 僱用一名新員工。
(D) 結帳。

Questions 44–46 三人對話

M	**How are you two doing** [45] **entering all the patient records into** [44] **our clinic's new database program?**
W1	We are about half done. Entering the basic information such as names and addresses is easy, but it takes time to include descriptions of all the [44] **dental work** each patient has received.
W2	She is absolutely correct. That part slows us down a lot.
M	I see. I was hoping we could finish transferring the records by the end of this week. [46] **Do you think you could get it done if I had one of my** [44] **dental assistants look after the descriptions?**
W1	Oh, definitely.

男	[45] 把所有病歷資料輸入我們 [44] 診所新資料庫的進度,妳們兩個進行得如何?
女1	我們大概完成一半了。輸入基本資料,像名字和地址很容易,但要包含每個病人做過的所有 [44] **牙科治療說明**,就很花時間。
女2	她說得一點也沒錯。那個部分大大拖累我們的進度。
男	我知道了。我本來希望可以在這個星期之內,把資料都轉換完畢。[46] 如果我讓一個 [44] 牙醫助理來處理說明的部分,妳們覺得妳們做得完嗎?
女1	噢,一定可以。

44. Where most likely do the speakers work?
(A) At a subway station
(B) At a dental clinic*
(C) At a travel agency
(D) At a marketing firm

44. 說話者最可能在哪裡工作?
(A) 在地下鐵車站。
(B) 在牙醫診所。
(C) 在旅行社。
(D) 在行銷公司。

45. What project have the women been working on?
(A) Drafting an employee's contract
(B) Creating a television advertisement
(C) Inputting details into a computer*
(D) Installing some audio equipment

45. 女子們正在進行什麼工作?
(A) 草擬員工的合約。
(B) 創作一支電視廣告。
(C) 把詳細資料輸入電腦。
(D) 安裝某個音響設備。

46. What does the man suggest?
(A) Working some overtime
(B) Moving the deadline
(C) Using different software
(D) Assigning more staff*

46. 男子有何建議?
(A) 加一下班。
(B) 更改截止期限。
(C) 使用不同的軟體。
(D) 指派更多人手。

Questions 47–49 對話

W Hello, ⁴⁷ **I'm calling about the promotion listed on your website for the month of March.** I'm interested in booking flight tickets for myself as well as below-cabin space for five large breed dogs from Boston to New York City.

M No problem. I can help you with that. Would you like to book return fare, and are there any preferred travel dates?

W ⁴⁸ **I'm bringing my dogs to compete in the National Dog Show,** so I have to arrive on March 13th and stay for at least five days. Can you give me an estimate of the cost?

M Well, with the March promotion, you'll receive a 20% discount on an economy seat. ⁴⁹ **Before I can determine the exact cost, can I get the exact size of the carriers for your dogs?**

女 哈囉，⁴⁷ 我打來是想問你們登在網站上的三月促銷活動。我對此有興趣，我想自己訂一張從波士頓到紐約市的機票，同時為五隻大型品種犬訂客艙下的位置。

男 沒問題。我可以幫您處理。您要訂來回機票嗎？有偏好的出發日期嗎？

女 ⁴⁸ 我要帶我的狗狗去參加全國狗展競賽，因此，我必須在 3 月 13 日到，並且至少待五天。你可以幫我估算一下費用嗎？

男 嗯，用三月的促銷活動，您訂經濟艙會打八折。⁴⁹ 方便知道您所有狗狗外出提籠的確切尺寸嗎？這樣我才能定下確切的費用。

47. Why is the woman calling?
(A) To request a reservation change
(B) To inquire about a special discount*
(C) To ask for a full refund
(D) To upgrade her flight ticket

47. 女子為何打這通電話？
(A) 要求更改預訂的資料。
(B) 詢問一個特別的折扣。
(C) 要求全額退費。
(D) 將她的機票升等。

48. What event does the woman mention?
(A) An animal competition*
(B) A veterinary seminar
(C) A tour of a city
(D) An art convention

48. 女子提到什麼活動？
(A) 一場動物競賽。
(B) 一場獸醫研討會。
(C) 一趟城市觀光之旅。
(D) 一場藝術大會。

49. What additional information does the man ask for?
(A) The number of passengers
(B) The dimension of the carriers*
(C) The preferred payment method
(D) A membership card number

49. 男子要求什麼額外資訊？
(A) 乘客的數量。
(B) 外出提籠的尺寸。
(C) 偏好的付款方式。
(D) 會員卡的號碼。

M	Hey, Monica. I wanted to sit down with you today to discuss the feedback that customers have submitted through our restaurant's website. **50 I just finished reading all of the comments.**
W	**51 I'm sorry. I've spent all day training the new cooks.** Did you find any useful tips?
M	Yes, one woman suggested **52 giving people the menus while they are waiting for a table.** They can also place their orders so that it will be ready by the time a table becomes available.
W	That's a wonderful idea! That would definitely save a lot of time.
M	I agree. **52 Let's have a quick meeting with the serving staff right now.**

男	嗨，莫妮卡。我今天一直想和妳坐下來討論，顧客在我們餐廳網站上提出的意見回饋。**50 我剛剛看完所有的意見了。**
女	**51 抱歉，我一整天都在訓練新來的廚師。** 你有找到任何有幫助的點子嗎？
男	有，有位女士建議，**52 在人們等候桌位時，提供菜單給他們看。** 他們也可以先點菜，這樣一來，等有座位時餐點也準備好了。
女	那點子真棒！那樣肯定能節省很多時間。
男	我同意。**52 我們現在和服務人員快速開個會吧。**

50. What did the man recently do?
(A) He had an oven repaired.
(B) He printed out a receipt.
(C) He looked at customer feedback.*
(D) He corrected an invoice error.

50. 男子最近做了何事？
(A) 他找人修好了爐子。
(B) 他印出了收據。
(C) 他看了顧客的意見回饋。
(D) 他更正了帳單上的錯誤。

51. Why does the woman say, "I've spent all day training the new cooks"?
(A) To express agreement
(B) To suggest a solution
(C) To request more details
(D) To provide an excuse*

51. 女子為何說「我一整天都在訓練新來的廚師」？
(A) 為了表示同意。
(B) 為了建議解決方法。
(C) 為了要求更多細節。
(D) 為了提出一個理由。

52. What will the man mention at the meeting?
(A) Taking orders from people who are waiting*
(B) Keeping the business open late on weekends
(C) Removing certain dishes from the menu
(D) Offering more specials during lunchtime

52. 男子將在會議上提及何事？
(A) 接受正在等座位的顧客點菜。
(B) 週末時，讓餐廳開晚一點。
(C) 把某些菜從菜單中刪去。
(D) 午餐時，提供更多特餐。

W	You're listening to Radio One with our special guest Tim Schwarz, a renowned consultant and an expert on how to succeed at a new job. Mr. Schwarz, would you be able to share your best tip for those who are starting a new job?	女	您現在收聽的是壹電台，我們的特別來賓是提姆‧許瓦茲，他是很有名的諮商師，也是如何做好新工作的專家。許瓦茲先生，您可不可以把你最棒的秘訣，分享給那些正開始從事新工作的聽眾？
M	Sure, I'd love to. ⁵³ **I think one of the easiest things you can do is to write everything down.** Take notes during training and keep a schedule book of all your deadlines and meetings.	男	當然，我很樂意。⁵³ **我認為，最容易做到的事就是把每件事都寫下來。**受訓時記筆記，並把你所有的截止期限和會議都記在記事本裡。
W	That's an excellent tip. You should consider publishing your thoughts in a self-help book.	女	真棒的建議。您應該考慮把您的想法出版成一本自助書。
M	It's funny you mention that. ⁵⁴ **I'm actually in the process of working with an editor on such a book.** ⁵⁵ **It's due to be out next October from Wayward Publishing.**	男	妳提到這件事，還真是有趣。⁵⁴ **我確實正和一位編輯合作，在寫這樣一本書。** ⁵⁵ 預計明年十月由威沃德出版社發行。

53. What suggestion does the man make?

(A) Organizing workspaces

(B) Being friendly

(C) Working extra hours

(D) Recording information*

54. What does the man mean when he says, "It's funny you mention that"?

(A) The woman's suggestion is already true.*

(B) He thinks the woman's comment is false.

(C) The woman's idea is strange.

(D) He refuses to answer the question.

55. According to the man, what will happen in October?

(A) A report will be distributed.

(B) A book will become available.*

(C) A company will be established.

(D) A project will be started.

53. 男子提出什麼建議？

(A) 整理工作場所。

(B) 待人友善。

(C) 加班。

(D) 記錄資訊。

54. 當男子說「你提到這件事，還真是有趣」，意指什麼？

(A) 女子的建議已然成真。

(B) 他認為女子的意見是錯的。

(C) 女子的主意很奇怪。

(D) 他拒絕回答問題。

55. 根據男子表示，十月會發生何事？

(A) 會發送一份報告。

(B) 一本書會上市。

(C) 一家公司會成立。

(D) 一項計畫會開始。

W Hi, Maxwell, ⁵⁶ **I've been trying to send some customer reports through the company e-mail, but it keeps telling me that the servers are down.** Have you been able to use your e-mail today?

M No, I've been having the same problem. ⁵⁷ **I already submitted a complaint to the IT department this morning,** but you should do the same if we want it to be fixed quickly.

W Okay, how should I go about sending a complaint? Should I contact the department head?

M No, you can just log on to the company message board and submit the complaint there. Here, ⁵⁸ **let me show you how to sign in.**

女 嗨,麥斯威爾,⁵⁶ 我一直試圖透過公司的電子郵件傳送一些顧客報告,但系統一直告訴我伺服器故障。你今天可以寄送電子郵件嗎?

男 不行,我遇到一樣的問題。⁵⁷ 我今天早上已經發了申訴信給資訊部門,不過,如果我們想要系統快點修好的話,妳也應該發申訴信。

女 好,我該怎麼發申訴信?我應該聯絡該部門的主管嗎?

男 不用,妳只需登入公司的布告欄,然後從那裡發出申訴信就可以了。來,⁵⁸ 我示範給妳看如何登入。

56. What is the woman unable to do?
(A) Print some documents
(B) Locate a file
(C) Send some work e-mails*
(D) Join the company dinner

56. 女子無法做什麼?
(A) 列印一些文件。
(B) 找出一份檔案。
(C) 傳送一些工作上的電子郵件。
(D) 參加公司的晚餐。

57. What did the man do this morning?
(A) Access a server
(B) Visit a department
(C) Fix a computer problem
(D) File a complaint*

57. 男子今天早上做了何事?
(A) 進入伺服器存取。
(B) 造訪一個部門。
(C) 解決一個電腦問題。
(D) 提出申訴。

58. What does the man say he will do?
(A) Demonstrate how to sign in*
(B) Submit another form
(C) Update a service request
(D) Reset a company password

58. 男子說他將會做什麼?
(A) 示範如何登入。
(B) 提交另一份表格。
(C) 更新一項服務要求。
(D) 重新設定電腦密碼。

W	Welcome back from Chicago, Ted. ⁵⁹ **I know you were visiting our current clients,** but I'm wondering if you managed to meet with any new companies that are interested in carrying out their advertising campaigns with us.
M	Yes, I found a potential new client for our firm. The company could be big business for us. ⁶⁰ **However, the CEO mentioned that their current advertising firm charges them 5% less than our standard rates.** If we want to sign his company, we'll need to match that cost.
W	Well, if the company is going to bring in a large amount of business for us, I think the 5% discount may be worthwhile. ⁶¹ **How about you draw up a proposal and then set up a conference call with the CEO?**

女　泰德，歡迎你從芝加哥歸來。⁵⁹ **我知道，你去拜訪我們現有的客戶，**但我想知道，你有沒有成功和一些新公司會面，使他們有意由我們來執行廣告宣傳活動？

男　有的，我幫公司找到一位潛在的新客戶。這家公司可能會帶給我們一筆大生意。⁶⁰ **但是，執行長提到，他們現在的廣告公司收費比我們的標準費率少5%。**如果我們想要簽下他的公司，我們的收費必須比得過才行。

女　嗯，如果這家公司會為我們帶進一大筆生意的話，我想，或許值得給 5% 的折扣。⁶¹ **你來草擬一份提案，然後安排和執行長開個電話會議如何？**

59. What did the man do in Chicago?
(A) Sign a new client
(B) Meet with some customers*
(C) Attend a workshop
(D) Deliver a sample order

59. 男子在芝加哥時做了何事？
(A) 簽了一個新客戶。
(B) 和一些客戶碰面。
(C) 參加一個工作坊。
(D) 送一份樣品。

60. What problem does the man mention?
(A) A client canceled a contract.
(B) A CEO was too busy to meet.
(C) A trip was delayed by a week.
(D) A price was not agreed upon.*

60. 男子提到什麼問題？
(A) 一名客戶中止了合約。
(B) 有位執行長太忙，無法碰面。
(C) 有項行程延後了一星期。
(D) 價格沒有談攏。

61. What does the woman suggest doing next?
(A) Flying back to Chicago
(B) Reading an article
(C) Writing a proposal*
(D) Reviewing a website

61. 女子建議接下來做什麼？
(A) 飛回芝加哥。
(B) 讀一篇文章。
(C) 寫一份提案。
(D) 細查一個網站。

Business	Suite
Jane, Baker, and Sons Law	601
Walder Tech Solutions	602
Sedwick International Trade	603
64 Martin Sound and Recording	604

公司	室
珍與貝克父子律師事務所	601
華德科技公司	602
賽德威國際貿易公司	603
64 馬丁音響錄音	604

W Hi, 62 I'm scheduled to see my dentist at 1:30 today. I parked in the underground parking garage, but I'm not sure where I should go to pay for parking.

M No problem, Ma'am. 63 Parking is free for paying visitors. Your dentist's office will stamp your ticket. Just show it to me when you leave and you'll be exempt from paying.

W That's great, thank you. Also, can you point me in the right direction? This is my first visit to Dr. Star, but I can't find his name on the directory.

M Ah, Dr. Star is new to this building, and we haven't been able to change the directory yet. 64 You'll find him in suite 604.

女 嗨，62 我排好今天一點半來看牙醫。我的車停在地下停車場，但我不確定要去哪裡付停車費。

男 好的，女士。63 付費訪客免停車費。您的牙醫診所會在你的停車卡上蓋章。您離開時，只要把卡給我看，就不用付費。

女 太好了，謝謝你。還有，你可以指給我正確的方向嗎？這是我第一次來看史達醫師的診，但我在公司名錄上找不到他的名字。

男 啊，史達醫師剛搬來這棟大樓，我們還沒有更改名錄。64 您可以在 604 室找到他。

62. What is the purpose of the woman's visit?
(A) To interview a lawyer
(B) To attend a medical appointment*
(C) To purchase a parking pass
(D) To meet with a client

62. 女子造訪的目的為何？
(A) 為了面試一位律師。
(B) 為了赴一場約診。
(C) 為了買停車入場證。
(D) 為了和客戶見面。

63. What does the man say about parking?
(A) It is free for paying customers.*
(B) It is cheaper than most places.
(C) It is only for employees
(D) It is located on the roof.

63. 關於停車，男子怎麼説？
(A) 付費的顧客可以免費停車。
(B) 停車費比大部分地方都便宜。
(C) 只有員工可以停車。
(D) 停車場在頂樓。

64. Look at the graphic. Which office name needs to be updated on the building directory?
(A) Jane, Baker, and Sons Law
(B) Walder Tech Solutions
(C) Sedwick International Trade
(D) Martin Sound and Recording*

64. 請見圖表。公司名錄上的哪一家公司名稱需要更新？
(A) 珍與貝克父子律師事務所。
(B) 華德科技公司。
(C) 賽德威國際貿易公司。
(D) 馬丁音響錄音。

CONFERENCE ROOM A: WEDNESDAY	
TIME	EVENT
10:00 A.M.	Graphic Design Meeting
11:00 A.M.	Conference Call
2:00 P.M.	Meeting with S&V Fashions
3:00 P.M.	Budget Review

會議室 A：星期三	
時間	活動
上午十點	平面設計會議
上午十一點	電話會議
下午兩點	與 S&V 服飾開會
下午三點	預算審查

W Rebecca Greenwood of Weston Pharmaceuticals just called. ⁶⁵ **Her company is looking to hire a new advertising firm** to sell their new line of vitamins. She'd like to come in Wednesday morning at ten to discuss our services.

M That's great. Weston Pharmaceuticals is a big international company. They could potentially become a large account for us. Can you reserve conference room A that day? It's the most comfortable room.

W Unfortunately, ⁶⁶ **that room is already booked at ten.**

M Let me check the schedule. Oh, ⁶⁶ **it's been reserved by Jim.** But I'm guessing Jim won't mind using another room instead.

W You're right. ⁶⁷ **I'll call him and ask if he's willing to switch rooms.**

女 韋斯頓製藥的蕾貝卡・葛林伍德剛剛打電話來。⁶⁵ **她的公司正想要找新的廣告公司來銷售他們的維他命系列新產品。** 她想要星期三早上十點過來，和我們討論服務內容。

男 太好了。韋斯頓製藥是國際大廠。他們可能會成為我們的大客戶。你可以預訂那天的會議室 A 嗎？那是最適宜的房間。

女 不巧，⁶⁶ 那間會議室十點已經有人訂了。

男 我來查一下時間表。噢，⁶⁶ **已經被吉姆預訂了。** 但我想，吉姆不會介意用另一間會議室。

女 你說得對。⁶⁷ **我會打給他，問問看他是否願意換場地。**

65. Where do the speakers work?
(A) At a fashion house
(B) At an advertising firm*
(C) At shipping business
(D) At a medical clinic

65. 說話者在哪裡工作？
(A) 在一家時裝公司。
(B) 在一家廣告公司。
(C) 在運輸公司。
(D) 在一家診所。

66. Look at the graphic. According to the man, what event is Jim in charge of?
(A) Graphic Design Meeting*
(B) Conference Call
(C) Meeting with S&V Fashions
(D) Budget Review

66. 請見圖表。根據男子所說，吉姆負責什麼活動？
(A) 平面設計會議。
(B) 電話會議。
(C) 與 S&V 服飾開會。
(D) 預算審查。

67. What does the woman say she will do?
(A) Upgrade a room
(B) Locate some files
(C) Postpone a meeting
(D) Ask for a room change*

67. 女子說她會做什麼？
(A) 把房間升等。
(B) 找出一些檔案。
(C) 延後會議。
(D) 要求換場地。

ITEM or SERVICE	PRICE
Inkspark 306 Printer	$399.00
2-year extended warranty	$69.00
306 color ink cartridge	$32.00
70 306 black ink cartridge	**$15.00**
Total:	$515.00

物品或服務	價格
Inkspark 306 印表機	$399.00
兩年延長保固	$69.00
306 彩色墨水匣	$32.00
70 306 黑色墨水匣	**$15.00**
總計	$515.00

W Is there anything else I can do for you, sir? **68 Or are you set with the new printer, cartridges, and extended warranty?**

M Actually, I have a question. **69 I was told that if I paid with my credit card at this store, I could split my payment into three monthly portions.** Is that service still available?

W Yes, of course. We accept all major credit cards, and they all have the three-month payment plan option.

M Okay, I think I'd like to try that. Also, **70 I just remembered that this printer comes with its own spare black ink cartridge, so I don't think I'll need this replacement cartridge.**

W Okay, I'll remove it from your bill before we proceed with payment.

女 還需要什麼服務嗎，先生？**68 還是，您需要新的印表機、墨水匣和延長保固就好？**

男 其實，我有個疑問。**69 有人告訴我，如果在這家店用信用卡付款，可以把款項分為三個月分期付款。**那項服務還有嗎？

女 當然還有。我們接受所有主要信用卡，它們都享有三個月分期付款方案。

男 好，我想我要用這個方案。還有，**70 我剛剛想起來，這台印表機附有備用黑色墨水匣，所以我想，我不需要這個替換墨水匣。**

女 好的，我會把它從您的帳單中刪除再結帳。

68. Who most likely is the woman?
(A) A hotel receptionist
(B) A sales clerk*
(C) A civil servant
(D) An artist

68. 女子最可能是誰？
(A) 飯店的櫃檯接待員。
(B) 售貨員。
(C) 公務員。
(D) 藝術家。

69. What does the man ask about?
(A) Payment plans*
(B) Special discounts
(C) Tax rebates
(D) New products

69. 男子詢問何事？
(A) 付款方式。
(B) 特別優惠。
(C) 退稅。
(D) 新產品。

70. Look at the graphic. Which amount will be removed from the bill?
(A) $399
(B) $69
(C) $32
(D) $15*

70. 請見圖表。哪一筆金額會從帳單中刪除？
(A) $399。
(B) $69。
(C) $32。
(D) $15。

Questions 71–73 電話留言

M Hello, Jim. **⁷¹ This is Ron Fuller calling from Fox Computers.** Everything looks fine with your computer except for the hard drive. It must be replaced, so **⁷² I've ordered a new one.** I was able to save some files from your old hard drive. **⁷³ If you'd like, I can transfer those files to your new hard drive when it arrives.** Please let me know how you'd like to proceed. You can reach me at 655-098-3334. Thanks.

男 哈囉，吉姆，**⁷¹ 我是福斯電腦的羅傳樂。** 除了硬碟之外，您的電腦看起來都還很好。硬碟必須要換，所以，**⁷² 我已經訂了一個新的。** 我把您舊硬碟的一些檔案存出來了。**⁷³ 如果您想要的話，等您的新硬碟來了，我可以把那些檔案轉存進去。** 請告訴我，接下來您想要怎麼做。您可以撥打 655-098-3334 找我。謝謝。

71. Where does the speaker work?
    (A) At a software company
    (B) At an electronics manufacturer
    (C) At a computer repair store*
    (D) At a shipping company

71. 說話者在哪裡工作？
    (A) 在一家軟體公司。
    (B) 在一家電子零件製造公司。
    (C) 在一家電腦維修店。
    (D) 在一家船運公司。

72. What does the speaker say he has done?
    (A) Ordered a component*
    (B) Refunded a fee
    (C) Replaced a part
    (D) Upgraded some software

72. 說話者說他做了何事？
    (A) 訂了一個零件。
    (B) 退還了一筆費用。
    (C) 更換了一個零件。
    (D) 把一些軟體升級。

73. What does the speaker offer?
    (A) To lend a computer
    (B) To move some information*
    (C) To extend a service warranty
    (D) To pay for a new computer

73. 說話者提議做何事？
    (A) 出借電腦。
    (B) 轉移一些資訊。
    (C) 延長服務保固。
    (D) 花錢買新電腦。

Questions 74–76 留言

M Good afternoon, Ms. Renolds. **⁷⁴ Thank you for visiting Star Insurance's website and filling out an online application form.** According to your application, you are interested in getting your tour company's new buses insured. You're in luck, because my company is currently having a two-for-one insurance sale for businesses. For every insurance policy you purchase, you'll receive a second policy absolutely free for the first year. **⁷⁵ If you'd like to take advantage of this sale, ⁷⁶ please contact me by June 23rd as the promotion expires the next day.**

男 雷諾女士，午安。**⁷⁴ 謝謝您造訪星辰保險公司網站，並填寫線上申請表。** 根據您的申請書，您有意為貴遊覽公司的新巴士投保。您真幸運，因為我們公司現正舉辦商務保險買一送一促銷活動。根據您所買的每一張保單，第二張保單首年完全免費。**⁷⁵ 若您想要享有這項促銷優惠，⁷⁶ 請於 6 月 23 日前和我聯絡，** 因為促銷在隔日截止。

74. Why did Ms. Renolds visit Star Insurance's website?

(A) To review a product

(B) To fill out a form*

(C) To set up a meeting

(D) To upgrade a service

74. 雷諾女士為何造訪星辰保險公司的網站？

(A) 為了看一項產品。

(B) 為了填寫一份表格。

(C) 為了安排一場會議。

(D) 為了升級一項服務。

75. What does the speaker offer Ms. Renolds?

(A) A membership card

(B) A full refund

(C) A discount*

(D) A new vehicle

75. 説話者提議給雷諾女士什麼服務？

(A) 一張會員卡。

(B) 全額退費。

(C) 折扣。

(D) 一輛新車。

76. According to the speaker, what must Ms. Renolds do by June 23rd?

(A) Sign up for a newsletter

(B) Visit Star Insurance in person

(C) Complete a training course

(D) Make a decision*

76. 根據説話者所述，雷諾女士必須在 6 月 23 日前做什麼？

(A) 登記訂閲電子報。

(B) 親自造訪星辰保險公司。

(C) 完成訓練課程。

(D) 做出決定。

Questions 77–79 導覽資訊

W Hello, everyone, and **[77] welcome to the Spartan Automotive Factory tour.** As I'm sure you're aware, Spartan Automotive was the first ever car manufacturer in the country. During this tour, you'll get to see some of the machinery used to make the first cars. **[78] Since there is currently another group taking this tour, we'll start in the show room instead of the assembly line.** You'll get to see some of the oldest cars ever manufactured. Then, we'll work our way into the assembly line area and conclude at the gift shop. **[79] Remember, gift shop purchases are on sale today only.**

女 大家好，**[77] 歡迎參觀斯巴坦汽車工廠。** 相信你們都知道，斯巴坦汽車是國內第一家汽車製造廠。在本次導覽中，你們會看到一些用來製造第一批汽車的機器。**[78] 由於現在有另一組正在參觀，所以，我們會先從展示廳、而不是裝配線開始參觀。** 你們會看到一些曾經生產的最古老車款。然後，我們會前往裝配區，最後到禮品部。**[79] 記得，禮品部的商品優惠只有今天。**

77. Where is the tour most likely taking place?

(A) At an automotive plant*

(B) At a car dealership

(C) At a toy outlet

(D) At a mechanic's shop

77. 這次導覽最可能在哪裡？

(A) 一間汽車廠。

(B) 一間汽車經銷商。

(C) 一間玩具暢貨中心。

(D) 一間修車行。

78. What does the speaker say has changed about the tour?
- (A) The number of guides
- (B) The outdoor sites
- (C) The cost of tickets
- **(D) The order of locations***

79. What does the speaker offer the listeners?
- **(A) A limited-time discount***
- (B) A hands-on workshop
- (C) A free membership
- (D) A map of the facility

Questions 80–82 會議摘錄

W　Before we conclude our meeting, I'd like to take this time to inform you of an important event. I've just found out that ⁸⁰ **the local mayor will be visiting our restaurant next Wednesday to celebrate his reelection.** As you know, the mayor often dines here, and he has requested his usual table for ten at 6:00 P.M. This shouldn't be any different than usual. ⁸¹ **There's no reason to get nervous.** However, I'd like to make sure that the new menus are finalized by the end of this week. I'd also like to distribute our new employee uniforms to ensure we all look our best. ⁸² **Please write down your size on this piece of paper by the end of the day.**

80. Why is the mayor visiting the restaurant?
- **(A) To hold a celebration***
- (B) To conduct an inspection
- (C) To give a speech
- (D) To host a birthday party

81. Why does the speaker say, "This shouldn't be any different than usual"?
- (A) To stress the importance of a meeting
- **(B) To reassure employees about an event***
- (C) To inform of the mayor's special request
- (D) To guess the duration of an inspection

78. 説話者説參觀行程的什麼部分改變了？
- (A) 導覽人員的數量。
- (B) 戶外的地點。
- (C) 票價。
- **(D) 地點的順序。**

79. 説話者提供什麼給聽眾？
- **(A) 限時折扣。**
- (B) 動手玩工作坊。
- (C) 免費會員資格。
- (D) 工廠的地圖。

女　在我們結束會議之前，我要利用這個時間通知各位一個重要活動。我剛剛發現，⁸⁰ **本市的市長下星期三會來我們餐廳慶祝連任。** 你們都知道，市長常來這裡用餐，他已經要求晚上六點保留他的老位子十位。這次應該和平常沒兩樣，⁸¹ **不必緊張。** 不過，我想確認新的菜單可以在這個星期內完成。我也要發放新的員工制服，以確保我們呈現最好的一面。⁸² **請在今天下班前，在這張紙上寫下你的衣服尺寸。**

80. 市長為何要造訪這家餐廳？
- **(A) 為了舉行慶祝會。**
- (B) 為了進行檢查。
- (C) 為了發表演説。
- (D) 為了主持生日派對。

81. 説話者為何説「這次應該和平常沒兩樣」？
- (A) 為了強調會議的重要性。
- **(B) 為了消除員工對活動的擔憂。**
- (C) 為了告知市長的特殊要求。
- (D) 為了推測檢查持續的時間。

04

82. What must listeners do before the end of the day?

(A) Check an updated schedule

(B) Fill out some information*

(C) Purchase some new clothing

(D) Print some new menus

82. 今天下班前，聽眾必須做何事？

(A) 檢查更新的時程表。

(B) 填寫一些資料。

(C) 購買一些新衣服。

(D) 列印一些新菜單。

Questions 83–85 電話留言

M Hi Jennifer. This is Timothy from Renton & Sons. **83 I'm calling in regards to the online order you submitted for laminate floor panels in white oak for your new office space.** I just want to double-check that your order is correct, because . . . well . . . ten thousand units is a bit excessive. **84 Even the biggest office spaces do not require more than five thousand units** because **85 our laminate panels are quite wide.** Please contact me by Friday to confirm your order. Thank you.

男 嗨，珍妮佛，我是連頓父子公司的提摩西。**83** 我打電話來，是關於您為了新辦公室，在線上訂購超耐磨白橡木地板一事。我只是想再次確認您的訂單沒錯，因為，呃，一萬片有點多。**84** 就連最大的辦公空間，最多也就需要五千片，因為 **85** 我們的超耐磨地板還蠻大片的。請在星期五之前與我聯絡，確認您的訂單。謝謝您。

83. What does Renton & Sons produce?

(A) Office furniture

(B) Flooring*

(C) Appliances

(D) Windows

83. 連頓父子公司生產什麼？

(A) 辦公室家具。

(B) 地板。

(C) 家用電器。

(D) 窗戶。

84. What does the man imply when he says, "ten thousand units is a bit excessive"?

(A) The customer's order may be wrong.*

(B) He will have to hire additional workers.

(C) The customer has canceled her order.

(D) He will deliver some materials late.

84. 當男子說「一萬片有點多」時，意指什麼？

(A) 顧客的訂單也許有錯。

(B) 他必須另外雇用工人。

(C) 顧客已經取消她的訂單。

(D) 有些材料，他會晚點送。

85. What does the man explain about his products?

(A) They are easy to clean.

(B) They are cheaper in summer.

(C) They are of high quality.

(D) They are large in size.*

85. 男子對他的產品做了什麼說明？

(A) 它們很容易清潔。

(B) 夏季比較便宜。

(C) 它們的品質很好。

(D) 它們的尺寸很大。

W　I'd like to take this time to say a few words about our fall internship program. Like last year, we've decided to recruit some of the highest achieving students from computer programming schools across the country. Over the next six months, [86] **these students will be helping us develop several new software programs** for public purchase. Like last year, one intern will be assigned to each team; however, I'd like to try something different this year. [87] **Instead of a single end of term intern assessment, I'd like team leaders to provide me with monthly progress reports.** [88] **This will help my colleagues and I make decisions about who will be offered permanent positions at the company.**

女　我想利用這個時間，談一下我們秋天的實習生計畫。就像去年一樣，我們決定從全國各地的電腦程式設計學院，招收一些表現最好的學生。接下來半年，[86] 這些學生會協助我們開發數個要公開販售的新軟體。像去年一樣，每個小組會指派一個實習生。不過，我今年想嘗試不一樣的做法。[87] 我不要實習結束時的單一評估報告，我想要小組長每個月交進度報告給我。[88] 這可以幫助我和同事決定，誰能得到公司的正職工作。

86. Where does the speaker most likely work?
　(A) At an employment agency
　(B) At a computer store
　(C) At a university
　(D) At a software company*

86. 說話者最可能在哪裡工作？
　(A) 在職業介紹所。
　(B) 在電腦商店。
　(C) 在大學。
　(D) 在軟體公司。

87. What change to the internship program does the speaker mention?
　(A) Employees will submit regular reports.*
　(B) Interns will be paid for their work.
　(C) Fewer students will be selected.
　(D) The program length will be extended.

87. 說話者提及實習生計畫有什麼改變？
　(A) 員工要定期提出報告。
　(B) 實習生的工作有酬勞。
　(C) 較少學生會獲選。
　(D) 計畫的時間要延長。

88. What is the purpose of the change?
　(A) To ensure interns follow all the rules
　(B) To make job candidate selection easier*
　(C) To provide team leaders with incentives
　(D) To allow managers to apply for funding

88. 改變的目的為何？
　(A) 為了確保實習生遵守所有規定。
　(B) 為了更容易挑選應徵者。
　(C) 為了提供小組長獎勵。
　(D) 為了讓經理申請資助。

M	Before we finish up, I'd like to announce a change in shipping procedures. **89 Starting next month, we will be offering free shipping to customers** who purchase products from our premium skincare line. As you know, interest in our premium line has grown significantly over the last year, but **90 many customers have complained about the high prices in addition to the cost of shipping.** To help offset product costs and encourage more purchases, we will offer shipping free of charge. **91 I have a meeting set up with Parcel Plus Shipping next week to finalize a deal** that will make shipping affordable for us.	男	在我們結束之前，我想宣布一項運送程序的變動。**89 從下個月開始，凡購買我們精選護膚產品的顧客，我們將提供免運費服務。** 你們都知道，對我們的高階產品感興趣的人，去年大幅增加，但是，**90 除了運費之外，很多顧客也抱怨定價太高。** 為了有助降低產品費用並促進消費，我們將提供免費送貨到府。**91 我下星期安排了和郵佳貨運公司的會議，確定我們能負擔的運費，以達成交易。**

89. According to the speaker, what service will the company begin offering next month?
(A) Discounted products
(B) Free shipping*
(C) Cheap memberships
(D) Complimentary samples

89. 根據說話者所述，公司下個月開始提供什麼服務？
(A) 折扣商品。
(B) 免運費。
(C) 收費低廉的會員資格。
(D) 免費贈送樣品。

90. Why has the company decided to add the new service?
(A) An advertisement failed.
(B) Business has dropped.
(C) Competition has increased.
(D) Some customers complained.*

90. 公司為何決定增加新服務？
(A) 廣告無效。
(B) 業績下滑。
(C) 競爭增加。
(D) 有些顧客抱怨。

91. What does the speaker say he will do next week?
(A) Conclude an important deal*
(B) Test a skincare product
(C) Update an online store
(D) Deliver some products himself

91. 說話者說，他下星期要做何事？
(A) 議定一筆重要的交易。
(B) 測試一項護膚產品。
(C) 升級線上商店。
(D) 親自運送一些產品。

W　Rebecca Strauss here, reporting for Channel 6 news. ⁹² **I'm standing just outside Smithview Mall, which is celebrating its grand opening.** Visitors are already lining up. ⁹³ **Everybody in town wants to shop in Smithview's two hundred brand new stores.** To celebrate its opening, all Smithview stores are having their own special sales. You can expect to receive as much as 30% off in some stores. Additionally, ⁹⁴ **the food court will be giving away free $5 vouchers** that can be used at any of the forty restaurants and coffee shops located within the mall. Come on down to Smithview Mall to take advantage of these great discounts.

女　我是第 6 台新聞記者蕾貝卡・史特勞斯，⁹² 我現在就在史密斯維購物中心外面，此刻正在慶祝盛大開幕。顧客已經在排隊了。⁹³ 鎮上的每個人都想逛逛史密斯維裡的兩百間全新商店。為了慶祝開幕，史密斯維的所有商店都推出自己的特賣活動。你可以預期有些商店會打到七折之多。此外，⁹⁴ **美食廣場將發送免費五元餐券**，購物中心內的 40 家餐廳和咖啡館都可使用。快來史密斯維購物中心，享受這些大優惠。

92. What type of business is being discussed?
(A) An electronics market
(B) A restaurant chain
(C) A shopping center*
(D) A coffee shop

92. 談話討論的是什麼型態的企業？
(A) 電器市集。
(B) 連鎖餐廳。
(C) 購物中心。
(D) 咖啡館。

93. Why does the speaker say, "Visitors are already lining up"?
(A) To emphasize interest in an event*
(B) To encourage listeners to stay home
(C) To discuss the size of a location
(D) To express concern about crowdedness

93. 說話者為何說「顧客已經在排隊了」？
(A) 為了強調對一項活動的興趣。
(B) 為了鼓勵聽眾留在家裡。
(C) 為了討論某個地區的面積大小。
(D) 為了表達對擁擠人群的擔憂。

94. What will customers receive if they visit the food court?
(A) A free beverage
(B) A 30% refund
(C) A discount coupon*
(D) A parking pass

94. 如果顧客去美食廣場，他們會得到什麼？
(A) 免費飲料。
(B) 30% 的退款。
(C) 折扣優待券。
(D) 停車通行證。

Schedule: *Thursday, March, 2nd*	
Time	**Event**
10:30 A.M.–11:30 A.M.	*Conference Call*
12:00 P.M.–1:20 P.M.	*Lunch Meeting*
1:30 P.M.–3:00 P.M.	*Staff Meeting*
4:00 P.M.–6:00 P.M.	*Meeting at ARF Technology*

時程表：**3 月 2 日**，**星期四**	
時間	**活動**
上午 10 點 30 分到 11 點 30 分	電話會議
中午 12 點到下午 1 點 20 分	午餐會議
下午 1 點 30 分到 3 點	員工會議
下午 4 點到 6 點	赴 ARF 科技開會

W Hello, Beth. This is Jennifer. I was really excited to hear that our two departments are going to be merging. I think it will really improve our efficiency if we're all on the same team. Since [95] **the merger will be taking place next week,** [96] **I thought it would be good to introduce both teams to each other.** [97] **I know you have a staff meeting this afternoon. How about I bring my team to your meeting and we can do a short introduction then?** I know you have to leave to visit a client right after, so let's keep the introductions short. Call me back and let me know what you think.

女 哈囉，貝絲。我是珍妮佛。聽到我們兩個部門要合併，我真的很興奮。如果我們都在同一個團隊，我想這確實會改善我們的效率。由於 [95] **下星期就要進行合併**，[96] **我認為介紹兩個團隊彼此認識會很有幫助。** [97] **我知道妳今天下午要開員工會議。我把我的團隊帶去妳的會議，然後，我們可以簡短介紹一下彼此，妳覺得如何？** 我知道，會議一結束妳就要去拜訪客戶，所以簡短介紹一下就好。再回我電話，讓我知道妳的想法。

95. What is planned for the next week?
(A) **A bigger team will be created.*
(B) A new product will be launched.
(C) Some managers will retire.
(D) Some meetings will be canceled.

96. Why does the speaker want to meet?
(A) To visit a client's store
(B) To go over some regulations
(C) **To introduce some employees***
(D) To explain a new contract

97. Look at the graphic. What time does the speaker want to meet?
(A) At 10:30
(B) At 12:00
(C) **At 1:30 ***
(D) At 4:00

95. 下星期規劃了何事？
(A) **將會產生一個較大的團隊。**
(B) 將發表一款新產品。
(C) 有幾位經理要退休。
(D) 有幾場會議要取消。

96. 說話者為何想要碰面？
(A) 為了拜訪客戶的商店。
(B) 為了審查一些規章。
(C) **為了介紹一些員工。**
(D) 為了解釋一份新合約。

97. 請見圖表。說話者想要什麼時間碰面？
(A) 10 點 30 分。
(B) 12 點。
(C) **1 點 30 分。**
(D) 4 點。

Questions 98–100 談話及地圖

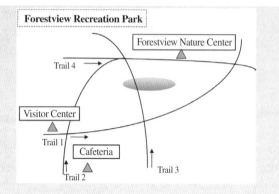

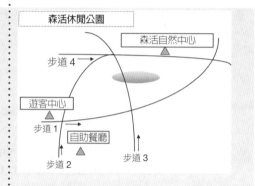

M **98 Welcome to Forestview Recreation Park.** We're happy that you chose Forestview for all your outdoor recreation needs. Today, we'll be offering some guided tours of our park. Please take a look at this map. We'll start on Trail 2 where a large chipmunk population lives. You can purchase peanuts to feed the chipmunks for this portion of the tour. From there, we'll travel on the remaining trails along the boardwalks and through the marsh. However, **99 this trail is currently off limits due to the construction taking place on our new nature center. 100 Once the center is complete, you'll be able to partake in our new Nature Education Program.** But for now, the construction area is too dangerous to visit.

男 **98 歡迎來到森活休閒公園。**很高興你們選擇森活，來滿足所有的戶外休閒需求。今天，我們會提供園區的導覽。請看一下這份地圖。我們會從步道 2 開始，那裡住著一大群花栗鼠。在這段行程，你們可以買花生餵花栗鼠。從那裡，我們會沿著木棧道，走完其他的步道並穿過沼澤。不過，**99 由於新的自然中心正在興建中，這條步道目前禁止進入。100 一旦中心完工後，你們就可以參加我們新的自然教育計畫。**但現在，工程區非常危險，無法參觀。

98. Who is the talk intended for?
(A) Park employees
(B) Botany students
(C) Construction workers
(D) Visitors at a park*

98. 這段話的對象是誰？
(A) 公園的員工。
(B) 植物學的學生。
(C) 營造工人。
(D) 公園的遊客。

99. Look at the graphic. Which trail is closed to visitors?
(A) Trail 1
(B) Trail 2
(C) Trail 3
(D) Trail 4*

99. 請見圖表。哪一條步道禁止遊客進入？
(A) 步道 1。
(B) 步道 2。
(C) 步道 3。
(D) 步道 4。

100. What project is the park developing?
(A) A bird-watching club
(B) A research foundation
(C) A study on chipmunks
(D) An educational program*

100. 公園正在進行什麼計畫？
(A) 賞鳥俱樂部。
(B) 研究基金會。
(C) 花栗鼠研究。
(D) 教育計畫。

101. 聘僱關係一終止，所有的員工都會拿到**推薦**函及遣散費。

102. 史蒂文斯先生**在**「文具與紙的世界」為公司挑了一些新用品。

103. 需要**有人**盡快來修影印機。

104. 公司的新軟體設計成可**自動**更新至最新的版本。

105. 新政策訂定的目的是要遏止遲到及**提升**員工責任感。

106. 大多數的員工以「正向的工作**環境**」作為他們續留公司的理由。

107. 到了明年夏天，馬汀咖啡在加拿大各地**將擁有**超過 300 家店面。

108. 這個法律的通過是為了保護擁有並經營小型企業**的公民**。

109. 與新供應商的會議已經重新安排，**提早**在週三舉行。

110. 哈沃史塔克公司作為電信電纜供應商，已建立了快速客戶服務的**聲譽**。

111. 員工手冊**簡要說明**了處理客訴的正確流程。

112. 藍道先生決定在休息室安裝新的自動販賣機，**供**大家使用。

113. 史密斯國際貿易公司的部門主管**定期**進行員工滿意度調查。

114. 顧問公司**提出**幾個異動程序的**建議**，以改善貨運公司的效率。

115. 志工的主要職責，就是協助遊客在展覽廳裡**找到**路。

116. 請保留本電子郵件，作為您款項資料已輸入本公司系統的**確認**依據。

117. 德拉果女士大約十年前就開始在這家銀行服務，**自此**一直擔任副經理的職位。

118. 巴恩斯先生正在嘗試取得一些**必要的**推薦函，以取得醫院的職務。

119. 在市區內進行營建工程的**法規**全都條列在市府的許可網頁上。

120. 在奧斯丁科技大學所進行的**研究**被認為是全國最先進的。

121. 柯文頓冰淇淋將最近銷售量的激增歸因於推出新口味，**而不是**廣告活動之故。

122. 在進行客戶滿意度調查後，華倫斯豪華禮車公司的服務**顯著地**改善了。

123. 這些電腦保留給那些在倫敦市中心**尋找**就業機會的人使用。

124. 請確認您已經**正確地**填寫所有資料，因為一個錯誤就可能導致手續的長期延誤。

125. 朱恩‧奧斯丁以前雇員的**角度**來書寫，因此她那篇有關 THP 電廠擴建計畫的文章相當獨特。

126. 人力資源部的職員能夠在不需部門主管的介入下，解決**他們**之間的問題。

127. 布朗先生**熟知**跨國企業政策，所以我們最好向他詢問。

128. 保單持有人**一**收到損壞修復帳單，**就**必須提出車險的索賠。

129. 艾德蘭鎮擁有漂亮的海灘和豐富的各類藝廊，是相當**棒的**景點。

130. 行銷部門安排了週會的舉行，以確保大家在新專案上**全力以赴**。

Questions 131–134 資訊

長假

所有在星辰包裝公司服務至少兩年以上的員工，都符合多休五天暑假的資格。同仁可填寫申請表，並繳回給主管。部門主管將負責審查這些申請表。符合資格的人選名單將投入抽獎系統中。在公司服務滿五年或五年以上者將給予優先考量。系統將抽出最多 15 個名額。

131. (A) 顯著的
(B) 合作的
(C) 獨家的
(D) 有資格做……的

132. **(A) 同仁可填寫申請表，並繳回給主管。**
(B) 舉例來說，所有長期員工將獲得額外的福利待遇。
(C) 但是，少數有功同仁才會獲得績優加薪。
(D) 管理部門很高興地宣布已經聘僱了新同仁。

133. **(A) 人選；候選者**
(B) 受獎者
(C) 供應商
(D) 居住者

134. (A) 更喜歡
(B) 更合意的
(C) 優先權
(D) 優惠的

Questions 135–138 通知

第八新聞頻道 60 歲了！

全市首要的新聞來源，第八新聞頻道將於 3 月 15 慶祝成立 60 週年紀念。這是電視公司與現場轉播節目的第 60 年。超過半世紀以來，第八新聞頻道為觀眾們提供了即時新聞報導、見解深刻的評論以及來自全市及各地的精采人文故事。我們想邀請身為忠實觀眾的您參加我們的慶祝活動。

3 月 15 日當天下午 4:30 至 6:30，我們將開放金斯利街的攝影棚供民眾參觀。來參加攝影棚導覽，第一線目睹幕後狀況，參觀我們最先進播放設備的操作示範。您甚至還有機會見到我們的新聞主播，並與他們對談。活動完全免費，但需登記報名。我們希望能在這個特別的時刻見到大家。

135. (A) 演唱會
(B) 討論
(C) (電視、廣播) 轉播
(D) 教學

136. (A) 提供
(B) 提供
(C) 將會提供
(D) 提供了

137. (A) 這個電視台在未來幾年，仍然會是全市重要的一份子。
(B) 您甚至還有機會見到我們的新聞主播，並與他們對談。
(C) 這個慶祝活動會是三月所舉辦的第三場。
(D) 第八新聞頻道在將來幾個月內將被一間全國新聞網收購。

138. **(A) 特別的**
(B) 專攻
(C) 尤其是
(D) 專門化

Questions 139–142 資訊

這通知是要提醒雅契府的住戶們，若要進行任何住家外圍整修必須先取得許可。屋內整修目前不需許可，但是所有外圍工程，不論大小，必須事先獲得批准。

過去，部分住戶認為承包商必須負責申請許可。這個普遍認定的想法其實是錯的。事實上，資產所有人必須自行取得必要的許可。建物檢查員將隨時走訪施工處，如果資產所有人未持許可，將處以罰款。

建物檢查員重要的職責就是執行許可法規。這個許可申請程序可確保施工整修符合所有必要的安全標準，進而保護整個社區免於房舍毀損及危險的隱憂。

欲察看各工程適用之許可清單，請上 renviewtown.com/permits 查詢。

139. (A) 即是，那就是
(B) 同樣地
(C) 因此
(D) 然而

140. (A) 承包商可因超時而加價。
(B) 這個普遍認定的想法其實是錯的。
(C) 大多數的建物檢查員也是承包商。
(D) 工程的費用可能隨季節調漲。

141. (A) 質疑
(B) 排除
(C) 執行
(D) 審閱

142. (A) 符合
(B) 符合
(C) 符合
(D) 已符合

Questions 143–146 網頁

星辰信用卡消費點數

星辰信用卡欲提供信用卡持卡人全球範圍最廣的集點專案。您使用星辰信用卡所進行的每一筆消費，最高可賺進 100 點。會員在 200 家特選商店中的任何一家購物，甚至可以得到雙倍點數。點數可於這 200 家商店中兌換成禮品卡。此外，點數還可用於 www.travelone.com 預訂班機、飯店房間及租車。欲申請星辰集點專案，只要填寫以下表格，並點擊「送出」即可。

143. (A) 理解
(B) 最全面的
(C) 全面的
(D) 最全面地

144. (A) 您使用星辰信用卡所進行的每一筆消費，最高可賺進 100 點。
(B) 點數僅可用於降低信用卡消費的月利率。
(C) 專案會員必須在以前從未申請過星辰信用卡。
(D) 此外，專案會員的所有消費均可享店內優惠折扣。

145. (A) 挑選
(B) 挑選
(C) 被挑選的
(D) 選集

146. (A) 因此
(B) 無論如何
(C) 此外
(D) 舉例來説

PART 7 P. 36–55

Questions 147–148 網站

http://www.premiuminsurance.com

| 首頁 | 保險單 | 我的帳戶 | 登出 |

湯姆·施瓦茲，歡迎回來！現在，**147 您可以使用優質保險公司的新網頁輕鬆地取得所有保單資料**。請用一點時間熟悉本網頁的特點。

- 更多付款方式及所有款項的線上收據

- **148(C) 在同一個地方就可輕鬆取得您所有的保單資料**

- **148(D) 升級的安全措施**及定時登出以保護您的機密資料

- **148(B) 全新客服工具**，像是最新的常見問答與即時客服通訊功能

- 簡單的線上表格，可更新地址與聯絡電話資料

147. 施瓦茲先生最有可能是誰？
(A) 保險業務員
(B) 保險客戶
(C) 網頁設計師
(D) 理賠專員

148. 下列何者不是文中所提到的新網頁特點？

(A) 團體保險的申請
(B) 新客服工具
(C) 整合的資料
(D) 加強的網路安全性

Questions 149–151 資訊

富裕製藥

曼努爾·羅德里格斯
首席研究員

羅德里格斯先生是現今製藥產業廣受歡迎的領導者，在過去的五年來一直督導富裕製藥所有主要的研究計畫。羅德里格斯先生在七年前加入富裕製藥，很快就以其優秀的才能與遠見獲得讚賞。**[149] 他被拔擢為首席研究員，[150(C)] 從此還大大地提高了20%以上的員工產能。**

[150(D)] 羅德里格斯先生已經受邀在多場的會議中演說，並於去年的藥理願景會議上榮任主講人。[150(A)] 他也擔任泰創大學醫學系的顧問，為許多學術計畫提供意見。在加入富裕製藥前，**[150(B)] 羅德里格斯先生移居自墨西哥，**於斯特拉福特大學求學，並在那以優等成績畢業。

149. 這份資料的目的是什麼？
(A) 概述一個大學課程
(B) 宣布員工升遷
(C) 介紹公司員工
(D) 慶祝員工退休

150. 關於羅德里格斯先生，沒有提到什麼事？
(A) 他受僱為大學教授。
(B) 他之前住在墨西哥。
(C) 他增進了員工績效。
(D) 他是位經驗豐富的演說者。

151. 關於羅德里格斯先生的職涯，文中提及了什麼？
(A) 他常因優異的職業道德而獲獎。
(B) 他在應徵工作前完成了兩個學位。
(C) 他在受聘為首席研究員之前擔任實習生。
(D) 他一開始並非以首席研究員身分受僱。

Questions 152–154 文章

3月7日一本地市長辦公室剛公布了給帕克縣學生的「嶄露未來實習計畫」的細節。**[152(C)(D)] 由專案主任米莉·安德魯斯所主導，這個計畫設計的目的就是為了提供高中學生從事公職的體驗。**

[152(B)] 史蒂芬·格林霍恩市長去年就發表了這個實習計畫。「我認為將青少年納入公共事務是很重要的。」他在一場訪談中說，**[153]**「這有助於他們決定想在大學進行的研究課程。」

[152(B)] 根據新公布的細節，米莉·安德魯斯將自全縣15所學校中挑選出15位學生。根據他們的興趣，獲選的學生將分配至市中心市長辦公室中擔任各種職務。這個計畫將於暑假期間持續進行八週。

本計畫的申請表於下週一開始即放在市長網站上。我們鼓勵學生事先準備至少一封的推薦函，將於五月初宣布獲選的實習生。

152. 關於「嶄露未來實習計畫」，提到了什麼事？
(A) 全國適用。
(B) 是全新的計畫。
(C) 提供給大學生。
(D) 由史蒂芬·格林霍恩主導。

153. 根據格林霍恩先生所言，這個實習計畫的主要目標是什麼？
(A) 教導學生有關選舉的事宜
(B) 建立志工社群
(C) 提供學生待遇優渥的工作
(D) 在學生未來的教育中引導他們

154. 下列句子最適合出現在 [1]、[2]、[3]、[4] 的哪個位置中？
「我們鼓勵學生事先準備至少一封的推薦函。」
(A) [1]
(B) [2]
(C) [3]
(D) [4]

Questions 155–156 網頁

嚮往無限公司

做為本公司客戶，您

- 可獲得日夜不斷的監控
- 支付合理月費，不需額外費用
- 能改善貴公司的保全需求

本公司提供

- [155] 監視攝影器材的客製化安裝
- 所有攝影機與警報系統的定期保養
- [155] 24 小時遠端監控貴公司
- [156] 所有入口的指紋掃描技術（需支付額外費用）
- 可使用嚮往公司網站，處理所有帳單

---

155. 下列何者是「嚮往無限公司」所提供的服務之一？
(A) 清理辦公室
(B) 監視攝影機的監視
(C) 網頁開發
(D) 暖氣系統維修

156. 文中提到何者與指紋掃描技術有關的事？
(A) 以每週支付方式購買。
(B) 嚮往公司獨特的服務之一。
(C) 可以額外費用購買。
(D) 可以電話告知方式加入帳戶中。

Questions 157–158 文章

胭脂鎮 3 月 3 日—胭脂鎮官員最近宣布了 [158(B)] **一個 4,000 公頃胭脂湖濱水區的遊樂園開發企劃案。**

[158(A)(C)] 這個新遊樂園預計有多座雲霄飛車、一座大型水族館、親水公園以及供現場音樂演奏的涼亭。數間當地商家，像是扶輪汽車，鬆餅屋餐館和小牛飲料都同意贊助遊樂園的開發。

---

[157] 在開發案宣布後，幾位當地激進分子對遊樂園的興建表達了關切，他們認為遊樂園會對濱水區脆弱的生態系統造成影響。「我們向大家保證將採取所有的預防措施。」開發負責人珍·佛德曼昨天在一場訪談中說，「這座遊樂園會與海灘及自行車道保持足夠的距離，所以對周遭野生動植物造成的影響極微。」

胭脂鎮其他居民，則對新遊樂園即將為胭脂湖區所帶來的潛在商機利益，表達了興奮之意。

---

157. 文中提到什麼與胭脂鎮有關的事？
(A) 目前有大規模的觀光產業。
(B) 是知名親水公園所在地。
(C) 部分居民反對該開發計畫。
(D) 大多數的當地野生動植物正瀕臨絕種。

158. 下列何者不是文中所提到的遊樂園特點？
(A) 大規模水族館
(B) 位於濱水區
(C) 有現場表演的場地
(D) 禮品店與售貨亭

Questions 159–161 資訊

維修服務

[159] 費爾斯維公寓大樓的維修部，專為您的公寓及所有公共空間提供定期修繕服務，大部分的服務可免費提供給住戶。以下的服務將不收取任何費用，但必須提早兩週預約。

- 浴室設備，像是蓮蓬頭、水龍頭與馬桶零件每兩年可更換一次。[160] **任何毀損零件每年可免費修理一次。**

- 門窗，包括紗窗，需要時，隨時可修理。

- 爐子上方的風扇濾網及煙霧偵測器每六個月可更換一次。冷氣機每年可享免費清理一次。

- 欲知完整服務清單，請參考網頁。[161] **預約可於網站 www.fairsviewcondos.com/maintenance 填寫申請表即可。**

159. 這則資訊最有可能是給誰看的？

   (A) 房地產仲介

   (B) 大樓管理公司的員工

   (C) 養老院的房東

   (D) 公寓大樓的住戶

160. 浴室的設備可多久免費修理一次？

   (A) 一個月一次

   (B) 每六個月一次

   (C) 一年一次

   (D) 隨時

161. 根據這則資訊，讀者要如何安排修繕事宜？

   (A) 填寫線上表格

   (B) 打電話給部門

   (C) 告訴房東

   (D) 在表單上簽名

Questions 162–163 簡訊

榮恩・帕克斯 [8:03]
吉姆，珍妮佛要我修改明天的簡報，可以請你幫我一下嗎？

吉姆・韋伯 [8:05]
當然。你需要什麼？

榮恩・帕克斯 [8:07]
[163] 我可以用電子郵件把新企畫案寄給你嗎？我已經把修改處用紅色標示出來了，但是 [162] 我不確定這些是否能呈現我們所有的廣告服務。

吉姆・韋伯 [8:08]
恐怕不行。[163] 我正要出門和客戶吃晚餐。那結束後，我到飯店找你好嗎？

榮恩・帕克斯 [8:09]
可以喔。那我剛好可以把已經做好的投影片簡報一起給你看。

吉姆・韋伯 [8:10]
好，那太好了。你的房號是？

榮恩・帕克斯 [8:10]
506 號房。到時候見！

162. 帕克斯先生最有可能是誰？

   (A) 廣告商

   (B) 飯店接待員

   (C) 藝術收藏家

   (D) 資訊科技專家

163. 在 8:08 時，韋伯先生說的「恐怕不行」是什麼意思？

   (A) 他擔心簡報。

   (B) 他沒有時間審視文件。

   (C) 他不認同一些修改。

   (D) 他沒有要求做修改。

Questions 164–167 電子郵件

收件者：staceymarshall@pressassociated.com
寄件者：htrander@themaxfestival.com
主旨：麥克斯夏日音樂祭
日期：6 月 5 日
附件：2-070406.pdf

親愛的馬歇爾女士，

[164, 167] 麥克斯夏日音樂季很高興您願意報導即將於大公園舉辦的三天音樂祭活動。這是我們的第一場音樂祭，我們安排了許多樂團。大公園可容納近 25,000 名遊客。我們希望在這三天中能達到全滿狀況。我已為您保留一張入場券，並 [165] 附上後臺全場通行證。您可以在抵達時於售票亭領取。

出入口將於 7 月 4 日下午一點開放，而 [166] 音樂祭將以 7 月 6 日晚間十點的煙火秀畫下句點。您可以隨意自由參加這三天的活動。您的媒體通行證可以讓您採訪任何樂團以及表演者。至於完整的表演者與演出時間表，可至我們的網站查詢並下載。最後，如果您在採訪期間有任何需要，都可以聯絡媒體服務處的莫莉，電話是 776-3333-6713。感謝您，希望您會喜歡麥克斯夏日音樂祭。

活動媒體統籌
哈利・崔德 敬上

164. 馬歇爾女士最有可能是誰？

(A) 顧客

(B) 記者

(C) 樂團經理

(D) 表演者

165. 這封電子郵件中還附上了什麼？

(A) 入場券

(B) 停車券

(C) 表演時間表

(D) 後臺全場通行證

166. 根據這封電子郵件，這個音樂祭顯著的特色是什麼？

(A) 可容納超過 25,000 人。

(B) 將包括爵士舞表演。

(C) 將以特殊煙火表演作為結束。

(D) 包含免費露營服務。

167. 下列句子最適合出現在 [1]、[2]、[3]、[4] 的哪個位置中？

「這是我們的第一場音樂祭，我們安排了許多樂團。」

(A) [1]

(B) [2]

(C) [3]

(D) [4]

Questions 168–171 線上聊天

潔西卡・賽門 [上午 10:32]
馬可仕，你有空嗎？ **168 我試著要進入我們的網路商店，但它無法載入。** 你的電腦可以載入嗎？

馬可仕・亞當斯 [上午 10:40]
我也一樣。昨天就這樣了嗎？

潔西卡・賽門 [上午 10:42]
我不這麼認為。我這裡有幾張昨天在網路下的訂單。不過 **168, 169 我收到一位老顧客的電子郵件，說我們的網頁當機了。** 你可以向資訊科技部詢問一下嗎？

傑夫・彼得斯加入聊天。

馬可仕・亞當斯 [上午 10:44]
傑夫，我們的網路商店有問題，好像無法載入。你可以弄清楚是怎麼回事嗎？

傑夫・彼得斯 [上午 10:48]
這就怪了。看起來好像是網路寄存網站當機了。

馬可仕・亞當斯 [上午 10:50]
你有他們的電話嗎？

傑夫・彼得斯 [上午 10:55]
170 有，我剛打電話給他們了。 他們說他們碰到了一些技術上的問題，應該明天早上前就可以修好。

潔西卡・賽門 [上午 11:00]
好，**171 我一會兒要和業務主管開會，我會告訴他這個問題的。**

168. 賽門女士呈報了什麼問題？

(A) 目前無法在網路上販賣商品。

(B) 網路商店有錯誤訊息。

(C) 一個顧客想要退還一些商品。

(D) 有一項產品不會再列在網站上了。

169. 賽門女士從誰那得知這個問題？

(A) 部門主管

(B) 顧客

(C) 資訊科技部主管

(D) 助理

170. 在 10:50 時，當亞當斯先生寫道：「你有他們的電話嗎？」，他的意思是？

(A) 他要求一些資料。

(B) 他要彼得斯先生打電話給一家公司。

(C) 他想要更新名錄。

(D) 他擔心他會迷路。

171. 賽門女士接下來最有可能做什麼？

(A) 打電話給一些顧客

(B) 在網路上買東西

(C) 參加會議

(D) 聯絡網路寄存網站

Questions 172–175 文章

每週就業專欄
就業博覽會

就業博覽會是一種快速又簡單招聘新員工的方法。但是，舉辦就業博覽會可能是非常花錢的活動，尤其是如果您只打算招聘幾位員工而已。**172 將以下的建議列入考量，再決定舉辦就業博覽會是不是適合貴公司。**

您打算招聘多少員工？

173 如果貴公司打算招聘一大群員工，那就業博覽會就很適合您了。 就業博覽會可以吸引許多應徵者，但如果您只有意找幾位新員工，那就業博覽會的應徵者數量可能會讓貴公司的人力資源部應接不暇，反而使整個招聘過程變得更麻煩。

有沒有適合舉辦就業博覽會的場地？

高中和大學都是舉辦就業博覽會很受歡迎的場地，但如果貴公司找的是經驗豐富的應徵者，那學校可能就不是適合之處了。在一個能吸引到合適應徵者的場所而舉辦的就業博覽會是 **174 很重要的**，像是商務會議。但遺憾的是，商務會議只在每年的特定時間舉行。

175 您可以透過其他方式招聘員工嗎？

175 線上就業廣告網站 已經改變了人們找工作的方式。在貴公司的招募季之前，人力資源部的人員可以在數個網站上貼出職缺公告。這可引起許多關注，也讓貴公司列出應徵者所必須符合的資歷條件。

這筆花費值得嗎？

在舉辦就業博覽會前，考慮一下活動的花費。您可能需要租借一個合適的場地，還得提供茶點和申請資料。如果免費網站就可以符合您的招聘需求，那舉辦就業博覽會就不值得了。

172. 這篇文章是有關什麼？
(A) 增進員工生產力的要訣
(B) 用來聘僱員工的網站
(C) 增進錄取機會的方法
(D) 有效率又省錢的招募策略

173. 根據這篇文章，要舉辦就業博覽會的原因是什麼？
(A) 招聘專業員工
(B) 填補大量職缺
(C) 提供員工經驗
(D) 宣傳公司品牌

174. 第三段、第二行的「critical」與下列哪一個意思最接近？
(A) 緊急的
(B) 重要的
(C) 有創造力的
(D) 負面的

175. 下列何者是找到求職者的另一種方式？
(A) 在當地報紙上刊廣告
(B) 利用就業網站
(C) 在公司舉辦就業博覽會
(D) 寄出大量電子郵件

Questions 176–180 文章及電子郵件

176 出版人指導下一代

1 月 10 日—出版商兼編輯吉姆・法蘭克從去年退休以來，就接掌了西部大學的出版研究學系。法蘭克以他在麥克斯威爾出版社所擔任的角色聞名，他在那裡擔任許多專案的資深編輯，其中包括了幾部暢銷套書的出版。

吉姆・法蘭克以系主任及教授之姿加入西部大學。**177 他開發了一些新課程，像是數位出版**，網頁寫作和國際版權管理。有意在出版界擔任編輯、圖書設計師或作家經紀人的學生都從他的學識中獲益良多。

由於法蘭克的努力，西部大學也創立了有史以來第一個出版實習職。**179 學生們在三週的實習計畫中和編輯、設計師及經紀人相**

互搭配。除此之外，法蘭克還安排了許多活動，讓業界專家在大學中發表各種不同主題的演說。因為法蘭克的創新與人脈，西部大學的出版課程已成了全國最棒的一門相關課程。

寄件者：beth@ricorspublishing.com
收件者：jimfrank@westernuniversity.com
日期：2 月 25 日
主旨：數位出版專題小組

親愛的法蘭克先生，

[179] 瑪格莉特・史蒂文森目前正在瑞克斯出版社實習。她提到您正在為學生安排下個月的客座講者。**[178] 如果您還有缺額的話，我很樂意加入這個專題小組。**身為瑞克斯出版的數位出版主管，我確信我能夠提供一些該領域工作的重要資訊。

[180] 下週我將忙於參加海外會議，但您可以跟我的助理留言，我將於隔週回覆。我的電話是 443-223-0911 轉分機 3367。

期待收到您的回信。

瑞克斯出版社數位出版主管
貝斯・史密斯敬上

176. 這篇文章主要是在討論什麼？
(A) 一家公司的業務活動
(B) 一位編輯的職涯變化
(C) 一家出版商的新套書
(D) 一個學生實習計畫

177. 下列何者是吉姆・法蘭克對大學的貢獻之一？
(A) 學生可修到更多課程。
(B) 開發學生就業網站。
(C) 建立獎學金基金會。
(D) 最近開設一間電腦室。

178. 史密斯女士為何要寄這封電子郵件？
(A) 她要回覆一通電話留言。
(B) 她想參加演講活動。
(C) 她在找更多實習生。
(D) 她想報名課程。

179. 史蒂文森小姐最有可能是誰？
(A) 瑞克斯出版社的主管
(B) 西部大學的學生
(C) 出版課程的客座講者
(D) 麥克斯威爾出版社的前編輯

180. 史密斯女士提到什麼有關她行程的事？
(A) 她可以重新安排會議。
(B) 她三月沒有時間出席客座講師小組。
(C) 只能在白天聯絡到她。
(D) 她下週將出差，不在公司。

Questions 181–185 備忘錄及電子郵件

備忘錄
免費雲端服務

正如各位所知，羅斯電腦最近與 L&B 科技合作，**[181] 以改善本公司的電腦效率及檔案儲存。**為了讓儲存檔案與分享檔案更便利，我們計畫在公司所有系統上安裝 L&B 雲端軟體。

L&B 雲端軟體可讓員工儲存各種容量的檔案，而不會佔據太多電腦記憶體的空間。**[183] 員工可以輕鬆地在短時間內傳送大型檔案，而不用擔心緩慢的上載速度。**除此之外，帶著筆記型電腦出差的員工也能夠自遠端讀取資料。再者，L&B 雲端軟體相當安全，所以員工可以放心任何 **[182] 敏感性**檔案都會安全無虞。

欲使用新軟體，只要完成設定，以您在公司的電子信箱註冊，即可開始儲存與傳送檔案。**[185] 這個服務將於 4 月 30 日上午九點起生效。**如果您對於設定或使用這個新軟體有任何問題或疑慮，請撥打分機 3342 或寄電子郵件到 michaelbrown@rothcomputers.com 與資訊科技部的麥可・布朗聯絡。

收件者：michaelbrown@rothcomputers.com
寄件者：sandrabell@rothcomputers.com
日期：4 月 12 日
主旨：雲端軟體

親愛的布朗先生，

我試著打分機電話給您，但您沒有接電話。我寫信是想請求關於新 L&B 雲端軟體的協助。**[185] 我在服務生效的第一天就設定了帳戶，但今天我的帳號內卻找不到任何**

檔案。**[184] 我所上傳的檔案好像全都被刪除了，因為我的帳戶裡是空的。** 由於這些檔案內含上一季很重要的銷售數據，我真的需要馬上取得。您可以告訴我該如何回復這些檔案嗎？如果您今天有空到我辦公室的話就太好了。

珊卓・貝爾

181. 這個備忘錄的目的是什麼？
(A) 宣布政策的異動
(B) 提醒員工備份電腦檔案
(C) 提供新軟體的資訊
(D) 說明一套新規定

182. 備忘錄中，第二段、第五行的「sensitive」與下列哪一個意思最接近？
(A) 小心的
(B) 反應的
(C) 令人驚訝的
(D) 機密的

183. 下列何者是 L&B 雲端軟體的優點之一？
(A) 減少成本。
(B) 節省公司時間。
(C) 免費安裝。
(D) 可審視出文件中的錯誤。

184. 貝爾女士正遭遇什麼問題？
(A) 她忘記自己的密碼。
(B) 她的電腦當機了。
(C) 所有檔案不見了。
(D) 她無法進入伺服器。

185. 貝爾女士何時設定她的帳戶？
(A) 4 月 10 日
(B) 4 月 11 日
(C) 4 月 12 日
(D) 4 月 13 日

Questions 186–190 電子郵件及表單

寄件者：oemerson@sommerfield.com
收件者：mfernandez@rkdistribution.br
主旨：展示
日期：8 月 5 日

親愛的費南德茲女士，

我的班機已降落於聖保羅，我正從機場的候機室寫這封電子郵件給您。很不幸地，我所託運的大行李被弄丟了。雖然我已經將隨身行李中的所有樣品一覽表列印出來，但是 **[188] 展示的商品樣本都在遺失的行李中。** 機場員工告訴我，他們至少需要三天的時間才能找到行李，並送到我住的地方。那也表示，我來不及在安排於後天的展示會前拿到它們了。

一旦我到了飯店，**[186] 就把樣品一覽表傳真到貴公司。** 如果不是太麻煩的話，**[187] 是不是可以將展示會延後兩天？** 請盡快與我聯絡。

奧斯卡・艾默生 敬上

行李遺失單

我們要為本公司不當處理您的物品，因而造成的不便表達最深的歉意。以下您所提供的資料將提供我們莫大的協助。請詳細描述每一件行李的外觀，以及行李內所有物品的清單，這將有助於 **[189] 加速**整個處理流程。

申請編號 3415673S/3

旅客姓名 奧斯卡・艾默生

電子信箱 oemerson@sommerfield.com

永久地址：美國俄亥俄州克里夫蘭市 44103 傑克森巷 409 號

暫時地址（至 8 月 12 日止）：01310-060 **[190] 巴西聖保羅**保利斯塔大道 1209 號 皮基里飯店

航班號碼	日期	起點	終點
MTC971	8 月 3 日	托雷多	布宜諾斯艾利斯
BTA302	8 月 5 日	布宜諾斯艾利斯	聖保羅

行李箱類型
大型皮革包，附拉鍊、肩帶

製造商　里格斯

顏色　棕色

內容物（請盡可能詳述）：

說明	數量
[188] 慢跑鞋、網球鞋、高爾夫球鞋、棒球鞋、高筒籃球鞋	12 雙
頂槍牌男士西裝	2
灰谷牌數位相機及充電器	1
長褲、短褲、襪子等	6
南美旅遊口袋指南手冊	2

寄件者：airportlostfoundoffice@spinternat.com

收件者：oemerson@sommerfield.com

主旨：341567S/3 申請

日期：8 月 6 日

親愛的艾默生先生，

我們很高興通知您，您所遺失的行李以及列舉的所有物品都已經找到了。將於 8 月 7 日下午一點至三點之間 [190] 送抵您所提供的暫時地址。

我們誠摯地感謝您的耐心等候與體諒。

聖保羅國際機場失物招領處 敬上

186. 關於樣品一覽表，艾默生先生提及了什麼事？

 (A) 將以傳真寄送。

 (B) 還沒寫好。

 (C) 比預期的要長。

 (D) 需要列印出來。

187. 艾默生先生要求費南德茲女士做什麼？

 (A) 遞送商品樣本

 (B) 送交訂單

 (C) 重新安排會議

 (D) 送他去飯店

188. 艾默生先生要展示的是什麼？

 (A) 腳踏車輪胎

 (B) 運動鞋

 (C) 影像軟體

 (D) 咖啡機

189. 表格中，第一段、第四行的「expedite」與下列哪一個意思最接近？

 (A) 發現

 (B) 修改

 (C) 詳述

 (D) 加快

190. 貨運要送到哪裡？

 (A) 克里夫蘭

 (B) 托雷多

 (C) 聖保羅

 (D) 布宜諾斯艾利斯

Questions 191–195 電子郵件、網頁及文章

收件者：傑若米・伯恩斯

寄件者：克莉絲汀・琳姆

日期：[195] 6 月 5 日

主旨：縫紉機

親愛的傑若米，

我剛收到您的電子郵件。我同意您的看法，我們應該考慮為服裝設計工作室添購新縫紉機。[195] 既然我們的事業剛起步，[193] 能買到堅固耐用，好清理又價格合理的機器應該是很棒的。因為我們每天都會使用縫紉機，具良好保固也是很重要的。頂尖評論 Topreviews.com 上有很多資訊，有助於我們挑選型號。您何不看一下網頁，再告訴我您認為哪一個型號符合我們的需求？

感恩

克莉絲汀

https://www.topreviews.com

類別：縫紉機

頂尖評論測試了四款適合家庭與商用的高檔縫紉機：

★★★★ 縫製大師 445 是 [193] 一款耐用，易清理的機器，具多種縫紉設定，適合縫紉各種不同布料。對部分家庭來說，機身可能太大，卻相當適合商業使用。[192, 193] 價格合理，還 [193] 附有五年保固。

★★★★設計系列 3019 是一款小巧，可攜式機器。適合作為行動式縫紉機。能縫製大多數車線款式，本機器以非常耐用的塑料製成。**[192] 價格合理，但無保固。**

★★★☆三倍縫製 88 善於縫製輕薄布料，處裡較厚重布料，如丹寧布可能略為不便。線上訂購可 **[192] 獲超低價格優惠。**

★★★☆ ZS 3000 是市面上最大型機器。需要精確的裝設，必須拆解才能清理。**[192] 價格特別低廉，但 [191] 該機器只能處理一些縫製技巧。**

帕克弗爾斯時裝秀

詹德・科奈里 撰稿

[195] 12 月 20 日—向來 **[194] 關注**最新時尚潮流的帕克佛爾斯居民，對於參加上週在帕克佛爾斯會議中心所舉辦的高級時尚活動，都感到興奮不已。多家自帕克佛爾斯發跡成長的公司都參與了第十屆帕克佛爾斯時尚季。超過 20 家服裝工作室在活動中亮相，其中數家工作室還是當地居民所開設的。

在當地超過 20 年的玫瑰設計，以絕美的冬季服飾揭開時尚秀序幕。緊接著登場的是永恆配件的老闆金・米勒的展示。**[195] 開業六個月的 In 潮流服飾與開業三年的湯布爾牛仔褲**，則是這場時尚秀的新人。時尚秀中展示的所有商品均在各公司網站上販售。

191. 關於 ZS 3000，提到了什麼事？
(A) 普遍在家庭中使用。
(B) 有延長保固。
(C) 容易搬運。
(D) 功能有限。

192. 網站上所提到的機器有什麼共同點？
(A) 都小巧可攜。
(B) 價格合理。
(C) 有各種顏色。
(D) 容易修理。

193. 伯恩斯先生最有可推薦琳姆女士哪一款縫紉機？
(A) 縫製大師 445
(B) 設計系列 3019
(C) 三倍縫製 88
(D) ZS 3000

194. 文章中，第一段、第一行的「monitor」與下列哪一個意思最接近？
(A) 相信
(B) 觀察
(C) 監督
(D) 依賴

195. 琳姆女士與伯恩斯先生最有可能在文章中的哪一家公司服務？
(A) 玫瑰設計
(B) 永恆配件
(C) In 潮流服飾
(D) 湯布爾牛仔褲

Questions 196–200 網頁、線上訂購單及電子郵件

Http://www.martinmovers.com

| 首頁 | 服務 | 估價 | 聯絡我們 |

馬丁搬家公司準備好提供您所有搬遷需求的協助。本搬家公司謹慎 **[196] 處理**大小搬遷工作上已有 20 年的經驗。不論您是搬新家，還是打算將公司遷至新大樓，我們都能提供您最具競爭力的價格。

我們的標準搬遷費用如下：

兩位搬運工人和一部中型卡車＝每小時 75 元

四位搬運工人和一部大型卡車＝每小時 150 元

[197(A)(B), 199] 辦公營業處所搬遷（六位工人和兩部大型卡車）＝均一價 400 元

關於辦公營業處所搬遷，顧客若於搬遷後要求搬運工人裝設影印機、電腦、印表機、投影機，將酌收額外費用。每裝設一台機器，將多收五元。**[197(C)] 欲申請免費估價，只要填寫線上表格，我們將盡快回覆給您。**

＊新年特別促銷活動：在 1 月 20 日前申請估價，將抵扣 30 元搬遷費。

馬丁搬家公司
估價申請表

日期	1 月 10 日
姓名	康納‧金史密斯
電子信箱	connor@goldsmithlegal.com
電話	409-333-3214
搬遷起始地：	紐約市第一大道 54 號
搬遷目的地：	紐約市秋景巷 889 號
200 搬遷日期	**2 月 23 日**
搬遷物品	八張書桌，八台電腦，三台印表機，一台影印機，一台冰箱，一張會議桌，25 張辦公椅。
其他意見	本律師事務所將搬至新址。因為 198 **本公司有自己的資訊科技員工**，所以我們不需要任何人員裝設設備。因此 199 **我相信應適用貴公司的標準均一價**。請以電子郵件與我聯繫以確認價格，並確認預約登記。

收件者：康納‧金史密斯
寄件者：史帝芬‧馬丁
日期：1 月 12 日
主旨：回覆：申請估價
附件：goldsmith_quote.pdf

親愛的金史密斯先生，

感謝您申請馬丁搬家公司估價。正如您於估價申請表所提到的，貴公司不需要任何的裝設服務，所以 199 **我相信我們的標準均一價應適用於貴公司。**

然而，遺憾的是，200 **您申請的當天，馬丁搬家公司已經登記額滿了。** 我不知道貴公司的搬遷是否可延後一天。當然，您是在我們促銷活動期間提出的估價申請，199 **我很樂意提供您 30 元的搬遷服務折扣。**

歡迎來電 409-555-8796 至本公司以進一步討論相關事宜。或者，我將於下週與您做後續連繫。

馬丁搬家公司
史帝芬‧馬丁 敬上

196. 網頁中，第一段、第二行的「tackling」與下列哪一個意思最接近？
(A) 修理
(B) 處理
(C) 考慮
(D) 款待

197. 關於辦公營業處所搬遷，沒有提到什麼？
(A) 將有六位搬運工人參與。
(B) 將使用一部以上的卡車。
(C) 免費提供估價。
(D) 必須提早兩週前預約。

198. 金史密斯先生提及有關他公司的什麼事？
(A) 將丟棄幾樣物品。
(B) 將縮減辦公空間。
(C) 需要多一名搬運工人。
(D) 聘用資訊科技專業人員。

199. 如果金史密斯先生聘用馬丁搬家公司，那他的搬遷費用是多少錢？
(A) 75 元
(B) 150 元
(C) 370 元
(D) 400 元

200. 關於馬丁搬家公司，提到了什麼事？
(A) 2 月 23 日的預約已額滿。
(B) 位於紐約市。
(C) 搬運車隊共有五部卡車。
(D) 週末加班需額外收費。

PART 1 P. 56–59   05

1. (A) She is trying on a necklace.
 (B) She is looking into a store window.*
 (C) She is folding a scarf.
 (D) She is cleaning a glass case.

2. (A) One of the men is placing his backpack on the floor.
 (B) One of the men is handing out brochures.
 (C) One of the women is holding a flag.*
 (D) One of the women is talking on the phone.

3. (A) There's a passenger on a platform.
 (B) The trains are stopped at a station.*
 (C) Tickets are being purchased from a machine.
 (D) Some tracks are being inspected.

4. (A) A woman is strolling on a beach.
 (B) A woman is mowing the grass.
 (C) A woman is pushing a wheelbarrow near the water.*
 (D) A woman is heading toward a bench.

5. (A) A piece of furniture is on display in a mall.
 (B) A vehicle is being parked in a garage.
 (C) Some men are stacking some containers.
 (D) Some movers are loading a sofa into a truck.*

6. (A) Some tables are being lined up on a stage.
 (B) Plants have been set on top of the tables.
 (C) A board has been placed next to the entrance.
 (D) Some decorations have been mounted on the walls.*

PART 2 P. 60   06

7. How many customers visited the store this morning?
 (A) Let's buy them.
 (B) The offer ends tomorrow.
 (C) Only about 10.*

1. (A) 她正在試戴項鍊。
 (B) 她正在看商店櫥窗。
 (C) 她正在摺一條圍巾。
 (D) 她正在清理一個玻璃櫃。

2. (A) 其中一位男子正把背包放到地上。
 (B) 其中一位男子正在分發小冊子。
 (C) 其中一位女子拿著一面旗子。
 (D) 其中一位女子正在講電話。

3. (A) 月台上有位旅客。
 (B) 火車停在車站。
 (C) 透過機器買車票。
 (D) 一些軌道正在檢查中。

4. (A) 一名女子正在海灘上散步。
 (B) 一名女子正在除草。
 (C) 一名女子在近水處推著獨輪手推車。
 (D) 一名女子正朝長椅走去。

5. (A) 購物中心裡展示著一件家具。
 (B) 一部車現在停在車庫裡。
 (C) 有些人正把一些貨櫃疊起來。
 (D) 有些搬家工人正把一張沙發裝上卡車。

6. (A) 一些桌子正在舞台上被排列。
 (B) 桌上放了一些植物。
 (C) 入口旁擺著一塊板子。
 (D) 一些裝飾品固定在牆上。

7. 今天早上有多少客人來過店裡？
 (A) 我們把它們買下來吧。
 (B) 報價的有效期到明天為止。
 (C) 只有大約十個人。

8. Where is your new cottage located?
   (A) It's just past this intersection.*
   (B) I haven't seen him today.
   (C) It's days from now.

9. Who did you talk to at the restaurant when making the reservation?
   (A) His name was Mark.*
   (B) Sure, we can book a table for you.
   (C) No, I haven't eaten there before.

10. Would you like to reserve a balcony seat?
   (A) Yes, that sounds good.*
   (B) No, she didn't.
   (C) The local opera house.

11. Who submitted these reimbursement forms?
   (A) By Tuesday at the latest.
   (B) The head of Marketing did.*
   (C) Sorry, I didn't go.

12. Which dates do you need the auditorium for?
   (A) From the 3rd to 5th, please.*
   (B) It's down the hall.
   (C) In the audio-visual room.

13. This lunch set includes a beverage, doesn't it?
   (A) A garage is included.
   (B) It was slightly undercooked.
   (C) That's correct.*

14. Aren't we traveling on the same bus?
   (A) The bag is over there.
   (B) No, I'm on an earlier one.*
   (C) He works for a travel agency.

15. Can you tell me who ordered the seafood spaghetti?
   (A) I prefer baked salmon.
   (B) In the cafeteria.
   (C) The man at table 5.*

16. Were you able to find the replacement part needed to fix the sink?
   (A) I am already working on the next job.*
   (B) Sixty words per minute.
   (C) Under 30 dollars.

---

8. 你新買的小屋位在哪裡？
   (A) 這個交叉路口過去就是了。
   (B) 我今天還沒見到他。
   (C) 離現在還有好幾天。

9. 您訂位時，是和餐廳的哪一位說的？
   (A) 他叫馬克。
   (B) 當然，我們可以為您預訂一個桌位。
   (C) 不，我沒在那裡用餐過。

10. 您要預訂包廂的位子嗎？
   (A) 好啊，聽起來不錯。
   (B) 不，她沒有。
   (C) 當地的歌劇院。

11. 這些請款單是誰提出的？
   (A) 最晚星期二前。
   (B) 行銷部門的主管。
   (C) 抱歉，我沒有去。

12. 你哪幾天需要使用禮堂？
   (A) 從 3 日到 5 日，麻煩你。
   (B) 在走廊盡頭。
   (C) 在視聽室。

13. 午餐的套餐包含飲料，不是嗎？
   (A) 包含車庫。
   (B) 有點不夠熟。
   (C) 沒錯。

14. 我們不是搭同一班公車嗎？
   (A) 袋子在那裡。
   (B) 不，我搭較早的一班。
   (C) 他在旅行社上班。

15. 你能告訴我是誰點了海鮮義大利麵嗎？
   (A) 我比較喜歡烤鮭魚。
   (B) 在自助餐廳。
   (C) 5 號桌的男子。

16. 你找到修理水槽所需的替換零件了嗎？
   (A) 我已經在進行下一個工作了。
   (B) 每分鐘 60 字。
   (C) 不到 30 元。

05

06

17. Please tell me when you're finished with the photocopier.
(A) For our online photos.
(B) Sure, this won't take long.*
(C) No, the page numbering is wrong.

18. Should we provide food at the workshop or just something to drink?
(A) Some snacks would be nice.*
(B) At 2:30, every day.
(C) He provided transportation for the participants.

19. What's the phone extension for the web designer?
(A) From the 11th of October.
(B) I'm afraid she has the day off.*
(C) By releasing the tension.

20. Jennifer Brown only paints in oil, right?
(A) Okay, we'll check if it's in stock.
(B) No, I've seen her watercolor pieces as well.*
(C) Boiled or fried?

21. How will the crew be able to fix the elevator if the building is locked?
(A) It stopped between the 9th and 10th floor.
(B) The security guard was told to let them in.*
(C) The safety inspection will happen on Monday.

22. Where should I hang the dentist's professional certification?
(A) Perhaps above his desk.*
(B) For Dr. Batica.
(C) Next Wednesday.

23. Why did the manager cancel the staff meeting?
(A) We don't have a meeting?*
(B) They will receive it soon.
(C) Almost half of the team members.

24. How often do you return to Montreal to visit?
(A) My parents don't live there anymore.*
(B) Yes, it is a huge city.
(C) I usually take the train.

25. Why isn't Mr. Borgald in his office?
(A) I think it started at 2:30.
(B) All division heads are in a meeting.*
(C) Take the stairs at the end of the hall.

17. 等你用完影印機，請告訴我一聲。
(A) 我們的網路照片要用。
(B) 當然，不會太久。
(C) 不，頁碼編錯了。

18. 我們的工作坊要提供餐點，還是只有飲料就好？
(A) 一些點心應該不錯。
(B) 每天兩點半。
(C) 他提供與會者交通接送。

19. 網頁設計師的分機是幾號？
(A) 從 10 月 11 日起。
(B) 抱歉，她休假。
(C) 透過釋放壓力。

20. 珍妮佛・布朗只畫油畫，對嗎？
(A) 好，我們會查查是否有存貨。
(B) 不是，我也看過她的水彩畫作品。
(C) 水煮的還是油炸的？

21. 如果大樓上鎖，工作人員要如何修理電梯？
(A) 它停在九樓和十樓中間。
(B) 警衛已接獲通知讓他們進來。
(C) 星期一將進行安全檢查。

22. 我該把牙醫師的執業證書掛在哪裡？
(A) 也許在他辦公桌的上方。
(B) 給巴緹卡醫師。
(C) 下星期三。

23. 經理為何取消員工會議？
(A) 我們不開會了？
(B) 他們很快就會收到。
(C) 幾乎一半的團隊成員。

24. 你多久回蒙特婁探訪一次？
(A) 我父母已經不住那裡了。
(B) 是啊，那是個大城市。
(C) 我通常搭火車。

25. 博高先生為何不在辦公室？
(A) 我想是兩點半開始的。
(B) 所有部門主管都在開會。
(C) 走通道盡頭的樓梯。

26. Which one of us should speak first?

(A) Yes, he did.

(B) Go ahead.*

(C) The first customer.

27. I can't reach the bulb to change it.

(A) Try standing on a chair.*

(B) The light bulbs are in the closet.

(C) This package is quite light.

28. Why don't we just postpone the job fair until April?

(A) Yes, we have a booth at the job fair.

(B) The convention center charges cancellation fees.*

(C) His interview is tomorrow morning.

29. How soon can I expect a reply to my loan application?

(A) No, it's a business loan.

(B) We will phone you in a few days.*

(C) Please reply by e-mail.

30. Are you almost finished packing or do you need more time?

(A) Our train doesn't leave until 4:00.*

(B) The package arrived yesterday.

(C) Is Diana finishing the report?

31. We don't have any more room in our Dalhousie warehouse.

(A) Yes, we have a room available on the second floor.

(B) That's why I suggested using the one in Hampstead.*

(C) Just two kilometers away from the main road.

26. 我們誰要先說？

(A) 是的，是他做的。

(B) 您先請。

(C) 第一個顧客。

27. 我手碰不到燈泡，沒辦法更換。

(A) 試試站在椅子上。

(B) 燈泡在櫃子裡。

(C) 這個包裹相當輕。

28. 我們何不把就業博覽會延到四月？

(A) 是的，我們在就業博覽會有攤位。

(B) 會議中心要索取取消的費用。

(C) 他的面試是在明天早上。

29. 我的貸款申請預計多快能得到回覆？

(A) 不是，是商業貸款。

(B) 我們幾天內會打電話給您。

(C) 請以電子郵件回覆。

30. 你差不多打包好了，還是要再多一點時間？

(A) 我們的火車四點才開。

(B) 包裹昨天送來的。

(C) 黛安娜要完成報告了嗎？

31. 我們在戴爾豪斯的倉庫已經沒有空位了。

(A) 是的，我們二樓有一間空房。

(B) 所以，我才建議用漢普斯德那個倉庫。

(C) 離主要道路只有兩公里。

Questions 32–34 對話

M	³² **I'm interested in buying a new T-pad tablet computer.** I've been waiting for it to be released.
W	Yes, many customers have inquired about the T-pad series recently.
M	³³ **What sizes does it come in?**
W	It comes in three sizes. 6 inch, 8 inch, and 11 inch. However, since we've had a lot of preorders for this tablet series, we don't have all the sizes in stock now.
M	Oh, I see. Well, what sizes do you have?
W	We have both the 6 inch and the 11 inch. If you'd like the 8 inch, though, I can order it from the warehouse for you.
M	No, that's okay. I'm interested in the 11 inch anyhow. I prefer a bigger screen.
W	Okay, great. ³⁴ **Let me calculate your total.**

男 ³² 我有意購買一台新的 T-pad 平板電腦。我一直在等產品發表。

女 好的,最近有許多顧客詢問 T-pad 系列。

男 ³³ 它有哪些尺寸?

女 有三種尺寸,6 吋、8 吋和 11 吋。不過,由於我們收到很多這系列平板電腦的預購單,現在不是所有尺寸都有現貨。

男 噢,了解。嗯,你們有哪些尺寸?

女 6 吋和 11 吋都有。不過,如果您想要 8 吋的,我可以幫您從倉庫訂。

男 不用,沒關係。反正我有興趣的是 11 吋。我比較喜歡大一點的螢幕。

女 好的,太好了。³⁴ 我算一下您的總金額。

32. What are the speakers discussing?
(A) A suitcase
(B) A printer
(C) A monitor
(D) A tablet computer*

33. What does the man ask about?
(A) The total cost
(B) The available sizes*
(C) The warranty options
(D) The free accessories

34. What will the woman most likely do next?
(A) Request payment*
(B) Consult a manager
(C) Register an ID
(D) Return an item

32. 說話者在討論什麼?
(A) 行李箱。
(B) 印表機。
(C) 螢幕。
(D) 平板電腦。

33. 男子詢問什麼?
(A) 總金額。
(B) 現有的尺寸。
(C) 保固的選項。
(D) 免費的配件。

34. 女子接下來最有可能做什麼?
(A) 要求付款。
(B) 請教經理。
(C) 註冊一個帳號。
(D) 退回一件物品。

Questions 35–37 對話

M	Hi, Jen. This is Ronald calling. Sorry, but I'm stuck in traffic now. There's an accident on the highway, so **35 I'm probably not going to be able to pick you up for the company dinner.**
W	Thanks for calling to let me know. I can take a taxi, then.
M	Well, **36 why don't you call Maxwell from Marketing to see if he can pick you up?** I think he lives near you.
W	Right. I heard he's going to pick up Lila, and I know where she lives. It's not far from here. **37 I'll call him right now and arrange something.**

男 嗨，珍，我是羅納德。抱歉，但我現在遇到塞車，路上有車禍發生，所以，**35 我很可能沒辦法去接妳參加公司的晚宴。**

女 謝謝你打電話告訴我。既然這樣，我可以搭計程車。

男 嗯，**36 妳何不打給行銷部的麥斯威爾，看看他能不能去接妳？**我想他就住在妳家附近。

女 沒錯。我聽說他要去接萊拉，我知道她住哪裡，離這裡不遠。**37 我馬上打給他，安排一下。**

35. Why did the man call the woman?
   (A) To inform of a change of plans*
   (B) To offer to call a car service
   (C) To explain an event schedule
   (D) To reschedule an appointment

35. 男子為何打電話給女子？
   (A) 通知計畫有變。
   (B) 提議打電話叫車。
   (C) 解釋活動的時程表。
   (D) 重新安排會面。

36. What does the man suggest?
   (A) Canceling an event
   (B) Using public transit
   (C) Asking a coworker for help*
   (D) Borrowing a neighbor's car

36. 男子有何建議？
   (A) 取消一個活動。
   (B) 利用公共交通運輸系統。
   (C) 請求同事的協助。
   (D) 借用鄰居的車。

37. What does the woman say she will do?
   (A) Change a reservation
   (B) Contact a colleague*
   (C) Call a tow truck
   (D) Pick up a coworker

37. 女子說她會做什麼？
   (A) 更改預約。
   (B) 聯絡同事。
   (C) 打電話叫拖吊車。
   (D) 開車去接同事。

Questions 38–40 對話

W	**38 I received a text message that a package was being delivered to my home, but when I checked, the package was not there.** My name is June Shane.
M	Let me check the computer system. Yes, it looks like the package is on its way back to this location. **39 The traffic was really bad because of the festival downtown, so we're a bit behind schedule,** but it should arrive by 3:30 P.M. You can pick it up then or wait for it to be delivered again tomorrow.

女 **38 我收到簡訊通知，有包裹送到我家，但當我查看時，家裡並沒有包裹。**我叫君萱。

男 我查一下電腦系統。是的，看來包裹正在運送的途中。**39 因為市中心的節慶活動，交通實在很擁擠，所以我們比預定時間晚了些，**但它應該在下午三點半前會到。你可以到時領取，或等包裹明天再送一次。

| W | Okay, ⁴⁰ **I have to get some groceries at the store next door, so I'll do that and then come back for the package later.** | 女 | 好，⁴⁰ 我必須去隔壁買些日用品，那我先去買東西，晚點再回來領包裹。 |

38. What are the speakers discussing?
    (A) A new office location
    (B) A store's hours
    (C) A package delivery*
    (D) A change of schedule

38. 說話者在討論何事？
    (A) 新的辦公室地點。
    (B) 商店的營業時間。
    (C) 包裹的遞送。
    (D) 時程表的變動。

39. Why is the man's company behind the schedule?
    (A) A new store was opened.
    (B) Some items were lost.
    (C) A few workers were sick.
    (D) Some roads were congested.*

39. 男子的公司為何比預定時間晚？
    (A) 新店面開幕。
    (B) 有些物品遺失。
    (C) 有些員工生病。
    (D) 有些道路擁塞。

40. What does the woman say she will do next?
    (A) Go to a supermarket*
    (B) Wait for an item at home
    (C) Cancel a purchase
    (D) Visit another post office

40. 女子說，她接下來要做什麼？
    (A) 去超市。
    (B) 在家等一件貨品。
    (C) 取消購買。
    (D) 去另一家郵局。

Questions 41–43 對話

M	Hi, ⁴¹ **this is Mark Stavros from Stavros Home Improvements.** Last year, you hired us to install new flooring in the main floor of your home. ⁴² **I'd like to let you know that we're currently having a special promotion and offering a 25% discount on all floor installations.**	男	嗨，⁴¹ 我是史達福居家裝修的馬克史達福。去年，您曾僱我們去您家裡一樓鋪設新地板。⁴² 我想通知您，我們目前有特別促銷，所有的地板安裝工程都打七五折。
W	Well, my main floor is still in great condition, but I've been thinking about installing carpeting in my upstairs bedrooms. Would that also be discounted?	女	嗯，我一樓的地板狀況還很良好，但我一直想在樓上的臥室鋪地毯。那也有打折嗎？
M	Yes, that would still be considered a floor installation. ⁴³ **If you'd like, I can send someone by next week to take measurements and discuss carpeting styles.**	男	有，那也視為地板安裝。⁴³ 如果您願意，我可以下星期派個人過去丈量並討論地毯的樣式。

41. What type of services does the man's company offer?

   (A) Vehicle upgrades

   (B) Home renovations*

   (C) Window cleaning

   (D) Appliance installations

42. Why is the man calling?

   (A) To return a phone call

   (B) To offer a free service

   (C) To discuss a payment plan

   (D) To advertise a promotion*

43. What does the man offer to do for the woman?

   (A) Provide a bigger discount

   (B) Mail some carpet samples

   (C) Send an employee*

   (D) Replace some old items

41. 男子的公司提供何種服務？

   (A) 車輛升級。

   (B) 住宅翻修。

   (C) 窗戶清潔。

   (D) 家電安裝。

42. 男子為何打這通電話？

   (A) 回一通電話。

   (B) 提供免費服務。

   (C) 討論付款方案。

   (D) 宣傳促銷活動。

43. 男子提議為女子做何事？

   (A) 提供更大的折扣。

   (B) 郵寄一些地毯的樣品。

   (C) 派一個員工來。

   (D) 更換一些舊的物品。

Questions 44–46 對話

W **44 Good afternoon, and thank you for calling Collingwood Insurance.** This is Samita speaking. How can I help you? M Hi, I'm interested in purchasing life insurance packages for me and my family members. **45 Can you give me a quote of how much it will cost to insure a family of five?** W Well, in order for us to determine your monthly rate, your family members will need to undergo a routine health exam. We have a staff doctor who visits our office every Thursday. Would next Thursday work for you? M Actually, I have a business meeting that day. **46 How about the following week?** W Sure. Does 2:30 work for you? M That would be fine. Thank you.	女 **44 午安**，謝謝您致電柯林伍德保險公司。我是莎米塔，請問需要什麼服務？ 男 嗨，我有興趣為我和我的家人購買壽險。**45 妳可以報價給我，一家五口投保的費用是多少嗎？** 女 嗯，為了確定你們的月付額，您的家人需要接受例行健康檢查。我們有位專任醫師，每星期四會到辦公室來。您下星期四方便嗎？ 男 其實，我那天有商務會議。**46 再下一個星期呢？** 女 當然可以。兩點半您方便嗎？ 男 可以。謝謝妳。

44. Where does the woman work?

   (A) At a doctor's office

   (B) At an insurance company*

   (C) At a sales office

   (D) At a dental clinic

44. 女子在哪裡工作？

   (A) 診所。

   (B) 保險公司。

   (C) 業務部。

   (D) 牙醫診所。

45. What information does the man ask for?

    (A) A list of services

    (B) A doctor's schedule

    (C) The location of a clinic

    (D) The price of a service*

46. What does the man imply when he says, "I have a business meeting that day"?

    (A) He needs another appointment.*

    (B) He will wear a formal suit.

    (C) He will visit another location.

    (D) He doesn't mind traveling far.

45. 男子詢問何項資訊？

    (A) 服務的清單。

    (B) 醫師的班表。

    (C) 診所的地點。

    (D) 服務的費用。

46. 當男子說「我那天有商務會議」，意指什麼？

    (A) 他需要約別的時間會面。

    (B) 他會穿正式的西裝。

    (C) 他會造訪另一個地點。

    (D) 他不介意長途旅程。

Questions 47–49 對話

M Hi, Jane. How is everything going?	**男** 嗨，珍。一切都順利嗎？
W Good. Hey, I wanted to ask you something. **⁴⁷ I'm thinking of taking a trip to Spain, and I heard you just got cheap tickets to France.**	**女** 很好。嘿，我想問你一件事。**⁴⁷ 我在考慮要去西班牙旅行，我聽說你剛剛買到前往法國的便宜機票。**
M Yes, **⁴⁸ the tickets were really cheap, because I used the new online ticket website tix4cheap.com.** I was able to save several hundred dollars and even got some vouchers for restaurants and hotels, too.	**男** 是的，**⁴⁸ 那機票真的很便宜，因為我上了新的線上機票網站 tix4cheap.com。** 我因此得以省下好幾百元，甚至還得到一些餐廳和旅館的優待券。
W Wow, that sounds great. Can anybody use that website?	**女** 哇，聽起來真棒。任何人都可以用那個網站嗎？
M Well, you have to sign up for a membership. If you pay to upgrade the membership, you get even more discounts.	**男** 嗯，妳必須註冊成為會員。如果妳付費升級會員資格，會得到更多折扣。
W **⁴⁹ Is it expensive? I don't know how often I will use it, so paying for the membership might not be worth it.**	**女** **⁴⁹ 會很貴嗎？我不知道我會多常用到，所以，付費會員也許不划算。**
M Well, you get the first six months free, so I think it'll be worth it in the end.	**男** 嗯，前六個月是免費的，所以我想最後是值得的。

47. What does the woman want to do?

    (A) Rent a house overseas

    (B) Sign up for a mailing list

    (C) Purchase airline tickets*

    (D) Upgrade a membership

47. 女子想要做什麼？

    (A) 在海外租房子。

    (B) 註冊加入郵寄名單。

    (C) 購買機票。

    (D) 升級會員資格。

48. What does the man recommend?

    (A) Going to a travel agency

    (B) Buying a lifetime membership

    (C) Using a new travel website*

    (D) Calling an airline directly

49. What is the woman concerned about?

    (A) A delay in payment

    (B) The price of a membership*

    (C) A missing coupon book

    (D) The location of an airport

48. 男子推薦什麼？

    (A) 去找旅行社。

    (B) 買終身會員。

    (C) 使用新的旅遊網站。

    (D) 直接打電話給航空公司。

49. 女子擔心什麼？

    (A) 付款延後。

    (B) 會員費。

    (C) 整本優惠券遺失。

    (D) 機場的位置。

Questions 50–52 對話

M Hello, Ms. Piper. It's Marcel Shumaker. **50 Did you get a chance to look at the design samples for your advertisement?** I e-mailed them yesterday. **W** Hi, Marcel. Yes, I'm looking at them now. I really like sample A. **51 I think the font is very attractive, and I especially love the new store logo you came up with.** **M** I agree. I think sample A fits **50 your store**'s style very well. **52 Would you like me to make the words "Summer Sale" a brighter color of red?** **W** Yes, that sounds like a good idea, especially since the advertisement is mainly to let people know about our big upcoming sale.	**男** 哈囉，派普太太，我是馬塞爾‧許梅克。**50 您抽空看過廣告的設計樣本了嗎？** 我昨天用電子郵件寄給您了。 **女** 嗨，馬塞爾。是的，我現在正在看。我真的很喜歡樣本 A。**51 我覺得字型很吸引人，尤其喜歡你們想出的新商標。** **男** 我也認同。我認為樣本 A 非常適合 **50 貴店**的風格。**52 您要我把「夏季特賣」的字樣，用比較亮的紅色嗎？** **女** 好啊，聽起來是個好主意，尤其是因為，這則廣告主要是讓人們知道我們即將開跑的夏季大特賣。

50. Who most likely is the woman?

    (A) A graphic designer

    (B) A store owner*

    (C) A newspaper reporter

    (D) A web developer

51. What is the woman pleased about?

    (A) Some seasonal discounts

    (B) A new logo design*

    (C) The price of a service

    (D) The annual sales results

50. 女子最有可能是誰？

    (A) 平面設計師。

    (B) 商店店主。

    (C) 報社記者。

    (D) 網頁開發工程師。

51. 女子對什麼感到滿意？

    (A) 一些季節性的折扣。

    (B) 新的商標設計。

    (C) 服務的費用。

    (D) 年度特賣的結果。

52. What does the man offer to do?

    (A) Move a company logo

    (B) Add a border to a design

    (C) Enlarge the size of a picture

    (D) Change the color of some words*

52. 男子提議做什麼？

    (A) 移除公司的商標。

    (B) 為設計加邊線。

    (C) 放大照片。

    (D) 更改某些字的顏色。

Questions 53–55 對話

M	Rebecca, why are you still in the office? It's after 6 P.M. **53 I thought you had dinner plans tonight?**
W	Yes, well, unfortunately I won't be able to leave for a while. I'm still working on some customer feedback reports, and it's not going well.
M	Oh no. What happened?
W	Well, the Rotary Golf Club has complained that some of our landscapers damaged their fountains last week when they were cutting the grass. **54 I'm so worried because I'm not sure how to convince them to remain our customer.**
M	That's too bad. Well, I'm on my way to see the manager now. **55 I'll bring it up with him and let you know what he says before I leave, okay?**

男	蕾貝卡，妳怎麼還在辦公室？已經過了六點，**53 我以為妳今晚有晚餐約會？**
女	是的，嗯，很遺憾，我暫時還無法離開。我還在忙著做顧客回饋意見報告，而且不太順利。
男	噢，不。怎麼回事？
女	嗯，扶輪高爾夫球社抱怨，我們的園藝設計師上星期除草時，弄壞了他們的噴水池。**54 我很擔心，因為我不確定要怎麼說服他們繼續作我們的客戶。**
男	那真是太糟了。嗯，我現在正要去找經理。**55 我會和他談這件事，並在我離開前，告訴妳他怎麼說，好嗎？**

53. What does the woman imply when she says, "I won't be able to leave for a while"?

    (A) She had to change her plans.*

    (B) She is waiting for someone.

    (C) She has already eaten dinner.

    (D) She doesn't have a car now.

53. 女子說「我暫時無法離開」，意指什麼？

    (A) 她必須改變她的計畫。

    (B) 她在等某個人。

    (C) 她已經吃過晚餐。

    (D) 她現在沒有車。

54. What is the woman worried about?

    (A) Presenting her findings to her boss

    (B) Finishing a report on time

    (C) Mending a business relationship*

    (D) Inspecting some damages

54. 女子擔心何事？

    (A) 把她的調查結果交給她的上司。

    (B) 準時完成報告。

    (C) 修補商業關係。

    (D) 檢查某些損害。

55. What does the man say he will do before he leaves?

    (A) Hold a monthly meeting

    (B) Pass on some information*

    (C) Visit a customer's office

    (D) Check the status of an order

55. 男子說他離開前會做什麼？

    (A) 舉行每月會議。

    (B) 傳達一些訊息。

    (C) 造訪顧客的公司。

    (D) 檢查一張訂單的進度。

Questions 56–58 三人對話

W1	Thank you for coming to our office for an interview, Mr. Bell. **56 I'm Jane Farrah, Human Resources Manager at Country Interior.**
W2	And I'm Shannon Rogers. **56 I'm the lead interior designer's assistant.**
M	Thanks for inviting me. It's nice to meet both of you.
W1	I've looked over your application package, and it seems that you have a lot of experience installing cabinets, flooring, and windows. I think you would make a great addition to our design crew, but **57 I'm curious about your ability to carry heavy materials.**
M	That shouldn't be a problem. I've worked several similar jobs and haven't had any problems with the physical demands.
W2	Okay, great. **58 Why don't you show us your references?** You mentioned in your e-mail that you would bring them.
M	**58 Sure**. They're right here.

女1	貝爾先生，謝謝你來我們公司參加面試。**56 我是舉國室內裝修的人事經理珍・法瑞。**
女2	我是夏儂・羅傑斯，**56 首席室內設計師的助理。**
男	謝謝妳們邀請我，很高興認識兩位。
女1	我仔細看過你的履歷資料，看來你在安裝櫥櫃、地板和窗戶方面經驗豐富。我想，你對我們的設計團隊會是很大的助力，但 **57 我想知道你搬運重物的能力。**
男	應該不成問題。我做過好幾個類似的工作，在體能需求上從來沒遇過任何問題。
女2	好的，好極了。**58 你何不給我們看看推薦信？** 你在電子郵件中提過，你會帶來。
男	**58 當然**，就在這裡。

56. Where do the interviewers most likely work?
    (A) At a furniture manufacturer
    (B) At an interior design company*
    (C) At an art gallery
    (D) At a moving company

57. What job requirement do the speakers discuss?
    (A) Meeting deadlines
    (B) Cooperating with others
    (C) Working long hours
    (D) Lifting heavy objects*

58. What does the man agree to do next?
    (A) Show some documents*
    (B) Fill out an application
    (C) Submit some design samples
    (D) Sign an employment contract

56. 面試官最可能在哪裡工作？
    (A) 家具製造廠。
    (B) 室內設計公司。
    (C) 藝廊。
    (D) 搬家公司。

57. 說話者在討論什麼工作條件？
    (A) 如期完成任務。
    (B) 和其他人合作。
    (C) 工時很長。
    (D) 抬起重物。

58. 男子同意接下來做什麼？
    (A) 出示一些文件。
    (B) 填寫一份申請書。
    (C) 提出一些設計的樣本。
    (D) 簽署一份僱傭合約。

W Hi, Michael. **59 Have you noticed the decrease in reservations lately?** We had a lot more reservations booked at this time last year. I think we need to do something to attract more guests. Do you have any suggestions? **M** Well, **60 what if we held a discount event next month?** We could send a mass e-mail to our regular visitors and offer them a voucher for 50% off the price of one night's stay. That way, they might book several nights. **W** Okay, that sounds like a great idea. **61 How about you design the voucher and draft the e-mail?** You can submit them to me by Friday for approval.	**女** 嗨,麥可。**59 你注意到最近訂房的人數減少了嗎?**去年這個時候,我們的訂房數多很多。我想,我們必須做點什麼來吸引更多房客。你有什麼建議嗎? **男** 嗯,**60 我們下個月舉行折扣優惠活動怎麼樣?**我們可以發送大量電子郵件給常客,提供他們一張住宿一晚的五折優惠券。那樣的話,他們可能會預訂幾個晚上。 **女** 好,聽起來是很棒的主意。**61 你來設計優惠券並草擬電子郵件如何?**你可以在星期五之前交給我批准。

59. What problem does the woman mention? (A) A room was damaged. (B) Some guests complained. (C) Some workers quit. **(D) A business is slow.***	**59.** 女子提及什麼問題? (A) 有個房間損壞。 (B) 有些客人抱怨。 (C) 有些員工辭職。 **(D) 生意下滑。**
60. What does the man suggest? (A) Offering free meals to guests **(B) Holding a promotional event*** (C) Upgrading room sizes (D) Merging with another business	**60.** 男子有何建議? (A) 免費供餐給客人。 **(B) 舉行促銷活動。** (C) 升等客房大小。 (D) 與另一家公司合併。
61. What does the woman ask the man to do? (A) Analyze customer feedback (B) Update a website (C) Make a mailing list **(D) Prepare some materials***	**61.** 女子要求男子何事? (A) 分析顧客的回饋意見。 (B) 更新網站。 (C) 列出郵寄名單。 **(D) 準備一些資料。**

Questions 62–64 對話

M Hi, Dara. **62 Do you have time to talk about my presentation for the Cosmetics Convention?**

W Yes. I'm terribly sorry I wasn't able to talk with you yesterday.

M That's not a problem. I know you've been busy filing patent applications.

W Yes, it's been so complicated, but **63 it looks like our new sunblock line will be ready for manufacturing next month.**

M Good to hear. Can I show you my PowerPoint presentation?

W Sure. You can use my computer.

M Okay, here it is. I just wanted to double-check that all of the diagrams are correct.

W It looks good so far. Wait a minute. **64 This diagram is from last year's convention.**

M Oh, no. You're right. I'm so glad you caught that.

男 嗨，黛拉。62 妳有空討論我要在化妝品大會發表的簡報嗎？

女 有的。我很抱歉昨天沒空和你討論。

男 沒關係。我知道妳一直在忙專利申請的事情。

女 是的，那很複雜。但是，63 看來我們新的防曬系列產品，下個月就可以投入生產。

男 很高興聽到這個消息。我可以把我的 PowerPoint 簡報給妳看嗎？

女 當然，你可以用我的電腦。

男 好，就是這個。我只是想要再檢查一次，確認所有圖表都正確。

女 目前看來都很好。等一下。64 這張圖是去年大會的。

男 噢，不妙。妳說得對。幸好妳發現了。

62. What industry do the speakers most likely work in?
(A) Cosmetics*
(B) Engineering
(C) Software
(D) Trade

63. What does the woman say will happen next month?
(A) A convention will take place.
(B) A new product will be manufactured.*
(C) A patent will expire.
(D) A new law will be enacted.

64. What does the woman imply when she says, "This diagram is from last year's convention"?
(A) A fee must be paid.
(B) Nothing needs to be done.
(C) This year's figures are not available yet.
(D) Some information is outdated.*

62. 說話者最可能在什麼行業工作？
(A) 化妝品。
(B) 工程。
(C) 軟體。
(D) 貿易。

63. 女子說，下個月會發生何事？
(A) 將舉行一場大會。
(B) 將生產一項新產品。
(C) 一項專利權將到期。
(D) 將實施一項新法規。

64. 當女子說「這張圖表是去年大會的」時，意指什麼？
(A) 必須支付費用。
(B) 沒有什麼事要做。
(C) 今年的數字還無法得知。
(D) 有些資訊已過期。

Office 4	Office 3	Office 2
Break Room	Office 1	

辦公室 4	辦公室 3	辦公室 2
茶水間	辦公室 1	

M Tracey, do you have time to take a look at the floor plan for our new office space at the Winslow building?

W Sure. **65 I have about ten minutes before I have to leave to meet with some new clients this afternoon.**

M Great. Here is the floor plan. Offices 3 and 4 will be for the sales and marketing departments, and **66 you'll be in the office next to the break room.** It's pretty large, so you'll have a lot of space to conduct meetings.

W That sounds like it'll work out great. Where will you be?

M I'll be in the corner office. That way I can be close to you and the sales department.

W Good idea. **67 How about I present this at the staff meeting tomorrow morning?**

男 崔西,你有空看一下我們在溫斯洛大樓新辦公室的平面圖嗎?

女 當然。**65 我大約有十分鐘,然後我就必須離開,去見今天下午的新客戶。**

男 太好了。這是平面圖。3 號和 4 號辦公室會給業務和行銷部門,**66 妳的辦公室會在茶水間隔壁。**那間相當大,所以妳會有充足的空間主持會議。

女 聽起來會進行得很順利。那你會在哪裡?

男 我會在轉角辦公室。那樣的話,我離妳和業務部都很近。

女 好主意。**67 我在明天早上的員工會議上簡報這件事如何?**

65. According to the woman, what will she be doing this afternoon?
   (A) Going on vacation
   (B) Moving to a new office
   (C) Meeting some customers*
   (D) Drawing up a floor plan

65. 根據女子所述,她今天下午會做何事?
   (A) 去度假。
   (B) 搬進一間新辦公室。
   (C) 會見一些新客戶。
   (D) 草擬一張平面圖。

66. Look at the graphic. Which office has been assigned to the woman?
   (A) Office 1*
   (B) Office 2
   (C) Office 3
   (D) Office 4

66. 請見圖表。哪一間辦公室分配給女子?
   (A) 辦公室 1。
   (B) 辦公室 2。
   (C) 辦公室 3。
   (D) 辦公室 4。

67. What does the woman say will take place tomorrow morning?
   (A) A visit with clients
   (B) An employee meeting*
   (C) A renovation
   (D) A company party

67. 女子說,明天早上會發生何事?
   (A) 拜訪客戶。
   (B) 員工會議。
   (C) 整修。
   (D) 公司派對。

Questions 68–70 對話及表單

Company	Location
Stanford Design	Chicago
Able Advertising	Miami
Renview Media	New York
70 Smart Style Design	**Atlanta**

公司	位置
史丹佛設計	芝加哥
艾波廣告	邁阿密
連威媒體	紐約
70 史邁特風格設計	**亞特蘭大**

M Hi, Jennifer. **68 I'm so pleased to hear that our company will host a charity gala** next month to raise money for the homeless.

W Yes, we can do something for the community and get great publicity. That reminds me. Did you get a chance to look over the list of firms we're considering hiring to advertise the event?

M Yes, I'm looking at it now. **69 I think Renview Media offers great discounts, but we might need somebody who works a bit faster.** The last time we hired them, there were many delays.

W Right. I remember that. **70 How about the one that's right here in Atlanta?** Their reviews all say they were fast and reasonably priced.

男 嗨，珍妮佛。**68 真高興聽到我們公司下個月要主辦慈善晚會**，為街友募款。

女 是的，我們可以為社區做點事情，並達到很好的公關宣傳。那提醒了我，你有空查看我們考慮要僱用來做活動宣傳的公司名單嗎？

男 有的，我現在正在看。**69 我認為「連威媒體」提供很大的優惠，但我們可能需要工作速度快些的公司**。我們上一次找他們，有許多事情都拖延了。

女 對，我記得。**70 同樣在亞特蘭大的這一家呢？** 他們的評價都說，他們動作很快而且收費合理。

---

68. What type of event is the company hosting?
   (A) A charity ball*
   (B) An art gallery opening
   (C) A retirement party
   (D) A professional conference

69. What is the man concerned about?
   (A) The cost of a project
   (B) The location of an event
   (C) A company's efficiency*
   (D) A worker's absence

70. Look at the graphic. Which company does the woman suggest?
   (A) Stanford Design
   (B) Able Advertising
   (C) Renview Media
   (D) Smart Style Design*

68. 公司將主辦哪一種活動？
   (A) 慈善晚會。
   (B) 藝廊開幕。
   (C) 退休派對。
   (D) 專業研討會。

69. 男子擔心何事？
   (A) 計畫的費用。
   (B) 活動的地點。
   (C) 公司的效率。
   (D) 某個員工缺席。

70. 請見圖表。女子建議的是哪一間公司？
   (A) 史丹佛設計。
   (B) 艾波廣告。
   (C) 連威媒體。
   (D) 史邁特風格設計。

Questions 71-73 宣告

W	Attention all travelers. **⁷¹ This announcement is for passengers of flight FR64 to Paris. ⁷² Due to unfavorable weather conditions in Paris, your flight has been delayed until further notice.** We expect the delay to last no more than two hours. You will be informed as soon as we have a new estimated departure. In the meantime, **⁷³ visit the International Flight Lounge and receive a free beverage** by showing your flight FR64 ticket. Thank you for your continued patience.	女 各位旅客請注意。**⁷¹ 搭乘 FR64 班機前往巴黎的旅客請注意**，**⁷² 由於巴黎天候不佳，班機已延後起飛，請待進一步通知**。我們預計班機延後時間不會超過兩小時。我們一得知新的預估起飛時間，就會通知您。在此期間，**⁷³ 您可以前往國際航班休息室**，出示您的 FR64 班機機票就可**享有免費飲料一杯**。感謝各位耐心等待。

71. Where most likely are the listeners?
   (A) At an airport*
   (B) On a ship
   (C) At a travel agency
   (D) In a shopping mall

71. 聽眾最有可能在何處？
   (A) 機場。
   (B) 船上。
   (C) 旅行社。
   (D) 購物中心。

72. What is the cause of the delay?
   (A) A security issue
   (B) Missing passengers
   (C) Mechanical problems
   (D) Poor weather*

72. 延誤的原因為何？
   (A) 安全問題。
   (B) 旅客行蹤不明。
   (C) 機械問題。
   (D) 天候不佳。

73. What does the speaker suggest listeners do?
   (A) Request a ticket refund
   (B) Obtain a complimentary drink*
   (C) Book hotel accommodation
   (D) Visit an information desk

73. 說話者建議聽眾做何事？
   (A) 要求機票退費。
   (B) 取得免費飲料。
   (C) 預訂飯店住宿。
   (D) 前往服務台。

Questions 74-76 會議摘錄

W	Today marks our first ever sales meeting since Glasco Merits merged with Summerview Metalworks. **⁷⁴ I'd like to go over the details of the company merger and what that means for the sales department.** As you know, **⁷⁵ we will be conducting regular meetings for all sales staff on the first Monday of every month.** Right now, I'd like to familiarize everybody with our new sales and billing procedures. I'll be distributing updated employee handbooks, which we will go over briefly. **⁷⁶ I know some of you have a training class this afternoon,** so I will try to keep this short.	女 今天是「格拉斯科・美利」與「賽摩威金屬製品」合併後的第一次業務會議。**⁷⁴ 我想要仔細檢視公司合併的細節，以及對業務部的意義。**你們都知道，**⁷⁵ 我們會在每月的第一個星期一，定期舉行全體業務同仁會議。**現在，我想讓各位熟悉新的業務與開立發票的流程。我會分發更新後的員工手冊，我們會從頭到尾簡單帶過。**⁷⁶ 我知道，你們有些人今天下午有訓練課程，**所以，我會努力讓會議簡明扼要。

74. What is the speaker mainly discussing?

    (A) A downsizing plan

    (B) A company merger*

    (C) A new office manager

    (D) A potential client

75. What does the speaker say will take place at the company once a month?

    (A) An employee review

    (B) A monthly bonus

    (C) A sales meeting*

    (D) A training course

76. Why will some employees be unavailable in the afternoon?

    (A) They are attending a training session.*

    (B) They are presenting at a trade show.

    (C) They are meeting with the head manager.

    (D) They are leaving for a company trip.

74. 說話者主要在討論何事？

    (A) 裁減員工計畫。

    (B) 公司的合併。

    (C) 新的公司經理。

    (D) 潛在客戶。

75. 說話者說，每個月公司會舉行何事？

    (A) 員工考核。

    (B) 每月紅利。

    (C) 業務會議。

    (D) 訓練課程。

76. 為何有些員工下午不在？

    (A) 他們要參加訓練課程。

    (B) 他們要出席貿易展。

    (C) 他們要和部門經理會面。

    (D) 他們要出發去員工旅遊。

Questions 77–79 會議摘錄

M As I'm sure you've heard, **⁷⁷ we're thinking of switching to a new company to supply all our restaurant's beverage needs.** Next week, a representative will visit the restaurant and bring samples of several different kinds of soda and juice. I'd like some of you to try as many as you can and fill out the feedback questionnaire they will provide. When you're finished, **⁷⁸ you can drop off your questionnaire in the head chef's office downstairs.** To show our appreciation for your participation, management will draw one questionnaire at random and **⁷⁹ give the winner a pair of movie passes.**

男 相信你們都聽說了，**⁷⁷ 我們正在考慮要換一家新公司供應我們餐廳的飲料。**有個業務代表下星期會來拜訪餐廳，並帶好幾種不同的汽水和果汁樣品來。我希望你們一些人盡量試喝，然後填寫他們提供的回饋意見調查問卷。等你們填完，**⁷⁸ 可以把問卷拿到樓下的總主廚辦公室。**為了感謝你們的參與，管理部會隨機抽出一份問卷，**⁷⁹ 贈送得獎者雙人電影入場券。**

77. What does the speaker say the business is considering?

    (A) Renovating a kitchen

    (B) Changing operation hours

    (C) Contracting a new chef

    (D) Hiring a new supplier*

77. 說話者說公司正在考慮何事？

    (A) 整修廚房。

    (B) 改變營業時間。

    (C) 與新主廚簽約。

    (D) 僱用新供應商。

78. Why should listeners visit the head chef's office?

    (A) To have an interview

    (B) To pick up a coupon

    (C) To sample some food

    (D) To submit a form*

79. What can listeners receive for participation?

    (A) Some movie tickets*

    (B) A vacation package

    (C) Some free food

    (D) A pay raise

Questions 80–82 電話留言

W Hi, Caroline. This is Trisha calling. **80 My flight was supposed to depart an hour ago, and they've just announced that it's been canceled due to poor weather conditions.** It looks like **81 I won't be home in time to attend the dinner to celebrate your promotion.** It's really too bad. To make it up to you, **82 I'd love to take you out for dinner next week, maybe on Thursday or Friday evening.** Call me and let me know if either of those days works for you.

80. Where most likely is the speaker?

    (A) At a bus station

    (B) At an airport*

    (C) At her home

    (D) In an airplane

81. What does the speaker imply when she says, "It's really too bad"?

    (A) She is not well.

    (B) She is disappointed.*

    (C) She lost a lot of money.

    (D) She regrets her decision.

82. What does the speaker ask the listener to do?

    (A) Drive to an airport

    (B) Reschedule a party

    (C) Unlock a door

    (D) Meet her for dinner*

78. 聽眾為何要去總主廚辦公室？

    (A) 為了進行面試。

    (B) 為了領取優惠券。

    (C) 為了試吃一些食物。

    (D) 為了交出一份表格。

79. 聽眾參與活動可以得到什麼？

    (A) 一些電影票。

    (B) 一次套裝旅行。

    (C) 一些免費食物。

    (D) 加薪。

女 嗨，卡洛琳，我是崔夏。**80 我的班機應該在一小時前起飛，但他們剛剛廣播，由於天候不佳，班機已取消。**看來 **81 我來不及回家參加妳的升職慶祝晚餐。**實在是太遺憾了。為了彌補，**82 我想下星期請妳出去吃飯，也許星期四或星期五晚上。**打電話給我，告訴我哪一天妳可以。

80. 說話者最有可能在何處？

    (A) 在巴士車站。

    (B) 在機場。

    (C) 在她家。

    (D) 在飛機上。

81. 當說話者說「實在是太遺憾了」，意指什麼？

    (A) 她不舒服。

    (B) 她很失望。

    (C) 她損失大筆金錢。

    (D) 她為她的決定感到懊悔。

82. 說話者要求聽者做何事？

    (A) 開車到機場。

    (B) 重新安排派對的時間。

    (C) 打開門鎖。

    (D) 和她碰面共進晚餐。

W Attention, all staff members. **84 A pipe burst in the stock room overnight and water has rushed into the back offices, 83 the frozen foods section, and the bakery aisles.** As of now, the managers think it's in our best interest not to open today. Instead, we'd like all available employees to help with the clean-up. If the mess is cleaned up by this evening, we will resume normal operations tomorrow. **85 Your managers will let you know about the schedule before you go home.**

女 所有工作人員請注意。**84 貯藏室裡有根水管昨晚爆裂，水湧進後勤辦公室、83 冷凍食品區和烘焙區走道。**現在，經理一致認為，今天最好不要營業。我們希望所有有空的員工轉而協助清理。如果今晚之前可以清理乾淨，我們明天就會恢復正常營運。**85 你們的經理會在下班時間前，告知日程安排。**

83. Where most likely is this announcement being made?
(A) At pastry shop
(B) At a bookstore
(C) At a supermarket*
(D) At a sports center

83. 這項通知最可能在哪裡發布？
(A) 在糕餅店。
(B) 在書店。
(C) 在超級市場。
(D) 在運動中心。

84. What problem does the speaker mention?
(A) Some employees are sick.
(B) Some items were misplaced.
(C) Some power cables are damaged.
(D) Some areas are flooded.*

84. 說話者提及什麼問題？
(A) 有些員工生病了。
(B) 有些物品放錯位置。
(C) 有些電纜受損。
(D) 有些區域淹水。

85. What will employees be informed about this evening?
(A) A store's schedule*
(B) A vacation plan
(C) A promotional sale
(D) A city inspection

85. 員工會在今天晚上收到什麼通知？
(A) 商店的時間表。
(B) 度假的計畫。
(C) 促銷拍賣。
(D) 市政府的檢查。

Questions 86-88 新聞報導

M	Welcome to News in Real Estate. I'm Chuck Thompson, and [86] **here is the latest news on how to sell your home quickly.** [87] **A recent survey on Channel 6's website** has shown that more and more home owners are using interior decorating services to quickly sell their homes. According to our survey, 75 percent of people who recently sold their home contracted a decorating service. These decorators are experts in giving your home some pleasing upgrades that will attract buyers. If you're on a budget, however, and can't afford a decorator, there are a few ways you can improve the look of your home. [88] **Designer Jen Bell will be joining me after the break to give you some tips.**	男 歡迎收看不動產新聞，我是查克・湯普森，[86] **這裡有如何快速出售你的房子的最新訊息。**[87] 近日，6 號電台網站上**有一項調查**顯示，有愈來愈多屋主善用室內裝潢來快速售出他們的家。根據我們的調查，近期賣出房子的人，有 75% 與裝潢服務的公司簽約。這些室內裝潢師是專家，帶給你一些令人滿意的升級項目，以吸引買家。不過，若你的預算有限，請不起室內裝潢設計師，有幾種你可以美化你家外觀的方法。[88] **廣告過後，設計師珍・貝爾會和我一起給大家一些建議。**

86. What is the news report about?
(A) Becoming an interior decorator
(B) Selling a home quickly*
(C) Taking an online survey
(D) Buying a home abroad

86. 這則快訊報導的主題為何？
(A) 成為一位室內裝潢設計師。
(B) 快速售出房子。
(C) 參加線上調查。
(D) 購買國外的房屋。

87. What did Channel 6 do on their website recently?
(A) Conduct a survey*
(B) Review a service
(C) Advertise a home
(D) Hold a contest

87. 6 號電台最近在網站上做了何事？
(A) 進行一項調查。
(B) 審核一項服務。
(C) 宣傳一間房子。
(D) 舉行一項競賽。

88. According to the speaker, what can listeners do after the break?
(A) View houses on the market
(B) Visit a designer's studio
(C) Hear some advice*
(D) Sign up for a newsletter

88. 根據說話者所述，廣告後聽眾可以做什麼？
(A) 查看市場上的房子。
(B) 造訪設計師的工作室。
(C) 聽到一些建議。
(D) 登記訂閱電子報。

M   To start today's meeting, ⁸⁹ **I'd like to discuss our new paperless policy.** Upper management feels it's important for Parker Refurbishing to be a leader in maintaining a green work environment. So from next week, ⁸⁹ **we're asking that all employees please refrain from using paper.** A new database has been set up to handle all our file saving needs. Now, I know what you must be thinking. ⁹⁰ **Last year, we tried and failed to go paperless, but this year,** I'm confident that our new database will make it possible. To show their appreciation for your efforts, ⁹¹ **upper management would like to reward you with a staff lunch** at the High Park Hotel Grill.

男   今天的會議一開始，⁸⁹ **我想討論我們新的無紙政策。**管理高層認為，「帕克翻新公司」要成為維護綠色工作環境的龍頭，這點很重要。因此，從下星期開始，⁸⁹ **我們要求所有員工節約用紙。**我們已經建立了一個新的資料庫，處理所有的檔案保存之需。我知道你們現在一定在想什麼。⁹⁰ **去年，我們嘗試無紙化卻失敗了，但今年**，我有信心，我們的新資料庫會讓這政策成功。為了感謝你們的努力，⁹¹ **管理高層會在「高公園飯店燒烤」舉辦員工午餐作為獎勵。**

89. According to the speaker, what is the company trying to do?
(A) Increase productivity
(B) Eliminate paper use*
(C) Upgrade a computer system
(D) Reduce electricity costs

89. 根據說話者所述，公司正努力做何事？
(A) 增加生產力。
(B) 淘汰紙張的使用。
(C) 升級電腦系統。
(D) 減少電費。

90. What does the speaker mean when he says, "I know what you must be thinking"?
(A) He wants to stress a key detail.
(B) He wants to caution against disobedience.
(C) He understands the listeners' concerns.*
(D) He acknowledges a listener's complaint.

90. 當說話者說，「我知道你們現在一定在想什麼」，意指什麼？
(A) 他想強調關鍵細節。
(B) 他想告誡大家，別不服從。
(C) 他了解聽者的掛慮。
(D) 他接受一位聽者的抱怨。

91. What will the listeners be rewarded with?
(A) A free meal*
(B) A new computer
(C) A gift card
(D) A promotion

91. 聽者會得到什麼獎勵？
(A) 免費的一餐。
(B) 一台新電腦。
(C) 一張禮物卡。
(D) 升職。

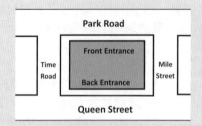

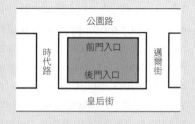

M Attention all businesses located in A&F Building! This is a reminder that ⁹² **the city's winter Christmas Parade will be taking place on Friday afternoon.** ⁹³ **As the street located in front of our building will be shut down from 11 A.M. to 6 P.M.,** please make sure to park on the street closest to the back entrance. Also, traffic is expected to be heavy that day, so please ensure you allow yourself enough time during your morning commute. ⁹⁴ **If possible, it might be a good idea to leave your cars at home and take the subway to work.**

男 A&F 大樓的所有公司,請注意!提醒大家,⁹² **本市的冬季耶誕節遊行將在星期五下午舉行。**⁹³ 由於本大樓前方道路將於上午十一點封閉到下午六點,請務必將車停在最接近後門入口的街上。此外,當天的交通流量預計將會很可觀,因此,請確保自己早晨通勤時間充裕。⁹⁴ 如果可以,把車留在家裡搭地下鐵來上班,或許是個好主意。

92. What will take place on Friday afternoon?
(A) A contest
(B) A parade*
(C) A repair
(D) A sale

92. 星期五下午會舉行什麼?
(A) 一場競賽。
(B) 一場遊行。
(C) 維修。
(D) 一場拍賣。

93. Look at the graphic. Which street will be closed?
(A) Time Road
(B) Park Road*
(C) Mile Street
(D) Queen Street

93. 請見圖表。哪一條街道將封閉?
(A) 時代路。
(B) 公園路。
(C) 邁爾街。
(D) 皇后街。

94. What does the speaker suggest?
(A) Staying home
(B) Attending an event
(C) Parking underground
(D) Taking public transportation*

94. 說話者有何建議?
(A) 留在家裡。
(B) 參加一場活動。
(C) 車停在地下樓層。
(D) 搭乘大眾交通運輸工具。

Questions 95–97 談話及圖表

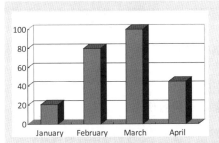

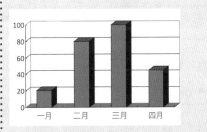

W Good afternoon, staff. ⁹⁵ **I'd like to start our monthly sales meeting by taking a look at our sales progress for our new Garden and Home Monthly Magazine.** As you can see, March has been our most successful month in attracting new ⁹⁵ **subscribers.** This is probably due to our new advertising campaign that was launched in mid-February. Additionally, ⁹⁶ **you can see that our second best sales month occurred during the month we offered subscribers a 20% discount on** ⁹⁵ **yearly subscriptions.** This month, I'd like to brainstorm ways to increase our subscription rate even more. ⁹⁷ **I'd like each of you to come up with a proposal for either a promotional event or an advertising campaign by next Friday.**

女 大家午安。⁹⁵ 每月業務會議的一開始，我想先讓各位看一下我們新出版《園藝家居月刊》的銷售進度。你們可以看到，三月是吸引新 ⁹⁵ 訂戶最為成功的月分。這很可能要歸功於我們在二月中推出的新一波促銷廣告。此外，⁹⁶ 你們可以看到，銷量次佳的月分，出現在我們提供訂戶 ⁹⁵ 訂閱一年八折優惠時。這個月，我要大家腦力激盪，想出讓我們的訂閱率大幅增加的方法。⁹⁷ 我希望你們每個人在下星期五前，想出一個促銷活動或廣告宣傳的提案。

---

95. Where most likely does the speaker work?
(A) At a home improvement store
(B) At an advertising firm
(C) At a publishing company*
(D) At a design company

96. Look at the graphic. When was the discount event held?
(A) In January
(B) In February*
(C) In March
(D) In April

97. According to the speaker, what should staff members do by next Friday?
(A) Edit some articles
(B) Prepare a report*
(C) Book train tickets
(D) Update a website

95. 說話者最可能在哪裡工作？
(A) 在居家裝修商店。
(B) 在廣告公司。
(C) 在出版公司。
(D) 在設計公司。

96. 請見圖表。折扣活動是何時舉行的？
(A) 一月。
(B) 二月。
(C) 三月。
(D) 四月。

97. 根據說話者所述，員工應該在下星期五之前做什麼？
(A) 編輯一些文章。
(B) 準備一份報告。
(C) 預訂火車票。
(D) 更新網站。

	Kimberly Shoe Outlet	Shoe Source Plus
Competitive prices	V	X
Free shipping	V	V
Innovative displays	V	X
100 Online orders	X	V

	金百利鞋子暢貨中心	鞋源加
價格有競爭力	V	X
免運費	V	V
創新的陳列方式	V	X
100 線上訂購服務	X	V

W　To start the meeting, 98 **I'd like to reiterate how impressed I am with our first year of business here at Kimberly Shoe Outlet.** 99 **When I started planning our opening a year ago,** I wasn't sure if we'd do well located near so many other shoe stores. But according to our sales figures, we've managed to beat the competition nearly every month. Now, we need to think of ways to keep that momentum going. Our biggest rival is Shoe Source Plus. As you can see on this chart, we have consistently lower prices than Shoe Source Plus, which has helped to attract customers. 100 **Next, I'd like to talk about what Shoe Source Plus launched last month and what we can do to start offering a similar service.**

女　會議一開始，98 **我想重申我對金百利鞋子暢貨中心第一年的業績，印象有多深刻。**99 **當我一年前開始規劃開店時，**我不確定在多家鞋店環伺之下，我們是否會成功。但從銷量來看，我們幾乎每個月都成功打敗了對手。現在，我們需要想辦法保持那股衝勁。我們最大的競爭對手是「鞋源加」。你們可以從這張表格看出來，我們的價格始終比「鞋源加」低，這有助吸引顧客。100 **接下來，我想談談「鞋源加」上個月推出的策略，以及我們可以怎麼做，以便開始提供類似的服務。**

98. What is the main topic of the meeting?
   (A) A new line of products
   (B) A manager's promotion
   (C) A company's location
   (D) **A business's success***

99. Who most likely is the speaker?
   (A) A shoe designer
   (B) **A store owner***
   (C) An advertiser
   (D) A financial planner

100. Look at the graphic. What will the speaker most likely discuss next?
   (A) Competitive prices
   (B) Free shipping
   (C) Innovative displays
   (D) **Online orders ***

98. 會議的主題為何？
   (A) 新系列產品。
   (B) 經理的升職。
   (C) 公司的地點。
   (D) **生意的成功。**

99. 說話者最可能是誰？
   (A) 鞋子設計師。
   (B) **商店所有人。**
   (C) 廣告客戶。
   (D) 理財專員。

100. 請見圖表。說話者接下來最有可能討論何事？
   (A) 有競爭力的價格。
   (B) 免運費。
   (C) 創新的陳列方式。
   (D) **線上訂購服務。**

◎ **PART 5 解答請見 P. 507 ANSWER KEY**

---

101. 帕克女士打算**自己**面試那些應徵者，因為她比任何人都了解這個職務。

102. 退稅將發還給**在**加州的公務員。

103. 有興趣的團體可以**方便地**在線上報名本週末不動產投資的研討會。

104. 本晉升將**提供**員工更優的福利、公司配車及更多的休假日。

105. 莫林法律事務所的員工**通常**一週工作四天，從週一到週四。

106. 如果商品在購買後一週內退還，均可換貨。

107. 根據這篇文章報導，BTR 電子上一季的利潤比預期**低**。

108. 除了店主**外**，每個人在去年夏季都休了一個禮拜的假。

109. 儘管桃樂絲‧克萊門特的風景畫都出自真實的地點，她仍在作品中投入了大量的**想像力**。

110. 接待員今天下午將會把**更新的**顧客名單交給所有的業務人員。

111. 春季培訓課程設立的目的是為了幫助業務同仁能更**創意地**思考。

112. 在試著組裝這張桌子前，你應該**查看**一下安裝說明。

113. 客服部主管雅內爾女士將在明天的員工會議上，**提出**公司於網路上收到的不良評價。

114. 拉森汽車**在**公關人員辛希亞‧莫里森和 M&T 公關公司的指導**下**努力改善公共形象。

115. 在和新客戶**談話**時，別忘了提到貝金漢下週的促銷活動。

116. 亞歷山大劇院週五晚上的演出票券很快就銷售一空了，因為這場演出是**由**本地兩位知名演員**主演**。

117. 湯普森藝廊將**自** 8 月 1 日**起**延長營業時間。

118. 唐諾‧馬哈尼負責將用品**分發**給所有格雷迪水管維修公司的水管工。

119. 由於這位執行長去年秋天在《今日商業雜誌》的訪談中表達了個人**觀點**，而以頗具雄心而聞名。

120.《財務月刊》的創刊編輯，安娜‧桑切斯很快就贏得了金融界中幾乎**所有人**的敬重。

121. 如評論中所述，劇院的新表演**顯然**大受歡迎。

122. 我們的招聘委員會**一**看完所有履歷表，**就**會編製出一份 20 位應徵者的名單，邀請參加面試。

123. 儘管天氣寒冷，這場音樂會仍然非常成功，吸引了超過 5,000 名的群眾到麋鹿公園暨休閒活動中心觀賞。

124. 寶福德製藥廠的研究同仁將**於**整修**期間**，把會議室當作辦公室使用。

125. 如公司網頁所述，客戶如欲**在**到期日**前**取消會員資格，必須付一筆費用。

126. 雖然該職務說明**與**其他家公司**類似**，但這份工作的薪資卻高出許多。

127. 為確保**遵守**安全規定，僅限資深員工才能進入研究室。

128. 如果窗戶在安裝期間損壞，萊立建材**會提供**免費更換。

129. 在具體審查**細節**前，市議會原則上同意這三個提案。

130. 班‧菲利浦醫院管理人堅持設備的**提升**，將使許多醫療程序更有效率。

Questions 131–134 文章

3月3日一經過將近三年的籌劃，哈普維爾最大的體育場即將動工。世博體育場將設於哈普維爾壯麗的海濱，可容量 10,000 個座位。同時，還有超過 100 個媒體採訪室，每間可容納 10 人之多。這項工程預計花三年的時間完工，即將座落於其他目前正在濱海區興建的新建築區中。根據哈普維爾運動協會理事長馬歇爾・湯瑪士表示，新體育場絕對是必要之建設。「我們需要一座大型體育場來容納逐漸增加的運動社團。」湯瑪士先生說，「另一方面，我們也能把體育場用在音樂會和馬戲團表演上。」

131. (A) 開發業者不確定要花多久時間才能完成這項工程。
(B) 體育場將從濱海區搬到市郊。
(C) 同時，還有超過 100 個媒體採訪室，每間可容納 10 人之多。
(D) 市長拒絕為市區開發計畫提供資金，就產生了延誤。

132. (A) 興建
(B) 正在興建
(C) 被興建
(D) 正在被興建

133. **(A) 必需品**
(B) 麻煩事
(C) 風險
(D) 便宜貨

134. **(A) 另一方面**
(B) 換句話說
(C) 起初
(D) 因此

Questions 135–138 新聞稿

翠登最早的家庭式餐飲加盟連鎖店—霍布森餐飲，其創辦人兼執行長梅雷迪斯・霍布森宣布，她將為市中心賈斯伯社區活動中心的整修工程捐贈 6,500 元。這筆款項來自上週五晚上在其餐館所舉辦的晚宴售票所得。霍布森女士將在預定於明天下午 2:00 所舉辦的特別典禮上將支票贈送給中心的管理人員。在過去的 25 年間來，霍布森女士已經為社區服務與慈善團體籌辦了多場成功的募款活動。但無疑地，上週五的活動是最成功的一場。

135. **(A) 將捐贈**
(B) 捐贈了
(C) 可能捐贈
(D) 捐贈

136. (A) 藝廊
(B) 飯店
(C) 學院
(D) 餐廳

137. (A) 儘管
(B) 在……期間
(C) 在……之間
(D) 在……下方

138. (A) 賈斯伯社區活動中心有針對小孩和大人的課程。
(B) 中心的開幕典禮將於下午 2:30 結束。
(C) 但無疑地，上週五的活動是最成功的一場。
(D) 霍布森女士計畫於明年某個時間在翠登上城開設分店。

Questions 139–142 會議摘要

我們的月會在下午 4:30 開始。這個會議的目的是為了討論 LGQ 國際貨運公司遷址的優缺點。麥克斯・鮑威爾以著眼於提升 LGQ 目前成長模式的重要性，帶領大家討論遷址的可能性。他解釋 LGQ 已經成長為最成功的分銷商之一，同時也配送全國最大量的電子產品。

鮑威爾先生也大致說明了 LGQ 因成長而正在經歷的挑戰。根據最近的報告顯示，就在 LGQ 開始成長時，往來最近港口的成本也變高了。員工們討論了一些可能的解決方案，但仍未達成最後決議。鮑威爾先生將進行更多研究，並於下次會議中報告他的研究結果。

139. (A) 取得
(B) 加入
(C) 宣傳
(D) 搬遷

140. (A) 分發
(B) 分發
(C) 分銷商
(D) 分發

141. (A) 鮑威爾先生也大致說明了 LGQ 因成長而正在經歷的挑戰。
(B) 執行長接著討論了新設施的優點。
(C) 接下來，股東受邀進行投票決定日期。
(D) 鮑威爾先生指示員工思考要如何進行運作。

142. (A) 現在
(B) 為什麼
(C) 就當，就在
(D) 自從

Questions 143–146 電子郵件

寄件者：tina@lindcosmetics.com
收件者：mia@mymailnow.com
日期：9 月 8 日
主旨：訂單 445009

親愛的克拉瑪女士，

感謝您來信詢問訂單狀況。根據我們的紀錄顯示，您在 9 月 1 日於本公司網站訂購了一條林德 SPF50 防曬乳，一瓶林德 500 護手霜，兩瓶超亮澤洗髮精。您的商品預定在 9 月 5 日送達。知道您還未收到商品，讓我深感驚訝。

我已經代您聯絡了運送公司。根據他們的行程表，您的商品將於 9 月 10 日送達。如果您所訂購的東西到那天仍未送抵，可以再次與我們聯繫。

本人衷心地為這次的不便致歉。本公司的配送方式通常快速又便宜。這次的狀況相當特殊，希望不會因此讓您對林德化妝品卻步。

感謝您

林德化妝品
蒂娜·史伯樂

143. (A) 它
(B) 一個
(C) 它們
(D) 一些

144. (A) 我們想邀請您光臨本店。
(B) 請在本公司網站上留下評論。
(C) 這個特定商品目前已售完。
(D) 我已經代您聯絡了運送公司。

145. (A) 聯絡了
(B) 聯絡
(C) 聯絡
(D) 聯絡

146. (A) 相似的
(B) 刺激的
(C) 特殊的，不尋常的
(D) 歡迎

Questions 147-148 廣告

商品待售	價格	地點
火焰鎮烤肉架 型號 A7000	450 元	加州洛杉磯

商品說明：

^{147(D)} **三年前全新購入。原價 700 元，附兩年保固。**

烤架組件已燒焦。^{147(B)} **買方可於火焰鎮網站上購買新品。**

外觀狀況良好（¹⁴⁸ **可應要求提供照片**）。

^{147(C)} **價錢可議。**可配送洛杉磯地區各處。若有疑問，可寄電子郵件至 rjohnson@mail.com。

147. 關於烤肉架，沒有提到什麼事？
 (A) 以原始的箱子包裝。
 (B) 需要新零件。
 (C) 價格未定。
 (D) 已逾保固期。

148. 賣方願意做什麼事？
 (A) 保留商品一個月
 (B) 提供商品使用說明
 (C) 配送至全國各地
 (D) 提供照片給可能的買方

Questions 149-150 通知

¹⁴⁹ **我們很高興宣布寇蒂莉亞・溫特斯加入 IPM 演藝經紀公司**，成為合夥經紀人。溫特斯女士畢業自羅丹大學公共關係學程。在羅丹就學時，她就創辦了該大學第一本由學生主辦的雜誌。畢業後，她在 UV 媒體暨演藝經紀公司實習，那是一家代理各方人才—音樂家、作家、職業運動員和演員的知名經紀公司。溫特斯女士受過優秀的訓練，將成為我們茁壯中的經紀團隊的一大資產。¹⁵⁰ **請於明天上午 10 點到 B 會議室一同歡迎她的加入。**

149. 這個公告最可能出現在哪裡？
 (A) 廣告公司
 (B) 大學
 (C) 錄音室
 (D) 演藝經紀公司

150. 員工受邀明天要做何事？
 (A) 參加會議
 (B) 歡迎新同事
 (C) 拜訪競爭對手
 (D) 與新客戶見面

Questions 151-152 簡訊

提姆・彼得森 [上午 11:03]
嗨，阿曼達。妳可以跟我報告桑普森・蘭恩那裡的最新工作進度嗎？

阿曼達・瑞 [上午 11:10]
我們已經清空主層樓和車庫。現在才剛開始屋子的二樓部分。

提姆・彼得森 [上午 11:12]
就這樣？¹⁵² 你們認為什麼時候可以做完？¹⁵¹ 我們在下午三點還有安排另一家要搬的。

阿曼達・瑞 [上午 11:15]
我們進度落後。當初估算時，沒有考慮到車庫裡的舊家具。

提姆・彼得森 [上午 11:20]
真的嗎？是誰做的估算。

阿曼達・瑞 [上午 11:21]
馬修在休假前做的。

提姆・彼得森 [上午 11:23]
好。下午一點時再跟我報告進度。到時候，我會決定要不要再找一組人幫忙下午的工作。

送出

輸入您的訊息……

151. 瑞女士在哪個行業服務？
 (A) 不動產仲介
 (B) 家具店
 (C) 搬家公司
 (D) 卡車租賃服務

152. 11:12 時，彼得森先生説的「就這樣？」是什麼意思？

(A) 他想知道房子的地址。

(B) 他認為員工工作進度緩慢。

(C) 他很驚訝，因為價格很便宜。

(D) 他想確認所有東西都裝上卡車了。

Questions 153–154 信件

拉賽福眼科診所
加州洛杉磯拉賽福大道 54 號

3 月 14 日

卡崔娜・薩若娃

加州洛杉磯上校巷 123 號

親愛的薩諾娃女士，

153 對拉賽福眼科診所來説，讓所有客戶提前收到本診所規定異動的通知，是非常重要的。自 8 月 1 日起，大多數主要的保險公司將不再給付所有年度例行視力檢查。為了補償這筆費用，本診所的每項檢查將減少 15 元的費用。請查看隨信附上受影響的保險公司名單。

154 在部分特定狀況下，如果您的家人曾在本診所檢查過，我們很樂意免費提供兒童視力檢查。若有任何問題，請來電 445-987-0023 與帳務管理員梅姬・威爾森洽詢該服務。

拉賽福眼科診所
娜迪亞・佛特尼醫師敬上

153. 這封信為什麼會寄給薩諾娃女士？

(A) 為了通知收費異動

(B) 為了宣傳新服務項目

(C) 為了確認預約

(D) 為了通知未做的檢查

154. 關於拉賽福眼科診所，提到了什麼事？

(A) 它想聘僱新員工。

(B) 它延長了營業時間。

(C) 它服務了來自全世界各地的客戶。

(D) 它為特定客戶提供免費服務。

Questions 155–157 文章

西點購物商場動工

撰稿人梅蘭妮・羅森伯格

3 月 23 日——昨天，在贊加市長市中心辦公室的記者會中，市長宣布市府通過了一個新購物商場的開發計畫。根據市長表示，**157 西點購物商場將座落在公園路與威爾森街上。**去年一場大火燒毀了該地的汽車製造廠，空下了那塊地供新開發案使用。

這個購物商場是福克斯市與私人開發企業——溫莎公司的一項合作計畫。這個商場將容納 200 多間新商店、55 家餐廳和一間百貨公司。溫莎公司將負責工程的執行，並監督初期的營運。

「福克斯市一直沒有大型的購物商場，」溫莎公司的強生先生在一場訪談中提到。「藉著建造這座最先進的商場，**155 福克斯的人們也會看到工作機會與觀光業的提升。**」

許多零售業者已經和溫莎公司簽約，以保留商場中的店面。**156 但是部分小型企業主也表達了商場一旦開幕，他們就會沒生意可做的憂慮。**「我的店面已經經營了兩代，」巴利茲鞋店的蜜雪兒・史蒂文斯説，「我的顧客都很忠實，但還是敵不過購物商場的價格。」

155. 溫莎公司希望為福克斯市帶來什麼？

(A) 外國學生

(B) 超市

(C) 更多觀光客

(D) 新小型企業

156. 蜜雪兒・史蒂文斯最有可能是誰？

(A) 報紙記者

(B) 零售店老闆

(C) 市府官員

(D) 土地開發業者

157. 下列句子最適合出現在 [1]、[2]、[3]、[4] 的哪個位置中？

「去年一場大火燒毀了該地的汽車製造廠，空下了那塊地供新開發案使用。」

(A) [1]
(B) [2]
(C) [3]
(D) [4]

Questions 158–160 資訊

西蒙·黛珂
《日落風箏》
行動裝置藝術，彩繪金屬片與金屬棒
1984

《日落風箏》是西蒙·黛珂最受歡迎的行動裝置藝術之一。**158 黛珂在 1970 年代時，運用可攜式馬達創造出行動感的方式，徹底顛覆了行動藝術。**《日落風箏》是黛珂在 1970 至 1988 年間，所創造的較大型系列中的其中一部分。**160(B) 曾於米蘭的抽象藝術美術館、紐約當代藝術美術館、倫敦新趨勢藝術美術館展出。160(C) 黛珂原本將《日落風箏》捐給蒙特內哥羅大學，159 它在那裡展示了十年**，最後由威爾森美術館的麥斯威爾·喬治購得，成為本館永久收藏品之一。在她離世前，160(A) 黛珂曾說《日落風箏》是「她畢生所創作出最充滿熱力的作品」。

158. 這份資料是如何描述西蒙·黛珂的？
(A) 她很留意細節。
(B) 她創作出很多作品。
(C) 她是個具創新風格的藝術家。
(D) 她為窮人服務。

159. 這份資料張貼在那裡？
(A) 抽象藝術美術館
(B) 威爾森美術館
(C) 當代藝術美術館
(D) 新趨勢藝術美術館

160. 關於《日落風箏》，沒有提到什麼事？
(A) 藝術家視其為她最佳作品之一。
(B) 已經流傳至數處。
(C) 曾被大學取得。
(D) 用了將近 20 年的時間完成這件作品。

Questions 161–163 電子郵件

收件者：珍·安德魯斯
寄件者：麥可·貝特利
日期：3 月 7 日
161 主旨：3 月 8 日最新情況

安德魯斯女士，

我為您明天的行程表做了些微的異動。您與潛在客戶傑夫·伍茲的會議已經取消了。**162 他的助理建議 3 月 10 日或許可以碰面。162 由於您當天早上即搭機返回**，當天下午有空。您要我敲定那個會面嗎？請看一下以下更新後的行程表。**163 我已經將伍茲先生的會議改成您的預算審查。**請告訴我這樣是否可行。

時間	會議	與會者
上午 8:30	員工會議	A 與 B 部門
上午 9:45	與華盛頓公司電話會議	潔西卡·鮑爾、湯姆·帕克
163 上午 10:30	**預算審查**	艾利·斯特倫斯基
下午 1:30	討論會議行程	約書亞·威爾森
下午 4:00	前往搭七點的 **162 班機至芝加哥**	

我已經將您的電子機票列印出來，放在公司的信箱了。旅途順利。

麥可敬上

161. 為什麼會寄這封電子郵件？
(A) 要取消下個月的會議
(B) 提供旅遊行程表
(C) 更新日常行程表
(D) 提供會議資料

162. 3 月 10 日會發生什麼事？
(A) 貝特利先生將飛到華盛頓。
(B) 安德魯斯女士要參加會議。
(C) 伍茲先生將舉行預算審查。
(D) 安德魯斯女士將自芝加哥返回。

163. 伍茲先生原本幾點要到？

    (A) 上午 8:35

    (B) 上午 9:45

    (C) 上午 10:30

    (D) 下午 1:30

Questions 164–167 電子郵件

收件者：溫弗雷德金融全體員工
寄件者：珊卓・伯恩斯
日期：10 月 24 日
[164] 主旨：新規定

親愛的全體同仁，

正如各位所知道的，為了減少冬季能源的消耗量，衛生暨環境部已經推行了一套適用於辦公場所的新法規。[164] **為配合新規定，溫弗雷德金融將於冬季期間設定暖氣系統。** 確切地來説，就是各位無法隨時調整辦公室的溫度。平日時，這個系統會讓整棟大樓的溫度上升到攝氏 19 度，然後一整天都 [165] **維持** 在 19 度的狀況下。到了每天下班時，就會降到攝氏 13 度。[166] **依循這個新規定，我們應該會看到電費減少了 10%。**

由於部分同仁會在週末時上班，管理部已經決定五樓的辦公室將可手動控溫。[167] **週末上班的同仁可向部門主管提出辦公室異動的申請。** 我們只要求辦公室的溫度不要超過攝氏 19 度即可。

總經理
珊卓・伯恩斯 敬上

164. 這封電子郵件的目的是什麼？

    (A) 宣布辦公場所即將出現的變動

    (B) 通知員工排定的檢測

    (C) 鼓勵員工挑選新辦公家具

    (D) 提供主管升遷機會

165. 第一段、第五行的「maintained」與下列哪一個意思最接近？

    (A) 確認

    (B) 修理

    (C) 拿取

    (D) 保持

166. 文中提到下列何者是新規定的好處？

    (A) 將改善員工工作效率。

    (B) 可讓公司聘用更多員工。

    (C) 幫公司省錢。

    (D) 可適用於公家與私人企業。

167. 週末上班的員工被建議做什麼事？

    (A) 直接寄電子郵件給伯恩斯女士

    (B) 提出更換辦公室的申請

    (C) 更動工作時間表

    (D) 週末在家工作

Questions 168–171 網路聊天

瑪莉・瑞諾德 [下午 2:02]
嗨，班。[168] **可以撥出點時間來嗎？我想要再跟你仔細核對一下庫存報告。**

班・傑傅瑞 [下午 2:03]
沒問題。

瑪莉・瑞諾德 [下午 2:04]
根據這份報告，[170] **我們只剩兩台康普 A75 筆記型電腦了。** 我們最近賣出很多台這型號的電腦。我要再多訂嗎？

班・傑傅瑞 [下午 2:06]
沒必要。新的型號 A76 剛推出。我們要改賣那個型號。[169] **我已經訂了 50 台新的。** 不過還沒到貨。

瑪莉・瑞諾德 [下午 2:10]
喔，好的。感謝你的説明。

班・傑傅瑞 [下午 2:11]
[171] **我們下禮拜開始就要在架上展示，所以一定要把產品資料印出來供展示用。**

瑪莉・瑞諾德 [下午 2:12]
好的。我馬上就著手進行。

168. 下午 2:03 時，傑傅瑞先生説的「沒問題」最可能是什麼意思？

    (A) 他贊同瑞諾德女士的想法。

    (B) 他方便回答瑞諾德女士的問題。

    (C) 他想要安排與瑞諾德女士的會議。

    (D) 他完全照著瑞諾德女士的要求做。

169. 關於傑傅瑞先生，提到了什麼事？
(A) 他已經訂購了一些商品。
(B) 他下載了一些資料。
(C) 他今天安置了一些產品。
(D) 他上週拜訪了一位供應商。

170. 傑傅瑞先生與瑞諾德女士從事哪一種行業？
(A) 電腦修理公司
(B) 貨運公司
(C) 電子用品店
(D) 軟體開發業者

171. 傑傅瑞先生與瑞諾德女士下週要做什麼？
(A) 整修店面
(B) 為新產品舉辦銷售會
(C) 退還過時的商品
(D) 擺設商品陳列

Questions 172–175 文章

6月15日—已故百萬富翁華特‧霍爾曼的家「華特‧霍爾曼莊園」最近被羅傑頓市府收購。根據羅傑頓歷史協會主任瑪莉卡‧崔頓表示，在轉型為在地博物館前，將對莊園進行小幅整修與修復。崔頓表示：**172「霍爾曼家擁有所有的原始裝潢與家具，可供遊客欣賞。」**

數十年來，「華特‧霍爾曼莊園」一直無人入住。倒是提供給私人宴會租用與婚禮使用。一些大型電影公司甚至將莊園當作拍攝場景。**173然而，讓莊園保持良好狀態的維護費用對該家族來說太高了。**華特‧霍爾曼的孫子，史蒂芬‧霍爾曼說：「這是個很困難的決定。我們家族已經擁有這個莊園好幾個世代了，但賣掉莊園才是確保它永續保存的最佳方式。」**175霍爾曼家族的其他人也對莊園將轉型為博物館表達滿意。**他們很高興華特‧霍爾曼的回憶能被保存下來。

174羅傑頓歷史協會打算開發莊園房舍的導覽之旅，同時也繼續提供花園舉辦私人宴會。來到莊園的遊客可以了解霍爾曼家族的歷史，從早期移民到成為全國第一波食品加工公司企業主之一的發跡史。

預計自明年春天起開放參觀。有興趣購買門票或了解莊園歷史的人，可至 www. walterhormanestate.com/info 查詢。

172. 關於華特‧霍爾曼莊園，提到了什麼事？
(A) 由華特霍爾曼的父親所建。
(B) 預約莊園作派對使用很昂貴。
(C) 其中設備將升級。
(D) 包含原有的家具。

173. 根據文章內容，霍爾曼家族覺得什麼很困難？
(A) 將房產改成公園
(B) 維護莊園
(C) 為房舍找家具
(D) 找到適當買主

174. 根據文章內容，莊園的哪個部分將維持不變？
(A) 仍為霍爾曼家族擁有。
(B) 外牆將做為防禦使用。
(C) 建築將做為客房使用。
(D) 外面的地產可供租用。

175. 下列句子最適合出現在 [1]、[2]、[3]、[4] 的哪個位置中？
「他們很高興華特‧霍爾曼的回憶能被保存下來。」
(A) [1]
(B) [2]
(C) [3]
(D) [4]

Questions 176–180 電子郵件

収件者：samadams@adamsroofing.com
寄件者：ginachoi@homeimprovementmonthly.com
日期：1月3日
主旨：《家居裝飾月刊》

親愛的亞當斯先生，

176 《家居裝飾月刊》將提供本雜誌新廣告商優惠價，做為新年促銷活動。《家居裝飾月刊》擁有超過 20,000 的紙本訂閱量。177 您的廣告將以平面形式傳達給所有訂閱戶，以及廣大電子訂閱戶。有了我們的服務，貴公司的業績絕對可以增加。

這個優惠只到 3 月 1 日有效。我們的優惠方案簡述如下。**178 本雜誌的美術設計已經準備好要根據您所需的規格設計出彩色廣告。**欲購買任何優惠套組，請以電子郵件回覆，或 上 網 www.homeimprovementmonthly.com/advertisements/orders。

套組	廣告格式	月費
1	一則全頁平面廣告加橫幅網頁廣告	300 元
2	一則半頁平面廣告加半橫幅網頁廣告	275 元
3	一則半頁平面廣告加網頁截角廣告	250 元
4	**180 一則 1/4 頁平面廣告加網頁截角廣告**	225 元

《家居裝飾月刊》

廣告統籌
吉娜‧崔敬上

収件者：ginachoi@homeimprovementmonthly.com
寄件者：samadams@adamsroofing.com
日期：1月5日
主旨：回覆：《家居裝飾月刊》

親愛的崔女士，

感謝您寄電子郵件告知貴雜誌的促銷活動。我的商業合夥人和我頗有興趣在貴雜誌 **179 刊登廣告。**不過，我對 **180 您的 1/4 頁平面**

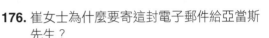

廣告有些疑問。我買了一份雜誌，也看了廣告。我發現有些廣告在雜誌的前頁，而有些卻刊在後頁。我想了解決定廣告刊登位置的因素是什麼。如果我們想把自己的廣告刊在前頁，是不是需要額外付費？

在此先感謝您的回答。

亞當斯屋頂工程 共同經營人
山姆‧亞當斯 敬上

176. 崔女士為什麼要寄這封電子郵件給亞當斯先生？
(A) 告知一個新的廣告機會
(B) 提供訂閱促銷優惠
(C) 鼓勵他僱用行銷公司
(D) 通知合約上的異動

177. 關於《家居裝飾月刊》，提到了什麼事？
(A) 有幾期晚送達。
(B) 廣告商可免費訂閱。
(C) 自明年起將每月發行兩期。
(D) 部分訂閱戶只訂電子版。

178. 關於《家居裝飾月刊》的美術設計，提到了什麼事？
(A) 他們可提供客製化服務。
(B) 他們要求額外費用。
(C) 他們也設計公司網頁。
(D) 他們要到三月才有空。

179. 在第二封電子郵件中，第一段、第二行的「placing」與下列哪一個意思最接近？
(A) 僱用
(B) 放置
(C) 分配
(D) 計算

180. 亞當斯先生最有可能採用哪一個方案？
(A) 第一套組
(B) 第二套組
(C) 第三套組
(D) 第四套組

Questions 181-185 電子郵件

收件者：mpordeski@mailme.com
寄件者：imranandal@pearsonmedicalresearch.com
日期：4 月 12 日
[181] **主旨**：培生醫學研究職位
附件：合約

親愛的波多斯基女士，

與您在電話面試中相談甚歡。我很高興能提供您本團隊研究助理一職。我想您知道，您將與全國最頂尖的醫學研究員合作，有機會使用最先進的設備。在六個月的合約期間中，您在生物與工程學中的教育背景將會是一大優勢。

正如我向您提過的，本公司與奧斯丁大學合作。因此您需要了解本公司總部與大學實驗室周邊的路徑。更確切地說，我將為您與其他新進研究員安排一場新進員工訓練。[185] 您提過您即將結束大四課程，所以我會安排一個不會妨礙到您行程的時間。麻煩您告訴我五月的哪一天是方便的。

[181] **請注意這個職位是實習職**。您的薪資是每週 200 元，偶爾職務上的支出也可核銷。不過在六個月實習期間後，[183] **我們將提供長期職位給表現優異的實習生**。[182] **請在附件中的合約上簽名並寄回，以確定您已接受這些條款**。若有任何問題，本公司人力資源部經理安德魯·百克斯特將與您聯絡。

感謝您，並期待與您共事。

培生醫學研究所 首席研究員
伊姆蘭·安鐸

收件者：實習生群組
寄件者：imranandal@pearsonmedicalresearch.com
日期：4 月 24 日
主旨：新進員工訓練

親愛的實習研究員，

由於您們當中有大多數人無法挪出同一時間來，我打算舉辦兩場新進員工訓練，一

場在 5 月 11 日，第二場在 5 月 16 日。[185] **5 月 16 日那場新進員工訓練之所以安排在週末，是為了給群組中的學生參加的**。若您不是學生身分，我們希望您參加 5 月 11 日的新進員工訓練。兩場訓練講習都將於當天上午九點在本公司總部舉行。在導覽後，我們將於巴夫小館用餐。之後，我們再走路到大學區。請攜帶附照片的證件，以方便進入大學實驗室。

感謝各位，期待見到大家。

培生醫學研究所 首席研究員
伊姆蘭·安鐸

---

181. 安鐸先生為什麼要寫信給波多斯基女士？
(A) 協商合約內容
(B) 邀她應徵工作
(C) 提供醫療協助
(D) 提供她實習職

182. 波多斯基女士被要求寄回什麼文件？
(A) 僱主推薦信
(B) 已簽名的合約
(C) 課程申請表
(D) 大學成績單

183. 提到什麼有關培生醫學研究所新職員的事？
(A) 他們可以在家工作。
(B) 他們的稅單必須上網提交。
(C) 他們無法獲得薪資。
(D) 他們的表現會受到評估。

184. 安德魯·百克斯特為什麼可能會聯絡波多斯基女士？
(A) 檢閱公司規定
(B) 解決合約問題
(C) 要求更多推薦信
(D) 說明付款流程

185. 波多斯基女士最有可能參加何時的新進員工訓練？
(A) 5 月 11 日
(B) 5 月 15 日
(C) 5 月 16 日
(D) 5 月 19 日

Questions 186–190 網頁及電子郵件

http://www.internationalspaceexplorationexpo.com

| 首頁 | 關於我們 | 活動 | 活動時間表 |

今年的國際太空探索博覽會（ISEE）將會是有史以來最棒的一場。**¹⁸⁶ 為了慶祝十週年紀念，ISEE 預計以五天的時間，推出最先進的太空探索科技展覽。** 將有 30 多位的業界領袖演講，並安排各種精彩的活動，包括：

V 會議中心展示導覽
V 新太空引擎科技展示
V 兒童工作坊，包括手作體驗
V **¹⁸⁸ 建造廢金屬太空船比賽**（成人可參加）
V 《太空旅行的未來》作者，**¹⁹⁰ 麥可 • 帕克斯維爾博士朗讀會**
V SEE 頒獎典禮，表揚太空科技中最傑出的成就

完整活動清單，請參考網頁活動時間表。

收件者：帕克 • 羅傑斯
寄件者：凱倫 • 沃克
主旨：博覽會事項更新
日期：10 月 27 日

¹⁸⁷ 我很高興您派我去採訪 ISEE。這是個很棒的經驗。 我在會議中心的導覽中度過了第一天。一些展示與新科技都讓我感到驚奇。**¹⁸⁸ 遺憾的是，導覽的時間有點長，我沒看到建造太空船的活動。** 不過我訪問了幾位博覽會的參與者，也拍到了孩子們品嚐太空食物的精彩照片。

我 **¹⁸⁹ 想**，**¹⁹⁰ 明天在帕克斯維爾博士讀完他書中一些摘錄後，我應該可以採訪到他。** 由於他剛榮獲年度最佳書籍獎，我想他的訪談或許可以成為下週刊號中，一則很棒的特別報導。我今晚會寄一份準備好的採訪問題給您過目。麻煩告訴我，您是否要增加任何訪談問題。

凱倫 敬上

收件者：麥可 • 帕克斯維爾
寄件者：凱倫 • 沃克
主旨：後續採訪問題
日期：10 月 29 日

親愛的帕克斯維爾博士，

昨天能與您對談，真是太棒了。我寄了一份訪談稿給我的編輯。他非常喜歡您的對答及照片。不過他還有一些問題想請教您。**¹⁹⁰ 我希望明天能在您的導讀後與您會面。** 應該不會超過 10 或 20 分鐘，請告訴我您是否可行。

凱倫 • 沃克 敬上

---

186. 關於 ISEE，提到了什麼事？
(A) 最初是為學生設計的。
(B) 一年舉辦多次。
(C) 已經存在多年。
(D) 遷至新會場。

187. 沃克女士最有可能是誰？
(A) 出版商
(B) 太空人
(C) 科學家
(D) 記者

188. 根據沃克女士表示，她沒有參加到哪一個會議活動？
(A) 展示
(B) 手工製作比賽
(C) 導覽
(D) 工作坊

189. 在第一封電子郵件中，第二段、第一行的「figured」與下列哪一個意思最接近？
(A) 決定
(B) 參與
(C) 代表
(D) 執行

190. 文中提到何者與帕克斯維爾博士有關的事？
(A) 他今年獲得了好幾個獎項。
(B) 他將在博覽會發表好幾場演講。
(C) 他是著名的報紙編輯。
(D) 他每年都做示範。

Questions 191–195 文章、報紙社論及電子郵件

布雷登伯里（6月11日）——布雷登伯里市鎮官員今天坐下來討論，數年來一直需要大規模維修的莫撒敏大橋的命運。今天的會議是該議題預訂議程中的第一場。雖然大規模的修復是其中一個選項，但幾個難題可能會迫使市鎮府拆除整座橋的結構。

192(B)「修復整座橋的成本太高了，」城市規畫師伊爾凱‧緹黛絲爾說，「我看到的是，汰換橋的結構是唯一財政上可行的方案。」

根據知名結構工程師麥爾坎‧汪達表示，交通流量也必須納入考量。191「209號高速公路即將增加兩線道，成為四線道公路，但莫撒敏大橋無法容納如此多的車輛增加。」汪達說，「除了建造一座更大更現代化的橋樑外，我看不出還有其他選擇。」

市鎮議會也希望廣納居民們對這個議題的看法。195 所有想要表達自己意見者，可以參加下週一下午4:30在市鎮府前阿克巴廣場所舉辦的公共論壇。

給編輯的信

192(C) 6月12日——昨天有關莫撒敏大橋的未來一文，促使我寫下這篇回應。這座橋不只是一座橋；192(D) 它是布雷登伯里文化不可或缺的一部分。為此，本鎮必須保留這座橋的結構是完整的。除此之外，考量觀光業每年所帶來的高收益，192(B) 修復這座地標的短期成本最終將證明是有利的。

布雷登伯里保護協會（BPS）創始會員 皮爾‧阿瑟頓

收件者：members@bredenburypressoc.org
寄件者：isabellecharlebois@bredenburypressoc.org
日期：6月23日
主旨：莫撒敏大橋的最新狀況

親愛的BPS會員，

恭喜大家！由於本會在市鎮議會上的強勢表現，加上193 無數的電子郵件、信件、與致電給市議會議員，看起來大橋免於被拆除的命運。根據今天《布雷登伯里先驅報》的一篇文章指出，市鎮府已經決定要將莫撒敏橋大重新安置到本鎮的最南端，僅供行人使用，而不開放給汽機車使用。

195 全體會員都該為上週一的勇於發聲、表達意見而自豪。194 各位的行動確實影響了市鎮府的決定。表現得太好了！

再次感謝各位

布雷登伯里保護協會會長
伊莎貝爾‧查爾鮑伊斯

191. 文章中，提到什麼與布雷登伯里市鎮有關的事？
(A) 它將增加年度預算。
(B) 它將提升一條道路品質。
(C) 它將實行本地停車規定。
(D) 它將提供特別導覽以吸引觀光客。

192. 關於阿瑟頓先生，沒有提到什麼事？
(A) 他和汪達先生共事。
(B) 他不認同緹黛絲爾女士的看法。
(C) 他看了6月11日報紙的報導。
(D) 他很重視市府地標。

193. 在電子郵件中，第一段、第二行的「countless」與下列哪一個意思最接近？
(A) 未經報導的
(B) 已登記的
(C) 許多的
(D) 含糊不清的

194. 查爾鮑伊斯女士為什麼要恭喜BPS會員？
(A) 他們影響了一個鎮的決定。
(B) 他們選出了一位新副會長。
(C) 他們是頭版新聞的主角。
(D) 他們為市鎮工程另外募款。

195. 關於 BPS 會員，提到了什麼事？

    (A) 他們協助修復了一座建築結構。

    (B) 其中很多人在阿克巴廣場發聲。

    (C) 其中很多人住在南端。

    (D) 他們在每個月的第一個星期一聚會。

Questions 196–200 網頁、收據及評論

http://www.grandcanyonexploreadventure.com

首頁	行程	預約	客戶服務

20 多年以來，我們經驗豐富的飛行員一直導覽著令人驚嘆、獨特的大峽谷觀光行程，讓遊客一覽無遺大峽谷絕佳的景緻。我們的行程可提供給高達六位乘客的團體，還可用英文、法文、西班牙文與中文進行導覽。請參考以下的行程表，再到我們的預約網頁了解更多價格相關的資訊。

- 大峽谷直升機之旅—每天下午 2:30 至 3:30。搭直升機飛越壯麗的大峽谷來度過您的午後時光。**196 您將可看到胡佛水壩，米德湖和周遭沙漠的絕妙景致。**

- 大峽谷直升機含午餐之旅—每天上午 11:30 至下午 3:00。**196 參觀「大峽谷直升機之旅」中所有驚人的空中景色。** 在這趟空中導覽之後，您將下降 4,000 英呎至峽谷底床，於科羅拉多河岸邊享用野餐式的午餐。

- **197 終極大峽谷套裝行程**—每天上午 **11:30 至晚上 6:00。** 享受我們其他行程的所有特點，包括空中之旅與野餐式午餐。午餐後，您可盡情探索歷史上美國原住民的家園，再次回到直升機進行第二趟飛行，觀賞美麗的夕陽。**199 參加本行程，還可獲贈探索與冒險小屋的牛排晚餐。**

客戶預約收據

購買日期： 8 月 3 日

客戶姓名： 瓊恩‧湯普森

編號： 877573999

預約細項	乘客數量	付款總額
197,200 終極大峽谷套裝行程（8 月 27 日出發）	6 X 80 元	480 元

199 付款方式： 信用卡

卡號： 111222-359229

持卡人姓名： 瓊恩‧湯普森

卡片到期日： 7 月 20 日

198 請保留一份收據作為記錄。 我們建議您影印一份，於行程當天隨身攜帶。此外，**197 我們也建議您在出發前一個小時抵達，以了解所有安全注意事項。**

http://www.grandcanyonexploreadventure.com/customerservice/customerreviews

首頁	行程	預約	**客戶服務**

大峽谷探索與冒險公司客戶評論：

整體來說，我對大峽谷探索與冒險公司的服務不是很滿意。我一開始訂了六個人的「終極大峽谷套裝行程」。但其中一位乘客意外地染上流行性感冒病倒了。**200 大峽谷探索與冒險公司卻拒絕退票，意思是，我們五個人被迫付了全額。** 除此之外，即使我們在要求的時間抵達，我們出發的時間還是延誤了半個小時，而且這還佔用到我們的探險時間。這趟旅程唯一的補償就是我們的導遊，貝絲‧李察斯，她談吐得體又親切。總而言之，我不推薦大峽谷探索與冒險公司給各位。

瓊恩‧湯普森 8 月 29 日

196. 有關大峽谷直升機含午餐的套裝行程，下列何者為真？

    (A) 為大型團體而設計。

    (B) 包含在餐廳用餐。

    (C) 最暢銷的行程。

    (D) 帶客人飛越胡佛水壩與米德湖。

197. 湯普森女士一行人必須在哪一天幾點到達出發地點？

    (A) 8 月 3 日上午 10:30

    (B) 8 月 3 日上午 11:30

    (C) 8 月 27 日上午 10:30

    (D) 8 月 27 日下午 2:30

198. 大峽谷探索與冒險公司建議湯普森女士做什麼？

(A) 在網站上寫評論

(B) 透過銀行轉帳付款

(C) 自行攜帶食物

(D) 保留一份收據

199. 有關湯普森女士的行程，提到了什麼事？

(A) 湯普森女士以現金付款。

(B) 主打河上獨木舟之旅。

(C) 導遊非常無禮又不專業。

(D) 以一份免費餐點畫下句點。

200. 根據湯普森女士表示，他們那團應該要收多少錢才對？

(A) 80 元

(B) 350 元

(C) 400 元

(D) 480 元

ACTUAL TEST ③

1. (A) He's trimming a tree.
   (B) He's wiping a machine.
   (C) He's opening a package.
   (D) He's holding a container.*

2. (A) Some cyclists are racing on a track.
   (B) Some cyclists are checking the tires.
   (C) Some cyclists are standing next to their bikes.*
   (D) Some cyclists are stopping at the traffic light.

3. **(A) Some laundry is hanging on the line.***
   (B) Towels are being folded.
   (C) The grass is being watered.
   (D) A man is washing some clothes.

4. (A) Customers are waiting around the cash register.
   (B) Some men are examining the vending machine.
   (C) One of the men is writing on a clipboard.
   (D) A woman is sitting with her knees over the armrest.*

5. (A) A man is opening the door to the garage.
   (B) Some crates are stacked in the back of a vehicle.*
   (C) A cart is being pushed up a ramp.
   (D) A trailer is being towed by a car.

6. (A) The steps are being repaired.
   (B) A tree is growing against the building.
   (C) Leaves are being swept out of the path.
   (D) A wooden handrail lines a staircase.*

PART 2 P. 102

7. When is the training session due to finish?
   (A) I am catching a train.
   (B) Not until 5.*
   (C) From the warehouse.

8. Where can I use a computer?
   (A) Two e-mail messages.
   (B) It's my pleasure.
   (C) In the business lounge downstairs.*

1. (A) 他在修剪樹木。
   (B) 他在擦拭機器。
   (C) 他正打開包裹。
   (D) 他正拿著一個容器。

2. (A) 有些自行車騎士正在賽道上比賽。
   (B) 有些自行車騎士正在檢查輪胎。
   (C) 有些自行車騎士站在他們的單車旁邊。
   (D) 有些自行車騎士停在紅綠燈前面。

3. **(A) 有些洗好的衣服掛在曬衣繩上。**
   (B) 正在摺毛巾。
   (C) 正在給草坪澆水。
   (D) 一名男子正在洗衣服。

4. (A) 顧客在收銀機周圍等候。
   (B) 有些男子正在檢查自動販賣機。
   (C) 其中一名男子正在板夾上寫字。
   (D) 一名女子坐著，膝蓋跨在椅子扶手上。

5. (A) 一名男子正打開車庫的門。
   (B) 一些板條箱堆放在車子的後車廂。
   (C) 正把一輛手推車推上斜坡。
   (D) 汽車拖著一輛拖車。

6. (A) 階梯正在整修。
   (B) 一棵樹緊靠著大樓生長。
   (C) 正把小徑上的樹葉掃到旁邊。
   (D) 木製欄杆沿著樓梯排成一列。

7. 訓練課程預計何時結束？
   (A) 我在趕火車。
   (B) 直到五點。
   (C) 來自倉庫。

8. 哪裡有電腦可用？
   (A) 兩封電子郵件訊息。
   (B) 別客氣。
   (C) 樓下的商務貴賓室。

9. What's the fee for the city bus tour?
   (A) I would recommend it to you.
   (B) A few famous museums.
   (C) **Twelve dollars per person.***

10. Where is the shareholder meeting taking place?
    (A) **On the 7th floor of the west wing.***
    (B) At the end of the month.
    (C) Yes, we invested in the new factory.

11. How much did sales drop last quarter?
    (A) At its headquarters.
    (B) **By almost 10%.***
    (C) Sorry, that's not for sale.

12. Would you like some magazines while you wait?
    (A) No, to buy a pair of jeans.
    (B) **Yes, that would be great.***
    (C) The room was too crowded.

13. Who's in charge of cleaning the copy room?
    (A) Next to the coffee machine.
    (B) **It's Daniel's job.***
    (C) I didn't expect it.

14. Isn't the elevator still being repaired?
    (A) **No, I just came up on it.***
    (B) It's made of aluminum.
    (C) I need some time to prepare.

15. The printer in my office is extremely slow.
    (A) **Make a request for a new one.***
    (B) It's not an easy choice.
    (C) Yes, the traffic was really bad this morning.

16. Which dining table did you buy?
    (A) After the holidays.
    (B) The restaurants on Green Edge Road.
    (C) **I chose the smallest one.***

17. Could we postpone the meeting until next week?
    (A) Yes, within 24 hours.
    (B) **I'll be attending a conference in Rochester.***
    (C) You can't miss it.

9. 市區觀光巴士的車資多少？
   (A) 我會推薦給你。
   (B) 一些有名的博物館。
   (C) **每人 12 元。**

10. 股東會議在哪裡舉行？
    (A) **在西側大樓的七樓。**
    (B) 在月底。
    (C) 是的，我們投資新工廠。

11. 上一季的銷量下跌多少？
    (A) 在總公司。
    (B) **將近 10%。**
    (C) 抱歉，那是非賣品。

12. 在你等候時，想看點雜誌嗎？
    (A) 不，去買一條牛仔褲。
    (B) **好啊，那太好了。**
    (C) 房間裡太擁擠了。

13. 誰負責打掃影印室？
    (A) 在咖啡機旁邊。
    (B) **那是丹尼爾的工作。**
    (C) 我沒料到會這樣。

14. 電梯不是還在修理嗎？
    (A) **沒有，我才剛搭電梯上來的。**
    (B) 是用鋁做的。
    (C) 我需要一些時間準備。

15. 我辦公室的印表機速度非常慢。
    (A) **要求換一台新的。**
    (B) 難以抉擇。
    (C) 是的，今天早上的交通狀況確實很糟。

16. 你買了哪一種餐桌？
    (A) 假期之後。
    (B) 在綠緣路的餐廳。
    (C) **我選了最小的那一張。**

17. 我們可以把會議延到下星期嗎？
    (A) 是的，24 小時之內。
    (B) **我到時要去羅徹斯特參加研討會。**
    (C) 你一定找得到。

18. The workers are installing the new heating system now, right?

    (A) Yes, we will have a warmer office soon.*

    (B) An installation art piece.

    (C) She's a software developer.

19. How do I subscribe to the journal?

    (A) On the paper.

    (B) They cost six dollars each.

    (C) You can simply sign up on this form.*

20. I can go to the print shop to collect the brochures.

    (A) Yes, many customers like it.

    (B) Thanks, that would save me some time.*

    (C) When did the designer quit?

21. Could you cover my shift tomorrow?

    (A) Some tables.

    (B) I have an appointment in the morning.*

    (C) They are in a café.

22. I think Nadia should deliver the lecture.

    (A) In the executive board room.

    (B) But Savitri is an expert on the subject.*

    (C) A few people were absent.

23. Your company advertises in several newspapers, doesn't it?

    (A) Not this year.*

    (B) A weekly report.

    (C) She's an editor.

24. Can I leave my car here overnight?

    (A) The engine sounds strange.

    (B) The owner has arrived.

    (C) You have to pay a fee.*

25. Who took the garbage out?

    (A) I can look after the plant.

    (B) I did in the morning.*

    (C) Several used batteries.

26. Let's practice our presentation.

    (A) The clients were impressed.

    (B) An award winner.

    (C) Room 305 has a projector.*

18. 工人現在正在裝設暖氣系統，對嗎？

    (A) 是的，我們的辦公室很快就會變暖和了。

    (B) 一件裝置藝術作品。

    (C) 她是軟體開發人員。

19. 我該如何訂閱那份期刊？

    (A) 在紙上。

    (B) 每一份六元。

    (C) 你只要在這張表格上登記就可以。

20. 我可以去影印店領取廣告小冊子。

    (A) 是的，很多顧客喜歡。

    (B) 謝謝，那會幫我省下一些時間。

    (C) 設計師何時辭職的？

21. 你明天可以幫我代班嗎？

    (A) 一些桌子。

    (B) 我早上有約。

    (C) 他們在咖啡館。

22. 我認為應該由娜迪亞發表演講。

    (A) 在執行董事會會議室。

    (B) 但莎薇翠是那個主題的專家。

    (C) 有些人缺席。

23. 你公司在好幾家報紙上登廣告，不是嗎？

    (A) 今年沒有。

    (B) 週報表。

    (C) 她是編輯。

24. 我可以把車停在這裡一整晚嗎？

    (A) 引擎聽起來有怪聲。

    (B) 車主已經到了。

    (C) 你必須付費。

25. 誰把垃圾拿出去倒了？

    (A) 我可以照顧植物。

    (B) 我今天早上倒的。

    (C) 好幾個用過的電池。

26. 我們來練習簡報吧。

    (A) 客戶印象深刻。

    (B) 得獎者。

    (C) 305 室有投影機。

27. Why did the taxi driver decide to make a detour?
  (A) After the trip.
  (B) He heard about an accident on the radio.*
  (C) Please be there by four.

28. My plane will depart two hours late.
  (A) I hope you don't miss your connecting flight.*
  (B) We have a new department.
  (C) Gate 7 is on your left.

29. Do you think we should bring an umbrella, or will the weather get better?
  (A) You can bring a friend.
  (B) I'd rather do it again.
  (C) We will mostly be in the car.*

30. I think my new landlord owns several apartments.
  (A) I like my neighborhood.
  (B) I didn't know you moved.*
  (C) We met a real estate agent.

31. Wasn't the swimming pool scheduled to open this week?
  (A) It failed the inspection.*
  (B) I'll schedule a pickup.
  (C) No, only for today.

27. 計程車司機為什麼決定繞道？
  (A) 旅行之後。
  (B) 他從收音機聽到有車禍。
  (C) 請在四點前到那裡。

28. 我的班機會晚兩個小時起飛。
  (A) 希望你不會錯過轉接的班機。
  (B) 我們有個新的部門。
  (C) 七號登機門在你的左邊。

29. 你覺得我們應該帶傘，還是天氣會好轉？
  (A) 你可以帶朋友來。
  (B) 我寧願再做一次。
  (C) 我們大部分時間會在車上。

30. 我想，我的新房東擁有好幾間公寓。
  (A) 我喜歡我住的那一帶。
  (B) 我不知道你搬家了。
  (C) 我們遇見一位不動產經紀人。

31. 游泳池不是預定這個星期開放嗎？
  (A) 它沒有通過檢驗。
  (B) 我會安排接機。
  (C) 沒有，只有今天。

PART 3   P. 103-107   🎧 11

Questions 32–34 對話

M	Hi, I'm wondering if you can help me with a return. **32 I bought this sweater here yesterday,** but it seems to be damaged.	男 嗨，不知道你是否可以幫我處理退貨。**32 我昨天在這裡買了這件毛衣**，但它似乎有瑕疵。
W	Oh, that's unfortunate. What seems to be the problem with it? May I have a look?	女 噢，很遺憾，是什麼問題呢？我可以看一下嗎？
M	Sure. I didn't notice it when I tried it on, but there is a white spot on the back of it. I'm hoping I can get a refund.	男 當然。我試穿的時候沒有注意到，但後面有一塊白色汙點。我希望可以退費。
W	I see what you mean. **33 It looks like a flaw that occurred during the dyeing process.** I can definitely help you with your return. **34 Just give me your receipt and membership card to start.**	女 我了解了。**33 看起來是染色過程產生的瑕疵**。沒問題，我會幫您處理退貨。**34 首先，請給我您的收據和會員卡。**

32. Where is the conversation most likely taking place?

    (A) At a clothing store*

    (B) At an outdoor market

    (C) At a second-hand shop

    (D) At a fabric store

33. What is the problem?

    (A) The price was not correct.

    (B) A receipt is missing.

    (C) An item is defective.*

    (D) A product is sold out.

34. What does the woman ask the man for?

    (A) A membership upgrade

    (B) His current address

    (C) A credit card number

    (D) Proof of payment*

Questions 35–37 對話

W	Hello, I'm calling about my tickets to the National Business Convention. I've just purchased them online. **35 I want to print the tickets,** but I can't seem to find them.
M	Yes, **36 we've been having trouble with our payment forms.** I'm sorry for the inconvenience. I can check your account for you. What's your full name?
W	Betty Miller. I'm a premium member of your website.
M	Okay, I see your information. It looks like your payment did not go through. **37 If you give me your credit card information, I can complete the transaction and send your tickets to you by e-mail.**

35. What is the woman trying to do?

    (A) Get a refund

    (B) Print some tickets*

    (C) Reserve a flight

    (D) Schedule an event

---

32. 這段對話最可能在哪裡發生？

    (A) 在服飾店。

    (B) 在露天市場。

    (C) 在二手商店。

    (D) 在布料行。

33. 出現了什麼問題？

    (A) 價錢不對。

    (B) 收據遺失。

    (C) 物品有瑕疵。

    (D) 有項產品售完。

34. 女子向男子要求什麼？

    (A) 會員升級。

    (B) 他目前的地址。

    (C) 信用卡卡號。

    (D) 付款證明。

女	哈囉，我打電話來是為了我買的全國商業大會入場券。我剛上網訂購，**35 想要把入場券列印出來**，但我似乎找不到票券。
男	是的，**36 我們的付款表格一直出問題。** 抱歉造成您的不便。我可以幫您查看帳戶。您的全名是？
女	貝蒂‧米勒。我是你們網站的尊爵會員。
男	好的，我看到您的資料了。看來您的付款沒有成功。**37 如果您給我信用卡資料，我可以完成交易，然後用電子郵件把票寄給您。**

35. 女子想要做什麼？

    (A) 拿到退款。

    (B) 列印一些票券。

    (C) 預訂航班。

    (D) 安排活動的時間。

36. What has caused a problem?

    (A) Some tickets are sold out.

    (B) An account has expired.

    (C) The printer is not working.

    (D) Some payment errors occurred.*

37. What information does the man ask the woman for?

    (A) An address

    (B) A credit card number*

    (C) An account password

    (D) A payment total

36. 造成問題的原因為何？

    (A) 有些票賣完了。

    (B) 有個帳戶到期了。

    (C) 印表機故障。

    (D) 付款出了問題。

37. 男子向女子要什麼資料？

    (A) 地址。

    (B) 信用卡的卡號。

    (C) 帳號密碼。

    (D) 付款總金額。

Questions 38–40 對話

W Mike, the district manager is flying back from Chicago today. I just got a call from the car company that was supposed to pick him up. Apparently, they won't be able to get him in time. **38 Can you go to the airport?** **M** Sure, but my car is out for repairs right now. **39 Could I use your car?** **W** That would be fine. I suggest leaving around 1:30 because it takes thirty minutes to get there. **40 Make sure to park in the free arrivals section so you don't need to pay for parking.** **M** No problem. I'm sure I can find it.	**女** 麥克，區經理今天從芝加哥搭飛機回來。我剛剛接到預定去接機的派車公司電話。看樣子，他們來不及去接他。**38 你可以去機場嗎？** **男** 當然，但我的車現在送修。**39 我可以借用妳的車嗎？** **女** 可以。因為到機場要 30 分鐘，我建議大約一點半出發。**40 務必把車停在免費入境區，那樣你才不需要付停車費。** **男** 沒問題，我相信我找得到。

38. What does the woman ask the man to do?

    (A) Cancel an appointment

    (B) Call a manager

    (C) Repair a vehicle

    (D) Pick up a coworker*

39. What does the man say he needs to do?

    (A) Borrow a car*

    (B) Delay a trip

    (C) Hire a driver

    (D) Meet a client

40. What does the woman remind the man to do?

    (A) Arrive an hour early

    (B) Park in the free area*

    (C) Call a car company

    (D) Carry some luggage

38. 女子要求男子何事？

    (A) 取消約會。

    (B) 打電話給經理。

    (C) 修理汽車。

    (D) 去接同事。

39. 男子說他需要做什麼？

    (A) 借車。

    (B) 延後行程。

    (C) 僱用一名司機。

    (D) 見一位客戶。

40. 女子提醒男子何事？

    (A) 提早一小時到達。

    (B) 停在免費的區域。

    (C) 打電話給派車公司。

    (D) 搬運一些行李。

Questions 41–43 對話

M   Hi, Anna. Congratulations on completing our new [41] **accessory** line. I was really impressed by all the **shoes** and **bags** you **designed** to go with our fall line.

W   Thank you. It was a lot of work, but very rewarding.

M   Would you consider joining my team for the winter line? I know our **designers** loved hearing your ideas. I think you could apply your thoughts to **outerwear** and **boots** as well.

W   That sounds like a great opportunity. I can't make any promises, though. [42] **I have a meeting with the director tomorrow to discuss where I'll be assigned.**

M   [43] **How about I call him today to make the suggestion?** Then you and he can discuss the idea tomorrow.

W   Great. I'd really appreciate that.

男   嗨，安娜。恭喜妳完成我們的新 [41] **配件**系列產品。我真的對你**設計**來搭配秋裝的所有**鞋包**印象深刻。

女   謝謝你。事情雖多，卻很值得。

男   妳要不要考慮加入我的團隊做冬裝？我知道我們的**設計師**很愛傾聽妳的構想。我認為，妳可以把妳的想法也應用在**外套**和**靴子**上。

女   聽起來是很棒的機會。不過我還無法答應。[42] **我明天要和總監開會，討論要指派我到哪個部門。**

男   [43] **我今天打電話給他，提個建議如何？**那麼，妳和他明天就可以討論這個想法。

女   太好了。非常感謝。

41. Where do the speakers most likely work?
    (A) At a law firm
    (B) At a department store
    (C) At an art gallery
    (D) At a fashion company*

42. What does the woman mean when she says, "I can't make any promises"?
    (A) She is unable to confirm her participation.*
    (B) She is busy with other projects.
    (C) She will leave her contract early.
    (D) She has to hire additional employees.

43. What does the man propose?
    (A) Attending a meeting
    (B) Calling a supervisor*
    (C) Delivering a report
    (D) Preparing a proposal

41. 説話者最可能在哪裡工作？
    (A) 在律師事務所。
    (B) 在百貨公司。
    (C) 在藝廊。
    (D) 在時裝公司。

42. 當女子説「我還無法答應」，意指什麼？
    (A) 她無法確定她能參與。
    (B) 她忙著做其他的計畫。
    (C) 她要提早解約。
    (D) 她必須另外僱用員工。

43. 男子提議什麼？
    (A) 參加會議。
    (B) 打電話聯絡主管。
    (C) 遞交一份報告。
    (D) 準備一份提案。

M	Hello, ⁴⁴ **I am expecting a package** from a branch of my company located in Manila. However, it hasn't arrived yet, and I haven't received any notices. My name is James Stone, and I work for Miller Fabric's head office down the street.	**男**	哈囉，⁴⁴ **我在等一件**從馬尼拉分公司寄來的**包裹**。但是，包裹還沒送來，而且我沒有收到任何通知。我是詹姆斯‧史東，在這條街的米勒織品總公司上班。
W	Yes, Mr. Stone. Your package arrived yesterday. We were planning to notify your company today. ⁴⁵ **As the import fee has not been paid, we cannot deliver it yet.**	**女**	是的，史東先生，您的包裹昨天送達。我們打算今天通知貴公司。⁴⁵ **因為進口費用尚未付清，我們便無法遞送。**
M	Oh, I wasn't aware there were any fees. Do I need to come in to pay it?	**男**	喔，我不知道有費用。我需要過去付款嗎？
W	No, ⁴⁶ **you can pay by credit card over the phone. Just let me pull up your file.**	**女**	不用，⁴⁶ **您可以在電話上用信用卡付款。我來找出您的檔案資料。**

44. What type of business is the man calling?
(A) A dental clinic
(B) A post office*
(C) A moving company
(D) A bookstore

44. 男子打電話到什麼類型的行業？
(A) 牙醫診所。
(B) 郵局。
(C) 搬家公司。
(D) 書店。

45. What problem does the woman mention?
(A) A payment was not made.*
(B) A package was sent back.
(C) An address is wrong.
(D) A form is missing.

45. 女子提及什麼問題？
(A) 有款項未付。
(B) 包裹被退回。
(C) 地址有誤。
(D) 表格遺失。

46. What will the man most likely do next?
(A) Make a phone call to a client
(B) Check the reverse side of an item
(C) E-mail a document to a colleague
(D) Provide payment information*

46. 男子接下來最有可能做何事？
(A) 打電話給客戶。
(B) 檢查一個物品的背面。
(C) 以電子郵寄一份文件給同事。
(D) 提供付款資訊。

W	Hello, Mr. Smith. ⁴⁷ **I'm doing a story for Channel 6's Local News at Five.** Can I ask you some questions about your company's new Pets at Work program? I've been hearing great things about it.	**女**	哈囉，史密斯先生。⁴⁷ **我正在為第6台的五點鐘地方新聞做專訪。**我可以請問您幾個與貴公司的寵物上班計畫有關的問題嗎？我一直聽到關於這個計畫的讚譽。

M	Sure. **48 We implemented the program last year.** Basically, **48 we've taken shelter cats and given them a home in our office buildings.** The cats are free to roam the office. Employees who interact with the cats have less stress and higher productivity.
W	It's also a great way to help out local shelters. But isn't it expensive to feed and maintain the cats?
M	Yes, it can get pricey. **49 But we've found the increased productivity more than makes up for it.**

男	當然。**48 我們去年開始實行這項計畫。** 基本上，**48 我們領養收容所裡的貓，給牠們一個家，就在我們辦公大樓裡。** 貓咪可以隨意在辦公室裡走動。和貓咪互動的員工壓力較小，生產力較高。
女	這也是一個幫助本地收容所的好方法。但是，飼養這些貓咪不會很貴嗎？
男	是的，可能很花錢。**49 但是我們發現，增加的產能遠超過這項花費。**

47. Who is the woman?
  (A) A veterinarian
  (B) A reporter*
  (C) A shelter owner
  (D) An artist

48. What has the man recently done?
  (A) Hired new summer employees
  (B) Appeared on a television program
  (C) Purchased a local animal shelter
  (D) Introduced animals to a workplace*

49. What does the man say about the cost of the program?
  (A) Employees cover most of the costs.
  (B) The benefits outweigh the costs.*
  (C) Donations help offset the costs.
  (D) The program does not cost anything.

47. 女子是誰？
  (A) 獸醫。
  (B) 記者。
  (C) 收容所持有人。
  (D) 藝術家。

48. 男子最近做了什麼？
  (A) 僱用新的夏季員工。
  (B) 出現在電視節目中。
  (C) 買下一間本地動物收容所。
  (D) 將動物帶進工作場所。

49. 關於計畫的費用，男子說了什麼？
  (A) 員工負擔大部分的費用。
  (B) 好處超過開銷。
  (C) 捐款有助抵銷開支。
  (D) 計畫沒有花任何錢。

Questions 50–52 對話

W	I'm so excited to be starting at Wilfred Law. It's one of the best law firms in the country, but **50 I'm a little nervous for the orientation.**
M	Don't worry. I'm sure everyone is nervous. It looks like the only seats left are in the corner.
W	In the corner? Are you sure that's okay? **51 I'd like to be close to the speakers in case I want to ask a question.**

女	我對於要開始在魏福德律師事務所上班感到很興奮。這是全國頂尖的律師事務所，但 **50 我對職前訓練感到有點緊張。**
男	別擔心，我相信每個人都很緊張。看來只有角落的位子還空著。
女	角落？你確定這樣沒問題嗎？ **51 我想要靠近講師一些，以防萬一我要問問題。**

M	Oh, there won't be any questions this time. But there are some comment cards on the table by the door. **52 You can write your questions and submit them at the end.** The questions will be addressed in tomorrow's presentation. Do you want me to get you a card?	**男**	喔，這一次不會有提問時間。但門邊的桌上有意見卡。**52 你可以把你的問題寫下來，結束時交出去。**問題會在明天的演講解決。你要我幫你拿張卡片嗎？

50. What type of event are the speakers attending?
    (A) A job orientation*
    (B) A staff party
    (C) A law conference
    (D) An orchestra performance

50. 說話者參加什麼活動？
    (A) 職前訓練。
    (B) 員工派對。
    (C) 法律研討會。
    (D) 交響樂團表演。

51. Why does the woman say, "Are you sure that's okay"?
    (A) She wants to leave a meeting early.
    (B) She thinks the speakers are too quiet.
    (C) She prefers to be in a larger room.
    (D) She does not like an option very much.*

51. 為何女子說「你確定這樣沒問題嗎？」
    (A) 她想要提前離開會議。
    (B) 她認為講師太安靜了。
    (C) 她比較喜歡大一點的空間。
    (D) 她不太喜歡某個選項。

52. What does the man say about the comment cards?
    (A) They include personal information.
    (B) They are too small to write on.
    (C) They can be handed in after the presentation.*
    (D) They are reserved for managers only.

52. 關於意見卡，男子說了什麼？
    (A) 它們包含個人資料。
    (B) 它們太小張，無法在上面寫字。
    (C) 它們可以在演講結束後交出去。
    (D) 它們只保留給經理用。

Questions 53–55 對話

M	Hi, **53 I'm calling to inquire about your rental cars. 54 I'll be in Chicago for a month on business** and I'd prefer to rent a car rather than take public transit.	**男**	嗨，**53 我打電話來詢問關於租車的事。54 我會到芝加哥出差一個月**，我比較喜歡租車，而不是搭乘公共交通運輸工具。
W	Okay, great. What kind of car are you looking for, and what is your price range?	**女**	好的，好極了。您在找什麼樣的車，還有您的價格範圍是？
M	Well, **54 I'll be picking up numerous clients and colleagues on our way to and from conferences,** so I'd like something roomy with four doors. Since I'll need the car for an entire month, I'd like something in the mid-price range.	**男**	嗯，**54 在我們往返研討會的路上，我會去接很多客戶和同事**，所以，我想要寬敞的四門汽車。既然我整整一個月都要用到車，我想要中價位的車款。
W	Okay, we have several cars that might fit your needs. I can e-mail you a list of cars with photos and prices, and you can get back to me when you've chosen one. **55 What's your e-mail address and phone number?**	**女**	好，我們有幾款車可能符合您的需求。我可以用電子郵件寄一份汽車清單給您，上面有照片和價格，等您選好後，可以回信給我。**55 您的電子郵件地址和電話號碼是？**

53. Where most likely does the woman work?

  (A) A travel agency

  (B) A taxi and limo service

  (C) A car rental company*

  (D) A conference center

54. What does the man say about his trip?

  (A) He needs to pick up many people.*

  (B) He will be traveling for two months.

  (C) His company pays for his expenses.

  (D) His colleagues are giving presentations.

55. What information does the woman request?

  (A) A hotel's location

  (B) The cost of flight

  (C) The dates of a trip

  (D) Some contact information*

Questions 56–58 三人對話

M1	⁵⁶ **I'd like to spend today's meeting talking about the bad reviews we've gotten online.** Several customers have complained about long wait times at our restaurant. Does anybody have any ideas?
W	Well, we have been short-staffed lately despite being very busy. ⁵⁷ **What about hiring some new part-time workers during peak hours?**
M1	That's a great idea. Max, you hired the last group of part-time workers, didn't you?
M2	Yes, I did. It wasn't hard. I just advertised on a student job board. We had a lot of applicants.
W	That's great, Max. ⁵⁸ **Would you be willing to collect some résumés that we could review together at the next meeting?**
M2	Sure. That shouldn't be a problem.

56. What problem does the restaurant have?

  (A) It lost some applications.

  (B) Its appliances are too old.

  (C) Its costs have increased.

  (D) It got some negative reviews.*

53. 女子最有可能在哪裡工作？

  (A) 旅行社。

  (B) 計程車與豪華禮車服務。

  (C) 租車公司。

  (D) 會議中心。

54. 關於旅程，男子說了什麼？

  (A) 他需要開車去接很多人。

  (B) 他會旅行兩個月。

  (C) 他的公司支付他的開支。

  (D) 他的同事要做簡報。

55. 女子要求什麼資訊？

  (A) 飯店的位置。

  (B) 機票的費用。

  (C) 旅程的日期。

  (D) 一些聯絡資訊。

男1	⁵⁶ 我想利用今天的會議談談我們最近得到的網路負面評價。好幾個顧客抱怨，在我們餐廳的等候時間很久。有人知道是怎麼回事嗎？
女	嗯，儘管很忙，我們最近人手卻一直不足。⁵⁷ 在尖峰時段僱用一些新的兼職人員如何？
男1	這真是個好主意。麥克斯，上一批兼職人員是你僱用的，不是嗎？
男2	對，是我。找人不會太難。我只是在學生打工板上打廣告。應徵的人很多。
女	那太好了，麥克斯。⁵⁸ 你願不願意收集一些履歷表，我們可以在下次會議時一起審核？
男2	當然，應該不成問題。

56. 餐廳有什麼問題？

  (A) 有些求職信遺失。

  (B) 設備太老舊。

  (C) 成本增加。

  (D) 收到一些負面評價。

57. What does the woman suggest?

    (A) Hiring some new employees*

    (B) Offering more menu options

    (C) Advertising online

    (D) Providing refunds

58. What does the woman ask Max to do?

    (A) Contact a store manager

    (B) Prepare for the next meeting*

    (C) Host a student job fair

    (D) Respond to online reviews

57. 女子有何建議？

    (A) 僱用一些新員工。

    (B) 提供更多菜單選擇。

    (C) 上網打廣告。

    (D) 提供退費。

58. 女子要求麥克斯何事？

    (A) 聯絡店面經理。

    (B) 為下次會議做準備。

    (C) 主持學生的就業博覽會。

    (D) 回應網路評語

Questions 59–61 對話

W Hi, Mr. Peters. **59 I remember you saying last time that you used Prime Employee Trainers to help train your new staff members.** Were you satisfied with their services?

M Yes. Prime has helped us during several hiring seasons. We're a small company, so we don't have the staff to do our own training.

W That's great. Well, **60 my home renovation company has just hired some new staff members.** I'd love to get their training done quickly and affordably.

M Actually, I think Prime only does training for IT and accounting departments. I'm not sure they would be able to help you. However, if you're looking to train your administrative workers, I know there are several companies that do that. **61 I'm sure you could find one if you search online.**

女 嗨，畢德斯先生。**59 我記得你上次說，你採用「一流員工訓練公司」協助訓練新進員工。**你對他們的服務滿意嗎？

男 是的，「一流」在好幾次招聘季幫上我們的忙。我們是間小公司，所以沒有人手自己訓練。

女 太好了。嗯，**60 我的居家裝修公司才剛僱用一些新員工。**我希望他們快點完成訓練，而且收費要公道。

男 事實上，我想「一流」只做 IT 和會計部門的訓練。我不確定他們是否能幫上你的忙。不過，如果妳是要訓練行政人員，我知道有幾家公司是做這方面的訓練。**61 如果妳上網搜尋，一定可以找到。**

59. What are the speakers discussing?

    (A) Hiring a training agency*

    (B) Advertising on the web

    (C) Launching a new product

    (D) Hosting a conference

60. What type of business does the woman own?

    (A) A trade corporation

    (B) A web development firm

    (C) A landscaping business

    (D) A home improvement company*

59. 說話者在討論什麼？

    (A) 僱用一個訓練機構。

    (B) 上網登廣告。

    (C) 發表新產品。

    (D) 主持研討會。

60. 女子擁有的是何種公司？

    (A) 貿易公司。

    (B) 網路開發公司。

    (C) 景觀美化公司。

    (D) 居家裝修公司。

61. What does the man suggest?

    (A) Developing a program

    (B) Interviewing some clients

    (C) Finding a company online*

    (D) Attending a meeting

61. 男子有何建議？

    (A) 開發一個程式。

    (B) 採訪一些客戶。

    (C) 上網找公司。

    (D) 參加會議。

Questions 62–64 對話及圖表

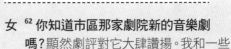

Admission Price per Person	
Students	$10
63 Groups of 6 or more	**$13**
Members	$17
Non-members	$20

單人門票	
學生	$10
63 6 人以上團體	$13
會員	$17
非會員	$20

W   **62 Have you heard about the new musical at the theater downtown?** Apparently it got rave reviews. Some coworkers and I are planning to go see it. Would you like to come?

M   Sure. I've actually been waiting to see it. How much are the tickets?

W   There are a few different prices. Here, look at this chart. **63 We already have six people who are interested, so we should be able to get this price.**

M   That sounds good. Are you planning to go this weekend?

W   No, probably on Thursday after work. Is that okay for you?

M   That sounds good. Are you going to order the tickets online?

W   No. Jenny in the Sales Department is going to stop by the theater today. **64 I'll call her and tell her to include you.**

女   62 你知道市區那家劇院新的音樂劇嗎？顯然劇評對它大肆讚揚。我和一些同事打算去看。你要一起去嗎？

男   當然，我其實在等待時機去看。門票多少？

女   有幾種不同的價位。來，看這張表。63 我們已經有六個人有興趣，所以我們應該可以適用這個價格。

男   聽起來很不賴。你們打算這個週末去看嗎？

女   不是，也許星期四下班之後。那個時間你可以嗎？

男   聽起來不錯。你們要上網訂票嗎？

女   不是。業務部的珍妮今天會順路去劇院。64 我會打電話給她，告訴她把你也算進去。

62. What type of event are the speakers discussing?

    (A) A film release

    (B) A restaurant opening

    (C) An academic seminar

    (D) A musical performance*

62. 說話者在討論什麼活動？

    (A) 電影上映。

    (B) 餐廳開幕。

    (C) 學術研討會。

    (D) 音樂劇演出。

63. Look at the graphic. What ticket price will the speakers probably pay?

    (A) $10

    (B) $13*

    (C) $17

    (D) $20

64. What does the woman offer to do?

    (A) Pick up some tickets

    (B) Make a purchase online

    (C) Contact a coworker*

    (D) Delay an event

63. 請見圖表。說話者最可能付哪種票價？

    (A) $10。

    (B) $13。

    (C) $17。

    (D) $20。

64. 女子提議做什麼？

    (A) 去拿票。

    (B) 上網購買。

    (C) 聯絡同事。

    (D) 延後活動。

Questions 65–67 對話及地圖

W Hi, Steve. I'm glad I ran into you. **65 This is my first time at Park Avenue Station**, and I'm so confused. I'm trying to get to the airport, but Line B is closed for repairs. Do you know of another way to get to the airport?

M Here, take a look at my subway map. I usually take this route. However, it's not an express route, so you'll have to transfer. **66 I think you can transfer at Center Station.** I don't think it'll take very long, though.

W Okay. Thank you so much. I hope I don't miss my flight to Florida.

M Oh, are you traveling for work again?

W No. Actually, **67 I'm visiting some family members for my vacation.**

M That'll be nice. I guess I won't see you at the office next week, then. Enjoy your trip!

女 嗨，史帝夫，真高興碰巧遇到你。**65 這是我第一次到公園大道站**，我完全搞糊塗了。我想要去機場，但 B 線正封閉整修。你知道其他去機場的路線嗎？

男 來，看一下我的地鐵路線圖。我通常搭這條路線。不過，這不是直達路線，所以妳必須轉車。**66 我想，妳可以在中央車站轉車。**不過我認為不會太久。

女 好的，非常感謝你。希望我不會錯過去佛羅里達的班機。

男 噢，妳又要出差了？

女 不是，其實 **67 我是休假去看家人。**

男 真好。那麼，我猜下星期不會在公司看到妳了。旅途愉快！

65. Where does the conversation take place?

    (A) At a bus stop

    (B) In a subway station*

    (C) At an airport

    (D) In an office

65. 這段對話發生在哪裡？

    (A) 在公車站。

    (B) 在地鐵站。

    (C) 在機場。

    (D) 在辦公室。

66. Look at the graphic. Which line does the man suggest the woman take first?

(A) Line A

(B) Line B

(C) Line C

(D) Line D*

67. Why is the woman going to Florida?

(A) To visit with family*

(B) To attend a seminar

(C) To go to an office

(D) To meet some clients

66. 請見圖表。男子建議女子先搭乘哪一條路線？

(A) A 線

(B) B 線

(C) C 線

(D) D 線

67. 女子為何要去佛羅里達？

(A) 去看家人。

(B) 去參加研討會。

(C) 去一家公司。

(D) 去見一些客戶。

Questions 68-70 對話及表單

FROM	發信人	SUBJECT:	主旨
[69]Andrew Webber	[69]安德魯·韋伯	ATTACHED: August Sales Figures	附件：八月銷售數據
Anna Stevens	安娜·史蒂文斯	Budget Projection for September	九月預算
David Skinner	大衛·史基納	Advertising Meeting Summary	廣告會議摘要
Janine Rogers	珍奈·羅傑斯	CANCELED: Dinner with Mr. Sampson	取消：與山普森先生的晚餐

M　Hi Trina. **[68] Are you having any trouble with your Internet connection?**

W　No, mine has been fine all morning.

M　I see. It must be my office then. I can't seem to access my e-mail or web browsers. **[69] Can you tell me if the e-mail with the latest sales figures came in yet?**

W　Let me check. Yes, it's right here. Do you want to see it on my computer?

M　No, that's okay. **[70] Can you forward a copy to my assistant?** I'll need it for the sales meeting with the CEO this afternoon.

男　嗨，崔娜。**[68] 妳的網路連線有任何問題嗎？**

女　沒有，我的網路整個早上都很順。

男　了解。那一定是我辦公室的問題。我似乎無法讀取電子郵件或連上瀏覽器。**[69] 妳可不可以告訴我，最新銷售數據的電子郵件寄來了沒？**

女　我查一下。有的，就在這裡。你要在我的電腦上看嗎？

男　不用，沒關係。**[70] 妳可以轉寄一份給我的助理嗎？**我今天下午和執行長開的業務會議上需要用到。

68. Why is the man unable to access his e-mail?

(A) The company servers are down.

(B) His office connection is not working.*

(C) He needs to upgrade his software.

(D) His computer has no battery power.

68. 男子為何無法讀取他的電子郵件？

(A) 公司的伺服器故障。

(B) 他的辦公室無法連上網路。

(C) 他需要升級他的軟體。

(D) 他電腦的電池沒電了。

361

69. Look at the graphic. Who sent the e-mail the speakers are referring to?

(A) Andrew Webber*

(B) Anna Stevens

(C) David Skinner

(D) Janine Rogers

70. What does the man ask the woman to do?

(A) Pass on an e-mail*

(B) Attend a meeting

(C) Scan a budget report

(D) Cancel a client dinner

69. 請見圖表。説話者提及的電子郵件是誰寄出的？

(A) 安德魯・韋伯。

(B) 安娜・史蒂文斯。

(C) 大衛・史基納。

(D) 珍奈・羅傑斯。

70. 男子請求女子何事？

(A) 傳一封電子郵件。

(B) 參加會議。

(C) 掃描一份預算報告。

(D) 取消與客戶的晚餐。

PART 4 P. 108-111 ◖12◗

Questions 71–73 介紹

W ⁷¹ **We're back with Dr. Ruth McKay on LRT radio.** As we heard before the break, Dr. McKay is president of the Natural Life Organization and author of the best-selling book *Eat Natural, Live Natural*. ⁷² **Dr. McKay has joined us to share her best advice on eliminating unnatural products from your life.** In just a moment, Dr. McKay will be reading excerpts from her book and then we'll have a question and answer session. ⁷³ **To ask a question, visit www.LRTradio.com and comment on Dr. McKay's profile.**

女 ⁷¹ 歡迎回到 LRT 電台，在現場的是茹絲・麥凱博士。我們在廣告之前已經知道，麥凱博士是全國生命組織的主席，並著有暢銷書《吃得天然，活得自然》。⁷² 麥凱博士要和我們分享她的最佳建議，告訴我們如何去除生活中的非天然產品。再過一會，麥凱博士會朗讀她書中的節選內容，接著我們會有問答時間。⁷³ 想問問題的話，請上 www.LRTradio.com 網站，在麥凱博士的個人簡介中留下意見。

71. Where does the speaker work?

(A) At a radio station*

(B) At a hospital

(C) At a university

(D) At a newspaper

72. What will Dr. McKay be discussing?

(A) Business finances

(B) Healthy living*

(C) Beauty products

(D) Political candidates

73. What does the speaker encourage listeners to do?

(A) Write down tips and information

(B) Call a receptionist with questions

(C) Purchase a new best-selling book

(D) Leave a comment on a website*

71. 説話者在哪裡工作？

(A) 廣播電台。

(B) 醫院。

(C) 大學。

(D) 報社。

72. 麥凱博士將討論什麼？

(A) 商業金融。

(B) 健康生活。

(C) 美容產品。

(D) 政黨候選人。

73. 説話者鼓勵聽眾做什麼？

(A) 寫下建議和資訊。

(B) 打電話給櫃台人員提問。

(C) 購買新的暢銷書。

(D) 在網站上留下意見。

Questions 74–76 會議摘錄

M Good afternoon, everyone. I called this meeting to talk about how we are serving tables during our dinner service. **74 I've noticed that some of the wait staff are very concerned with taking orders and expediting food quickly.** However, **75 it's important to interact with our customers. We should make an effort to chat with them and ask how their day has been going.** This will make them feel more at home and more likely to dine at our restaurant in the future. **76 Now, I'd like to play a short video that will give you some tips about how to interact with customers.**

男 大家午安。我召集這次會議,是為了談談我們在晚餐時段的服務方式。**74 我注意到,有些服務人員的工作內容高度涉及點餐以及快速送餐。**但是,**75 和顧客互動很重要。我們應該努力和他們聊天,問問他們今天過得如何。**這會讓他們感覺比較自在,將來比較可能來我們餐廳用餐。**76 現在,我想放一段短短的影片,給你們一些如何和顧客互動的訣竅。**

74. Who most likely are the listeners?
- (A) Hotel guests
- (B) Supermarket employees
- (C) Business managers
- **(D) Restaurant workers***

74. 聽眾最有可能是誰?
- (A) 飯店的房客。
- (B) 超市員工。
- (C) 商務經理。
- **(D) 餐廳員工。**

75. What is the topic of the meeting?
- (A) Introducing new menus
- **(B) Being friendly with customers***
- (C) Wearing company uniforms
- (D) Policies for cleaning workspaces

75. 會議的主題為何?
- (A) 介紹新菜單。
- **(B) 待客友善。**
- (C) 穿公司制服。
- (D) 清潔工作空間的政策。

76. What will the listeners do next?
- **(A) Watch a film***
- (B) Complete a survey
- (C) Practice a dialogue
- (D) Study a pamphlet

76. 聽眾接下來會做何事?
- **(A) 觀看影片。**
- (B) 完成調查報告。
- (C) 練習對話。
- (D) 研究一份小冊子。

W　Good afternoon, and [77] **welcome to the product launch of ISD Social, a new app designed by software developer Steven Jones.** In just a moment, [77] **Mr. Jones will introduce his new app and show us some of its features.** Mr. Jones is currently lead software designer at Issac Stanford Development. [78] **Over the last three years, Mr. Jones has headed several projects** at Issac Stanford, the most noteworthy of which is the popular ISD Photo Sharer. Mr. Jones will also be available for a question and answer session later today. [79] **Anyone interested in attending can fill out a question card and submit it to me after the presentation.** Now, here's Mr. Jones to tell you a bit about his new app.

女　午安，[77] 歡迎參加「ISD 社交」的產品發表會，這是由軟體開發者史蒂芬・瓊斯所設計的新應用程式。再過一會，[77] 瓊斯先生就會介紹他新開發的應用程式，並為我們展示它的一些特色。瓊斯先生目前是艾薩克・史丹佛開發公司的首席軟體設計工程師。[78] **過去三年來，瓊斯先生領導艾薩克・史丹佛的多項專案**，最值得注意的是流行的 ISD 照片分享。瓊斯先生今天稍晚也有留時間進行問與答。[79] 有興趣參加的人可以填寫一張提問卡，在簡報之後交給我。現在，就讓瓊斯先生來告訴你，關於他的新應用程式的二三事。

77. What event is being introduced?
(A) A store opening
(B) A charity marathon
(C) A product demonstration*
(D) A technology sale

77. 談話中介紹的是什麼活動？
(A) 商店開幕。
(B) 慈善馬拉松。
(C) 產品發表。
(D) 科技產品特賣。

78. What did Steven Jones do over the last three years?
(A) Lead several development projects*
(B) Review new products in the market
(C) Acquire a few small companies
(D) Coordinate marketing campaigns

78. 過去三年來，史蒂芬・瓊斯做了什麼？
(A) 領導數個開發計畫。
(B) 細察市場上的新產品。
(C) 收購一些小公司。
(D) 協調行銷活動。

79. What should listeners do if they want to attend the question and answer session?
(A) Install a new app
(B) Visit a press room
(C) Log into a website
(D) Hand in a question card*

79. 聽眾若想參加問答活動，應該做什麼？
(A) 安裝新的應用程式。
(B) 造訪媒體新聞室。
(C) 登入網站。
(D) 遞交提問卡。

Questions 80–82 電話留言

M Hello, Anna. This is Max calling. **80 I just found out that the hotel has lost our reservation** for **81 our business conference next Friday.** I've called a few other hotels, but they're all booked on account of the conference. I remembered your sister is a manager at the Booker Valley Hotel. Is there any way you can call her and see if she can help find us rooms? I know you're busy preparing your presentation. **82 But we really need a place to stay.**

男 哈囉，安娜，我是麥克斯。**80 我剛剛得知，飯店遺失了 81 我們下星期五為了參加商務研討會的訂房資料**。我已經打給其他幾家飯店，但是因為研討會的關係，它們都客滿了。我記得妳的姊姊是布客谷飯店的經理。妳有沒有辦法打給她，看看她是否能幫我們訂到房間？我知道妳正忙著準備簡報，**82 但是我們真的需要下榻的地方。**

80. What did the speaker find out?
(A) His conference was canceled.
(B) His luggage was misplaced.
(C) His reservation was lost.*
(D) His speech is too long.

80. 說話者得知了什麼？
(A) 他的研討會取消了。
(B) 他的行李放錯地方了。
(C) 他的訂房資料不見了。
(D) 他的演講太長了。

81. What is the speaker scheduled to do on Friday?
(A) Take a vacation
(B) Meet some clients
(C) Review a proposal
(D) Attend a conference*

81. 說話者預定星期五要做什麼？
(A) 度假。
(B) 會見一些客戶。
(C) 審核一個提案。
(D) 參加研討會。

82. Why does the man say, "I know you're busy preparing your presentation"?
(A) To reschedule a trip date
(B) To acknowledge an inconvenience*
(C) To offer help with a project
(D) To provide feedback on some work

82. 男子為何說「我知道妳在忙著準備妳的簡報？」
(A) 為了重新安排旅程的日期。
(B) 以承認造成不便。
(C) 為了提議幫忙一個專案。
(D) 為了提出工作的回饋意見。

Questions 83–85 新聞報導

M Yesterday, the State of Mississippi announced that **83 it will build a new express highway over the next five years.** The new highway will connect the City of Bradford with Greenwich County. According to the announcement, the new express highway is the first to connect these cities and will **84 lessen driving times by up to six hours.** To help sponsor the highway, drivers can purchase **85 express passes that will allow unlimited access to the new highway once it's built.** Vicki Brookes, mayor of the City of Bradford, said her community has been waiting a long time for the development of this highway and hopes more routes will be planned.

男 昨天，密西西比州宣布 **83 將在五年內興建一條新的快速公路**。新的公路將連接布拉福市與格林威治郡。根據公告內容，新的快速公路將是第一條連接這兩地的公路，並能 **84 將開車時間大幅縮短六個小時**。為了贊助公路的經費，駕駛人可以購買 **85 快速通行證**，等公路興建完成就可不限次數使用新公路。布拉福市市長薇琪・布魯克斯表示，她的市民等這條公路開發，已經等了很長一段時間，希望日後能規劃更多路線。

83. According to the news report, what will happen over the next five years?
(A) A city will be planned and developed.
(B) A new highway route will be completed.*
(C) A new location for the city hall will be sought.
(D) A tourism sector will be revamped.

84. What benefit to travelers does the speaker mention?
(A) Safer ways to travel
(B) Discounts for families
(C) Beautiful natural landscapes
(D) Shorter travel times*

85. What does the speaker say about express passes?
(A) They can be used repeatedly.*
(B) They can be ordered online.
(C) They will be distributed free of charge.
(D) They will expire every six months.

83. 根據新聞報導,未來五年會發生何事?
(A) 會規劃並開發一座城市。
(B) 會完成一條新的公路。
(C) 會尋找新的市政府位址。
(D) 會改組觀光部門。

84. 説話者提及旅客會得到什麼好處?
(A) 行車更安全。
(B) 家庭有優惠。
(C) 美麗的大自然景色。
(D) 更短的車程 。

85. 關於快速通行證,説話者説了什麼?
(A) 它們可以重複使用。
(B) 它們可以上網訂購。
(C) 它們將免費發送。
(D) 六個月就會失效。

Questions 86–88 宣告

W ⁸⁶ **Welcome to today's seminar for elementary school teachers.** Today, we're going to discuss classroom management strategies. I know some people are running late due to traffic, but we have another group scheduled after lunch. ⁸⁷ **While we're waiting for them, let's introduce ourselves.** As I'm sure you know, ⁸⁸ **a free workbook** is included with your registration fee. ⁸⁸ **I'll hand those out now while you introduce yourselves.** You'll notice a complimentary e-book CD in the back of the book. This is in case you want to review the topics we're covering today.

女 ⁸⁶ 歡迎來到今天的國小教師研討會,我們今天要討論課堂管理策略。我知道有些人因為交通的關係會晚點到,但午餐時間後已排定另一組上課。⁸⁷ 在等他們的同時,我們來自我介紹。相信你們都知道,報名費包含 ⁸⁸ 免費的練習手冊。⁸⁸ 我會趁你們自我介紹時,把這些手冊發下去。你們會發現手冊封底附有免費的電子書 CD。這是考量到你們想要複習今天討論的主題之用。

86. Who most likely are the listeners?
(A) Librarians
(B) Educators*
(C) Nurses
(D) Professors

87. What does the woman mean when she says, "we have another group scheduled after lunch"?
(A) A meeting will take place later.
(B) Some refunds will be given.
(C) An event will be canceled.
(D) She cannot wait any longer.*

86. 聽眾最有可能是誰?
(A) 圖書館員。
(B) 教育工作者。
(C) 護士。
(D) 教授。

87. 當女子説「午餐時間後已排定另一組上課」,意指什麼?
(A) 稍晚會舉行會議。
(B) 將退還一些款項。
(C) 有個活動會取消。
(D) 她不能再等了。

88. What will the speaker distribute to the listeners?

(A) A sign-up form

(B) Music CDs

(C) Training materials*

(D) Payment requests

88. 說話者會發給聽眾什麼？

(A) 報名表。

(B) 音樂 CD。

(C) 訓練教材。

(D) 請款單。

Questions 89–91 會議摘錄

W Today, I'd like to discuss our law firm's summer vacation period. As you know, [89] **we've just picked up several new cases** that will go to trial in the next six months. However, it's important that all full-time staff have a summer vacation. To help deal with the workload during the summer, [90] **we've decided to hire some temporary workers.** We feel that five part-time workers would help cover some of the administrative work. I posted the job listings online, but um . . . we'd like to fill these positions as soon as possible. If you know anyone who is qualified, [91] **please pass their résumé to me.**

女 今天我想討論我們律師事務所的夏季休假。你們都知道，[89] **我們剛剛接了幾個會在半年內開庭審理的新案子。**然而，重要的是，所有的全職員工夏季都有休假。為了協助處理夏季的工作量，[90] **我們決定僱用一些臨時人員。**我們認為，五名兼職人員將有助處理部分行政工作。我把朝聘啟示貼上網，但是，嗯……我們希望這些職缺能盡快補齊。如果你們知道任何適任人選，[91] **請把他們的履歷表傳給我。**

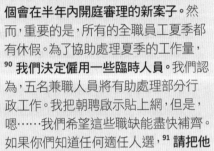

89. What does the speaker say about the law firm?

(A) It hired some full-time employees.

(B) It has donated to a local charity.

(C) It will merge with another firm.

(D) It acquired some new cases.*

89. 關於這間律師事務所，說話者說了什麼？

(A) 事務所僱用了一些全職員工。

(B) 事務所捐款給當地的慈善團體。

(C) 事務所會和另一家事務所合併。

(D) 事務所接到一些新案子。

90. According to the speaker, what decision was recently made?

(A) To hire temporary staff*

(B) To cancel summer vacations

(C) To increase some rates

(D) To renovate a conference room

90. 根據說話者所述，最近公司做了什麼決定？

(A) 僱用臨時員工。

(B) 取消夏季休假。

(C) 調升一些費用。

(D) 整修會議室。

91. What does the speaker ask the listeners to do?

(A) Host a training session

(B) Interview candidates

(C) Submit résumés*

(D) Fill out a questionnaire

91. 說話者要求聽眾做何事？

(A) 主持訓練課程。

(B) 面試應徵者。

(C) 呈交履歷表。

(D) 填寫問卷。

Questions 92–94 廣播

M We're back with SSB Radio. [92] **I'd just like to remind our listeners in the Smithside area that we're hosting our first summer music competition at the Smithside waterfront next week.** [93] **The competition will feature numerous local bands and will conclude with a performance by world-famous country music singer Sally Jones.** You won't want to miss it! The show starts at 3 P.M. at the northeast pavilion. Make sure to arrive early for free parking. Tickets will be available for a small fee, but children and seniors can enter at no charge. [94] **For a complete list of participating bands, please visit www. ssbradio.com/musiccompetition.**

男 歡迎回到 SSB 電台現場。[92] 我想要提醒史密斯塞德地區的聽眾，下星期我們將在史密斯塞德水岸舉行第一屆夏季音樂大賽。[93] 競賽的亮點將是許多當地樂團，壓軸演出的是世界知名的鄉村歌手莎莉・瓊斯。你絕對不想錯過！表演下午三點在東北館展開。務必提早抵達，才有免費停位。門票費用極低廉，但兒童與年長者還是可以免費入場。[94] 完整的參賽樂團名單，請上 www.ssbradio.com/musiccompetition 查詢。

92. What is the talk mostly about?
(A) An awards ceremony
(B) A film festival
(C) A local competition*
(D) A political speech

92. 這段話的主題為何？
(A) 頒獎典禮。
(B) 電影節。
(C) 地方性賽事。
(D) 政治演說。

93. What does the speaker imply when he says, "You won't want to miss it"?
(A) A local event will be sold out soon.
(B) Some performances will start early.
(C) The show was very popular last year.
(D) A schedule of events is very exciting.*

93. 說話者說「你一定不想錯過」，意指什麼？
(A) 一項當地活動的門票很快就會賣完。
(B) 有些表演會提早開始。
(C) 這場表演去年很受歡迎。
(D) 排定的活動非常令人興奮。

94. Why does the speaker suggest that listeners visit a website?
(A) To get a free parking pass
(B) To see a full list of contestants*
(C) To find a map of the event
(D) To sign up to be a performer

94. 說話者為何建議聽眾造訪網站？
(A) 以取得免費停車證。
(B) 為了看到完整的參賽者名單。
(C) 為了找到活動的地圖。
(D) 為了登記成為表演者。

Questions 95–97 資訊及樓層平面圖

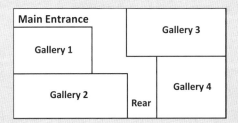

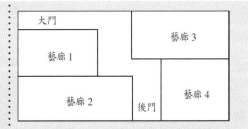

W Thank you for visiting Rutherford's National Art Gallery. [95] **This month, we're featuring a wide variety of classic watercolor paintings.** I highly recommend visiting the [96] **Monet exhibit located in gallery four, as it will only be available for a limited time. Here is a map of the art gallery.** [96] **We also feature a wide variety of art from the Cubist period, which you can find located near the rear entrance across from the Monet exhibit.** Should you like to register for a guided tour of the art gallery, they are held at 11:00 A.M., 2:00 P.M., and 4:00 P.M. every day. [97] **Simply sign up on this sheet and return to the front desk at your desired time.**

女 謝謝你們來參觀盧瑟福國家美術館。[95] 我們本月特展是各式各樣的經典水彩畫。我大力推薦觀賞 [96] 在四號藝廊展出的莫內展，因為它的展出時間有限。這裡是美術館的地圖。[96] 我們的特展還有立體派時期的許多藝術作品，你們可以在靠近後門的地方看到，就在莫內展的對面。如果你們想要報名參加美術館的導覽，活動時間是每天上午 11 點、下午兩點和四點。[97] 只要在這張表格上簽名登記，然後在你想參加導覽的時間回到櫃台處就可以了。

95. What is the gallery featuring this month?
(A) Landscape photography
(B) Watercolor paintings*
(C) Abstract installations
(D) Pencil sketches

95. 美術館的本月特展為何？
(A) 風景照。
(B) 水彩畫。
(C) 抽象裝置。
(D) 鉛筆素描。

96. Look at the graphic. In which room is the Cubist art exhibit?
(A) Gallery 1.
(B) Gallery 2*
(C) Gallery 3.
(D) Gallery 4

96. 請見圖表。立體派展覽在哪一間藝廊？
(A) 藝廊 1。
(B) 藝廊 2。
(C) 藝廊 3。
(D) 藝廊 4。

97. How can listeners attend a guided tour?
(A) By paying a fee
(B) By calling a tour guide
(C) By registering on a website
(D) By signing up on a sheet*

97. 聽眾要如何參加導覽？
(A) 支付費用。
(B) 打電話給導遊。
(C) 上網登記。
(D) 在表格上簽名登記。

Questions 98–100 留言及費用報告

September 1 9 月 1 日	Taxi to Airport: $45 機場計程車：$45	Client Dinner: $98 客戶晚餐：$98
September 2 9 月 2 日	Car Rental: $55 租車：$55	Convention Ticket: $35 研討會門票：$35

M Hello, Mary. This is Jeff from the Accounting Department. I've just gotten a chance to review the expense report you submitted after your trip last week. **98 Unfortunately, it seems that one of your receipts is missing from the envelope. 99 Your expense report requests reimbursement for an expense of 35 dollars on September 2,** but you did not submit that particular receipt. In order for me to process the payment, I'll need to see the receipt. However, if you've misplaced it and no longer have it, **100 please e-mail me and I'll forward you the Request for Reimbursement Without a Receipt form.**

男 哈囉，瑪莉，我是會計部的傑夫。我剛剛才有空檢視妳上星期出差後，送來的費用報告。**98 不巧的是，似乎有張收據遺失了，不在信封裡。99 妳的費用報告中，申請核銷一筆 9 月 2 日的 35 元**，但妳並沒有附上那張收據。為了讓我可以處理付款，我需要看到收據。不過，如果妳一時找不到，而且手頭上已經沒有單據，**100 請寄電子郵件給我，我會轉寄「無收據核銷申請表」給妳。**

98. Why is the speaker calling?
(A) An application has been lost.
(B) A submission is incomplete.*
(C) A trip has been delayed.
(D) A file is damaged.

98. 說話者為何打這通電話？
(A) 申請書遺失了。
(B) 提出的文件不完整。
(C) 旅程延後了。
(D) 檔案毀損。

99. Look at the graphic. Which expense is the man referring to?
(A) Taxi to Airport
(B) Car Rental
(C) Client Dinner
(D) Convention Ticket*

99. 請見圖表。男子提及的是哪一筆費用？
(A) 機場計程車。
(B) 租車。
(C) 客戶晚餐。
(D) 研討會門票。

100. What does the speaker say he can do?
(A) Send a form*
(B) Pay a fee
(C) Reject a request
(D) Submit a proposal

100. 說話者說他可以做何事？
(A) 寄送表格。
(B) 支付費用。
(C) 拒絕請求。
(D) 提出計畫。

PART 5　P.112-115

◎ **PART 5 解答請見 P. 508 ANSWER KEY**

---

101. 明年初將舉行增額市議員的**任命**。

102. 北星鞋業董事長表示**他**正在草擬一份企業合併的企劃案。

103. 威爾森女士在**出國**旅遊前應更新她的旅遊行程。

104. 根據報導，最近與市長辦公室的**協商**進行得並不順利。

105. 好幾位應徵者接受面試，但只有**我們**幾位獲得了那個職位。

106. 因為所有夥伴都在**策略性地**規劃交易中扮演要角，合併才能成功。

107. 在美國大學取得學位之後，保羅·布查德**回到**巴黎，在當地學校任教。

108. 請確保所有運送的貨物都送到超市的側**門**。

109. 城市規畫師每週碰面數次，討論即將進行的市中心開發**計畫**。

110. 銷售職位將開放給應屆畢業生應徵，**這**表示求職者必須已經完成學位。

111. 公司課程均**提供**給季節性聘用人員與長期聘僱員工。

112. 班森音樂學校就位於鮑伊德大道上，會**經過**羅蘭牙醫診所。

113. 全職員工通過規定的試用期後，就**有資格**享有福利。

114. 威斯頓獎學金**表揚**在科學和科技領域的傑出研究。

115. 每位員工都給予一本員工手冊，這樣就可以**輕鬆地**提醒自己作業程序。

116. 山福鞋店是本市最受歡迎的商店，因為它的產品耐穿、價錢**合理**而且款式流行。

117. 布倫南全體員工都很**樂意**當面，或在電話中與您討論居家裝潢需求。

118. 玫瑰紡織廠使用的**正是**最新的生產設備和材料。

119. **除非**另有說明，否則所有立比品牌冰箱都享有兩年保固。

120. 社區感謝您**參與**維持橡實谷公寓的清潔與安全。

121. 利率是總裁決定要轉換到綠寶石銀行的關鍵**因素**。

122. 衛生檢測員將不定期來訪，**以**確保檢測狀況是公平的。

123. 溫斯頓電影製片公司在取得彼得·努甘特孫子的**同意**後，於兩年前將他的小說拍成冒險片。

124. 市長辦公室發表了明年將以稅收來修補道路的**相關**聲明。

125. 戴伯特公寓塔樓位於兩個地鐵站步行距離內的**便利**之處。

126. 實習生若想應徵任何新的全職工作，都需要**繳交**新的申請表。

127. 胡拉漢女士修改的雷諾製造使命聲明的草稿中，**精確地**表達了公司的目標。

128. **雖然**公園在夏季月分開放，但民眾仍然不得進入某些特定區域。

129. **有鑑於**保羅·羅傑斯的學歷，難怪他是會議中演講費最高的講者。

130. 考量到我們面臨的炎熱天氣，使用公共泳池的人數**勢必會**增加。

TEST 3

PART 4

PART 5

12

Questions 131-134 資訊

在回音文具用品公司，我們努力盡快配送您所訂購的商品。如果您擔心貨物已延遲寄送，請注意本公司的運送規定。依據顧客於結帳時所選擇的運送方式，本公司預計的運送時間會自四天至四週不等。預估的運送日期會明列於收據上。我們盡力確保預估的運送時間是準確的。但是，有些訂單運送時間會較久。若您發現您的訂單延遲過久，請立即與我們聯絡。我們承諾會找出問題所在，並告知配送進度。

131. (A) 注意
　　(B) 傳送
　　(C) 準備
　　(D) 要求

132. (A) 退換物品只能更換，無法退款。
　　(B) 聯絡專員，以取得更新後的新產品清單。
　　(C) 預估的運送日期會明列於您的收據上。
　　(D) 查看線上回饋專區，告訴我們您有多滿意本公司的服務。

133. (A) 長度
　　(B) 冗長的
　　(C) 較長的
　　(D) 最長的

134. (A) 不同的
　　(B) 延遲的
　　(C) 訂價過高的
　　(D) 更好的

Questions 135-138 文章

4月24日

經過數月的討論，納卡維克市市鎮議會終於通過與 DRTL 企業的協議。依據協議條款，DRTL 將會開發巴雷特街東邊街尾的那塊 30 英畝的空地。詳細的企劃案需要取得該區零售商店與辦公室的屋舍才能訂定。納卡維克市市長里奧納‧哈維對於這

個計畫能對全市與周遭區域所帶來的經濟利益感到樂觀。「本開發案預期將創造 300 個全職職缺。」哈維說，「有一度我以為持續的延宕會迫使我們取消這整個計畫。」雖然全鎮都渴望能進行這個案子，但像這類的大型開發案，延遲是不可避免的。DRTL 發言人，傑夫‧柏金斯認為這個開發案將花上三年才能完工。同時，他警告大家可能會有更多的挫折發生。柏金斯說：「當然，我們把最好的預測結果提供給鎮議會參考，但即便如此，我們還是無法預期任何可能會發生的事。」

135. (A) 開發
　　(B) 將會開發
　　(C) 已開發
　　(D) 可以開發

136. (A) 經濟的
　　(B) 無法預料的
　　(C) 環境的
　　(D) 頻繁的

137. (A) 雖然全市都渴望能進行這個案子，但像這類的大型開發案，延遲是不可避免的。
　　(B) 然而，當地居民以合理的懷疑與我們討論工程將帶來的強烈噪音。
　　(C) 鎮議會成員將針對知名建築師所提出的四個企劃案來投票。
　　(D) 雖然市鎮府承諾授予開發者一紙合約，但他們現在仍須看看其他的選擇。

138. (A) 爭論
　　(B) 背景
　　(C) 預測
　　(D) 結合

Questions 139-142 文章

羅德里克歌劇院宣布將延長梅蘭妮‧貝克的新音樂劇《爵士之生》的演出時間。由於門票需求增加，直至八月底前，每天晚上都將演出。這突如其來的宣布，讓音樂劇受到知名音樂劇評論家傑佛瑞‧歐普瑞的嚴厲批評。在評論後，門票的銷售量急

遽地下滑。然而，上週連續三晚的票都銷售一空。根據歌劇院代表的説法，這個演出吸引了一群原本不看音樂劇的長者。而新觀眾也顯然對於能聽到貝克重新創作的絕美爵士樂曲感到興奮不已。

139. (A) 要求
(B) 要求了
(C) 苛求的
(D) 要求

140. (A) 傑出的
(B) 深的
(C) 嚴厲的
(D) 迅速的

141. (A) 音樂劇的來賓大多數都是從外地來的。
(B) 最後一場演出將於 8 月 24 日舉行。
(C) 在評論後，門票的銷售量急遽地下滑。
(D) 同樣地，劇院也受害多年。

142. (A) 明顯的
(B) 更明顯的
(C) 明顯
(D) 顯然地

Questions 143–146 電子郵件

寄件者：顧客服務部
收件者：保羅 · 神奈川
日期：10 月 16 日
主旨：歡迎加入大西洋音樂趨勢
附件：表格

親愛的神奈川先生，

感謝您訂閱《大西洋音樂趨勢》！您現在將獲得所有關於音樂活動的詳細資訊，像是即將到來的音樂課程、音樂節以及在加拿大大西洋沿岸各地所舉辦的演唱會。您將於 20 號收到您的第一期刊物。若未於該天送達，請通知我們。之後，每期刊物將於當月的第一週寄出。藉著訂閱本刊，您也可以無限地觀看線上影片、唱片、文

章、時程表，甚至是演唱會的售票資訊。您只需要用帳號及附件註冊申請表末的八位數密碼登入網站即可。

顧客服務部代表
維若妮卡 · 范澤 敬上

143. **(A) 現在，從此刻起**
(B) 之後
(C) 然後
(D) 同時

144. **(A) 若未於該天送達，請通知我們。**
(B) 如欲訂購，請於上班時間來電。
(C) 下個慶典將於 11 月中在蒙克頓舉行
(D) 我們邀請讀者投稿演唱會的評論以供刊登。

145. (A) 使用
(B) 使用權
(C) 使用
(D) 使用權

146. (A) 為了
(B) 有關
(C) 在……上方
(D) 在

PART 7　P.120–139

Questions 147–148 通知

珍的水療沙龍	假日公告

- 自 11 月 20 日至 1 月 20 日將延長水療時間。（星期一至星期六上午 10 點至晚上 10 點）

- 請注意，水療將於 12 月 24 日至 29 日期間暫停營業。

- 如同以往，**[148] 取消需於 24 小時前提出，以免產生取消費用。**

147. 這則公告的目的是什麼？

(A) 為新的服務打廣告

(B) 說明時間表

(C) 宣布促銷

(D) 提供退款

148. 關於取消，提到了什麼事？

(A) 取消水療要事先告知。

(B) 顧客可以線上取消預約。

(C) 取消皆需支付服務費。

(D) 假日預約無法取消。

Questions 149–150 通知

東點社區居民公告

[149] 自下個月起，本社區週訊將改為無紙化。為致力保護環境及減少用紙量，週訊僅提供數位版。

[150] 任何目前在週訊上刊登小型商業廣告的人，請來電 900-555-3434 與週訊編輯聯絡以更新合約。第一份線上週訊預定於 11 月 1 日上傳至 www.eastpointcommunity.com/newsletter。希望您會喜歡以這新穎便利的方式收到您的週訊。

東點社區週訊團隊 敬上

149. 週訊將有何種改變？

(A) 將與另一份刊物合併。

(B) 寄送速度會更快。

(C) 較不頻繁出刊。

(D) 不再印出紙本。

150. 根據公告，廣告客戶為什麼要和編輯聯絡？

(A) 簽署新合約

(B) 獲得優惠折扣

(C) 會員升級

(D) 修改清單

Questions 151–153 議程

[153(A)(B)] **春季免費教育訓練講習**
上午 9:30 至下午 4:30

上午 9:30：相見歡

[151] 與主管以及新同事見面。在觀看公司介紹短片的同時，可享用咖啡和甜甜圈。

上午 10:30：規章與程序

領取員工手冊，和部門主管一起檢閱規章與程序。包含簡短問答時間。

中午 12:00： [153(D)] **午休**

將於會議室提供三明治、沙拉和甜點的輕食自助式午餐，並提供素食餐。

下午 1:00：部門觀摩

員工將參觀各自部門，由指派的資深員工進行實務訓練。

下午 3:30：辦公桌分配

員工將被帶往個人辦公桌，設定公司帳號與電子郵件。[152] 任何疑問可隨時詢問資訊工程人員。

151. 這個講習最可能針對的對象是誰？

(A) 公司執行長

(B) 電腦技術員

(C) 新任辦公室員工

(D) 調動部門的員工

152. 講習中的哪一部分與資訊工程人員有關？

(A) 相見歡

(B) 規章與程序

(C) 部門觀摩

(D) 辦公桌分配

153. 關於講習，沒有提到什麼事？

(A) 是免費的活動。

(B) 時間為一個工作天。

(C) 由人力資源部主管負責。

(D) 包含茶點。

Questions 154–157 報告

倫格魯寢具

每週狀況報告：9 月 5 日至 9 日

撰寫人：專案統籌 亞歷山卓‧科賓

155, 157 本週成果：

- 與墨西哥目前生產寢具產品的四間製造商聯繫。**154 以電子郵件將我們新寢具的設計規格與生產價格、交貨時間、布料取得以及運費等相關問題寄給對方。**

- 根據回覆，看起來 **157 P&M 紡織廠**應是最佳選擇。它的地理位置比大多數公司偏南許多，但生產力可滿足我們的供應需求。此外，客戶服務部主管珊米‧露意茲回覆電子郵件的速度迅速。**156 對於問題的回覆既詳盡又專業。我相信她能確保過渡時期進行得平順又有效率。**

- 其他三間公司不是無法取得我們想要的布料，就是無法達到供應的要求。所以，就不再將其列入考慮。

下週規畫：

- 與 P&M 紡織廠聯繫，以電話會議的方式討論付款與運送期限。

- 檢視所有產品的最後設計，且於必要時要求修改。與設計團隊開會討論修改。

154. 關於倫格魯寢具，提到了什麼事？
(A) 剛聘僱一位新主管。
(B) 在墨西哥是間全新的公司。
(C) 有自己的工廠。
(D) 準備好要推出新產品。

155. 根據報告，科賓先生在 9 月 5 日那週做了什麼？
(A) 定案一些設計資料
(B) 評估可能的生意伙伴
(C) 親自參觀工廠
(D) 申請延後付款

156. 文中提到什麼與露意茲女士有關的事？
(A) 她剛到 P&M 紡織廠上班。
(B) 她提出了變更的建議。
(C) 她聯絡了一些公司。
(D) 好共事。

157. 下列句子最適合出現在 [1]、[2]、[3]、[4] 的哪個位置中？
「它的地理位置比大多數公司偏南許多，但生產力可滿足我們的供應需求。」
(A) [1]
(B) [2]
(C) [3]
(D) [4]

Questions 158–159 表單

格蘭大道飯店：宴會服務

感謝您選擇格蘭大道飯店為宴會地點。請填寫以下資料。**158 本公司客戶服務代表人員將與您聯絡，以確認預約及請求付款資訊。**

預約姓名：＿＿＿＿＿
活動日期：＿＿＿＿＿
電子郵件：＿＿＿＿＿
公司電話：＿＿＿＿＿
個人電話：＿＿＿＿＿

宴會廳偏好：
[ ] 鑽石廳（人數上限 100 人）
[ ] 玫瑰廳（人數上限 150 人）
[ ] 星光廳（人數上限 200 人）

159 需要的布置：
[ ] 晚宴（圓桌與椅子）
[ ] 晚宴與舞會（餐桌與舞池）
[ ] 晚宴與致詞（餐桌與舞台）
[ ] 其他：＿＿＿＿＿

餐點與飲料：
[ ] 全套服務自助餐與甜點吧
[ ] 三道菜式晚餐

視聽設備需求：[ ] 是　[ ] 否
說明：＿＿＿＿＿

賓客飯店住宿：[ ] 是　[ ] 否
房間數：＿＿＿＿＿

158. 根據表單，格蘭大道飯店的員工將做什麼事？
(A) 以電子郵件寄出含房間照片的手冊
(B) 協助客戶布置與清理
(C) 提供賓客免費住宿券
(D) 聯絡客戶有關付款資訊

159. 關於格蘭大道飯店的服務，提到了什麼事？
(A) 要求支付視聽器材使用費。
(B) 將安排適合活動的場地。
(C) 提供宴會賓客飯店住宿折扣。
(D) 於晚宴和舞會提供免費現場音樂演奏。

Questions 160–162 職務廣告

http://www.employmentfind.com

線上求職
今天就打造您的事業！

當您單打獨鬥時，房地產這一行會是艱辛的。在團隊房地產，您不孤單！

本公司大型房地產仲介網絡，讓房地產的展示與銷售變簡單了。**160 藉由分享資料庫中潛在買家的資訊，我們比國內其他仲介賣出更多的房地產。** 我們共享的佣金鼓勵團隊成員一同努力完成工作。

161 完成我們新的房地產教育訓練研習，並申請房地產執照。 如果成功地申請到執照，那您就可以獲得一份附有完整福利的全職合約職位。

在您獲得合約之前，學歷與經歷將列入考量。大學學歷尤佳，但是高中畢業生亦可應徵。應徵者必須自備交通工具，因為開車來回當地房產為工作所需。

請點選以下按鍵來應徵職位。您需要輸入電子郵件信箱、電話號碼並上傳履歷表。只有通過書面篩選者會獲得通知。面試前，建議所有應徵者先自行了解本公司法規。更多資訊，**162 請至公司網址 www.teamrealestate.com 查詢。**

立即申請

160. 下列何者為這份工作的職責之一？
(A) 將客戶名單分享至共用資料庫中
(B) 提供改進宅第的建議
(C) 以電話方式吸引客戶
(D) 協調督導計畫

161. 根據廣告，下列何者為合約職位所要求的條件？
(A) 大學文憑
(B) 房地產執照
(C) 行銷經驗
(D) 推薦函

162. 根據廣告，求職者為什麼要上團隊房地產公司的網站？
(A) 了解團隊房地產公司的常規
(B) 應徵具福利的合約職位
(C) 上傳履歷表與推薦函
(D) 詢問教育訓練講習的時間

Questions 163–166 文章

163 社區服務 50 年

3 月 27 日— **163, 165(B) 亞伯拉罕·德魯教授**在當地頗負盛名，不是因為他擔任心理學教授多年，或於學術期刊發表許多論文，而是因為他致力於社區擴展的緣故。50 年前，德魯先生為當地孩童創辦了第一個課後計畫，幫助了全市許多孩童。**165(A) 該計畫以為問題男童創立的棒球營起，** 現在已經發展成「國小學童的作業幫手」、「給青少年的街頭藝術」以及「回饋」，一個個人與企業為遊民籌辦食物募捐行動的慈善機構。「我從沒想過自己的課後計畫可以發展成這些獨特的計畫。」德魯先生說，「而是 **165(D) 有太多來自社區的關注。到處都有人在尋求幫助他人擺脫困難的方法。」**

在服務 50 年後，德魯先生即將自教職與計畫統籌的職位上退休。他的孫子麥可·德魯 **164 繼續**管理這些計畫。「我很開心能延續祖父所創立的一切。」麥可·德魯説，「他是個很棒的人，而社區需要他所做的這一切。」

下個月，**¹⁶⁵⁽ᴰ⁾ 德魯先生的志工群，將於威爾弗瑞德公園舉辦一個退休派對來表揚他**。派對將包括當地樂團的表演、當地餐廳所提供的美食以及一場小型煙火秀。**¹⁶⁶ 市長將頒發終身服務成就獎給德魯先生，以感謝他多年來對社區的貢獻。**更多活動相關資訊，請上網站 www.wilfredpark.com/events/april 查詢。

163. 撰寫這篇文章最可能的原因是？
- (A) 慶祝城市的創立
- (B) 鼓勵讀者捐款給慈善機構
- (C) 宣布當地社區企業的結束營業
- **(D) 彰顯當地人物的成就**

164. 第二段、第二行的「retain」與下列哪一個意思最接近？
- (A) 貢獻
- (B) 同意
- (C) 記住
- **(D) 保持**

165. 關於亞伯拉罕・德魯，沒有提到什麼事？
- (A) 他創立了男童棒球營。
- (B) 他在大學教學。
- **(C) 明年將開設另一間學校。**
- (D) 他啟發他人進行慈善工作。

166. 有關威爾弗瑞德公園所舉辦的派對，提到了什麼事？
- (A) 當地喜劇節目將演出。
- (B) 市府將主辦慶祝活動。
- (C) 參加者需支付小額費用。
- **(D) 將頒獎給德魯先生。**

Questions 167–168 簡訊

佩德羅・艾倫多 [上午 11:00]：
威爾森女士，請查看您的電子信箱。我已經將更新後的合約寄給您了。

蒂娜・威爾森 [上午 11:02]：
好的，謝謝您。**¹⁶⁷ 酬勞等級也更新了嗎？**

佩德羅・艾倫多 [上午 11:03]：
¹⁶⁷ 當然。因為您已經和我們合作超過一年，所以 **¹⁶⁸ 您現在為本雜誌所拍攝的彩色照片，每張費用將從 80 元調為 100 元。**

蒂娜・威爾森 [上午 11:05]：
太棒了。感謝您弄清楚這部分。我會看看合約，簽名後盡快寄回。

佩德羅・艾倫多 [上午 11:08]：
太好了。很高興您明年能繼續和我們一起合作。

送出

167. 在上午 11:03 時，艾倫多先生所寫的「當然」是什麼意思？
- (A) 他會再寄一次電子郵件。
- (B) 他確定計畫成功。
- (C) 他願意分享一些資訊。
- **(D) 他做了先前商議的修訂。**

168. 威爾森女士最有可能是誰？
- (A) 合約律師
- (B) 雜誌編輯
- **(C) 攝影師**
- (D) 記者

Questions 169–171 電子郵件

收件者：珍妮・羅賓森 (jrobertson@wetrainyou.com)
寄件者：溫戴爾・史帕克斯 (wbsparks@consumerconventioncenter.com)
日期：1 月 4 日
主旨：年度小型企業會議

親愛的羅賓森女士，

¹⁶⁹ 很開心聽到您將出席即將於 2 月 3 日舉辦的第三屆年度小型企業會議。¹⁷⁰ 我知道時間已經逼近了，所以非常感謝您那麼熱心地頂替提姆・布維爾斯。您在管理小型教育訓練公司上的經驗，絕對會引起與會者的興趣。若您能夠概述新公司在訓練新員工時，必須採取的基本步驟，一定會深受歡迎。

若您有意提供貴公司的宣傳手冊，請至少於演講前一週送來。同時，也請告知我們您演講時所需的視聽器材。此外，**171 我可以將您網站上的個人簡介用為會議活動的資料嗎？**若您偏好使用不同的簡介，請以電子郵件寄給我。

再次感謝您所做的一切。

會議統籌
溫戴爾‧史帕克斯敬上

---

169. 史帕克斯先生最可能寄這封電子郵件的原因是？

(A) 提出行程異動

(B) 要求更新後的時程表

(C) 寄一封過時的邀請函

(D) 接受對方同意參與

---

170. 有關布維爾斯先生，提到了什麼事？

(A) 他每年都出席會議。

(B) 他無法在會議中演講。

(C) 他擔任活動統籌。

(D) 他創立了自己的小型公司。

---

171. 下列句子最適合出現在 [1]、[2]、[3]、[4] 的哪個位置中？

「若您偏好使用不同的簡介，請以電子郵件寄給我。」

(A) [1]

(B) [2]

(C) [3]

(D) [4]

Questions 172–175 簡訊

珍‧史雲森 9 月 4 日 2:35
強納森，你把訂單編號 2256 的東西送去寄了嗎？
如果還沒，**172, 174 我們需要再加一套一樣的客製化原子筆和紙。**

強納森‧格魯爾 9 月 4 日 2:37
這張訂單還在儲藏室，但是生產客製化的原子筆和紙，需要再花至少兩天的時間。

珍‧史雲森 9 月 4 日 2:38
有可能盡快完成嗎？客戶說急著要。

強納森‧格魯爾 9 月 4 日 2:40
要跟生產部的人確認一下。

羅溫娜‧麥克阿瑟加入談話。

強納森‧格魯爾 9 月 4 日 2:41
173 羅溫娜，妳有空處理一張緊急訂單嗎？
174 和訂單編號 2256 是一樣的東西。

羅溫娜‧麥克阿瑟 9 月 4 日 2:43
175 我想我明天早上可以做好。這樣可以嗎？

珍‧史雲森 9 月 4 日 2:44
好，**175 可以的。**太感謝了！

---

172. 這間公司販售哪一類商品？

(A) 手錶

(B) 文具

(C) 家具

(D) 電器

---

173. 格魯爾先生為什麼和麥克阿瑟女士聯絡？

(A) 轉告顧客投訴

(B) 查詢員工會議的開會地點

(C) 確定訂單物品運送地點

(D) 詢問一些工作的期限

---

174. 客戶想要做什麼？

(A) 訂單加倍

(B) 取消運送

(C) 退還受損商品

(D) 更新付款資料

---

175. 在 2:44 時，史雲森女士說「可以的」是什麼意思？

(A) 她可以重新安排預約時間。

(B) 她對於新產品印象深刻。

(C) 完工時間對顧客來說是可接受的。

(D) 有些新產品將在網路上打廣告。

Questions 176–180 電子郵件

收件者：msimpson@tristarinternational.com
寄件者：bookings@stonewallhotel.com
日期：5 月 17 日
176 主旨：**訂房號 CV1124**

親愛的辛普森女士，

感謝您選擇石牆飯店舉辦貴公司的年度研習。**176 如同您在線上預約時所指示，已經為貴公司預訂了 12 間特大床海景套房。**由於您來訪的目的是辦理企業研習，我也已經預約了免費貴賓休息室與會議廳。

根據線上預約顯示，**179 您的入住日期為 8 月 5 日，退房則是 8 月 8 日。**每晚單房的費用是 109 元，將於最終帳單一併結算。您的訂房號碼是 CV1124。請記下這個號碼，若您要求任何異動，需要提供這個號碼。

如您所知，石牆飯店涵蓋許多其他的特點與活動。**177 若貴公司有意參加免費衝浪課程，建議您事先預約。**再者，我們提供免費早餐、客房服務套餐，還有大廳旁全新開幕的牛排餐廳—石牆燒烤餐廳。

感謝您選擇石牆飯店。期待為您服務。

石牆飯店 訂房服務部

收件者：bookings@stonewallhotel.com
寄件者：msimpson@tristarinternational.com
日期：5 月 19 日
主旨：回覆：訂房號 CV1124

訂房服務部，您好：

寫這封信是為了告知我的訂單出現了一些錯誤。我的訂房編號是 CV1124。在線上預約時，**179 我所指定的是 10 間小套房，**但您信中所說的卻不是這樣。除此之外，**178 我已經支付了 179 本公司 8 月 6 日健行行程的午餐，您卻未在信中提到此事。**除了更新正確的房型外，也請確認這項服務已經預約完成。若您能盡快告知這 **180 問題**的後續處理狀況，本人將非常感激。

感謝您的協助。

三星國際公司
執行長辦公室 馬柯‧辛普森敬上

---

176. 第一封電子郵件的目的是什麼？
(A) 確認團體預約
(B) 告知新規定
(C) 協助預約
(D) 提供免費升等

177. 關於石牆的衝浪課程，提到了什麼事？
(A) 只提供上午時段。
(B) 是新服務項目。
(C) 只是暫時提供。
(D) 是受歡迎的主打項目。

178. 飯店的記錄遺漏了什麼資料？
(A) 已經預約了休息室。
(B) 將於 8 月 5 號抵達。
(C) 已經預訂了餐食服務。
(D) 已經預付了房費。

179. 關於三星國際公司，可推論出什麼？
(A) 由 12 位成員組成。
(B) 研習第二天要去健行。
(C) 將於石牆燒烤餐廳吃晚餐。
(D) 會比預約時間晚一天抵達。

180. 在第二封電子郵件中，第一段、第六行的「issue」與下列哪一個意思最接近？
(A) 變更
(B) 選擇
(C) 價格
(D) 問題

Questions 181–185 通知及時程表

賀伯賞鳥社

4 月 2 日 — **181 諾斯維爾休閒處最近宣布，在賀伯野生動物園創立了賀伯公園賞鳥社。**賞鳥社聚會時間為週五至週日下午 1:00 至 3:00。社團聚會將 **182 持續整個夏季，**並以賀伯步道上多處賞鳥點為主要特色。每位參加者需穿著適合步道健行的服裝，並自行攜帶飲用水。參加者欲拍攝賀伯野生動物園中的各種鳥類，可攜帶相機。參加上限人數為 10 人，有意參加者，可向社團統籌明蒂‧貝克特報名（334-998-0034）。

賀伯野生動物園六月週末活動表

- **星期五**
  — [185] **中午 12:00 兒童野餐**
    （營地與休閒公園）
  — [183] **下午 2:00** 賀伯賞鳥社（松鼠步道）
  — 下午 4:00 T&V 企業每週棒球賽
    （鑽石球場）

- **星期六**
  — [183] **下午 2:00** 賀伯賞鳥社（松鼠步道）
  — [184] **下午 4:00 瘋燒烤**
    （東亭，僅限 6 月 10 日與 6 月 24 日）

- **星期日**
  — 上午 10:00 自然水彩畫
    （美術館大樓，每人 15 元）
  — [183] **下午 2:00** 賀伯賞鳥社（松鼠步道）
  — 下午 4:00 A 級足球（足球場）
  — 下午 6:00 公園音樂會（西亭）

更多與上述活動相關資訊，請上網站 www.heberwildlifepark.com 或來電 556-332-0989。

---

181. 這則公告的目的是什麼？
(A) **告知賀伯野生動物園的新活動**
(B) 宣布賀伯賞鳥社的新統籌人員
(C) 為賀伯野生動物園取消的活動致歉
(D) 宣傳諾斯維爾休閒處的新職缺

182. 在公告中，第一段、第三行的「run」與下列哪一個意思最接近？
(A) 慢跑
(B) **持續**
(C) 漫步
(D) 成長

183. 關於六月的賞鳥社，提到了什麼事？
(A) 有 12 位成員。
(B) 要求參加者攜帶相機。
(C) **見面時間有異動。**
(D) 社團統籌將不會出席。

184. 下列哪一項活動只在六月舉辦兩次？
(A) T&V 企業棒球賽
(B) **瘋燒烤**
(C) 自然水彩畫
(D) 公園音樂會

185. 關於賀伯野生動物園，提到了什麼事？
(A) 它的涼亭全都改善了。
(B) 營區全年開放。
(C) 有湖和噴水池。
(D) **有給小朋友的特別活動。**

Questions 186–190 廣告、電子郵件及網站評論

多倫多旅行社

★★★★★
安大略省多倫多

[186] 為慶祝創業第一年，[188] 只要在 4 月 5 日至 5 月 5 日間訂購多倫多文化團之旅，多倫多旅行社就提供八折的特別優惠。[186] 這是本旅行社最受歡迎的行程，每週五開團。以下是標準行程的細目說明。

→ 安大略皇家博物館：以著名的安大略皇家博物館為起點。在安大略皇家博物館多個現代美術館內，享受世界絕美的藝術品。參觀展出中的最新考古發現與許多大型恐龍物種。四月特別展：18 世紀地圖。

→ 曲棍球名人堂：前進曲棍球名人堂，觀賞影片中深受世人懷念的加拿大最佳曲棍球傳奇人物。了解加拿大最受歡迎運動的歷史，看看過往球員的重要收藏品。

→ [190] **丹福斯節：在丹福斯節為旅程畫下句點。** 在活力四射的街道派對感受希臘文化。當你享受現場演奏音樂與舞蹈的同時，品嚐由多倫多多家希臘餐館所提供的餐點。（至 4 月 20 日止）

備註：旅遊的最後一項行程，將視市中心舉辦的慶典活動有所異動。另外，[187] 套裝行程費用僅含全部門票，餐點及飲料需自付。

寄件者：蘇珊・梅勒克
收件者：山謬・帕克
188 日期：**4 月 10 日**
回覆：確認預約

親愛的帕克先生，

感謝您訂購多倫多旅行社的行程。以下是您的行程摘要。若有任何問題或疑慮，請來電 416-888-3232 與我聯絡。

行程名稱：多倫多文化之旅
行程日期：4 月 12 日
出發時間：上午 9:00，多倫多聯合車站
返回聯合車站時間：晚上 11:30
信用卡支付金額：190 元

感謝您，祝您旅途愉快！

旅遊統籌
蘇珊・梅勒克 敬上

顧客意見回饋：

這是我第一次參加多倫多旅行社的行程，我發現本次旅遊比我上回到多倫多參加的觀光巴士行程，更令我印象深刻。這家旅行社的確了解如何 **189 滿足**遊客在這座城市中，對其獨特的歷史與文化的興趣。我們的導遊法蘭西斯・威爾茲在往返地點的接送上幫了很大的忙，也讓大家能快速進入行程上列出的景點。**190 行程中唯一掃興的是雨天，讓大家無法好好的享受最後一個行程。**因此，我希望貴公司能規劃一個天氣不佳時的備案景點。

張貼者：山謬・帕克

---

186. 關於多倫多旅行社，提到了什麼事？
(A) 它有好幾個旅遊行程。
(B) 已經營業數年了。
(C) 不再提供夏季旅遊行程。
(D) 新增了一個觀光旅遊行程。

187. 根據廣告，多倫多旅行社提供給顧客什麼？
(A) 餐點與飲料券
(B) 升級的旅遊項目
(C) 團體旅遊行程的優惠折扣
(D) 博物館的門票

188. 關於帕克先生，提到了什麼事？
(A) 包含從希臘回來的機票。
(B) 參觀了四個主要的景點。
(C) 以折扣價購買。
(D) 原本是為了當地藝術家而開發的。

189. 在網站的回饋意見中，第一段、第三行的「treat」與下列哪一個意思最接近？
(A) 款待
(B) 增加
(C) 決定
(D) 忽略

190. 帕克先生不滿意哪一部分的行程？
(A) 在聯合車站送別
(B) 安大略皇家博物館
(C) 曲棍球名人堂
(D) 丹福斯節

Questions 191–195 時程表、電子郵件及評論

歐洲製造業委員會

第四屆年度大會
德國柏林
羅文斯堡會議中心
10 月 10 日星期六

暫定時程表	
時間	**地點**
上午 9:00-上午 9:30	相見歡及開幕演講。主講人：EMC 主席艾立克・碩文斯基，地點為克蘭茲宴會廳
上午 10:00-上午 11:30	史特勞斯廳　　　惠特曼廳 **191 紡織工廠**管理技巧 —漢斯・提斯卡威特　　高階 **191 染色與漂白科技** —蜜雪兒・普爾德

下午 1:00-下午 2:30	外包與海外管理—羅威納·溫特沃斯	¹⁹³ **機具升級與保養**—史賓賽·德斐歐雷
下午 3:00-下午 4:30	聯繫國際服飾大盤商—安妮塔·皮特里	國際寄送策略—李紹

- ¹⁹² 主講人須於 8 月 28 日前與喬漢娜·史華茲 (jswartz@emc.com) 確認可出席時間。若未確認可出席時間，將自動更換講者。

- 將提供主講人 ¹⁹⁵ 豪華大飯店免費住宿一晚。請填寫附件表格，並於 9 月 5 日前回傳給柏塔·喬文。¹⁹⁵ 若與同事或助理同行，需自行支付額外的房間費用。請於表格上註明。

寄件者：詹姆斯·華森
<jwatson@hampshiretextiles.com>
收件者：喬漢娜·史華茲
<jswartz@emc.com>
日期：9 月 1 日
主旨：EMC 時程表

親愛的史華茲女士，

很抱歉這麼晚才寄這封信，但是我剛剛才發現我的事業夥伴史賓賽·德斐歐雷今年無法出席 EMC 大會。我知道他已經確認出席，但是一件無法預期的事情讓他無法出席。¹⁹³ **由於我們兩人對演講主題都很了解，所以我很樂意代替他發表演說。** 為解決這個事情，請盡速與我聯絡。

詹姆斯·華森 敬上

http://www.emc.org

日程	歷史	捐款	**評論**

我對最近舉辦的 EMC 大會出席人數感到非常欣喜。不只有許多與會者聆聽我的演講，在演講的結尾還能進行問答座談。與會者對於講題都非常熟悉，也能進行深入的對談。同時，講者的 ¹⁹⁴ **身分**也讓我能在整場研討會中與許多國際人士有所接觸。這些接觸對於我自身未來的事業發展非常重要。另外，¹⁹⁵ **我和助理也十分滿意下榻的飯店。** 整體來說，能在 EMC 大會中演講是個很棒的經驗。

詹姆斯·華森

191. 這場會議的重點是哪個產業？
(A) 貨運
(B) 乳製品
(C) 電器
(D) 紡織

192. 根據時程表，演說者必須做什麼事？
(A) 支付飯店費用
(B) 於 10 月 8 日前抵達柏林
(C) 寄送一些演講資料
(D) 確認能否出席

193. 華森先生的演講主題最可能與何者有關？
(A) 紡織工廠管理技巧
(B) 外包與海外管理
(C) 機具升級與保養
(D) 國際寄送策略

194. 在評論中，第一段、第四行的「capacity」與下列哪一個意思最接近？
(A) 角色
(B) 時間
(C) 觀點
(D) 經驗

195. 關於華森先生，下列何者可能為真？
(A) 他在德國經營了好幾間製造廠。
(B) 他在豪華大飯店訂了第二個房間。
(C) 他每年都出席 EMC 大會。
(D) 他將講題更改為較難的題目。

Questions 196–200 表格、電子郵件及信件

http://www.abi.org

亞洲企業內幕

當期號	聯絡我們	訂閱	常見問題

姓名：克莉絲塔・廖
電子郵件：clao@rejuvenateproperties.com
城市與國家：越南胡志明市
主旨：建議

訊息：如您所知，《亞洲企業內幕》是平面季刊。但是將印刷流程搬到東京後，有些客戶得在幾週之後才能收到雜誌。我的雜誌寄送通常就延誤三週的時間。這讓我的公司，回春地產，錯失在《亞洲企業內幕》中一些重要地產出售的消息。**196 因此，我認為《亞洲企業內幕》應該提供客戶線上訂閱，提供可下載的電子書。這將有助我們這類的客戶，了解所有目前市場上有的交易。**

提交

收件者：ABI 編輯部員工
寄件者：編輯助理永田明美
日期：10 月 23 日星期三
主旨：會議摘要

以下是 10 月 23 日編輯部全體同仁出席的編輯會議所討論的事項摘要。

196 編輯主任後藤寬貴宣布，《亞洲企業內幕》將免費提供所有訂閱者可下載的電子書。另外，新訂閱讀者也能選擇以較低的訂閱價單獨訂購電子版。設計部已經聘請了兩名電子書設計人員來籌備每一期刊物。

編輯部員工討論了哪些文章要放進 ABI 的下一期季刊中。員工同意該期將報導哈普翠克國際公司與全球基金的合併案，該報導由山謬・帕克所採訪。**197 印度武士科技與台灣三星製造公司的新聞將依序由珍・杜貝和山謬・帕克分別報導。**編輯部的矢野愛子仍在等自由撰述所報導的北京新世界會議中心的最新情況。**198 如果他們無法在截稿日期前交稿，那報導將納入下一期的內容。**

《亞洲企業內幕》
1 月 ・ 第七卷 ・ 第一期

編輯的話：

本期將慶賀《亞洲企業內幕》電子版的發行。訂閱者可下載精心設計的電子書，其中包含紙本期刊的所有內容。一月號將報導許多在亞洲發生的企業交易。**199 同時也包含新的編輯評論專區，編輯部員工將於線上回覆提問與評論。**

198 記得留意我們的下一期，在下一期中我們將報導北京世界會議中心計畫的所有相關細節。200 記得登入網站，就有機會贏得明年會議中心開幕商業研討會議的免費門票。

後藤寬貴

---

196. 關於廖女士，下列何者為真？
(A) 她只在越南購買房地產。
(B) ABI 執行了她的構想。
(C) 她訂閱了幾本日本雜誌。
(D) 她的文章常刊登在 ABI 上。

197. 誰將報導武士科技公司？
(A) 後藤寬貴
(B) 山謬・帕克
(C) 珍・杜貝
(D) 永田明美

198. 關於矢野愛子，提到了什麼事？
(A) 她以電子書設計人員的身分加入 ABI。
(B) 她沒有按時收到一些文章。
(C) 她和山謬・帕克一起撰寫文章。
(D) 她沒有出席 6 月 1 日的會議。

199. 關於《亞洲企業內幕》，文中提及了什麼？
(A) 開發了新專欄。
(B) 大部分的訂閱者都在越南。
(C) 將遷至中國北京。
(D) 每年發行六期。

200. 關於 ABI 網站，提到了什麼事？
(A) 只提供給 ABI 訂閱者。
(B) 將於明年升級。
(C) 提供七種不同語言的版本。
(D) 將為訂閱者舉辦贈品活動。

ACTUAL TEST ④

1. **(A) He's seated in a waiting area.***
   (B) He's picking up a book from the table.
   (C) He's arranging the chairs.
   (D) He's hanging a picture.

2. **(A) A woman's working on a flower arrangement.***
   (B) A woman's choosing a vase from the shelf.
   (C) A woman's carrying a bouquet to a party room.
   (D) A woman's lining up some plants on the table.

3. (A) The counter has been cleared of objects.
   (B) A man is watering a potted plant.
   (C) The faucet is being repaired.
   (D) Some plates are piled on the countertop.*

4. (A) A display case has been set up on the floor.
   (B) Tables have been set up under canopies.*
   (C) One of the men is trying on a shirt.
   (D) Two vendors are shaking hands.

5. **(A) Some trees are making shadows.***
   (B) A field of grass is being mowed.
   (C) Some bushes are being trimmed.
   (D) Some benches are being removed.

6. (A) Some pedestrians are stepping onto a curb.
   (B) A cyclist is examining the wheels.
   (C) A bicycle is locked to a pole.*
   (D) A road is closed for construction.

1. (A) 他坐在等候區。
   (B) 他從桌上拿起一本書。
   (C) 他正在排椅子。
   (D) 他正在掛一幅畫。

2. (A) 女子正在插花。
   (B) 女子正從架子上挑選花瓶。
   (C) 女子正拿著一束花進入派對。
   (D) 女子正在排好桌上一些植物。

3. (A) 櫃台上的物品都清除了。
   (B) 男子正在給盆栽澆水。
   (C) 正在修理水龍頭。
   (D) 櫃台檯面上堆著一些盤子。

4. (A) 展示櫃擺放在地板上。
   (B) 遮篷下面放置著桌子。
   (C) 其中一名男子正在試穿襯衫。
   (D) 兩名小販在握手。

5. **(A) 有些樹投下陰影。**
   (B) 正在除一大片草地。
   (C) 正在修剪一些灌木叢。
   (D) 正在移走一些長椅。

6. (A) 有些行人踩上人行道的路緣。
   (B) 自行車騎士正在檢查車輪。
   (C) 一輛自行車鎖在柱子旁。
   (D) 有條路封閉整建。

7. Where is the meeting being held today?
   (A) It was boring.
   (B) The downtown office.*
   (C) No, she hasn't said.

8. Do you need another ticket for the baseball game?
   (A) Yes, I'd like one more.*
   (B) Please come here.
   (C) The players are out of town.

7. 今天的會議在哪裡舉行？
   (A) 很無聊。
   (B) 市區的辦公室。
   (C) 不，她沒說。

8. 你需要另一張棒球賽的門票嗎？
   (A) 是的，我想再要一張。
   (B) 請過來這裡。
   (C) 球員出城去了。

9. Who will pick up Mr. Kim from the station?
   (A) I live in that area.*
   (B) He is from Korea.
   (C) On the express route.

10. How did the package from England arrive so quickly?
   (A) No, he's a delivery man.
   (B) They used express shipping.*
   (C) I'm going there on vacation.

11. Who repaired the projector in this room?
   (A) Early this morning.
   (B) Our technology specialist.*
   (C) The presentation at noon.

12. Your parcel should arrive at 4:30 P.M. today.
   (A) Yes, I passed the test.
   (B) The delivery truck.
   (C) I'll be in the office then.*

13. When will the employee promotions be announced?
   (A) I doubt it is true.
   (B) Several other candidates.
   (C) Next week at the earliest.*

14. Are you ready to go get some coffee?
   (A) I've been running for twenty minutes.
   (B) I have a meeting soon.*
   (C) One cup is $5.99.

15. Why are you waiting outside?
   (A) I forgot it at home.
   (B) Twenty more minutes.
   (C) The café is closed already.*

16. How should we arrange the new desks?
   (A) Let's make some rows.*
   (B) Yes, they were expensive.
   (C) No, they are too long.

17. Do you need some help hanging these posters?
   (A) They are posted on this site.
   (B) Did she design it?
   (C) Yes, I'd appreciate it.*

18. Which teams are using this room today?
   (A) They are working well.
   (B) No, it's the fourteenth.
   (C) Just the Accounting Department.*

9. 誰會去車站接金先生？
   (A) 我住在那一區。
   (B) 他是韓國人。
   (C) 在快速公路上。

10. 英國寄來的包裹怎麼這麼快就到了？
   (A) 不，他是送貨員。
   (B) 他們用快捷貨運。
   (C) 我會去那裡度假。

11. 這個房間的投影機是誰修好的？
   (A) 今天早上稍早。
   (B) 我們的技術專員。
   (C) 中午的簡報。

12. 你的包裹應該在今天下午四點半送到。
   (A) 是的，我通過測驗了。
   (B) 送貨卡車。
   (C) 那個時間，我會在辦公室。

13. 何時會宣布人事升遷？
   (A) 我懷疑是真的。
   (B) 其他幾個應徵者。
   (C) 最快下星期。

14. 你要喝點咖啡嗎？
   (A) 我跑步跑了 20 分鐘。
   (B) 我很快就要去開會。
   (C) 一杯 $5.99。

15. 你為何在外面等？
   (A) 我忘在家裡了。
   (B) 再 20 分鐘。
   (C) 咖啡館已經打烊了。

16. 我們要怎麼排這些新書桌？
   (A) 我們排成幾列吧。
   (B) 是的，它們很貴。
   (C) 不，它們太長了。

17. 你需要人幫忙掛這些海報嗎？
   (A) 它們貼在這個地方。
   (B) 是她設計的嗎？
   (C) 是的，非常感謝。

18. 哪些單位今天要用這間房間？
   (A) 他們進展得很順利。
   (B) 不，是第 14 個。
   (C) 只有會計部門。

19. Are the replacement parts going to get here in time?
    (A) In the mail room.
    (B) The cost has increased.
    (C) I paid for express shipping.*

20. Why is the mall open so late today?
    (A) No, I've bought it already.
    (B) There's a holiday sale.*
    (C) Until 9:00 at night.

21. Should I talk to the manager about my vacation plans now or before I leave tonight?
    (A) In the conference room.
    (B) The sales pitch was very successful.
    (C) I heard he is going home before lunch.*

22. I'm not sure where the conference will be held.
    (A) Ask at the front desk.*
    (B) It lasts three days.
    (C) For all participants.

23. I need some more details about the museum opening.
    (A) At the main entrance.
    (B) No problem. Here is the web address.*
    (C) Twelve adult passes.

24. Where will we go after the plant tour?
    (A) Janice has the full itinerary.*
    (B) Only the managers, I think.
    (C) We plan to hire a few more guides.

25. You can come in for a checkup at 11 o'clock.
    (A) What other times are available?*
    (B) The dentist was very gentle.
    (C) This procedure was cheaper.

26. Should I get another chair for the meeting?
    (A) Tom is home sick today.*
    (B) I called the meeting.
    (C) Yes, it is very comfortable.

27. I forgot my scarf at home.
    (A) It is a house with seven rooms.
    (B) I am scared, too.
    (C) It's pretty warm out today.*

19. 替換的零件會及時送到這裡嗎？
    (A) 在收發室。
    (B) 成本增加了。
    (C) 我付錢叫了快捷貨運。

20. 購物商場今天為何開到這麼晚？
    (A) 不，我已經買了。
    (B) 有假期大特賣。
    (C) 直到晚上九點。

21. 我應該現在和經理談我的休假計畫，還是今晚離開前再說？
    (A) 在會議室。
    (B) 這套推銷用語非常有效。
    (C) 我聽說，他在中午之前就會回家。

22. 我不確定會議在哪裡舉行。
    (A) 問一下櫃台。
    (B) 它持續三天。
    (C) 給所有的參加者。

23. 我需要知道更多關於博物館開幕的詳情。
    (A) 在大門口。
    (B) 沒問題，這是網址。
    (C) 12張成人票。

24. 參觀完工廠後，我們要去哪裡？
    (A) 珍妮絲有完整的行程表。
    (B) 我想，只有經理。
    (C) 我們打算再多僱一些嚮導。

25. 你可以十一點來接受檢查。
    (A) 還有其他時間可選嗎？
    (B) 牙醫很溫和。
    (C) 這種療程比較便宜。

26. 我應該再去拿張椅子以供開會時用嗎？
    (A) 湯姆今天請病假。
    (B) 是我召集會議的。
    (C) 是的，椅子非常舒服。

27. 我把圍巾忘在家裡了。
    (A) 那棟房子有七間房間。
    (B) 我也很害怕。
    (C) 今天外面相當溫暖。

28. The concert tickets for tonight are sold out, aren't they?
    (A) The venue is located downtown.
    (B) Yes, but you can attend the one tomorrow.*
    (C) Two singers have cancelled.

29. Do you know where the application packages are?
    (A) Not too many.
    (B) For external application only.
    (C) You can get them from the manager.*

30. How often do we need to service the copy machine?
    (A) I think I threw out the handbook.*
    (B) The toner cartridges.
    (C) I installed it on Friday.

31. Which floor is my hotel room on?
    (A) The elevator is over there.
    (B) I wish I had a key.
    (C) Didn't the clerk tell you?*

28. 今晚音樂會的票已售完，不是嗎？
    (A) 表演場地位於市中心的鬧區。
    (B) 是的，但你可以看明天那一場。
    (C) 有兩位歌手取消了。

29. 你知道申請文件在哪裡嗎？
    (A) 不太多。
    (B) 只供外部申請之用。
    (C) 你可以跟經理拿。

30. 影印機需要多久維修一次？
    (A) 我想我把說明書扔了。
    (B) 碳粉匣。
    (C) 我星期五安裝好的。

31. 我的房間在飯店幾樓？
    (A) 電梯在那裡。
    (B) 希望我有鑰匙。
    (C) 接待員沒告訴你嗎？

PART 3   P. 145–149   15

Questions 32–34 對話

M	Hello, I'm Samuel Morgan. **32 I have an appointment with Dr. Baker to have a cavity filled.**
W	Yes, you're next on the waiting list. **33 However, he's running behind schedule, so it'll be another thirty minutes.**
M	Oh, I see. Well, I need to stop by the bank across the street, so maybe I'll do that first.
W	Sure, **34 just make sure you go out the exit on the left.** The elevators on the north side of the building are down for repairs, so you won't be able to use them.

男　哈囉，我是山繆‧摩根。**32 我向貝克醫師預約了要補蛀牙。**

女　是的，你是等候名單上的下一位。**33 不過，他的看診延誤了，所以還要再等 30 分鐘。**

男　喔，我知道了。嗯，我得去一下對面的銀行，不然我先去銀行一下。

女　當然好，**34 只是要確認是從左邊的出口出去。** 由於大樓北側的電梯待修中，停止運轉，所以你無法搭乘那邊的電梯。

32. Where most likely are the speakers?
    (A) In a bank
    (B) In a dental clinic*
    (C) In a shopping mall
    (D) In a bookstore

32. 說話者最可能在哪裡？
    (A) 在銀行。
    (B) 在牙醫診所。
    (C) 在購物商場。
    (D) 在書店。

33. What problem does the woman mention?

    (A) An appointment will be delayed.*

    (B) A patient file was misplaced.

    (C) An employee called in sick.

    (D) A bill was not paid.

34. What does the woman advise the man to do?

    (A) Reschedule an appointment

    (B) Stay in the office

    (C) Take the stairs

    (D) Use a specific door*

Questions 35–37 對話

M	Hello, ³⁵ **I'm interested in picking up a refrigeration unit for my truck.** ³⁶ **I run a small catering business** and the fridge I currently have is broken.
W	Great, we have several different models that may suit your needs. And they all come with free installation and a two-year warranty.
M	That sounds good. But my truck is actually quite small, so I'm worried you might not have a unit small enough for it.
W	Our A4000 series is very compact. I have a few in the back storage room. ³⁷ **Why don't you come take a look at them?**

35. What is the purpose of the man's visit?

    (A) To extend a warranty

    (B) To request a repair

    (C) To do some shopping*

    (D) To deliver an appliance

36. What is the man's job?

    (A) Caterer*

    (B) Architect

    (C) Engineer

    (D) Farmer

37. What does the woman suggest the man do?

    (A) Look at a catalogue

    (B) Inspect some merchandise*

    (C) Shop on a website

    (D) Provide an address

---

33. 女子提及什麼問題？

    (A) 有個約診時間會延後。

    (B) 有位病人的檔案放錯地方。

    (C) 有位員工打電話請病假。

    (D) 有張帳單未付。

34. 女子建議男子何事？

    (A) 重新安排預約時間。

    (B) 留在辦公室裡。

    (C) 走樓梯。

    (D) 使用特定的出入口。

男	哈囉，³⁵ 我想要為我的卡車買冷藏設備。³⁶ 我經營小型的外燴生意，平時在用的冰箱壞了。
女	好的，我們有幾種款式可能符合您的需求，而且含免費安裝以及兩年保固。
男	聽起來很不錯。可是我的卡車其實相當小，所以我擔心，妳也許沒有夠小的款式。
女	我們的 A4000 系列非常小巧。我後面的貯藏室裡有幾台。³⁷ 您何不過來看看？

35. 男子造訪的目的為何？

    (A) 延長保固。

    (B) 要求修理。

    (C) 購物。

    (D) 運送一件家電。

36. 男子的工作為何？

    (A) 外燴業者。

    (B) 建築師。

    (C) 工程師。

    (D) 農夫。

37. 女子建議男子何事？

    (A) 看型錄。

    (B) 查看一些商品。

    (C) 上網購物。

    (D) 提供住址。

Questions 38–40 對話

M Hello, this is James calling from the features department. Today is the deadline for the story on the new downtown sports center, but **38 I think I'll need another day or two to finish the piece.**

W Oh no. What's the reason? We don't normally allow extensions.

M Well, unfortunately, **39 my computer crashed** and I lost the latest edits on the article. I need to redo a lot of work.

W Okay, **40 I'll have to talk with the editorial director about this.** In the meantime, please try to get as much done as possible so the proofreaders can get started.

男 哈囉，我是特寫組的詹姆士。今天是那篇市區新運動中心報導的截稿日，但 **38 我想，我還需要一、二天才能完成這篇報導。**

女 喔，不。是什麼原因？我們通常不允許延期。

男 嗯，很不幸，**39 我的電腦當機**，我最後修訂的文章不見了。很多工作我必須重來。

女 好，**40 我得和總編輯談這件事。**在這期間，請努力能做多少是多少，如此一來，校對人員才可以開始作業。

38. What does the man ask the woman for?
 (A) A later deadline*
 (B) An updated contract
 (C) A credit card number
 (D) A coworker's e-mail

38. 男子向女子要求何事？
 (A) 較晚的截稿日期。
 (B) 更新的合約。
 (C) 信用卡卡號。
 (D) 同事的電子郵地址。

39. What problem does the man mention?
 (A) He lost some client information.
 (B) He forgot his login password.
 (C) He did not understand some directions.
 (D) He had some technical difficulties.*

39. 男子提及什麼問題？
 (A) 他弄丟了一些客戶資料。
 (B) 他忘記他的登入密碼。
 (C) 他不了解某些指令。
 (D) 他遇到一些技術問題。

40. What does the woman say she will do?
 (A) Send some forms
 (B) Contact a manager*
 (C) Hire some workers
 (D) Locate a file

40. 女子説，她會做什麼？
 (A) 寄送一些表格。
 (B) 聯絡一位管理人員。
 (C) 僱用一些人手。
 (D) 找出一份檔案。

Questions 41–43 對話

M Hello, Michelle? This is Andrew Parsons calling. Last week, **41 you interviewed for the legal assistant position at our company.** Are you available to come in for a training session this week?

W Thank you for contacting me, Mr. Parsons. I'd love to come in for training. However, **42 I'm still working for my current employer, so I'm not available during the day.**

男 哈囉，蜜雪兒？我是安德魯・帕森斯。上星期 **41 妳來我們公司面試法務助理的工作。**這星期妳有空來參加訓練課程嗎？

女 謝謝你打給我，帕森斯先生。我很樂意參加訓練。不過，**42 我還在目前的公司上班，因此我白天沒有空。**

389

M	You could always come in after hours. **43 I'd like to make sure you're familiar with our reporting and communication systems before you start.** How does 6:30 P.M. on Wednesday evening sound? I think it will take two to three hours.	男	妳可以下班後隨時過來。**43 我想確定妳在到任之前，已熟悉我們的通報與通訊系統。** 星期三下午六點半，這時間聽起來可行嗎？我想會花兩到三個小時。

41. Where does the man most likely work?
(A) At a library
(B) At a bakery
(C) At a pharmacy
(D) At a law office*

42. Why is the woman unavailable during the day?
(A) She is working for a company.*
(B) She is taking a college course.
(C) She is traveling out of town.
(D) She is attending a conference.

43. What does the man ask the woman to do?
(A) Submit an updated application
(B) Learn about company systems*
(C) Conduct an online survey
(D) Provide written references

41. 男子最可能在哪裡工作？
(A) 在圖書館。
(B) 在烘焙坊。
(C) 在藥局。
(D) 在律師事務所。

42. 女子為何白天沒空？
(A) 她在一家公司上班。
(B) 她在修習大學課程。
(C) 她去外地旅行。
(D) 她去參加研討會。

43. 男子要求女子何事？
(A) 提出更新的應徵資料。
(B) 學習公司的系統。
(C) 執行線上調查。
(D) 提供書面推薦信。

Questions 44–46 對話

M	Hello, **44 I'm interested in purchasing some new chairs for my office.** A colleague mentioned to me that you provide a discount on bulk orders. Does that apply to the Deluxe 500 faux leather model?	男	哈囉，**44 我想為我的辦公室買一些新椅子。** 有個同事跟我提到，你們提供大批採購折扣優惠。這適用於 Deluxe 500 人造皮款嗎？
W	I'm sorry but, **45 because that is our newest model, our discounts do not apply.** However, the Grand 400 faux leather model is available to receive the ten percent discount on bulk orders.	女	很抱歉，**45 因為那是我們的最新款式，不適用於折扣優惠。** 不過，Grand 400 人造皮款，大批採購可享有 10% 的折扣。
M	Oh, I see. Well, I haven't looked at that specific model. Is it listed on the website?	男	噢，了解。嗯，我還沒看過那一款。它有列在網站上嗎？
W	It is, and if you purchase today, I can give you an additional 50 percent off the cost of shipping.	女	有的，而且如果您今天購買，我可以額外替您的運費打五折。
M	Oh, that sounds great. **46 Let me check the website and call you back.**	男	喔，聽起來很棒。**46 我看一下網站，再打電話給妳。**

44. What does the man want to buy?

    (A) A refrigerator

    (B) Some shoes

    (C) A copy machine

    (D) Some office furniture*

45. Why does the woman apologize?

    (A) A discount cannot be used.*

    (B) Some products are sold out.

    (C) A store is closed for renovations.

    (D) Some customers complained.

46. What does the man say he will do?

    (A) Discuss an issue with a colleague

    (B) Visit an online store*

    (C) Provide an address

    (D) Send some measurements

Questions 47–49 對話

M	Hi, Jan. **⁴⁷ I've updated the employee handbook that we'll be using this year.** Can you check the changes before I send the file to everyone in the office?
W	Okay, this all looks good. Oh, wait a minute. The company address you've used is wrong. **⁴⁸ This is the old office address before the city changed the street name.**
M	Oh, wow. I'm so glad you caught that. **⁴⁹ I can't believe I missed it.**
W	It happens to us all. Let's send the file to Tina and have her check all the information just to be sure nothing else is wrong.

47. What are the speakers mainly talking about?

    (A) Moving to a new building

    (B) Hiring a designer

    (C) Updating a customer profile

    (D) Editing a document*

48. What problem does the woman notice?

    (A) An address is outdated.*

    (B) A form was misplaced.

    (C) An employee was late.

    (D) A phone number is wrong.

---

44. 男子想要買什麼？

    (A) 冰箱。

    (B) 鞋子。

    (C) 影印機。

    (D) 辦公家具。

45. 女子為何致歉？

    (A) 有項折扣無法使用。

    (B) 有些產品已售完。

    (C) 有間店關閉整修。

    (D) 有些客戶抱怨。

46. 男子說，他要做什麼？

    (A) 和同事討論一個問題。

    (B) 造訪線上商店。

    (C) 提供地址。

    (D) 寄送測量尺寸。

男	嗨，珍。**⁴⁷ 我已經更新了今年要用的員工手冊。** 妳可以檢查一下修改的地方，我再把檔案寄給大家嗎？
女	好，整體看來很好。噢，等一下。你用的公司地址是錯的。**⁴⁸ 這是本市更改街道名稱之前的舊辦公地址。**
男	噢，哇。幸好妳抓到那個錯誤。**⁴⁹ 簡直不敢相信我竟然沒發現。**
女	我們難免會遇到這種事。那我們把檔案寄給緹娜，請她檢查所有資料，確認沒有其他錯漏之處。

47. 說話者主要在談何事？

    (A) 搬進新大樓。

    (B) 僱用一位設計師。

    (C) 更新客戶檔案。

    (D) 編輯一份文件。

48. 女子注意到什麼問題？

    (A) 有個地址是舊的。

    (B) 有份表格放錯地方。

    (C) 有個員工遲到。

    (D) 有串電話號碼是錯的。

49. Why does the woman say, "It happens to us all"?
   (A) To explain a problem
   (B) To provide clarification
   (C) To prevent an accident
   (D) To show compassion*

49. 女子為何說「我們難免會遇到這種事」？
   (A) 以解釋一個問題。
   (B) 以澄清意思。
   (C) 以防意外事故發生。
   (D) 以示同理心。

Questions 50–52 對話

W　Hi, this is Becky Hill calling. **50 I need to reschedule my appointment with Dr. Miller.** Do you have anything available next week?

M　Let me check our schedule. It looks like Dr. Miller is available next Wednesday morning. Can you come in at 10:00 A.M.?

W　No, **51 I'll be out of town that day for a business convention.** Are there any appointments available on Friday?

M　Possibly. Oh, here we go. I see there was a cancellation on Friday, so there's an opening at 3:00 P.M. Does that work?

W　That's perfect. **52 I'll write it down in my planner.**

女　嗨，我是貝琪・希爾，**50 我需要重新安排和米勒醫師的約診時間。**下星期什麼時段可以？

男　我查一下時間表。看上去，米勒醫師下星期三上午有空。你可以上午十點過來嗎？

女　沒辦法，**51 我那一天要出城去參加商務研討會。**星期五有任何時段空著嗎？

男　可能有。喔，有了。我看到星期五個約診取消了，所以，下午三點有個空檔。那個時間可以嗎？

女　太好了。**52 我會寫在記事本上。**

50. What is the purpose of the woman's call?
   (A) To inquire about test results
   (B) To make a payment
   (C) To change an appointment*
   (D) To update insurance information

50. 女子打電話的目的為何？
   (A) 詢問檢驗的結果。
   (B) 付款。
   (C) 更改約診。
   (D) 更新保險資料。

51. What is the woman doing on Wednesday morning?
   (A) Visiting a clinic
   (B) Traveling to another city*
   (C) Meeting a client
   (D) Hosting a local event

51. 女子星期三早上要做何事？
   (A) 去診所就診。
   (B) 到另一個城市出差。
   (C) 與客戶碰面。
   (D) 主持一個本地活動。

52. What will the woman most likely do next?
   (A) Contact a coworker
   (B) Record some information*
   (C) Go to a hospital
   (D) Meet with a consultant

52. 女子接下來最可能做何事？
   (A) 聯絡同事。
   (B) 記錄一些資訊。
   (C) 前往醫院。
   (D) 與諮詢顧問會面。

M	Before we go, let's discuss our office lease. ⁵³ **As you know our lease expires next year**, which would be a good time to move to a larger office. However, I'd like to get everyone's input before we decide on a location.
W1	Betina and I were talking about this yesterday, and she mentioned she saw a sign at the new Roger's building downtown. What did it say, Betina?
W2	Well, apparently the new building will open next year and they're looking for businesses to rent spaces. ⁵⁴ **We could make an appointment to see the spaces.**
M	That sounds good. ⁵⁵ **Can you get me the contact number listed on the sign?**
W2	⁵⁵ **Sure.** I'll stop by there on my way home.

男	在開始之前,我們先來討論一下辦公室的租約。⁵³ **你們都知道,我們的租約到明年**,這會是搬到較寬敞辦公室的好時機。不過,在我們決定地點之前,我想聽聽各位的意見。
女 1	貝緹娜和我昨天才在談這件事,她提到,她看到市中心的新羅傑大樓外有個告示牌。上面寫什麼,貝緹娜?
女 2	嗯,看起來那棟新大樓明年會啟用,而他們現在正在找公司承租。⁵⁴ **我們可以約個時間去現場看看。**
男	聽起來還不賴。⁵⁵ 妳可以給我告示牌上的聯絡電話嗎?
女 2	⁵⁵ 當然可以。我會在回家的路上順道去看。

53. According to the man, what will happen next year?
　(A) A CEO will visit.
　(B) A business will fail.
　(C) A renovation will occur.
　(D) A contract will expire.*

54. What does Betina suggest?
　(A) Checking a website
　(B) Taking a building tour*
　(C) Extending a lease
　(D) Purchasing a building

55. What does Betina agree to do?
　(A) Pass on a phone number*
　(B) Call a real estate agent
　(C) Revise a contract
　(D) Create a company sign

53. 根據男子所言,明年會發生何事?
　(A) 有位執行長會來訪。
　(B) 有間公司要倒閉。
　(C) 要進行整修。
　(D) 有份合約要到期。

54. 貝緹娜建議什麼?
　(A) 查看一個網站。
　(B) 參觀一棟大樓。
　(C) 延長租約。
　(D) 買下一棟大樓。

55. 貝緹娜同意做什麼?
　(A) 轉達一串電話號碼。
　(B) 打電話給不動產經紀人。
　(C) 修改一份合約。
　(D) 創作公司招牌。

M	Beth, take a look at these hairpins.
W	They're really pretty, aren't they? I bought one a while ago. They're made with real pearls from Florida. **56 No two pins are the same.** See, they all have different colors.
M	I don't remember you ever wearing a hairpin like this.
W	Actually, **57 I lost it while I was on vacation.**
M	That's too bad. I'd love to get one of these for my sister. Her birthday is next week, but, well, I don't get paid for ten days.
W	**58 I can lend you the money.** You can pay me back when you get paid.
M	Wow, that's so generous of you.

男	貝絲，看看這些髮夾。
女	真漂亮，不是嗎？我不久前買了一個。它們是用佛羅里達產的真珠製成的，**56 每隻髮夾都獨一無二**。你看，它們的顏色都不一樣。
男	我不記得妳戴過像這樣的髮夾。
女	事實上，**57 我去度假時弄丟了**。
男	真慘。我想要買一個這種的給我妹妹。她下星期生日，但是，呃，我已經有十天沒領到薪水了。
女	**58 我可以借你錢**。等你領到薪水時再還我就好。
男	哇，妳真慷慨。

56. What does the woman say is special about the hairpins?
(A) They are made of gold.
(B) They are inexpensive.
(C) They are made in France.
(D) They are all unique.*

56. 女子說，這髮夾特別之處為何？
(A) 它們是用黃金做的。
(B) 它們不貴。
(C) 它們是法國製的。
(D) 它們每個都獨一無二。

57. Why does the woman say she no longer wears her hairpin?
(A) She lost it.*
(B) She broke it.
(C) She dislikes it.
(D) She gifted it.

57. 女子為何說，她不再戴她的髮夾？
(A) 她遺失了。
(B) 她打破了。
(C) 她不喜歡。
(D) 她送人了。

58. What does the man imply when he says, "I don't get paid for ten days"?
(A) He usually gets paid every week.
(B) He forgot to pick up his paycheck.
(C) He doesn't have enough money right now.*
(D) He recently got a pay increase.

58. 當男子說「我已經有十天沒領到薪水了」，意指什麼？
(A) 他通常每星期領薪水。
(B) 他忘記去領薪水支票。
(C) 他現在沒有足夠的錢。
(D) 他最近加薪。

Questions 59–61 對話

W	Welcome to Paxton Pharmaceuticals. **59 How may I help you?**
M	I'm with Kent Shipping Services. **60 I have a delivery for Dr. Alex Strummer.** Can you ask him to come down and sign for it?
W	Is it all right if I sign for him?
M	Actually, this delivery contains sensitive materials. Only Dr. Strummer is authorized to sign for them.
W	I see. Well, **61 Dr. Strummer is at our Swanson Road laboratory right now.**
M	Okay. **61 I'll come back tomorrow.**

女	歡迎光臨帕克斯頓製藥。**59 需要什麼服務？**
男	我是肯特貨運。**60 我有件貨品要給艾力克斯・史楚默博士。** 你可以請他下來簽收嗎？
女	我幫他簽收，可以嗎？
男	事實上，這件貨物內含敏感資料，只有史楚默博士有權利簽收。
女	我明白了。嗯，**61 史楚默博士目前在我們位於史旺生路的實驗室。**
男	好的，**61 我明天再來。**

59. Who most likely is the woman?
(A) A sales clerk
(B) A web designer
(C) A company receptionist*
(D) A post office manager

59. 女子最可能是誰？
(A) 銷售員。
(B) 網頁設計師。
(C) 公司的櫃檯人員。
(D) 郵局的經理。

60. Why does the man visit the office?
(A) To make a delivery*
(B) To have a meeting
(C) To inspect a lab
(D) To collect a payment

60. 男子為何造訪這家公司？
(A) 為了遞送貨物。
(B) 為了開會。
(C) 為了視察實驗室。
(D) 為了收取款項。

61. What does the woman imply when she says, "Well, Dr. Strummer is at our Swanson Road laboratory right now"?
(A) Dr. Strummer is a medical scientist.
(B) A storage room is available.
(C) Dr. Strummer cannot sign a form.*
(D) An urgent prescription request must be made.

61. 當女子說「嗯，史楚默博士目前在我們位於史旺生路的實驗室」，意指什麼？
(A) 史楚默博士是位醫學科學家。
(B) 有一間貯藏室空著可用。
(C) 史楚默博士無法簽文件。
(D) 必須要求緊急處方。

W	Hi, Marco. **62 Our company's 10th anniversary party is just a month away.** Did you get a chance to call the hotel yet?
M	Yes, and unfortunately, the Hill Park Hotel's banquet rooms are all booked. **63 I was thinking of contacting the Royal Hotel.** I believe their banquet rentals are even cheaper and they include a fully catered buffet.
W	Oh, that sounds good. But wait, isn't the hotel too far for most people to drive to? Aren't there any hotels closer to the office?
M	Yes, but they are quite expensive. I'm not sure we can afford them on our budget. **64 I will e-mail the office manager this afternoon and get his opinion.**

女	嗨,馬可。**62 再一個月就是我們公司的十週年派對**,你撥出時間打電話給飯店了嗎?
男	有,但遺憾的是,希爾公園飯店的宴會廳全都被訂走了。**63 我想聯絡皇家飯店。** 我相信他們的宴會廳租金還更便宜些,而且包含全套自助餐。
女	喔,聽起來很好。但是,等一下,那家飯店對大部分的人來說,要開車去不是太遠了嗎?沒有任何離公司比較近的飯店嗎?
男	有,但他們收費相當昂貴。我不確定以我們的預算能否負擔得起。**64 我今天下午會寫電子郵件給經理,詢問他的意見。**

62. What type of event are the speakers discussing?
(A) A store's grand opening
(B) An award ceremony
(C) A company anniversary*
(D) A retirement party

62. 説話者在討論何種活動?
(A) 商店的盛大開幕。
(B) 頒獎典禮。
(C) 公司的週年紀念。
(D) 退休派對。

63. What is the man considering?
(A) Whether to send invitations
(B) Who to hire as a caterer
(C) When to schedule an event
(D) Where to hold an event*

63. 男子在考慮何事?
(A) 是否要寄送邀請函。
(B) 僱用誰承辦酒席。
(C) 把活動安排在何時。
(D) 在哪裡舉行活動。

64. What does the man say he will do?
(A) Visit a venue
(B) Update a menu
(C) Cancel a reservation
(D) Consult a supervisor*

64. 男子説他會做何事?
(A) 去看一個場地。
(B) 更新菜單。
(C) 取消預訂。
(D) 請教主管。

Questions 65–67 對話及裝箱單

PREMIUM HOME DÉCOR		
Item	Quantity	Total Price
Panel Curtains	4	$160.00
[67] **Cushions**	**4**	**$40.00**
Shag Rug	1	$79.00
Lamp Shade	2	$44.00

優質居家裝潢		
項目	數量	總計
片簾	4	$160.00
[67] **靠墊**	**4**	**$40.00**
長絨地毯	1	$79.00
燈罩	2	$44.00

M Hello, Ma'am. How can I help you?

W Hi, [65] **I bought a new sofa recently** and found that most of my décor no longer matches. So, I ordered several furnishings from your online store. [66] **They arrived yesterday, but only two of the cushions I ordered were delivered instead of four.**

M Oh, I'm sorry to hear that. May I have a look at your packing slip?

W Sure. It's right here.

M Hmm. Unfortunately, the color you ordered is out of stock. You seem to have gotten the last two. I'm not sure when we'll get more, so [67] **how about I refund the full cost of the cushions,** and you can keep the two you did get for free.

W That would be great. Thank you!

男 哈囉，女士，需要什麼服務？

女 嗨，[65] 我最近買了張新沙發，卻發現大部分的裝潢都不搭了。所以我在你們的線上商店訂了一些家具。[66] 昨天送來了，但我訂的靠墊只送來兩個，而不是四個。

男 喔，發生這種狀況真的很抱歉。我可以看一下您的裝箱單嗎？

女 當然，就在這裡。

男 嗯。很不巧，您訂的顏色缺貨。您似乎買到最後兩個。我不確定我們何時會有貨。那麼，[67] 我把靠墊的費用全額退給您，已經收到的那兩個您可以自己留著，等同免費，這樣好嗎？

女 太好了，謝謝你！

65. What does the woman say she did recently?
(A) She stained her carpet.
(B) She moved to a new house.
(C) She misplaced some items.
(D) She purchased some new furniture.*

66. Why does the woman need assistance?
(A) Her order arrived incomplete.*
(B) She was charged too much for an item.
(C) She does not like some items.
(D) Her receipt was not in the box.

67. Look at the graphic. How much money will the woman be refunded?
(A) $160.00
(B) $40.00*
(C) $79.00
(D) $44.00

65. 女子說她最近做了何事？
(A) 她弄髒了地毯。
(B) 她搬新家。
(C) 有些東西她放錯地方了。
(D) 她買了新家具。

66. 女子為何需要協助？
(A) 她訂的貨沒有全部送來。
(B) 某件貨品的收費太高。
(C) 有些物品她不喜歡。
(D) 她的收據不在盒子裡。

67. 請見圖表。女子可以收到多少退款？
(A) $160.00。
(B) $40.00。
(C) $79.00。
(D) $44.00。

Questions 68–70 對話及標示

Flight	Destination	Gate
AV13	70 Los Angeles	A56
CP03	Miami	B45
PS55	Paris	B13
AA01	Beijing	A32

航班	目的地	登機門
AVI3	70 洛杉磯	A56
CP03	邁阿密	B45
P555	巴黎	BI3
AA0I	北京	A32

W Where are your bags, Steve? Did you already take them to the baggage drop off?

M No. I'm only bringing this carry-on. I packed light because 68 **I won't be staying for the entire workshop.**

W Oh? Why not?

M 69 **I have an important marketing meeting in the middle of the week. I couldn't reschedule it, so I'll only be attending the first two days of the workshop.**

W That's too bad. You're going to miss out on a lot of the presentations by the regional managers. Oh, look at the time! We'd better get to our departure gate.

M Right. 70 **The departure board says we're at A56.** We still have to go through airport security, so let's hurry.

女 史帝夫，你的行李在哪裡？你已經送去托運了嗎？

男 沒有，我只帶了這個手提行李。我的行李很輕便，因為 68 我不會待到整個工作坊結束。

女 哦？為什麼不？

男 69 這星期到一半時，我有個很重要的行銷會議。我無法重新安排時間，所以我只會參加前兩天的工作坊。

女 真是太掃興了。你會錯過很多地區經理的報告。噢，你看時間！我們最好過去登機門。

男 是啊。70 班機起飛看板上說，我們是 A56。我們還必須通過機場的安檢，所以我們趕快吧。

---

68. What type of event are the speakers traveling to?
 (A) A holiday vacation
 (B) A sales conference
 (C) A training session
 (D) A corporate workshop*

69. Why is the man staying just a short time?
 (A) He was unable to get a flight.
 (B) He could not reserve a hotel.
 (C) He has a conflicting schedule.*
 (D) He is not well.

70. Look at the graphic. What city are the speakers flying to?
 (A) Los Angeles*
 (B) Miami
 (C) Paris
 (D) Beijing

---

68. 說話者要飛去參加的是哪種活動？
 (A) 休假。
 (B) 銷售研討會。
 (C) 訓練課程。
 (D) 企業的工作坊。

69. 男子為何只會停留短暫的時間？
 (A) 他無法搭上飛機。
 (B) 他訂不到飯店。
 (C) 他的行程有衝突。
 (D) 他不舒服。

70. 請見圖表。說話者要飛往哪座城市？
 (A) 洛杉磯。
 (B) 邁阿密。
 (C) 巴黎。
 (D) 北京。

398

Questions 71–73 廣播

M   Welcome back to KTM radio, and thank you for listening to our new program, Travel Talk. **71, 72 Respected travel writer, Samuel Berkley, has joined us to talk about his new travel book series titled** *A Trekker's Guide to the World,* **which will be published early next year.** Each book focuses on one popular tourist country and includes useful information, such as where to eat, where to stay, and what to see. **73 Those of you who are interested in learning more about Berkley's new series can check it out online at <u>www. trekkersguide.com</u>.**

男   歡迎回到 KTM 電台，感謝您收聽我們的新節目「旅遊閒談」。**71, 72 備受景仰的旅遊作家山繆‧柏克利來到節目，和我們談談他將於明年初出版的新系列旅遊叢書《背包客的世界指南》。**每一本書各聚焦在一個受歡迎的旅遊國家，並包含實用的資訊，像是去哪裡吃、去哪裡住宿和要看什麼。**73 若您有興趣瞭解柏克利新系列叢書，詳情請上 www.trekkersguide.com 查詢。**

71. Who is Samuel Berkley?
 (A) A radio host
 (B) A publisher
 (C) A writer*
 (D) A diplomat

72. What is Samuel Berkley planning on doing?
 (A) Launching a travel website
 (B) Taking a trip around the world
 (C) Releasing a book series*
 (D) Giving a talk about hotels

73. What are listeners instructed to do?
 (A) Go to a website*
 (B) Book a trip
 (C) Purchase a book
 (D) Post questions online

71. 山繆‧柏克利是誰？
 (A) 電台主持人。
 (B) 出版商。
 (C) 作家。
 (D) 外交官。

72. 山繆‧柏克利打算做何事？
 (A) 推出旅遊網站。
 (B) 環遊世界。
 (C) 發行系列書籍。
 (D) 分享有關飯店的談話。

73. 聽眾被告知要做何事？
 (A) 造訪網站。
 (B) 預訂旅程。
 (C) 買書。
 (D) 上網提問。

Questions 74–76 談話

M Hello everyone. Welcome to the Audio Visual Technology Exhibition here in San Francisco. My name is Jackson, and I'm an employee at Southern Tech. **74 Today, I'd like to introduce you to a new type of headphones my company just released. 75 What sets our design apart from others is its wireless capability.** You can actually upload music into the headphones and wear them without using another device. Everyone here today is eligible to win a free set. **76 All you need to do is fill out a survey telling us about the devices you currently own.**

男 大家好,歡迎來到舊金山的視聽科技展。我是傑克生,南方科技的員工。**74 今天要為各位介紹我們公司才剛發表的新型耳機。75 我們的設計與眾不同之處在於它的無線功能。**你真的可以不必使用別的裝置,就能上傳音樂到耳機並且戴著聽。今天在場的各位都可以免費贏得一副耳機,**76 只需填寫一份調查,告訴我們你現在擁有的裝置就可以了。**

74. What product is being discussed?
- (A) A stereo system
- **(B) An audio device***
- (C) A television set
- (D) A software program

74. 談話討論的是什麼產品?
- (A) 立體音響系統。
- **(B) 音訊裝置。**
- (C) 電視機。
- (D) 軟體程式。

75. How does the product differ from competitors' products?
- (A) It is cheaper to repair.
- (B) It is more durable.
- (C) It is less expensive.
- **(D) It has a unique feature.***

75. 這項產品與競爭對手的產品有何不同?
- (A) 修理費用較便宜。
- (B) 比較持久耐用。
- (C) 價格較低廉。
- **(D) 有一項獨有的特色。**

76. How can listeners win a free product?
- (A) By testing out a model
- **(B) By completing a survey***
- (C) By visiting a website
- (D) By purchasing an item

76. 聽眾要如何贏得免費產品?
- (A) 充分檢測一個款式。
- **(B) 完成一份調查。**
- (C) 造訪一個網站。
- (D) 購買一個物品。

M Hello, Ms. Choi. This is Mike Burton calling from Burton and Sons properties. **77 It was nice speaking with you on the phone yesterday,** and I hope you're still interested in seeing the restaurant space on Miller Road. You asked about basement storage space, and I wanted to let you know **78 that storage rooms can be rented for a monthly fee.** Anyway, several people are interested in the space, **79 so we should probably go see it as soon as possible.** That way, we can sign a lease before someone else does.

男 哈囉，崔女士。我是博頓父子房地產公司的麥克‧博頓。**77 很高興昨天和您通電話**，希望您還有興趣看米勒路上的那間餐廳。您詢問了地下室貯藏空間的問題，我想通知您，**78 貯藏室可以月租。**不過，有好幾個人都對這個空間感興趣，**79 因此我們應該盡快去看看。**那樣的話，我們就可以趕在其他人之前簽下租約。

77. What did the speaker do yesterday?
(A) He went to a restaurant.
**(B) He talked to the listener.*
(C) He purchased a storage unit.
(D) He signed a lease.

77. 説話者昨天做了何事？
(A) 他去了一家餐廳。
(B) 他和聽者談話。
(C) 他買下一個貯藏空間。
(D) 他簽了一份租約。

78. What does the speaker say about storage rooms?
(A) They have shelving units inside.
(B) They are an added bonus.
(C) They have security systems.
**(D) They are available for a fee.*

78. 關於貯藏室，説話者怎麼説？
(A) 裡面有層架。
(B) 是額外的好處。
(C) 有保全系統。
(D) 可付費使用。

79. Why does the speaker say, "Several people are interested in the space"?
(A) To explain why the space is no longer available
**(B) To encourage the listener to see the space quickly*
(C) To request the listener to give up the space
(D) To describe the size and price of the space

79. 説話者為何説「有好幾個人都對這個空間感興趣」？
(A) 解釋這個空間為何不再能租。
(B) 鼓勵聽者趕快點去看這個地點。
(C) 要求聽者放棄這個地點。
(D) 形容這個空間的大小與價格。

Questions 80–82 電話留言

W Hi, this is a message for David Taylor. **80 This is Beatrice calling from Eastside Homeless Shelter.** Thank you very much for signing up to help out at our annual concert fundraiser downtown. As of now we have enough volunteers for the event. **81 However, we are looking for volunteers to work one Sunday a month in our soup kitchen.** We really need the extra help there, so you'd be doing your community a great service. If you're interested, **82 please e-mail me at beatrice@ eastsideshelter.com, so I can send you an application.**	**女** 嗨，這是給大衛・泰勒的訊息。**80 我是東岸街友庇護所的畢翠絲**，非常感謝您報名要當我們於市中心舉行的年度募款音樂會的義工。目前，我們已有足夠的活動義工。**81 不過，我們正在尋找能一個月抽出一個星期日，在我們的慈善廚房幫忙的義工。**我們那裡真的很需要額外的幫手，所以，您會幫上社區很大的忙。如果您有興趣，**82 請寄電子郵件到 beatrice@eastsideshelter.com 給我**，好讓我能寄申請書給您。

80. Where does the speaker work?
    (A) At a job agency
    (B) At a charity*
    (C) At a concert hall
    (D) At a city park

81. Why does the speaker say, "As of now we have enough volunteers for the event"?
    (A) To turn down an offer*
    (B) To stress the success of an event
    (C) To voice a concern about a policy
    (D) To request more funding

82. What does the speaker ask the listener to do?
    (A) Attend a concert
    (B) Send an e-mail*
    (C) Visit a website
    (D) Record some information

80. 說話者在哪裡工作？
    (A) 職業介紹所。
    (B) 慈善團體。
    (C) 音樂廳。
    (D) 市立公園。

81. 說話者為何說「目前，我們已有足夠的活動義工」？
    (A) 以回絕一個提議。
    (B) 以強調一場活動的成功。
    (C) 以表達對一項政策的關心。
    (D) 以要求更多資金。

82. 說話者要求聽者做何事？
    (A) 參加一場音樂會。
    (B) 寄送電子郵件。
    (C) 造訪一個網站。
    (D) 記錄一些資訊。

W   **[83] Now that we've had a chance to view the yacht club banquet hall, I'd like to take everyone out onto the docks, where we will see a variety of boats owned by the club. [84] Our entire collection of vessels was donated to us by retired engineer Samuel Welsh last year.** Mr. Welsh designed these boats himself and has graciously given them to us to host private events on. If you'd like to learn more about Mr. Welsh's work, **[85] I highly recommend picking up a pamphlet near the exit, which details his amazing career.**

女   [83] 現在，既然我們已經參觀過遊艇俱樂部的宴會廳，我想帶大家出去到碼頭上，在那裡，我們可以看到俱樂部擁有的各種不同船隻。[84] 我們的所有船隻都是退休工程師山繆・韋爾許去年捐贈的。韋爾許先生親自設計這些船隻，並好心送給了我們，以便遊艇俱樂部在上面舉辦私人活動。如果你們想更了解韋爾許先生的作品，[85] 我極力推薦各位拿一份出口附近的小冊子，上面詳述他令人嘖嘖稱奇的生涯。

83. Where is the talk taking place?
(A) At a factory
(B) At a yacht club*
(C) At a museum
(D) At a travel agency

84. According to the speaker, what did Samuel Welsh do last year?
(A) He made a donation.*
(B) He hired an assistant.
(C) He went on a sailing trip.
(D) He opened a gallery.

85. What does the speaker recommend that the listeners do?
(A) Read a booklet*
(B) Book a cruise
(C) Go for a swim
(D) Buy a membership

83. 這段談話發生在哪裡？
(A) 在一間工廠。
(B) 在一個遊艇俱樂部。
(C) 在一間博物館。
(D) 在一家旅行社。

84. 根據說話者所述，山繆・韋爾許去年做了何事？
(A) 他捐贈了東西。
(B) 他請了一個助理。
(C) 他去航海旅行。
(D) 他開了一家藝廊。

85. 說話者推薦聽者何事？
(A) 閱讀一份小冊子。
(B) 預訂搭船遊覽。
(C) 去游泳。
(D) 購買會員資格。

M **⁸⁶ Do you have a difficult time keeping your office space and lobby clean?** Is it hard to find trustworthy and affordable after-hours cleaners? Corporate Custodian Services is a reliable and cheap way to keep your office clean and tidy. **⁸⁷ We understand your busy schedule, which is why all our cleaners start work after you've gone home for the day.** Imagine arriving at work to a freshly cleaned office every morning. With Corporate Custodian Services, you never have to worry about taking out the trash or sweeping again. Don't believe us? **⁸⁸ Visit www.corporatecustodianservices.com/feedback to read postings from our satisfied customers.**

男 ⁸⁶ 要保持辦公室與大廳整潔，是否有困難？要找到值得信任而且負擔得起，在下班之後來的清潔人員是不是很難？「企業守衛服務」是維持您辦公室潔淨整齊、既可靠又價廉的方式。**⁸⁷ 我們了解您的時程表很忙碌，所以，我們所有清潔人員會在你們下班回家後才開始工作。**想像一下，每天早上到一個剛打掃乾淨的辦公室來上班。有了「企業守衛服務」，您再也不必煩惱要把垃圾拿出去倒或者打掃了。難以置信嗎？⁸⁸ **請至 www.corporatecustodianservices.com/feedback**，看看我們的客戶滿意意見回饋。

86. Who is the advertisement intended for?
(A) Hotel staff
(B) Security guards
(C) Office managers*
(D) Bus drivers

86. 這則廣告的對象是誰？
(A) 飯店員工。
(B) 保全人員。
(C) 辦公室經理。
(D) 公車司機。

87. What does the speaker say is special about the service?
(A) It is offered every day.
(B) It can be booked online.
(C) It can be cancelled easily.
(D) It is done in the evenings.*

87. 說話者說，這項服務的特別之處為何？
(A) 每天提供。
(B) 可以上網預約。
(C) 可以輕鬆取消。
(D) 在傍晚履行。

88. What are listeners encouraged to do?
(A) Ask for an estimate
(B) Call a telephone number
(C) Read some client reviews*
(D) Purchase new equipment

88. 廣告鼓勵聽眾做何事？
(A) 要求估價。
(B) 打某個電話號碼。
(C) 看一些客戶意見。
(D) 購買新設備。

W Before we wrap up, **89 I'd like to let you all know about a change in our company's travel expense reimbursement.** Currently, employees are only allowed to ask for expense reimbursement when they travel out of town. However, **90 many of our employees who travel within the city for client meetings have expressed displeasure about the lack of reimbursement for their expenses.** In the interest of keeping things fair, the company will begin expense reimbursement for all employees regardless of where they are traveling. **91 Please distribute the new expense handbooks by the end of this month and be prepared to explain them to your respective departments.**

女 在我們結束之前，**89 我想要讓你們所有人知道，我們公司交通旅資報銷的改變。** 目前，只有到外地的費用，員工才准予報銷。不過，**90 有許多員工在城裡往來，是為了與客戶會面，他們對於費用無法報銷表示不滿。** 為了公平起見，公司會開始讓所有員工報銷費用，不論目的地是哪裡。**91 請在本月底前將新的費用手冊發下去，並準備好向你們各自的部門解釋更動內容。**

TEST 4

PART 4

 16

89. What is the main topic of the announcement?
(A) Booking flights online
(B) Paying for travel costs*
(C) Training new employees
(D) Canceling out of town travel

89. 這項聲明的主題為何？
(A) 上網預訂航班。
(B) 支付旅費。
(C) 訓練新員工。
(D) 取消外地旅行。

90. According to the speaker, why is the change being made?
(A) To respond to employee complaints*
(B) To improve employee work efficiency
(C) To make up for a lack of pay raises
(D) To follow a government regulation

90. 根據說話者所述，公司為何做出這項改變？
(A) 為了回應員工的抱怨。
(B) 為了改善員工的工作效率。
(C) 為了補償未能加薪。
(D) 為了遵守政府規定。

91. What are the listeners reminded to do?
(A) Update employee contracts
(B) Pass out new information booklets*
(C) Gather reports from employees
(D) Speak with department managers

91. 說話者提醒聽眾做何事？
(A) 更新員工合約。
(B) 分發新的資訊小冊子。
(C) 收集員工的報告。
(D) 和部門經理談話。

Tour Date	Departure Time
Monday, May 2	10:30 A.M. / 2:30 P.M.
Tuesday, May 3	11:30 A.M. / 3:30 P.M.
Wednesday, May 4	10:30 A.M. / 2:30 P.M.
93 Thursday, May 5	**11:30 A.M. / 3:30 P.M.**

旅行日期	出發時間
5月2日，星期一	10:30 A.M. / 2:30 P.M.
5月3日，星期二	11:30 A.M. / 3:30 P.M.
5月4日，星期三	10:30 A.M. / 2:30 P.M.
93 5月5日，星期四	**11:30 A.M. / 3:30 P.M.**

M Attention, all passengers of Barbados Boat Tours. **92 Due to an approaching tropical storm, all tours have been canceled for today, Tuesday, and Wednesday.** We expect the storm to have passed by the following day, and **93 our business will resume Thursday morning.** We would like to offer all ticket holders complete refunds. Simply **94 visit the front desk to have your ticket refunded or changed for another day.** Thank you very much for your understanding, and we apologize for the inconvenience.

男 巴巴多輪船旅遊的乘客請注意，**92 由於熱帶暴風雨即將來襲，今天、星期二和星期三的所有行程皆已取消。**暴風雨預計在第二天會經過，而 **93 我們會在星期四早上恢復營業。**我們會提供所有購票的旅客全額退費。您只需要 **94 到櫃台退票或更改日期。**非常感謝您的諒解，造成您的不便，敬請見諒。

92. What has caused a cancelation?
(A) An absent ship captain
(B) Missing passengers
(C) Poor weather conditions*
(D) A damaged boat

92. 什麼原因導致取消？
(A) 輪船船長缺席。
(B) 乘客失蹤。
(C) 天候不佳。
(D) 輪船受損。

93. Look at the graphic. What time will the next boat tour take place?
(A) 10:30 A.M.
(B) 11:30 A.M.*
(C) 2:30 P.M.
(D) 3:30 P.M.

93. 請見圖表。下一班輪船旅程是何時？
(A) 上午10點30分。
(B) 上午11點30分。
(C) 下午2點30分。
(D) 下午3點30分。

94. What does the speaker ask listeners to do?
(A) Wait for a few hours
(B) Try a new restaurant
(C) Stay away from the dock
(D) Visit the front desk*

94. 說話者要求聽眾做什麼？
(A) 等幾個小時。
(B) 試試新餐廳。
(C) 遠離碼頭。
(D) 前往櫃台。

Questions 95–97 會議摘錄及問卷調查結果

Question:
What improvement would you most like to see?

Answer Option	Number of Votes
A. A reduction in fares	105
96 **B. Shorter wait times**	**87**
C. More payment options	55
D. Online reservations	32

問題：您最想看到什麼樣的改進？

答案選項	票數
A. 票價調降	105
96**B. 候車時間縮短**	**87**
C. 更多付款方式選擇	55
D. 線上訂票	32

W Let's start the meeting by looking at the results of ⁹⁵ **a survey we recently conducted with the passengers onboard our express buses.** First, let's look at the answers to the first question, "What improvement would you most like to see?" As you can see, most survey participants said they would prefer fare decreases. However, we are really not in a position to offer discounts at this point. But, ⁹⁶ **we could hire a few more drivers in order to implement the second-most popular answer.** ⁹⁷ **If you know of any websites we could post advertisements on, please let me know at the end of the meeting.**

女 ⁹⁵ **最近針對搭乘我們快捷巴士的旅客，我們做了調查**，會議一開始，先來看看結果。首先，來看第一題的答案：「您最想看到什麼樣的改進？」正如你們所見，大部分參與調查的人說，他們比較希望票價調降。不過，我們目前真的無法提供折扣。不過，⁹⁶ **我們倒是可以僱用更多司機，實現票數第二高的答案。** ⁹⁷ **如果你們知道哪些網站可以張貼廣告，請在會議之後告訴我。**

95. Where most likely does the speaker work?
(A) At a travel agency
(B) At an airline
(C) At a marketing agency
(D) At a bus company*

96. Look at the graphic. What survey result does the speaker want to implement?
(A) A reduction in fares
(B) Shorter wait times*
(C) More payment options
(D) Online reservations

97. What does the speaker ask the listeners to do?
(A) Recommend employment websites*
(B) Interview potential candidates
(C) Review customer information
(D) Upgrade a company system

95. 說話者最可能在哪裡工作？
(A) 旅行社。
(B) 航空公司。
(C) 行銷公司。
(D) 巴士公司。

96. 請見圖表。說話者打算執行哪一項調查結果？
(A) 調降票價。
(B) 縮短候車時間。
(C) 更多付款方式選擇。
(D) 線上訂票。

97. 說話者要求聽者何事？
(A) 推薦求職網站。
(B) 面試可能的人選。
(C) 檢閱顧客資料。
(D) 升級公司的系統。

Ristorante Catoria
50% Off Group Discount Coupon

[99] * *Groups may not exceed 15 patrons.*
* *Valid until December 31st.*

卡多麗亞餐廳
團體 5 折優惠券

[99]* **團體不得超過** 15 人。
*12 月 31 日前有效。

W Hello, this is Jan. [98] **I'm calling about the holiday party we're organizing for our department this year.** Now . . . we've already decided the party will be on December 22nd, and it's great to hear that [99] **the number of guests has been jumped to twenty.** However, it looks like we won't be able to use the coupon for Ristorante Catoria. We might want to make a reservation at a cheaper buffet. Also, it would be nice to find a place that has a party room available that can accommodate all our guests. [100] **Can you do some research and prepare a list of potential places?**

女 哈囉，我是珍。[98] **我打電話來問關於正在籌備的今年度部門佳期派對。** 那麼，我們已經決定派對在 12 月 22 日舉行，而且很高興聽到 [99] **賓客人數已激增到 20 人。** 不過，這樣看來我們無法使用卡多麗亞餐廳的優惠券了。我們可能要預訂較低廉的自助餐。還有，如果能找到一個備有派對室的場地，足以容納我們所有賓客的話就更好了。[100] **你可以調查一下，準備一份可能行得通的場地清單嗎？**

98. Why is the event being held?
    (A) To launch a product line
    (B) To host an award ceremony
    (C) To announce a promotion
    (D) To celebrate a holiday*

98. 為何舉行這個活動？
    (A) 為了推出一條產品線。
    (B) 為了主辦頒獎典禮。
    (C) 為了宣布升遷。
    (D) 為了慶祝假期。

99. Look at the graphic. Why is the speaker unable to use the coupon for the event?
    (A) Not enough guests will attend the event.
    (B) The event will occur after the expiration date.
    (C) The event will take place on a weekend.
    (D) Too many people will be present at the event.*

99. 請見圖表。說話者為何無法將優惠券用於本次活動？
    (A) 參加活動的賓客人數不足。
    (B) 活動會在有效日期之後舉行。
    (C) 活動在週末舉行。
    (D) 活動的出席人數太多。

100. What does the speaker ask the listener to do?
    (A) Make a list of other restaurants*
    (B) Call Ristorante Catoria
    (C) Change the date of an event
    (D) Ask management for more funds

100. 說話者要求聽者做什麼？
    (A) 列一張其他餐廳的清單。
    (B) 打電話給卡多麗亞餐廳。
    (C) 更改活動日期。
    (D) 向管理階層要求更多資金。

101. 由於前僱主的推薦函**令人印象深刻**,德瑞克立刻得到了那個管理職。

102. 納米斯航空不再**獲准**運送貨物到北部地區。

103. 傑洛米設法要拿到明天比賽的入場券,但它們已經**完全**售完了。

104. **未經**正式許可,任何人不得進入這間辦公室。

105. 弗雷德里克頓兒童扶助協會所舉辦的年度慈善晚宴,**預定在** 12 月 7 日於大瑪麗安飯店舉行。

106. 擁有者的使用手冊中,包含了如何清潔這台微波爐的詳細**說明**。

107. 市府買下了巴萊納街上的**閒置**大樓,將它改成一所國小。

108. 顧客必須在櫃檯付**款**,否則無法領取處方箋的藥。

109. 除非員工在一回來就**立刻**出示原始收據,否則公司將不核銷差旅費用。

110. 《斯蒂克尼娛樂指南》肯定**是**找到本地最佳用餐處最可靠的資訊來源。

111. 今天早上總技師托利弗先生**自己**開始修理工作,不過午餐後有兩位職員可以來幫他。

112. 為了達到最佳效果,製造商**建議**晴天時再塗上外部漆料。

113. 達特茅斯學院的教師必須**於**本月最後一天**前**交出學生期末成績。

114. 費茲傑羅戲院正在進行整修,因此樂蘭·甘農樂團演唱會的籌辦者正在**積極**尋找另一個場地。

115. 一旦傳送帶修好,工廠就**可以**繼續生產了。

116. 應該有人告訴西諾波利先生,**他的**車停在給購物中心顧客的預留車位了。

117. 拉森柏格機車將**自**謝佛維爾汽車公司提出的收購大幅獲利。

118. 我們昨天收到的申請表,**仍**需由一位部門主管審查。

119. 如果惡劣天氣迫使棒球賽取消,已購票**的人**將獲得全額退款。

120. 雖然這個地區的觀光收入在冬季月分時通常會**減少**,但在溫暖的春天就會回復。

121. 新人事經理所負責的一個重要**措施**就是定期和工廠員工開會討論安全事宜。

122. 蓋特女士的**功勞**是實施讓顧客數量顯著增加的策略。

123. 美術館的門票可以在網路上以**稍微**便宜的價格購得。

124. 本部門**原本要參加**上週的政策會議,但時間上卻撞期而無法參加。

125. 格利森先生**偏好**湖景,因此選擇租用皇后街的辦公室,而不是在茉雷巷的。

126. 選拔委員會必須在三月底前收到格倫丁文學獎明年的**提名**。

127. 為了讓小組減少**浪費**,經理沒有將所有的銷售圖表印成紙本,而是以電子郵件的附件寄給大家。

128. 如果威爾森女士需要多一點時間付款,就必須和銀行經理聯繫。

129. 卡隆快遞除了迅速運送外,親切的服務也是他們的管理部所重視**的**。

130. 運動版的編輯對她自己所核准的文章比其他編輯更**嚴格**。

Questions 131–134 文章

人氣店家的大膽之舉

卡斯爾巴一因為愈來愈多的客訴，卡斯爾巴最具歷史，也最受歡迎的優格餐廳「趣味餐廳」推出了一個確實令人意外的改變。餐廳老闆決定採用一個許多人都覺得很特別的規定。在過去的兩週以來，顧客在餐廳用餐時，不得使用筆記型電腦做事。趣味餐廳是本市中第一家，也是唯一一家實施這種規定的餐廳，目的是鼓勵顧客在用餐後隨即離開餐廳。藉由讓顧客在餐桌上耗費較短的時間，這家餐廳每日業績量增加了 20%以上。顧客也不用等位子。新規定已經證明受到顧客們的歡迎。現在，卡斯爾巴其他受歡迎的餐飲業者也在考慮進行類似的調整。

131. (A) 員工
(B) 價格
(C) 抱怨
(D) 運送，遞送

132. (A) 一些
(B) 較少的
(C) 任何
(D) 很多

133. (A) 顧客在試賣期間可獲得免費咖啡。
(B) 新規定已經證明受到顧客們的歡迎。
(C) 趣味餐廳也有戶外用餐區。
(D) 老闆們相信新員工在開始工作前，需要更多的訓練。

134. (A) 考慮
(B) 考慮
(C) 正在被考慮
(D) 正在考慮

Questions 135–138 信件

您使用助聽器嗎？
今天就聯絡納普頓科技公司吧！

八月份，納普頓科技公司將代表聽力 1000 開始進行一項詳盡的消費者研究計畫。為了這個大型計劃，本團隊正徵求 300 百多名佩戴助聽器的民眾。所有參與者必須配戴醫生囑咐的器具。配戴時間距本研究計畫起不得超過三年。需出示紙本處方箋，作為確證。如有興趣，請上本公司網站 www.knaptontechnologies.com/hearingaidstudy，並填寫簡短問卷調查。我們的人員將與合格參與者聯絡。每位參與者將於研究完成後獲贈價值 200 元的禮券。

135. **(A) 尋找**
(B) 為……投保
(C) 升遷
(D) 展示

136. (A) 除了……外
(B) 當作
(C) 因為
(D) 在

137. **(A) 需出示紙本處方箋，作為確證。**
(B) 將提供新電池給所有參加者。
(C) 我們要求處方箋的款項必須當場給付。
(D) 送交後將立即根據處方箋配藥。

138. **(A) 將得到**
(B) 已得到
(C) 得到
(D) 被得到

Questions 139–142 新聞稿

下個月，日本電器製造業龍頭崎企業將搬遷至青柳街 117 號，該處最近剛翻修完成的現代化辦公大樓。崎企業將佔用青柳大樓最上面的七個樓層。在這個新址中，員工們將享用超過 90,000 平方公尺的漂亮辦公空間及便利的設施。崎企業也計劃另外租下大樓一樓的零售空間。「那是展示我們最新高科技冰箱與烤箱的最佳地點。」崎企業的發言人秋葉香織說。秋葉女士提到，設計與工程師部門將留在他們位於小川大樓的原址。

139. (A) 家具
(B) 服裝
(C) 壁紙
(D) 家用電器

140. (A) 賣
(B) 油漆
(C) 佔用
(D) 攝影；照相

141. (A) 崎企業的產品以尖端設計與省電聞名。
(B) 崎企業也計劃另外租下大樓一樓的零售空間。
(C) 崎企業以亞洲前 20 名最佳工作場域列於《東京時報》上。
(D) 崎企業的股票在公告後隨即價值倍增。

142. (A) 它
(B) 他們的
(C) 什麼
(D) 任何

Questions 143–146 電子郵件

收件者：佐佐木香織
　　　　<ssawaki601@e-mail.com.jp>
寄件者：客戶服務部
　　　　<customerserv@elsworth.co.uk>
日期：10 月 16 日星期四晚上 8:56
主旨：查問網站

親愛的佐佐木女士，

我們要感謝您在本公司網站上的回饋欄上，留下有關 EW2500 數位相機使用手冊的意見。您表示，在如何上傳影像到手機或行動裝置的相關說明非常複雜難懂。我們完全認同您對這一點的看法。其他客戶也對同一問題提出了回饋。因此，本公司出版部已經針對相機轉傳影像所需要的特定軟體與傳輸線的說明做出修訂。我們

已將更新版的使用手冊放在本公司的網站上。您可以在「新數位相機區」中找到。如果您偏好紙本說明，我們也很樂意以平信寄送給您，但寄送最少需要一週的時間。

埃爾斯沃斯相機公司
客戶服務部專員
立倫·基爾戈 敬上

143. (A) 所有的
(B) 對於
(C) 什麼
(D) 的

144. (A) EW2500 數位相機目前是我們最受歡迎的商品。
(B) 如果您需要，我們可以透過電子郵件將完整的使用說明寄給您。
(C) 其他客戶也對同一問題提出了回饋。
(D) 我們大多數的客戶來自亞洲的南部地區。

145. (A) 替代
(B) 同樣地
(C) 因此
(D) 儘管如此

146. (A) 最初的
(B) 更新的
(C) 絕對的
(D) 專心的

PART 7 P.162-181

Questions 147–148 簡訊

傳訊者：榮恩·卡浦爾，553-0304
收訊者：薩爾達·文森蒂

薩爾達，我把我的日誌本留在辦公室了。我必須在兩點和客戶碰面，但我忘記確切地點了。[148] 我正要離開丹尼燒烤店，打算直接去開會。[147] 妳可以看一下我的日誌本，把地址傳給我嗎？

147. 卡浦爾先生為什麼傳簡訊給文森蒂女士？

(A) 詢問她是否找到了他的公事包

(B) 詢問一個取消的會議

(C) 要她傳一個地址給他

(D) 預約餐廳

148. 卡浦爾先生接下來可能會做什麼？

(A) 離開餐廳

(B) 去辦公室

(C) 查網站

(D) 打電話給客戶

Questions 149–150 廣告

¹⁴⁹ **古世界考古基金會美國分會徵求兩位全職實習生，協助柬埔寨暹粒附近的考古挖掘工作。**

¹⁵⁰⁽ᴬ⁾ **應徵者須取得大學考古學位，或現為考古學系大四學生。**

需具研究經驗。¹⁵⁰⁽ᶜ⁾ **具考古現場實際操作經驗者尤佳。**

¹⁵⁰⁽ᴮ⁾ **應徵者須願意於八月至十月間遠赴至挖掘現場。** 基金會將提供住宿與機票。

實習生將於行程結束時領取全額薪水。實習生將於挖掘工作結束後，由專案統籌決定是否獲聘為全職員工。

149. 關於古世界考古基金會美國分會，提到了什麼事？

(A) 它想要聘僱一位兼職實習生。

(B) 它在外國進行挖掘工作。

(C) 除了旅費外不另給付實習生薪資。

(D) 在三年前創立。

150. 下列何者不是該職務的資格條件？

(A) 大學教育

(B) 旅行意願

(C) 實地訓練

(D) 電腦知識

Questions 151–153 備忘錄

收件者：蒂蒙斯醫學研究人員
寄件者：員工關係部主任安德森・巴斯特
回覆：演講
日期：4 月 5 日

所有人員，請注意，

4 月 13 日下週四，我們將在 203 號禮堂舉辦一場特別的演講。¹⁵¹ **瑪麗亞・賽喬斯是西木大學的資深研究員。** 過去的五年來，她在那裡進行研究。除了和英國倫敦的研究者合作進行幾項癌症新療法的研發外，她還負責一系列新疫苗的開發。在加入西木大學前，賽喬斯成名於澳洲雪梨的醫學研究院。在那裡，¹⁵³ **我剛好有機會在幾項開創性的專案中受教於她。** ¹⁵² **賽喬斯女士下週將到溫哥華，並同意與我們分享實驗室技術上的最新成果發表。** 所有人員都必須參加這場演講。

151. 這個備忘錄討論的是什麼？

(A) 創立新實驗室的計畫

(B) 新職缺

(C) 一位科學家的職涯

(D) 專案計畫的截止日期

152. 蒂蒙斯醫學研究位於何處？

(A) 倫敦

(B) 雪梨

(C) 西木

(D) 溫哥華

153. 巴斯特先生提到什麼有關賽喬斯女士的事？

(A) 她是他以前的導師。

(B) 她將搬到溫哥華。

(C) 她將加入他的研究團隊。

(D) 她將開設自己的實驗室。

Questions 154–155 簡訊

賈邁爾・麥爾斯 上午 [10:30]
嗨，弗格森。我還在戴維斯影印店等兩幅橫旗。你可以先去前往布置嗎？¹⁵⁴ **我把房間鑰匙放在辦公桌右上的抽屜裡。**

弗格森・博伊德 上午 [10:33]
找到了。我現在就去。

賈邁爾・麥爾斯 上午 [10:35]
太感謝了。我知道頒獎典禮 1:30 才開始，但我們需要仔細檢查所有設備。

弗格森・博伊德 上午 [10:40]
只是確定一下，**155** 我們的頒獎典禮是在埃利奧特街的前市政大樓，對吧？不是皇后街上新的這棟。

賈邁爾・麥爾斯 上午 [10:42]
155 沒錯。典禮後攝影師會在前面的草地上為獲獎者拍照。這就是我多訂一幅橫旗在外面使用的原因。我一拿到橫旗就趕到前市政大樓跟你會合。

弗格森・博伊德 上午 [10:45]
好。待會兒見！

---

154. 上午 10:33 時，博伊德先生說的「找到了」是什麼意思？
(A) 他會把客戶需要的資料傳過去。
(B) 他在開車時有看到戴維斯影印店。
(C) 他拿到了會場的鑰匙。
(D) 他正在找通訊錄上的電話號碼。

155. 博伊德先生接下來最有可能去哪裡？
(A) 火車站
(B) 公司總部
(C) 影印店
(D) 舊市政廳

Questions 156–158 信件

> **霍爾特高爾夫暨鄉村俱樂部**
> **亞伯達省埃德蒙頓**
> **羅西特大道 34 號**
> **www.holtgolf.ca**
>
> 4 月 24 日
> 亨利・麥克阿瑟先生
> 亞伯達省埃德蒙頓
> 華盛頓大道 220 號

親愛的麥克阿瑟先生：
感謝您購買霍爾特高爾夫暨鄉村俱樂部會員。本年度內，您可以享用我們所有的優質服務。自 5 月 1 日起至 9 月 30 日，除了可自選開球時間外，您還可以盡情地使用我們的休息室、餐廳和水療設備。除此之外，**156** 我們所有的小餐館都附贈碳酸飲料，您只要在點餐時，出示會員卡即可。

除了這些極佳的服務外，霍爾特高爾夫暨鄉村俱樂部正宣布另一項專屬會員的服務。**157** 從現在起至八月底，所有的會員都可以邀請賓客到我們廣闊的球場上打一場高爾夫球。這個特別優惠只限上午八點至下午四點。該服務需提早於 24 小時前預約。

若您有任何問題或疑慮，請來電客服熱線900-555-3344。

米切爾・沃克 敬上

156. 關於霍爾特高爾夫暨鄉村俱樂部，下列何者為真？
(A) 它提供會員免費飲料。
(B) 它只在春季開放。
(C) 它提供優惠的會員資格。
(D) 它舉辦季節性派對。

157. 根據信件內容，八月後會有什麼變動？
(A) 會員無法使用水療。
(B) 會員不能帶賓客入場。
(C) 高爾夫球開球時間會提早。
(D) 有高爾夫球課程。

158. 下列句子最適合出現在 [1]、[2]、[3]、[4] 的哪個位置中？
「本年度內，您可以享用我們所有的優質服務。」
(A) [1]
(B) [2]
(C) [3]
(D) [4]

Questions 159–162 文章

米蘭（7月14日）—— [159] 歐洲頂尖設計公司之一的馬軒可時尚，其首席設計師羅伯特‧佩利尼已經宣布將自公司的職位退休。

自10年前首次接掌該職，羅伯特‧佩利尼一直努力讓馬軒可時尚成為業界最知名的品牌之一。由於佩利尼的熱情與設計眼光，馬軒可已經成為名流間最受歡迎的品牌。而佩利尼的設計也常見於伸展台與紅毯上。[160] 公司的成功甚至促成了姊妹公司馬軒可飾品的成立。

里維拉設計公司的前任設計師伊莉娜‧莫羅娃將接掌馬軒可首席設計師一職。莫羅娃擁有管理大型時尚企業十多年的經驗。[161] 她的作品在許多時尚季、雜誌中成為焦點，也曾為一些歐洲頂尖歌手與演員提供服裝。

在離開馬軒可後，[162] 羅伯特‧佩利尼將與蘇菲亞‧伯蘇斯基合夥創立新的獨立時尚坊。引述佩利尼自己說的話，[162]「我很期待與蘇菲亞合作。她頗具創意的眼光與我相近。」至於佩利尼的新時裝作品何時發表，至今尚未有消息傳出。

159. 這篇文章的目的是什麼？
(A) 報導一家公司的倒閉
(B) 宣布公司領導權的變動
(C) 宣傳公司的新職缺
(D) 公布新系列產品

160. 關於馬軒可，提到了什麼事？
(A) 總部在北美洲。
(B) 被佩利尼收購。
(C) 擁有里維拉設計公司。
(D) 設立了第二家公司。

161. 關於伊莉娜‧莫羅娃，提到了什麼事？
(A) 她將成為佩利尼的事業夥伴。
(B) 她在里維拉設計公司的事業很成功。
(C) 她原本是一位伸展台模特兒。
(D) 她的設計是提供給一般消費者。

162. 下列句子最適合出現在 [1]、[2]、[3]、[4] 的哪個位置中？
「至於佩利尼的新時裝作品何時發表，至今尚未有消息傳出。」
(A) [1]
(B) [2]
(C) [3]
(D) [4]

Questions 163–165 廣告

[163] **第一屆年度海濱餐車祭**

愛捷克斯餐飲協會很高興宣布有史以來的第一場海濱餐車祭。自8月8日星期一至8月14日星期日，愛捷克斯海濱區將邀請許多本地餐車參與。來賓在上午11:00至下午6:00間可享現場音樂演奏、獎品以及兒童遊樂活動。並 [164] **可以優惠價試吃餐車上的食物。**

與會的知名餐車：

★ 里約墨西哥捲餅——可享新鮮開胃小點，及各式墨西哥捲餅和玉米片

★ 瘋狂燒烤——滷豬肋排、雞翅及手撕豬肉

★ 邦妮薯條——配上您喜愛食材沾醬的薯條

所有入場均免費。[165] **停車位有限，請盡早到場。**

欲知與會餐車完整名單，請上網站 www.ajaxwaterfront.com/foodtruckfestival。

163. 這則廣告是在宣傳什麼？
(A) 餐廳的盛大開幕
(B) 公園的音樂會
(C) 汽車展
(D) 新社區活動

164. 關於參加的餐車，提到了什麼事？
(A) 將開至各個城市。
(B) 將分發免費禮物。
(C) 全天營業。
(D) 將降價販售食物。

165. 參加者被鼓勵做什麼事？

(A) 盡早到場

(B) 把自己的車子留在家裡

(C) 付入場費

(D) 在海濱區露營

Questions 166–169 電子郵件

寄件者：馬庫斯・潘次
收件者：塔瑪拉・伍茲
日期：10 月 10 日
主旨：資料

嗨，塔瑪拉：

167 非常感謝妳在莎米拉探視家人時頂替她的職務。在她出國前，她正在做兩家本地房產的廣告。根據她的文件顯示，她已經將下述的説明整理好了：

馬歇爾大道 776 號是一棟位於史古葛湖的三層樓住家。有四間臥房，升級的廚具電器，家具完備的地下室與一座木造壁爐。地處閒靜地區，步行即可抵達本地學校。

芬頓街 9902 號是一棟三房住家，**168(A) 配有大庭院及游泳池。168(C)** 車庫是最近增建的，可容納兩部車。**168(D)** 這棟住屋鄰近所有大型購物商場與大學。

我會傳送塔瑪拉的文件過去，這樣妳就可以更新內容，加上相關的資料了。**169 這些房產資料和照片必須在週五前，交給《史古葛週報》的不動產編輯。**如果妳有任何問題或疑慮，請告訴我。

潘次不動產
馬庫斯・潘次 敬上

166. 為什麼會寄這封電子郵件？

(A) 要求一些文件

(B) 提供工作指令

(C) 提供付款資訊

(D) 要求與本地聯絡人聯繫

167. 關於莎米拉，提到了什麼事？

(A) 她常出國。

(B) 她買了一棟新屋。

(C) 她為報社工作。

(D) 她去度假了。

168. 有關芬頓街的住屋，沒有提到什麼事？

(A) 它有大庭院和一座游泳池。

(B) 它之前刊於網站中。

(C) 它有一間新蓋的車庫。

(D) 它接近許多重要的設施。

169. 根據電子郵件的內容，提到了什麼有關《史古葛週報》的事？

(A) 它會介紹伍茲女士須更新資料的精選房產物件。

(B) 它每週五發行。

(C) 它會依房地產價格收費。

(D) 免費發送給本地居民。

Questions 170–173 簡訊

布萊克・懷特 [下午 3:23]
帕克女士，**170 我剛發現第一街將舉辦遊行。**該區會非常的擁擠，**172 所以貴餐廳停車場的地面重鋪工程要再等等了。**

珍妮斯・帕克 [下午 3:26]
那表示你們不會進來了嗎？

布萊克・懷特 [下午 3:28]
不，我們還是會到。我們會協助完工地下室的儲藏室。

珍妮斯・帕克 [下午 3:31]
好，那太好了。你認為那裡全部弄好要多久時間？

布萊克・懷特 [下午 3:32]
我現在確認一下。

提姆・羅賓斯加入對話。

布萊克・懷特 [下午 3:35]
提姆，地下室的工程，你們做好多少了？

提姆・羅賓斯 [下午 3:40]

嗯，**171** 開始一切都很順利，一直到我們發現東南邊角落有幾處進水。那看起來會是個很大的清理工程。

布萊克・懷特 [下午 3:42]

如果我的工作人員明天過去幫你呢？

提姆・羅賓斯 [下午 3:44]

那可以幫我們回歸到預定的進度。我們甚至可能可以安裝新冰箱。

珍妮斯・帕克 [下午 3:45]

如果你要搬動冰箱，就需要使用大樓後面的廠商專用出入口。我想你還留有鑰匙吧？

布萊克・懷特 [下午 3:47]

是的，我有。**173** 大樓後面有任何地方可以讓我們的人員在那天停車嗎？

珍妮斯・帕克 [下午 3:50]

如果有遊行的話，恐怕就沒有空位了。你們可能要停到第五大道的空地上。

170. 懷特先生提到什麼會打斷明天的工作？

(A) 國定假日

(B) 街頭活動

(C) 遺失的貨運商品

(D) 設備不足

171. 下午 3:40 時，羅賓斯先生說：「那看起來會是個很大的清理工程。」是什麼意思？

(A) 他的組員通常都在做清理工作。

(B) 有些損害很嚴重。

(C) 他不喜歡自己目前的工作。

(D) 他的組員的工程太複雜了。

172. 帕克女士最有可能是誰？

(A) 餐廳老闆

(B) 營建工人

(C) 停車場服務員

(D) 電器製造商

173. 懷特先生詢問的其中一個問題是什麼？

(A) 到另一個入口的路線

(B) 大樓鑰匙的下落

(C) 當地活動的時間

(D) 停車位的位置

Questions 174–175 網頁

http://www.hamptonoutsourcing.org

首頁	聯絡我們	沿革	服務項目

漢普頓外包公司

漢普頓外包公司，對所有希望將生產工作委外至海外各地的公司而言，是所有外包公司的首選。在今日日益縮小的地球村中，**174** 幾乎在全世界各地都可以便宜又有效率地完成電子零件的生產。我們知識廣博的同仁藉由幫您連結海外事業夥伴，來協助貴公司成長、**175(B)** 輔佐您取得適當的授權、並確保您的海外事業利益以合乎道德的方式進行。**175(C)** 我們的客戶在立足於國際的同時，也以維護環保著名。除此之外，**175(A)** 我們還向您保證，您所有的潛在事業夥伴都能獲得貴公司所有產品檢修相關的高階訓練。

今天就來電漢普頓外包公司，與我們的代表人員聯絡吧。

174. 誰最有可能是漢普頓外包公司的客戶？

(A) 客戶服務中心的人員

(B) 保險經紀人

(C) 環境保護局

(D) 家電用品公司

175. 下列何者不是漢普頓外包公司的強項？

(A) 優質的員工訓練

(B) 對授權的了解

(C) 環保流程

(D) 熟悉出口稅制

Questions 176–180 信件及優惠券

收件者：拉斐爾・羅薩里奧
　　　　<rosario@ebookmail.com>

寄件者：賈奈兒・帕里克
　　　　<jparik@alliancepremiumairways.com>

主旨：您的航班

180 日期：1 月 6 日

180 附件：優惠券

親愛的羅薩里奧先生，

[176] 感謝您與高優聯盟航空客戶服務部分享您的個人經驗。[176,177] 本人對您在 1 月 2 日不愉快的經驗深感抱歉。[177] 根據您所填寫的線上表格，您於第三方網站上預訂了商務艙的座位，但由於預約紀錄遺失，只好被迫搭乘經濟艙。

我已聯絡您之前預約班機的網站。顯然地，由於電腦故障，造成早先的預約被刪除。很不幸地，這已經造成了部分座位被轉售。[178] 我了解您已獲得部分退款，但我想為您的不便另外提供優惠券。更多資訊，請您參考附件。

高優聯盟航空客戶服務部經理
賈奈兒·帕里克 敬上

高優聯盟航空優惠券
下一趟航班可折扣 200 元

詳細說明：高優聯盟航空很樂意為您的下一趟航班提供 200 元的折扣。請注意，本優惠券僅可用於國際回程航班。[179] 有效使用期限於本年度 12 月 31 日止。您可於所有高優聯盟航空自動服務機，或線上 www.alliancepremiumairways.com 使用本優惠券。

票號： YY7732999938
核發日期： 1 月 6 日
[180] **簽發單位：** _____ 溫哥華 _____ 艾德蒙頓
_____ 蒙特婁 **X** 多倫多

176. 帕里克女士為什麼會寄這封電子郵件？
(A) 回覆線上客訴
(B) 提供工作合約
(C) 取消機票
(D) 詢問旅程

177. 帕里克女士提到 1 月 2 日發生什麼事？
(A) 她解決了一個座位問題。
(B) 一架班機沒有理由地延誤了。
(C) 很多商務艙座位是空的。
(D) 羅薩里奧先生拿到了較低艙等的座位。

178. 關於羅薩里奧先生，提到了什麼事？
(A) 他在最後一刻要求更換航班。
(B) 他從溫哥華飛到多倫多。
(C) 他預先支付了航班的錢。
(D) 他通常搭乘經濟艙。

179. 在優惠券中，第一段、第二行的「good」與下列哪一個意思最接近？
(A) 高品質
(B) 幸運的
(C) 表現良好
(D) 有效的

180. 帕里克女士的辦公室最有可能在哪裡？
(A) 溫哥華
(B) 艾德蒙頓
(C) 蒙特婁
(D) 多倫多

TEST 4

PART 7

Questions 181–185 網頁及顧客評論

| 評論 | 首頁 | 設計工具 | 聯絡我們 |

狂傳單，大小公司行號最佳線上傳單製作器。

有了狂傳單，您可以為自己的公司行號創作客製化傳單。不論您是要宣傳門市的開幕，或只是要吸引大眾對貴公司服務的注意。狂傳單有您設計絕佳傳單所需的一切。

步驟一：設計您的傳單
我們的線上製作器有許多可客製的樣板。瀏覽我們的目錄，選出適合您的樣板。只要按一下滑鼠，就可以更改所有字體。[181] 如果您想要加上圖像突顯設計，我們有超過 10,000 個庫存圖片可供免費使用。此外，你也可以上傳自己的設計圖像與商標，搭配我們的字體。

步驟二：選擇數量
在狂傳單，每筆訂單最少有 25 張傳單。但您訂購的傳單數量愈多，每張的單價就愈便宜。

數量	每張單價
25-300	20 分錢
[183] **301-1,000**	**15 分錢**
1,001-1,500	10 分錢
1,501 以上	5 分錢

步驟三：購買數位版
182 只要額外支付單一價 **50 元**，就可以下載您個人設計的數位版。這個設計非常適合使用於公司的網站上，也可當作電子商訊郵件的一部分，或作為平面廣告。

步驟四：結單
訂單需五天時間處理。但大型訂單將耗費更長的準備時間。若有任何延誤，將以電子郵件通知。

評論	首頁	設計工具	聯絡我們

★★★★★ 狂傳單有超棒的服務！

我在市中心開設鞋店，老覺得要把即將舉辦的拍賣活動傳播出去是件很難的事。我決定利用狂傳單的線上製作器來設計傳單。我發現它很容易操作，而且設計也很優美。**183** 我最後訂了 **1,000 張傳單**，還購買了自己設計的數位版，把它用在我的網站上。我們的拍賣活動很成功。**184** 很多客人都說，他們是從鎮上到處張貼的傳單上得知我們的活動。我對狂傳單的服務真的很滿意。**185** 它比一些我瀏覽過的線上製作器還要好，而且它們的樣板也精緻很多。未來我絕對會再使用狂傳單！

貞・崔斯坦

181. 根據網頁內容，線上製作器可以讓使用者做什麼？
(A) 增加圖像
(B) 包含網路連結
(C) 選擇紙張種類
(D) 設計商標

182. 網頁中提到什麼與狂傳單有關的事？
(A) 它免費寄送產品。
(B) 額外付費就提供電子檔案。
(C) 它讓使用者看到他人的設計。
(D) 它只接受到店現場訂單。

183. 關於崔斯坦女士，提到了什麼事？
(A) 她收到的傳單比訂購的更多。
(B) 她的訂單延誤了幾天。
(C) 她收到 50 塊錢的折扣。
(D) 她為每張傳單付了 15 分錢。

184. 關於崔斯坦女士，提到了什麼事？
(A) 它只在網路上打廣告。
(B) 它在全鎮貼傳單。
(C) 它每個月都舉辦拍賣。
(D) 它提供線上訂購折扣。

185. 根據評論，崔斯坦女士為什麼喜歡狂傳單勝於其他公司？
(A) 它們的運送時間較快。
(B) 它們有較佳的設計。
(C) 它們使用品質較好的紙張。
(D) 它們比較便宜。

Questions 186–190 電子郵件及記錄表

寄件者：linda@mailmail.com
收件者：billing@startelecom.com
日期：4 月 23 日
主旨：帳單編號 3788292

親愛的客服人員：

我寫這封信是想告知，我在三月時收到了一封異常高額的手機帳單。列在手機帳單上的金額是 155.33 元。之前，我的帳單金額每個月都在 80 元至 90 元之間。

為了避免延遲繳納費用，我已經繳付帳款了，但 **186** 我想知道為什麼我會被收取這麼高的金額。我的帳單並未顯示任何明細說明這些費用。我知道我最近提高了使用流量，這會增加費用。但我也取消了所有裝置的保險契約。**187** 如果我的取消申請處理得當，那這兩筆費用應該會相互抵消才是。

請來電 333-0967-5563 與我聯繫這件事。**188** 我要在下午 **3:30** 之後才能接電話。

琳達・艾伯特 敬上

客戶服務聯絡紀錄表

日期：4 月 24 日

代表人員	帳號	來電時間	解決與否
麥可·帕克	BG44532	上午 9:33	是
朱恩·巴索勒迪	GH30993	上午 10:42	是
娜迪亞·卡普爾	TZ33221	下午 3:23	否
188 布魯克林·史密斯	GS17649	**下午 3:45**	否

收件者：linda@mailmail.com
寄件者：tristan@startelecom.com
日期：4 月 25 日
主旨：回覆：帳單編號 3788292

親愛的艾伯特女士，

感謝您來信星辰電信提出您的疑慮。昨天我們一位代表人員在您指定的時間試著打電話給您，但您並沒有接電話。我親自研究了您的問題，發現您的保險取消並未正式通過。因此，**187 您的帳戶同時 189 記錄了保險契約和流量升級方案的費用。**

為修正這問題，**190 我已經取消了您的保險計畫，將 63.98 元存入到您的帳戶中，應可轉用到下一次的帳單。**

如果您還有其他的疑慮或問題，請直接回覆這封電子郵件。

星辰電信客戶服務部
崔斯坦·馬修斯 敬上

186. 為什麼會寄第一封電子郵件？
　　(A) 取消服務
　　(B) 申請另一張帳單
　　(C) 詢問費用清單問題
　　(D) 註冊帳戶

187. 關於艾伯特女士，提到了什麼？
　　(A) 她之前在星辰電信工作。
　　(B) 她打電話給星辰電信客服代表人員。
　　(C) 她正確地辨識出星辰電信的失誤。
　　(D) 她想結束在星辰電信的帳戶。

188. 誰在 4 月 24 當天打電話給艾伯特女士？
　　(A) 麥可·帕克
　　(B) 朱恩·巴索勒迪
　　(C) 娜迪亞·卡普爾
　　(D) 布魯克林·史密斯

189. 在第二封電子郵件中，第一段、第四行的「registered」與下列哪一個意思最接近？
　　(A) 註冊入學
　　(B) 記錄
　　(C) 相配
　　(D) 允許

190. 在馬修斯先生的電子郵件中提及了什麼？
　　(A) 有些服務將免費提供。
　　(B) 卡普爾女士明天會打電話給艾伯特女士。
　　(C) 艾伯特女士的帳單下個月會減少。
　　(D) 客戶會因取消而被收費。

Questions 191–195 電子郵件、傳單及簡訊

收件者：**195 研究生**
寄件者：費迪南·蒙哥馬利
主旨：系列講座
日期：3 月 10 日

親愛的學生們，

我有個好消息。菲利浦·奧尚先生已經答應，他會在我們時尚職涯系列講座中發表演說。身為研究生，你們的工作就是安排他在 6 月 1 日至 2 日間的差旅住宿，以及往返校園的交通。另外，請預約供他演講的場地。**191 我想貝爾福德大禮堂會是最佳選擇。奧尚先生的演講應該會大受歡迎，所以我們需要有最大容納空間的場地，但如果無法使用那間，請預約另一間。**

此外，一旦奧尚先生提供了他的資料，我需要你們設計，並列印出另一份傳單。我希望你們五個能在沒有什麼太大的 ¹⁹² 爭議下分擔這些工作。但若有任何問題，一定要告訴我。

時尚設計教授
費迪南·蒙哥馬利

時尚設計學院
時尚職涯系列講座邀請到：

菲利浦·奧尚先生
¹⁹³ **貝斯時裝公司執行長暨首席設計師**

時尚設計與科技
6 月 1 日下午 3:30
¹⁹¹ **維斯蒙特禮堂**

這幾年來，許多時裝公司已經將手繪設計的方式，轉換為時裝設計軟體程式。身為前景備受矚目的設計師們，你們必須了解 ¹⁹³ **時裝設計軟體中所有最新的創新發展。** 各位要如何了解 ¹⁹³ **最新的軟體趨勢**呢？其中一個可能的方法，就是對每個新程式都知之甚詳。但這可能要付出很大的代價，也很耗時。有幾個方式可以預測哪些程式將成為時裝設計中的主流，而我也將分享自己對時尚業中科技趨勢的見解。

傳訊者：羅伯特·帕克
收訊者：羅莎·赫南德茲
日期：5 月 28 日

羅莎，我在赫茲大樓的影印中心印傳單。但我發現有個東西遺漏了。¹⁹⁴ 奧尚先生的照片好像被刪除了。¹⁹⁵ 妳可以盡快修復傳單，把新版本寄給我嗎？影印中心再不到一個小時就要打烊了。¹⁹⁵ 蒙哥馬利博士要我今晚把傳單送到他的辦公室。

---

191. 關於維斯蒙特禮堂，提到了什麼事？
(A) 它無法在 6 月 1 日使用。
(B) 是所有研討會演講的場所。
(C) 它的座位比貝爾福德大禮堂少。
(D) 有新的投影機。

192. 在電子郵件中，第二段、第三行的「issues」與下列哪一個意思最接近？
(A) 衝突
(B) 期刊
(C) 分發
(D) 宣告

193. 奧尚先生的演講和什麼有關？
(A) 設計軟體的新趨勢
(B) 縫紉機的發展
(C) 繪畫技巧的學習
(D) 時尚公司的特色

194. 帕克先生提到了什麼問題？
(A) 地點已經更改了。
(B) 傳單上漏了一個圖像。
(C) 工作經歷是錯的。
(D) 活動時間是錯的。

195. 赫南德茲女士最有可能是誰？
(A) 貝斯時裝公司的首席設計師
(B) 時尚設計軟體開發者
(C) 時尚設計學院教授
(D) 時尚設計學院研究生

Questions 196–200 廣告、線上表單及評論

翠登空調
空調設備

超過 15 年來，翠登空調一直為公司行號提供合理價格的空調設備。我們提供給許多本地咖啡館、餐廳與超市值得信賴的空調冷卻系統。我們所有的設備可應貴公司要求提供清理服務與修繕。若您對設備有任何的不滿，我們將免費更換。雪梨地區各地的運送與裝設亦免費。企業主須簽訂兩年期合約，我們也提供每月支付方案。

空調設備方案：

合約方案	196(D) 型號	類型	196(C) 房型（平方公尺）	196(B) 每月費用
銅	GP-A3000	天花板式	9-25	55.00 元
199 銀	GP-A4000	**直立式**	26-55	75.00 元
金	GP-A9999	天花板式	55-100	95.00 元
白金	GP-AR300	天花板式	100-200	115.00 元

洽詢免費報價，可上網 www.trentonaircon. com 或來電 1-800-444-2323 聯絡我們內行的客服專員。

翠登空調—客服報價單

姓名：麥迪娜‧皮拉斯
行號：麥迪娜咖啡
電子郵件：medina@mailme.com
日期：4 月 23 日
註記：我填寫這份表單是想詢問貴公司的空調設備。我咖啡店隔壁的餐廳目前就是使用貴公司的設備。**197 該餐廳老闆，史密斯先生非常推薦貴公司的服務。**

目前我餐廳的空調機已經將近 10 年了。光是維修和清理就要花一大筆錢。我想如果向貴公司承租，還比較划算。因為我的咖啡店很小，只有 22 平方公尺，我想應該適用貴公司較便宜的方案，但這部分我還是會依貴公司的建議為主。另外，您可以確認您所推薦的設備是附遙控器的嗎？我目前的空調機並沒有。感謝您，期待您的回覆。

顧客評論

我成為翠登空調公司的客戶已經一年了。我必須說，我對他們的服務非常滿意。因為翠登的轉介方案，我很驚訝在第一年的保養服務中，就收到了百分之十的優惠折扣。看來，**197 如果你提供了推薦者的姓名，雙方都會自動收到折扣**。另外，我也對合約條款非常滿意，條約內容讓我可以根據業務需求變更設備。**198 在我的店面擴大後，**我打電話給翠登，客服代表答應將我的設備升級成較大型的套組。兩天後新設備就**200 送來了，199 雖然型式從天花板式換成直立式，但安裝居然免費**。因為他們絕佳的經營方式與客服，我極度推薦翠登。

麥迪娜咖啡店主 麥迪娜‧皮拉斯

---

196. 下列有關翠登空調的資訊，何者未出現在廣告中？
(A) 節能
(B) 月費
(C) 房間大小
(D) 型號

197. 有關史密斯先生，下列何者可能為真？
(A) 他幫他的餐廳在空調上省錢。
(B) 他買下了餐廳旁邊的咖啡店。
(C) 他獲得翠登空調一年免費服務。
(D) 他明年要升級空調設備。

198. 關於麥迪娜咖啡，提到了什麼事？
(A) 為史密斯先生所擁有。
(B) 搬到新址。
(C) 提供夜間娛樂活動。
(D) 最近擴大規模。

199. 皮拉斯女士目前採用的是哪一個合約方案？
(A) 銅
(B) 銀
(C) 金
(D) 白金

200. 在評論中，第一段、第七行的「turned up」與下列哪一個意思最接近？
(A) 移除
(B) 考慮
(C) 設計
(D) 抵達

TEST 4

PART 7

ACTUAL TEST ⑤

1. (A) He's checking in at an airport.
   (B) He's pulling a suitcase.*
   (C) He's packing for a trip.
   (D) He's opening his luggage.

2. (A) They are making a dish.
   (B) They are cleaning the kitchen.
   (C) They are spraying water on the floor.
   (D) They are wearing aprons.*

3. (A) A man is taking an order.
   (B) A woman is trying on a pair of sunglasses.
   (C) Some merchandise is arranged on the table.*
   (D) Some posters are being put up.

4. **(A) People are seated on the stairs.***
   (B) People are stepping down from the platform.
   (C) People are walking beneath the tree.
   (D) People are moving across the showroom.

5. (A) A lecture is being given outdoors.
   (B) Some people are watching a demonstration.*
   (C) A man is filling a container with some tools.
   (D) Some bottles are being cleared off the table.

6. (A) A man is backing a vehicle into a garage.
   (B) Workers are unloading some supplies.
   (C) A vehicle is being examined.*
   (D) Equipment is being loaded onto a cart.

1. (A) 他正在機場辦理登機手續。
   (B) 他正拉著行李箱。
   (C) 他正在為旅行打包。
   (D) 他正打開他的行李箱。

2. (A) 他們正在做菜。
   (B) 他們正在清理廚房。
   (C) 他們把水灑在地上。
   (D) 他們穿著圍裙。

3. (A) 男子正在接受點單。
   (B) 女子正在試戴太陽眼鏡。
   (C) 桌上排列著一些商品。
   (D) 一些海報正被掛上。

4. **(A) 人們坐在台階上。**
   (B) 人們正走下月台。
   (C) 人們正走在樹下。
   (D) 人們正穿越展示廳。

5. (A) 課程正在戶外進行。
   (B) 一些人正在觀看操作示範。
   (C) 男子正利用一些工具把容器裝滿。
   (D) 正桌上一些瓶子正被清掉。

6. (A) 男子正倒車進入車庫。
   (B) 工人正卸下一些日用品。
   (C) 一輛車正被檢查。
   (D) 設備正被裝上手推車。

7. How long does it take to reach Paris?
   (A) Seven hours in the air.*
   (B) To go sightseeing.
   (C) The plane landed.

8. Where should I hang these pictures in the office?
   (A) We need to take a picture.
   (B) I prefer them in the break room.*
   (C) No, he's not in the office.

7. 到巴黎要多久？
   (A) 搭飛機七個小時。
   (B) 去觀光遊覽。
   (C) 飛機降落了。

8. 我該把這些畫掛在辦公室的哪裡？
   (A) 我們需要拍張照片。
   (B) 我比較喜歡掛在休息室。
   (C) 不，他不在辦公室。

9. Who will be in charge of organizing the company picnic?
(A) The office manager.*
(B) In the park.
(C) One day this weekend.

10. Would you like a hamburger or a hotdog?
(A) In the frozen foods section.
(B) I'm not all that hungry now.*
(C) A package of twelve.

11. Don't we need a key to get into the building?
(A) Her response is key.
(B) She's already in her room.
(C) Yes, but I forgot mine.*

12. Where did you save the insurance files?
(A) I saved you some time.
(B) She called the insurance company.
(C) On your desktop.*

13. Why have we ordered the team T-shirts from a different website?
(A) By next Monday.
(B) From the online store.
(C) The colors were better.*

14. How did you get such a good interest rate?
(A) I visited the bank in person.*
(B) It's 2% each month.
(C) No, I'm not buying a house.

15. How is he going to finish his project on time?
(A) Has he fixed the projector?
(B) He needs to stay late.*
(C) It's six o'clock now.

16. Does this school offer any classes on finance?
(A) Have a look at one of the brochures.*
(B) The financial analysis was wrong.
(C) Classes start in September.

17. When did they build a fountain in front of the hospital?
(A) A large amount of water.
(B) Three or four months ago.*
(C) The architects.

---

9. 誰要負責籌劃公司的野餐？
(A) 辦公室經理。
(B) 在公園。
(C) 這個週末的其中一天。

10. 你要漢堡還是熱狗？
(A) 在冷凍食品區。
(B) 我現在還不是很餓。
(C) 一袋十二個。

11. 我們進入大樓不需要用鑰匙嗎？
(A) 她的回應是關鍵。
(B) 她已經在她的房間了。
(C) 要，但我忘記帶我的了。

12. 你把保險檔案存在哪裡了？
(A) 我替你省了些時間。
(B) 她打電話給保險公司。
(C) 在你的桌面。

13. 我們為什麼從不同的網站訂購團隊 T 恤？
(A) 下星期一之前。
(B) 從線上商店。
(C) 顏色比較好看。

14. 你是怎麼獲得這麼好的利率的？
(A) 我親自去銀行拜訪。
(B) 每個月 2%。
(C) 不，我沒有要買房子。

15. 他要如何及時完成他的計畫？
(A) 他修好投影機了嗎？
(B) 他必須留到很晚。
(C) 現在是六點。

16. 這間學校有提供任何金融課程嗎？
(A) 看一下那些冊子。
(B) 那份財務分析是錯的。
(C) 九月開學。

17. 他們何時在醫院前面蓋了噴水池？
(A) 大量的水。
(B) 三、四個月前。
(C) 幾位建築師。

18. Is Mr. Sampson going to arrive today or tomorrow?
   (A) It's okay. He doesn't want to.
   (B) A flight schedule.
   (C) He arrived late last night.*

19. You can change the meeting time, can't you?
   (A) Remember to change your clothes.
   (B) The directors are already on their way.*
   (C) He was not present.

20. Do you need help cleaning up this mess?
   (A) The cleaners are new.
   (B) The containers were empty.
   (C) I can just use the vacuum.*

21. Why don't you ask the Sales Department for some advice?
   (A) I hadn't thought of that.*
   (B) The figures from last month.
   (C) I won't leave my job.

22. How do I get downtown from here?
   (A) It's expensive to live there.
   (B) Yes, she works at a shop.
   (C) There's a subway map on the wall.*

23. Which client signed our contract?
   (A) At the conference.
   (B) The increase in rent.
   (C) The one from New York City.*

24. Aren't you retiring at the end of the year?
   (A) No, early next year.*
   (B) A retirement party.
   (C) Three full-time employees.

25. Didn't you say the renovation would be done by today?
   (A) I did, but we ran into a problem.*
   (B) The workers are over there.
   (C) No, we didn't order the appliances.

26. Have they announced the nominees for the award yet?
   (A) The picks are as expected.*
   (B) To honor the company president.
   (C) The first award ceremony.

18. 山普森先生是今天還是明天抵達？
   (A) 沒關係，他不想要。
   (B) 航班時刻表。
   (C) 他昨天很晚才抵達。

19. 你可以更改會議的時間，不是嗎？
   (A) 記得換衣服。
   (B) 幾位總監已經在路上了。
   (C) 他不在場。

20. 你需要人幫忙清理這團混亂嗎？
   (A) 清潔人員是新來的。
   (B) 容器是空的。
   (C) 我用吸塵器就可以了。

21. 你何不要求業務部提一些建議？
   (A) 我沒有想到。
   (B) 上個月的數據。
   (C) 我不會辭職。

22. 我如何從這裡去市中心？
   (A) 住那裡，花費很高。
   (B) 是的，她在一間商店工作。
   (C) 牆上有張地鐵的路線圖。

23. 哪一位客戶簽了合約？
   (A) 在研討會上。
   (B) 租金上漲。
   (C) 來自紐約市的那位。

24. 你不是年底要退休嗎？
   (A) 不是，是明年初。
   (B) 退休派對。
   (C) 三名全職員工。

25. 你不是說，整修工作今天會完成？
   (A) 我是說過，但我們遇到了問題。
   (B) 工人在那裡。
   (C) 不，我們沒有訂電產品。

26. 他們宣布獎項的入圍者了嗎？
   (A) 挑出的人選一如預期。
   (B) 為了向公司總裁致敬。
   (C) 第一屆頒獎典禮。

27. Do you want me to pick you up at the station?
  (A) It's almost 5 o'clock.
  (B) A discounted ticket.
  (C) I'm not coming today.*

28. I think this seat is already taken.
  (A) Sit down, please.
  (B) Where do the chairs go?
  (C) Sorry. I'll move in a second.*

29. Have you seen my bag around here?
  (A) We need to buy shopping bags.
  (B) Yes, it's a textbook.
  (C) Didn't you leave it in your car?*

30. We need to find a faster way to get to the airport.
  (A) Some delicious pastries.
  (B) He'll be traveling all week.
  (C) Sorry, but this is the best route.*

31. What time does the conference start tomorrow?
  (A) Oh, I thought you weren't going.*
  (B) A very good business deal.
  (C) In the convention center.

27. 你要我去車站接你嗎？
  (A) 快要五點了。
  (B) 打折的車票。
  (C) 我今天不去。

28. 我想這個位子有人坐了。
  (A) 請坐。
  (B) 椅子到哪裡去了？
  (C) 對不起，我馬上換位子。

29. 你有沒有在這附近看到我的包包？
  (A) 我們需要買購物袋。
  (B) 是的，是一本教科書。
  (C) 你不是留在你的車上了嗎？

30. 我們必須找到較快能抵達機場的路線。
  (A) 一些美味的糕點。
  (B) 他整個星期都在旅行。
  (C) 抱歉，但這是最便捷的路線了。

31. 明天的研討會幾點開始？
  (A) 噢，我以為你不會去。
  (B) 一次很成功的交易。
  (C) 在會議中心。

PART 3 P. 187-191

Questions 32–34 對話

W Hello. This is Margaret Brown calling. **³² I recently mailed the paperwork to update my car insurance policy,** but I never received a call from your company.

M Sorry to hear that, Ms. Brown. I'll have a look at our records. Can you remember the date you sent the forms?

W Ummm . . . Actually, I don't know the date, but I think it was a month ago.

M Well, ³³ **unfortunately, it seems that your forms never arrived here.** However, ³⁴ **I can give you our website** and you can complete the paperwork online. It's a brand new system, but it's much easier than sending in mail.

女 哈囉，我是瑪格麗特・布朗。³² **我最近寄了文件，要更新我的汽車保險**，但一直沒接到你們公司的電話。

男 很抱歉發生這種事，布朗女士。我會查看一下我們的紀錄。您還記得寄出表格的日期嗎？

女 嗯，其實，我不知道日期，但我想是一個月前的事。

男 呃，³³ **很遺憾，您的文件似乎沒有寄到這裡。**不過，³⁴ **我可以給您我們的網站**，您可以上網完成文書處理。這是全新的系統，但是比寄送郵件要簡單多了。

32. What is the woman trying to do?

    (A) Lease a new car

    (B) Purchase an appliance

    (C) Renew an insurance policy*

    (D) Apply for a credit card

33. What has caused a problem?

    (A) An application was rejected.

    (B) Some mail did not arrive.*

    (C) A payment method failed.

    (D) Some information was wrong.

34. What does the man offer to do?

    (A) Complete a profile

    (B) Send a new contract

    (C) Cancel a policy

    (D) Provide a web address*

Questions 35–37 對話

W	Hi, Ben. Did you have a nice holiday?
M	It was excellent. **35 I spent a lot of time in the brand new stores uptown.**
W	Oh, really? Did you buy anything nice?
M	A few things, but a lot of the best stuff was sold out. **36 There were so many sales at the time.**
W	That's too bad. At least you got to browse the new stores.
M	Yeah, but I'm glad to be back. What did I miss while I was away?
W	Well, **37 we just got a new client who wants us to install new telephone systems for her company.** I'd better fill you in on the details of her company.

35. What did the man do on his holiday?

    (A) He threw parties.

    (B) He visited a farm.

    (C) He camped.

    (D) He shopped.*

32. 女子試圖做何事？

    (A) 租一輛新車。

    (B) 購買一件家電。

    (C) 更新保單。

    (D) 申請信用卡。

33. 什麼原因導致問題？

    (A) 申請被拒。

    (B) 有個郵件沒有送到。

    (C) 付款方式無效。

    (D) 有些資料是錯的。

34. 男子提議為何？

    (A) 讓檔案完整。

    (B) 寄送新的合約。

    (C) 取消一份保單。

    (D) 提供網址。

女	嗨，班，你的假期過得好嗎？
男	棒極了。**35 我在城北新開的店逛了好久。**
女	噢，真的嗎？你有買什麼好東西嗎？
男	有一些，但很多最好的東西都賣光了。**36 那段時間有好多拍賣。**
女	太糟了。至少你逛了那些新開的店。
男	是啊，不過我很高興回來。我不在時，錯過什麼了嗎？
女	嗯，**37 我們剛接到一個新客戶，她要我們幫她的公司安裝新的電話系統。** 我最好告訴你她公司的詳細資料。

35. 男子休假時做了何事？

    (A) 他舉行派對。

    (B) 他去農場。

    (C) 他去露營。

    (D) 他去逛街。

36. What does the man say about the places he visited?
- (A) They served free food.
- **(B) They had many discounts.***
- (C) They were hard to find.
- (D) They were next to a park.

37. According to the woman, what did the company do recently?
- **(A) They gained a client.***
- (B) They held a sale.
- (C) They took a vacation.
- (D) They changed management.

36. 關於造訪的地方，男子說了什麼？
- (A) 它們供應免費食物。
- **(B) 它們有許多折扣。**
- (C) 它們很難找。
- (D) 它們在公園旁邊。

37. 根據女子所述，公司最近做了何事？
- **(A) 他們得到一個客戶。**
- (B) 他們舉行了拍賣。
- (C) 他們去度假。
- (D) 他們改變了管理方式。

Questions 38–40 對話

M	Jane, I just got an e-mail from our clients in Taiwan. **38 They're visiting at the end of the month to inspect some of their factories.** They asked if they could stop by our office since we're in the area.
W	Oh, that's great. **39 This could be a good time to pitch them the new European advertisement campaign we've been working on.** Do you think the designers can finish the samples in time?
M	I believe so. However, **40 I should let them know right away that their deadline is moving up by a few weeks.** They thought there was more time to finish up.

男　珍，我剛收到台灣客戶的電子郵件。**38 他們月底要來拜訪，視察一些他們的工廠。**他們問到，因為我們也在這一區，是否可以順道來我們公司一趟。

女　喔，那太好了。**39 這會是一個好時機，向他們大力推銷我們持續在進行的歐洲新廣告。**你覺得設計師能及時完成樣本嗎？

男　我相信可以。不過 **40 我得立刻知會他們，截稿日期提前了幾個星期。**他們原本以為還有很多時間可以完成工作。

TEST 5
PART 3

38. What are the speakers mainly discussing?
- (A) An office inspection
- (B) A factory opening
- **(C) A client visit***
- (D) An advertising launch

38. 說話者討論的主題為何？
- (A) 視察辦公室。
- (B) 工廠開幕。
- **(C) 客戶來訪。**
- (D) 展開廣告活動。

39. What does the woman suggest doing?
- **(A) Presenting a new campaign***
- (B) Signing a contract
- (C) Organizing an inspection
- (D) Having some equipment repaired

39. 女子提議做何事？
- **(A) 展現新的活動。**
- (B) 簽署合約。
- (C) 安排視察。
- (D) 修理一些設備。

40. What does the man say he will do?
- **(A) Pass on some information***
- (B) E-mail some samples
- (C) Update a website
- (D) Prepare an itinerary

40. 男子說他將做何事？
- **(A) 傳達一些訊息。**
- (B) 以電子郵件傳送一些樣本。
- (C) 更新網站。
- (D) 規劃行程。

M1 Thank you both for coming in today. I think we've covered just about everything regarding the International Cultural Expo.	**男1** 謝謝你們倆今天來。我想我們已經處理了所有關於國際文化展的事情。
W Yes, ⁴¹ **I'm really looking forward to taking over.** I think James has done a great job organizing the event so far.	**女** 是的，⁴¹ **我真的很期待接手。**我認為，詹姆士把到目前為止的活動籌劃工作做得非常好。
M1 James, can you think of anything else Trisha might need to know?	**男1** 詹姆士，你還能想到任何崔夏可能需要知道的事情嗎？
M2 Ah, yes. One more thing; ⁴² **the vendors will need receipts for their participation fees for tax purposes. It's okay to send them by e-mail.**	**男2** 啊，有的，還有一件事，⁴² **攤販會需要報名費的收據以便報稅。可以用電子郵件寄給他們。**
W I understand. So James, I heard you're going to be working on the east coast.	**女** 了解了。那麼，詹姆士，我聽説你要去東岸工作。
M2 Yes, ⁴³ **I'm moving to Florida, so I'll be working at the Orlando Expo Center. I'm excited about the change.**	**男2** 是的，⁴³ **我要搬到佛羅里達**，所以我會到奧蘭多展覽中心工作。我對這個改變感到很興奮。

41. What are the speakers discussing?

(A) Moving a business

(B) Negotiating a contract

(C) Traveling for business

(D) Changing event management*

41. 説話者在討論何事？

(A) 搬遷一家公司。

(B) 協商一份合約。

(C) 出差。

(D) 更換活動管理人。

42. What does James advise the woman to do?

(A) Schedule another meeting

(B) Make a list of vendors

(C) Hire an assistant

(D) Send receipts by e-mail*

42. 詹姆士建議女子做何事？

(A) 安排另一次會議。

(B) 列出攤販的名單。

(C) 僱用一位助理。

(D) 用電子郵件寄送收據。

43. What does James say he is excited about?

(A) Moving to a new city*

(B) Managing more projects

(C) Earning more money

(D) Learning a new sport

43. 詹姆士説，他對何事感到很興奮？

(A) 搬到新的城市。

(B) 管理更多專案。

(C) 賺更多錢。

(D) 學習新的運動。

Questions 44–46 對話

W Hi, Mitchell. This is Reba from the Sales Department. **44 I'm not sure if you know this, but the air conditioning in conference room B isn't working.** Do you think you'd be able to fix it at some point today?

M Oh, sorry to hear that. This happened with conference room A, too, but it was easy to fix. I can come take a look at it.

W Right now? **45 Well, umm, I'm actually meeting a client here in a few minutes.** We don't really need the air conditioning today.

M Yes, **46 it is oddly cool for this time of the year.** How about I come up and take a look at it when you're finished?

W Sure. That would be great. Thanks!

女 嗨,米契爾,我是業務部的芮芭。**44** 我不確定你是否知道這件事,但會議室 B 的空調故障了。你覺得你今天能找個時間來修嗎?

男 喔,很遺憾聽到這事。會議室 A 也是如此,不過很容易就能修好。我可以過來看看。

女 現在嗎? **45** 嗯,其實我馬上要和一位客戶在這裡開會。我們今天不是非開空調不可。

男 是啊,**46** 一年的這個時候,天氣異常涼爽。等你們結束後,我再過來看看,如何?

女 當然,那太好了,謝謝!

44. Why is the woman calling the man?
   (A) To provide directions to an office
   (B) To request a room change
   (C) To report a malfunction in equipment*
   (D) To inquire about a missing file

45. What does the woman mean when she says, "Right now"?
   (A) She feels sorry about bothering the man.
   (B) She will cancel a meeting.
   (C) She wants to delay a repair.*
   (D) She is pleased with a plan.

46. What does the man say is unusual?
   (A) The weather is unseasonably cold.*
   (B) The office is experiencing many problems.
   (C) The meetings have been cancelled.
   (D) The woman's schedule is busy.

44. 女子為何打電話給男子?
   (A) 提供到某個辦公室的方向指引。
   (B) 要求換房間。
   (C) 報告設備故障。
   (D) 詢問一個遺失的檔案。

45. 當女子說「現在嗎」,意指什麼?
   (A) 她對於打擾男子感到抱歉。
   (B) 她將取消會議。
   (C) 她想要延後修理的時間。
   (D) 她對計畫很滿意。

46. 男子說何事很不尋常?
   (A) 天氣不合時宜地冷。
   (B) 辦公室經歷許多問題。
   (C) 會議取消了。
   (D) 女子的時程表很忙碌。

M	Alice, I just called the box office and ⁴⁷ **apparently the last showing of the musical downtown has been canceled.** Do you have any other ideas about where we can take our clients when they visit from Italy?
W	That's too bad about the musical. Hmm. Well, ⁴⁸ **I've heard the Harbor Ship Tour is really good. It takes place on a yacht** and there's music and fine dining. Also, the night view of the coast must be spectacular.
M	Oh, right! I've heard about those yachts. They serve fresh seafood, which is supposed to be really incredible. ⁴⁹ **Can you look up the number and call to find out how much tickets are?**

男	艾莉絲，我剛打電話給劇院售票處，⁴⁷ 看起來，市區音樂劇的最後一場表演取消了。對於客戶從義大利來訪時，可以帶他們去哪裡，妳有沒有其他點子？
女	關於音樂劇的事，真是太糟了。嗯，這樣的話，⁴⁸ 我聽說港口輪船之旅實在很棒。旅程是搭乘遊艇，遊艇上還有音樂和精緻的晚餐。此外，海岸的夜景一定很令人讚嘆。
男	喔，對！我聽說過那些遊艇。遊艇上供應新鮮的海鮮，應該真的非常美味。⁴⁹ 妳可以查一下電話號碼，然後打去問票價多少嗎？

47. What problem does the man mention?
(A) A telephone number was lost.
(B) A ticket price was wrong.
(C) A trip was postponed.
(D) An event was canceled.*

48. What does the woman suggest?
(A) A visit to a museum
(B) An evening on a boat*
(C) A vacation to Italy
(D) A night at the opera

49. What does the man ask the woman to do?
(A) Inquire about a price*
(B) Contact some clients
(C) Refund some tickets
(D) Make a reservation

47. 男子提及什麼問題？
(A) 有串電話號碼遺失了。
(B) 有個票價是錯的。
(C) 有個旅程延後了。
(D) 有個活動取消了。

48. 女子有何建議？
(A) 參觀博物館。
(B) 船上之夜。
(C) 去義大利度假。
(D) 歌劇之夜。

49. 男子要求女子做何事？
(A) 詢問價錢。
(B) 聯絡一些客戶。
(C) 退還一些票券的錢。
(D) 預訂。

Questions 50–52 三人對話

M1	Please come in, Micha and Jennifer. Have a look around the rooms. As I mentioned, **50 the previous couple has recently vacated the space.**
W	I really like the size of the rooms and the windows, but there are a few things we're worried about.
M2	Yes, **51 we're wondering about the cost of heating the place in the winter.** Does this building have good insulation?
M1	Yes, it was all replaced last year. Also, a new energy efficient furnace was installed, so it's actually quite cheap to heat the apartments.
M2	Wow, in that case, I'm surprised the previous couple decided to leave.
M1	Well, **52 they just retired and decided to move to a smaller place.**

男1	請進，米卡和珍妮佛，四處看看房間吧。正如我提過的，**50 之前的那對夫妻最近搬離這個地方。**
女	我真的很喜歡這些房間的大小和窗戶，但我們有一些疑慮。
男2	對，**51 我們想知道這裡冬天的暖氣費用。**這棟大樓的保暖效果好嗎？
男1	是的，去年全都更換過了。除此之外，還安裝了新的節能暖爐，所以要讓公寓暖和起來，其實費用相當低廉。
男2	哇，那樣的話，我很驚訝，之前那對夫妻竟然決定搬走。
男1	嗯，**52 他們剛退休，決定搬到小一點的房子。**

50. Who most likely are Micha and Jennifer?
(A) City inspectors
(B) Potential tenants*
(C) Interior designers
(D) Hotel receptionists

50. 米卡和珍妮佛最可能是誰？
(A) 市府檢查員。
(B) 可能的房客。
(C) 室內設計師。
(D) 飯店接待人員。

51. What are Micha and Jennifer concerned about?
(A) The location of the windows
(B) The size of the rooms
(C) The cost of heating*
(D) The noise of the city

51. 米卡和珍妮佛擔心什麼？
(A) 窗戶的位置。
(B) 房間的大小。
(C) 暖氣的費用。
(D) 城市的噪音。

52. What is mentioned about the previous couple?
(A) They are no longer working.*
(B) They own the whole building.
(C) They prefer warmer climates.
(D) They have not moved yet.

52. 關於之前那對夫妻，文中提到什麼？
(A) 他們已經不再工作了。
(B) 他們擁有整棟大樓。
(C) 他們比較喜歡溫暖的氣候。
(D) 他們還沒搬走。

Questions 53–55 對話

M	Tammy, [53] **is everything all set for our trade show next Monday?**
W	Yes, I've had all our products and banners packed into the van, and I've just finished printing out the new flyers.
M	Did you ask some staff if they could come to the convention center on Monday to help us set up?
W	Oh . . . [54] **thanks for the reminder. I'm sure I can find some people who are willing to help out.** But how will they get into the convention center? I only have one pass for myself.
M	[55] **We have bought extra passes just in case we wanted to invite our clients to the show.** I'll go get a few for you now.

男	譚美，[53] 我們下星期一的貿易展都準備好了嗎？
女	是的，我已經把所有的產品和廣告布條都裝上卡車了，而且剛剛把新的傳單都印好了。
男	妳有沒有問過一些員工，他們能否星期一到會議中心來幫我們布置攤位？
女	噢……，[54] 謝謝你提醒。我確定我可以找到一些願意來幫忙的人。但他們要如何進入會議中心？我只有一張自己的通行證。
男	[55] 我們多買了一些通行證，以防萬一要邀請客戶進去會場。我現在去拿幾張給妳。

53. What will happen on Monday?
   (A) A vehicle will be repaired.
   (B) A training session will continue.
   (C) A trade show will start.*
   (D) A new product will launch.

54. What did the woman forget to do?
   (A) Find some volunteers*
   (B) Contact a convention center
   (C) Set up some tables
   (D) Update an itinerary

55. What does the man say is available?
   (A) Extra passes into a show*
   (B) A company banner
   (C) Free refreshments
   (D) Product samples

53. 星期一將發生何事？
   (A) 有車要修理。
   (B) 訓練課程會繼續。
   (C) 貿易展將開始。
   (D) 新產品要發表。

54. 女子忘記做何事？
   (A) 找一些義工。
   (B) 聯絡會議中心。
   (C) 擺放桌子。
   (D) 更新行程。

55. 男子說有什麼可用？
   (A) 額外的展場通行證。
   (B) 公司的廣告布條。
   (C) 免費茶點。
   (D) 產品的樣本。

Questions 56–58 對話

W This is Carole Strauss calling from Rubin Marketing. **56 I understand you left a message about contracting us to advertise your new store.**

M Yes, **56 thanks for getting back to me.** **57 I opened a new hair salon,** and I'd love to start advertising in local newspapers and maybe on a billboard downtown.

W Okay, great. I'd love to set up a meeting with you to get a sense about what you'd like to include in your ads and what price range you're comfortable with. **58 Are you available to come to our office tomorrow afternoon?**

M That would work great for me. I'll actually be in that area picking up supplies, so **58 I can stop by around 2:00 P.M.**

女 我是盧賓行銷公司的卡蘿‧史特勞斯。**56 我聽說您留了訊息，要和我們簽約宣傳新店面。**

男 是的，**56 謝謝妳回我電話。57 我新開了一家美髮沙龍**，想要開始在地方報紙上，還有，也許在鬧區的廣告看板上刊登廣告。

女 好的，很好。我想要安排和您開個會，了解您的廣告內容要包含什麼，還有哪個價位區間是您覺得可以輕鬆負擔的。**58 您明天下午有空來我們辦公室嗎？**

男 那個時間很好。事實上，我正好要去那一帶補貨，所以 **58 我可以大約下午兩點順路過去。**

---

56. Why does the woman call the man?
(A) To ask for a payment
(B) To return a phone call*
(C) To cancel a meeting
(D) To make a hair appointment

57. What did the man recently do?
(A) Hired a graphic designer
(B) Cancelled a subscription
(C) Started a new business*
(D) Purchased a billboard

58. What does the man say he will do tomorrow?
(A) Attend a lunch
(B) Get a haircut
(C) Sell some products
(D) Go to an office*

56. 女子為何打電話給男子？
(A) 要求付款。
(B) 回撥電話。
(C) 取消會議。
(D) 預約美髮。

57. 男子最近做了何事？
(A) 僱用一位平面設計師。
(B) 取消訂閱。
(C) 展開新事業。
(D) 購買廣告看板。

58. 男子說，他明天有何事？
(A) 出席午餐餐會。
(B) 剪頭髮。
(C) 販售一些產品。
(D) 去一家公司。

W	David, [59] **how did your editorial meeting go this morning?** You were planning to ask the senior editor to hire some more contract workers, correct?
M	Yes. The senior editor agreed to allocate funds for three additional employees during our busy periods.
W	Wow, isn't that too many? [60] **Last year, we were only allowed to hire one.**
M	Well, actually, they've only agreed to hire part-time freelancers. Still, having a few extra writers will really help us tackle the workload. [61] **The Human Resources Department is planning to place some online ads next week,** so we should have help soon.

女	大衛，[59] **今天早上的編輯會議結果如何？** 你打算要求資深編輯多找一些約聘人員，對嗎？
男	是的。資深編輯同意撥專款，在我們工作高峰期多請三個人。
女	哇，不會太多嗎？[60] **去年只准我們請一個人。**
男	嗯，事實上，他們只同意僱用兼職的自由工作者。儘管如此，多幾個撰稿人員的確有助於我們應付工作量。[61] **人力資源部計劃下星期上網刊登廣告**，所以我們應該很快就有幫手了。

59. What department do the speakers work in?
(A) Finance
(B) Editorial*
(C) Advertising
(D) Design

59. 說話者在哪個部門工作？
(A) 財務。
(B) 編輯。
(C) 廣告。
(D) 設計。

60. Why does the woman say, "Wow, isn't that too many"?
(A) To express surprise about a decision*
(B) To suggest another option
(C) To correct a management mistake
(D) To request a change of policy

60. 女子為何說「哇，不會太多嗎」？
(A) 為了對某個決定表達驚訝。
(B) 為了建議另一個選項。
(C) 為了改正一個管理上的錯誤。
(D) 為了要求政策上的改變。

61. According to the man, what does the Human Resources Department plan to do?
(A) Prepare a new manual
(B) Host a job fair at an office
(C) Hold a training workshop
(D) Run an advertisement online*

61. 根據男子所述，人力資源部計劃做什麼？
(A) 準備新的手冊。
(B) 在辦公室主辦就業博覽會。
(C) 舉行訓練工作坊。
(D) 上網刊登廣告。

Questions 62–64 對話及圖表

Package	Rate per Day
All Star Coverage	$35.00
64 Premium Coverage	**$20.00**
Advanced Coverage	$15.00
Basic Coverage	$10.00

套裝產品	每日費用
全星級保險	$35.00
64 優質保險	**$20.00**
高階保險	$15.00
基本保險	$10.00

W Hi, my name is Jane Simpson, and I'm calling from Redman Enterprises. One of our sales teams will be traveling abroad, and 62 **I'd like to purchase travel insurance for them.** I've heard that you have excellent rates.

M Yes, that's correct. We have a few main packages. Our All Star Coverage package is our most comprehensive. 63 **Will your team be trying any extreme sports during their free time?**

W No, I don't believe they'll have time for that during the trip.

M 64 **Then, I recommend our Premium package.** It includes health and accident insurance, but is much cheaper without the sports coverage.

W Okay. That sounds great. Can you e-mail me the paperwork I'll need to fill out?

女 嗨,我是瑞德曼企業的珍·辛普森。我們有個業務團隊要出國,62 **我想幫他們保旅遊險。**我聽說你們的費用非常超值。

男 是的,沒錯。我們有幾個主要的套裝產品。我們的全星級套裝保險是保障最全面的產品。63 **您的團隊在空閒時間,會嘗試任何極限運動嗎?**

女 不,我相信他們的旅程中沒有時間從事那個。

男 64 **那麼我推薦我們的優質保險。**它包含健康與意外險,但不包含運動保險項目,因此要便宜得多。

女 好,聽起來很棒。你可以把我需要填寫的文件,用電子郵件寄給我嗎?

62. What is the purpose of the phone call?
(A) To inquire about a discount
(B) To apply for a service*
(C) To make a reservation
(D) To schedule a meeting

63. Why does the man ask if the employees will do any sports?
(A) To offer some free gifts
(B) To decide on the most suitable package*
(C) To recommend a travel destination
(D) To request some medical information

64. Look at the graphic. How much will each employee likely pay per day?
(A) $35
(B) $20*
(C) $15
(D) $10

62. 這通電話的目的為何?
(A) 要求折扣。
(B) 申請某項服務。
(C) 預訂。
(D) 安排會議的時間。

63. 男子為何問,員工是否將會從事任何運動?
(A) 以提供免費禮物。
(B) 以選定最適合的套裝產品。
(C) 以推薦旅遊的目的地。
(D) 以詢問一些醫學資訊。

64. 請見圖表。每位員工每天可能要付多少錢?
(A) $35。
(B) $20。
(C) $15。
(D) $10。

Questions 65–67 對話及航班時刻表

Flight Number 班機編號	Departure City 出發地		On Time/Delayed 準時／誤點	Est. Arrival Time 預計抵達時間
BT091	Toronto	多倫多	Landed　已降落	11:00
AC550	Alberta	亞伯達	On Time　準時	11:35
HG330	Vancouver	溫哥華	On Time　準時	12:00
DT302	⁶⁵ Montreal	⁶⁵ 蒙特婁	**Delayed　誤點**	13:20

W I just had a look at the airport website. ⁶⁵ **It seems that Michael Park won't arrive on time.**

M Yeah, I heard his city is experiencing a big storm, so ⁶⁵ **many flights had their takeoff times delayed.**

W That's too bad. I suppose we should go pick him up later then.

M Actually, ⁶⁶ **traffic is supposed to be terrible today with all the construction around the airport.** How about we just leave now?

W You're right. We don't want to be late. ⁶⁷ **If we get there too early, we can browse the gift shops.**

女 我剛看了機場的網站。⁶⁵ 看來麥可‧帕克無法準時抵達。

男 是啊,我聽說他的城市正遭受強勁暴風雨侵襲,因此 ⁶⁵ 許多班機的起飛時間都延後了。

女 真是太糟了。那我猜想我們要晚一點去接他了。

男 事實上,⁶⁶ 機場周邊在施工,今天的交通狀況應該很糟。我們現在就出發怎麼樣?

女 你說得對。我們可不想遲到。⁶⁷ 如果太早到,我們可以逛逛禮品店。

65. Look at the graphic. Which city is Michael Park traveling from?
(A) Toronto
(B) Alberta
(C) Vancouver
(D) Montreal*

66. According to the man, why should the speakers leave now?
(A) Traffic may cause delays.*
(B) The airport is far away.
(C) They need to take the bus.
(D) A flight was early.

67. What does the woman suggest doing while they wait?
(A) Getting some food
(B) Looking in some stores*
(C) Seeing a film
(D) Having coffee

65. 請見圖表。麥可‧帕克從哪個城市過來?
(A) 多倫多。
(B) 亞伯達。
(C) 溫哥華。
(D) 蒙特婁。

66. 根據男子所述,說話者為何應該現在動身?
(A) 交通可能導致延誤。
(B) 機場很遠。
(C) 他們必須搭公車。
(D) 有班機提早抵達。

67. 女子建議在等待時做什麼?
(A) 吃點東西。
(B) 看看商店。
(C) 看場電影。
(D) 喝咖啡。

Questions 68–70 對話及圖表

Plan	Contract Length	Monthly Payment
Bronze	6 months	$140.00
Silver	**70 12 months**	**$100.00**
Gold	24 months	$60.00
Platinum	36 months	$30.00

方案	合約期間	月費
銅	6 個月	$140.00
銀	**70 12 個月**	**$100.00**
金	24 個月	$60.00
白金	36 個月	$30.00

M Hello, I'm looking to purchase a new service plan for my cell phone, so I thought I'd drop in and ask about your plans.

W Of course. Well, we offer several different plans. Have a look at this chart. Obviously, you will pay the lowest monthly fee for the longest contract but ⁶⁸ **we charge a cancelation fee if a contract is cancelled before it ends.**

M Umm . . . Okay, ⁶⁹ **I'm planning to do an exchange program abroad next year,** so I don't think a two-year or three-year plan is right for me.

W All right, ⁷⁰ **I think the one-year plan would be best for your needs.** Are you interested in signing a contract today?

M Yes, sure. I have some time now.

男 哈囉,我想購買新的手機方案,所以,我想就順路過來,詢問你們的方案。

女 當然。嗯,我們提供好幾種不同的方案。請看一下這張表。顯然合約期間最長,您付的月費也就最低,但是,⁶⁸ 如果合約還沒到期便要取消,我們會收取違約金。

男 嗯……是這樣的,⁶⁹ 我計畫明年出國當交換生,所以我覺得兩年或三年的方案不適合我。

女 好的,⁷⁰ 我認為一年的方案最符合您的需求。您想今天簽約嗎?

男 好,當然。我現在有時間。

68. According to the woman, when is an extra fee charged?
(A) When a product is delivered
(B) When a device gets broken
(C) When a client doesn't pay a bill
(D) When a service is canceled early*

69. What does the man say he might do next year?
(A) Purchase a new phone
(B) Go overseas*
(C) Sign a new contract
(D) Lease a device

70. Look at the graphic. How much has the man agreed to pay per month?
(A) $140.00
(B) $100.00*
(C) $60.00
(D) $30.00

68. 根據女子所述,何時會收取額外的費用?
(A) 當產品交貨時。
(B) 當設備損壞時。
(C) 當客戶未付賬單時。
(D) 當服務提早取消時。

69. 男子說他明年可能會做何事?
(A) 買新的手機。
(B) 出國。
(C) 簽一份新合約。
(D) 租一個設備。

70. 請見圖表。男子同意每月付多少錢?
(A) $140.00。
(B) $100.00。
(C) $60.00。
(D) $30.00。

437

Questions 71–73 談話

M **71 Welcome to the Ancient Civilizations Museum.** We're so pleased you could attend the opening of our new Cultures of Egypt exhibit and see some of the rarest and oldest artifacts discovered along the Nile River. **71 Before we start, 72 I'd like to offer you each a headset.** This will allow you to hear me over the hum of the conversation in the museum. Additionally, **73 if you're interested in ancient pottery making techniques, there is a presentation at 3:30 in the auditorium.** Follow me, so we can begin.

男 **71 歡迎來到古文明博物館。**很高興你們能參加埃及文明新展覽的開幕,看到一些在尼羅河沿岸發掘的最罕見且最古老的工藝品。**71 在開始之前,72 我要發給你們每人一副耳機。**這會讓你們在博物館的嘈雜交談聲中聽到我說的話。此外,**73 如果你們對古代的陶器製作技術有興趣,三點半在禮堂有演講介紹。**跟我來,我們可以開始了。

71. What is the purpose of the talk?
(A) To explain the rules
(B) To name some key features
(C) To ask for payment
(D) To begin a tour*

71. 這段話的目的為何?
(A) 解釋規則。
(B) 列舉一些重要的特徵。
(C) 要求付款。
(D) 開始一趟導覽。

72. What will the speaker distribute?
(A) Some headphones*
(B) A museum program
(C) Tickets to a performance
(D) A map of nearby galleries

72. 說話者會分發何物?
(A) 一些耳機。
(B) 博物館的節目單。
(C) 表演的門票。
(D) 附近藝廊的地圖。

73. According to the speaker, what will begin at 3:30?
(A) A question and answer session
(B) A classical music concert
(C) An antiques auction
(D) An educational presentation*

73. 根據說話者所述,什麼會在 3 點半開始?
(A) 問答時間。
(B) 古典音樂會。
(C) 古董拍賣。
(D) 教育主題演講。

M **⁷⁴ I'd like to take this opportunity to talk about our company's expense policies.** I know that many of you in the sales department frequently need to take clients out to lunch. However, some of you have not been submitting your expense reports on time. It's very important to submit your reports and receipts within one month of the expenses. It is also important to make sure the forms are filled out properly. **⁷⁵ Veronica, our expense manager, will contact you if you've filled out a form incorrectly. ⁷⁶ From next month, the company will be implementing a new policy.** Expense reports that are submitted late will no longer be reimbursed.

男 **⁷⁴ 我想利用這個機會談談我們公司的費用規定。**我知道，有很多業務部的人經常需要帶客戶出去吃午餐。不過，你們有些人並未準時交出你們的費用報告。要在支出後的一個月內，交出你們的報告和收據，這很重要。確定表格都填寫正確也很重要。**⁷⁵ 如果你們的表格未填寫正確，我們的財務經理，薇若妮卡會和你們聯絡。⁷⁶ 從下個月開始，公司將實施新的政策。**遲交的費用報告將不再核銷。

74. What is being discussed?
  (A) Company expense regulations*
  (B) Training new sales employees
  (C) Hiring an office manager
  (D) Filling out insurance forms

75. Why will Veronica contact listeners?
  (A) To provide payment
  (B) To request receipts
  (C) To review a policy
  (D) To resolve an error*

76. What will the company do next month?
  (A) Stop using a form system
  (B) Begin using a new policy*
  (C) Lengthen a project deadline
  (D) Deposit payments electronically

74. 談話在討論何事？
  (A) 公司的費用規定。
  (B) 訓練新的業務人員。
  (C) 僱用辦公室經理。
  (D) 填寫保險表格。

75. 薇若妮卡為何聯絡聽者？
  (A) 為了付款。
  (B) 為了要求收據。
  (C) 為了審核一項政策。
  (D) 為了解決錯誤。

76. 公司下個月會做何事？
  (A) 不再使用表格系統。
  (B) 開始採用新政策。
  (C) 延長一個計畫的最後期限。
  (D) 以電子方式存款。

439

W **⁷⁷ May I have your attention, Smithside Mall shoppers.** Thank you for visiting our brand new location. Today, we have a special promotion happening for customers who fill out a customer satisfaction survey. We have two stations set up – ⁷⁸ **one at the north entrance and one at the east entrance.** Please stop by and let us know how your shopping experience was today. Your participation is greatly appreciated.
⁷⁹ **All participants will have their name entered into a draw for a $100 gift card that can be used at any Smithside Mall stores.** Thank you and enjoy your day!

女 ⁷⁷ 史密斯塞德商場的各位顧客，請注意。謝謝你們光臨我們新開的分店。今天，我們為填寫滿意度調查的顧客推出特別促銷。我們設了兩個調查站，⁷⁸ 一個在北側入口，一個在東側入口。請順路前往，讓我們知道您今天的購物經驗。非常感謝您的參與。⁷⁹ 所有參加者都可以參加一百元禮物卡的抽獎，禮物卡可在任何一家史密斯塞德商場使用。謝謝各位，並祝您今天愉快！

77. Where is the announcement taking place?
(A) At an outdoor market
(B) At a shopping center*
(C) At a bus station
(D) At an art gallery

78. Why does the speaker say, "We have two stations set up"?
(A) To correct a mistake
(B) To explain some locations*
(C) To apologize for a delay
(D) To express disappointment

79. What does the speaker offer?
(A) Entrance into a contest*
(B) A book of discount coupons
(C) Free beverages at a café
(D) A discount on a purchase

77. 這項通知在何處發布？
(A) 露天市場。
(B) 購物中心。
(C) 公車站。
(D) 藝廊。

78. 説話者為何説，「我們設了兩個調查站」？
(A) 為了改正錯誤。
(B) 為了解釋地點。
(C) 為延誤道歉。
(D) 為了表達失望。

79. 説話者提供何物？
(A) 進入比賽場地的權利。
(B) 一本折扣券。
(C) 咖啡館的免費飲料。
(D) 購物折扣。

M Good afternoon, Edge Radio listeners. Thank you for tuning into Business Talk with Tom Wiser. Today, I'll be talking to **⁸⁰ professional employment counselor Michelle Bernstein.** Over next half hour, Ms. Bernstein will be talking about strategies for landing a job that suits your education, interests, and lifestyle. During the last ten minutes of the show, we'll be taking questions from listeners, so **⁸¹ visit our website at www.edgeradio.com/businesstalk and leave a comment with your question.** Let me kick off the show by welcoming our guest! Ms. Bernstein, **⁸² I heard you released a series of digital books last month.**	**男** 優勢電台的聽眾午安,感謝您收聽湯姆‧魏瑟主持的商業講座。今天,我會和 **⁸⁰ 專業求職顧問蜜雪兒‧伯恩斯坦**對談。接下來半小時,伯恩斯坦女士會談論一些策略,教你如何找到一份符合你的學歷、興趣和生活方式的工作。在節目的最後 10 分鐘,我們會回答聽眾的問題,所以,**⁸¹ 請上我們的網站,www.edgeradio.com/businesstalk,**在留言處寫下你的問題。節目一開始,讓我先歡迎我們的來賓!伯恩斯坦女士,**⁸² 我聽說妳上個月推出了一系列電子書。**

80. What is Ms. Bernstein's area of expertise?
(A) Web development
(B) Entertainment
(C) Career guidance*
(D) Finance

81. What are the listeners encouraged to do?
(A) Send in résumés
(B) Call Ms. Bernstein
(C) Purchase an e-book
(D) Leave a comment online*

82. What does the speaker say happened last month?
(A) A group interview was conducted.
(B) A radio schedule changed.
(C) A free seminar took place.
(D) A line of books was released.*

80. 伯恩斯坦女士的專業領域是什麼?
(A) 網頁開發。
(B) 娛樂業。
(C) 生涯輔導。
(D) 金融業。

81. 說話者鼓勵聽眾做何事?
(A) 寄送履歷表。
(B) 打電話給伯恩斯坦女士。
(C) 購買電子書。
(D) 上網留下意見。

82. 說話者說上個月發生何事?
(A) 進行團體面試。
(B) 電台的節目表更改。
(C) 舉辦免費研討會。
(D) 發行一系列書籍。

W We're just about finished for today, but I have one final thought to add. **83 I want to remind all the cashiers present that we've added another feature to our customer transactions here at Park Road Café and Bakery.** As you know, many stores are now allowing customers to pay with the cell phone app, Pay Smart. **84 Our systems have just been upgraded to include this payment method,** and **85 we've put signs at all our cash registers announcing the new feature.** We will have a general training session about how to use the new system. Can everyone meet tomorrow afternoon for that?

女 我們即將結束今天的營業,但我還有最後一點意見要補充。**83 我要提醒在場的所有收銀員,我們已經在「帕克路咖啡烘焙坊」的顧客交易流程中,增加了另一個功能。**你們知道,現在有許多商店都允許顧客用手機 app「智慧付」來付款。**84 我們的系統剛剛升級來含括這種付款方式,**而且 **85 我們在所有的收銀機上都貼了告示,宣布這項新功能。**我們會有一個關於如何使用新系統的一般訓練課程。大家明天下午可以集合上課嗎?

83. Who most likely are the listeners?
   (A) Restaurant chefs
   (B) Café workers*
   (C) Software designers
   (D) Employee trainers

84. What is the purpose of the talk?
   (A) To explain a customer complaint
   (B) To announce a new sales procedure*
   (C) To begin a training session
   (D) To demonstrate some new equipment

85. What can be found at each cash register?
   (A) Announcement signs*
   (B) Membership cards
   (C) Promotional coupons
   (D) Updated menus

83. 聽眾最可能是誰?
   (A) 餐廳主廚。
   (B) 咖啡館員工。
   (C) 軟體設計師。
   (D) 員工訓練講師。

84. 這段談話的目的為何?
   (A) 解釋顧客的抱怨。
   (B) 宣布新的銷售步驟。
   (C) 開始一項訓練課程。
   (D) 展示一項新設備。

85. 每一台收銀機上有什麼?
   (A) 通知的告示。
   (B) 會員卡。
   (C) 促銷優惠券。
   (D) 更新的菜單。

M Hello, Ms. Wilford. This is Mike Drew calling. I just received your e-mail about the package that was delivered to you yesterday. **86 I'm sorry to hear** that **87 the box was water damaged.** I agree with you that you should not try to use the products in the box, as they are electrical and water damage could be dangerous. To remedy this problem, **88 I am going to send a brand new order at no charge to you.** Please repackage the original order and give it to the deliveryman when he brings your new order. Again, I'm very sorry for the inconvenience.

男 哈囉，魏爾福女士，我是麥克德魯。我剛剛收到您關於昨天遞送包裹的電子郵件。**86 很抱歉聽聞 87 盒子浸水損壞。** 我同意您所說的，您不應該嘗試使用盒內的產品，因為它們是電器用品，而泡水損傷可能很危險。為了補救這個問題，**88 我打算免費送一個全新的貨品過去。** 請將原來的貨品重新包裝好，當送貨員把新的貨品送過去時，把舊的交給他。再次為造成您的不便致上歉意。

86. What is the purpose of the telephone message?
   (A) To order some electronics
   (B) To purchase insurance
   (C) To apologize for a problem*
   (D) To ask for a shipping address

86. 這段電話留言的目的為何？
   (A) 訂購一些電器。
   (B) 購買保險。
   (C) 為問題致歉。
   (D) 詢問送貨地址。

87. What problem does the speaker mention?
   (A) Some electronics are broken.
   (B) Some packaging is damaged.*
   (C) A payment has been delayed.
   (D) A new item is sold out.

87. 說話者提及什麼問題？
   (A) 有些電器用品故障。
   (B) 有個外盒破損。
   (C) 有筆款項延後。
   (D) 有個新產品售完。

88. What does the speaker say he will do?
   (A) Pick up an item
   (B) Contact a manager
   (C) Provide a refund
   (D) Send another package*

88. 說話者說他會做何事？
   (A) 拾起一件物品。
   (B) 聯絡經理。
   (C) 提供退款。
   (D) 寄送另一個包裹。

M Hi, Divia. This is Jeff calling. [89] **I've just had a chance to look at your design for Sampson Real Estate's online advertisement, and I wanted to give you some feedback.** Actually, the design has a few issues. Sampson Real Estate is one of the oldest companies in the area and they focus mostly on high-end properties. I'm sorry I didn't explain this better to you, but Sampson usually prefers more traditional graphics. [90] **The ones you've used are a bit too young and casual.** [91] **How about I send you some of Sampson's previous advertisements so you can review them and get an idea about what they want?** Call me back when you get a chance.

男 嗨，蒂薇亞，我是傑夫。[89] 我剛剛才有時間看妳為山普生不動產設計的線上廣告，我想給妳些意見。實際上，這個設計有幾個問題。山普生不動產是業界最老的公司之一，他們主要聚焦在高檔的房地產上。抱歉沒有把這一點跟妳解釋得更清楚些，但山普生通常偏愛較傳統的圖樣。[90] 妳所使用的圖，有點太過於年輕且不夠正式。[91] 我寄一些山普生之前的廣告給妳如何？這樣妳可以仔細看看，對他們想要什麼有個概念。等妳有空時，回我電話。

89. What industry does the speaker work in?
   (A) Internet sales
   (B) Fashion retail
   (C) Advertising*
   (D) Publishing

89. 說話者在哪個行業工作？
   (A) 網路銷售。
   (B) 服飾零售。
   (C) 廣告業。
   (D) 出版業。

90. Why does the speaker say, "Actually, the design has a few issues"?
   (A) To outline the survey results about a design
   (B) To suggest that their budget is limited
   (C) To indicate a problem with some finished work*
   (D) To express some safety concerns

90. 說話者為何說「實際上這個設計有幾個問題」？
   (A) 為了概述一個設計的調查結果。
   (B) 為了暗示他們的預算有限。
   (C) 為了指出某項已完成作品的問題。
   (D) 為了表達一些安全疑慮。

91. What does the speaker suggest the listener do?
   (A) Study some prior designs*
   (B) Work on another project
   (C) Contact a client directly
   (D) Consult a coworker

91. 說話者建議聽者何事？
   (A) 研究一些之前的設計。
   (B) 進行另一項專案。
   (C) 直接與客戶聯絡。
   (D) 請教同事。

Questions 92–94 會議摘錄

W   Hello, everyone. Thanks for attending this editorial meeting on such short notice. Some of our new publications were set to be released early next year. Unfortunately, the release dates have been pushed back again. This means those who have preordered books will now have to wait even longer to receive their copies. Who knows how many will cancel their orders? [92] **I suggest we run another preorder promotion to ensure we don't lose sales.** [93] **I'd like everyone to come up with some promotional ideas.** [94] **I am available throughout this morning to discuss any concerns you might have about what kind of promotions are appropriate.**

女   大家好，謝謝各位一接到通知就趕來參加編輯會議。我們有些新書本來預定明年初要發行，遺憾的是，發行日期已再度延後。這意謂著那些已經預訂新書的人，現在必須等更久才能收到他們的書。誰知道會有多少人取消訂單？[92] **我建議，我們進行另一波預購促銷，以確保我們不會損失銷量。**[93] **我想要每個人想出一些促銷的點子。**[94] **我今天整個上午都有空，任何有關何種促銷可能適合的疑慮，都可以找我討論。**

92. What does the woman imply when she says, "Who knows how many will cancel their orders"?
 (A) She wants someone to report an exact figure.
 (B) She is worried about a loss of business.*
 (C) She would prefer to receive online orders.
 (D) She was not expecting any problems to occur.

92. 當女子說「誰知道會有多少人取消訂單」，意指什麼？
 (A) 她想要有人報告確實的數字。
 (B) 她擔心生意損失。
 (C) 她比較喜歡接到線上訂單。
 (D) 她不希望發生任何問題。

93. What is the topic of the meeting?
 (A) Redesigning a book cover
 (B) Reducing production costs
 (C) Developing a marketing strategy*
 (D) Attracting new authors

93. 會議的主題為何？
 (A) 重新設計一本書的封面。
 (B) 降低生產成本。
 (C) 發展行銷策略。
 (D) 吸引新的作者。

94. What will the speaker probably do this morning?
 (A) Attend a weekly meeting
 (B) Conduct a telephone consultation
 (C) Visit a broadcasting station
 (D) Address employee questions*

94. 說話者今天早上可能會做何事？
 (A) 參加週會。
 (B) 進行電話諮詢會議。
 (C) 拜訪廣播電台。
 (D) 處理下屬的問題。

Questions 95–97 指示及座位圖

section 1	section 3	96 section 4	Exit aisle
section 2			

stage

第一區	第三區	96 第四區	出口 走道
第二區			

舞台

W Hello, everyone. I'm so excited ⁹⁵ **you were all able to attend our audition for a part in the International Ballet.** Before we start the auditions, I'd like to let everyone know how things are going to happen today. Everyone has been given a number. When your number is close to being called, please make your way backstage. Everyone is free to watch the auditions. However, since many families are also here to watch, ⁹⁶ **we ask that you sit in the section closest to the aisle,** so you do not disturb anyone when you are moving to and from your audition. ⁹⁷ **We also ask that you be quiet and courteous during performances.** Following the auditions, our lead choreographers will make decisions and invite selected dancers to a second audition next week.

女 大家好。很高興 ⁹⁵ **你們都能來參加我們國際芭蕾舞團的甄選。**在開始之前，我想告訴各位今天的流程。每個人都拿到了一個號碼。快要叫到你的號碼時，請前往後台。各位都可以隨意觀賞甄選過程。不過，由於有許多人的家人也來這裡觀賞，因此，⁹⁶ **要請你們坐在最靠近走道的區域，**這樣的話，你們要上下台時，才不會干擾到其他人。⁹⁷ **同時要求你們，演出進行時請保持安靜且遵守禮節。**甄選之後，我們的首席舞蹈指導會作出決定，並邀請獲選的舞者參加下星期的第二輪甄選。

95. Who most likely are the listeners?
    (A) Directors
    (B) Writers
    (C) Performers*
    (D) Reporters

96. Look at the graphic. What section does the speaker want the listeners to sit in?
    (A) Section 1
    (B) Section 2
    (C) Section 3
    (D) Section 4*

97. What are listeners asked to do during the audition?
    (A) Remain quiet*
    (B) Take photographs
    (C) Avoid cellphone use
    (D) Speak to choreographers

95. 聽眾最可能是誰？
    (A) 導演。
    (B) 作家。
    (C) 表演者。
    (D) 記者。

96. 請見圖表。説話者要聽眾坐在哪個區域？
    (A) 第一區。
    (B) 第二區。
    (C) 第三區。
    (D) 第四區。

97. 在甄選時，聽眾被要求做何事？
    (A) 保持安靜。
    (B) 拍照。
    (C) 不要使用手機。
    (D) 和舞蹈指導談話。

Create a digital design	創建數位設計
99 **Present your idea**	99 **展示你的概念**
Construct a physical model	建造實體模型
Submit for feedback and revisions	交出作品以接受意見與修正

M   Let's start with some great news. 98 **Thanks to our recent merger, Frontier Architecture managed to pick up numerous contracts with private and city developers.** As a result, we're going to have a lot of building designs to work on in the coming year. Now, I'd like to talk about our design development process. Take a look at this flowchart. 99 **Notice that we've added a step between create a digital design and construct a physical model.** This new step means you will need to get approval from a senior designer before constructing a model. Because we have so many projects to work on, we need to make sure we're not wasting our time building models that won't be approved. 100 **This new process will help you focus your time and should ensure that we are able to meet our deadlines.**

男   我們用一些很棒的消息來開始會議吧。 98 **由於我們最近的合併,「新領域建築」設法簽下了許多私人及市府開發單位的合約。** 因此,接下來一年,我們會有很多建物的設計要忙。現在,我想談談我們的設計發展步驟。請看這張流程圖。 99 **請注意,我們在創建數位設計與建造實體模型之間增加了一個步驟。** 這個新步驟,代表你在建造模型之前,必須得到資深設計師的認可。因為有那麼多專案要進行,我們必須確定沒有把時間浪費在建造不會得到認可的模型上。 100 **這個新的程序有助於你們集中時間,而且應該能確保我們在截止日前完成。**

20

98. What does the speaker say about Frontier Architecture?
(A) They lost several important clients.
(B) They recently merged with another company.*
(C) They hired a new design team.
(D) They won an international award.

99. Look at the graphic. According to the speaker, which step was recently added?
(A) Create a digital design
(B) Present your idea*
(C) Construct a physical model
(D) Submit for feedback and revisions

100. What problem will the speaker's plan prevent?
(A) Losing digital files
(B) Paying overtime wages
(C) Working in a crowded office
(D) Not finishing work on time*

98. 關於新領域建築,說話者說了什麼?
(A) 他們失去好幾個重要的客戶。
(B) 他們最近和另一家公司合併。
(C) 他們僱用了新的設計團隊。
(D) 他們贏得一項國際大獎。

99. 請見圖表。根據說話者所述,哪個步驟是最近增加的?
(A) 創建數位設計。
(B) 展示你的概念。
(C) 建造實體模型。
(D) 交出作品以接受意見與修正。

100. 說話者的計畫能預防什麼問題?
(A) 遺失電子檔案。
(B) 付加班費。
(C) 在擁擠的辦公室工作。
(D) 未準時完成工作。

◎ **PART 5** 解答請見 P. 509　ANSWER KEY

101. 這些彩色團體制服是由**我們的**子公司，丹徹斯特輪胎所提供的。

102. 一旦收到所有旅行必要**文件**後，將盡快處理這一家的簽證。

103. 在演講中，格蘭史達製藥廠執行長**特別**提到研究部主管對於公司成功貢獻良多。

104. 喬安的管理方法與她的前任大**不**相同。

105. 對戴伯特承建公司的屋頂工人來說，配戴安全背帶不是一個選擇而是**規定**。

106. 本公司水電工人將**示範**如何又快又輕鬆地更換莫爾頓 DR 水槽排水管。

107. 布拉姆威爾地毯公司不核發任何商品退款，因此在購買前務必**仔細地**丈量地板空間大小。

108. **不論**年度獲利高低，他們仍然為商業分析師提供重要的經濟資訊。

109. 在舊設計的亞果機車與新款的格蘭福特機車之間，這份報告提供了詳細的**比較**。

110. 如欲與客服專員通話，請勿掛斷。

111. 新倉庫的儲存空間存放三百台腳踏車**綽綽有餘**。

112. 在這國家申請家庭簽證是一段漫長又**複雜**的過程。

113. 那些頂尖的汽車專家堅稱，渥宜津石油公司的過濾器能產生**絕佳的**成效。

114. 信用卡帳單明細或電話帳單可做為居住**證明**。

115. 博爾達克先生**最初**要求加布里埃拉籌辦研討會，但是後來又把這工作分配給露意絲。

116. 求職者需附上三份推薦信，**連同**完成的申請文件**一起**繳交。

117. 雖然博諾先生從來沒做過冰箱維修，但他對冷藏系統的知識卻非常**淵博**。

118. 第六頁的流程圖說明了各專案主管間的職務**分配**。

119. 這些種子會長出最大、卻不**一定**是最健康的番茄。

120. 雖然店家不提供退款，但顧客可更換與原價**等值**的任何商品。

121. 從新聞照片中看出奧塔貝里市市長坐在首相**對面**。

122. 新鞋款的推出決定，是**根據**市場研究結果而訂的。

123. 埃爾德柏恩就業中心是這一區中，唯一一間方便輪椅人士**出入**的大樓。

124. 戴流士醫生努力**提升**診所的門面，將於候診室擺放畫作。

125. 未進入決賽**的**球隊球員可免費觀賞比賽。

126. 當地官員**向**農民**保證**，噴灑在馬鈴薯作物上的殺蟲劑對人體無害。

127. 藍福製造的工廠員工**同意**每天多上班 30 分鐘，以抵銷上升的生產成本。

128. **考慮到**山繆曾在三大洲的工作經驗，難怪執行長讓他負責海外計畫。

129. 不是在這個社區長大的人，可能無法理解史坦荷爾街大橋在歷史上的**重要性**。

130. **雖然**珍妮佛比比爾年輕很多，但在公司裡珍妮佛比他還資深。

Questions 131–134 電子郵件

收件者：<nina_haidara@kmail.net>
寄件者：
<duron_charette@wrnpharmaceuticals.com>
日期：9月7日
主旨：研究主管職缺

親愛的海德拉女士，

WRN 製藥廠很樂意邀請您下週至本公司進行第二次面試。因為這已經是第二階段，本公司招聘委員會只面談前五名應徵者，這五位是我們認為最適合這個具挑戰性職位的人選。委員會一致同意，您幾乎擁有我們所需的一切特質。我們相信您仍對這個職位感到興趣。若是如此，您下週三下午 2:30 是否有空會面？另外，做為本次面試內容的一部分，希望您可以準備一份書面研究計畫，內容為第一次面試中討論到的其中一個主題，以及一場十分鐘的簡報。很期待能聽到您對於未來計畫的願景。

WRN 製藥廠
杜倫・夏爾特 敬上
304-677-2426 轉分機 18

131. (A) 適合
(B) 適合的
(C) 適合
(D) 適合

132. (A) 協議
(B) 表現；成果
(C) 特質
(D) 晉升

133. (A) 儘管
(B) 若是這樣
(C) 然而
(D) 例如，舉例來説

134. (A) 我們現任研究主管將針對您的新職務進行培訓。
(B) 執行長很樂意幫您寫推薦信。
(C) 您需要在星期三之前完成目前的研究計畫。
(D) 很期待能聽到您對於未來計畫的願景。

Questions 135–138 信件

香岱爾・瑤頓
61735 伊利諾州德拉凡市莫林街 302 號

親愛的瑤頓女士，

要提醒您另一次眼睛檢查的時間快到了。本所紀錄顯示，自您上回讓霍班醫生檢查距今已經 11 個月了。眼科專家建議您至少每年檢查視力一次。如此一來，可以盡早檢查出眼睛的問題，也能更新眼鏡度數。本診所的首要考量，就是盡力維持病患最佳視力狀態。過幾天我們將致電以作為本函的後續追蹤。如欲預約，請來電（309）754-3231。感謝您。

赫林街眼科診所 護眼團隊

135. (A) 本所最近擴大候診室，增添孩童更大的遊戲區。
(B) 本所記錄顯示，自您上回讓霍班醫生檢查已經 11 個月了。
(C) 運動及健康飲食也會影響您的眼睛狀況。
(D) 本所更新了官網，包含便利的線上預約系統。

136. (A) 建議
(B) 已建議
(C) 建議
(D) 將會建議

137. (A) 然而
(B) 如此一來
(C) 例如，舉例來説
(D) 同樣地

138. (A) 方式
(B) 意見
(C) 條件；狀況
(D) 優先（事項）

Questions 139–142 文章

《帕斯波羅先趨報》
本地新聞

（6月12日）一星期二下午，帕斯波羅市市長黛博拉·密道頓宣布市議會決定，將為想成為市區公車司機的民眾，進行一對一的培訓計畫。她特別說明年底前需要 20 名新司機。在記者會談話中，市長強調了聘請新司機來代替即將退休人力的緊急需求。這個宣布獲得多數市府官員的認同。然而，特魯羅區議員史帝芬·迪格比不斷地公開反對市府大筆地提供資金在培訓計畫上，因為離帕斯波羅市西方 50 公里遠的沃夫維爾汽車營運大學，其畢業生都具備填補該缺額的資格。他要市府聘用熟悉該領域的人才。

139. (A) 特別地
(B) 毫無疑問地
(C) 無論如何
(D) 除此之外

140. (A) 解決
(B) 減少
(C) 要求，需求
(D) 困難

141. (A) 將獲得
(B) 獲得
(C) 一直獲得
(D) 獲得

142. (A) 他相信可以以增加座位來改善目前公車狀況。
(B) 他要市府聘用已熟悉該領域的人才。
(C) 他覺得司機的合格測驗太容易通過。
(D) 他預期高油價將造成較高的公車費用。

Questions 143–146 信件

收件者：法蘭絲·凡奈克
寄件者：蜜雪兒·薩克拉
日期：7月14日

主旨：早安

我從同事那得知你即將升職。雖然奧斯陸新設辦公室的招募主管一職，將於 8 月 2 日才正式開始，還是先祝福你新工作一切順利。如果需要任何協助，歡迎與我聯絡，我很清楚這種過渡期，雖然令人興奮，卻也是相當具挑戰性。你在巴黎查拉時尚擔任副招募總監一職時，工作表現一向都很傑出。我相信你在新職位上的表現也會很成功的。恭喜你，也祝你一切順利！

蜜雪兒·薩克拉敬上

143. (A) 旅程
(B) 事件
(C) 獎項
(D) 晉升，升職

144. (A) 開始
(B) 開始了
(C) 已開始
(D) 可以開始

145. (A) 有挑戰性的
(B) 挑戰
(C) 挑戰者
(D) 挑戰

146. (A) 奧斯陸辦公室比較小，但有個大停車場。
(B) 我還在進行所有新職缺的面試事宜。
(C) 你可以問問服飾店的員工折扣。
(D) 我相信你在新職位上的表現也會很成功的。

Questions 147–148 收據

公園家戶外活動用品店

亞伯達省艾德蒙頓，公園路南區 229 號

(777) 223-4455

日期：5 月 12 日

時間：10:37

品項

3345 [147] 樂路克斯 四人座沙發		$499.00
3348 樂路克斯 扶手椅		$199.00
3355 樂路克斯 腳凳		$99.00
4489 D&F 六入抽屜櫃		
四座（79 元／座）		$316.00
1223 明星設計款枕頭		
兩個（19 元／個）		$38.00

小計	$1151.00
稅（5%）	$57.55
總計	$1208.55
信用卡支付金額	$1208.55

總購買件數：9

非特價商品於購買後 60 天內，皆可接受退貨。退貨規定請至 www.parkhomeoutfitters. ca/returns. 查閱。

****

[148] **上官網加入會員，即可以最高五折優惠購買線上特定商品**，優惠至 6 月 28 日。

****

感謝您購買公園家戶外活動用品店商品。

147. 公園家戶外用品店最可能是哪一種商店？

    (A) 家具行

    (B) 紡織品商店

    (C) 建設公司

    (D) 服飾店

148. 根據收據，顧客要如何獲得折扣？

    (A) 申請會員

    (B) 出示折價券

    (C) 填寫問卷調查

    (D) 購買兩項以上商品

Questions 149–150 電子郵件

收件者：蓋瑞·洪

<garyhong@songendepartmentstore.co.au>

寄件者：派翠西亞·圖倫斯基

<songendepartmentstore.co.au>

主旨：頌恩百貨公司十週年慶

日期：10 月 14 日

附件：新聞稿

親愛的洪先生，

[149] 有關我們在雪梨的十週年慶祝活動新聞稿，已聯絡了數家電視台。週年慶將以音樂會為開幕活動，將於 11 月 24 日在市中心門市外舉辦。[149] 自下週起到整個活動期間，我們也在所有分店安排了幾場週年慶特賣會。[150] 待分店主管確認後，我會將完整的時程表寄給您。

同時，請參閱附件的新聞稿，若宣傳部需要增添任何資料，再請告知。

頌恩百貨公司行銷經理

派翠西亞·圖倫斯基 敬上

149. 這封電子郵件的目的是什麼？

    (A) 列出出售商品清單

    (B) 重新安排現場音樂演奏節目時間

    (C) 邀請同事出席活動

    (D) 報告宣傳計畫的最新狀況

150. 圖倫斯基女士答應稍後要寄什麼？

    (A) 最近的一篇新聞文章

    (B) 商店優惠折扣的時程表

    (C) 電視台清單

    (D) 修改後的新聞稿

Questions 151–152 文章

大城小事

[151, 152] 城鎮書店老闆辛西亞‧普戴爾宣布，她將於布魯克賽德大道 667 號開設第二間書店的計畫。地點就在布魯克賽德小學對面，之前是史密斯頓麵包店的所在地。普戴爾女士的新書店尚未命名，但預計於明年春天開幕。書店將有寬廣的童書區，[152] 普戴爾女士希望可以藉此吸引許多布魯克賽德小學的小客人。普戴爾女士原本位於第五大道上的城鎮書店，其藏書類型與營業型態則鎖定成人讀者。

151. 這篇文章的目的是什麼？
(A) 討論商店結束營業
(B) 介紹一位成功的烘培業者
(C) 報告店家搬遷
(D) 宣布新店家開幕

152. 關於布魯克賽德大道，提到了什麼事？
(A) 位在一家受歡迎的麵包店的對面。
(B) 預計今年開幕。
(C) 是普戴爾女士的首次創業。
(D) 預期客源為學生。

Questions 153–155 通知

聖麥克醫院研究盛會

聖麥克醫院將舉辦一場盛會幫助持續性醫療研究。盛會將於大復興飯店舉行，但是 [153] 由於飯店預約錯誤，必須更動活動日期。活動將由原訂的 9 月 20 日改到 10 月 5 日晚上 5:00 至 8:00。出席前請注意以下資訊。

[154] 從中央車站到大復興飯店的交通路線如下：[154] 帕歇爾大道往北行，右轉彌督路。左轉貝絲大街，經過五條街後右轉史密斯維路。大復興飯店就位於瑪莉蘿絲戲院對面。盛會將於 IA 宴會廳舉行。

停車資訊：
[155] 地下停車場可免費停車。請確認您攜帶連同盛會入場券一同核發的停車證。否則您須自行支付停車費用。

153. 這項活動變更了什麼？
(A) 費用
(B) 位置
(C) 贊助商
(D) 日期

154. 中央車站位於何處？
(A) 彌督路
(B) 貝絲大街
(C) 帕歇爾大道
(D) 史密斯維路

155. 關於在大復興飯店停車，提到了什麼事？
(A) 盛會貴賓必須支付停車費。
(B) 停車場位於對街。
(C) 有來賓停車證者可免費停車。
(D) 飯店有共用的停車場。

Questions 156–157 簡訊

史蒂芬‧尹　下午 4:45
珍妮佛來電要跟你說有關明天和執行長開會的事。[156] 她想知道你是否可以回電給她。

羅傑‧馬丁尼茲　下午 4:50
我現在在倉庫。你覺得她是在擔心報告無法及時完成嗎？

史蒂芬‧尹　下午 4:52
有可能。

羅傑‧馬丁尼茲　下午 4:54
嗯，我正在檢查倉庫的警報系統。我被叫來，因為系統似乎又出問題了。

史蒂芬‧尹　下午 4:57
要我打電話給保全公司嗎？

羅傑‧馬丁尼茲　下午 5:00
我想我可以自己修好。[157] 你可以告訴珍妮佛，請她 5:30 到我辦公室來一趟嗎？我想，我們應該在今晚下班前討論一下她所擔心的事。

史蒂芬‧尹　下午 5:01
好，沒問題。

156. 下午 4:50 時，馬丁尼茲先生說，「我現在在倉庫。」他的意思最有可能是？

(A) 他明天不在。

(B) 他要送貨。

(C) 他需要和尹先生說話。

(D) 他無法打電話給珍妮佛。

157. 尹先生被要求做什麼事？

(A) 和執行長聯絡

(B) 籌備會議

(C) 打電話給技術員

(D) 離開辦公室

Questions 158–160 信件

10 月 10 日

彼得・史帝文森

俄亥俄州克里夫蘭拉姆齊大道 45 號

親愛的史帝文森先生，

十分感謝您決定參加在法國巴黎舉辦的第一屆國際雜誌節。**158 我們已經收到您的報名。**如您所要求的，我們已將展場入場費及預約展示席位所需的額外費用刷入您的信用卡帳上。當您抵達時，我們將立即引領您至攤位，並發給您一張名牌，讓您在展場中的任何飲料及食物攤位都能享有折扣。

要提醒您活動報名費並不含住宿費。欲於鄰近地區訂房，請查看 www.parishotels.com。**160 藉由出示參加本雜誌展的證明，您可以以定價 75 折的價格訂房。**本信函可為適當證明，當您入住時只需向櫃檯人員出示本函即可。

159 隨信附上本次巴黎會區地圖，有助於您熟悉附近環境。地圖內容也包含了該區最受歡迎的餐廳與飯店。

再次感謝您，希望本次的國際雜誌展能成為您收穫滿載的一個經驗。

會展統籌

妮可・德雅爾丹司 敬上

158. 為什麼會寄這封信？

(A) 提供部分退款

(B) 告知地址變更

(C) 說明流程

(D) 告知收到報名

159. 史帝文森先生被建議事先檢閱什麼？

(A) 當地地圖

(B) 會議議程

(C) 合約條款

(D) 班機時間

160. 下列句子最適合出現在 [1]、[2]、[3]、[4] 的哪個位置中？

「本信函可為適當證明，當您入住時只需向櫃檯人員出示本函即可。」

(A) [1]

(B) [2]

(C) [3]

(D) [4]

Questions 161–164 文章

漢默電子 8000 系列不可預期的延誤
蘇菲亞・米亞琪 撰稿

上週，**161 全世界主要智慧型手機製造商—漢默電子，**宣布了新智慧型手機 8000 系列延後上市的消息。業界專家與顧客們對此消息同感震驚。漢默電子的擁護者在社群媒體上，對深受期待的 8000 系列手機取消一事，表達了失望之情。

根據漢默電子代表表示，由三種個別模型及各種伴生技術所組成的 8000 系列，由於公司新款螢幕設計上不可預期的問題而延誤了。雖然一開始原型被核准了，但第一批生產的裝置卻無法通過安全檢測。**162(A)** **(B) 這可能是因為用來製作螢幕的玻璃有瑕疵，使得內部組件容易過熱。**

除了無法通過檢測外，**164 漢默的新系列已證實它並不如公司預期地持久。**162(D) 由於材質的瑕疵，**8000 型被證實是相當脆弱的。**對於一家以生產耐用產品而自豪的公司來說，推出這系列的產品將會是非常難堪的一件事。

161, 163 漢默電子正在探尋其他替代材料，計畫明年推出 8000 系列。但是，該公司或許已經流失許多渴望新產品的顧客了。

161. 關於漢默電子，提到了什麼事？
(A) 是智慧型手機科技的頂尖製造商。
(B) 將以折扣價來銷售 8000 系列。
(C) 要把總部遷至另一個城市。
(D) 將持續生產有瑕疵的產品。

162. 下列何者不是 8000 系列設計上的問題？
(A) 螢幕是有瑕疵的玻璃。
(B) 產品會過熱。
(C) 材料太貴。
(D) 裝置是脆弱的。

163. 漢默電子為什麼要到明年才會推出 8000 系列？
(A) 他們需要處理專利權的問題。
(B) 檢測已經重新安排時間。
(C) 有些工廠需要升級。
(D) 他們需要足夠的時間來找新原料。

164. 下列句子最適合出現在 [1],[2],[3],[4] 的哪個位置中？
「對於一家以生產耐用產品而自豪的公司來說，推出這系列的產品將會是非常難堪的一件事。」
(A) [1]
(B) [2]
(C) [3]
(D) [4]

Questions 165–168 簡訊

訊息		編輯

萊斯特·吉伯斯 [9:00]
嗨，蜜雪兒，妳在辦公室嗎？

蜜雪兒·鍾 [9:01]
快到了。怎麼了？

萊斯特·吉伯斯 [9:03]
165, 166 我正在進行肯辛頓大道上一棟房子的工程，剛剛才發現我沒有足夠的紅色室外漆，來粉刷門窗邊框。我們店裡還有油漆嗎？沒有的話，我就要開車去安德斯公園的商店買一罐了。

蜜雪兒·鍾 [9:04]
賈斯汀現在在辦公室。我現在加他進來。你需要幾罐？

賈斯汀·惠特克被加入對話。

萊斯特·吉伯斯 [9:05]
167 我需要兩罐紅色室外漆。賈斯汀，你可以去倉庫查看一下嗎？

賈斯汀·惠特克 [9:07]
你今天運氣真好。

萊斯特·吉伯斯 [9:10]
太好了！我必須先塗完房子東側的油漆，至少要一個小時後才會開始粉刷邊框，所以我十點之後回來拿。

蜜雪兒·鍾 [9:11]
事實上，我才剛把我的卡車倒車到卸貨區，為了尼爾森大道和比克斯街轉角的工作，我要去拿所需的東西。**166** 你離那一區不遠，所以我可以順便先把紅色室外漆拿給你。

萊斯特·吉伯斯 [9:15]
那太棒了。非常感謝！**168** 賈斯汀，麻煩在庫存記錄單上添上我的名字和現在的時間。午餐後，我一定會回去在表格上簽名。

賈斯汀·惠特克 [9:17]
沒問題。

165. 吉伯斯先生可能從事哪一個行業？
(A) 房屋修繕承包商
(B) 網路供應商
(C) 塑膠製品製造商
(D) 速食餐廳

166. 鍾女士說她接下來要去哪裡？
(A) 安德斯公園
(B) 肯辛頓大道
(C) 比克斯街
(D) 尼爾森大道

167. 上午 9:07，當惠特克先生說：「你今天運氣真好」是什麼意思？

    (A) 有足夠的錢可以執行新計畫。

    (B) 到那房子的路線很容易理解。

    (C) 庫存裡正好有所需要的油漆罐數量。

    (D) 他傍晚可以幫吉伯斯先生的忙。

168. 吉伯斯先生請惠特克先生做什麼事？

    (A) 在表格上填入重要細節

    (B) 把一些物品放到架上

    (C) 安排與客戶諮商

    (D) 寄送發票給當地店家

Questions 169–171 廣告

> ### 商業網絡
> ### 滑鼠一點就能建立關係網絡！
>
> 商業網絡是線上網絡服務的最新發展。快速，價格合理，又容易使用，[169] **商業網絡可以讓您與業界專業人士建立良好關係，幫助您找到夢想中的工作。** 本公司的線上服務可以讓您追蹤就業市場的潮流，同時也能獲得您領域中企業會議的最新資訊。
>
> 與 [170] **本公司姊妹網絡——研讀網合作，** 您可以獲得許多進階功能，例如：
>
> - [171(B)] **簡便履歷建立器，** 讓您可以在幾分鐘內就做出一份完美的履歷表
>
> - 龐大的企業名單與 [171(D)] **搜尋工具，尋找適當職缺**
>
> - 應有盡有的 [171(A)] **影音圖書館，** 主題從申請到面試理想的工作應有盡有
>
> - 每週配對服務，依據您的技能來媒合新工作
>
> 更多資訊，請至網站 www.biznet.com 查詢。

169. 客戶最可能怎樣運用商業網絡？

    (A) 購買線上服務

    (B) 找到公司的職缺

    (C) 完成稅務資料

    (D) 宣傳公司服務項目

170. 關於開發商業網絡的公司，提到了什麼事？

    (A) 可以去電和公司代表人員聯繫。

    (B) 在幫助家庭事業上頗具聲譽。

    (C) 是由一間大型的銷售企業所創立的。

    (D) 擁有不只一個網絡網站。

171. 下列何者不是商業網絡的特色？

    (A) 影音圖書館

    (B) 履歷表產生器

    (C) 會議門票

    (D) 職缺搜尋工具

Questions 172–175 通知

> ### 波帝歌湖海灘與營地（LPBC）
>
> [172] **波帝歌湖海灘與營地於今年春夏兩季開放時間，為自 4 月 10 日起至 9 月 1 日。** 但請注意，LPBC 將保留對露營者施加其他限制的權力。[173] **由於連續的乾燥氣候，露營者將禁止在特定時間內使用露天營火。** 以野營爐和烤肉方式烹煮食物則不在此限。一旦開放用火，露營者必須向公園購買預先砍好的木柴。任何時間都不得砍伐樹木。
>
> 非露營者可於白天造訪波帝歌湖海灘，但需酌收費用。海灘遊客可於早上八點待到下午五點。[174] **團體票可事先預訂，以享優惠。** 另外，公園還提供波帝歌湖博物館導覽服務，是一座原由威廉·馬克斯爵士所擁有的歷史莊園。博物館門票可於導覽當天在前門購買。
>
> **付款與預約**
>
> - 預約營地，請撥打 888-341-0867。營地每晚 65 元。[175] **預約時，需繳納 30 元訂金，訂金恕不退還。** 訂金可抵露營費用。
>
> - 非露營者的海灘一日卷可於抵達時購買，每人八元。15 人以上的團體事先預約可享八折優惠。
>
> - 波帝哥湖博物館門票每人七元。每天三次導覽，分別為上午 11 點、下午 1 點及下午 3 點。

172. 這則通知公告的內容是什麼？
    (A) 新規定
    (B) 結束營業
    (C) 費用調漲
    (D) 營業時間表

173. 關於到訪波帝歌湖營地，提到了什麼事？
    (A) 露營者在森林亂丟垃圾會被罰。
    (B) 露營者可能無法使用營火。
    (C) 露營者必須加入團體才能參觀博物館。
    (D) 露營者需另外付費才能進入海灘。

174. 關於波帝歌湖非露營服務，提到了什麼事？
    (A) 可預約博物館門票。
    (B) 海灘遊客在週末時可留下過夜。
    (C) 海灘遊客可免費使用陽傘。
    (D) 團體於造訪海灘時可享有折扣。

175. 取消營區預約會發生什麼事？
    (A) 損失訂金。
    (B) 款項可退還。
    (C) 會收到帳單。
    (D) 會員資格會被降級。

Questions 176–180 信件及電子郵件

¹⁸⁰3 月 10 日

凱莉．諾斯翠女士
辛普森出版社
人力資源部
澳洲雪梨中心街 55 號

親愛的諾斯翠女士，

我想利用這個機會遞上我的求職函，以應徵辛普森出版社於雪梨新辦公室的編輯主任一職。¹⁷⁶ 正如您可從我所附上的履歷表看到的，我在編輯領域有相當豐富的經驗，包括五年在《樂序雜誌》擔任主編以及在《雪梨時代》報紙擔任三年的編輯助理。

¹⁷⁶ 除了這些經驗外，我還擁有新聞學士學位及出版研究碩士學位。此外，有鑑於我也是出版過七本童書的作家，我相信自己可以為主編一職增添新 ¹⁷⁷ 亮點。我相信我個人獨特的經歷將帶給公司極大的貢獻。

非常感謝您撥冗。期待能與您會談。

艾德利安．柏杜 敬上

收件者：辛普森出版社編輯同仁
寄件者：艾德利安．柏杜
¹⁸⁰ 日期：4 月 30 日
主旨：¹⁷⁸ 提醒事項

編輯同仁：

¹⁸⁰ 從我們第一次提出兒童教育新系列書籍的企畫至今將近一年了。我要稱許大家在這一系列上的辛苦付出。隨著出版時間的逼近，¹⁷⁸ 我想要提醒大家幾件事。

首先，請務必每週和設計師討論書本的整體設計。在實現大家共同的願景中，讓設計師看到各位的投入，並提供指引是很重要的。

再者，部分自由校對人員的進度已經落後。請確實定期與他們保持聯繫，必要的話，增聘更多自由校對人員來完成工作。

最後，¹⁷⁹ 由於套書出版時將包括網站的發行，在「關於我們」的部分，希望大家都能繳交一份小篇的自我介紹。大約 100 字的簡單小傳就夠了。

感謝大家一直以來的努力，期待發行那一天的到來！

艾德利安

---

176. 這封信的目的是什麼？
    (A) 詢問起薪
    (B) 列出一些專業能力
    (C) 提供就業推薦函
    (D) 詢問工作地點

177. 在信件中，第二段、第二行的「dimension」與下列哪一個意思最接近？
    (A) 要求
    (B) 前例
    (C) 問題
    (D) 特點

178. 柏杜先生為什麼會寫這封電子郵件？
    (A) 稱讚員工完成工作
    (B) 強調一些工作的重要性
    (C) 激勵員工接受額外的工作
    (D) 告知新進員工特別程序

179. 關於辛普森出版社，提到了什麼事？

    (A) 主要出版電子書。

    (B) 在七個國家聘用編輯。

    (C) 將停止出版部分書籍。

    (D) 將於網站上介紹員工。

180. 關於柏杜先生，提到了什麼事？

    (A) 之前擔任圖書設計師。

    (B) 一年前受僱於辛普森出版社。

    (C) 因為工作機會搬到雪梨。

    (D) 他不再寫童書。

Questions 181–185 電子郵件及經營計畫書

收件者：汪達・威利斯

        <willis@utcbankandloans.com>

寄件者：傑佛瑞・湯瑪斯

        <jthomas@mailmail.com>

日期：3 月 12 日

回覆：經營企畫書

[183] 附件：修訂版企畫書

親愛的威利斯女士，

感謝您這麼快就回覆。很高興您能幫我 **[182]** 取得新事業的資金支持。**[181]** 我已經看過您寄給我的所有回饋意見，也依其編寫我的經營企畫書。如您所建議的，**[183]** 我已經在企畫書內加上詳述潛在客戶的部分，隨信附上修改後的版本。

我想這是申請企業貸款所需完成的全部文件。但若還有其他需要填寫的文件，再請您與我聯繫。

期待您的消息。

傑佛瑞・湯瑪斯 敬上

修訂後的經營企畫書：布理恩咖啡

第一部份：目的

市中心港口區已經成為活躍的商業區，到處都有許多辦公大樓、銀行和百貨公司。本店—布理恩咖啡鄰近著名法院，為市中心繁忙核心地帶。**[184]** 希望以合理價格提供各種國際精品咖啡，同時也提供一個可以享受美味午餐的輕鬆氛圍。

[183] 第二部分：目標市場

布理恩咖啡將為在市中心上班的商業專業人士提供服務。由於在步行距離內就有多家法律事務所與銀行，我們的顧客可能在早上、休息時間及午餐時到咖啡店來。另外，週末的顧客也包含到附近港區百貨公司的購物者。

第三部分：時間表

布理恩咖啡預定於 6 月 1 日開幕。希望以下前置作業能於這些日期前完成：

3 月 28 日 簽訂租約與申請商業許可證

4 月 10 日 整修用餐區與提升廚房設備

4 月 20 日 聘用員工並完成員工訓練

5 月 15 日 確定菜單、預訂存貨以及規劃開幕

第四部分：行銷計畫

[185] 開幕前與開幕後的詳細行銷計畫，請見附件試算表。

181. 這封電子郵件的目的是什麼？

    (A) 審閱許可證的指導方針

    (B) 送出有關財務資料的回饋意見

    (C) 要求撰寫商業計畫的建議

    (D) 回覆對方所要求的修訂版

182. 在電子郵件中，第一段、第一行的「secure」與下列哪一個意思最接近？

    (A) 護衛

    (B) 取得

    (C) 節省

    (D) 繫牢

183. 經營企畫書新增了哪一個部分？

    (A) 第一部分

    (B) 第二部分

    (C) 第三部分

    (D) 第四部分

184. 湯瑪斯先生計劃要做什麼生意？

    (A) 貸款公司

    (B) 百貨公司

    (C) 法律事務所

    (D) 咖啡店

185. 根據經營企畫書，何種資料被另外繳交？

(A) 預期獲利的詳細估算表

(B) 求職推薦人的聯絡資訊

(C) 公司的宣傳方式

(D) 整修公司的介紹

Questions 186–190 網頁、電子郵件及表單

http://www.partysuppliers.com

產品陳列館	首頁	辦派對訣竅	訂購表	聯絡我們

派對商品供應網

歡迎來到本公司線上購物網站。瞧瞧我們的產品陳列館有 1,000 多種不同的派對產品。**186** 為了讓您的派對大受歡迎，一定要看看本公司的派對布置訣竅！

最新促銷方案：

2 月至 3 月：購買一件，即享第二件半價優惠（適用於所有現貨商品）

187 4 月至 8 月：訂購滿 30 元可享免運

寄件者：馬修·史帕克斯
<msparks@stantonautomotive.com>

收件者：裘恩·貝司特
<juneb@stantonautomotive.com>

187 日期：4 月 27 日

主旨：更新開幕活動

嗨，裘恩：

我比較了派對商品供應網與開普伯納派對商場兩家店，並選擇了前者，以添購我們在四號開幕派對當天所需要的東西。看起來他們提供了許多擺設自家產品的好方法，這樣應該不用花太多功夫就能讓展示間看起來很棒。

我想我們應該為展示間訂購客製旗幟，以及飾帶與氣球。**189 我們還可以做一個較大的旗幟掛在門前。**

若你也同意的話，我想要盡快下訂。工作區域還是一團亂，但是 **188 油漆工應該很快就可以完工，這讓我們在大日子來臨前，還有足夠的時間可以布置。**

有空時，告訴我你的看法。

馬修

訂單編號：112233265

聯絡資訊：馬修·史帕克斯
(444) 232-0916

寄送地址：史丹頓汽車經銷商，大西洋城布魯克斯巷 14 號

187 配送時段：5 月 1 日至 2 日，上午 9 點至下午 1 點

數量	產品編號	產品敘述
1	YZ0933	訂製旗幟（3 呎長）
1	YZ0955	**189 訂製旗幟（6 呎長）**
12	GH3345	彩虹氣球每組 12 個
2	BB2300	飾帶（白色）
		187 總計：104.50 元

備註：**190 所有訂製旗幟皆於巴爾的摩生產總部印製。這些商品將直接從巴爾的摩寄送至大西洋城，而不是從艾德華港店寄出，這表示您將收到兩件不同的包裹。** 若有任何疑問，歡迎立即與我們聯絡。

186. 關於派對商品供應網，提到了什麼事？

(A) 提供免費的產品樣本。

(B) 提供顧客布置建議。

(C) 最近開了另一間分店。

(D) 明年將擴展產品線。

187. 關於史丹頓汽車經銷商的訂單，下列何者可能為真？

(A) 將免費寄送。

(B) 包含外國商品。

(C) 包含半價商品。

(D) 五月將可退費。

188. 為何史帕克斯先生想要盡快安排寄送？

(A) 需要時間購買更多東西。

(B) 想要利用促銷優惠的機會。

(C) 需要更多人手來幫忙清理。

(D) 想要有足夠的時間布置。

189. 史丹頓汽車經銷商大門外最可能擺放哪種產品？

(A) 3 呎長的訂製旗幟

(B) 6 呎長的訂製旗幟

(C) 彩虹氣球

(D) 飾帶

190. 根據表格內容，氣球最可能從哪裡寄送出去？

(A) 巴爾的摩
(B) 大西洋城
(C) 開普伯納
(D) 艾德華港

Questions 191–195 電子郵件、菜單及意見卡

寄件者：吉米 · 普特利
<jpertelli@jimmysitalianrestaurant.com>
收件者：蘇 · 漢彌頓
<suehamilton@jimmysialianrestaurant.com>
日期：1 月 10 日星期日
主旨：菜單測試活動

嗨，蘇，

很難相信離重新營業已經不到一個月了。**191 既然我們還沒敲定最終菜單，就讓我們花點時間來為吉米義大利餐廳想些最棒的餐點吧。**我覺得下週六舉辦一場專屬親朋好友的非公開試菜活動，會是個不錯的主意。

對於試菜會上可以提供哪些餐點，我有一些構想。來做一道 **192 豐盛的**深盤素食披薩如何？這真的可以突顯我們新的素食菜單選擇。**193 我認為烤龍蝦拼盤是另一道絕佳的主菜。195 我也想要提供一些新的甜點，但這全得取決於糕點區是否已經完工。**如果還沒有的話，是不是就提供一些新口味的有機冰淇淋，再淋上你迷人的巧克力醬？不過，這讓你決定。身為主廚，你有絕對的自主權。

最後，試菜完後，我想要展示冰淇淋製作過程給賓客們看。告訴我你覺得這個想法是否可行。

謝謝

吉米

吉米義大利餐廳試菜菜單
1 月 15 日星期六

卡布里沙拉佐莫扎瑞拉起司與新鮮巴西里

椰汁蝦

烤大蒜麵包

紅醬素食義大利麵

奶油悶 **193 烤龍蝦拼盤**

肋眼火烤牛排佐烤馬鈴薯

195 吉米著名泡芙甜點

試菜意見卡

姓名：法蘭 · 漢普瑞

請針對您在吉米義大利餐廳的試菜經驗提供意見。

我非常喜歡開胃菜。但是，對我來說，沙拉淋了太多的義大利老醋醬。素食義大利麵相當不錯，但是我覺得麵條有點煮過頭了。**194 另一方面，烤龍蝦是我吃過最好吃的。**我覺得牛排有點生，但是馬鈴薯調味調得非常好。甜點對我來說可能太甜了點，但是糕點烘焙得很完美。我也喜歡冰淇淋製作示範，但我希望可以吃到當中的一些口味。

191. 菜單測試的目的是什麼？

(A) 挑選新菜單的餐點
(B) 為餐廳查驗做準備
(C) 測試新廚師
(D) 決定誰是主廚

192. 在電子郵件中，第二段、第一行的「hearty」與下列哪一個意思最接近？

(A) 誠摯的
(B) 芳香的
(C) 滿足的
(D) 原始的

TEST
5

PART 7

193. 關於試菜單，下列何者為真？
    (A) 只展現舊菜單上的餐點。
    (B) 列出幾個冰淇淋新口味。
    (C) 只在週末供應給顧客。
    (D) 包含了普特利先生建議的主菜。

194. 漢普瑞女士最喜歡的餐點最可能是哪一道？
    (A) 沙拉
    (B) 義大利麵
    (C) 龍蝦
    (D) 牛排

195. 關於糕點區，提到了什麼？
    (A) 對廚房來説太大了。
    (B) 搬到另一個位置。
    (C) 在整修過程中損壞了。
    (D) 準時完工了。

Questions 196–200 廣告、電子郵件及簡訊

哈特佛德歌劇院
紐約市貝爾韋街 45 號

www.hartfordoperahouse.com

哈特佛德歌劇院很高興宣布，今年夏天本院將有精彩的活動時程表。**[196] 我們將提供從演唱會到舞台劇的各項演出，所以我們相信一定有適合您的活動。**所有活動門票皆可於本院網站購買，也可一次購買季票。**[200] 持有季票者能依自己喜好參加各項活動，還可免費攜伴，每場以三位為限。**

活動節目表：
6 月 23 日—米勒兄弟古典樂團
7 月 3 日—亞倫・布魯爾的單人喜劇脱口秀
[198] 7 月 4 日—《走入叢林》，由卡崔娜・貝爾芙德所寫的得獎音樂劇
7 月 10 日—《埃及女人》，由湯米・威爾森所執導的舞台劇

完整夏季節目表，請上
www.hartfordoperahouse.com 查詢。

收件者：里拉・山普森
寄件者：羅德里克・凱利
副本：瓊恩・凡瑞克
主旨：密德華斯紙業與包裝公司之行
日期：6 月 2 日

親愛的山普森女士，

密德華斯紙業與包裝公司期待您於 7 月 2 日至 **[198] 7 月 4 日**至本公司總部參觀。**[197] 很高興貴公司同意討論我們兩家企業可能合併的條件。**

除了提供工廠和辦公室導覽外，我們還為您規劃了一個很棒的行程，包括與本公司執行長共進午餐、西花高爾夫球俱樂部之旅以及港口遊艇俱樂部之行。**[198] 我們也在您行程的最後一晚，安排了本地歌劇院現場演出的娛樂活動。**希望您會喜歡這趟旅程，若有任何需要，請告訴我。

密德華斯紙業與包裝公司

羅德利克・凱利 敬上

寄件者：凡瑞克
收件者：凱利

下週我們與山普森女士進行高爾夫球俱樂部之行時，天氣預報預測會下雨。**[199] 我想若能對調高爾夫球俱樂部參訪行程與歌劇院活動會比較好。**這會更動到我們參加的歌劇院活動，但不需重新購票。**[200] 我可以免費攜帶數位賓客入場。**

196. 關於哈特佛德歌劇院，提到了什麼？
    (A) 要和另一間公司合併。
    (B) 贈送免費季票。
    (C) 位於高爾夫球俱樂部旁。
    (D) 安排各式各樣的活動。

197. 山普森女士預計在參訪中做什麼？
    (A) 討論新的交易
    (B) 檢視合約
    (C) 諮詢律師
    (D) 展示產品

198. 山普森女士原本預定出席哪一個歌劇院
活動？

(A) 古典樂表演

(B) 現場喜劇表演

(C) 受歡迎的音樂劇

(D) 有關埃及的舞台劇

199. 凱利先生需要重新安排什麼？

(A) 搭船之旅

(B) 高爾夫球賽

(C) 午餐會報

(D) 工廠導覽

200. 凡瑞克女士最可能不需要購買入場券的
原因為何？

(A) 他們要參加的活動是免費的。

(B) 山普森女士尚未同意行程表。

(C) 凡瑞克女士已經有歌劇院的季票。

(D) 凱利先生必須等票券退費。

ACTUAL TEST ⑥

PART 1　P. 226–229　　　　　　　　　　🎧 21

1. (A) They are putting on their helmets.
(B) They are passing by a bike.
(C) They are gathering on a bridge.
(D) They are riding next to the water.*

2. (A) A woman is buying some bread.
(B) A woman is wearing a pair of gloves.*
(C) A woman is carrying a tray.
(D) A woman is opening a container.

3. (A) Some people are operating a machine.
(B) Some people are standing in rows.
(C) A man is speaking to a group of people.*
(D) A woman is examining her tools.

4. (A) A musician is performing on a stage.
(B) Some musical instruments are on display.*
(C) Some music stands have been set up.
(D) A guitar is being tuned.

5. (A) A plant is blocking the doorway.
(B) A ladder is propped against the shelves.*
(C) Books have been piled on the floor.
(D) A framed photograph is being hung up.

6. (A) The workstations are illuminated by some lamps.*
(B) The desks are positioned in a circle.
(C) A computer has been taken apart.
(D) Some cables are coiled around a pole.

1. (A) 他們正在戴頭盔。
(B) 他們正經過一輛腳踏車。
(C) 他們正在橋上集合。
(D) 他們正在水邊騎車。

2. (A) 女子正在買麵包。
(B) 女子戴著手套。
(C) 女子正端著托盤。
(D) 女子正打開容器。

3. (A) 一些人正在操作機器。
(B) 一些人正成排站著。
(C) 一名男子正對著一群人講話。
(D) 女子正在檢查她的工具。

4. (A) 音樂家正在舞台上表演。
(B) 陳列著一些樂器。
(C) 一些譜架被架好。
(D) 一把吉他正被調音。

5. (A) 一棵植物擋在門口。
(B) 一把梯子靠著架子。
(C) 書堆放在地上。
(D) 正掛起一張裝在相框裡的照片。

6. (A) 工作站靠一些燈照亮。
(B) 書桌排成一個圓。
(C) 電腦被拆開。
(D) 一些電纜捲在一根柱子上。

PART 2　P. 230　　　　　　　　　　🎧 22

7. Where is the bus station located?
(A) It departs at six o'clock.
(B) Downtown across from the arena.*
(C) We bought tickets today.

8. I think the new manager is very nice, don't you?
(A) I can't meet him this afternoon.
(B) No, they hired him last month.
(C) Yes, he tells great jokes.*

7. 公車站位在哪裡？
(A) 它六點出發。
(B) 市區的體育場對面。
(C) 我們今天買了票。

8. 我覺得新來的經理很親切，你不覺得嗎？
(A) 我今天下午見不到他。
(B) 不，他們上個月僱用了他。
(C) 是啊，他很會講笑話。

9. Didn't we receive the new shipment on June 1?
(A) **No, there's been a delay.***
(B) To inspect the new merchandise.
(C) You should have canceled it by now.

10. Where can I post this notice about the lecture?
(A) No, I didn't notice the change.
(B) **Give it to the receptionist.***
(C) The lecturer has not replied yet.

11. Why is the office so cold this morning?
(A) Have you seen the movie yet?
(B) **They're repairing the furnace.***
(C) Another room, please.

12. The CEO will arrive on September 10, right?
(A) Yes, that's the deadline.
(B) **No, she rescheduled her trip.***
(C) I went there two days ago.

13. The window in the conference room is broken.
(A) **I'll notify maintenance.***
(B) An international conference.
(C) I will open the door for you.

14. When does the modern art exhibit begin?
(A) Over twenty famous artists.
(B) No, I don't enjoy galleries.
(C) **The show kicks off this weekend.***

15. Can you tell me who the project leader will be?
(A) **Barry MacDonald.***
(B) Beside Jacob's office.
(C) He suggested it in the meeting.

16. Can you bring the report to the budget meeting tomorrow morning?
(A) It starts at ten o'clock every day.
(B) **I'm off all day tomorrow.***
(C) We just finished the presentation.

17. Which company takes care of the shipping?
(A) Within two to five days.
(B) **The one located in Chicago.***
(C) No, they won't sail today.

9. 我們不是 6 月 1 日收到新來的貨了嗎?
(A) **不,延後了。**
(B) 為了檢查新商品。
(C) 你在這之前就該取消了。

10. 我可以把這張演講的告示貼在哪裡?
(A) 不,我沒有注意到改變。
(B) **把它交給櫃檯人員。**
(C) 演講者還沒有回覆。

11. 辦公室今天早上為什麼這麼冷?
(A) 你看過電影了嗎?
(B) **他們正在修暖氣。**
(C) 另一個房間,謝謝。

12. 執行長會在 9 月 10 日抵達,對吧?
(A) 是的,那是截止日期。
(B) **不,她更改了旅程的時間。**
(C) 我兩天前去過那裡。

13. 會議室的窗戶破了。
(A) **我會通知維修人員。**
(B) 一場國際會議。
(C) 我會幫你開門。

14. 當代藝術展何時開始?
(A) 超過 20 位知名藝術家。
(B) 不,我不喜歡藝廊。
(C) **展覽本週末開始。**

15. 你可以告訴我,專案主持人是誰嗎?
(A) **貝瑞·麥唐諾德。**
(B) 在雅各的辦公室旁邊。
(C) 他在會議上提出的。

16. 明天早上的預算會議,你可以把報告帶來嗎?
(A) 每天十點開始。
(B) **我明天休假。**
(C) 我們剛結束演講。

17. 哪一家公司負責運送?
(A) 二到五天之內。
(B) **位在芝加哥的公司。**
(C) 不,他們今天不開船。

18. Doesn't the manager usually arrive by nine o'clock?

    (A) It usually finishes quickly.

    (B) Unfortunately, he doesn't have any.

    (C) Yes, but he's meeting with clients.*

19. Should we drive to the restaurant or take the subway?

    (A) A new train schedule.

    (B) It's just across the street.*

    (C) I'll give you a new invoice.

20. Do you know what Dr. Pike said about the research results?

    (A) He hasn't reviewed them yet.*

    (B) At least three more tests.

    (C) During the medical conference.

21. How frequently do you take a vacation?

    (A) First Class seats, please.

    (B) Once or twice a year.*

    (C) Yes, she's already left.

22. Will you apply for a new job or take some more classes?

    (A) He will graduate in the fall.

    (B) My updated résumé.

    (C) I have an interview next week.*

23. Why did the packages arrive so damaged?

    (A) He will reimburse the costs.

    (B) There was heavy rain.*

    (C) A new delivery company.

24. Maybe you could print the graphs in color this time.

    (A) That would be better.*

    (B) The computer is new.

    (C) It's too big for the copy room.

25. Where should we hold the awards dinner?

    (A) Beef and vegetables.

    (B) He is the HR manager.

    (C) We should check the budget first.*

26. Would you mind sending me a copy of your report?

    (A) How much paper is left over?

    (B) Oh, I just turned off my computer.*

    (C) They sent the receipt to my office.

---

18. 經理不是通常九點會到嗎？

    (A) 通常很快就完成。

    (B) 不巧，他一個都沒有。

    (C) 是的，但他正在見客戶。

19. 我們應該開車去餐廳還是搭地鐵去？

    (A) 一張新的火車時刻表。

    (B) 餐廳就在街道對面。

    (C) 我會開張新的發票給你。

20. 你知不知道，關於研究結果，派克博士怎麼說？

    (A) 他還沒看過。

    (B) 至少還要檢驗三次。

    (C) 在醫學研討會時。

21. 你多久會度假一次？

    (A) 頭等艙，謝謝。

    (B) 一年一到兩次。

    (C) 是的，她已經離開了。

22. 你會應徵新工作還是再多修一些課？

    (A) 他今年秋天畢業。

    (B) 我更新過的履歷表。

    (C) 我下星期有個面試。

23. 包裹送來時，為何受損這麼嚴重？

    (A) 他會退還費用。

    (B) 之前下大雨。

    (C) 一家新的貨運公司。

24. 也許這一次，你可以把圖表印成彩色的。

    (A) 那會好很多。

    (B) 電腦是新的。

    (C) 太大，放不進影印室。

25. 我們應該在哪裡舉行頒獎晚宴？

    (A) 牛肉與蔬菜。

    (B) 他是人資部經理。

    (C) 我們應該先核對預算。

26. 寄一份你的報告給我，好嗎？

    (A) 還剩多少紙？

    (B) 噢，我剛剛關了電腦。

    (C) 他們把收據寄到我的辦公室。

27. Was the client pleased with the photos we took?

    (A) On the company website.

    (B) I haven't spoken to her.*

    (C) A new set of cameras.

28. Who is checking the financial figures?

    (A) Early next Monday morning.

    (B) At least three charts, I'm sure.

    (C) All of the team members, actually.*

29. Did you attend the ice sculpture show downtown?

    (A) They're still in the museum.

    (B) I don't really enjoy the cold.*

    (C) What time will you go?

30. Can you help me with this new software?

    (A) How long have we been waiting for it?

    (B) The program is called "Easy Accounting."

    (C) Bill was the one who installed it.*

31. Do you think these sausages have gone bad?

    (A) Check the date on the package.*

    (B) From the butcher next door.

    (C) I prefer bacon and eggs.

---

27. 客戶對我們拍的照片滿意嗎？

    (A) 在公司的網站上。

    (B) 我還沒機會和她說話。

    (C) 一組新相機。

28. 誰在核對財務數字？

    (A) 下星期一一大早。

    (B) 我確定，至少有三張圖表。

    (C) 實際上是整個團隊。

29. 你參觀過市區的冰雕展了嗎？

    (A) 他們還在博物館裡。

    (B) 我不是很喜歡寒冷。

    (C) 你何時要去？

30. 你可以幫我看這個新軟體嗎？

    (A) 我們已經等多久了？

    (B) 這個軟體叫「輕鬆搞定會計」。

    (C) 那是比爾安裝的。

31. 你覺得，這些香腸已經壞了嗎？

    (A) 查看包裝上的日期。

    (B) 向隔壁的肉販買的。

    (C) 我比較喜歡培根和蛋。

PART 3   P. 231–235

Questions 32–34 對話

M Hi, **³² I got an e-mail about a big sale happening at this outlet this week.** The sale starts today, right? Does it apply to the leather winter jackets?

W Yes, of course. Everything in the store is 50% off the tag price. **³³ Did you bring the coupon included in the e-mail for an additional 10% off for members?**

M No, my home printer ran out of ink. **³⁴ I'll print it at the office and then come back in the evening.** I'm hoping to get all my winter clothes shopping done today.

男 嗨，**³² 我收到一封電子郵件，說這家暢貨中心本週有大拍賣。**拍賣是從今天開始，對嗎？包含冬季的皮外套嗎？

女 是的，當然。店裡所有商品，都照標價打對折。**³³ 您帶了電子郵件所附的優惠券嗎？會員憑券可以再打九折。**

男 沒有，我家裡的印表機沒有墨水了。**³⁴ 我會到辦公室列印，傍晚再帶過來。**我希望今天可以把冬裝買齊。

---

32. Why did the man choose to shop at the store?

    (A) The store is next to his home.

    (B) He received an e-mail notification.*

    (C) His friend recommended the store.

    (D) The store's selection is very large.

32. 男子為何選擇到這家店購物？

    (A) 這家店在他家隔壁。

    (B) 他收到電子郵件發送的通知。

    (C) 他的朋友推薦這家店。

    (D) 這家店的選擇非常多元。

33. What does the woman ask for?
    (A) A credit card number
    (B) A purchase receipt
    (C) A membership card
    (D) A discount voucher*

34. Why does the man say he will return at a later time?
    (A) He left his wallet at the office.
    (B) He wants to bring his wife.
    (C) He needs to print something.*
    (D) He has an urgent meeting.

Questions 35–37 對話

W Hi, Mr. Witz. **35 I'm wondering if these blankets can be dry-cleaned.** I spilled grape juice on them and I'm afraid I won't be able to remove the stains myself.

M It shouldn't be too hard to get them out. They'll be ready for pick up on Friday. Oh, and the dress you dropped off yesterday will be done that day as well.

W I see. Actually, **36 I was planning on wearing that dress to a work dinner on Wednesday.** Is it possible you could have it cleaned by then?

M That's perfectly fine. **37 I'll have the staff get to work on it today, so you can pick it up Wednesday morning.**

35. Where is this conversation most likely taking place?
    (A) At a fabric store
    (B) At a supermarket
    (C) At a restaurant
    (D) At a dry cleaner*

36. What is the woman doing on Wednesday?
    (A) Traveling out of town
    (B) Attending a company event*
    (C) Making a presentation
    (D) Going to a conference

37. What does the man offer to do?
    (A) Refund a service
    (B) Replace an item
    (C) Rush an order*
    (D) Rent out a garment

33. 女子要求何物？
    (A) 信用卡卡號。
    (B) 購物收據。
    (C) 會員卡。
    (D) 折扣優惠券。

34. 男子為何說他稍晚再來？
    (A) 他把皮夾留在辦公室沒帶。
    (B) 他想帶他太太來。
    (C) 他需要列印東西。
    (D) 他有緊急會議要開。

女 嗨，魏茲先生。**35 我不知道這些毯子能不能乾洗。** 我把葡萄汁灑在上面了，我擔心光靠自己沒辦法把汙漬去掉。

男 要去除汙漬應該不會太難。毯子星期五就可以來拿。喔，還有，您昨天送來的洋裝，那天也會洗好。

女 了解。其實 **36 我原本打算星期三要穿那件洋裝去應酬晚餐。** 你有可能在那之前把它洗好嗎？

男 完全沒問題。**37 我會請員工今天就做，** 這樣您星期三早上就可以來拿。

35. 這段對話最可能發生在哪裡？
    (A) 布料行。
    (B) 超級市場。
    (C) 餐廳。
    (D) 乾洗店。

36. 女子星期三有何事？
    (A) 出城去外地。
    (B) 參加公司的活動。
    (C) 做簡報。
    (D) 去研討會。

37. 男子提議何事？
    (A) 退還某項服務的費用。
    (B) 更換一項物品。
    (C) 趕一個訂單。
    (D) 出租一件衣服。

Questions 38–40 對話

M	Hello, this is Mark calling from Direct Car Rentals. **38 My coworker and I are scheduled to come to your workplace to pick up the car you rented.** However, we're running late, because traffic is really bad. We won't get there until after 7 P.M.
W	Okay, thanks for notifying me. I usually leave at 6:30, but **39 I can leave the keys with the security guard.**
M	That sounds great. **40 I also have your updated membership forms** I was going to give you. Should I give them to the security guard?
W	You can just slip them into my mailbox next to the entrance. It's box number 101A.

男	哈囉,我是汽車直租公司的馬克。**38 我和同事排定要到貴公司取回您租的車。**不過,因為交通狀況實在很糟,我們會晚一點到。晚上七點以後才會到。
女	好,謝謝你通知我。我通常六點半下班,不過,**39 我可以把鑰匙留給警衛。**
男	聽起來很不錯。**40 我還帶了您最新的會員表**要給您。我該交給警衛嗎?
女	你可以直接把它投進我的信箱,就在入口旁邊,號碼是 101A。

38. Why will the man visit the woman's office?
(A) To deliver an invoice
(B) To apply for a job
(C) To install some equipment
(D) To pick up a vehicle*

39. What does the woman say she will do?
(A) Wait for a worker to arrive
(B) Give a key to an employee*
(C) Pay for a service online
(D) Use a discount coupon

40. What does the woman ask the man to put in her mailbox?
(A) Some client paperwork*
(B) A tax receipt
(C) A user's manual
(D) Some promotional vouchers

38. 男子為何造訪女子的辦公室?
(A) 為了送一張發票。
(B) 為了應徵工作。
(C) 為了安裝某個設備。
(D) 為了取一輛車。

39. 女子說她會做何事?
(A) 等一位同事到來。
(B) 把鑰匙交給一位員工。
(C) 在線上支付服務費用。
(D) 使用折扣優惠券。

40. 女子要求男子把什麼放進她的信箱?
(A) 一些客戶文件。
(B) 稅賦憑證。
(C) 使用手冊。
(D) 一些優惠券。

Questions 41–43 三人對話

M1	Hello, welcome to Paper and Things. What can I do for you today?
W	Hi, **41 I can't seem to find any folders.** I'm looking for some plastic A4 size folders that will hold a few sheets of paper. I'm preparing some training materials for my new interns.
M1	Well, I'm sure we sell those, but they might be out of stock. I'll ask my coworker. Hey, Tim! **42 Do we have clear A4 size folders in stock?**
M2	Yeah, but **42 they're in boxes in the stock room.** I can go get you some. How many do you need?
W	Fifteen. Also, do you know if there's a print shop nearby? I'd like to get these training booklets printed today.
M2	**43 We run a print shop here as well.** Just head to the back of the store after I give you your folders and place your order at the counter.
W	How convenient. Thank you.

男 1	哈囉，歡迎光臨「紙與用品」。您今天需要什麼服務？
女	嗨，**41 我似乎找不到任何資料夾**。我在找 A4 大小的塑膠資料夾，可以裝好幾張紙的那種。我在準備訓練教材給新來的實習生。
男 1	嗯，我確定我們有賣，但可能缺貨。我問一下同事。嘿，提姆！**42 我們的透明 A4 大小資料夾還有嗎？**
男 2	有，但是 **42 在倉庫的箱子裡**。我可以去幫你拿一些。你需要多少？
女	15 個。還有，你知道附近有沒有影印店嗎？我想要今天就把這些訓練手冊印出來。
男 2	**43 我們這裡也有影印服務**。等我把資料夾給您後，您只要走到店後方，把訂單放在櫃台上就可以。
女	真方便，謝謝你。

41. What is the woman shopping for?
(A) Books
(B) Printer ink
(C) Paper
(D) Folders*

41. 女子要買什麼？
(A) 書。
(B) 印表機墨水。
(C) 紙。
(D) 資料夾。

42. What does Tim say about some items?
(A) They are still in storage.*
(B) They are out of stock.
(C) They are available at another store.
(D) They are currently on sale.

42. 關於某些物品，提姆說了什麼？
(A) 它們仍有存貨。
(B) 它們缺貨。
(C) 另一家店還有。
(D) 它們目前在促銷。

43. What additional service does Tim mention?
(A) Free shipping
(B) In-store printing*
(C) Discounted membership
(D) Free book binding

43. 提姆提到什麼額外的服務？
(A) 免費運送。
(B) 店內列印。
(C) 會費打折。
(D) 書籍免費裝訂。

W	I just got a call from the Birch Hotel. **44 We booked their banquet room for our upcoming fundraiser,** but **45 it seems the room has some electrical problems that cannot be fixed in time.** Unfortunately, we won't be able to hold the event there.
M	Really? That's too bad. Well, we should try to find an alternate location as soon as possible. The invitations are going to be printed early next week.
W	Can you research some possible locations and call them about prices and availability?
M	Actually, I think I have the perfect place—the new Fort Albert Hotel downtown. It's a brand new hotel and the architecture is stunning. Plus, it has multiple banquet rooms, so there will probably be something available when we need it. **46 I'll look up the number now.**

女	我剛接到樺木飯店打來的電話。**44** 我們訂了他們的宴會廳來舉辦即將到來的募款活動，但 **45** 宴會廳的電路似乎出了問題，無法及時修好。很不幸，我們無法在那裡舉行活動。
男	真的嗎？真是太糟糕了。這樣的話，我們應該盡快找到替換的地點。邀請函下星期初就會印好。
女	你可不可以研究一下可能的地點，然後打電話問價格和是否接受預訂？
男	其實，我想，有個理想的地點——市區新開的艾伯特堡飯店。那是間全新的飯店，建築樣式迷人至極。不只如此，它有好幾間宴會廳，因此，在我們需要的時段，可能還有空房間。**46** 我現在查電話號碼。

44. What are the speakers organizing?

(A) A company trip

(B) A holiday event

(C) An awards dinner

(D) A fundraiser*

44. 說話者在籌備何事？

(A) 公司旅遊。

(B) 假期的活動。

(C) 頒獎晚宴。

(D) 募款活動。

45. What problem does the woman mention?

(A) A hotel is in need of repair.*

(B) A reservation was lost.

(C) Some invitations were misplaced.

(D) Some customers complained.

45. 女子提及什麼問題？

(A) 飯店需要整修。

(B) 預訂資料遺失。

(C) 有些邀請函放錯地方。

(D) 有些顧客抱怨。

46. What most likely will the man do next?

(A) Cancel an event

(B) Visit a hotel

(C) Find a contact number*

(D) Make a reservation

46. 男子接下來最可能做何事？

(A) 取消一個活動。

(B) 造訪一家飯店。

(C) 找到聯絡電話號碼。

(D) 預訂。

W	Hi, Pierre. Have you checked out the new timetable for next month? **47 I put you on the schedule to teach two sculpture classes in the afternoon.**
M	Oh, hmmm. Do these classes need to be back-to-back?
W	Why? Will that be a problem?
M	Well, sculpture classes can be quite messy. It takes about 15 to 20 minutes to clean up after, but with only a five-minute break, it would probably be impossible.
W	Ah. **48 I see your point. 49 What if we hold the next class in another room?** We have two more classrooms available at that time.

女	嗨，畢耶。你看過下個月的新課表了嗎？ **47 我幫你排了兩堂下午的雕塑課。**
男	噢，嗯……這些課必須連著上嗎？
女	怎麼了？會有問題嗎？
男	嗯，雕塑教室可能會弄得很亂。下課後，要花將近 15 到 20 分鐘清理，但下課時間只有五分鐘，很可能無法清理完畢。
女	啊，**48 我懂你的意思。49 如果我們把第二堂課換到另一間教室呢？** 那個時段，我們還有兩間教室空著。

47. Where most likely do the speakers work?
- (A) A dance academy
- **(B) An art school***
- (C) A paint supply shop
- (D) A restaurant

47. 說話者最可能在哪裡工作？
- (A) 舞團。
- **(B) 藝術學校。**
- (C) 美術用品店。
- (D) 餐廳。

48. What does the woman imply when she says, "Will that be a problem"?
- (A) She disagrees with the man's statement.
- (B) She does not want to edit a schedule.
- **(C) She wants to know what she has overlooked.***
- (D) She is eager to take the man's class.

48. 當女子說「會有問題嗎」，意指什麼？
- (A) 她不同意男子的說法。
- (B) 她不想修訂課表。
- **(C) 她想知道哪裡疏忽了。**
- (D) 她渴望接男子的課。

49. What does the woman offer to do?
- **(A) Change a classroom***
- (B) Hire a cleaner
- (C) Recruit some students
- (D) Pay for art supplies

49. 女子提議做什麼？
- **(A) 換教室。**
- (B) 僱一個清潔工。
- (C) 招收一些學生。
- (D) 付錢買美術用品。

Questions 50–52 對話

W Maxwell, **50 I need the results of the e-survey we conducted for the marketing presentation next Monday.** Have you downloaded all the results yet?

M I'm having trouble getting them. **51 The survey company website is down.** I'm waiting for a call back from them. When do you need the results by?

W By tomorrow morning at the latest. **52 I have to print a report of the figures on Friday,** so I'd like to get all the design work done by Thursday night.

50. What are the speakers discussing?
- **(A) Preparing for a presentation***
- (B) Building a new website
- (C) Submitting a budget review
- (D) Hiring a new advertiser

51. Why was the man unable to complete a task?
- (A) A meeting lasted all day.
- **(B) A website was not working.***
- (C) Some files went missing.
- (D) Some fees were not paid.

52. What does the woman say she will do on Friday?
- (A) Meet with a client
- (B) Give a presentation
- (C) Design a brochure
- **(D) Print a document***

Questions 53–55 三人對話

M1 Hello, I'm Mitch Holland. I called yesterday about a repair quote for the damage done to my vehicle. **53 I need it to file my insurance claim.**

W Okay, sure. Who did you speak with yesterday?

M1 The mechanic's name was Kevin Rogers.

W Okay, yes, **54 I think Kevin completed the quote yesterday.** Just a moment. Kevin?

M2 Yes, what is it?

W Did you finish the quote for Mr. Holland? I can't seem to find it.

M2 Yes, it's on your computer. **55 I just need you to print it out.**

W No problem.

女 麥斯威爾，**50 我需要我們線上調查的結果，下星期一的簡報要用。**你下載所有結果了嗎？

男 我下載時遇到困難。**51 民調公司的網站掛點。**我在等他們回我電話。你什麼時間以前需要這些結果？

女 最晚明天早上。**52 我必須在星期五印出一份這些數字的報告，**所以，我希望所有的版面設計在星期四晚上之前完成。

50. 說話者在討論何事？
- **(A) 準備簡報。**
- (B) 建立新的網站。
- (C) 提出預算審核。
- (D) 僱請新的廣告公司。

51. 男子為何無法完成任務？
- (A) 會議開了一整天。
- **(B) 網站無法運作。**
- (C) 有些檔案遺失了。
- (D) 有些費用未付。

52. 女子說，她星期五要做何事？
- (A) 和客戶見面。
- (B) 發表簡報。
- (C) 設計宣傳手冊。
- **(D) 列印文件。**

男1 哈囉，我是米契·霍蘭德。我昨天打過電話來要我車子受損修理費的報價。**53 我需要報價單申請保險理賠。**

女 好的，當然。您昨天和誰通電話？

男1 技工的名字是凱文·羅傑斯。

女 好，有的，**54 我想凱文昨天就完成報價了。**請稍等一下。凱文？

男2 是，有什麼事？

女 你完成霍蘭德先生的報價單了嗎？我似乎找不到。

男2 有，在妳的電腦裡。**55 只是需要妳把它印出來。**

女 沒問題。

53. What is Mr. Holland planning to do?

    (A) Purchase a new car

    (B) Make an insurance claim*

    (C) Apply for a license

    (D) Rent a vehicle

54. According to the conversation, what did Kevin do yesterday?

    (A) He had a car towed.

    (B) He ordered some new parts.

    (C) He prepared a price quote.*

    (D) He witnessed a car accident.

55. What does Kevin ask the woman to do?

    (A) Process a payment

    (B) Call an insurance company

    (C) Fill out a form

    (D) Print a document*

53. 霍蘭德先生計劃做何事？

    (A) 買一輛新車。

    (B) 申請保險理賠。

    (C) 申請執照。

    (D) 租一輛車。

54. 根據這段對話，凱文昨天做了何事？

    (A) 他叫人來把車拖走。

    (B) 他訂購了一些新零件。

    (C) 他做了一份報價單。

    (D) 他目擊一場車輛。

55. 凱文要求女子何事？

    (A) 處理一筆款項。

    (B) 打電話給保險公司。

    (C) 填寫一份表格。

    (D) 列印一份文件。

Questions 56–58 對話

M Hi, I purchased some new boots from your online store on December 2 during your half-price event. **⁵⁶ I just got them now, but the invoice says I was charged full price.**	**男** 嗨，我在 12 月 2 日半價活動期間，在你們的網路商店買了幾雙新靴子。**⁵⁶ 我現在剛收到貨，但發票上說，要收我全額。**
W I'm sorry to hear that. **⁵⁷ It seems there was an error on our website that day.** Several customers reported the same problem.	**女** 很遺憾聽到這事。**⁵⁷ 看來好像那天我們的網站出了錯。**好幾位顧客都遇到同樣的問題。
M Oh, that's too bad.	**男** 喔，那太糟了。
W Yes, we're planning to refund the extra cost, but since I have you on the line, I can do that directly right now.	**女** 是啊，我們打算退回多收的費用，但既然您在線上，我可以現在直接幫您處理。
M I'd appreciate that. Thank you.	**男** 太感謝了。
W You're welcome. **⁵⁸ I also noticed your membership is about to expire. Would you like to renew it now?**	**女** 不客氣。**⁵⁸ 我還注意到，您的會員資格快到期了。您要現在更新嗎？**
M Sure. That's a good idea.	**男** 當然，真是個好主意。

56. Why is the man calling?

    (A) He received the wrong order.

    (B) He wants to return an item.

    (C) He would like to visit the store.

    (D) He was charged too much for an item.*

56. 男子為何打這通電話？

    (A) 他收到的貨品是錯的。

    (B) 他想退一件貨品。

    (C) 他想造訪這家店。

    (D) 他有件貨品被收了太多費用。

57. What does the woman explain?

(A) **A technical malfunction***

(B) A discount policy

(C) A delivery failure

(D) A change in supplier

58. What does the woman ask the man to do?

(A) Send an order back

(B) Locate an invoice

(C) **Renew a membership***

(D) Describe an item

Questions 59–61 對話

W　Hi, Max. This is Tracy. **59 I'm downstairs trying to park in the parking garage, but I forgot my pass in my office last night, so I can't open the gates to get in.**

M　Oh, sorry to hear that. Can you ask the parking attendant to let you in?

W　He's not at his desk right now. I've been waiting for ten minutes but he hasn't come back. **60 Would you be able to bring my pass down to me?** It's on my desk next to my computer.

M　I'm just heading into a meeting. **61 I'll send Patty down with your pass in just a moment.**

W　Okay, thanks for your help!

59. Where most likely is the woman?

(A) **At a parking entrance***

(B) On a bus

(C) In an office

(D) In a stairwell

60. What does the woman ask the man to do?

(A) Call the parking attendant

(B) **Deliver a parking pass***

(C) Cancel a meeting

(D) Recommend a venue

61. Why does the man say, "I'm just heading into a meeting"?

(A) To acknowledge a problem

(B) To ask for permission

(C) To suggest an option

(D) **To decline a request***

---

57. 女子作何解釋？

(A) **技術性故障。**

(B) 折扣政策。

(C) 運送失敗。

(D) 更換供應商。

58. 女子要求男子何事？

(A) 把訂的貨送回去。

(B) 找出發票。

(C) **更新會員資格。**

(D) 描述一項物品。

女　嗨，麥克斯，我是崔西。**59 我在樓下，想把車停進停車場，但我昨天晚上把停車證忘在辦公室沒帶，所以，我沒辦法開啟柵欄進去。**

男　喔，很遺憾聽到這事。妳可以請停車場管理員放妳進去嗎？

女　他現在不在位子上。我已經等了十分鐘，但他還沒回來。**60 你可以把我的停車證拿下來給我嗎？** 在我桌上，電腦的旁邊。

男　我正要去開會。**61 我馬上派佩蒂拿妳的停車證下去。**

女　好的，謝謝你的幫忙！

59. 女子最可能在哪裡？

(A) **在停車場入口。**

(B) 在公車上。

(C) 在辦公室裡。

(D) 在樓梯間。

60. 女子要求男子何事？

(A) 打電話給停車場管理員。

(B) **送停車證來。**

(C) 取消會議。

(D) 推薦一個場地。

61. 男子為何說「我正要去開會」？

(A) 為了承認有問題。

(B) 為了請求許可。

(C) 為了建議一個選項。

(D) **為了拒絕一個請求。**

Questions 62–64 對話及座位表

```
========== Front ==========
        ┌──────────┬──────────┐
        │⁶³ seat 25C│ seat 25D │
  ┌─────┤          │          ├──────────┐
  │Aisle│          │          │  Window  │
  └─────┤ seat 26C │ seat 26D ├──────────┘
        └──────────┴──────────┘
```

```
========== 前面 ==========
        ┌──────────┬──────────┐
        │⁶³ 座位 25C│ 座位 25D │
  ┌─────┤          │          ├──────────┐
  │ 走道│          │          │   窗戶   │
  └─────┤ 座位 26C │ 座位 26D ├──────────┘
        └──────────┴──────────┘
```

W　Excuse me. ⁶² **Sorry, but I think you might be in my seat.** ⁶³ **The flight attendant said I'm in seat C next to the aisle.**

M　Oh, really? I was pretty sure this was my seat. ⁶² **Let's compare our boarding passes.** Oh . . . I see the mistake. ⁶³ **I should be in seat 26C.** Sorry about that. I'll move to the back now.

W　Oh, that's okay. If you'd like to sit here, I could take your seat. Actually, my friend will be sitting in that row, so it would be better for us to sit together during the flight.

M　Okay, that sounds good.

W　Great, thanks. ⁶⁴ **I'll go let the flight attendant know about the change now.**

女　不好意思，⁶² 抱歉打擾了，但我想你可能坐到我的位子了。⁶³ 空服員說，我的位子是靠走道的 C。

男　噢，真的嗎？我很確定，這是我的位子。⁶² 那我們來比對一下各自的登機證。噢，我發現問題出在哪了。⁶³ 我應該坐 26C。抱歉，我現在就移到後面那排。

女　噢，沒關係。如果你想坐這裡，我可以坐你的位子。其實，我朋友會坐在那一排，所以，飛航途中，我們坐在一起會更好。

男　好的，聽起來不錯。

女　太好了，謝謝。⁶⁴ 我去告訴空服員換位子的事。

62. What is the purpose of the conversation?
   (A) To determine a cost
   (B) To request a service
   (C) To correct a mistake*
   (D) To explain a process

62. 這段對話的目的為何？
   (A) 決定費用。
   (B) 要求服務。
   (C) 改正錯誤。
   (D) 解釋流程。

63. Look at the graphic. Which seat was the woman originally assigned to?
   (A) 25C*
   (B) 25D
   (C) 26C
   (D) 26D

63. 請見圖表。女子原先分配到的是哪個位子？
   (A) 25C。
   (B) 25D。
   (C) 26C。
   (D) 26D。

64. What will the woman most likely do next?
   (A) File a complaint with the airline
   (B) Report a change to the flight staff*
   (C) Get off the plane
   (D) Request a vegetarian meal

64. 女子接下來最可能做何事？
   (A) 向航空公司申訴。
   (B) 向機組人員報告換位子一事。
   (C) 下飛機。
   (D) 要求素食餐。

Questions 65–67 對話及時程表

Stage	Project Type
1	In-ground swimming pool installation
2	**66 Backyard landscaping and gardens**
3	Veranda reconstruction (front and back)
4	Final roof repairs

階段	工程類型
1	地面泳池裝設
2	**66 後院造景與園藝**
3	陽臺重建（前、後）
4	最後的屋頂修補

W Hello, Andrew. **65 How is the construction on the Park Road house coming along?**

M Very well. The house interior is in great condition, so we've been able to start on the exterior improvements right away.

W That's good to hear. I'm thinking of listing it for sale at the end of May. A lot of people will be looking for new homes at that time. Do you think your team can finish up by then?

M Let's have a look at the schedule. Well, we've managed to complete the in-ground pool and **66 we're going to start the backyard landscaping in a couple days.** I think we'll be able to put the finishing touches on everything else by mid-May.

W That's great. **67 Just make sure to record all your labor hours for our cost analysis.** That way, we can determine the price of the home in May.

女 哈囉，安德魯。**65 公園路的房屋工程進展如何？**

男 很順利。屋內的裝潢還很好，所以，我們可以立刻進行外部改善工程。

女 很高興聽到這個消息。我正考慮在五月底把它列入出售名單。到時候會有很多人在找房子。你覺得你的團隊可以在那之前完成嗎？

男 來看一下進度表。嗯，我們已設法完成地面泳池，**66 過幾天要開始後院造景工程。**我想我們可以在五月中以前，完成其他部分的收尾工作。

女 太好了。**67 你要確定記錄下你們所有的工時，以便我們進行成本分析。**那樣的話，我們五月可以決定房價。

65. What most likely is the man's profession?
   (A) Interior decorator
   (B) Delivery man
   (C) Real estate agent
   (D) Contractor*

66. Look at the graphic. What stage of the improvements will begin in a couple days?
   (A) Stage 1
   (B) Stage 2*
   (C) Stage 3
   (D) Stage 4

67. What does the woman ask the man to keep?
   (A) Receipts of all costs
   (B) A list of available homes
   (C) A record of time worked*
   (D) Photos of his progress

65. 男子的職業最可能為何？
   (A) 室內裝潢人員。
   (B) 送貨員。
   (C) 不動產經紀人。
   (D) 承包商。

66. 請見圖表。幾天內會開始哪個階段的改善工程？
   (A) 階段 1。
   (B) 階段 2。
   (C) 階段 3。
   (D) 階段 4。

67. 女子要求男子要保留什麼？
   (A) 所有費用的收據。
   (B) 可買到的房子清單。
   (C) 工時紀錄。
   (D) 工程進度的照片。

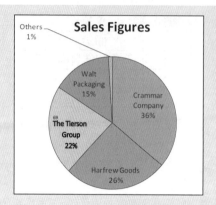

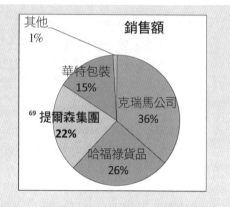

M	Hi, Jane. **⁶⁸ Did you hear the board is thinking of merging with Walt Packaging?** I just got the e-mail report. Have you had a chance to look at it?
W	No, I've been too busy with conference calls. What did the report say?
M	Here, I printed it off. **⁶⁹ We're already the third largest packaging company in the country,** but if we merge with Walt Packaging, that should move us up to first place.
W	Hmm. I'm not sure it would be a smart move, though. **⁷⁰ Walt Packaging's sales figures for last year look pretty low.** They could be even lower this year.
M	Yes, but with our company's policies, I think we could increase their sales and maybe even surpass Crammar Company's figures by next year.

男	嗨，珍。**⁶⁸ 妳有沒有聽說，董事會正考慮併購「華特包裝」？**我剛收到電子郵件寄來的報告。妳看過了嗎？
女	沒有，我忙著開電話會議。報告上說了什麼？
男	這裡，我印出來了。**⁶⁹ 我們已經是國內第三大包裝公司，**但如果我們併購「華特包裝」，會讓我們升到第一名。
女	嗯。不過，我不確定這是不是聰明的一步棋。**⁷⁰「華特包裝」去年的銷售額看起來相當低。**今年甚至可能更低。
男	是的，但有了我們公司的策略，我認為我們可以提升他們的業績，明年甚至有可能超越「克瑞馬公司」的銷售額。

68. What are the speakers mainly discussing?
(A) **A company merger***
(B) A budget report
(C) Department productivity
(D) Hiring a financial analyst

69. Look at the graphic. Where do the speakers work?
(A) Walt Packaging
(B) Harfrew Goods
(C) **The Tierson Group***
(D) Crammar Company

70. Why does the woman say she has doubts?
(A) The man did not understand some figures.
(B) A company was excluded from a report.
(C) Her company is located in another state.
(D) **A company has not made many sales.***

68. 說話者討論的主題為何？
(A) **公司的併購。**
(B) 預算報告。
(C) 部門的產能。
(D) 僱用財務分析師。

69. 請見圖表。說話者在哪裡工作？
(A) 華特包裝。
(B) 哈福祿貨品。
(C) **提爾森集團。**
(D) 克瑞馬公司。

70. 女子為何說她有疑慮？
(A) 男子不了解一些數字。
(B) 報告不包括某家公司。
(C) 她的公司位在另一個州。
(D) **有家公司的銷售額並不高。**

Questions 71–73 廣告

W Do you have an old leather jacket or coat you don't wear anymore? Why not call New Again Leather? **71 We'll arrange to pick up your used leather clothes and recycle them.** When you call, inquire about our Trade-In Program. **72 By signing up for a membership, you can get a discount** on the purchase of recycled clothing items of your choice. **73 For more details or to schedule a pick-up, call 800-555-2222.**	**女** 您有再也不穿的皮夾克或皮外套嗎？何不打電話給「重新皮件」？**71 我們會安排人手去取您的舊皮衣，回收再利用。**當您打電話來，請詢問我們的舊衣換現金活動。**72 註冊加入會員後，您可以在購買所選的二手衣物時，享有折扣優惠。73 更多詳情或安排取件，請電洽800-555-2222。**

71. What service is being advertised?
(A) Dry cleaning
(B) Furniture delivery
(C) A clothing recycling program*
(D) A cooking course

72. How can listeners receive a discount?
(A) By becoming a member*
(B) By ordering two items
(C) By registering online
(D) By entering a contest

73. What does the speaker say is available over the phone?
(A) A customer survey
(B) A list of stores
(C) The best discount
(D) An appointment*

71. 廣告了何種服務？
(A) 乾洗。
(B) 家具運送。
(C) 衣物回收活動。
(D) 烹飪課程。

72. 聽眾要如何獲得折扣優惠？
(A) 成為會員。
(B) 訂購兩件物品。
(C) 在線上註冊。
(D) 參加比賽。

73. 說話者說，透過電話可以取得什麼？
(A) 顧客意見調查。
(B) 商店名單。
(C) 最好的折扣。
(D) 預約。

Questions 74-76 宣告

M   **⁷⁴ Attention all travelers.** The 4 P.M. bus to St. Ellen has been canceled due to heavy snow fall. We apologize for this inconvenience and urge you to go to ticket booth 2 to get a refund for your ticket. **⁷⁵ Those who are traveling to St. Ellen are encouraged to purchase a ticket for the 6 P.M. train instead.** While you're waiting for the train, **⁷⁶ please visit Coffee Madness for a free beverage and Wi-Fi access.** Again, we're very sorry for the delays and thank you for visiting **⁷⁴ Central Bus and Train Station.**

男   **⁷⁴ 各位旅客請注意**。由於下大雪，下午四點開往聖艾倫的巴士已取消。造成您的不便，敬請見諒，並請您盡速前往2 號票口辦理退票。**⁷⁵ 欲前往聖艾倫的旅客，建議您改買六點的火車票。** 在您等候火車時，**⁷⁶ 請到瘋咖啡享用免費飲料及 Wi-Fi 上網。** 我們再次為造成延誤致上歉意，並感謝您造訪 **⁷⁴ 中央巴士暨火車站。**

74. Where is the announcement being made?
  (A) At a city hall
  (B) At a shopping mall
  (C) At a transit station*
  (D) At a concert venue

74. 這個廣播在哪裡發布？
  (A) 市政府。
  (B) 購物商場。
  (C) 轉運站。
  (D) 音樂會會場。

75. What does the speaker ask listeners to do?
  (A) Proceed to a boarding gate
  (B) Keep an original receipt
  (C) Use a bank machine
  (D) Purchase another ticket*

75. 說話者要求聽眾何事？
  (A) 前往登機門。
  (B) 保留原始收據。
  (C) 使用自動提款機。
  (D) 購買另一張車票。

76. According to the speaker, what can customers get at Coffee Madness?
  (A) A train ticket
  (B) A complimentary drink*
  (C) A loaned computer
  (D) An updated bus schedule

76. 根據說話者所述，顧客可以在瘋咖啡得到什麼？
  (A) 一張火車票。
  (B) 一杯免費飲料。
  (C) 一台出租的電腦。
  (D) 一張更新的巴士時刻表。

Questions 77-79 電話留言

W   Hi, Anna. It's Bethany calling. **⁷⁷ Are you able to come to the store this afternoon? ⁷⁸ I think we need to get some of the decorating decisions finalized.** The boss is getting impatient. There are a lot of paint and flooring samples to look through, so **⁷⁹ I'm going to choose the best ones now and bring them to the store.** When we meet, we should see how the samples look in the actual store space. Please call me back. Thank you.

女   嗨，安娜，我是伯達妮。**⁷⁷ 妳今天下午能來店裡嗎？⁷⁸ 我想我們必須對一些裝潢作出最後決定。** 老闆不耐煩了。有好多油漆和地板的樣本要看，所以 **⁷⁹ 我現在會選出些最好的，帶到店裡。** 等我們碰面，我們可以看看這些樣本在實際店面空間裡看起來如何。請回我電話，謝謝妳。

77. What is the purpose of the message?

    (A) To locate some materials

    (B) To request a meeting*

    (C) To hire a designer

    (D) To ask about a product

78. What does the speaker imply when she says, "The boss is getting impatient"?

    (A) Her boss needs to reschedule a project.

    (B) She needs to change some paint colors.

    (C) The designers will start working soon.

    (D) Some selections must be confirmed quickly.*

79. What most likely will the speaker do next?

    (A) Decide on design samples*

    (B) Contact a manager

    (C) Visit a manufacturing site

    (D) Go to a paint supply store

77. 這段留言的目的為何？

    (A) 找出一些材料。

    (B) 要求碰面。

    (C) 僱用一位設計師。

    (D) 詢問一個產品。

78. 當説話者説「老闆不耐煩了」，意指什麼？

    (A) 她的老闆需要重新編排一個專案的時間表。

    (B) 她需要更換一些油漆的顏色。

    (C) 設計師會很快開始工作。

    (D) 有些選擇必須趕快確定。

79. 説話者接下來最可能做何事？

    (A) 選定設計的樣本。

    (B) 聯絡一位經理。

    (C) 拜訪工廠。

    (D) 去油漆行。

Questions 80–82 談話

M Good afternoon, interns. Thanks for coming to this meeting on such short notice. **80 I hope everyone is enjoying their interning experience at Parson Real Estate. 81 Tomorrow is the launch of our new branch office downtown, and I'd like you all to help out with the event.** As you know, we'll be setting up tables outside with brochures about our services. **81 I'd like you to stay at the tables all morning and hand out brochures to people on the street. 82 I've had T-shirts made for you to wear so don't worry about dressing up.** I'll be distributing them at the end of the meeting.	男 午安，各位實習生。謝謝大家一接到通知就趕來參加會議。**80 希望大家在帕爾森不動產的實習都很愉快。81 我們在市區的分公司明天開幕，希望大家都來幫忙這次活動。**你們都知道，我們要在外面擺桌子，放上關於公司業務的小冊子。**81 我希望你們整個早上都留守桌邊，並向路人發放廣告小冊。82 我幫你們訂做了 T 恤穿，所以不用擔心要穿著正式服裝。**會議結束時，我會分發 T 恤。

80. Where do the listeners work?

    (A) At a bank

    (B) At a fashion house

    (C) At a university

    (D) At a real estate agency*

80. 聽者在哪裡工作？

    (A) 銀行。

    (B) 服裝設計公司。

    (C) 大學。

    (D) 不動產仲介公司。

81. What will the listeners be doing tomorrow?
(A) Conducting surveys
(B) Interviewing interns
(C) Distributing pamphlets*
(D) Cleaning up an office

82. What has the speaker done for the listeners?
(A) Prepared uniforms*
(B) Bought some chairs
(C) Shortened a schedule
(D) Paid for a trip

Questions 83–85 會議摘錄

W **83 I'm very pleased to announce that Sampson National Bank will be awarded the Outstanding Community Outreach Award this year.** This is truly a reflection of how much work we've done to improve our local community. I especially want to recognize the work of Mona Ruiz. **84 She arranged the fundraiser we sponsored to rebuild our city's youth club in June** and was responsible for the success of our mentorship program. **85 Because of her work, our bank has doubled its charitable outreach.** I'd like to ask Ms. Ruiz to say a few words now about what she foresees us doing next year.

83. What is the speaker announcing?
(A) Hiring a new employee
(B) A company fundraiser
(C) An upcoming mentorship program
(D) The winning of an award*

84. What did the company sponsor in June?
(A) A sports club
(B) A fundraising event*
(C) A financial convention
(D) A university scholarship

85. What does the speaker say about Mona Ruiz's work?
(A) It improved the company image.
(B) It is outlined on the company's website.
(C) It increased the company's charity work.*
(D) It doubled the number of clients.

---

81. 聽者明天有何事要做？
(A) 進行調查。
(B) 面試實習生。
(C) 分發傳單。*
(D) 打掃辦公室。

82. 說話者為聽者做了何事？
(A) 準備制服。*
(B) 買了些椅子。
(C) 縮短時程表。
(D) 支付旅費。

女 **83** 很高興宣布，山普生國家銀行榮獲今年的傑出社會服務獎。這真實反映出我們為改善本地社區盡了多少心力。我尤其要表彰蒙娜‧露薏絲的工作。**84** 為了我們重建本市青年俱樂部的贊助計畫，她於六月安排了募款活動，而我們的導師計畫之所以成功也要歸功於她。**85** 因為她的工作成果，我們銀行的慈善服務範圍得以加倍擴展。現在，我想邀請露薏絲女士來談談，她預測我們明年要做什麼。

83. 說話者宣布何事？
(A) 僱用一位新員工。
(B) 公司的募款活動。
(C) 即將來臨的導師計畫。
(D) 獲得獎項。*

84. 公司在六月贊助主辦了什麼？
(A) 運動俱樂部。
(B) 募款活動。*
(C) 金融研討會。
(D) 大學獎學金。

85. 關於蒙娜‧露薏絲的工作，說話者說了什麼？
(A) 它改善了公司形象。
(B) 公司的網站概述了內容。
(C) 它增加了公司的慈善工作。*
(D) 它讓客戶人數加倍。

Questions 86–88 談話

M **86 Let's start off the meeting by looking at an analysis of the online reviews for our new outdoor barbeque, the Grill Master 2000.** As I'm sure you know, this barbeque has numerous features, and it seems our customers really love it. Based on the reviews, the aesthetic appeal appears to be the most popular feature. **87 The customers love that they have five colors to choose from,** meaning they can match their barbeque to their lawn furniture. However, our website does not display images of each color. **88 The web designers are going to work on updating the website with that information.**

男 **86 會議一開始，先來看看我們新戶外烤肉爐，「烤肉大師 2000」的線上調查分析。**相信你們都知道，這個烤肉爐有許多特色，而且看起來，我們的顧客真的很喜歡它。根據評論，美學的吸引力似乎是最受歡迎的特色。**87 顧客喜歡有五個顏色可選，**表示他們可以讓烤肉爐和草地上的家具互相搭配。不過，我們的網站並未列出每種顏色的圖片。**88 網頁設計師將會更新網頁，加入這個資訊。**

86. What is the main topic of the meeting?
   (A) Restructuring plans
   (B) A new delivery method
   (C) A product prototype
   (D) Customer feedback*

86. 會議的主題為何？
   (A) 重建計畫。
   (B) 新的運送方式。
   (C) 某個產品的原型。
   (D) 顧客的意見回饋。

87. What feature of the product does the speaker mention?
   (A) Removable grills
   (B) Portability
   (C) Color options*
   (D) Energy efficiency

87. 說話者提到產品的何項特色？
   (A) 可拆卸烤肉架。
   (B) 可攜帶。
   (C) 顏色的選擇。
   (D) 節能。

88. What does the speaker imply when he says, "Our website does not display images of each color"?
   (A) A website should be edited.*
   (B) Images have been removed from a website.
   (C) A photographer needs to be hired.
   (D) Customers mostly chose one color.

88. 當說話者說「我們的網站並未列出每種顏色的圖片」，意指什麼？
   (A) 網站應該修改。
   (B) 圖片已從網站移除。
   (C) 需要僱用攝影師。
   (D) 顧客大部分選某種顏色。

TEST 6

PART 4

24

Questions 89–91 會議摘錄

W Hello, and welcome to our monthly Hamilton Township meeting. ⁸⁹ **I'm sure most of you are aware that we've been trying to persuade state officials to build a new community center downtown.** ⁹⁰ **However, we're still short on signatures from local residents,** and we'd like to plan a few events this summer to raise awareness. The Hamilton Restaurant Alliance has already agreed to host a street party near the waterfront to help us spread the word about the event. I think this will generate a lot of publicity and we'll reach our goal of 50,000 signatures. ⁹¹ **I'd like everyone to schedule to work a shift and distribute flyers at the party.**

女 哈囉，歡迎參加漢彌爾頓鎮的月會。⁸⁹ 相信你們大部分人都知道，我們持續致力於說服州政府官員在市區蓋一座新的社區中心。⁹⁰ 不過，本地居民的簽署人數還不夠，我們想在今年夏天規劃一些活動，喚起大家的注意。漢彌爾頓餐廳聯盟已經同意在靠近碼頭區的地方舉行一場街頭派對，協助我們把關於這個活動的訊息傳播出去。我認為，這會產生很大的宣傳效果，我們會達成五萬個簽名連署的目標。⁹¹ 希望大家可以安排輪班並在派對上發傳單。

89. What is the talk mainly about?
(A) Electing a new town mayor
(B) Planning a city anniversary
(C) Convincing state officials*
(D) Forming a charity group

90. What problem does the speaker mention?
(A) Lack of public support*
(B) A delay in the release of funds
(C) Damaged facilities
(D) Lost signatures

91. What are listeners asked to do?
(A) E-mail state officials
(B) Volunteer at an event*
(C) Sample some food
(D) Contact local media

89. 這段談話的主題是什麼？
(A) 選出新的鎮長。
(B) 籌劃市府週年紀念日。
(C) 說服州政府官員。
(D) 組織慈善團體。

90. 說話者提及什麼問題？
(A) 缺乏公眾支持。
(B) 延後發放專款。
(C) 設備受損。
(D) 簽名遺失。

91. 聽眾被要求做什麼？
(A) 寫電子郵件給州政府官員。
(B) 當活動的義工。
(C) 試吃一些食物。
(D) 聯絡本地媒體。

Questions 92–94 宣告

M Good morning, everyone. Thanks for attending [92] **Parker Hospital**'s administrative new-hire training. We hope you'll have a long career in Parker Hospital's many award-winning medical departments. Today, we'll go over hospital policies and then you'll meet with your department heads for more specific training. We're sure you'll gain a lot of useful information today, but don't worry if you forget something. We'll be handing out employee conduct manuals for you to review when you go home today. Not all seats are full right now, so [93] **we'll wait a few more minutes for the rest of the group to arrive. [94] In the meantime, I'll pass out the handbooks. Please read through the introduction page.**

男 大家早。感謝大家參加 [92] **帕克醫院**的行政新人訓練。我們希望你們在帕克醫院的許多得獎醫學部門都能有長久的職業生涯。我們今天要細看醫院的政策,接著,你們會和所屬部門主管見面,接受更精確的訓練。我們確信,你們今天會獲得許多實用的資訊,如果你忘記了某些內容,也別擔心。在你們今天回家前,我們會分發員工指導手冊讓你們複習。現在,還有座位是空的,所以,[93] **我們再多等幾分鐘,等其他人到來。[94] 在這期間,我會分發手冊。請讀完引言。**

92. What type of business does the speaker work for?
(A) A transit company
(B) A medical facility*
(C) An advertising firm
(D) A pharmacy

92. 說話者在何種行業工作?
(A) 運輸公司。
(B) 醫療機構。
(C) 廣告公司。
(D) 藥局。

93. What does the speaker imply when he says, "Not all seats are full right now"?
(A) Some participants have not arrived.*
(B) The chairs can be rearranged.
(C) The venue will be changed.
(D) The event is not successful.

93. 當說話者說「現在,還有座位是空的」,意指什麼?
(A) 有些參加者還沒到。
(B) 椅子可以重排。
(C) 場地要換。
(D) 活動不成功。

94. What does the speaker ask the listeners to do?
(A) Write down their medical history
(B) Go to their assigned departments
(C) Fill out contact information
(D) Review some materials*

94. 說話者要求聽眾何事?
(A) 寫下他們的病史。
(B) 前往指定部門。
(C) 填寫聯絡資料。
(D) 仔細看一些資料。

Questions 95–97 留言錄音及訂購單

Quantity	Item Description
10	Ballpoint Pens (10 per package)
20	Black toner cartridge
35	Clear plastic A4 file
95 60	**Glossy copy paper (1000 sheets per box)**

數量	品名
10	原子筆（一盒十隻）
20	黑色碳粉
35	A4 透明塑膠資料夾
95 60	光面影印紙（一箱一千張）

W Hi, I'm calling to leave a message for Mike Wentz. I've just reviewed your monthly order, and I wanted to confirm something with you. 95 **It seems you've listed ten times the amount of paper you usually order.** I think it may be a mistake. I'd be happy to correct it for you. 96 **Just call me back and give me the okay, and I'll process your order.** Also, I wanted to let you know that 97 **we're using a new courier** starting next week, but your order should arrive within the same timeframe. 97 **If you have any problems, though, feel free to call Tina in Customer Service.**

女 嗨，我打來留言給麥克・溫茲。我剛看過您的每月訂單，想和您確認一件事。95 您似乎列了平常訂購量十倍的紙張。我想也許是寫錯了。我很樂意為您更正。96 只要回電給我，表示同意，我就會處理您的訂單。此外，我想告訴您，我們從下星期開始換成新的快遞公司，但您訂的貨應該會在同樣的時間送達。97 不過，若您有任何問題，請隨時打給客服部的緹娜。

95. Look at the graphic. Which quantity on the order form will probably be changed?
   (A) 10
   (B) 20
   (C) 35
   (D) 60*

95. 請見圖表。訂單上的哪個數量最可能會修改？
   (A) 10。
   (B) 20。
   (C) 35。
   (D) 60。

96. What will the speaker do before processing the order?
   (A) Wait for a confirmation*
   (B) Give a phone number
   (C) Inspect a package
   (D) Review a product manual

96. 說話者在處理訂單之前會做何事？
   (A) 等候確認。
   (B) 給一個電話號碼。
   (C) 檢查一個包裹。
   (D) 檢閱產品使用手冊。

97. What does the speaker say about Tina?
   (A) She will not be in the office.
   (B) She will deliver some items herself.
   (C) She will take care of shipping problems.*
   (D) She will refund some purchases.

97. 關於緹娜，說話者說了什麼？
   (A) 她不會在辦公室。
   (B) 她會親自送一些物品。
   (C) 她會處理貨運的問題。
   (D) 有些購買的東西，她會退款。

Questions 98–100 宣告及圖表

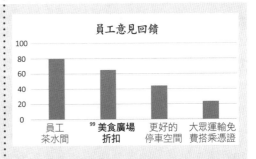

M　Thank you so much for filling out our employee feedback comment cards. **98 At Rodsmart Shopping Center, we value your opinions** and will try to make changes to ensure a happy and productive work environment. Many of you offered suggestions about employee break rooms. I'm sure everyone would love a quiet place to spend their breaks, but unfortunately, we just don't have rooms available for this. **99 However, the second most popular suggestion seems more feasible.** I will be speaking with upper management in the next few days to see if we can get working on that. **100 For participating in this feedback session, you can all collect a mall gift card on your way out.**

男　非常感謝你們填寫員工意見卡。**98 羅德史邁特購物商場重視你們的意見**,並會努力改變以確保有個愉快且具生產力的工作環境。你們許多人都建議設置員工茶水間。我確信每個人都愛安靜的地方休息,但是,很不湊巧,我們沒有空間可用。**99 不過,第二多人提的建議似乎比較可行。**這幾天,我會和管理高層談,看看我們是否能開始進行。**100 因為參與了這次意見反應,你們離開時都可以拿到一張商場的禮物卡。**

98. Where does the talk take place?
(A) At a museum
(B) At a restaurant
(C) At a shopping mall*
(D) At an office

99. Look at the graphic. Which suggestion will the company begin to work on?
(A) Employee break rooms
(B) Food court discounts*
(C) Better parking spaces
(D) Free transit passes

100. What will employees receive for completing comment cards?
(A) A gift card for the mall*
(B) Entrance into a contest
(C) A voucher for a free drink
(D) A new work uniform

98. 這段談話發生在哪裡?
(A) 在博物館。
(B) 在餐廳。
(C) 在購物商場。
(D) 在辦公室。

99. 請見圖表。公司會開始進行哪一項建議?
(A) 員工茶水間。
(B) 美食廣場折扣。
(C) 更好的停車空間。
(D) 大眾運輸免費搭乘憑證。

100. 員工完成意見表會收到什麼?
(A) 商場的禮物卡。
(B) 參加比賽的資格。
(C) 免費飲料券。
(D) 新的員工制服。

◎ PART 5 解答請見 P. 509 ANSWER KEY

101. 東側倉庫裡的架子一定塞**滿**了節慶季節的東西。

102. 游泳池是保留給住在高級套房裡的賓客**使用**的。

103. 隆先生承認**他**被期待能接下更多管理工作。

104. 達維斯維爾企業將於月底**更換**網路供應商。

105. 尤佳城市旅行社以非常實惠的價格,提供史基夫湖**環**湖自行車之旅。

106. 馬頓新款 MR-200 型無疑地是所有的雪胎中最耐用的**輪胎**。

107. 隨著訂單量顯著地增加,勞福咖啡廳得以和供應商**洽談**新協議。

108. 潘朵拉髮型設計提供員工**許多**提升職涯的機會。

109. 格林維爾和崔頓之間的 56 號高速公路,**因為**電線杆倒塌而封閉。

110. 沒有現任房客的**轉介**,是不可能在多切斯特大樓租到公寓的。

111. **只有**在車輛檢查完成後,才會在擋風玻璃上貼上綠色貼紙。

112. 由於兩位主管決定提早退休,**必須**在 7 月 30 日前找到替代人選。

113. **要等到**進一步的通知,大樓南側底部的載貨電梯才能使用。

114. 這個包裹外面所標示的重量**相當**準確。

115. 大衛傳了一個含有**大量**引擎維修資訊的網站連結。

116. 為了找出到西門子、達思茅斯和附近城鎮最便捷的路線,一定要查看**更新後的**地圖。

117. **既然**申請截止日期已過,招聘委員會將開始審視履歷表。

118. 知名藝術評論家葛羅莉亞·汎·辛格爾在她的電視節目裡**分析**許多時期的畫作。

119. 瑞福超市安裝數座自助結帳機,預期將**對**員工數量造成異動。

120. 與其他人相比,唐諾準備房地產證照考試的時間短的**驚人**。

121. 葛利森鞋業的製造部主管,對於工廠所有的運作情況都很**清楚**。

122. 自從港口去年重新開放以來,布雷頓角島的觀光**經濟**明顯地改善了。

123. 藍福建築供應商的人員要求我們**具體說明**工程所需的木材種類。

124. 費茲傑羅航空提供 200 多個**飛遍**北加拿大各處的航班。

125. 賴斯特維爾學院的吉他初級班很快就額滿了,所以我們建議填寫線上**報名**表格。

126. 蘭卡斯特企業新**任命**的副總裁,將於週五向員工發表第一次的談話。

127. 公共關係部的主管必須不斷地與媒體聯絡,所以藍道夫企業**正在尋找**具優秀溝通技巧的人選。

128. 拉波特女士籌劃募款活動的方式**明顯地**與哈洛威女士不同。

129. 最近金斯頓居民人數大幅增加,**其中大多數**是國際學生。

130. 為協助卡林頓旅社的員工讓您的住宿更**愉快**,請填寫賓客回饋表,並留置於櫃台。

Questions 131–134 電子郵件

收件者：sandrabae@gladstoneresearch.com.au
寄件者：markjohnson@sydneyunienergy.au
日期：5 月 15 日
主旨：感謝您！

親愛的貝博士，

非常感謝您上週五造訪我們主要的研究中心。正如以往，我們非常感激您專業的建議。您的演說，關於工業設備能源生產與消耗系統的最新發展，讓我們全體工程團隊獲益良多。今年秋季，本部門打算增聘五位工程研究員。您是否願意主持一個與上週演講主題相關的訓練？如果您方便，那無疑地會對新員工大有幫助。我們期待您能盡快回覆，以便討論相關細節。

馬克‧強生 敬上

131. (A) 打電話
(B) 開設
(C) 拜訪
(D) 成為員工；（為機構）提供人員

132. (A) 感謝，感激
(B) 將被感激
(C) 正在感激
(D) 被感激

133. (A) 他的
(B) 你的東西
(C) 你
(D) 他

134. (A) 所有工程師都必須遵守本中心嚴格的規定。
(B) 許多應徵者有令人印象深刻的履歷。
(C) 如果您方便，那無疑地會對新員工大有幫助。
(D) 有了您的回饋意見，我們將能很快建造起來。

Questions 135–138 文章

基爾瑞（4 月 5 日）—今天上午，國家交通管理局宣布，將提供威斯頓谷航空網 4100 萬的補助金。有了這筆資金，威斯頓谷有兩座機場的夢想很快就可以實現了。該地區許多居民歡迎這個針對現有航空服務的增建消息。這次的開發預計將在兩座機場創造超過 500 個工作機會。整個威斯頓谷的企業主都非常開心。一位當地企業主，珍妮佛‧羅西尼奧今天稍早表達了她對這筆補助金的欣喜之情。「這對像我這樣必須頻繁出差到多倫多的人來說，是個非常棒的消息。」羅西尼奧表示，「多年來，我們毫無選擇，只能忍受四個小時的公車車程進城。但很快地，我就可以在一小時內搭上飛機到那裡了。」

135. **(A) 資金**
(B) 政策
(C) 設計
(D) 策略

136. (A) 威斯頓谷航空網確認這個計畫必須延緩。
(B) 其中一個機場會有更多的停車位供旅客可使用。
(C) 這次的開發預計將在兩座機場創造超過 500 個工作機會。
(D) 但是，大多數的地區性航班票價有可能提高。

137. (A) 同樣地
(B) 另一個
(C) 然後
(D) 的人

138. **(A) 達……時間**
(B) 和……一起
(C) 有關
(D) 在……之上

Questions 139–142 電子郵件

收件者：阿諾·馬洛里
                     <amallory@channel6news.net>
寄件者：米蘭達·卡爾霍恩
                     <mcalhoun@channel6news.net>
回覆：超棒的評論
日期：3 月 21 日

親愛的阿諾，

第六頻道新聞管理部很高興看到《蒙克頓公報》與《上城娛樂》對本節目的精采評論。我們所有人都同意您在此的表現只能用傑出形容。為此，第六頻道新聞很樂意在您下個月 3 月 30 日的薪資中增發一筆年度獎金。此外，您目前的薪資也將自 4 月 1 日起增加百分之 12%。自去年 11 月您接掌頭條新聞主播以來，我們固定收看的觀眾量已經增加三倍。第六頻道也得到了全國各報紙的好評。沒有您卓越的表現，我們無法達到這個成就。謹代表第六頻道新聞的全體同仁，感謝您的辛勤工作與付出。

瑪琳達

139. (A) 孤僻的，沉默寡言的
    (B) 相符的
    (C) 負擔得起的
    (D) 傑出的，優秀的

140. (A) 給予
    (B) 一個獎項
    (C) 它給予
    (D) 它給予

141. (A 例如，舉例來説
    (B) 此外
    (C) 然而，不過
    (D) 另一方面

142. (A) 第六新聞頻道也得到了全國各報紙的好評。
    (B) 下個月某一天將聘用一位助理新聞主播。
    (C) 我們團隊將於下週開會討論為您的節目做些改變。
    (D) 您是其中一位有資格獲得年度獎金的員工。

Questions 143–146 文章

電子產品貿易展

（8 月 25 日）全球電子產品年度貿易展連續第五年來到東京，於 8 月 23 日星期六展開。這場盛會有來自全世界各地超過 500 家公司參與。跟去年一樣，中國是出席最踴躍的國家。再者，主辦單位報告説，參加的南美洲企業數量也較往年明顯提高。今年活動另一項明顯的變化是，大多數公司展示的是廚房電器，而非以往的電子娛樂產品。

143. (A) 活動志工不需付報名費。
    (B) 產品展示將於三個不同的禮堂舉行。
    (C) 這場盛會有來自全世界各地超過 500 家公司參與。
    (D) 招聘人員收取與會的大學生履歷。

144. (A) 沉重的
    (B) 大量地；沉重地
    (C) 更重的
    (D) 沉重

145. (A) 此外
    (B) 取而代之的是
    (C) 取而代之的是
    (D) 因此

146. (A) 課程
    (B) 示範
    (C) 活動
    (D) 典禮

Questions 147–148 通知

147 致親愛的顧客：

我們很高興宣布，自十月起本店將舉辦每週才藝之夜。這個活動將於每週三晚間 6:00 至 8:00 舉行，**147 舞台將設置於本餐館的一樓。**

參加者可唱歌、彈奏樂器或朗誦詩歌。務必提早到場以便報名 20 分鐘的場次。**148 所有參加者於活動期間可免費享用咖啡或茶。**

更多資訊，請上本店網站 www.cafemaria.com 或來電 777-4367。

147. 這則公告最有可能出現在哪裡？
(A) 地鐵站
(B) 音樂書籍
(C) 咖啡館
(D) 醫生診所

148. 根據公告，參加者可獲得什麼？
(A) 優惠折價券
(B) 小額款項
(C) 參賽證明
(D) 免費飲料

Questions 149–150 帳單

東景會議中心
華盛頓州西雅圖湖景路 55 號

日期：	帳單收件者：
4 月 12 日	特麗莎・巴克斯特
帳單編號：	道地機車
9800032	佛羅里達州奧蘭多亞莫街 90 號

6 月 25 日至 6 月 27 日
東景會議中心年度汽車展發票

品項：	單價：	總計：
會議展位（30 平方英尺）	100.00 元／天	300 元
149 額外服務：		
3 張展示桌	10 元／張	30 元
倉儲	30 元／單位	120 元
電腦租用	20 元／台	20 元
55 吋電視租用	30 元／台	30 元
展場通行證	20 元／人	200 元

	小計：	700 元
	稅：	45.5 元
	總額：	745.5 元 *

150 * 請於 4 月 20 日前至線上帳戶繳費

149. 下列何者未包含在本次活動費用中？
(A) 展場的通行證
(B) 展示桌
(C) 電視租用
(D) 擺設與清理

150. 巴克斯特女士被要求做什麼？
(A) 登記會員
(B) 寄支票到會場
(C) 支付帳單款項
(D) 確認參加者數量

Questions 151–152 簡訊

珍妮佛・波特 [上午 11:23]
嗨，拉斐爾。你這週末有去瑞奇特大道的辦公場所嗎？

拉斐爾・莫雷茲 [上午 11:25]
有，我星期六去的。**151 既然我們大多數的攝影師每天將忙於活動**，妳確定我們需要這麼大的空間嗎？

珍妮佛・波特 [上午 11:27]
那些房間是很大，但如果我們擴大規模的話，就會需要那些空間了。

拉斐爾・莫雷茲 [上午 11:28]
但這件事應該近幾年都還不會發生吧。

珍妮佛・波特 [上午 11:30]
是沒錯，但我們還是應該為公司的長程目標著想。**152 瑞奇特大道的空間讓我們我們最終有機會設置 151 實地攝影棚。**

拉斐爾・莫雷茲 [上午 11:32]
妳說的沒錯。一旦 **151 我們開始提供人像攝影服務**，我們肯定需要額外的空間。

489

151. 這些人最有可能從事何種行業？
    (A) 攝影公司
    (B) 時尚設計坊
    (C) 活動規畫公司
    (D) 藝廊

152. 在上午 11:32 時，莫雷茲先生說的「妳說的沒錯。」是什麼意思？
    (A) 那個地點離市區太遠。
    (B) 那棟大樓將有助公司達成目標。
    (C) 那棟大樓內需要進行大規模的室內設計工程。
    (D) 那處所有一些明顯的缺陷。

Questions 153–155 電子郵件

收件者：崔斯坦．斯塔爾
寄件者：艾蜜莉亞．辛普森
日期：6 月 2 日
回覆：沃爾頓購物中心合約

嗨，崔斯坦，

我剛收到馬克思．潘恩的電子郵件，提到你昨天寄給他的預算企畫案。**153 很明顯地，有些數字是錯的。154 你沒有寫進我們後來在 5 月 20 號協商時所同意的數字，**而是寫上我們在 5 月 6 號首次廣告比稿時跟他報告的原始數字。

潘恩先生希望在 6 月 5 日把這個廣告企畫向他的主管報告。他提到還有其他幾家公司也向他提出企畫案。如果我們無法在 6 月 3 號前處理好這份文件，他就會從它們當中挑選一家。因為我正要飛往芝加哥的辦公室，我希望你能立刻處理這件事。**155 請把修訂後的企畫案寄給潘恩先生，**並在收到他的回覆後寄電子郵件給我。

艾蜜莉亞 敬上

153. 為什麼會寫這封電子郵件？
    (A) 要求休假
    (B) 介紹一位應徵者
    (C) 公告規定變動
    (D) 指出一些錯誤

154. 企畫案是何時修改的？
    (A) 5 月 6 日
    (B) 5 月 20 日
    (C) 6 月 3 日
    (D) 6 月 5 日

155. 辛普森女士要斯塔爾先生做什麼？
    (A) 打電話
    (B) 退一筆款項
    (C) 寄送一份文件
    (D) 和經理談話

Questions 156–157 文章

普利茅斯縣的餐廳業績正在下滑。根據《普利茅斯日報》的報導，今年冬季業績已經下滑了超過 15%。這個下滑幅度已經讓許多餐廳老闆深感震撼，特別是冬季假期一般餐廳業績是提升的。**156 小義大利餐館的老闆，鮑伯．富爾頓認為，這個衰退現象的因素之一就是批發價格的提高。**「隨著所有東西價格提高，我們也必須提高自己的餐飲售價。」富爾頓先生在一場訪問中提到，「但大多數的客人不想為一頓飯付那麼多錢。」**157 為了刺激更多營業額，許多當地餐廳已經協力研擬會員方案。**這些方案將提供顧客在全縣許多餐廳的消費折扣。

156. 根據這篇文章，餐廳業績為什麼會下滑？
    (A) 天氣變得很不舒適。
    (B) 成本上升得太高。
    (C) 蓋了更新的餐廳。
    (D) 許多當地工作機會消失。

157. 餐廳老闆如何回應這個趨勢？
    (A) 改善食物品質
    (B) 減少員工數量
    (C) 與其他餐廳合作
    (D) 推出電視廣告

Questions 158–161 網路聊天

瑞塔・弗雷澤 [下午 2:23]
諾頓女士,您有空嗎?湯瑪士和我不太清楚我們的工作。去年我負責開發每一季的訓練課程,但湯瑪士今年被分配了一模一樣的工作。

派翠琳娜・諾頓 [下午 2:25]
是的,[158] 每個人都需要有為人資部開發他們自己課程的機會。

瑞塔・弗雷澤 [下午 2:26]
所以公司不再使用我去年研製的資料了嗎?

派翠琳娜・諾頓 [下午 2:28]
沒錯,湯瑪士應該要研製出今年使用的新資料。

湯瑪士・伍茲 [下午 2:30]
但是 [160] 如果我想使用瑞塔部分的構想呢?

派翠琳娜・諾頓 [下午 2:33]
課程研發是這個工作的一部分。

湯瑪士・伍茲 [下午 2:35]
是,[159] 但瑞塔去年的課程很棒。[161] 我不想她所有的心血都浪費了。

派翠琳娜・諾頓 [下午 2:39]
如果瑞塔同意的話,只要你把適用的部分更新,我想你是可以使用她部分的資料。[161] 先讓我審閱去年的資料後,再回覆你。

瑞塔・弗雷澤 [下午 2:41]
如果湯瑪士和我一起合作這個專案呢?

派翠琳娜・諾頓 [下午 2:44]
[158] 我覺得沒這個必要。

瑞塔・弗雷澤 [下午 2:45]
好,我了解。

湯瑪士・伍茲 [下午 2:46]
當您決定後,請通知我們。謝謝。

158. 諾頓女士最有可能是誰?
(A) 財務規畫師
(B) 人力資源部主管
(C) 企業實習生
(D) 廣告顧問

159. 關於弗雷澤女士,提到了什麼?
(A) 她去年開發一個很成功的訓練課程。
(B) 她通常和伍茲先生一起合作專案。
(C) 她對今年所分配的工作很滿意。
(D) 她明年將接管諾頓女士的工作。

160. 在下午 2:33,當諾頓女士說:「課程研發是這個工作的一部分」時,她是什麼意思?
(A) 她的工作職責包括了課程開發。
(B) 她相信弗雷澤女士更適合這份工作。
(C) 她不認同伍茲先生的建議。
(D) 她與公司的合約需要修改。

161. 接下來最有可能發生什麼事?
(A) 弗雷澤女士將連絡主管。
(B) 伍茲先生將開始進行一項專案。
(C) 伍茲先生和弗雷澤女士將開會。
(D) 諾頓女士將檢視一些舊資料。

Questions 162–165 電子郵件

收件者:塔米卡・凱恩斯
寄件者:馬賽爾・凡卓
回覆:資料
日期:4 月 22 日

[162] 我來信是有關您在本公司網站所申請的服務項目報價。很高興您對草坪與庭園管理的多項服務有興趣。我可以向您保證,我們是本市最佳造景公司。我們為本地許多商家維護景觀,像是飯店與鄉村俱樂部。我們還負責維護市中心紀念體育場的大草坪。

我已經附上您所申請的服務項目報價單。[163] 這個報價是依據雷諾茲藝廊的每週草坪保養服務而訂的。[165] 但如果您要求額外服務,像是庭園植栽或是移除樹木,則將另行收費。但如果您與本公司簽訂兩年期的合約,那所有的額外服務將可享優惠折扣。請參考報價單,[164] 我將於下週初與您聯繫,回答您可能有的疑問。

馬賽爾・凡卓 敬上

TEST **6**

PART 7

162. 這封電子郵件的目的是什麼？
- (A) 更動時程表
- **(B) 回覆一項請求**
- (C) 寄設計圖
- (D) 繳交申請書

163. 凱恩斯女士最可能從事何種行業？
- **(A) 藝廊工作**
- (B) 體育館事務
- (C) 鄉村俱樂部
- (D) 飯店業

164. 電子郵件提及了什麼？
- (A) 凱恩斯女士是草坪與庭園管理的新職員。
- (B) 草坪與庭園管理是新開的公司。
- **(C) 凱恩斯女士將於下週收到凡卓先生的聯繫。**
- (D) 凡卓先生參觀了凱恩斯女士的公司。

165. 下列句子最適合出現在 [1]、[2]、[3]、[4] 的哪個位置中？
「但如果您與本公司簽訂兩年期的合約，那所有的額外服務將可享優惠折扣。」
- (A) [1]
- (B) [2]
- (C) [3]
- **(D) [4]**

Questions 166–168 文章

帕克·華倫斯加入冒險軟體
《每日漫談》 [166] 艾咪·史旺森撰稿

紐約（2 月 24 日）—帕克·華倫斯已經宣布他將加入新創公司「冒險軟體」。華倫斯先生至今已從事軟體應用程式開發五年。他最廣為人知的身分，便是音樂分享應用程式—大理石 FM 的創造者。大理石 FM 在兩年內就累積了超過三百萬的下載量，讓華倫斯成為業界最搶手的軟體程式開發者之一。

儘管拒絕了流體應用程式與 T&B 開發者兩間公司的工作，華倫斯卻跨出了驚人的一步，接受一家成立不到兩年的公司的工作

機會。「當我見到 [166] 冒險軟體的亞倫·派克時，我就知道他和我有共同的目標。」 [167] 華倫斯最近在他最新應用程式的發表會上說道，「他和我都熱愛音樂。他對未來的工作有一些很棒的點子。我非常有信心明年我們就會發行熱門新產品。」

[167] 華倫斯最新的應用軟體—大理石影片在不到一個月的時間，就造成了超過 500,000 次的下載量。科技世界正引領期盼，華倫斯與派克的合作會帶來大創舉，打頭陣的便是兩人將於 3 月 30 日再次發表的 [168] 更新版派克智慧交響樂。

166. 派克先生最有可能是誰？
- (A) 影片導演
- (B) 交響樂作曲家
- (C) 音樂影片製作人
- **(D) 軟體公司老闆**

167. 關於史旺森女士，下列何者最可能為真？
- (A) 她之前任職於流體應用程式。
- **(B) 她出席了大理石影片的發表會。**
- (C) 她購買了一份大理石 FM。
- (D) 她在活動上與派克先生碰面。

168. 關於智慧交響樂，提到了什麼事？
- **(A) 是一個已經存在的應用程式。**
- (B) 原本由 T&B 開發者所開發的。
- (C) 下載量將限制在 500,000 次。
- (D) 將展現出大理石 FM 的特點。

Questions 169–171 手冊

節能戰士

您是在夏季還是冬季支付高額的水電帳單呢？ [169] 有了節能戰士，您就可以找到幫您省錢的節能方法。聯絡我們，就提供您免費的四步驟諮詢。

1. 判斷您的用電需求
本公司合格的能源顧問將造訪貴府，以決定您的用電需求。 [170(A), (B)] 您需要填寫一張詳細的調查表，表中會問您在家的時數，您在每個季節希望的室溫，以及您烹飪與打掃的習慣。

2. 居家檢測

一旦本公司的顧問決定您的用電需求後，他們將檢測貴府的窗戶、牆壁和門，以確保適當的隔絕效果。**170(C) 他們也會測試您的暖氣、冷卻與照明系統以找出它們的缺點。**與其他公司不同的是，節能戰士將準備一份詳細的缺失報告，並提出改善建議。

3. 選擇您的升級方案

我們的顧問將以您的預算為考量，為您的住家討論出推薦的升級方案。我們將協助您選擇並安裝所有設備，從窗戶的雙層玻璃到屋頂的太陽能面板。

4. 安裝服務

我們的團隊會配合您的行程來安裝所有的升級配備。**171 但大多數的安裝工作都需要花上數天才能完工。**您會看到帳單上立即省下的錢，而且最棒的是這些錢會一直省下去。接下來幾年您可以不斷地省錢。若您在第一年間對升級的設備有任何使用上的問題，節能戰士都將免費為您維修。

169. 這個手冊的目的是什麼？
- (A) 公告一項新能源
- (B) 比較兩家能源公司
- **(C) 宣傳公司服務**
- (D) 討論隔熱的好處

170. 在居家諮詢服務中，下列何者不會被檢測？
- (A) 住家使用的時數
- (B) 住家主人偏好的室溫
- (C) 暖氣設備的效能
- **(D) 目前每月的水電費用**

171. 手冊中提到升級設備的什麼缺點？
- (A) 購買升級設備要花不少錢。
- **(B) 安裝所有的設備要花一些時間。**
- (C) 安裝期間，住家主人必須在家。
- (D) 有一年的時間，每月帳單都不會減少。

Questions 172–175 文章

紐蒙特科技會議展開世界巡迴之旅

3 月 5 日一紐蒙特科技會議（NTC）預定於下個月展開世界巡展的第一站。這個會議是世界最大科技展之一，展出涵蓋了醫療科技到航空工程展示。**172 NTC 由紐蒙特企業及其執行長巴雷特‧麥可斯於澳洲雪梨所創辦。173 每年有超過 30,000 名民眾到訪雪梨會場，參觀尚未上市的最新創新科技。**

NTC 通常接待來自世界各地的科學家，而這是它第一年成為國際巡展。麥可斯先生在一場訪問中提到，「我們對擴辦感到非常興奮。當我們在十年前開辦這場會議時，絲毫沒有想到它會成為世界最大的科技盛會。**174 我們真的很開心下個月就要在英國倫敦展開六國之旅。**我們已經開始期待大批與會人潮了。」

美國、巴西、日本、德國和南非也將在這趟巡展中。巡展大多數日期的入場券已經銷售一空。如果 NTC 全球巡迴之旅成功的話，麥可斯先生打算在明年的巡展中增加更多展點。**175 「加拿大和法國的專業人士已經向我們提出企畫書了，」**麥可斯先生說。「我們很樂觀其他國家也將提出類似的企畫。」

TEST 6

PART 7

172. 有關紐蒙特企業，下列何者為真？
- **(A) 協助成立紐蒙特科技會議。**
- (B) 在英國、巴西和日本都有分公司。
- (C) 是醫療科技業的主要開發商。
- (D) 買賣航太工程設備。

173. 關於雪梨的會議，提到了什麼事？
- (A) 花了五年的時間才受到歡迎。
- (B) 僱用超過 30,000 名員工。
- **(C) 展出還無法購買的科技技術。**
- (D) 是第二個展出地點。

174. 下一場紐蒙特科技會議將於何處舉行？
- (A) 法國
- **(B) 英國**
- (C) 巴西
- (D) 日本

175. 下列句子最適合出現在 [1]、[2]、[3]、[4] 的哪個位置中？

「如果 NTC 全球巡迴之旅成功的話，麥可斯先生打算在明年的巡展中增加更多展點。」？

(A) [1]

(B) [2]

(C) [3]

(D) [4]

Questions 176–180 信件及問卷調查

大皇宮酒店
泰國蘇美島

貝戴妮·斯帕克斯

LIT 4W2 安大略省多倫多布洛克路 44 號

親愛的斯帕克斯女士：

感謝您選擇大皇宮酒店作為 10 月 12 日至 10 月 25 日的住宿地點。根據我們的紀錄，**177 您的住宿含在本酒店泰國假期套裝行程中，以慶祝我們 50 周年紀念。我們正在 178 進行該套裝行程的簡短問卷調查。176 如果您能填寫這份隨信附上的問卷，並以回郵信封寄回，我們將非常感激。179 如果您於 1 月 2 日前寄回，將可獲得下次旅程的九折優惠折扣**，作為本酒店的謝禮。但如果您在該截止日期後寄回，我們仍提供您抽獎機會，獎項為免費入住本酒店旗下任何一家飯店。

大皇宮酒店
瑞塔·劉 敬上

泰國大皇宮酒店
參加問卷活動，您就可以協助我們為所有賓客提供最佳服務

姓名：貝戴妮·斯帕克斯	179 日期：11 月 28 日

1. 本酒店可否致電您，以進一步針對您的回答進行討論？

• 可，電話號碼 ＿＿＿＿＿＿＿＿＿

• 不方便

2. 您對本酒店的設備與服務品質的評價為何？

• 很差　　　• 略差　　　• 普通

• 好　　　• 很好

請說明您的回答：我覺得我的房間十分舒適也很乾淨。餐廳的食物也很棒。但是當我點客房服務時，食物總是很晚才送到。

3. 您對本酒店的設施評價為何？

• 很差　　　　• 略差

• 普通 • 好　　　• 很好

請說明您的回答：**180 我很喜歡貴酒店提供的各種活動。**在住宿期間，我可以去潛水，參加洞穴探險，上舞蹈課，甚至還可以遊覽當地市場。有好多刺激的事可做！

---

176. 劉女士為什麼要寫信給斯帕克斯女士？

(A) 通知遲付的款項

(B) 重新安排飯店住宿時間

(C) 要求顧客回饋意見

(D) 回覆投訴

177. 關於大皇宮酒店，提到了什麼事？

(A) 它的總部位在泰國。

(B) 它打算在多倫多蓋飯店。

(C) 它想要拓展休閒娛樂活動。

(D) 它推出促銷活動以慶祝週年紀念。

178. 在信件中，第三行的「conducting」與下列哪一個意思最接近？

(A) 執行

(B) 授權

(C) 表現

(D) 轉調

179. 斯帕克斯女士最有可能收到大皇宮酒店提供的什麼？

(A) 折價券

(B) 比賽入場許可

(C) 進入比賽現場

(D) 免費住宿一晚

180. 斯帕克斯女士提到了有關大皇宮酒店的什麼事？

(A) 它的員工沒有幫她解決問題。

(B) 它提供賓客許多各種不同的活動。

(C) 它的食物品質不佳。

(D) 它位於大都市的地點很棒。

Questions 181–185 通知及表單

> 收件者：《圖姆斯金融月刊》全體員工
> 寄件者：圖姆斯出版收購委員會
> 回覆：圖姆斯——派克商業與金融
> 日期：3 月 6 日
>
> 正如各位已經知道的，《圖姆斯金融月刊》計劃於 4 月 27 日正式與《派克商業雜誌》合併。[181] 這個合併案對兩家公司來說，都是很棒的機會。[182]《派克商業雜誌》是前三大商業刊物之一，專門報導國際商業議題與趨勢。這次的合併將讓我們創造出史上第一本的商業與金融雜誌，相信絕對可以將我們的雜誌推向第一名的位置。此外，有了更大型的編制，我們就可以推出雙週刊號，創造出更高的銷售量。
>
> [183] 部門主管將於 4 月 2 日那週會面，以處理合併及市中心全新辦公室翻修的部分細節。[184] 如果各位有任何想在會議中提出的疑問，請提早以電子郵件寄給相關部門主管。
>
> 圖姆斯出版收購委員會

部門	日期／時間	部門主管
編輯部	4 月 2 日 星期一 上午 9:00 — 下午 1:00	編輯部主任 瓊安·絲蒂爾（《圖姆斯金融月刊》）／總編輯 湯米·雷納多（《派克商業雜誌》）
設計部	4 月 3 日 星期二 上午 10:00 — 下午 2:00	[184] 首席設計師 山謬·韋斯特福德（《圖姆斯金融月刊》）／設計主管溫蒂·史凱勒（《派克商業雜誌》）
行政部	4 月 4 日 星期三 上午 11:00 — 下午 4:00	部門主管 安娜貝爾·科代爾（《圖姆斯金融月刊》）／部門主管 史蒂芬·貝里昂（《派克商業雜誌》）
公關部	4 月 5 日 星期四 上午 9:30 — 中午 12:00	首席廣告企劃 拉伊尼·彼得森（《圖姆斯金融月刊》）／廣告部主管 珊蒂·巴克斯特（《派克商業雜誌》）

> ★ 所有會議均於《圖姆斯金融月刊》相關部門舉行。
>
> ★ 史蒂芬·貝里昂將於合併前退休。安娜貝爾·科代爾已經獲選在合併後管理新部門。[184, 185] 所有部門主管須出席 4 月 4 日的會議，該會議將於 A 會議室舉行，該會議室可容納所有出席者。

181. 這個備忘錄的其中一個目的是什麼？
(A) 提醒一項財務計畫的變更
(B) 說明為什麼解僱部分員工
(C) 公告一位部門主管的退休
(D) 論及即將進行的合併案益處

182. 根據備忘錄，《派克商業雜誌》專長的領域是什麼？
(A) 當地金融
(B) 公司合併
(C) 政府政策
(D) 國際商務

183. 關於圖姆斯派克商業與金融的員工，提到了什麼事？
(A) 他們被要求提早退休。
(B) 他們可以申請管理職。
(C) 他們將搬到新辦公大樓。
(D) 他們全都需要參加 4 月 6 日的會議。

184. 關於韋斯特福德先生，提到了什麼事？
(A) 他計劃接管部門主管一職。
(B) 他將在會議中討論電子郵件寄來的問題。
(C) 他安排了兩家雜誌的合併案。
(D) 他為新公司總部挑選地點。

185. 4 月 4 日的會議將發生什麼事？
(A) 將有更多的參加者出席。
(B) 貝里昂先生不會出席討論。
(C)《派克商業雜誌》的執行長將發表演說。
(D) 員工會被告知新工作職務。

迷你焦點團體誠徵人員

艾德蒙頓最大的市場研究公司,杜斯勒行銷公司正在招募 21 歲至 70 歲的民眾參加一場以旅遊為主題的研究。這個活動將於 6 月第二個禮拜,在艾麥里大道 48 號的桑德森飯店會議中心舉行。這個研究將以觀賞一連串旅遊相關短片開始,接著由我們的主持人協助進行小組討論。整場會議將持續三個小時。**[186(A)] 將提供所有參與者津貼。**有興趣者,可致電杜斯勒行銷公司 409-5321-8082。請務必聲明是 73 號研究。**[186(B)] 為確定來電者是否符合參與本研究的資格,請勿掛斷電話,並回答一些篩選問題。**

樂藍:

杜斯勒行銷公司真的很感謝您從忙碌的工作中,撥冗協助本公司於桑德森飯店為太平洋探險公司所進行的市場研究專案。**[188] 您將協助四組迷你焦點團體的討論,每組會由五人所組成。**由於這次主題是漫遊加拿大西海岸,**[186(C)] 我們的客戶堅持要求我們將對象[187]設定於該地區中,具豐富旅遊經驗(不限於商旅或休閒為目的)的人選。**

會議預定自下午 3:00 至 6:00

年齡組/日期
21-35,6 月 9 日星期二
36-45,6 月 10 日星期三
46-60,6 月 11 日星期四
61-70,6 月 12 日星期五

一抵達會場,參與者將發給黃色名牌。請確保研究進行期間,特別是在錄影成員們討論的影片時,名牌上的名字清晰可辨。這樣我們把研究結果與建議交給太平洋探險公司時,**[189] 可方便杜斯勒公司以姓名來提及這些參與研究的人員。**

以下這四部影片,每一部關注在太平洋探險公司不同的旅遊主題面向。

影片一:賞鯨之旅小組討論
影片二:單日獨木舟之旅
[190] 影片三:受歡迎的山區度假中心
影片四:惠斯勒山峰的健行之旅

妮娜・赫南德茲

收件者:rothschild@pactificadventures.ca
寄件者:nhernandez@dressler.ca
日期:6 月 28 日
主旨:73 號研究
附件:73 號研究結果

親愛的羅斯柴爾德先生:

我要通知您,您上個月要求針對特定目標市場的研究已經完成了。如附件報告指出,其中一個主題獲得所有焦點團體的喜愛。**[190] 這個主題概述了旅行者最喜歡的住宿地點。**為了確定我們的研究結果涵蓋了所有的重要項目,我們想與您以及貴公司代表一同觀看影片,並進行長談。請告知我們方便碰面的日期與時間。

杜勒斯行銷公司 客戶服務部主管
妮娜・赫南德茲 敬上

---

186. 關於迷你焦點團體參與者,沒有提到什麼事?
(A) 他們會收到付款。
(B) 他們在來電時需要回答一些問題。
(C) 他們必須是有經驗的旅行者。
(D) 他們是飯店員工。

187. 在說明中,第一段、第四行的「locate」與下列哪一個意思最接近?
(A) 評論
(B) 相信
(C) 找到
(D) 確認

188. 關於 73 號研究,提到了什麼事?
(A) 將於杜勒斯總部舉行。
(B) 包含四個相同規模人數的小組。
(C) 只著重水上休閒活動。
(D) 將於兩天內完成。

189. 根據說明,參與者為什麼會配發名牌?
(A) 這樣行銷公司才能輕易地辨認參與者。
(B) 這樣每個登記號碼才能搭配正確的名字。
(C) 這樣他們才能快速找到自己的座位。
(D) 這樣他們才得以進入會議中心。

190. 根據研究結果，那一個影片最受歡迎？
(A) 影片一
(B) 影片二
(C) 影片三
(D) 影片四

Questions 191–195 時程表及兩封電子郵件

聖約翰美術館 即將展出的展覽

日期	展覽名稱	簡介
4 月 11 日— 8 月 20 日	回收物也可以是雕刻品	人們通常把回收物看成是破銅爛鐵。然而，正如這 10 位 **[191] 南美洲**各地藝術家作品的展覽所呈現的，任何素材都可以改造成美得令人屏息的雕刻品。
4 月 28 日— 10 月 3 日	運動員百相	這場水彩畫展示了 **[191] 來自世界各地藝術家**的作品，其畫作展現了專業運動員美麗的肖像。
6 月 5 日— 11 月 29 日	不只是樹	這場來自 **[191] 非洲各地與地中海數國**藝術家的非凡攝影與畫作展捕捉了森林迷人的力量。
[193]6 月 11 日— 7 月 14 日	**藝術中的食物史**	透過影像記錄、雕塑、攝影與繪畫，這個特別的展覽追溯了 15 世紀至 19 世紀歐洲的食物沿革。

購票可至本館網站或寄電子郵件至 banderson@stjohnartgallery.org。欲了解本館精彩的會員專案，只要上本館網站，點選「成為聖約翰美術館會員！」即可。**[192] 會員可免費獲得兩張自選展覽的入場券。**

寄件者： 謝汶・賈巴爾
　　　　　<CJabar@rogerstalent.ca>
收件者： 貝琳達・安德森
　　　　　<banderson@stjohnartgallery.org>
主旨： 感謝您
日期： 3 月 10 日

[192] 我來信的目的，是要謝謝您那兩張「藝術中的食物史」的免費門票。我還需要一張該展覽的門票給我的部門主管，海蓮娜・拉弗勒。我想，美術館應該有我的信用卡記錄，因此請將款項刷入同一張信用卡帳上，將票寄到同一地址即可。

感謝您們的人員提供這麼棒的展覽。

謝汶・賈巴爾

寄件者： 貝琳達・安德森
　　　　　<banderson@stjohnartgallery.org>
收件者： 謝汶・賈巴爾
　　　　　<CJabar@rogerstalent.ca>
主旨： 展覽取消
日期： 3 月 14 日

親愛的賈巴爾先生：

聖約翰美術館感謝您過去七年來的惠顧。我們深感抱歉，由於不可抗拒因素，您與貴同事打算參觀的展覽已經取消了。然而，本館已經安排了一場黑白攝影展代替展出。**[193] 預定於相同日期（6 月 11 日— 7 月 14 日）進行 [194] 展出，定名為「拉丁美洲的勞工階級」。[195] 我已經將新的展覽指南郵寄至貴公司。**麻煩再告訴我，您想改看哪場展覽。

感謝您對此事的諒解。

聖約翰美術館
貝琳達・安德森 敬上

191. 根據網站內容，所有展覽的共同點是什麼？
(A) 它們展出來自各國的作品。
(B) 它們展出來自地中海國家的作品。
(C) 都有影片播出。
(D) 都有雕刻品。

192. 關於賈巴爾先生，提到了什麼事？

    (A) 他捐了一組收藏品供展覽。

    (B) 他目前擔任美術指導員。

    (C) 他已經看過其中三場展出。

    (D) 他是美術館的付費會員。

193. 哪一場展覽已經被取消了？

    (A) 回收物也可以是雕刻品

    (B) 運動員百相

    (C) 不只是樹

    (D) 藝術中的食物史

194. 在第二封電子郵件中，第一段、第四行的「run」與下列哪一個意思最接近？

    (A) 指揮

    (B) 移除

    (C) 被展示

    (D) 被宣告

195. 安德森女士為賈巴爾先生做了什麼？

    (A) 將款項刷入他的信用卡帳上

    (B) 郵寄更新後的節目手冊

    (C) 升級他的會員資格

    (D) 重新安排一場社交活動

Questions 196–200 電子郵件及附件

收件者：馬克思・朗恩，加布里埃拉・
        桑切斯，丹尼爾・威爾克斯
寄件者：莎莉・多卡斯
日期：7 月 16 日上午 9:09
主旨：辦公空間
附件：可用地產

大家好，

198 我真的很開心上週五和大家在戴維思微爾燒烤共進午餐。我對我們埃貝特營建機具租賃於邁阿密開設的第一家分公司深感興奮。由於邁阿密的住房市場日益成長，我相信我們都摩拳擦掌準備吸引第一批顧客，並開始推薦各公司最適合他們工程與目標的設備。

我很感謝各位對最合宜的辦公地點所投入的心力。利用各位所建議的預算與標準，我在 www.vanzylerealty.com. 上搜尋，找到了幾個可能的地點，並編成一張清單。我已附上該檔案。請大家查看，並提供意見。

196 埃貝特營建機具租賃

莎莉・多卡斯

基爾福特路 13990 號
郊區兩層樓出租房產。二樓辦公處室。停車場可容納 100 部汽車之多。位於丹蒙市公車總站對面，鄰近許多出差旅客投宿的商務飯店。距離邁阿密市中心半小時。
月租：975 元

蘇格登公路 1389 號
200 邁阿密市中心大型零售空間。大樓大型標示對公路上駕駛人而言清楚可識。大樓包括大型存放空間，可放置零件與機具。新安裝的空調設備保證讓您在炎夏中保持舒適。
月租：1150 元

貝克福德大道 7643 號
位於三樓的商業與辦公空間。坐落於邁阿密主要商業區的住宅地段。與兩座大型購物中心位於同一條街上。設備包括最先進的保全警報系統。現場提供列表機、掃描器、傳真機及彩色影印機，供公司行號使用。
月租：1050 元

威爾莫特路 6094 號
單層樓建築，附小型辦公空間。土地契約亦立即適用於建築後方的地產。**197 坐落於城市東側，懷德遜公園中，為邁阿密公寓塔樓首要開發位置。**
月租：825 元

收件者：莎莉・多卡斯，馬克思・朗恩，
        加布里埃拉・桑切斯
寄件者：丹尼爾・威爾克斯
日期：7 月 20 日上午 11:23
主旨：回覆：辦公空間

大家好：

莎莉，非常感謝妳將搜尋結果縮小至所提供的清單範圍。我確信上週五所舉行的策略會議相當地有收穫。**198 很抱歉，因為一個緊急的業務問題臨時被叫到波士頓，讓我無法到場。** 我同時也要謝謝各位，這麼有耐心地等候我回覆這封重要的電郵討論。

馬克思，雖然我也了解在便宜的郊區設置辦公場所，有其省錢的必要，但 **200 我們公司也不該忽略在市中心設置辦公室的重要性與便捷，畢竟那個區域的房子愈蓋愈多。**

199 我也同意加布里埃拉的看法。我們公司需要在即將到來的邁阿密住房博覽會擺設攤位。 下週我將飛往邁阿密探訪親人，屆時我會了解一下這事。同時，在邁阿密期間，我計劃與一位當地的房地產經紀人共進午餐，他一直在我們公司服務直到兩年前才離開。莎莉，謝謝妳提醒我，海倫·李察遜現在就住在邁阿密。我相信她一定可以為我們提供一些實用的見解。

埃貝特營建機具租賃 丹尼爾·威爾克斯

196. 多卡斯女士最有可能是誰？
(A) 房地產專家
(B) 邁阿密住宅局官員
(C) 營造機具的專業人員
(D) 戴維思微爾燒烤的廚師

197. 哪一個是附件中提到的地產特色？
(A) 省電暖氣系統
(B) 辦公室新鋪設的地毯
(C) 給員工的大型自助餐廳
(D) 鄰近住房開發地

198. 關於威爾克斯先生，提到了什麼事？
(A) 他明天一早將飛往邁阿密。
(B) 他在波士頓承租了一些地產。
(C) 他沒有出席戴維思微爾燒烤的會議。
(D) 他打算應徵管理職。

199. 關於桑切斯女士，提到了什麼事？
(A) 她用電子郵件向同事提出一個點子。
(B) 她以前住在邁阿密市中心。
(C) 她將與前同事碰面。
(D) 她開設自己的機具租賃公司。

200. 威爾克斯先生最有可能中意哪一塊地產？
(A) 基爾福特路 13990 號
(B) 蘇格登公路 1389 號
(C) 貝克福德大道 7643 號
(D) 威爾莫特路 6094 號

TEST 6

PART 7

TOEIC® TEST (1) Answer Sheet

LISTENING SECTION

(Answer bubbles A B C D for questions 1–100)

READING SECTION

(Answer bubbles A B C D for questions 101–200)

TOEIC® TEST (2) Answer Sheet

READING SECTION

(Answer bubbles A B C D for questions 101–200)

LISTENING SECTION

(Answer bubbles A B C D for questions 1–100)

TOEIC® TEST (3) Answer Sheet

READING SECTION

101–200 (answer bubbles A B C D)

LISTENING SECTION

1–100 (answer bubbles A B C D)

TOEIC® TEST (4) Answer Sheet

READING SECTION

Questions 101–200, each with answer choices Ⓐ Ⓑ Ⓒ Ⓓ

LISTENING SECTION

Questions 1–100, each with answer choices Ⓐ Ⓑ Ⓒ Ⓓ

TOEIC® TEST (5) Answer Sheet

LISTENING SECTION

READING SECTION

TOEIC® TEST (6) Answer Sheet

READING SECTION

#	A	B	C	D
101	Ⓐ	Ⓑ	Ⓒ	Ⓓ
102	Ⓐ	Ⓑ	Ⓒ	Ⓓ
103	Ⓐ	Ⓑ	Ⓒ	Ⓓ
104	Ⓐ	Ⓑ	Ⓒ	Ⓓ
105	Ⓐ	Ⓑ	Ⓒ	Ⓓ
106	Ⓐ	Ⓑ	Ⓒ	Ⓓ
107	Ⓐ	Ⓑ	Ⓒ	Ⓓ
108	Ⓐ	Ⓑ	Ⓒ	Ⓓ
109	Ⓐ	Ⓑ	Ⓒ	Ⓓ
110	Ⓐ	Ⓑ	Ⓒ	Ⓓ
111	Ⓐ	Ⓑ	Ⓒ	Ⓓ
112	Ⓐ	Ⓑ	Ⓒ	Ⓓ
113	Ⓐ	Ⓑ	Ⓒ	Ⓓ
114	Ⓐ	Ⓑ	Ⓒ	Ⓓ
115	Ⓐ	Ⓑ	Ⓒ	Ⓓ
116	Ⓐ	Ⓑ	Ⓒ	Ⓓ
117	Ⓐ	Ⓑ	Ⓒ	Ⓓ
118	Ⓐ	Ⓑ	Ⓒ	Ⓓ
119	Ⓐ	Ⓑ	Ⓒ	Ⓓ
120	Ⓐ	Ⓑ	Ⓒ	Ⓓ
121	Ⓐ	Ⓑ	Ⓒ	Ⓓ
122	Ⓐ	Ⓑ	Ⓒ	Ⓓ
123	Ⓐ	Ⓑ	Ⓒ	Ⓓ
124	Ⓐ	Ⓑ	Ⓒ	Ⓓ
125	Ⓐ	Ⓑ	Ⓒ	Ⓓ
126	Ⓐ	Ⓑ	Ⓒ	Ⓓ
127	Ⓐ	Ⓑ	Ⓒ	Ⓓ
128	Ⓐ	Ⓑ	Ⓒ	Ⓓ
129	Ⓐ	Ⓑ	Ⓒ	Ⓓ
130	Ⓐ	Ⓑ	Ⓒ	Ⓓ
131	Ⓐ	Ⓑ	Ⓒ	Ⓓ
132	Ⓐ	Ⓑ	Ⓒ	Ⓓ
133	Ⓐ	Ⓑ	Ⓒ	Ⓓ
134	Ⓐ	Ⓑ	Ⓒ	Ⓓ
135	Ⓐ	Ⓑ	Ⓒ	Ⓓ
136	Ⓐ	Ⓑ	Ⓒ	Ⓓ
137	Ⓐ	Ⓑ	Ⓒ	Ⓓ
138	Ⓐ	Ⓑ	Ⓒ	Ⓓ
139	Ⓐ	Ⓑ	Ⓒ	Ⓓ
140	Ⓐ	Ⓑ	Ⓒ	Ⓓ
141	Ⓐ	Ⓑ	Ⓒ	Ⓓ
142	Ⓐ	Ⓑ	Ⓒ	Ⓓ
143	Ⓐ	Ⓑ	Ⓒ	Ⓓ
144	Ⓐ	Ⓑ	Ⓒ	Ⓓ
145	Ⓐ	Ⓑ	Ⓒ	Ⓓ
146	Ⓐ	Ⓑ	Ⓒ	Ⓓ
147	Ⓐ	Ⓑ	Ⓒ	Ⓓ
148	Ⓐ	Ⓑ	Ⓒ	Ⓓ
149	Ⓐ	Ⓑ	Ⓒ	Ⓓ
150	Ⓐ	Ⓑ	Ⓒ	Ⓓ
151	Ⓐ	Ⓑ	Ⓒ	Ⓓ
152	Ⓐ	Ⓑ	Ⓒ	Ⓓ
153	Ⓐ	Ⓑ	Ⓒ	Ⓓ
154	Ⓐ	Ⓑ	Ⓒ	Ⓓ
155	Ⓐ	Ⓑ	Ⓒ	Ⓓ
156	Ⓐ	Ⓑ	Ⓒ	Ⓓ
157	Ⓐ	Ⓑ	Ⓒ	Ⓓ
158	Ⓐ	Ⓑ	Ⓒ	Ⓓ
159	Ⓐ	Ⓑ	Ⓒ	Ⓓ
160	Ⓐ	Ⓑ	Ⓒ	Ⓓ
161	Ⓐ	Ⓑ	Ⓒ	Ⓓ
162	Ⓐ	Ⓑ	Ⓒ	Ⓓ
163	Ⓐ	Ⓑ	Ⓒ	Ⓓ
164	Ⓐ	Ⓑ	Ⓒ	Ⓓ
165	Ⓐ	Ⓑ	Ⓒ	Ⓓ
166	Ⓐ	Ⓑ	Ⓒ	Ⓓ
167	Ⓐ	Ⓑ	Ⓒ	Ⓓ
168	Ⓐ	Ⓑ	Ⓒ	Ⓓ
169	Ⓐ	Ⓑ	Ⓒ	Ⓓ
170	Ⓐ	Ⓑ	Ⓒ	Ⓓ
171	Ⓐ	Ⓑ	Ⓒ	Ⓓ
172	Ⓐ	Ⓑ	Ⓒ	Ⓓ
173	Ⓐ	Ⓑ	Ⓒ	Ⓓ
174	Ⓐ	Ⓑ	Ⓒ	Ⓓ
175	Ⓐ	Ⓑ	Ⓒ	Ⓓ
176	Ⓐ	Ⓑ	Ⓒ	Ⓓ
177	Ⓐ	Ⓑ	Ⓒ	Ⓓ
178	Ⓐ	Ⓑ	Ⓒ	Ⓓ
179	Ⓐ	Ⓑ	Ⓒ	Ⓓ
180	Ⓐ	Ⓑ	Ⓒ	Ⓓ
181	Ⓐ	Ⓑ	Ⓒ	Ⓓ
182	Ⓐ	Ⓑ	Ⓒ	Ⓓ
183	Ⓐ	Ⓑ	Ⓒ	Ⓓ
184	Ⓐ	Ⓑ	Ⓒ	Ⓓ
185	Ⓐ	Ⓑ	Ⓒ	Ⓓ
186	Ⓐ	Ⓑ	Ⓒ	Ⓓ
187	Ⓐ	Ⓑ	Ⓒ	Ⓓ
188	Ⓐ	Ⓑ	Ⓒ	Ⓓ
189	Ⓐ	Ⓑ	Ⓒ	Ⓓ
190	Ⓐ	Ⓑ	Ⓒ	Ⓓ
191	Ⓐ	Ⓑ	Ⓒ	Ⓓ
192	Ⓐ	Ⓑ	Ⓒ	Ⓓ
193	Ⓐ	Ⓑ	Ⓒ	Ⓓ
194	Ⓐ	Ⓑ	Ⓒ	Ⓓ
195	Ⓐ	Ⓑ	Ⓒ	Ⓓ
196	Ⓐ	Ⓑ	Ⓒ	Ⓓ
197	Ⓐ	Ⓑ	Ⓒ	Ⓓ
198	Ⓐ	Ⓑ	Ⓒ	Ⓓ
199	Ⓐ	Ⓑ	Ⓒ	Ⓓ
200	Ⓐ	Ⓑ	Ⓒ	Ⓓ

LISTENING SECTION

#	A	B	C	D
1	Ⓐ	Ⓑ	Ⓒ	Ⓓ
2	Ⓐ	Ⓑ	Ⓒ	Ⓓ
3	Ⓐ	Ⓑ	Ⓒ	Ⓓ
4	Ⓐ	Ⓑ	Ⓒ	Ⓓ
5	Ⓐ	Ⓑ	Ⓒ	Ⓓ
6	Ⓐ	Ⓑ	Ⓒ	Ⓓ
7	Ⓐ	Ⓑ	Ⓒ	Ⓓ
8	Ⓐ	Ⓑ	Ⓒ	Ⓓ
9	Ⓐ	Ⓑ	Ⓒ	Ⓓ
10	Ⓐ	Ⓑ	Ⓒ	Ⓓ
11	Ⓐ	Ⓑ	Ⓒ	Ⓓ
12	Ⓐ	Ⓑ	Ⓒ	Ⓓ
13	Ⓐ	Ⓑ	Ⓒ	Ⓓ
14	Ⓐ	Ⓑ	Ⓒ	Ⓓ
15	Ⓐ	Ⓑ	Ⓒ	Ⓓ
16	Ⓐ	Ⓑ	Ⓒ	Ⓓ
17	Ⓐ	Ⓑ	Ⓒ	Ⓓ
18	Ⓐ	Ⓑ	Ⓒ	Ⓓ
19	Ⓐ	Ⓑ	Ⓒ	Ⓓ
20	Ⓐ	Ⓑ	Ⓒ	Ⓓ
21	Ⓐ	Ⓑ	Ⓒ	Ⓓ
22	Ⓐ	Ⓑ	Ⓒ	Ⓓ
23	Ⓐ	Ⓑ	Ⓒ	Ⓓ
24	Ⓐ	Ⓑ	Ⓒ	Ⓓ
25	Ⓐ	Ⓑ	Ⓒ	Ⓓ
26	Ⓐ	Ⓑ	Ⓒ	Ⓓ
27	Ⓐ	Ⓑ	Ⓒ	Ⓓ
28	Ⓐ	Ⓑ	Ⓒ	Ⓓ
29	Ⓐ	Ⓑ	Ⓒ	Ⓓ
30	Ⓐ	Ⓑ	Ⓒ	Ⓓ
31	Ⓐ	Ⓑ	Ⓒ	Ⓓ
32	Ⓐ	Ⓑ	Ⓒ	Ⓓ
33	Ⓐ	Ⓑ	Ⓒ	Ⓓ
34	Ⓐ	Ⓑ	Ⓒ	Ⓓ
35	Ⓐ	Ⓑ	Ⓒ	Ⓓ
36	Ⓐ	Ⓑ	Ⓒ	Ⓓ
37	Ⓐ	Ⓑ	Ⓒ	Ⓓ
38	Ⓐ	Ⓑ	Ⓒ	Ⓓ
39	Ⓐ	Ⓑ	Ⓒ	Ⓓ
40	Ⓐ	Ⓑ	Ⓒ	Ⓓ
41	Ⓐ	Ⓑ	Ⓒ	Ⓓ
42	Ⓐ	Ⓑ	Ⓒ	Ⓓ
43	Ⓐ	Ⓑ	Ⓒ	Ⓓ
44	Ⓐ	Ⓑ	Ⓒ	Ⓓ
45	Ⓐ	Ⓑ	Ⓒ	Ⓓ
46	Ⓐ	Ⓑ	Ⓒ	Ⓓ
47	Ⓐ	Ⓑ	Ⓒ	Ⓓ
48	Ⓐ	Ⓑ	Ⓒ	Ⓓ
49	Ⓐ	Ⓑ	Ⓒ	Ⓓ
50	Ⓐ	Ⓑ	Ⓒ	Ⓓ
51	Ⓐ	Ⓑ	Ⓒ	Ⓓ
52	Ⓐ	Ⓑ	Ⓒ	Ⓓ
53	Ⓐ	Ⓑ	Ⓒ	Ⓓ
54	Ⓐ	Ⓑ	Ⓒ	Ⓓ
55	Ⓐ	Ⓑ	Ⓒ	Ⓓ
56	Ⓐ	Ⓑ	Ⓒ	Ⓓ
57	Ⓐ	Ⓑ	Ⓒ	Ⓓ
58	Ⓐ	Ⓑ	Ⓒ	Ⓓ
59	Ⓐ	Ⓑ	Ⓒ	Ⓓ
60	Ⓐ	Ⓑ	Ⓒ	Ⓓ
61	Ⓐ	Ⓑ	Ⓒ	Ⓓ
62	Ⓐ	Ⓑ	Ⓒ	Ⓓ
63	Ⓐ	Ⓑ	Ⓒ	Ⓓ
64	Ⓐ	Ⓑ	Ⓒ	Ⓓ
65	Ⓐ	Ⓑ	Ⓒ	Ⓓ
66	Ⓐ	Ⓑ	Ⓒ	Ⓓ
67	Ⓐ	Ⓑ	Ⓒ	Ⓓ
68	Ⓐ	Ⓑ	Ⓒ	Ⓓ
69	Ⓐ	Ⓑ	Ⓒ	Ⓓ
70	Ⓐ	Ⓑ	Ⓒ	Ⓓ
71	Ⓐ	Ⓑ	Ⓒ	Ⓓ
72	Ⓐ	Ⓑ	Ⓒ	Ⓓ
73	Ⓐ	Ⓑ	Ⓒ	Ⓓ
74	Ⓐ	Ⓑ	Ⓒ	Ⓓ
75	Ⓐ	Ⓑ	Ⓒ	Ⓓ
76	Ⓐ	Ⓑ	Ⓒ	Ⓓ
77	Ⓐ	Ⓑ	Ⓒ	Ⓓ
78	Ⓐ	Ⓑ	Ⓒ	Ⓓ
79	Ⓐ	Ⓑ	Ⓒ	Ⓓ
80	Ⓐ	Ⓑ	Ⓒ	Ⓓ
81	Ⓐ	Ⓑ	Ⓒ	Ⓓ
82	Ⓐ	Ⓑ	Ⓒ	Ⓓ
83	Ⓐ	Ⓑ	Ⓒ	Ⓓ
84	Ⓐ	Ⓑ	Ⓒ	Ⓓ
85	Ⓐ	Ⓑ	Ⓒ	Ⓓ
86	Ⓐ	Ⓑ	Ⓒ	Ⓓ
87	Ⓐ	Ⓑ	Ⓒ	Ⓓ
88	Ⓐ	Ⓑ	Ⓒ	Ⓓ
89	Ⓐ	Ⓑ	Ⓒ	Ⓓ
90	Ⓐ	Ⓑ	Ⓒ	Ⓓ
91	Ⓐ	Ⓑ	Ⓒ	Ⓓ
92	Ⓐ	Ⓑ	Ⓒ	Ⓓ
93	Ⓐ	Ⓑ	Ⓒ	Ⓓ
94	Ⓐ	Ⓑ	Ⓒ	Ⓓ
95	Ⓐ	Ⓑ	Ⓒ	Ⓓ
96	Ⓐ	Ⓑ	Ⓒ	Ⓓ
97	Ⓐ	Ⓑ	Ⓒ	Ⓓ
98	Ⓐ	Ⓑ	Ⓒ	Ⓓ
99	Ⓐ	Ⓑ	Ⓒ	Ⓓ
100	Ⓐ	Ⓑ	Ⓒ	Ⓓ

ANSWER KEY

Actual Test 01

#	Ans	#	Ans	#	Ans	#	Ans	#	Ans	#	Ans	#	Ans	#	Ans
1	(A)	26	(B)	51	(D)	76	(D)	101	(B)	126	(A)	151	(D)	176	(B)
2	(A)	27	(C)	52	(A)	77	(A)	102	(C)	127	(B)	152	(B)	177	(A)
3	(D)	28	(A)	53	(D)	78	(D)	103	(A)	128	(B)	153	(D)	178	(B)
4	(C)	29	(A)	54	(A)	79	(A)	104	(D)	129	(C)	154	(D)	179	(B)
5	(B)	30	(A)	55	(B)	80	(A)	105	(A)	130	(D)	155	(B)	180	(D)
6	(D)	31	(C)	56	(C)	81	(B)	106	(B)	131	(D)	156	(C)	181	(C)
7	(B)	32	(B)	57	(D)	82	(B)	107	(A)	132	(A)	157	(C)	182	(D)
8	(A)	33	(A)	58	(A)	83	(B)	108	(B)	133	(A)	158	(D)	183	(B)
9	(A)	34	(D)	59	(B)	84	(A)	109	(C)	134	(C)	159	(D)	184	(C)
10	(C)	35	(B)	60	(D)	85	(D)	110	(C)	135	(C)	160	(C)	185	(A)
11	(B)	36	(A)	61	(C)	86	(D)	111	(B)	136	(D)	161	(A)	186	(A)
12	(C)	37	(A)	62	(B)	87	(A)	112	(C)	137	(B)	162	(A)	187	(C)
13	(B)	38	(D)	63	(A)	88	(B)	113	(C)	138	(A)	163	(B)	188	(B)
14	(B)	39	(D)	64	(D)	89	(B)	114	(B)	139	(D)	164	(B)	189	(D)
15	(A)	40	(B)	65	(B)	90	(D)	115	(B)	140	(B)	165	(D)	190	(C)
16	(C)	41	(B)	66	(A)	91	(A)	116	(D)	141	(C)	166	(C)	191	(D)
17	(B)	42	(C)	67	(D)	92	(C)	117	(D)	142	(A)	167	(A)	192	(B)
18	(C)	43	(A)	68	(B)	93	(A)	118	(A)	143	(B)	168	(A)	193	(A)
19	(C)	44	(B)	69	(A)	94	(C)	119	(C)	144	(A)	169	(B)	194	(B)
20	(A)	45	(C)	70	(D)	95	(A)	120	(A)	145	(C)	170	(B)	195	(C)
21	(B)	46	(D)	71	(C)	96	(C)	121	(C)	146	(C)	171	(C)	196	(B)
22	(A)	47	(B)	72	(A)	97	(C)	122	(B)	147	(B)	172	(D)	197	(D)
23	(B)	48	(A)	73	(B)	98	(D)	123	(A)	148	(A)	173	(B)	198	(D)
24	(A)	49	(B)	74	(B)	99	(D)	124	(B)	149	(C)	174	(B)	199	(C)
25	(C)	50	(C)	75	(C)	100	(D)	125	(D)	150	(A)	175	(B)	200	(A)

Actual Test 02

#	Ans	#	Ans	#	Ans	#	Ans	#	Ans	#	Ans	#	Ans	#	Ans
1	(B)	26	(B)	51	(B)	76	(A)	101	(B)	126	(A)	151	(C)	176	(A)
2	(C)	27	(A)	52	(D)	77	(D)	102	(A)	127	(C)	152	(B)	177	(D)
3	(B)	28	(B)	53	(A)	78	(D)	103	(C)	128	(A)	153	(A)	178	(A)
4	(C)	29	(B)	54	(C)	79	(A)	104	(A)	129	(A)	154	(D)	179	(B)
5	(D)	30	(A)	55	(B)	80	(B)	105	(D)	130	(D)	155	(C)	180	(D)
6	(D)	31	(B)	56	(B)	81	(B)	106	(B)	131	(C)	156	(B)	181	(D)
7	(C)	32	(D)	57	(D)	82	(D)	107	(C)	132	(D)	157	(A)	182	(B)
8	(A)	33	(B)	58	(A)	83	(C)	108	(C)	133	(A)	158	(C)	183	(D)
9	(A)	34	(A)	59	(D)	84	(D)	109	(C)	134	(A)	159	(B)	184	(B)
10	(A)	35	(A)	60	(B)	85	(A)	110	(B)	135	(A)	160	(D)	185	(C)
11	(B)	36	(C)	61	(D)	86	(B)	111	(D)	136	(D)	161	(C)	186	(C)
12	(A)	37	(B)	62	(A)	87	(A)	112	(B)	137	(B)	162	(D)	187	(D)
13	(C)	38	(C)	63	(B)	88	(C)	113	(B)	138	(C)	163	(C)	188	(B)
14	(B)	39	(D)	64	(D)	89	(B)	114	(A)	139	(D)	164	(A)	189	(A)
15	(C)	40	(A)	65	(C)	90	(C)	115	(B)	140	(C)	165	(D)	190	(B)
16	(A)	41	(B)	66	(A)	91	(A)	116	(B)	141	(A)	166	(C)	191	(B)
17	(B)	42	(D)	67	(B)	92	(B)	117	(D)	142	(C)	167	(B)	192	(A)
18	(A)	43	(C)	68	(A)	93	(B)	118	(B)	143	(C)	168	(B)	193	(C)
19	(B)	44	(B)	69	(C)	94	(D)	119	(C)	144	(D)	169	(A)	194	(A)
20	(B)	45	(D)	70	(D)	95	(C)	120	(A)	145	(B)	170	(C)	195	(B)
21	(B)	46	(A)	71	(A)	96	(B)	121	(B)	146	(C)	171	(D)	196	(D)
22	(A)	47	(C)	72	(D)	97	(B)	122	(B)	147	(A)	172	(D)	197	(C)
23	(A)	48	(C)	73	(B)	98	(D)	123	(C)	148	(D)	173	(B)	198	(D)
24	(A)	49	(B)	74	(B)	99	(B)	124	(C)	149	(D)	174	(D)	199	(D)
25	(B)	50	(B)	75	(C)	100	(D)	125	(A)	150	(B)	175	(C)	200	(C)

Actual Test 03

1 (D)	26 (C)	51 (D)	76 (A)	101 (D)	126 (B)	151 (C)	176 (A)
2 (C)	27 (B)	52 (C)	77 (C)	102 (B)	127 (D)	152 (D)	177 (D)
3 (A)	28 (A)	53 (C)	78 (A)	103 (B)	128 (A)	153 (C)	178 (C)
4 (D)	29 (C)	54 (A)	79 (D)	104 (B)	129 (B)	154 (D)	179 (B)
5 (B)	30 (B)	55 (D)	80 (C)	105 (B)	130 (D)	155 (B)	180 (D)
6 (D)	31 (A)	56 (D)	81 (D)	106 (D)	131 (A)	156 (D)	181 (A)
7 (B)	32 (A)	57 (A)	82 (B)	107 (B)	132 (C)	157 (B)	182 (B)
8 (C)	33 (C)	58 (B)	83 (B)	108 (D)	133 (C)	158 (D)	183 (C)
9 (C)	34 (D)	59 (A)	84 (D)	109 (C)	134 (B)	159 (B)	184 (B)
10 (A)	35 (B)	60 (D)	85 (A)	110 (C)	135 (B)	160 (A)	185 (D)
11 (B)	36 (D)	61 (C)	86 (B)	111 (A)	136 (A)	161 (B)	186 (A)
12 (B)	37 (B)	62 (D)	87 (D)	112 (D)	137 (A)	162 (A)	187 (D)
13 (B)	38 (D)	63 (B)	88 (C)	113 (B)	138 (C)	163 (D)	188 (C)
14 (A)	39 (A)	64 (C)	89 (D)	114 (A)	139 (A)	164 (D)	189 (A)
15 (A)	40 (B)	65 (B)	90 (A)	115 (D)	140 (C)	165 (C)	190 (D)
16 (C)	41 (D)	66 (D)	91 (C)	116 (D)	141 (C)	166 (D)	191 (D)
17 (B)	42 (A)	67 (A)	92 (C)	117 (B)	142 (D)	167 (D)	192 (D)
18 (A)	43 (B)	68 (B)	93 (D)	118 (C)	143 (A)	168 (C)	193 (C)
19 (C)	44 (B)	69 (A)	94 (B)	119 (D)	144 (A)	169 (D)	194 (A)
20 (B)	45 (A)	70 (A)	95 (B)	120 (B)	145 (D)	170 (B)	195 (B)
21 (B)	46 (D)	71 (A)	96 (B)	121 (A)	146 (C)	171 (D)	196 (B)
22 (B)	47 (B)	72 (B)	97 (D)	122 (B)	147 (B)	172 (B)	197 (C)
23 (A)	48 (D)	73 (D)	98 (B)	123 (A)	148 (A)	173 (D)	198 (B)
24 (C)	49 (B)	74 (D)	99 (D)	124 (D)	149 (D)	174 (A)	199 (A)
25 (B)	50 (A)	75 (B)	100 (A)	125 (A)	150 (A)	175 (C)	200 (D)

Actual Test 04

1 (A)	26 (A)	51 (B)	76 (B)	101 (C)	126 (B)	151 (C)	176 (A)
2 (A)	27 (C)	52 (B)	77 (B)	102 (B)	127 (B)	152 (D)	177 (D)
3 (D)	28 (B)	53 (D)	78 (D)	103 (D)	128 (A)	153 (A)	178 (C)
4 (B)	29 (C)	54 (B)	79 (B)	104 (A)	129 (B)	154 (C)	179 (D)
5 (A)	30 (A)	55 (A)	80 (B)	105 (B)	130 (D)	155 (D)	180 (D)
6 (C)	31 (C)	56 (D)	81 (A)	106 (A)	131 (C)	156 (A)	181 (A)
7 (B)	32 (B)	57 (A)	82 (B)	107 (C)	132 (B)	157 (B)	182 (B)
8 (A)	33 (A)	58 (C)	83 (B)	108 (C)	133 (B)	158 (A)	183 (D)
9 (A)	34 (D)	59 (C)	84 (A)	109 (D)	134 (D)	159 (B)	184 (B)
10 (B)	35 (C)	60 (A)	85 (A)	110 (B)	135 (A)	160 (D)	185 (B)
11 (B)	36 (A)	61 (C)	86 (C)	111 (D)	136 (D)	161 (B)	186 (C)
12 (C)	37 (B)	62 (C)	87 (D)	112 (C)	137 (A)	162 (D)	187 (C)
13 (C)	38 (A)	63 (D)	88 (C)	113 (C)	138 (A)	163 (D)	188 (D)
14 (B)	39 (D)	64 (D)	89 (B)	114 (A)	139 (D)	164 (D)	189 (B)
15 (C)	40 (B)	65 (D)	90 (A)	115 (C)	140 (C)	165 (A)	190 (C)
16 (A)	41 (D)	66 (A)	91 (B)	116 (C)	141 (B)	166 (B)	191 (C)
17 (C)	42 (A)	67 (B)	92 (C)	117 (A)	142 (B)	167 (D)	192 (A)
18 (C)	43 (B)	68 (D)	93 (B)	118 (D)	143 (B)	168 (B)	193 (A)
19 (C)	44 (D)	69 (C)	94 (D)	119 (A)	144 (C)	169 (A)	194 (B)
20 (B)	45 (A)	70 (A)	95 (D)	120 (A)	145 (C)	170 (B)	195 (D)
21 (C)	46 (B)	71 (C)	96 (B)	121 (A)	146 (B)	171 (B)	196 (A)
22 (A)	47 (D)	72 (C)	97 (A)	122 (A)	147 (C)	172 (A)	197 (A)
23 (B)	48 (A)	73 (A)	98 (D)	123 (D)	148 (A)	173 (D)	198 (D)
24 (A)	49 (D)	74 (B)	99 (D)	124 (D)	149 (B)	174 (D)	199 (B)
25 (A)	50 (C)	75 (D)	100 (A)	125 (B)	150 (D)	175 (D)	200 (D)

Actual Test 05

1	(B)	26	(A)	51	(C)	76	(B)	101	(B)	126	(A)	151	(D)	176	(B)
2	(D)	27	(C)	52	(A)	77	(B)	102	(B)	127	(D)	152	(D)	177	(D)
3	(C)	28	(C)	53	(C)	78	(B)	103	(C)	128	(B)	153	(D)	178	(B)
4	(A)	29	(C)	54	(A)	79	(A)	104	(A)	129	(C)	154	(C)	179	(D)
5	(B)	30	(C)	55	(A)	80	(C)	105	(D)	130	(D)	155	(C)	180	(B)
6	(C)	31	(A)	56	(B)	81	(D)	106	(A)	131	(B)	156	(D)	181	(D)
7	(A)	32	(C)	57	(C)	82	(D)	107	(C)	132	(C)	157	(B)	182	(B)
8	(B)	33	(B)	58	(D)	83	(B)	108	(A)	133	(B)	158	(D)	183	(B)
9	(A)	34	(D)	59	(B)	84	(B)	109	(B)	134	(D)	159	(A)	184	(D)
10	(B)	35	(D)	60	(A)	85	(A)	110	(D)	135	(B)	160	(C)	185	(C)
11	(C)	36	(B)	61	(D)	86	(C)	111	(D)	136	(C)	161	(A)	186	(B)
12	(C)	37	(A)	62	(B)	87	(B)	112	(B)	137	(B)	162	(C)	187	(A)
13	(C)	38	(C)	63	(B)	88	(D)	113	(B)	138	(D)	163	(D)	188	(D)
14	(A)	39	(A)	64	(B)	89	(C)	114	(C)	139	(A)	164	(C)	189	(B)
15	(B)	40	(A)	65	(D)	90	(C)	115	(B)	140	(C)	165	(A)	190	(D)
16	(A)	41	(D)	66	(A)	91	(A)	116	(D)	141	(D)	166	(B)	191	(A)
17	(B)	42	(D)	67	(B)	92	(B)	117	(A)	142	(B)	167	(C)	192	(C)
18	(C)	43	(A)	68	(D)	93	(C)	118	(C)	143	(D)	168	(A)	193	(D)
19	(B)	44	(C)	69	(B)	94	(D)	119	(B)	144	(A)	169	(B)	194	(C)
20	(C)	45	(C)	70	(B)	95	(C)	120	(A)	145	(A)	170	(D)	195	(D)
21	(A)	46	(A)	71	(D)	96	(D)	121	(C)	146	(D)	171	(C)	196	(D)
22	(C)	47	(D)	72	(A)	97	(A)	122	(D)	147	(A)	172	(D)	197	(A)
23	(C)	48	(B)	73	(D)	98	(B)	123	(C)	148	(A)	173	(B)	198	(C)
24	(A)	49	(A)	74	(A)	99	(B)	124	(A)	149	(D)	174	(D)	199	(B)
25	(A)	50	(B)	75	(D)	100	(D)	125	(C)	150	(B)	175	(A)	200	(C)

Actual Test 06

1	(D)	26	(B)	51	(B)	76	(B)	101	(B)	126	(C)	151	(A)	176	(C)
2	(B)	27	(B)	52	(D)	77	(B)	102	(A)	127	(B)	152	(B)	177	(D)
3	(C)	28	(C)	53	(B)	78	(D)	103	(A)	128	(D)	153	(D)	178	(A)
4	(B)	29	(B)	54	(C)	79	(A)	104	(A)	129	(D)	154	(B)	179	(A)
5	(B)	30	(C)	55	(D)	80	(D)	105	(B)	130	(C)	155	(C)	180	(B)
6	(A)	31	(A)	56	(D)	81	(C)	106	(C)	131	(C)	156	(B)	181	(D)
7	(B)	32	(B)	57	(A)	82	(A)	107	(D)	132	(D)	157	(C)	182	(D)
8	(C)	33	(D)	58	(C)	83	(D)	108	(D)	133	(C)	158	(B)	183	(C)
9	(A)	34	(C)	59	(A)	84	(B)	109	(D)	134	(C)	159	(A)	184	(B)
10	(B)	35	(D)	60	(B)	85	(C)	110	(C)	135	(A)	160	(C)	185	(A)
11	(B)	36	(B)	61	(D)	86	(D)	111	(B)	136	(C)	161	(D)	186	(D)
12	(B)	37	(C)	62	(C)	87	(C)	112	(B)	137	(D)	162	(B)	187	(C)
13	(A)	38	(D)	63	(A)	88	(A)	113	(A)	138	(A)	163	(A)	188	(B)
14	(C)	39	(B)	64	(B)	89	(C)	114	(C)	139	(D)	164	(C)	189	(A)
15	(A)	40	(A)	65	(D)	90	(A)	115	(A)	140	(A)	165	(D)	190	(C)
16	(B)	41	(D)	66	(B)	91	(B)	116	(B)	141	(B)	166	(D)	191	(A)
17	(B)	42	(A)	67	(C)	92	(B)	117	(C)	142	(A)	167	(B)	192	(D)
18	(C)	43	(B)	68	(A)	93	(A)	118	(C)	143	(C)	168	(A)	193	(D)
19	(B)	44	(D)	69	(C)	94	(D)	119	(A)	144	(B)	169	(C)	194	(C)
20	(A)	45	(A)	70	(D)	95	(D)	120	(C)	145	(A)	170	(D)	195	(B)
21	(B)	46	(C)	71	(C)	96	(A)	121	(A)	146	(C)	171	(B)	196	(C)
22	(C)	47	(B)	72	(A)	97	(C)	122	(D)	147	(C)	172	(A)	197	(D)
23	(B)	48	(C)	73	(D)	98	(C)	123	(C)	148	(D)	173	(C)	198	(C)
24	(A)	49	(A)	74	(C)	99	(B)	124	(B)	149	(D)	174	(B)	199	(A)
25	(C)	50	(A)	75	(D)	100	(A)	125	(A)	150	(C)	175	(D)	200	(B)

決勝
新制多益

聽力閱讀6回模擬試題

作 者	Kim dae Kyun
譯 者	林育珊／蔡裴驊／關亭薇（前言）
編 輯	呂敏如／林晨禾／賴祖兒
校 對	黃詩韻／林蜜琪／陳妍希
主 編	丁宥暄
內文排版	林書玉
封面設計	林書玉
製程管理	洪巧玲
負責人	黃朝萍
出 版 者	寂天文化事業股份有限公司
電 話	+886-(0)2-2365-9739
傳 真	+886-(0)2-2365-9835
網 址	www.icosmos.com.tw
讀者服務	onlineservice@icosmos.com.tw
出版日期	2022 年 3 月 初版二刷 （寂天雲隨身聽APP版）

國家圖書館出版品預行編目(CIP)資料

決勝新制多益：聽力閱讀6回模擬試題 (寂天雲隨
身聽APP版) / Kim dae Kyun著. -- 初版. -- 臺北
市：寂天文化, 2022.03
　　面；　公分
ISBN 978-626-300-113-8 (16K平裝)

1.多益測驗

805.1895

Copyright © 2017 by Kim dae Kyun
All rights reserved.
Traditional Chinese copyright © 2022 by Cosmos Culture Ltd.
This traditional Chinese edition was published by arrangement with Saramin through Agency Liang.

版權所有　請勿翻印
郵撥帳號1998620-0 寂天文化事業股份有限公司
劃撥金額600 元（含）以上者，郵資免費。
訂購金額600 元以下者，請外加郵資65 元。
〔若有破損，請寄回更換，謝謝。〕